Marilyn Durham was born on the edge of the Central Plains in southern Indiana, where she still lives. She has written a couple of novels about the American West, as well as many speeches about writing. She has two grown-up children and three grandchildren, and is fond of Gary Oldman, *Monty Python*, *Blackadder* and *Buffy the Vampire Slayer*.

By Marilyn Durham

The Man Who Loved Cat Dancing
Dutch Uncle
Flambard's Confession

FLAMBARD'S CONFESSION

Marilyn Durham

PHOENIX

A PHOENIX PRESS PAPERBACK

First published in the United States in 1982
by Harcourt Brace Jovanovich, Publishers
This paperback edition published in 2003
by Phoenix,
an imprint of Orion Books Ltd,
Orion House, 5 Upper St Martin's Lane,
London WC2H 9EA

Published by arrangement with Harcourt, Inc.

A CIP catalogue record for this book
is available from the British Library.

ISBN 1 84212 518 4

Typeset by Deltatype Ltd, Birkenhead, Merseyside
Printed and bound in Great Britain by
Clays Ltd, St Ives plc

For Ann, for Dan,
and for Hilda

© 1983 A harij. J. Kemp

FLAMBARD IN EXTREMIS

September 1128

I

Algar the prior was in his lodging, listening to the complaints of his bursar about the cellarer's extravagance, when they were disturbed by a cautious opening of the door. There entered the head of the third prior and guardian of St. Cuthbert's shrine. The event was unprecedented; Brother Edwin had never been known to leave his post when pilgrims might be expected.

'Yes, Brother?' Algar recognized him with a frown.

Brother Edwin came in stealthily and closed the chamber door with reverential care. 'Reverend Father Prior, His Grace the Bishop has just come into the sanctuary in a most unusual state. I thought perhaps you might wish to come and speak to him.'

Algar's face tightened at mention of his bishop, but his light voice expressed only polite surprise. 'A most unusual state, Brother? What can that mean? I don't suppose you're implying His Grace is sober?'

The bursar snorted and tried to cover the indiscretion with a cough. Brother Edwin advanced another step and whispered earnestly:

'He's wearing a monk's habit, Reverend Father Prior, a very old, torn one. He's barefooted, too.'

The bursar let forth another small sound of amusement. Algar studied Edwin severely for a moment, as if he had been the transgressor, then laid down his stylus and rose from his seat.

'You will ask pardon for your levity in the chapter tonight, Brother,' he remarked to his bursar. He came from behind his large study table and motioned Brother Edwin to precede him through the chamber door.

A brisk wind fluttered the hems of their gowns as they came into the cloister. The stone of the cloister walk was striped with sun and shadow of a perfect September day.

'I truly didn't recognize him at first, Reverend Father Prior,' Edwin confided in his thready voice. 'I knew no one of our house could be so poorly clad, so naturally I took him for a pilgrim to the shrine. It was only – ' He stopped, flustered to find he had inadvertently trotted ahead of the prior's more deliberate step. His walk was typical of Prior Algar, a safe, solemn man with the clear grey eyes of his northern breed and the calm of an anchorite.

'It was only when he laughed that I knew him,' Edwin said in surprise at himself. 'It's quite a distinctive sound, if you'll forgive my saying so, Reverend Father.'

'He laughed? He came into the sanctuary, dressed in rags, and laughed? Well, of course he's drunk, Brother.' Algar knew that laugh too well; it had often been turned on him. It was like that of a Danish pirate come to burn the roof over your head. 'We'll call for his attendants at the palace to come for him,' he added, 'but not before I've had a word with him.'

'Reverend Father, I don't believe he's intoxicated.'

'No? What, then? Imbecile? Senile? Did he speak to you sensibly?'

'No, Reverend Father, but he was – he was praying when I left him. He seemed – exalted.'

Algar stopped walking. His lean face became more severe. 'He's preparing another one of his coarse jokes for us, then, no doubt?'

'Jokes, Reverend Father Prior?'

Algar stepped to the next arcade of the cloister walk and squinted at the unblemished sky above the open garth. Before him rose the long south wall of the still unfinished nave of the great church which bishops and monks of Durham had been building for forty years. The first work had been accomplished by his predecessor, Prior Turgot of blessed memory, and by the soldierly Bishop William de St. Carileph. Ranulph, the present bishop, had finished the transepts and extended the nave to its full length at the expense of great hardship to the monks and people of Durham alike. Algar prayed dutifully every day that he would live long enough to see the nave vaulted and roofed, but it seemed unlikely.

He turned back to Edwin, almost blind from the sun, and asked: 'Can you believe it's anything else? Is there anything else in Ranulph Flambard's heart but levity and greed, Brother? He returned to us four and twenty years ago, after being driven out by King Henry. He began his new reign by making an unwarranted feast for the brothers in his palace. Some might construe that as an act of love and humility if he hadn't also let loose women, musicians, tumblers, and beggars into his court to sit with us and entertain us. Prior Turgot had the courage to rebuke him openly – and found an ivy wreath placed on his head even as he spoke, as if he were a pagan!'

Brother Edwin ducked his head as if he were accused of placing that wreath. But he was smiling.

'Forgive me, Reverend Father, if I seem frivolous, but I remember

Prior Turgot' – he checked himself and made a hasty blessing – 'may he rest in peace. I was only a novice then, but I remember how His Grace explained the matter. He said – '

'I know what he said, Brother. He compared himself to Christ, breaking bread with sinners!' Algar thrust his hands into his sleeves again and walked on.

'He may have meant it in all innocence, Reverend Father, and surely no harm came from it. Just as when he wanted the brothers to wash the feet of girl children from the village as well as those of the boys one year on Holy Thursday. In the sight of God, he said, there is no difference between the sexes.'

'Are you attempting to instruct me, Brother?'

'Oh, no, Reverend Father Prior!'

'I believe no one can accuse me of neglecting any part of that duty and reverence we owe to Ranulph Flambard as our nominal abbot and our consecrated bishop. But Ranulph *the man is* another matter, and it is the man I suspect at the moment, Brother, the corrupt and worldly man who bought his office from a greedy and godless king. The man who spent his life in the enjoyment of every vice, who now loves nothing better than to disturb the souls of others.'

Brother Edwin couldn't stop himself from adding:

'But the holy hermit of Finchale, our Godric, says he has a good heart.' He faltered under Algar's cold stare. 'Forgive me, Reverend Father. I know you've had much to bear with from His Grace. I pray for him daily, that he should repent of his worldliness and lead a more holy life. I pray for you, too, of course, Reverend Father Prior.'

'Thank you,' Algar said dryly. 'Now, let us see what mystery hides behind this penitent's guise of His Grace's, shall we?'

Their slippers made light clappings on the floor as they passed the transept arch. The empty nave behind them was like a roofless cavern, set with great piers tall as trees and twice as thick, its floor strewn with the paraphernalia of the builder's craft.

They passed along the south alley of the choir, their footsteps multiplied by echoes until Algar stopped by the entry to the choir next to the bishop's throne. There was a cresset set before a pillar there, its many cups filled with tallow from the kitchen and kept burning night and day to give light to the choir as the monks came in to sing their service. By the wavering light of those many wicks he made out the form of a man writhing slowly on the floor just below the altar.

Brother Edwin whispered, 'Oh, Blessed Savior!'

Algar felt a moment of unreasoned dread, even as he realized it was the movement of the cresset flames that made the figure seem to writhe. The man was motionless, stretched out face down on the floor with his arms spread like a penitent. Shuddering from a brief chill, Algar started forward.

'My lord Bishop! Your Grace! How is it with you? Edwin, is he alive?' Ranulph was in his seventy-first year. A sudden seizure might be expected.

As Edwin hurried to kneel by him, the bishop moved his head so that he was resting on one cheek rather than on his brow. One of his deep-set dark eyes blinked against the cresset flare.

Algar knelt too and bent over him. 'Your Grace, you gave us a fright. What are you doing?'

'I'm praying, for Christ's Sweet Sake! Or I was until you gave such a yell. What's the matter with *you*?' He struggled to rise; he was a heavy man. Algar and Edwin helped him, seizing his trembling arms.

'Forgive my intrusion, Your Grace, but it isn't your usual manner of prayer.' The prior sniffed for the odor of spirits on the old man's breath, but found none. 'My lord, why are you wearing those strange ra— that monk's gown?'

'Why shouldn't I wear it? It's mine. I've had it with me for more than thirty years – to remind me where I came from. You may take that for a lesson if you like, one way or another.'

Algar lifted his thin brows. 'Why, it's a fair lesson indeed, Your Grace. Penance kept hidden benefits only the worm. This is moth-eaten. Allow me to find you something more fitting.' He was astonished to see Brother Edwin frown at him and shake his head.

The bishop snorted and pulled his arm free of Algar's bony hand. 'Offering a subtle thought to a monk is like trying to teach a cat to sing. She can't do it very well, but she will not have a tutor.' Erect, he was steady-footed, but his swarthy skin, gone sallow with age, was pale and glazed with sweat even in the cool of the chancel.

Algar said: 'I fear you're ill after all, Your Grace. Let us help you to a seat.' He glanced at the throne, rejected the notion of boosting Ranulph up into it, and led him to his own choir stall near it. Ranulph leaned against the misericord panting.

'Go and find the infirmarian,' Algar told Edwin, and when the little man had hurried to obey, the prior leaned toward the bishop and asked in a kinder voice: 'My lord, what ails you?'

Ranulph's eyes in their old age were the more intimidating for their contrast to his pale face, which was usually florid with high temper and wine. He gazed thoughtfully at Algar. 'I've had a visitor in the night.'

'He must have brought sorry news to make you – did he come from the king?'

The bishop smiled slightly and eased his posture in the stall. 'No, he wasn't from the king, at least not from King Henry. Nor did he bring me bad news. Quite the contrary. But, Prior, I think he would have made even your heart shake if you had seen him.'

'What do you mean, Your Grace? Who was he? Where was he from?'

The bishop turned his eyes to the eastern end of the church and gestured briefly with an upward-pointing finger that indicated the hidden apse, not the altar and screen which hid it. 'From up there, I suppose, where he sleeps.'

Algar drew back involuntarily and blessed himself. 'What, St. Cuthbert?'

'So he said.'

A silence. Algar collected himself. So this was the joke, prepared for with such care. Ranulph doubted the legend of the saint, as everyone knew. But to take this method of dishonoring it!

Algar said coldly: 'My lord, you must have been dreaming. Why should the holy patron of our house come to you?'

Ranulph sighed. 'I thought it might be a dream, too. But I was broad awake. I was sitting at my desk writing a letter. I pricked my wrist with my pen a few times, to make certain of it.' He showed Algar dark marks of blood or ink on his left arm. 'No, it was – he.' He swayed his head in the direction of the shrine, but kept his eyes on Algar.

'I knew him, from the day we took him from the old shrine and put him up there, remember? Or were you here then? A scrawny old corpse with sunken mouth and white hair, wrapped in a linen shroud – the one the old virgin of Tiningham made for him, I suppose. Skin, bones; toothless; and he stank! Not like roses, I tell you, but all the sheep he ever herded in his youth in the Lothians. Jesu!'

In spite of himself, Algar cast a swift glance in the direction of the shrine. Ranulph made a vivid picture, but Algar, too, had seen the saint when they had enshrined him there twenty-four years ago. He'd been a chorister, only a boy, but he remembered the old shepherd's frizz of hair and the round *O* of a fallen, lipless mouth. He made himself remember, too, that this was all a farce.

'And what did he say, my lord? Was there some dire warning or prophecy? Some rebuke for the brothers of the house?'

Ranulph wheezed out a laugh. 'It was I he came to see, not you or your rustic brothers, you conceited man!' Laughter made him cough, and coughing made him breathless for a time.

'He came to chide me for dawdling. Oh, he was hopping mad – hopping – and snapping his gums together like an old mad toad! At me! I'm to blame for not getting the work finished, you understand. Tell that to your parsimonious brethren at the next chapter, will you? I've – failed – to build his church in time. His church! I've spent the third part of my life at the task, but I get no thanks and it isn't even my own I've poured out a fortune for. No, it's his! My labor was only for his gratification, you see.'

Algar studied him, purse-mouthed. 'Surely that isn't what the saint would say, my lord.'

'Oh, isn't it? Well, I couldn't tell you the half of all he said between Lauds and cock-crow. He speaks Latin in the most abominable way, and he kept shaking that filthy severed head about – '

'What?'

'The head of that king – Oswald, was it? Yes, it was put in the coffin with him by some fool at his first enshrinement. Well, he doesn't like its company. He wonders what Christ will say to him when he comes wagging it up to the Judgment Seat.' A fit of coughing interrupted him.

Algar said in a frigid voice: 'But surely, my lord, the Blessed Cuthbert has been with Christ all this time.' Ranulph's pitiful grasp of dogma appalled him almost as much as his blasphemy. He straightened his back. 'I believe you have had either a sick fancy or a most vivid dream, which you must take as a warning to change your life.'

'I took it as a warning,' Ranulph muttered.

Brother Edwin returned with the infirmarian, Brother Fergus, who put his practiced hand on Ranulph's brow to test him for fever, then searched his eyes for signs of delirium. But the bishop rejected his ministry.

'Get your dirty finger out of my eye, you fool. You'll be wanting to count my teeth next, as if I were a horse, which is an animal you're better fit to physic than a man. If you want a diagnosis, I'll furnish one: I am sick. I'll soon die. There!'

'My lord Bishop,' said Fergus in a wounded voice, 'I have already sent word to your palace for your own physician to come and tend to you. But if you want to be well again, you'll leave off taking his vile

Italian concoctions and let me bleed you in the infirmary.'

'Let me be, Fergus, you butcher. I came here to make my peace and die quietly. Otherwise, I'd never come so near you and your filthy leeches!'

Algar said: 'If you are truly ill, as I believe you must be, you'd do well not to mock your benefactor. But if you won't have his help, go home and rest in your own good bed, my lord. Prayers will be said for your recovery at Vespers and at every other Hour, both here and in the chapel of your own house. If you – '

'THIS is my *house*!'

The startled monks stared at him as the mighty cavern of the choir vault caught up Ranulph's shout and gave it back in response: THIS-my-HOUSE-this-house-my-house-house-house.'

Ranulph Flambard fell back against the choir stall, gasping. 'If your precious patron could elect to crawl into a cave – to die – on a whim – then I – may die *here*. *I* am the Bishop of Durham!' His eyes squeezed shut suddenly; his dark brows contracted in pain; his breath wheezed in his throat.

Brother Edwin whispered: 'Perhaps, Reverend Father Prior, until this seizure passes, we could make him more comfortable with a pallet here?'

'Bring him a pallet,' Algar said curtly.

By midday when the brothers came to celebrate the High Mass, Ranulph the bishop was lying comfortably on a sheeted straw paillasse such as pilgrims and those taken into sanctuary were offered for their rest. The whole priory and those in the town below it now knew he was dying. Only Algar had heard the tale of his interview with the good saint of Lindisfarne.

If the general populace got word of that story, they would be crowding into the church, miring its aisles with their muddy feet, abusing its holy silence with fatuous questions. Algar thanked God Ranulph had not chosen to reveal his 'vision' to anyone else; but it troubled him, and had he not had a severe sense of his own duty, Algar might have mentioned it to someone. Half of him still clung to the belief there was some planned mockery on Ranulph's part, though the bishop had now lain for several hours at the foot of the high altar and looked as clear of conscience as a suckling babe. He had his hands clasped so firmly in prayer that they remained locked together even when he napped.

If the tale were true, thought the prior, what a glorious lesson it would make! Yet he could say nothing even to his own chancellor, who was like a blood brother to him.

The few stonemasons who dared to take leave of their work on the heights of the walls and descend their ladders in hope of discovering what went on were driven out at once by Algar and his doorkeepers.

While Mass was sung, Algar could look down from his stall to where Ranulph lay, broad head and silvered hair gleaming under the candlelight. He seemed alert for a man who was at the point of death, Algar thought. Two candles were set upon the floor, one on either side of his head; he gazed at them, blinking, or he turned his head, following the movements of the priest and his deacons in the Divine Service. Occasionally he joined with the monks in some brief phrase, his voice still surprisingly strong, though slightly off pitch.

When the Mass was concluded, two of the younger monks stepped out of the departing company and fell to their knees to aid him with prayer. Waiting on the far side of the choir screen in the nave were certain members of the bishop's family and household who were forbidden – like all who were not brothers of St. Cuthbert's – to come beyond the Jesus Altar. In his own good time Algar came out to them, and seated himself on a faldstool before the altar, as if to hear confessions. He ignored the bishop's sons, the archdeacon and his brother, when they crept past him to interview their father in defiance of the Rule. In a few moments they returned.

'This is ridiculous!' said Martin, the bishop's eldest son. 'He isn't going to die from a mere pain in the arm. He's had that for years.'

'Still, old men will die of something,' Algar answered.

'And to say he's had a vision – '

'Who says that?' Algar asked.

'He does, by God! That alone should tell us he's senile. Someone's been putting ideas in his head. My father never had a vision in his life!'

'Nor have I. Nor have most men,' Algar said coolly. 'But I do not dispute with a bishop when he says he has.'

He disliked this bastard of the bishop's more than the rest. Some of the sons and nephews were decent enough men, like Ranulph the archdeacon. Some were incompetent but harmless, like Thomas. Thomas had once been made the child Bishop of Lisieux during his father's time of exile, but the people of that Norman city had rejected him, the Archbishop of Rouen had finally deposed him, and now he was a simple parish priest.

Martin fitz Ranulph was his father's secretary, the only one of his sons not in Holy Orders, by all accounts his favorite, though he was a constant complainer and railer against his father. As much as Algar detested Ranulph for his vices, he could almost pity him for having a son like Martin.

'I say, I think someone's been putting nonsense into my father's head, Prior, in order to humiliate him and disgrace our family,' Martin said with heavy inflection on the 'someone.'

Algar turned a glacial gaze to meet and match Martin's glare. 'If His Grace is humbled here, God alone does it for the salvation of his soul. What other humiliations he suffers are at the hands of those who purport to love him. Surely you wouldn't number me among his sycophants, would you?'

Martin's heavy face flushed to the hairline. 'Do you judge me, Prior? Don't attempt it. You know nothing of humiliation, unless you know what I've suffered at his hands.'

'No man may tell the sins of another,' Algar said, and dismissed the man by blessing himself in preparation for silent prayer.

Another voice spoke in his ear after a respectful pause. Algar opened his eyes, then stood up to honor the presence of Osbert, sheriff of Durham and the bishop's nephew, who held the fee of Bishop Middleham and was a most worthy friend of the abbey.

Osbert said: 'I'll clear these rascals out for you, Prior, and give you a rest, but first, answer me a question.'

Algar nodded.

'Is he really in danger of dying?'

'His Grace says he is dying. When I was speaking to him this morning he was seized with a sudden pain. He clutched his left arm and his chest, and complained of pains such as he has suffered before. He has trouble in breathing and his extremities are cold. I believe he knows the state of his own health as well as his physician, whom he has refused to let examine him.'

Osbert grinned. 'Well, his wits haven't fled altogether, then, have they? But why won't he go home to bed? I never knew him to pass up feathers for straw before.'

'Have you spoken to him about it?'

'I have.'

Ranulph the archdeacon came forward. 'He said something odd, about wanting to make certain his soul was properly lodged. I told him he could pray himself to Heaven as well from a good bed, but he said he didn't mean that. What do you make of it?'

'Senility!' said Martin from behind them.

Algar bowed his head. 'He is both bishop and abbot here. If he wishes to make his peace with God on a pallet before the altar, there is no man to say he may not.'

Osbert nodded and, being a busy man, took his leave. After a time the rest of the household reluctantly began to slip out of the nave, followed by their servants, who had been waiting near the baptismal font. Algar was left alone. He decided it was no part of his duty to spend the day in personal watch over the penitent. He returned to his work and didn't come to the chancel again until just before Vespers.

He found Ranulph awake and the two novices praying for him, weeping. He dismissed them. He knelt, said a brief prayer, and spoke to the bishop.

'It will be dark soon, Your Grace, and there will be no one in the sanctuary until Compline, after which it will certainly be too cold here for a man in your state of health. Let me have the infirmarian carry you to a more comfortable bed, or let us take you home.'

Ranulph studied him. 'No, I like it here. This is the most beautiful choir vault in the world, if I say so myself. I want to hear the brothers sing Vespers, Compline, and Matins against it just once more. As for the cold, I'm always cold these days, but have them bring me a blanket and I'll do well enough.'

'You haven't eaten. Shall you want food brought into the sanctuary as well?'

Ranulph smiled at the rebuke. 'I'm finished with eating, except what's lawful here. Before they come for Vespers I'll confess myself and take the Sacrament. My pain is gone now and I can speak.'

'I'll send for your confessor.'

'Why? He's a fool. Besides, I haven't made a full confession to him in the whole time I've had him. No use to flatter him now. Does that shock you? It shouldn't. You're a priest. You know our worst temptation is to conceal in ourselves what we'd force out of others. We're the greatest temporizers, prevaricators, and self-deceivers in the world, aren't we? Worse even than kings. All reason and no feeling in the end. I haven't made a complete confession with my tongue for nearly forty years and it would weary me to try now. But hear what I can manage, and I'll see you know the rest before I die.'

'I cannot absolve what I do not know, my lord.'

'Oh, God, how tedious it must be to be righteous!' Ranulph sighed, put his hand to his throat, and tugged at something under his gown. 'Here, help me pull it off.'

Algar felt the chain and pulled it until a small key came out of the monkish robe. He lifted Ranulph's head to draw it off him. The key was of iron, but the chain was gold, and, though fine, quite heavy for its size.

'There you have it,' said the bishop, 'the key to my unrighteous life. When I am dead you may paw through my vices to your heart's content, but now believe that I am heartily sorry for all my sins, remembered or otherwise, because most of them gave me more trouble and less pleasure than I could believe before I committed them. God hear me, amen. Is that enough for now? Then hear my confession.'

Algar nodded.

2

When Algar asked after a pause, 'Is there anything else?' Ranulph gave him such a wry look of amusement the prior suspected once again that all could yet be revealed as a morbid prank. He imagined a merry, wine-besotted Ranulph regaling dinner guests with his droll description of how monks and relatives scurried at the prospect of his dying – of his prior's gullibility in particular.

'I can remember no more that I have leisure to tell,' Ranulph said. 'But I'd think you'd heard enough for now. My sins are as multitudinous as the lawsuits of the English. God forgive me them, as I hope for His mercy, in Jesus' Name, amen.'

Algar gave him conditional absolution, then administered the Sacrament. The bishop continued to fix his eyes on him strangely as he received the Bread on his tongue, the Wine to his dry lips, and the holy oil to his head and hands. When the prior had put away the sacred Articles, removed his stole, kissed its emblem, and folded it, he picked up the chain and key from the floor to weigh them in his palm again.

'What am I to do with this, Your Grace, if you don't require it of me again?'

'Deal justly with that which it brings you. Keep it, or throw it away. I don't suppose it really matters, though once I thought it might. Algar – have you ever considered what is the worst aspect of dying?'

'The pains of Hell, which we must suffer if we die in our sins. So we are taught.'

'Oh, well. Perhaps. Frankly, Hell and all its provinces have been so embellished by the human imagination, I find some difficulty understanding how that country can be administered. No disrespect to your belief, but I have a more personal one.'

'Yes, I should think you would.'

'It's really so simple that – no, *you'd* not laugh. You'd only think me the same wicked ignoramus as before. I'll tell you anyway. It is: just not to be here, after.'

Algar considered the proposition and shrugged.

'Oh, I can well imagine the dying,' said Ranulph. 'And being shrouded, put into the tomb, and all that. It doesn't frighten me. I've seen it too often. I can even imagine being roused to take part in some Divine courtroom procedure without fear. I'm a fairly good attorney, you know. I can hold my own with the Devil if the law is clear. And it will be, because I do believe in the mercy of God. I've seen it demonstrated, though in some peculiar ways.

'What I can't take in is – not *being* – between the two events, burial and judgment; not being aware of anything, especially anything that was of interest to me in life.

'For example, where are you going to get the money to finish this work, once you don't have me grubbing it out shilling by shilling? I never will know that. Do you see? Where'll you get it, Algar, if the king keeps the see vacant and pockets my rents? He will, you know.'

He sighed impatiently. 'God knows, the horror of death to me isn't that it imposes the worm, as old Turgot liked to say at funerals, but that it imposes *absolute* ignorance and impotence.'

'Those who live in Christ may look down on the world and even on Hell, as Lazarus looked on the rich man who thirsted.'

'A loathsome story, I always thought. Why would the saints get any pleasure from that? I wouldn't. I'm too squeamish. What I want to know about isn't the general doings of Earth, but what happens here. What will my eventual successor do to my church? Will he complete it according to my plan, or will he want to put minarets on it because he's been to the Holy Land and fallen in love with the temples of the heathen?'

He snorted. 'That's possible, you know. I could name a man in France right now who says the heathen pointed arch is more elegant than our good Roman ones. So who's to say some future bishop won't think little twisted spires more elegant than honest towers?

'Ah, God, but I want to know how this land, this country, will survive without me! Lift your brows if you will, but when the king makes one of his slab-faced bastards Earl of Durham, who'll spend *his* life and our revenues in France, you'll see my point. And there's more: will the Scots leave us in peace? I doubt it. The present King of the Scots longs to enter Heaven a hero. He must have his wars and his slaughters, or his thanes will grow bored and turn to their favorite occupation, which is the murder of Scottish kings, eh?'

Algar nodded in spite of himself. He was an implacable foe of all Scots, save the royal and the sanctified. But he temporized for conscience' sake.

'My lord, your fears are unfounded. You have an ample host at your disposal and good captains to lead them. The King of England is also a famous soldier who won't let his kinsman rob him. Besides, King David is half English. He holds an earldom of our king, and he has sworn to uphold him and his daughter when that lady becomes our rightful queen. We will fight no more wars with Scotland. We're Christian countries both, now.'

'Oh, Algar, what a babe you are! That oath was forced on the Scot as it was on everyone else. Nobody will support Maud but her bastard brother, who'd like to rule through her. There'll be no queens here. The English don't like the title and the French don't like Maud's airs, calling herself empress. When Henry dies, all who were sworn will throw that oath out the window and take to the old ways of choosing a king, by treachery and by battle. You'll have wars, Algar.'

He was becoming more excited as he spoke and began to rub his breast with a clenched fist again. 'Lord God, if bishops were permitted to name their successors as kings do, I'd choose mine better than Henry Beauclerk will.'

He sighed. 'Well, it's past grieving for, I suppose, but not past hope.' He smiled at Algar in his secret, irritating way. 'I didn't tell you this morning, did I? It's not as good as a fresh life in good health, but I had it revealed to me by my *visitor* that there's a way I may be spared what I most dread.'

'God grant Your Grace is spared for many years,' Algar said without conviction.

'No, no, I mean after I die.' His dark eyes sparkled in the old manner. 'Why, man, I speak good news for you as well as myself, if you love this place as I do. I've seen the proof with my own eyes, heard it with my ears, and confirmed it with logic as I lay here today. It isn't a matter of sanctity; only one of desire, desire surpassing the desire for Heaven.' He reached for Algar's arm and gripped it.

'I may remain here, watch over my treasure, see my work

completed, see the future come to pass. You could, too, if you desired it enough.'

'Oh, my lord, for shame! That's blasphemous! Don't think such things. If you fancy you can linger in the spirit at your will, you put your soul in danger. God is the only warden of our souls. When He calls us, we must go to Him. Only the damned are left on Earth to wander, or those who are buried in unhallowed ground to walk about. It's horrible to imagine such a fate, let alone desire it!'

'Nonsense! *Then why does Cuthbert walk?*'

Algar tore his arm free from the bishop's grip and rose unsteadily. His face was as pale as Ranulph's.

'Answer me that, Algar! If only the damned or unchurched linger, how is he free to pay calls on the living when he chooses? He does! I haven't been the only recipient of his visitations. I never credited the rumors before, but now I've seen him, just as others have done. He came to my chamber in the night and spoke to me.'

'No!' Algar cried angrily. He stumbled toward the altar, above which the crucified Christ hung in perpetual anguish that Man need fear the mouth of Hell no more. The prior communed with that Figure for a moment, then said in a somewhat calmer voice:

'No, my lord, it isn't so. The common people may say it, but I have been a watcher in this place for thirty years and I have never seen' – he made himself turn from the gloom of the apse where Cuthbert lay sleeping under stone – 'anything.

'My lord, legend and suggestion are insidious. Tell a man a ghostly tale at a late hour and he's more apt to believe it than if you told it him at cock-crow. You were ill. You dread death as do all men. Your mind was weary, dwelling on the cares of your office. Somehow you were reminded of St. Cuthbert and – ' A shudder took him unexpectedly, and for a fraction of time he lost his grasp on certainty. There had been a shadow in the apse, darker than the rest. 'It is the late hour that calls phantoms to our brain.'

'Nothing calls them. They come when they will, not because of suggestion, or the hour, but because they will, damn it! In spite of Heaven, Hell, or the dungeons of Purgatory, they are here, Algar. Whether by the grace of God or the strength of his own will, Cuthbert does it. And soon so shall I.' The look on Ranulph's face when he uttered that prediction made Algar want to rush from the sanctuary into the last of the day's warm light, but he said firmly:

'Your Grace, I am bound to believe in the life to come and in the power of the saints to perform miracles – '

'But not in my doubtful witness, eh?' Ranulph rolled over onto his hands and knees, making an effort to rise. He flung up one hand, and Algar caught it and helped him to his feet. For a moment Ranulph's face was screwed tight with pain, then his brow cleared. He pushed Algar away and stood alone. His laughter was almost silent.

'Prior, your precious saint came to me last night with his unjust complaints, and I was too thunderstruck by the revelation to answer him, but now I shall. I lay all his charges at your feet. It was you I've had to contend with all these years when I tried to make our work here proceed at some better pace than a crawl. You've bewailed and begrudged me every penny spent, including what I gave from my own treasury. You've cried extravagance at every load of stone, at the hire of every stonecutter. I think you wouldn't mind if the work here lasted a thousand years, so long as the intent to finish it was registered with the Almighty.

'You can't see the need for beauty in anything but a psalter. You won't appreciate a brave man, a fair woman, a fine horse, a lustrous jewel, or a splendid church. You think yourself above all things of this world, yet you worship money. Yes, you do! You won't spend it, but you love to see it stored up in a checker roll, neat and final. That's a kind of avarice, my friend. The old visitor had something to say to me on that score last night – maybe he has a message for you, too.'

'I'll not stay with you if you take to ranting, my lord. I have better use for my time.' Algar made a move to leave, but Ranulph caught him by both arms.

'No! You say you believe the dead are called up by fevers in the brain? Well, I'm warm enough; let me call Cuthbert and see if he comes again.' He spun Algar around to face the apse. 'Cuthbert! Cuthbert, rise up, do you hear me? Here's a doubter. Come out of your marble bed where I once put you! Unwind your stale sheets and show yourself to this miserable man!'

The whole vault of the choir took up the cry and made an antiphony of it. The sub-sacrist coming into the church to light the candles for Vespers heard the din and rushed into the choir to see his prior wrestling with his bishop, like Jacob with the angel.

'What is it? What is it? Reverend Father! Your Grace!'

Algar shouted: 'Bishop, this is infamous! You alarm the brothers and offend the sanctity – '

'Look!' Ranulph cried at the same moment. 'There! There he comes again! Tell him, old man! In the Name of Christ on the Damascus road. Intelligence from beyond the tomb! Elias and

Elijah! Oh, wonderful – ' The last word was uttered in sudden reverence. Surprise stiffened Ranulph's face. He let his arms fall from Algar's neck. Algar, staring into his face, saw a joy reflected there that made him almost shriek with terror. He dreaded to look behind him for its source, but his head turned without his volition, and as it did, Ranulph slumped against him and slid to his knees, stayed for an instant, then fell full length with a groan.

'No – more – then.'

There was no one in the twilit apse, but there was a sound in the prior's head, like the echo of sound that has stopped.

With the sub-sacristan's help he rolled Ranulph over just under the shrine of the Blessed Virgin, where her devotional candles were guttering in the breeze that at sundown always sighed through the church. Ranulph opened his eyes.

'Oh, Lady of Stone – '

'Be silent! You're killing yourself!'

'I who have been a lover of earth's women, have loved you long and well; take me in your arms and do not spurn your most – constant lover.' His voice came on a thread of breath. 'I wasn't addressing the Virgin, Algar.'

To his dismay, Algar found his eyes smarting with tears, though they might well have started from rage. He followed the bishop's anguished gaze up to the dark vaulting overhead.

'Get the infirmarian, Brother,' he said to the sub-sacristan. 'Tell him to bring a litter.'

'Take my ring,' Ranulph gasped. 'Put it there – on the altar.' So, he truly believed himself to be dying and now relinquished his symbol of authority, gave it back to God as was proper. Algar worked the thick gold band with the large uncut sapphire off the old man's middle finger. He cupped the ring in his palm, then raised Ranulph's head to ease his harsh breathing. The prior turned to the apse again for a brief look, but flinched away to gaze instead at the massive piers flanking the choir and presbytery. They were variously carved with chevrons, checkers, spiraling, and fluting, and they stood up like trees to the branching arches they supported, tier upon tier, to the ribbed vaults. It was like no other in England or in the world.

Lady of Stone; yes, that was what the bishop meant in his babbling. Not the Lady of Heaven, but this abiding matron of a church, dedicated to the Blessed Virgin's name. Lady of Stone that would stand eternally, beholding and beheld of God and Man.

'She might have another lover if he would let himself bend to it,' murmured Ranulph, whose eyes had opened again.

Algar didn't reply. Of all the bishop's traits, his sentimentality offended the prior almost as much as his pride, his avarice, and his un-Christian temper. He composed his mind to a prayer for the bishop's soul. In such men as Ranulph sentiment could be as beguiling as the *ignis fatuus* and as dangerous to take for a guide.

Fergus came with his assistant to take up the old man and carry him to his palace. The brothers shuffled their feet to the choir aisle, waiting for a sign to come in and begin the Vespers service.

Algar turned away to lay the bishop's ring on the altar. He remained there to make sure there were no tears on his face before he took his place in the stalls. He didn't fear to let the brothers see him weeping, but he did fear they might think him distraught for other reasons. The tale of his wrestling with Ranulph had undoubtedly burned through the little community like wildfire.

Ranulph Flambard came to his mortal illness on the feast day of St. Giles, Helper of Cripples, which was also the calends of September. Removed to his palace, he fell into the hands of his Italian physician, who hung over him with fumigations, brewed him potions, bled him copiously, and on his behalf consulted books of astrological prognostication. In spite of these ministrations Ranulph seemed to recover. He was sitting up in bed within a few days, drinking a clary of wine, honey, and pepper and receiving the powerful men of his county who came to pay probable last respects to their spiritual and temporal lord.

Algar was one of those called to the palace by the command of the bishop. He stood in the sumptuous presence hall, disdainful of its comforts, which, for the rougher north country, were considerable. Padded benches and cushioned, painted arm stools in the Roman style were set around a well-banked hearth. The floors were strewn thick with white oat straw, of which the bishop was very extravagant. He had it swept up and renewed weekly when he was in residence and liked to have it sprinkled with sweet herbs and lavender, as if it were a lady's bower.

Standing apart, Algar watched the other guests covertly. All the heavy-landed lords were there: the Amundvilles, the Bonnevilles, the Conyers, Escollands, and such. They drank their lord's honeyed wine and talked, not of his imminent death, but rather of the affairs of King Henry which kept him so long abroad in his Norman country. With more relish they also spoke of their brood mares, their stud bulls, or their grandchildren.

Among them stood the bishop's bastards and nephews: Martin,

scowling into his wine cup; Thomas the priest, smiling at nothing; his twin, Ralph, parson of Middleham, chatting with his lame brother, Elias, canon of Lincoln. The last born, William, was the only one among them who looked as if he might weep at the funeral, and then perhaps only for the smallness of his legacy.

The nephews were more favored than the sons. Osbert was sheriff; Ranulph was archdeacon; Robert and Richard held wealthy manors in plenty. Strange, but then it must be conceded they had more initiative than their cousins, too. All of them, sons and nephews alike, were made in the bishop's mold: dark-eyed, sallow, handsome, and portly, except Elias, who was thin, and young William, who was fair and mild-eyed.

After an hour's wait, Algar was on the point of returning to his priory when the bishop's chamberlain called out his name with those of several others and beckoned them to follow him to the bedchamber.

The bishop sat up in his kingly bed, leaning on a pile of wool-stuffed pillows and clad in a shirt white as his fringe of hair. His eyes acknowledged Algar's presence, but he spoke first to the others, and at length. By the time they were instructed, blessed, and dismissed, Algar was bored and impatient to be gone. But he advanced to the bedside and bent to kiss the bishop's ring, which son Martin had come to recover no more than an hour after it had been laid upon the altar.

Ranulph smiled and patted the bed with its rich coverlet of indigo wool backed with hares' skins. 'Sit down, Brother. You look weary.'

'Thank you, Your Grace, but I prefer to stand.'

'Sit, Algar.'

Algar obeyed, stiff as a lance shaft.

Ranulph rested on his pillows and studied him.

'I see you're still offended with me, Prior. As you should be, of course. Forgive me for mocking you that day. You showed no more skepticism than I would have displayed myself if the Bishop of Winchester told me he'd been seeing St. Swithin. Forgive me for charging you with the worship of treasure, too. You have a task to do, which is to keep a tight grip on the purse strings of your house, and you do it well. Whatever our differences in the past, I've never thought you unfit for your office.'

'Thank you, Your Grace.' There was a little silence. Algar was unaccustomed to hearing apologies from his superior, equally unaccustomed to framing graceful acknowledgments.

'Your Grace gave me a valuable chain with a key when you were ill. I would prefer to return it, lest you should want it later.' Like the ring, he thought.

'No, keep it. And take away with you what goes with it. My chamberlain will give you the red box when you leave.'

'The red box, my lord?' he asked, but he was unmoved and incurious.

The bishop smiled and shrugged, almost defensively. 'Yes. Nothing of value, really. Some writings of mine, kept over the years. It's a chronicle of sorts. I began it in the London Keep, to pass the time. It's a boring business, being a prisoner. I'm no scholar, but I took some part in the affairs of the world. I thought history might someday give me a bad report. And so it may – it's a gloomy tale bearer. Now, I care only if the muse remembers I did some little work here.' His deep eyes fixed on Algar for a moment, as if hoping for some agreement on that point. Then, in a swift change, the eyes sparkled and he smiled.

'It's not fit reading for children at any event, so take it away with you, for the sake of my "innocents." It would please me if you could find a place for it. There may be a day when someone makes use of it.'

Algar said: 'Very well, Your Grace, I shall take your generous gift to the priory. Have I your permission to read these writings, or shall I simply put them in safekeeping?'

Ranulph grinned. 'Why, Algar, do you mean you could avoid the temptation to peep into that box, even if I should say no? I was the friend of William the Red and may have recorded a crime or two still uncharged to him – or to myself. I told you I'd let you have my whole confession in good time. Don't you want to know all you've absolved me of, confessor?'

Algar felt the prod and responded: 'I do as my lord requires, no more, no less. But I won't have your – relatives – saying I overreached my authority. As to your confession, you made a general one. It's between you and God whether you stand truly absolved.'

'Spoken like a true monk! Well done! I believe you, by St. Michael and all his angels, I do, Prior! Very well, I'll charge you with only two things: don't read my chronicle until I'm dead, and don't let it fall into the hands of my eldest son. Destroy it tonight, if you like, but don't let Martin have it. Is that injunction enough for you?'

Another man might have felt pleased to have his suspicion confirmed, but not Algar. He said dryly, 'In all that Your Grace commands I am your obedient servant.' He nodded and left the chamber.

Downstairs he saw William the chamberlain and raised his finger to summon him, then waited at a distance from the company until the man brought him the box.

Martin slouched in grim meditation over his wine cup, not taking part in the talk, but he kept his eye on Algar and roused himself when the chamberlain returned from the bishop's scriptorium with a vermilion-stained, large flat box.

'Here, what's this? Are we dividing spoils already?' Martin lurched from his stool to confront Algar. 'That's my lord's writing box, which he's very particular about. What're you doing with it, Prior?'

'Obeying His Grace's wish that it be taken to the priory,' Algar replied calmly.

'In the Devil's name! When he's dead, maybe, but it's early times to be ransacking the house. Give it to me.'

Algar stared at him without either defending himself or giving up the box, which he found to be quite heavy.

'Martin, for the love of God, the prior's no thief,' said Elias, but Martin turned on him.

'No thief, maybe, but the old man's in his dotage. He doesn't know what he says half the time. If he did, he'd never give this up. It's one of his peculiar treasures and he doesn't let anybody touch it, not even me, so he'd be damned unlikely to give it to this dry stick, wouldn't he?' He took it from Algar, who didn't resist him.

'Let him have it back, Martin,' said Osbert.

Martin glared at him. 'Hold your tongue, too, Cousin. We may all be bastards here, but I'm the eldest of them and the natural heir, at least until the will is read. I won't have my property carried off piecemeal.'

'Algar, are you carrying off a great treasure of jewels?' Elias drawled. 'My esteemed half brother is right. We can't let any rarities slip from our grasp, since none of us is likely to earn a bishop's miter like Father's.' He smiled apologetically at Algar, lifting one shoulder slightly. 'Chamberlain, take this fabulous strongbox and lock it up safe again, until we know what wonders it holds.'

Algar returned to the priory in a vile mood. It wasn't within his capacity to relieve his heart by damning Martin to Hell aloud or in his mind, but he made the afternoon a torment to his sub-prior and dean. By Vespers he was deeply aware of his mistreatment of them and spent an extra hour on his knees by way of penance after the service, giving his thin shoulders in addition a dozen ritual lashes with his cincture.

Following chapter he was in his lodge that evening, determined to add to his penance by remaining wakeful from Compline to Matins, in order to pray for the souls of the bishop and his sons. Beyond putting himself to the lash the whole time, he could imagine no more rigorous self-discipline.

He was disturbed when he had been at his prayers no more than a quarter of an hour. He rose from his calloused knees and opened the door, expecting to see the night porter, but it was Elias, holding the unwieldy red box. He entered the lodge hurriedly and with a gasp of relief set the box on a table.

'Heavy! The old man must have it well packed. I took the liberty of asking him about it when you'd gone, and he told me to bring it to you.'

'What will your brother say when he finds it missing?'

'Don't worry about Martin. Nobody else does, really. He's in his cups now. He probably won't remember the matter tomorrow, but if he does we shall all simply look bemused until he gives it up and is drunk again, which never takes long, the fool.' He rubbed the weary arm that had carried the box.

'Can you believe, Algar, knowing my own many virtues and those of my siblings, that Martin is the only one of us Father ever gave a shaved farthing for?' He smiled. 'Well, parenthood is astounding, isn't it? In spite of its popularity with the masses, I'm glad I never experienced it.'

He glanced around the room as if hoping to be offered some token of hospitality for his trouble, but there was neither fire nor wine flagon and none was forthcoming. He took it easily, as he took everything.

'Well, I won't detain you from your bed any longer, Prior. God keep you. Tell me if there really are any jewels in the box, won't you? I'd deserve a finder's fee, mightn't I?' He waved casually as he went out the door.

With the grim knowledge that he was breaking his pledge to the bishop, Algar went at once to the box and opened it. If there was a single jewel, a bitten penny, or a grain of gold in it, he would return the whole thing at once. Not even the pearls from King Solomon's crown would he keep if it left him open to another accusation from the detestable Martin. Besides, any treasure hidden by the bishop must be illbegotten indeed, or he would have adorned his stout person with it, as he had done with a king's ransom in heavy rings and ornaments throughout his reign over Durham.

3

The box was a portable desk, which the bishop had used in his travels about the realm when he was chief executor of justice in the royal courts. Once it might have held the records of his fierce extortions from the people, English and French alike, when he drove them to penury and distraction with his demands for money to stuff the war chest of his master, the greedy and ambitious King of the English. Now it appeared almost empty.

The thin lid was hinged in the middle, to fold back and provide a place for a book or letter that was being copied. Under it were lidded compartments for sealing wax, flint, candles, pumice, talc, ink powder. The smell of old wood and old parchment was not unpleasant. There were pens blunted with use, a penknife, and a few parchment scraps.

Algar lifted out the scraps, under which were one or two trinkets, including a holy medal hung from an age-stiffened thong, such as hawkers at fairs sell to country people. Its face was so battered it was impossible to identify which saint was represented on the tin stamping. It was utterly worthless.

He studied the surface of the desk, then ran his fingers along the front inner edge until he found two leather tabs, which he pulled carefully because they felt brittle. The writing board lifted to reveal the inner compartment, stuffed with parchment. There were two bundles tied with faded red ribbon of the sort used to fix under seals.

Algar made a wry mouth as he gauged the thickness of each sheaf. The bishop hadn't merely scribbled his apologia; he had written a book, even trimmed it to size for a binding press. Yet it was unreadable to the ordinary lettered man, as it was written in a court cipher familiar only to those clerks of the chancel who made use of it.

Algar would have denied he felt any disappointment in that discovery. He closed the inner lid and began to gather up the scraps and pens to replace them. One piece caught his eye out of all those with scrawled computations. It was a note written in French, which he was capable of reading.

But in a moment he crumpled it in his hand as if he were crushing vermin, then flung it from him and wiped his palm on his gown. A filthy testimony of carnal love, and the object was not even a woman!

'I found him that is my soul's lover. I held him and would not let him go until I had brought him to my mother's house . . . '

Algar snatched up the note from the floor again, threw it into the writing box, closed the lid, and returned to his grim prayers. The next day, convinced that he had done all that could be required of him, he sent the box to the script room to be stored and resolved to put the bishop entirely out of mind for the day.

On the morning following the feast day of the holy martyrs Marcellus and Valerian, Ranulph Flambard died and was brought to be buried under the floor of the chapter house by the side of his predecessor, according to custom. A message was sent overseas to Caen, advising King Henry that his border country was in need of a new shepherd. Ranulph's will was opened and read. It directed that all his worldly goods be sold and the money divided between the poor and his creditors. His sons and nephews heard the news without surprise; they returned to their homes, except for Martin, who took ship for France, where he had relatives to support him.

In time Algar bethought himself of the writing box and told his chancellor to make such use of the parchment as he could.

'It's old, but you may still be able to use it if you scrape it carefully.'

Algar had no interest in reading any more of the lies or vile adventures that the bishop may have recorded for his vain amusement, but because he neglected to forbid his chancellor to do so, the chancellor did. He was a man of greater experience but less rectitude than Algar, having served William de St. Carileph at the royal court in his youth.

He put the sheaves of parchment in a convenient place, but one that his young clerk would be unlikely to find, promising himself the pleasure of reading old Ranulph's confessions at his leisure. The pen stubs, holy medal, and other scraps he dumped out of the box after a brief examination of their content. He was amused to find the bishop had whiled away idle moments in court making free translations into the vernacular of the Song of Songs. He wondered the more that a portion of it had been so roughly rejected, then preserved after all.

THE CUCKOO'S CHILD

4

Now God help Ranulph Flambard, his servant, and the King's!

I write this in the royal keep of London on the morrow of the nones of September, in the year of Our Lord the eleven hundredth. It is also the forty-third year of my own life, I may add, and may well be my last. Is that possible? Will I end here? Dear God, I fear I may, since I am a prisoner in the hands of desperate men.

I was brought here two weeks since by six of Prince Henry's men – I must remember to name him King Henry hereafter – and shut up in this highest chamber of the southeast tower by no less a person than the constable, William de Mandeville, a man I have known for more years than I have teeth, but who looked on me then as if I had slain his father. There is no bar to my door, but there is a guard outside it and I have been warned: being charged with treason, any attempt I make to escape or to suborn my guard will be taken as a sure sign of my guilt, and my death upon the discovery of the action will be instant.

I demanded to see my accusers. I was told they were legion. I demanded to see my friend and mentor the Bishop of London. I was denied. Most grudgingly I was finally granted writing materials, so that I might send a message to Maurice at his seat at St. Paul's. The chivalrous de Mandeville permitted me to write a letter, but he would not positively swear he would see it was delivered. There is the knightly mind at work again: incomprehensible!

Under pressure of my incessant urging, my letter was at last taken to the bishop, though little good it did me. Maurice, my beloved old half-wit, sent me a typical reply, begging me to be patient! As if I were a child wheedling him for a taste of honeycomb, rather than for my life. Ah, God! But what use is it to rail against him here?

He sent me, of his goodness, a supply of ink and parchment fit to record the history of the world and urged me to begin preparing my defense, which is both ridiculous and impossible. How can I defend myself when I haven't been told what I stand accused of? Maurice, for the love of God, come and explain it to me!

How gray, damp, and barren it is in this place which I helped to build to the king's greater glory. The September rains have made the walls of my chamber to sparkle with an evil moisture. From the Thames the air comes up thick and damp in the mornings and blows sharp and chill through my window at night. I'm beginning to feel its effect in my bones as Maurice does, though he's twenty years my senior.

I cannot write my defense! I waste parchment. I waste it on this scribbling, too, yet it keeps me from going mad and shouting at the walls. If I stand on my stool, I can just see the sails of ships at anchor below in the river. I get no exercise, except I'm allowed to go down to the chapel to hear Mass. It's one of de Mandeville's ridiculous notions that I'm safe in hearing Mass, but may not celebrate it. He fears, I suppose, that I'll try to suborn Our Lord to my cause if I'm allowed to handle the Divine Substance! There's no telling what a fool thinks.

For lack of a barber my beard has grown, along with my hair, so I must resemble an ecclesiastical version of that grim and treacherous bear Robert de Mowbray, who betrayed Rufus. He's still alive somewhere, in some oubliette far worse than mine. Blind, they say; probably mad by now. He's had no trial after five years. His wife was given a papal dispensation to consider herself a widow and seek another husband, though it's certain her lord still lives. He deserved his fate. But God forgive him, I can pity him now. I'm his brother in oblivion.

How long have I been here? A month? Two? All my days run together lately and I dream, waking and sleeping. It's become difficult to tell the difference between the two. I must take care I don't jabber to myself like a dotard.

When I feel the urge to mutter I come, instead, to this table and write something: another appeal to the king, which won't be answered; the argument for my innocence, which won't be read. But my mind is cluttered with strife, and I sit instead and dream. I think of my family as they soon may be: my mother outcast and starving, my brothers disgraced, my children evicted from the cloister and sold into bondage, while I sit helpless. It is horrible what a man will think of when he has no occupation.

Oddly, my dreams are less terrible when I sleep, for then I often find myself in some moment of my past. I woke laughing last week from seeing the snow falling thick as goose down on the cloister garth at St. Vigor, where I grew up. The other oblates and I were sent out with brooms to brush it from the carrels before it turned to ice, but swept it wildly up in clouds to cover each other instead. The pure joy of the cold and our folly seemed more intense to me in that dream, or in the first waking moment after it, than the real experience, which ended in our getting arse-thumped with a cincture by the dean of order for disturbing the peace of the brothers inside.

Last night I dreamed strangely of my own begetting, which took place in a horse stall in Falaise, according to my mother, who's given to making such disclosures. I remember protesting to her: 'But, Mother, a person would have to be delirious with lust to get down to it in a horse stall, mucked out or not!'

'We were,' she said serenely.

And so they must have been, because they were an ill-matched pair on which neither the Church nor Fortune could ever be expected to smile.

Thurstin, my father, was a poor priest of the Bessin, that marshy country around Bayeux, where his family had lived in honorable penury since King Clovis was made a Christian. He had been devoted to the Church by his own father when he was about ten years old – in gratitude to God that our family hadn't been touched by the great fever sweeping France that year.

He grew up in the cathedral school of Bayeux, took Holy Orders, and served Bishop Odo fitz Herluin, Duke William Bastard's half brother. Unlike most other priests of modest birth, Thurstin could read and write. His ambition was to end his days at some great abbey in study and prayer.

My mother in her youth was a beautiful woman, filled with that peculiar fire the Bretons engender, which makes them so damned treacherous and interesting. She was the daughter of a medical mountebank who gathered herbs and sold them at fairs from Brest to Paris. To draw the crowds to him, she danced before his stall.

Most Bretons are of Gaelic stock, descended from Welshmen who took refuge in Brittany hundreds of years ago to escape Saxon pirates who invaded their land. They are, generally, fair-skinned and blue-eyed, as Thurstin my father was. But my mother was so dark, some people in our parish put it about, none too quietly, that she wasn't of Christian stock at all, but descended from heathen people who slipped into France from Moorish Spain. She was small and agile, with coarse black hair and large, fierce black eyes that could melt with sudden love or tears. My brothers and I have inherited her un-Christian color and, for us, that same inconvenient lachrymal weakness.

My parents were unlike in estate and humor and might never have glanced at each other, let alone conceived me in a horse stall, if it hadn't been for the doings of great men. In the summer of 1057 Henry le Gros, King of France, and his vassal, the perfidious Count of Anjou, made an invasion of Normandy to revenge themselves. Our duke had given them a humiliating defeat three years earlier. Duke William Bastard was then in his prime and had been our lord since he was a boy of eight. He was already a famous soldier: daring, hardy, astonishingly strong, and impassively cruel (in the manner of his family) when cruelty served him best. His tutors taught him it was better to rule by bribe and bargain than by the sword's edge alone, and he would spend freely to save breaking heads, if he could. But he could also break heads and flay backs, saving the coin, when the mood took him. Rather than rush to defend his borders with hastily arrayed men at the first news of his enemies' movements, he chose to sit in his castle at Falaise with his wife and babes, while his spies brought him intelligence of his foes.

My father, Thurstin, was one of his spies, lent to him by his brother, Odo, as casually as a good host offers his guest a hunting dog. Thurstin, terrified but obedient to his lord's wish, went through the pillaged border country posing as a seller of pilgrim's trinkets from the Holy Land. He observed that the French and Angevins, glutted from easy victories, had let discipline falter and were lumbering toward the river near Varaville, thinking to surprise the Bastard at Caen.

He gave report of them to the duke. William listened with that chill attention he gave to any hearing, then made swift plans. As the vandals struggled to pull their booty-laden wagons across the gravel riverbed – as Count Geoffrey Martel boasted to his knights that now only the sea should be an obstacle to their march – Duke William and his host fell on the flounderers. They slaughtered them in the water like boys spearing frogs.

The sodden remnant of the French who gained the riverbank tried to re-form and give battle, but they were scattered like mice, chased through the fields, and slain like hares. The King of France fled the field before the battle was well begun, and it was said of him that until he died he still dreamed and wept over the bloody waters at Varaville.

My parents must have met somewhere before that battle and celebrated its victory in the manner I have described. When the armies were dispersed and there was peace again, Thurstin brought Jehanne, my mother, home to Bayeux. Either in compensation for his good services, or as punishment for having taken a wife, Lord Odo dismissed him from his chancel, but gave him the cure of St.

Loup, a parish outside the walls of Bayeux, where I was born the following spring. In time they also bred my two brothers, Fulcher and Osbern.

As his children grew in stature and appetite, my father was hard pressed to keep his family fed and clothed, not to say respectable. Our family was poor but not base-born, as some of my enemies have said. Still, Thurstin's situation was this: he could leave us no inheritance, yet he couldn't have us slipping down into the ranks of the common villein. It became his dream to place us where the Gospel would nourish our souls and an abbey or monastery our bodies with ample and regular meals.

But the religious life is not without expense if one wants to be respectable, not just a mere lay brother consigned to fieldwork or kitchen drudgery. Most decent houses wanted as much as thirty deniers for the trouble of making a boy a monk. From Thurstin they might as well have asked the ransom of a king.

Fortune ransomed me in a strange manner. When I was about eight, Bishop Odo of Bayeux fell in love with the wit and learning of a certain scholar of the Abbey of St. Michel-sur-Mer, named Robert de Tombelene. Brother Robert was a writer of glosses on the Scriptures, with particular attention given to the Canticles of Solomon. A copy of his commentaries was presented to Lord Odo by the abbot of St. Michel.

In return for this gift and for the delight it gave him, Odo presented Robert with an old church near Bayeux called St. Vigor-le-Grand. It lay in ruins from the wars fought during the childhood of William Bastard and was little better than my father's own church at St. Loup. Nevertheless, Odo granted Robert de Tombelene a charter to make it into an abbey, and himself its abbot.

De Tombelene was of a noble family and had fully expected to be an abbot someday. St. Vigor was small for his particular ambition, but it was available, and its charter cut short the years of waiting for some better place. He gathered a dozen monks from St. Michel and other houses, and together they quickly set to work to establish themselves, aided by additional grants of land from Odo.

Now, about this same time a sign appeared in the sky at night, rapidly growing from a puzzling blur no more distinct than a smudge of ash on a dark cloth to a soul-shaking, star-dimming, three-tailed comet, streaming in mute glory across more than half the heavens.

Everyone in our village was dazzled and frightened by the size and mystery of it. Was it sent to destroy the world with its fiery tail, because we were idle and had let the Holy Sepulcher go unrescued from the heathen, in spite of the urgings of the Holy Father in Rome to a holy war? Or was it the foretelling of some great birth, or the death of some famous man like the English monk-king, Edward, who died about this time?

For Duke William Bastard the comet appeared as a promise from Heaven that he should be king in England when his pious cousin died. For his English rival, Harold Godwinson, the portent must have seemed the same.

But a common man can believe God's messages are meant for him as well as a duke or a king. My simple father took the comet as a reminder that he had once pledged me to God in atonement for having lain with my mother. Fearing that all St. Loup might be engulfed in flames for his lapse, he hurried me to St. Vigor to offer me either as oblate or hod carrier.

Abbot Robert had at the time more need of hod carriers than of indigent oblates. He needed oblates of good family who brought accompanying donations to allay the expense of his building plan. The pity was, I was almost too small to make even a laborer. He shook his head at my father.

Yet my father wouldn't retreat. He was under the inspiration of the long-haired star. He told the scholar that for seven nights he had dreamed how I would become the most famous pupil of a famous man; how I would someday grow to sit among shepherds, yet take my place in council with kings.

Naturally, de Tombelene was skeptical about premonitions, aware of how good priests are inclined to dream to their own advantage. But in the season of the comet even a skeptic could be swayed by omens. He consented to take me as a free scholar, if I proved myself both a good student and a willing laborer. I should be kept until I was twelve, at which time my father must pay him thirty deniers – or take me back again.

I scarcely knew of all this haggling. I'd been roused from my bed with my brothers in the house loft, hastily washed, crammed with bread, and pulled from my mother's arms just as I saw she was weeping. On our way to St. Vigor my fears were stopped for a time by my father's hopeful chatter on the wonderful life that awaited, the honor that might be mine. Somehow I got the notion he was taking me off to be a soldier. When we came to the abbey, I thought it was only to rest and take a meal. I was left kicking my bare heels outside the abbot's lodging for a while, then brought in for a cursory viewing.

When we came from the lodge, Thurstin took me around to the

cloister gate and rang the bell. The wall about the new abbey was just being built, and Father's application at its gate was a fiction of good manners. The bell was answered by a large, rawboned man wearing a mason's apron over a mortar-spattered black gown.

'This is my son,' my father blurted in a suddenly loud voice. 'He's to be taught here. The abbot gave permission.' He thrust me through the gate. 'Raf, remember the prayers I've taught you. Obey your masters. Love God. Never shame me.' His voice broke, and choking on some final word, he turned and fled home across the fields.

I quite naturally began to shriek out for him to take me with him, but the big monk caught me up in one arm and put a calloused, lime-caked hand over my mouth. When I didn't stop crying at once, he pinched my nostrils shut and pulled up my chin so that he could look into my face.

'Short farewells are best, boy, and silence is the Rule we live by here.' His pale eyes and sun-reddened face were as strange and terrible as a lion's. Fear and the threat of suffocation made me silent. When he loosened his grip and let my feet touch ground again, I was mute, as much from shame, and rage against my father, as from fear.

In the cloister garth the monks paused in their labors to look at me.

'So, you're to be a scholar here, are you? Come along, then, you're just in time. In the heat of the day the young ones rest and say their lessons.'

He seized me by the nape, gathering up a handful of my ragged tunic in his broad fist, and trotted me briskly across the open ground that wasn't yet a proper cloister. On the south side of the church there was a long bench set against the wall. A group of boys sat on it, their thin legs dangling. As we approached them they suddenly broke out in a caterwauling, worse than that of the legions of the damned protesting Judgment.

I balked in terror at the noise, but the big monk lifted my tunic higher, until I was forced to hop along beside him on my toes. When we reached the bench he spoke to the monk who stood confronting the howling, his back turned to us. How he could hear my captor's voice above that din I couldn't imagine, but his hand came up stiffly and made a horizontal slash through the air. The bellowing stopped as if he'd just slit a dozen throats.

'Here's another scholar for you, Cormac,' the big monk said with a grin, and propelled me forward toward the most beautiful human being I had ever seen.

5

His hair was red-hued such as I'd never seen before. His skin was so fair that even though it was mottled with freckles it gave the impression of an unblemished whiteness. His eyes were a warm, pale brown under reddish lashes; his lips were long, well-formed, and firmly set. I had never seen a religious painting or an illuminated manuscript that showed the angel of the Annunciation, but when at last I did, I recognized him.

'I'm Cormac, the schoolmaster,' he said in a musical moan, an accent strange to my ear. 'And who would you be?'

'Ranulph,' I whispered when the big monk prodded me. His name was as strange as his face and voice, so that I half believed he might be a woman, though his voice was not like my mother's, nor had I ever seen a woman so radiant.

'Ranulph? Ranulph fitz – what?'

'Just Ranulph. Thurstin's my father.'

He glanced at the big monk. 'Well, that's a simple answer. Are you simple?'

'No, my lord.'

He frowned very slightly. 'Do you mock me, boy? Do not call me "my lord."' There was a little stir of amusement among the boys on the bench, which he quelled with half a glance. 'I am Cormac, the schoolmaster. Until you are a monk and thus my brother, you will call me "master." Now, has anyone ever taught you a prayer, I wonder?'

'I know the Ave, the Pater Noster, and the Kyrie,' I burst out proudly. I might be simple, abandoned, and ugly, but I had learning. Few other boys in St. Loup knew three prayers by heart.

Master Cormac seemed amused by my claim. His eyes took in my mended shirt, ragged tunic, and bare feet. 'Very good. No doubt you have a pious mother.'

'My father taught me. He is the priest of St. Loup.' I was expecting a commendation for that, and was preparing to tell him how many proverbs I knew as well, when his face warned me to silence.

'Are you an innocent, or a bastard, that you name the priest of your village as your father?'

'I'm not a bastard!' I knew the low esteem in which such folk were held. My mother's enemies in the village were bastards, some of them the progeny of pigs and demons as well. 'He is my father! My mother is his wife!'

'A married priest is an abomination in the sight of God,' he mewed disdainfully. 'A priest who consorts with women is a burden to the righteous. Like cuckoos when their mating is done, they leave their eggs in another's nest to be hatched and fed.' His hound's eyes dwelt on me in scornful amusement. 'Do you understand my meaning, boy? You have no leave to speak proudly here because a priest damned himself for a night's pleasure and thinks he's made amends by teaching his brat a few prayers.'

I was so hot with shame and rage that my head swam. I shook it stupidly from side to side like a bull.

Cormac smiled faintly. 'You'll understand in time. Take a seat at the end of the bench now. Do not speak or fidget.'

I slunk to the bench, past the strange boys, who all dropped their glance into their laps as I passed, except one, who smiled at me slightly and lifted one shoulder. Cormac strode two steps forward and cuffed him over the head with the heel of his hand. The boy squeezed his eyes shut but didn't make a sound.

'Keep your opinions off your face, Ugo.'

I sat down heavily on the bench, at odds with myself over whether to curse Cormac in my mother's fashion and be beaten, or to make a sudden escape over the half-built cloister wall.

Cormac stepped back into his place and lifted his hand. 'Pater Noster.' His hand descended. The boys began to shout:

'Pater-Noster-qui-es-in-caelis!—Sanctificetur-nomen-tuum!—Adveniat-regnum-tuum!—Fiat-voluntas-Tua!—Sicut-in-Caelo!—Et-in-terra!

I recognized the howling this time but sat, sullen and critical of its pronunciation. Cormac cut them off sharply and pointed his finger at me.

'We have a learned cantor here who won't sing. Come forth, little David. Let us hear you alone. Perhaps you sing to a different canon.'

I wasn't going to let a lady-faced foreigner make a fool of me a second time. 'No.'

His head went up like a stallion's. 'Come forward to me on the instant!'

'No!'

He loomed over me without seeming to have passed through intervening space. He snatched me up by the nape of the neck, and his knee hit me in the stomach, bending me over it. My shirt was jerked over my head along with my tunic, while with his other hand he loosed the cincture around his waist, doubled it, and flailed my bare back and buttocks.

When his last blow was struck, he immediately removed the support of his knee and I fell on my stomach, but an instant later I was brought aloft again, my face within an inch of his. 'Recite to me, boy.'

Thus began my life at St. Vigor as an oblate in the choristers' school. The Abbey of St. Vigor-le-Grand was under the Rule of St. Benedict, but the choristers' school was under the Rule of Cormac. Between the two I was caught, as between the arms of a vise. I learned:

Never to speak to another monk or to another boy without the master's permission.

Never to touch another person, never to come so near him as to let the hems of our gowns touch, while speaking, singing in the chapel, studying, taking meals, or washing in the lavatory, unless for humanitarian reasons.

Not to scratch myself unduly, or to touch myself privately, especially while in bed.

Not to ask for more food than was offered, or to refuse to eat what was given, or to make an unseemly noise while eating or drinking without asking pardon of all who were near.

To guard my own speech and deportment, but also to be watchful and report truly the imprudence of the other boys. If I did not, and what I concealed should be of consequence, I would suffer along with the offender, if it were a punishable matter.

To bear all accusations and rebukes with a serene countenance and thank my accuser humbly for his charity for admonishing me.

Never to take particular notice of another person, to stare at him fixedly, vainly, or out of mere idleness.

Never to avoid instruction by masking ignorance with silence, but rather to seek further enlightenment. On the other hand, to remember it is a waste of the instructor's time to ask vain, silly questions only to gain attention.

For such shortcomings the punishment was light: swift blows, insults, sarcastic raillery from my instructor. Serious offenses merited stronger rebuke. To wit:

For yawning or falling asleep in the choir during service: three stripes with a cincture (or whip) to the offender's bare back, on his shirt if it be a hard winter. (Adamant refusal to obey, such as mine, was so rare there wasn't a rule for it. Cormac was to be congratulated for making such a quick decision on the gravity of the offense.)

For coughing at the beginning of a psalm (a pernicious habit), for smiling during service, for striking one's teeth against the chalice while taking the Sacrament, for choking on the Wafer: six stripes with the scourge.

For omitting grace before a meal: twelve stripes.

For engaging in vain disputes, fighting, or speaking familiarly with a female: fifty stripes.

When I learned of the last two rules, I gave thanks to God there were at least two for which I could never be punished, since it was obviously impossible to commit them. Occasion taught me otherwise.

That first day I learned most of the Rule by painful example, so vivid that by the time we were herded from our light supper on one side of the refectory to our beds on the other (the dorter was still under construction), I was ablaze with welts from Cormac's belt and my ears rang with his imprecations.

Until the dorter was built, we slept on pallets in the refectory, monks and boys alike, which was otherwise highly irregular. Boys were stuffed between monks at table and in choir, to discourage frivolity among us. At night when we knelt and said our prayers, a monk sat on his pallet by us, listening. He continued to watch over us until we were asleep, then slipped away to the chapter, which had temporary quarters in the abbot's little lodge.

At regular intervals along the refectory wall there were cresset lamps set in brackets, malodorous with kitchen grease. These were kept lighted until the brothers came to bed after Compline. One lamp at the doorway was kept alight all night, in case someone needed to thread his way through the bodies to go out to the privies.

The rule of silence was heavily imposed at bedtime. If a boy wriggled too much, snuffled over his griefs too loudly, or scratched too persistently, he might be struck lightly with a willow wand held for that purpose in the hand of his monk. No matter that the flicker of the lamps, the threat of the rod, and the very presence of so many monks made it all but impossible not to writhe, sniff, or be wakeful; woe to that oblate who, for the sake of searching out a flea, caused his guardian to be late for chapter!

When I was at last stretched out on my belly, my sore back was laced with welts and covered by nothing but an itching blanket. My shirt and tunic had been ripped apart in one of my grapplings with

Cormac. I couldn't lie still and I wouldn't be silent. I was struck several times, mere taps, really, but the last token of rebuke burst open my dam of sorrow and I began to sob aloud like a robbed Jew.

In a moment I felt someone kneel beside me. Brother Placidus, my watcher, said, 'I'll leave him to you, Brother.'

A strong, smooth hand passed over my head as I wept. It stroked my back and shoulders, pushing aside the rough cover. I felt the coolness of an unguent being applied to my burning welts; then the same firm palm continued to massage me until my sobs abated.

'It is a vain and selfish thing, to give way to tears,' Cormac murmured in his peculiar, cadenced speech, as if he were chanting a lay. 'God, Who has seen the agony of His own Son and the sufferings of the martyrs, cannot but despise the easy tears of a soft, petted boy. You have been offered food, shelter, and the precious gift of learning here, yet you whimper at the little discipline needed to make you worthy of it.'

I lay mute under the spell of his hands and his voice. I hated him, but his touch was as healing as my mother's.

'What use are tears to anyone, for that matter?' he murmured. 'They shame a man. They grieve his friends and bring joy to his enemies. They change nothing that is past, prevent nothing that will be.

'If you're weeping for your wickedness, pray God to make you better. If you weep for your bruises, harden your spirit. But if you weep to be let out of this house of learning, which seeks to lift you above the common lot of men, who are little better than beasts, then no one will keep you here against your wish. It is unlawful to do so.' His hands worked down my thin ribs and back again.

'Tomorrow you may go home. Our abbot will have less expense. There will be more soup and bread for everyone.

'Your parents will no doubt be glad to see their darling return to them with good appetite. I expect your father can apprentice you to some laborer, to keep you from starving. So, why delay? There are enough priests in your family already, one might say.'

He left me paralyzed by the doleful music of his voice and the despair it invoked. To go home was my only desire, but he had made me see it was impossible, even while he seemed to encourage it. My father's last words had been: never shame me. I would shame him by coming home again. The cuckoo's child has no nest to go home to.

Lest I grow too sentimental, let me acknowledge that my early sufferings were no worse than those any boy of my upbringing suffered under good discipline. I soon recovered my spirits and became tame to all the customs of the house – except Cormac's. I learned the psaltery by heart, though the words meant nothing to me; I learned to sing and to do simple sums; I carried mortar for the builders of our cloister walls and swept up after their labors.

Not every day was confined to lessons and hod carrying. To the abbey's fields and orchards we boys of the school might go under the guardianship of old Brother Ambrose to pick berries, harvest apples, or help bring in the hay. On those brief holidays we were allowed a little freedom to talk, laugh, run, roll in the long grass, and behave as a boy must do sometimes, if he's to keep his sanity.

It was pleasant to come in from such a day, wash the sweat and chaff from our bodies, then go to the cool church to succumb to the peace and beauty of Vespers, to be followed by a light meal of bread, cheese, and buttermilk before bed.

But the next day I would be under Cormac's tyranny again, listening to the catalogue of my character as he cuffed me repeatedly on the side of the head:

'You're an idiot! You're an idiot, bred of a whole race of brain-rotted malingerers, but I'm going to cure you of all that. By St. Kessog and his Bow, when I'm finished with you, your kinsmen will sniff you like a strange dog, you'll be so changed. Now! Recite to me: *Bonitatem facisti . . .* '

It might be supposed that once out of Cormac's grasp, we boys would want to put him from our minds as well, but when we were in the orchards or fields and found Brother Ambrose in a garrulous vein, there was no subject we were more curious to explore than our schoolmaster. I loathed Cormac; I devised imaginary plots by which I might be revenged someday for the abuse he gave me. But I, too, wanted to hear all about the monster, as if he were a camelopard, an oliphant, or some strange serpent from the ultimate seas. Where had he come from? Why did the abbot dote on him, as he most unashamedly did in the presence of the brothers?

'Cormac's an Irishman, of course, as you might tell from his name. He was a gentleman in that land, according to him, though one needn't believe much else he has to say on that score.'

'What do you mean, Brother?' asked one of the boys. 'Does he boast and tell lies?' Cormac, soiling his musical lips with a lie? Preposterous!

'Why, no, he doesn't tell lies. That's a vile sin.' Ambrose tried to amend his choice of words. 'When he first came to us, he was fevered and babbled out of his head. I've heard no more talk of royalty since then.

'I daresay it's easier being royal in his country than in other places. There, a man with a sword and a few cattle may call himself a king if he likes.'

We exchanged wise looks, but we were impressed. Cormac, a foreign prince, reduced to teaching us!

'But if he's royal, why is he a monk? I know I'd rather be a prince, if I had the choice,' Ugo said.

'Then you show your ignorance, young heathen. There's more to life than wearing fine garments and eating dainty meats. God sent our brother to teach us that; and it should be a lesson to you all.'

'How did He send him?'

'Why, as He sent Jonah: the sea spewed him up to our door. It was two years before we came to this place. He was on his way to Rome, he said, but a storm swept his ship away and left him more dead than alive on Mont St. Michel's shore. He was half drowned, with nothing on his back but a torn shirt and that harp of his, trussed in a leather bag.

'He was burning with fever when the brothers brought him to our infirmary. The Father Abbot was still only Brother Robert then, but he was ever the scholar and came down to see the boy said to be foreign. He always liked to talk to odd people, but he has a good heart. When he bent over Cormac and laid his hand on his head, the boy grabbed it and wept, thanking God for casting him among such kindly people.

'Father Abbot took to the lad as if he were his own kin, out of sheer pity, I suppose. He taught him his letters. He still gives him instruction, you know, and our Cormac's a credit to his teacher, as you should be to him.'

I took this tale to bed on many a night, savoring its strangeness. Cormac was a prince of Ireland. No wonder he despised me for my low birth. But no, he was an impostor, and someday he would be found out and dismissed by the abbot.

Someday, I would be like Father Abbot, renowned for my wisdom and learning, and the head of that very house. Cormac would return from his exile, an old and broken man. I would go to look at him as he begged for shelter within our walls. He would recognize me and fall at my feet, sniveling and whining for forgiveness. How would I reply?

In some dreams I would let him stay on as a penitent, sweeping the cloisters and cleaning the privies to earn his keep. He would bless me every time I passed and scourge himself in the sanctuary for having once been cruel to me.

In other dreams I would reject him, after reminding him of his perfidy; he would froth and rave until my flock drove him out the gate to starve on the roads as he deserved.

I couldn't say which of those dreams gave me the greater satisfaction.

When I was eleven a famine spread through England and France. In England it was owing in part to the ruin inflicted by King William Bastard and his enemy, Harold the Usurper. Our duke, now king, won his victory with the blessings of God and all His saints, we were told, but soon afterward was forced to put down a great insurrection by Scots and Danes combined with discontented English who affected to support the last English heir, Edgar Atheling.

The shire of York gave these miscreants shelter and substance while they plotted their treasons, so King William chastised the men of York by burning their houses, fields, barns, even their farming tools. He hanged every man and boy of them he could catch. All that shire and much of the country north of it were laid to utter ruin.

I remember how we in the abbey cheered when the abbot told us of the scourging of York. We of course prayed daily for the deliverance of the poor, yet those English, however poor, had betrayed our lord and so received their just punishment.

But in Normandy we soon suffered bad weather and ruined crops, too. Prices soared and poor men starved, though our land was glutted with the golden booty stripped from the English churches and religious houses by worthy men, among them Odo, our own dear bishop, who was now Earl of Kent. He had enriched our simple old church with altar vessels of gold and silver and embroidered hangings.

Lord Odo was generous to my father as well. In an expansive mood during one of his brief returns to his diocese, he heard petitions from his flock. One of the petitioners was Thurstin, who had finally screwed up his courage to remind his old master that he had once done him and his noble brother a small service. Odo embraced him, affected to remember the service, and offered my father a better living in an English church. My honest, stupid father refused it, asking instead only for thirty deniers with which to endow me as a monk of St. Vigor. As an afterthought he begged that my brothers be enrolled in the cathedral school as charity scholars.

So I was assured of a permanent cell in my prison. I felt little joy at the sight of my father the day he came to put the money in the abbot's hand and tell me his good news. I didn't want to be a monk, yet I was rapidly becoming unfit for anything else. I neither protested nor even sighed, but heard my fate with a face I had learned to model on Cormac's: serene, watchful, with the ends of my mouth turned up in a meaningless smile. It is not courteous to Our Lord and the Virgin to serve Them with a doleful face.

When my father left, I climbed up into the church tower. I was supposed to be sweeping the cloister aisles; but as it was a warm summer afternoon, most of the brothers were reading or napping in the carrels there, and my activity would have disturbed them. I excused myself.

The oblates were forbidden to climb into the tower, not so much for fear of mischief as of accident. The church was nearly a century old, and our abbot was already considering how to pull it down and build a more gracious one with twin towers and a central lantern.

In spite of the prohibition, I would gaze down on the bald pates of the brothers in the garth, out over the Joseph's-coat pattern of tilled fields, the orchards, cow pastures, and meadows where rose-thorn plows were pulled by oxen no bigger than mice.

I also liked to spy on the abbot's garden, where a little wilderness of flowers and herbs grew for the beautification of the altar and use in the kitchen and infirmary, but also for his own pleasure. He liked to sit there on a sunny day, reading, a plump, smooth man, very dainty and sparing of his movements.

Mostly I favored the tower as a place to torment the birds, not those of a dovecote attached to the abbey, but wild doves living in the tower, improvident as beggars lodged against a castle wall. They built no true nests, but laid a paltry arrangement of twigs and straws haphazardly on the belfry ledges and trustingly put their eggs among them, to hatch or be blown off by a vagrant wind. Once one of them had fallen and cracked on the head of the sacristan as he was tolling his bell. I liked to examine the eggs to see if chicks were forming inside them. The doves would swoop through the tower around my head, complaining, while I hissed and waved them off.

That was the occupation I sought to soothe my troubled mind that day. But when I came near the top I heard a more diverting sound. Music was coming from the abbot's garden. I crept around the ledge to see who made it, though I really knew. It was Cormac with the only token from his strange country, a little brass-stringed harp no longer than his forearm. At the abbot's pleasure he was sometimes allowed to neglect his studies and play in the garden.

I always thought it strange Cormac should have learned to handle anything so lovely and frivolous as the harp. In my mind he had been born with a psaltery in one hand and a scourge in the other. No one in the abbey seemed more devoted to grim duty.

I was told he had other talents. He was getting to be a respectable penman, though he still took private instruction from the abbot, and he was a good singer. His strong tenor was the foundation of the upper voices of our choir, though he had a tendency sometimes to embellish a line, which threw us off and provoked the precentor.

For me, to see him in the abbot's garth, plucking the bell-toned strings with his long fingernails and singing like David to King Saul, was such a novel and diverting sight, I forgot the birds' eggs and crept along the mossy edges of the tower ledge to watch him.

Abbot Robert sat on the stone bench next to him, their backs to the lodge wall, thick with some flowering vine. I couldn't understand the words of the song Cormac uttered; they were plainly sad. It was his native tongue, perhaps, for it had the same melancholy music as his speech.

When it was finished he tuned his strings. The abbot absently pulled at the vine by his shoulder until a piece of it came loose. He made a circlet of it and put it on his head, then laughed almost ashamedly. Cormac laughed, too, and struck up a local tune about the Leafy Man, a figure in the country folk's Maytime frolics. I wrapped my arms about the corner pier and buried my mouth in my sleeve to keep from laughing, because the words were bawdy and I knew their meaning. Also, the abbot, a sober man and famous scholar, appeared a bit of a fool in his wreath.

'Oh, I'm not the man for that song,' he said merrily when it was over. 'But, you – ' He took the wreath and put it on Cormac's head. It wasn't bound, so it came loose and fell around his face instead, the tendriled ends curling at his mouth as if they had sprung from it.

The abbot brushed them away so that they curled in the other direction, then he touched Cormac's cheek with a lingering finger. Cormac stopped smiling. They sat gazing at each other, as if turned to stone. I held my breath as I watched them, not understanding their silence, but with an instinct that this was the prologue to something I would not like but must see.

Abbot Robert took Cormac's long, sun-spattered, fair face between his fingers and kissed him on the mouth. I expected Cormac to pull back, be shocked, even perhaps to strike the abbot, but he sat quietly, only carefully putting his harp aside on the bench beside him. I was frozen in anticipation of the moment when he would act or speak.

Suddenly the bell moved beneath me, uttering its first response to the pull of its rope. I jumped at the sound and lost my grip on the pier. My feet slipped and scrambled at the ledge as the bell swung and pealed louder. I felt myself drop a sickening few inches before my hands caught at the arch abutments. I shrieked in mortal fear, but my voice was nearly lost in the noise of the Vespers bell, until it swung again and the bell ringer caught the dissonance.

'Who's there?' he cried.

I couldn't answer, only yell.

'Jesus bless us!' he bellowed. 'Devil, be gone! Oh, Lord bless the bell! Devil, be gone!' He began to ring it furiously, thinking I was one of those envious demons who liked to chew on bell ropes to keep them from summoning the monks to their prayers. I began to slide again. One of my feet had crushed an egg and was too slimy to get a fresh purchase on the stones. My fingers were growing numb, and while the sacristan continued to aroint me and jangle the bell, I could do nothing more than scream.

Then the bell stopped and someone was clattering up the ancient ladder to rescue me. I could hear his harsh breath as he neared the top. He reached out and grabbed me by the wrist. I couldn't see him because my eyes were squeezed shut and my scholar's gown had pulled up over my nose in my fall.

'Stop that noise!' he said shortly. 'Open your eyes, you fool. Do you think you can come down blind?'

I obeyed fearfully, one eye at a time. He was still wearing his remnant of wreath, though now it hung around his neck. His frown was so fierce I had a moment's doubt whether he had come to rescue me or throw me down the tower shaft.

'Get your foot out farther along the ledge. Straighten your knee!' I did so, but I couldn't shift my weight to the foot in that position. 'Now, let go with your other hand.'

'No!' Only his grip on my wrist would keep me from plummeting to the base of the tower and smashing on the floor like an egg. I began to cry again.

Cormac jerked at my arm. 'Let go your hand!'

My fingers scraped stone until they bled as he pulled, but at last they came away and he hauled me suddenly to him on the ladder, which groaned like an old tree limb in a high wind. I dangled, shrieked, clawed for support; he swayed out and somehow pulled me between himself and the ladder, pinning me there with his own body.

We stood there trembling for an endless time. The ladder felt ominously loose above us. I was two rungs over him, with his arms barring me on either side and his head just below mine. I could feel the shudder of his breath on my shoulder as I sobbed from exhaustion and terror.

At last he said: 'Now, we'll go down. One step at a time. You cannot fall, do you understand? I'll take a step, then you'll take one. One at a time.'

I think he must have repeated that instruction half a dozen times before I could respond. I kept expecting him to lose his temper and cuff me, or just leave me to get down as best I could. There were shouts of encouragement from below each time he took the initial step, then returned to coax me again until at last I could make my muscles move.

As we crept downward I saw nothing, not even the wall three inches from my nose; I heard nothing but my own heartbeat and Cormac's insistent whispers. Once my sandal slipped again, and for another long while we paused while his hard body pressed me so tightly against the ladder that I couldn't breathe, but it gave me courage to descend again.

When Cormac's feet touched the floor, he took me under the arms and set me down, then I collapsed like an empty sack at his feet. I heard a clamor of voices above me from the brothers, who had come in to Vespers and discovered us there. Cormac was praised and I was scolded. I was expecting a flogging – deserved it – but when I tried to struggle to my feet to meet my punishment, I fainted.

I came to my senses in the infirmary, alone. It was so quiet there I could hear the distant singing from the church. I had evidently passed from a faint into natural sleep, during which time all the elements of my unnerving day had combined to make one incomprehensible nightmare: my father was holding me by the wrists as I hung over the edge of the tower, which was more like a deep well. With tears in his eyes, he spoke of his love for me and his great hopes, then let go his grip, and I fell and fell into the darkness until someone caught me, crushing me painfully in his arms. I heard a voice saying: 'I'll save you now. One step at a time.' But it was Abbot Robert's voice I heard as I jerked awake.

The dream still rotated silently in my head, like a child's wooden top. I was bruised from chin to shin; my fingers were raw. I tried to rise from the bed, but fell out of it instead, weeping and incontinent.

When the infirmarian returned from service, he found me in such a state of delayed hysteria, he declared me to be the victim of a brain fever. I was kept in the infirmary for a week, suffering his purges by day and my incomprehensible dreams by night.

When I was pronounced recovered and returned, whey-faced and dizzy, to the school, I found that for the first time I was loath to meet Cormac's gaze from some feeling other than hatred. I was slack in my responses and feared he might think me made permanently a simpleton, but he seemed to take no notice. When we were dismissed I lingered in his presence, summoning the courage to repent my folly and thank him for my life. It was perhaps the longest and most difficult speech I had made till then.

He heard me with only cursory attention, with a brief nod acknowledged my debt, and dismissed me. I retired to the cloister garth in relief; then, to my own surprise and the dismay of the postulant master, I began to weep like a foolish girl – until I was on the point of being declared invalid again.

I could understand my weeping no more than the postulant master. My feelings, it seemed, were bruised because Cormac had merely been cool to me. Yet I no longer hated him, even when he later returned to cuffing and insulting me for inattention.

6

Upon my father's payment of the thirty deniers, I ceased to be a charity student and became eligible for the abbot's chief enthusiasm, the school of the scriptorium.

As a respected scholar, Robert de Tombelene wished to rule over a house of learning, as well as of religion, at St. Vigor. He encouraged every member of our community to learn his letters and the use of the pen. Most of the older brothers could read after a fashion, at least well enough to study their psaltery, but to master writing was time-consuming and of little use to them. Most gave up the effort after having been taught to scratch their alpha-beta-gammas with a reed, in Roman capitals.

It was a pity for the abbot's ambitions; more so for his master of the writing office, Brother Herlo, who was a skilled penman with a zeal to teach his art. Instead of a whole community of literate, scrivening monks, Herlo got only those few pressed to the art by the abbot and four or five boys such as myself.

Under Herlo's eye we learned first to cut reed pens without slashing our thumbs; then, painfully, we learned our letters, first in the Roman style, with a reed big enough to find use in the infirmary as a clyster. In time we were taught to style the flowing uncial letters with a pen.

In time. My own uncials didn't begin to flow for at least two years, but there were other things to learn. Herlo taught us how to read our psalteries, not recite them, and he introduced us to the first principles of mathematics we'd known beyond counting on our ink-stained fingers.

I was now turned into a willing scholar, for a fresh hope had come into my life: I might one day escape the cloister if I studied. Cormac provided the example.

In my fourteenth year Abbot Robert attended the synod held in Rouen, where the Mystery of the Holy Trinity was to be discussed by the learned – along with other articles of faith and discipline. It was an exciting conference, though not in the way its leaders expected, for they fell into such a passionate argument on the impropriety of a married clergy that Archbishop John, who detested the practice, barely escaped with his life from those who were husbands. A row ensued when he said that those with wives or concubines should be deprived of their offices and revenues.

We heard much of the doings of that synod when the abbot returned, but little was said of another matter, which was the absence of Cormac, who had gone with de Tombelene to Rouen as his clerk. It leaked out by way of carrel gossip in the cloister that Cormac had been sent to Paris, to study illumination of manuscript.

This made sense, as our abbot hoped to draw wealthy patrons to take an interest in our still-new house. The copying and illuminating of works suitable for rich men to give to churches they endowed was his chief ambition for our little scriptorium. His own Commentaries on the Canticles of Solomon was to be a suitable example of such works, which even Bishop Odo might be pleased to accept. Cormac would be the jewel in our community's crown if he mastered the art of laying on gold leaf.

But, on the other hand, it was whispered that he might not come back, having once sampled life in the court of Paris. Furthermore, there was a mystery connected with his going. In the normal way of things, our abbot having conceived the notion, he would have brought it before the brothers in chapter, asking for their advice and prayers on the matter. He would of course do as he liked with Cormac in any event, but it was courtesy to his household to ask their guidance.

Instead of that formality, there was an almost incidental mention of Cormac's departure several chapter meetings after it took place; then the abbot abruptly asked us to pray for his own mysterious frailties of the flesh and of the spirit and to grant him our compassion steadfastly, so that he might overcome all his errors and rule us according to the manner prescribed by our holy founder, St. Benedict. He wept as he spoke, as did several of his friends, who gave him the kiss of peace afterward.

I hadn't the least idea what he meant, and no one offered to enlighten me. But I wasn't as much interested in what sins the abbot might have committed as in the possibility that he might one day send me, as he had Cormac, out into the bright world.

Fortunate Irishman! He had gone to dwell in the court of the King of France, in Paris, that Eden for scholars who lived on the royal bounty. Kings and dukes kept clerks as well as did cloisters, to write their letters for them, account for their rents, and make for their delight beautiful books.

If that sounds like the discovery of a simpleton, it was. I was entirely dependent on hearsay for my knowledge of the outer world, having come to St. Vigor with my mother's milk scarcely dry on my lips. But now I knew my true destiny. I would give up my sluggish ways and become so adept a pupil of Master Herlo that he would recommend the abbot send me away to a greater master. I would do wonders! Become a prodigy!

Now, it wasn't because I wished to follow Cormac; to the contrary. Since his rescue of me, I had been most awkward with him, avoided him. He might have noticed that and made some comment on my change of character, if he had me still for a pupil, but he didn't. Another brother took the psaltery school in hand, while Cormac spent more and more time in the abbot's lodge, studying his own letters or playing his harp for his master's recreation – that is, until he was suddenly translated to Paris.

Coupled with my new ambition was another reason, no less faulty, for leaving St. Vigor. Brother Ambrose, the schoolboys' confidant and gossip of the hay meadows, had died that spring. He was the first in our house to do so since its foundation, which was rather remarkable, but he was also the first person I knew intimately who had died. The event filled me with a new terror.

Children have a sense of immortality, much as animals must have, I think, and in their ignorance cannot conceive of death until they see it near to hand. Brother Ambrose died in his sleep quite peacefully, but for weeks afterward I was disturbed by dreams of death coming for me in my sleep, so that I strove to keep awake and was punished for my restlessness. I greatly feared to die and to be buried in the long grass of the little cemetery north of the church, forgotten except in the brothers' prayers for the dead, before my life had truly begun. I made a secret bargain with the Almighty to be a source of pride to Him, if He would only let me live to old age.

So, in the year that King William invaded Scotland and made Malcolm Canmore submit to him and give him as hostage his son, I became a devoted scholar, surpassing all others of my age in desire for learning. Modesty forbids me to say I became the prodigy I wished to be, but in truth I found the work not as unpleasant as I feared. Latin grammar came slowly, but mathematics was more play than work once I was introduced to the checker.

For two years I think I was truly Brother Herlo's delight, so that by the time I was sixteen he recommended to the abbot that I be taken into minor orders as an encouragement. I became a porter for a short time, then advanced to the rank of lector.

I was proud as a cockerel the day I first read to the brothers as they sat in the refectory. My voice had gained its manhood the year before, but I thought that never until that day had I truly heard it. I was entranced with myself, so much so that I failed to hear the signal given for the end of the reading and went chanting on until the abbot coughed.

He did me the honor to compliment my reading, then abashed me by correcting some of my rustic pronunciation. I had never liked him overmuch, but I forgave him all his peculiarities when he said I had a good accent. I was jealous of the other lectors who shared the reading times with me and prayed nightly that it should be my turn to read when we came to the Canticles and other more poetic portions of Scripture.

I had been reveling in the sound of my own voice and in my scholastic preeminence for only about six months when two flies fell into the unguent. They were cousins: Richard and Baldwin de Fourneaux, a delicate pair of nobleman's sons who had been fluttering around the candle of monastic life for years without coming close enough to be tonsured.

They had been entered in the sacred lists at Bec and at Fontanelles in childhood and youth, but poor health, or doubts about their readiness, had kept them from taking vows. The younger, Baldwin, was very frail; but they were both well educated, and Richard was, I grudgingly admit even after all these years, a brilliant scholar in matters of the Old Testament.

Why they chose to come at last to our poor, unfinished house I never knew, unless it was our abbot's reputation that drew Richard, while poor, pale Baldwin followed – or was pushed after him by his exasperated family.

When they came I was cast out of favor before a dog could lick its backside. Richard took his vows at once and became the abbot's new pet, while fragile Baldwin, with his hectic cheeks and child's gaze, was everyone's darling. Even Brother Herlo began to find fault with my accent when I read after Richard and thought me impatient and rude compared to the lamblike Baldwin.

Only in mathematics could I still hope to shine over them. They were both dolts at anything but the simplest of sums. But that was poor consolation to me, as mathematics was a skill boasted by a thousand clerks who never bothered to take minor orders at all.

Then, as if to lay the final burden on my apprehensive shoulders, fate sent Cormac home to us, and there were now three prodigies between me and the light that shone through the cloister gate.

Cormac's reappearance coincided with the departure of Brother Herlo, who abruptly returned to St. Michel. The reason given was that Herlo felt age advancing on him and wished to spend his declining years in the house where he first took his vows. But as Cormac took his place in the scriptorium, gossip whispered that Herlo had been asked to share the rule of his little kingdom and had refused. A less kind version was that Cormac refused to return unless he had the whole rule of the scriptorium. Opinion was divided on the abbot's wisdom in the matter, and I was in the second rank of the anti-Cormac faction.

The first day I entered the writing room after Cormac had taken charge of it, I was both haughty and apprehensive. I half expected him to seize me by the neck as he'd done so many years before. I sat down to my work with a bare nod to him. When he came to look over my shoulder, half my expectations were granted: he found fault with my work.

'You're too stiff,' he said. 'You're cramping your letters. They look as if they're all backed up for fear of falling off your margin.' He took my pen away before I could utter a word of defense and handed me one of his small brushes. 'Write with this and with nothing but this, until your wrist loosens. You'll soon see the difference.'

I was dumb with mortification. Baldwin and several of my peers sat with fixed smiles as they heard me being humiliated. I held the foolish little brush in my fingers, on the point of tears and of half a mind to fling it and my ink bottle at Cormac's head. I'd be beaten for it; everyone would despise me; but it would ease my heart. And after that, what? I swallowed my rage and dipped the brush in ink.

For the first hour all I made were ink puddles; then I began to get the feeling of the brush. By the end of the week I could make as fine a letter with it as if it were my quill. When Cormac returned my pen to me, I saw my letters flow in a way I'd never dreamed before. But I wouldn't yet forgive him for the manner in which he'd forced improvement on my hand.

He had changed. Though he was still harsh with those who loitered, whispered, or forgot, he was no more the cruel despot who had haunted my dreams. The magic of his voice had not changed. When we made copy, then proved it by repeating it aloud, he would sometimes read it over again in such a way as to make even obscure or boring passages clear. He dictated to our pens from the works of St. Augustine, and his mutable voice gave such animation to the words, I could almost believe it was the young profligate of Hippo himself, describing his wayward youth before God claimed him.

While we worked, he might sit in silence, staring out the window or reading. I would steal glances at his long, pure profile, envying him his fairness, which my brown hands told me would never be mine. I was guilty of a hundred petty sins, not the least of which was that I longed to be fair and handsome; also learned, royally employed, and famous in the world. I even envied Baldwin's pallor, which was the result of weak lungs.

I envied him his disposition, too: uncomplaining and meek. He was always more agreeable to Cormac than I. He never took umbrage when slighted, never frowned at a correction – but then he needed few of them. And if he coughed too much, he begged our pardon for it as humbly as if he'd let fly a fart at the opening of the Gospel. I detested him. Cormac seemed to favor him above all the rest.

I began to curry favor in the most despicable way, by offering to tutor Baldwin in mathematics. Cormac agreed to it, and Baldwin was so amenable to my haughty instructions that I had almost forgiven him for being better favored than myself, when he spoiled it with what was undoubtedly meant to be a compliment.

'Ranulph, with your talent for accounting, you'll be the bursar here someday.'

I would rather have died than to live only to be the bursar of St. Vigor, so I pretended I had no further time for instructing him and petitioned Cormac instead to teach me the use of the brush.

What a vile, miserable young rascal I had become, all in the name of ambition – and love. I had passed from wariness of Cormac, to rapture, to imbecility, never knowing when the change occurred. Between suspicion and blind adoration there should have been some middle ground, but it was a confusion to me. Once he had filled my dreams with apprehension of abuse. Now I dreamed of doing him some immeasurable service that would make him love me. I would save his life, perhaps, though how I might do that at St. Vigor, unless he fell into the jakes, I had no notion. Yet in my head I saved him daily from a raging bull, or pulled him from dark waters, and each time he was grateful and suddenly aware of me. I'd come to my wits from one of these fantasies and go hot and cold by turns when he glanced at me – as if he might read my foolish mind.

Why did I suddenly love him? God knows. It might only have been because I had reached an age to comprehend the emotion. But I wasn't his only worshiper; Baldwin's sheep eyes followed him with the same devotion. There were others, old, half-toothless brothers who had known him since he was a boy, who forgot their meditations when he passed their carrels, as if he were the reincarnation of St. John the Beloved.

He had been a part of us, as familiar as our daily bread, but he had been renewed by his absence. There was a new assurance that differed from his old hauteur; his robe seemed of a closer cut and better cloth than ours, though it was the same wool. Was it his travels? His maturity? Did the old brothers dream of saving him from wild bulls, or nursing him through an illness?

Even Abbot Robert forgot his resolves and favored him again as before. Cormac now spent long hours shut up with the abbot in his lodge, where they were making a superlative copy of some book the abbot had borrowed from a friend in Rouen which he meant to give to Bishop Odo on his next pastoral visit. While they so labored, we in Cormac's writing room would wait in idleness.

Sometimes when they had worked for hours, there would suddenly come the sound of a harp from behind the abbot's garden wall, fainter than the melodious hum of bees or the snores of sleeping monks in the cloister garth. Those who heard it would stir and sigh, lifting their heads as if they smelled sweet odors, and I would steal a glance at Baldwin, or he at me.

Other times we would wait for our master only to have him enter in a dark mood, give short answers to mild questions, and then sit paring away the edge of his thumbnail with his jagged bottom teeth as he stared out the window with unseeing eyes. We would bend our necks to our work and fear to trouble him, wondering what dispute could take place beyond those walls to make him look so ill contented.

Once I saw him in that mood turn his gaze upon Baldwin, in such a manner that the poor fellow all but fell from his stool in a faint. Envy made a meal of me until Cormac's eye switched to me and he said sharply, 'What are you gaping at?'

Whatever his mood, if he came at last to my desk with a harsh word for inattention, or if he bent over to find fault and, finding none, gave me one of his wolfish smiles and tapped my shoulder in approval, my blood would race and my heart would swell and pulse at his voice, like his harp in the corner of the room when the church bell caused it to sing.

Baldwin, on the other hand, looked more and more unhappy and distracted no matter what mood Cormac displayed. I began to feel I was drawing near some obscure victory, though what it could consist of I had absolutely no idea.

Outside our walls the great world ran on, as indifferent to us as we to it. In England there was a rebellion against the rule of King William Bastard, while he was himself in Maine, conquering it and making his eldest son its count. The men who rebelled were not the broken English, but those very Normans the king had so richly rewarded with treasure and honors, who earlier had helped him win his kingdom there. Because they were Normans, no reward was great enough to keep them loyal for very long, if there was an opportunity to do mischief. Every earl in England, save old Roger of Montgomery and the king's brother Odo, Earl of Kent, took part in the conspiracy to put him off his throne. The treason was concocted, of all places, at a wedding feast, where it is assumed they were all very drunk.

This 'Earls' Revolt' was put down by Archbishop Lanfranc of Canterbury, King William Bastard's regent in the realm and his most trusted friend. When it was over, the miscreants were dealt with according to the king's generosity. Some were banished, some fined;

most were generously forgiven. Only one was beheaded, and that was an Englishman, the last English earl among his people. His name was Waltheof, and our abbot said the king wept when he heard of his treason, because he had loved him as a son.

A Breton, Ralph Bigod, who was one of the chief instigators, was banished to his native land, which was small punishment for him, being a man of great wealth in both places. But at home in Brittany he stirred up a war against us from his fortress at Dol. King William marched against him and suffered the first military defeat of his adult life. After a long and humiliating siege of the castle, he was forced to return home, unable to break his enemy's strength, though he had challenged Ralph to single combat to settle their dispute honorably. It was said by many men that after that campaign William Bastard was never the same man.

As the abbot told it to us, the king had other griefs that bore him down. His second son, Richard, a brave young man and more like his father than any of his other sons, was killed in a foolish accident while hunting in the New Forest, which the king had recently enlarged in Hampshire for his own pleasure. Some ignorant folk took Richard's death as a sign of God's disapproval of the wasting of that land, though the king wasn't the first lord to drive off a few shepherds and plowmen in order to make a decent deer park out of what could never be good farm or pastureland.

It was a great pity the boy Richard died so young, said our abbot, because he would have been our duke someday, the kingdom falling to his elder brother, Robert.

Also, a daughter of the king's who had been betrothed to one of the Spanish kings had died on her way to her wedding, to the great sorrow of all her family, but especially her mother, the Lady Matilda, who was said to be distracted with her double grief. Sad tidings from beyond the walls on a bad year.

My own day of grief was as sudden, though it came two years later. Brother Rollo, that rawboned porter who had first hauled me by the neck of my shirt from my father's arms to Cormac's feet, stood up in chapter one evening and accused Cormac and Baldwin de Fourneaux of harboring an unnatural affection for each other, which he said they had consummated with a criminal act in the cemetery garth by dead of night. He used a harsher word than *consummate,* stunning the chapter with the charge uttered in his bull's voice.

We sat like stones from the shock of it. We had heard every other accusation of sin – short of murder – charged in the chapter but that.

Brothers had indicted themselves or others for greed, envy, sloth, covetousness, theft – with hardness of heart surpassing Pharaoh's and charity less than Herod's – but this was different. This was a crime worthy of expulsion from the community, expulsion from the grace of the Church.

In the silence that followed, Cormac stood up, as an accused person must do when another rebukes him. Like the rest of us, he wore his cowl to keep his eyes from wandering, so that his ears might better hear the admonitions or instructions of the abbot. He pushed the cowl back now, to identify himself, and fixed his eyes, not on his accuser, but on Abbot Robert, who gripped the arms of his faldstool and stared at him in turn.

'This is a grave charge, Brother,' the abbot said in a faint, prim voice, showing neither surprise nor horror, though his face was very pale. 'If it is made in vain or out of spite, it will be to your peril. What does Brother Cormac say to this charge of his brother in Christ?' His small mouth pursed and his fat chin trembled a little.

Cormac sighed, then said very evenly: 'That my brother in Christ is much mistaken. Or blind. Or drunk. Or both.' Still he looked only at the abbot.

'Not so, Father Abbot!' shouted Rollo. 'I saw them together there in their filthy lust with my own eyes! But rather than match my tongue to a liar's, I call on other witnesses!'

Witnesses he had in plenty, though not to the same scene. One by one they sprang up and damned Cormac from the shadow of their cowls.

'I was just going to the jakes, being somewhat taken with a colic from eating green pears, Father Abbot. It was between Lauds and Prime, when all the brothers should have been in their proper beds, so I thought. But I saw Cormac and Baldwin sitting in the carrel nearest the laving bowl, their backs to me. They were very close – embracing or touching. I accuse myself that I didn't report it at once.'

Another: 'When we come down from the dorter for Matins, Father Abbot, I am accustomed to being the last, being bedded farthest from the night stair; but of late, Cormac and Baldwin have lingered behind me, as if they were slow to throw off sleep. They come running a few moments later to catch up to us before we reach the church door.'

Another had seen the two go into the privies one after the other, where it seemed to him they lingered overlong. This, too, was at night. Such childish, spiteful tales! Why hadn't they reported them at the time – if indeed they had truly happened? Why didn't Cormac denounce them for what they were? Why did he merely stand there? What was the use of that silent communication with the abbot, who hadn't said a word in his defense or demanded that he speak again? I could bear it no longer and jumped up, throwing back my cowl.

'Father Abbot, since I came here ten years ago I've never been aware there was so much trotting forth by moonlight. It seems everyone in the house has the colic. I begin to wonder if any in this house has ever slept the night through but myself.'

For an instant Cormac shifted his attention from the abbot to me. The corners of his mouth pulled down slightly, as if he were amused.

'Sit down, Brother,' the abbot told me huskily. 'You have no part in this, unless you can offer additional proof to the charge, or against it. And if you sleep soundly, you can hardly do either.'

'What proof? These are no proofs of anything but someone's spite!' I yelled.

'Sit down, Brother!' cried the abbot, slamming his hand on the stool.

Cormac gave me a bare nod and I collapsed on the bench, the lump of anger and grief in my throat about to choke me. Baldwin, who had been hunched on his seat throughout the business with his face buried in his hands, now leaped to his feet.

'Does no one think to ask me? Am I forgotten in all this?'

His cousin pulled at his gown to make him sit, but he jerked away, tearing off his cowl and mangling it in his hands as he fell on his knees.

'Father Abbot, Brothers in Christ, have mercy on me! I am at fault here, not Cormac. I accuse myself of being the sole cause – '

'Sit down and be quiet,' Cormac said in a low voice without bothering to look at Baldwin.

' – the sole cause of the appearance of sin in my master! No! I am accused too, Cormac, and I must speak!'

'My cousin is ill, Father Abbot,' said Richard quickly. 'He's had a fever these last two days that he's told no one of but me. He speaks out of his head.'

'No!' shrieked Baldwin.

'Let him speak,' said the abbot.

Richard sat down. Cormac folded his arms.

Baldwin spoke as if he were being strangled: 'I have been afflicted with doubts of late – about my fitness for life in the cloister. I came here – not entirely of my own will, as my cousin knows, though I don't blame him for that, or any other, for I found the life here to my

– to my liking, at first. But of late I have doubted – again – and so could not sleep. I told my fears to my good master; I begged him to help me resolve my confusion. He spoke to me, but I wouldn't take his advice. I was running – yes, running away that night. He followed me – into the cemetery, where he – where I led him – into that semblance of sin, for which I take all blame – and pray the good Father Abbot will now punish me for what has come of my – confusion and disobedience.' He sighed, shuddered, and looked as if he might faint.

'If you had doubts about your profession, why didn't you speak to the novice master or to your confessor?' asked the abbot sternly.

'I am at fault again. I didn't believe they would understand – my reasons. I beg – ' He began to cough, then to sob. The impassive Cormac frowned for the first time then, as if he heard a dog whining without cause.

Brother Rollo gave his great peasant's laugh. 'He didn't think they'd understand it wasn't shriving he wanted, but *swiving*!'

There was an outburst of laughter from some and angry shouts of reproof from others for that obscenity. Baldwin and Richard both yelled 'No!' in unison and scrambled to their feet. The abbot cried for order, but now some of Cormac's friends at last confronted the porter, shaking their fists in his face. Rollo took his own big fists out of his sleeves and struck in the nose one of them who came too close to him. With that the fists began to fly all around the chamber. The doorkeepers came forward swinging their staves, but they did little beyond inflaming the quarrel. Not everyone was enraged by Cormac's sin or Rollo's vulgarity. There were many who took the opportunity to poke their fingers in a brother's eye for the sake of a private grudge.

I sprang up, wanting to maul Baldwin, whose womanish denial had been the most damning evidence against my master, but no sooner was I up than I was knocked sprawling by a monk named Ulf, who fell on me and pummeled me until someone leaped on him in turn and began twisting his ears. Someone knocked over the candlesticks that stood by the abbot's chair, and as we rolled and thrashed in the dark I could hear him crying for lights and order, shrill with rage or fear. Cressets appeared in the door, brought by one of the doorkeepers, and exposed us to our own disreputable shadows lurching and quavering on the walls. There was weeping and groaning. The great candlesticks were set up and lighted again.

The abbot cursed us for animals, crying that we would all be whipped out of God's house. Some brothers fell into their seats again; others crawled weeping, beating their heads against the floor, lashing themselves with their cinctures. I had a lump the size of an egg behind my ear, a bloody nose, and scraped knuckles. Baldwin was huddled on the floor at the abbot's feet, wailing like a widow. De Tombelene, scarlet-faced and wild-eyed, looked at him as if he might kick him. I looked about for Cormac.

He was gone.

The porters were sent to search for him, while the rest of us heard the abbot wheeze out pronouncement of our punishment: scourging by pairs, no man escaping; bread and water for our one meal for a week; and a month's silence, save for our prayers, with anathema for those who broke the least letter of the sentence.

After a time the porters came back to report that Cormac couldn't be found. Then Robert de Tombelene spoke the words that cast him out of our community, made him an outlaw for any man's taking, after which he bent and slapped Baldwin across the head to make him stop howling. We assembled ourselves as best we could and tottered off to say a ragged Compline.

The peace and brotherhood of our house were broken for more than that one night. We were commanded to silence, but nothing could stop our growls and groans. My head was near to splitting, and I ground my teeth in an agony of frustrated rage and grief until my jaw would hardly unhinge for prayers in the morning. My temple was shattered and my idol fled, made an outlaw, an excommunicate. If thieves fell on him and murdered him, he would go to Hell and they to Heaven.

Rollo was confined to prison for a week for creating general discord with intemperate language. False accusation wasn't a charge lodged against him, because Baldwin confirmed his cruel witness on the same night as Cormac's flight. While the rest of us finally slept in the last hour before Prime, Baldwin rose and went quietly to the jakes, threw his cincture over a rafter beam, put the other end about his neck, and stepped off the stool with just enough space between it and his feet to let himself swing free.

7

The summer that followed Cormac's flight was hot and dry beyond the natural. Crops withered in the fields under a remorseless sun. The air was so dry in August that wildfire sprang up in the barns and fields, wantonly scorching everything that hadn't already died of the drought. Where the fields met the forest the trees burned, too, then the hovels of the poor folk who tilled the sorry fields. As always when such weather comes, the cattle sickened and died. It was as if all the earth had turned phoenix and sought her own destruction.

We were besieged by desperate people wanting food, even water, as the region's wells began to fail and the lesser streams dried to muddy trickles.

We had a good well at St. Vigor and our outlying barns were well stocked with grain, yet we suffered a famine of a different kind, that of the spirit. In spite of fasts and penances, quarrels erupted among us with ever greater frequence and ferocity. The brothers no longer hesitated to complain to the abbot because of the food, or some division of labor, or any petty difference they imagined lay between them, until he retired more and more to his lodge and let his prior bear the burden of an unruly house.

Having grain to share, he was afraid to dispense it to the poor, for fear the discontented monks would complain to the bishop that he used poor management. He may have reasoned, too, that since famine will always follow drought and lasts even beyond it, it would be foolish to empty all our granaries at once to satisfy empty bellies, then suffer for it more in a harsh winter. So he consented to feed only our tenants and turned others away to find their remedy where they could. He was not an uncharitable man, whatever else his faults, only sensible. It hurt him to deny the poor.

In the end it hurt us as much. One after another our tithe barns were either destroyed by wildfire or pillaged by the ravenous poor. They in turn were scoured by the Comte de Bessin's constabulary, who were commanded to restore order. Between burning and looting, trampling and being trampled, all who lived in that country were destined to grow thinner before another harvest, including the monks of St. Vigor.

Fever followed famine. The cattle languished first, then the pigs, then the men. Again, as in the year of the Great Comet, men disputed the cause of God's displeasure with His Creation. It was because the king, who was our duke, had failed to finish building the abbey he had promised to the Almighty thirty years before, to expiate the sin of having married his cousin without Rome's dispensation. Or it was because he had fought an unjust war against one of his sworn vassals. Or he had allowed his eldest son, Robert, to defy him successfully, and to bolt when he failed to take Rouen by siege.

When disaster falls on the human race, every man becomes a philosopher and can find good reason in the blowing of an oat straw. If anyone had asked me at the time, I would probably have said the famine was Robert de Tombelene's fault for condemning Cormac without a proper hearing, thereby causing at once Baldwin's suicide, my heartache, and a general holocaust. How he solely was to blame I could not prove; I only knew it was true whenever I looked at his face.

No one at St. Vigor knew what a private blow I had suffered that night, though the kindly prior once or twice questioned me about my lack of spirit and noticed the dark circles under my eyes. I made some untruthful answer and he dropped the inquiry, for surely to God in that house everyone was suffering from lack of spirit and dark circles. A squint-eyed Fleming became master of the writing office in Cormac's place. He'd come to us after an unrewarding career in the service of some minor lord. He wrote a barbarous hand, but he was able to give me some practical instruction in account keeping, so we got along well enough. Two of our younger members ran away when the barn burning began. I took further minor orders, grimly advancing toward the priesthood, which would set me free. I would ask for a parish and live in poverty, like my father, though I would breed no hungry sons. On the surface of my daily life I seemed to have recovered better than some, but privately I had little peace.

At times as I worked or studied, my eyes would blur with memories of past scenes in the writing room that now seemed like an Eden, barred and lost. I kept my countenance, but inside I was twisted with a confusion of feeling, now grief, now disgust, for Cormac. I pitied or felt self-pity, seeing I was now condemned to a life of privation in a place where I had no friend and the only acceptable object of love was a Being at once implacable, invisible, and remote.

I vowed I would not love God, then. If He could approve the service of a brainless brute like Rollo while condemning Cormac, whatever his faults, He was beyond my knowing, and what cannot be known cannot be loved.

It could be feared, however, and It was. My resolve cost me many a night's sleep, since it made me vulnerable to Divine retribution. Those who cast out God let in something in His place. Invisible fingers plucked at my bedclothes when I was half asleep, reminding me that I had gone to bed in a state of mortal sin and was now fair game to be shriveled with malignant disease, driven mad, possessed, or handled in some worse way as a horrible example to others.

In time the terror was too much. I broke, succumbed, told my confessor every rankling thought I could bear to name, and so achieved a degree of ease. I put my mind to trying to love the Blessed Virgin by way of restitution, since I could still only fear God.

Then winter came and a fever with it. Nearly half the men in our house died within a month and another fourth were made invalid by watery bowels and famished bodies. It seemed our Divine Service must lapse for want of celebrants. Of those within the house in Holy Orders, one was fled, four were dead, and three were so weak with the flux it wasn't certain they could live.

We met in chapter to discuss the crisis. Since I was young and the fever had so far not touched me, and because my new devotion to the Virgin gave my superiors reason to believe me a very pious fellow, I was chosen along with Richard de Fourneaux to be examined for ordination. I, at least, was too young for the priesthood, but I wasn't the first that dreadful year to be made a deacon on a Wednesday and a priest on a Sunday.

Bishop Odo himself would administer that greatest of the Sacraments to us in his cathedral at Bayeux. He was expected to ordain as many as fifty priests during his brief return to his diocese. Richard de Fourneaux was already in deacon's orders and need not go to Bayeux so early, but I was sent ahead of my time and given leave to visit my parents between ordinations.

I had not seen my father for six years, or my mother for ten. My brothers were no more than distant childhood memories. Even the home and village I had lived in were so faded from my memory that I could remember the people there only in the vaguest way. What would they think of me? I was grateful to be given a new gown for my ordination, along with sandals and breeches, which we didn't ordinarily wear. My old gown I had outgrown so that its hem hung above my ankles by several inches.

I reached Bayeux quickly, amazed at how much shorter the distance seemed than the last time I had traveled it. All my minor orders had been taken in the abbey church from Bishop Odo's suffragan. When I reached the streets of Bayeux, I was like any gaping yokel, staring at the housewives and their bawling children, at the bakeshops, wineshops, fish market, and the shambles as if I'd never heard of such things.

Famine and sickness had touched Bayeux, too, but not so harshly as in the country. The men-at-arms of the castle strutted the narrow streets looking well fed, while ships laden with merchandise lay at anchor in the river.

The smell of the food shops made my stomach contract with hunger. I had come to Bayeux fasting, and when I reached the cathedral I found I must remain in that condition, in readiness for the ceremony on the morrow. I was ushered into a small chamber in the bishop's palace where, along with all the other ordinands, I must prepare my soul for the Sacrament. Bishop Odo and his household guests prepared themselves in another way, feasting on all manner of luscious meats in the dining hall below us and hearing pleasant music while they laughed and drank.

The next morning I was brought before Odo, almost fainting with hunger, to be examined for intent and readiness. When we came to the blessing, the Eucharist stuck to the roof of my mouth and the Wine could barely dislodge it. I struggled not to gag or choke, which is a very bad omen for one taking Holy Orders. When the ceremony was finished, I was much relieved and hurried away to find my family.

The village of St. Loup in my father's time was a rutted road with five or six houses and a public well. My father's church was no bigger than our chapter house, and its thatched roof wanted repair. The rectory seemed no better than a sheepcote. I had to stoop to enter its door.

I saw a woman, shriveled and all but toothless, a hag who bent over the hearth stirring a mess of something in a small pot that smelled mostly of onions. She looked up as I entered. I saw she was half blind as well as shrunken. One eyelid quivered over an empty socket.

'Mother?' I asked, half hoping I was wrong.

She gave me a great cry and flung herself on me, leaving her spoon to sink into the stew. 'Thurstin! Old man! Look who's come to see us!'

My father came in from the hen yard, so frail and grey that I began to weep as I embraced my mother, who wouldn't let me go to greet him. I put out my arm to take him into our circle and we all wept, they for the joy of seeing me, I for the horror of seeing them.

When Mother was calm enough, we sat down to eat her stew and tell our news. Mine was soon told, and it made them weep again. Theirs was stranger to me. My brothers, Osbern and Fulcher, were in the cathedral school at Bayeux and considered very promising clerks by the dean of order. They came home once or twice a year.

My mother had miscarried of two more children after I was sent away. I was told of the births of cousins and the deaths of people I had forgotten existed. My bowl of stew was finished before it had half appeased my hunger, but I denied to my mother that I could eat more; there was so little in the pot.

When we had exhausted all our talk it had not yet struck None. I was free to spend the rest of the week with them, yet the rest of that day seemed endless. My father took me to the church with him at Vespers and presented me to all the village, then gave me the honor of assisting him at the altar as his deacon. My mother killed half her scrawny hens while we were celebrating Vespers and made a feast for all the village, to honor me.

I lay in my old bed above the rafters that night, miserable beyond words and ashamed of my misery. This was the life of a parish priest without family or friends in high places, the life I chose for myself over life in the cloister. This was the existence I had planned to petition the bishop for, as soon as I was sanctified a priest. I couldn't endure it. I had thought that life in the abbey the past year had toughened me for anything, but I was soft; soft and useless for any work but penwork. My parents were all but starving and I was useless to them. I should have been kept at home and put to work in the fields, or sent to be a soldier. Both those lives would have been equally hateful to me, but I might have felt more worthy of my parents' pride.

I swore to myself that somehow I would escape from the two lives open to me; I would find some occupation that would let me raise up my family a little from the muck. Before they died I would see that they tasted some luxury, if I had to sell myself to the Devil for it. That pitiful crone who had been my beautiful mother would wear a decent coif and a fine woolen gown.

Little mice, working through the roof thatch, sent a shower of straw bits down through the roof laths to drift over my face.

I remember little else about the rest of my time in St. Loup. It was all of a piece, I suppose. I may have repented my resolve to sell myself to the Devil for gain, but when I entered the church in Bayeux that Sunday morning to be made a priest, my eyes were dazzled by the gold of its candlesticks, its silver basins, jeweled patens, the rich robes of the bishop – I remembered my resolve to find a better life.

When the time came for me to prostrate myself before the altar, I could think of nothing but the bishop. Odo was glorious in his miter and chasuble: tall, handsome, and open of countenance, his hair still golden, his face ruddy. He had a generous, humorous mouth, with a voice that could roar or drip honey. For all his elegance, he wasn't a soft-looking man like our abbot. His hand, when he placed it on my head, seemed as firm and heavy as if it were encased in the warrior's glove that was as familiar to him as the episcopal one. He was about my father's age, but looked twenty years younger.

When he placed that hand on my head, I could see nothing but the thickly embroidered hem of his alb, the edge of his golden chasuble, and the embossed green leather tips of his shoes. A shudder went over me. He was a priest whose hand had been sanctified by another to sanctify me. That other had been so blessed in turn by another, and all those ghostly hands extended back to the hand of Christ, laid on Peter's head, now blessed me that I might someday wear such power and do such office for other men, some yet unborn. I felt what it might be to stand in his shoes; felt I wore them, now; was being presented to myself, blessed by myself. The paradox made my head swim.

Fulcher and Osbern were there in the nave afterward to greet me, sallow, pustular boys I couldn't recognize. I had leave to spend a little more time with them before I took my way back to St. Vigor, but I was loath to leave the splendid church, whose trappings, looted from Kent by Odo, drew me like a lodestone.

My father saw the bishop coming toward us and timidly approached him to pay his respects. I followed him, my nostrils filled with incense, my eyes with candle glow and gold shine. I heard my father thank great Odo, weeping. On impulse I fell at the bishop's feet.

'Gracious lord and father, you have done me high honor today and have given my father his dearest dream. I am nothing, except what you have made me, but if I can ever serve you in any manner, in whatever cause, even to the laying down of my life, then behold your ready servant.'

It was a green speech. I was already his servant whether I liked it or not. As soon as the words were uttered they embarrassed me. I flushed, expecting him to laugh. One of his priests did snicker, but Odo silenced him with a noble gesture of his broad, calloused hand.

'Stand up, my son, and let me look at you.'

I obeyed. His scrutiny was very candid, with no hint of scorn, though with a touch of amusement. 'Why, it's a handsome sacrifice,' he murmured, and my ears burned pleasantly. 'Beware, my son, how you pledge yourself to men of this world. You've a ready tongue in your head, but too often the tongue is the only valiant organ in a man's body. How's your heart?'

'My tongue hardly knows how to speak yet, Your Grace. It was my heart that gave it words.'

'Oho, I see! Very well, I'll remember. See that you do the same.' He waved me away with a blessing and returned to his conversation.

With my family surrounding me and my father praising me for my speech, we went into the bishop's palace along with all the rest of the new-made celebrants and ate of Odo's food, which was in bountiful supply, after which my kinsmen followed me to the west gate of the city. I kissed them all good-bye there as if for forever and returned to St. Vigor across the open fields. As soon as its gate closed behind me, my life returned to its normal state of dull despair, so that I almost forgot my naive speech to the Bishop of Bayeux.

But he had not. Before he returned to his earldom in England, he made a visitation of the churches and convents in his care. Those among us who had survived the terrible year, who lived to see our green fields turn golden and our apples blush scarlet, greeted him as he entered our church:

> 'Sacerdos et Pontifex
> Et Virtutem opifex,
> Pastor, bone in Populo
> Sic Placuisti Domino . . .'

He said Mass at our altar, then feasted with us later, delighting Abbot Robert with a gift of wine from Italy. He brought a train of followers with him, but his own presence more than theirs seemed to fill our refectory to the walls. We neglected our food to stare at him and try to hear his conversation with the abbot.

I had been permitted to assist him at the celebration of Mass and was still shivering a bit with the honor, though he hadn't recognized me, or seemed not to. But now, as he smiled at some remark the abbot made in his ear, his ever roaming eyes glanced on me and in a moment he beckoned to me to approach him.

I got up in confusion and went to the abbot's table like a peasant with an unpaid tax on his conscience. Odo let me stand while he spoke privately to the abbot.

'I have need of a courier to take some letters to Rouen. He must stay there for a time for such instructions as I may send, afterward,' he said. 'I would send one of my own clerks, but their appetites are already whetted for English ale and English weather. It would be a shame to disappoint them.' This was evidently a jest, because several of his retinue at the table made wry, humorous faces.

Then he said to me: 'I remember a word you spoke to me recently, young man. Do you recall it?'

'Yes, Your Grace,' I whispered.

He turned again to the abbot. 'Is he reliable? Discreet?' They must already have covered *that* ground, else he would never have called for me.

Abbot Robert said: 'Sound enough, Your Grace. For one of his years, steady and quiet.'

That was a fair judgment, I thought. God knew I had been quiet lately from lack of hope.

Odo dismissed me then, as if it were no great matter. 'Very well, then. Attend me before I leave and you will be given your commission, my son.'

I bowed and withdrew. It was hard to take my seat again quietly and not alarm the whole munching, staring company at my table by beating my hands together and shouting out my joy: I'm leaving St. Vigor! But I sat down quietly, already practicing discretion.

Odo received me later in the abbot's walled garden, sitting on the same bench where Cormac had once played his harp and exchanged a lover's kiss with de Tombelene. He put a leather bag into my hands – a clerk's budget – with the letters inside, rolled and sealed.

'You will deliver these to the priest William de St. Carileph. He is one of the king's chaplains, who serves for the moment in the Lady Matilda's chancel. He will see to their further delivery.'

He smiled at me. I held the budget in my arms as if it were a precious child. 'For love of me, you will tell no one what you carry, or whose business you're about, and you will do William de St. Carileph any other service which he might require of you. That will be no hardship. The court of Rouen is a pleasant place for a young priest to find himself in. Our lady the queen is fond of those in Holy Orders and treats them generously.' His brow creased slightly. 'You won't mind leaving your home here, for a time?'

'Oh, no, Your Grace. I would gladly go to the ends of the earth for your sake!'

He laughed, picking up another, smaller pouch from the bench beside him. 'Here's a purse. It won't take you to the ends of the earth, but it should keep you from starving on the road you do travel. There will be a further reward, perhaps, if you are faithful.' He rose and signed to one of his chaplains who stood at the garden gate and who came forward to us at Odo's gesture, with a rich cloak folded over his arm.

'The brothers of St. Vigor are commendably plain, but their gowns seem too thin. Take this cloak for your journey, my son. It's fur-lined and of some value, so don't neglect it, even as you sleep.'

I fell at his feet and kissed his ring. I would have kissed his feet, but he suddenly became conscious of the hours passing and strode into the abbot's lodge to make his farewells.

His chaplain folded the beautiful cloak around my shoulders and fastened the silver-gilt clasp at my throat.

'This is one of his own, young bumpkin, and it's worth more than you and a mule together, so see you keep it well.'

Very shortly after the bishop and all his retinue rode out our gates thunderously, I was left to make swift preparations. I received a nearly new pair of stout sandals and some braies to save me from shame if I needed to remove my gown for any reason. I was given a loaf of waybread, a leather bottle of watered wine, a staff, and my abbot's blessing.

'Remember, Ranulph, you are a courier, not a herald. No need to cry your business in any man's ear, not even that of another brother. But you must neither carry yourself so as to seem too secret, either. You could give temptation to a thief who thinks you carry treasure beyond mere letters. Here is a map for your journey. Stay on the high road running north that lies east of here. You'll have no trouble finding Rouen.'

The map seemed accurate enough to guide a donkey. It consisted of a heavy line drawn on a scrap of parchment, with the names of towns I should pass through: Caen, Lisieux, Brionne, Elbeuf, and Rouen, the last two separated by a wavy line representing the Seine River. Caen should be no more than two hours' journey – I could amble from St. Vigor to St. Loup in an hour. The whole journey would take no more than a day. They had given me an overgenerous loaf of bread.

But after two hours' walking I could still see the castle tower of Bayeux behind me when I stood on high ground, and there was no sign of Caen ahead. After four hours my feet were raw from the chafing of my sandal straps, so I took them off and hung them by their thongs around my neck. When the sun sank behind the trees to my left, I sat down to say a prayer and to refresh myself with a bit of bread and a sip of wine, but a quarter of the loaf was hardly enough to diminish the appetite raised by my exertion. The world was bigger than I thought.

I saw Caen before I slept, yet mindful of thieves, I didn't go to St. Stephen's for a bed, but slept in a grassy ditch instead. The next morning at dawn I skirted Caen, eager to find Lisieux and make up lost time. I walked until I thought I had left Europe and wandered into Asia by mistake, but Lisieux evaded me, though I could hear church bells in the distance. My high road became a cow path, led me to a little stream, and vanished once I'd crossed the water. I tried to recover my direction as the second night fell, but the road to Lisieux had shifted like a serpent in the dark. I was lost. I fell down under a tree about midnight, my bread and wine exhausted, my legs nearly paralyzed with fatigue.

Rain woke me, lashing rain and wind, which I might have seen coming if I hadn't been so engrossed in finding the road again. I huddled on the leeward side of the tree, but the squall made a mockery of its shelter. With water pouring down my neck I got up and once again trotted away, praying for the sight of a peasant's hut or even a sheepfold to take refuge in – but there was nothing. The dark woods grew nearer to the road, cutting some of the fury of the storm but making it seem more terrible because of the closeness. By dawn I was weary to the point of delirium, and the weight of the bishop's rain-soaked cloak hung on my shoulders like a dead man. I knew I would never see Lisieux. I would die first.

The rain abated at dawn, but came back in full force by midmorning, before it settled into a steady pour. I found a road of some sort but was too dazed to rejoice. Its ditches brimmed with brown water; the road itself was a pudding of soft mud. I walked mindlessly. I walked in pain. My legs were like logs; my thighs could hardly lift the weight of my gown to take a step. There was nowhere to lie down or even to sit and rest. The land rose and fell, but there was no change in it. There were no people in the sodden fields, no smoke rising from a roof hole.

My mother had an old tale about the fairy folk of Brittany who could enchant the ground a man walked on, so that no matter how his legs moved, he couldn't leave that piece of earth until the demons had had their sport with him. I began to believe such a thing had happened to me and was sorry I had no salt or a piece of iron to protect myself from dark spirits of the forest and field.

As the numbing water ran down my face, I closed my eyes, opening them only to keep from straying too near the ditch. In a moment I fell into a kind of dream, wherein I was dry and the sun was shining on me. I jerked awake, but in a few steps nodded and another dream took me: I was floating toward a huge, clean feather bed, hovering over it with weightless limbs, sinking like a thistle toward it to rest and rest.

I fell forward on hands and knees in the squelching mud and came to my senses with such a wrench of despair that I might have lain down to drown in the mire if I hadn't smelled smoke.

A cluster of low buildings sat on a hill beyond the trees to the right; a rutted track, streaming yellow water, led up to the place no more than a few paces from my nose.

I clutched my muddy bag and wet cloak and ran crazily up that slippery path, sliding back a step for every two I went forward. A low stone wall surrounded the manor; the gate was missing, but slivers of candlelight showed through the window shutters of the house, which must be the home of some comfortable knight, I thought, or some freeman not too careful of his safety.

'Ho, in the house! In the barn! Will someone aid a poor traveler? Bailiff! Stableman! Help! God's peace on all within! Will someone answer?' I slipped then and fell into ooze particularly viscous and stinking.

'Help! Help in God's Name!'

The barn looked half ruined, its thatch burned off, only black rafters showing. Ill luck was truly mine. Was the place deserted after all and the lights only a trick of my mind? No, there was a light. It grew wider.

'Thank God for His mercy! Help for a poor traveler!'

A pack of short-coated, starveling dogs rushed out of the house and flung themselves on me, yelping and snarling. I pulled the cloak over my head and fell face down to save myself from their fangs. The mud beneath me was as ripe as the dippings from a privy, but the desire to preserve my throat from dog fangs made me burrow in it. Wolfish teeth snapped at my legs and buttocks. I was challenged by barks; a cold nose found its way under the cloak to snuffle my ear. I heard a human voice and raised my appeal to it:

'For the love of God, call off your dogs!'

But the voice, torn by the wind or by great anger, answered shrill and hard:

'Hold him, dog! Hold him! I'll put a pitchfork into the whoreson thief!'

8

'No, no! In the name of God, have mercy on one of his poor priests!'

My voice broke with anguish and a cur's teeth snicked me on the rump in reproof.

'Hold, dogs!' The voice was high enough to be the piping of a churlish stableboy, hoping to earn his master's approval for his valor. 'So, you're a priest, are you, vermin? Say something to me in Latin!'

'*Quare tristis incedo dum affligit me inimicus?* Why do I go sorrowful, while the enemy afflicts me! Now, call off your dogs, *boy!*'

He gave me a sharp laugh. 'Let me see your tonsure, first, holy man. Move too quick and I'll run this hayfork up your arse!'

To the profound misgivings of the whining hounds I uncovered my head. A great, slavering muzzle lolled its tongue before my face, either to kiss or to devour me. Behind the beast's pleated brow rose the windtorn human shape, poised with lifted hayfork, grim as Hell's own usher. The wind whipped at its long, unbound hair and ample skirts.

'You're a woman!' I croaked.

'And you're a priest – I think. Let me see more of you.'

The dogs jumped back in alarm as I rose, then rushed forward again savagely.

'Hold there! Get off, Gris!' She thumped the brute's lean ribs with her fork handle. 'Jesu, Father, but you stink like something three weeks dead – and no wonder! You've fallen in the pig's paddle. Marie!'

The house door opened wider to let out a coiffed head.

'My lady?'

'Call the dogs in. It's nothing but a wayfaring priest they've run to earth. Go on up to the house, Father. You're saved from being eaten.'

I went, closely accompanied by the sniffing, bristling dogs. The woman walked behind us with her hayfork over her shoulder. I could see the house was a decent, small country manor, built of stone and with heavily barred shutters and a thick door. But where were all its people?

'God's blessing on all within,' I said devoutly as we entered.

An elderly man crouched on a stool by the central hearth. The woman who had peered at us from the door was a fat, matronly servant, who held a child protectively in her arms, a wan-faced little girl about four years old. None of them spoke in answer to my civil greeting. I turned to the woman, who had brought her hayfork into the house as if still on guard against me. Her tangled mass of pale brown hair flowed over her shoulders and partly obscured her face, but one long, dark-rimmed eye like a sparrow hawk's regarded me. She swept the hair back with one hand and threw her chin up at the same time.

'So, you're a priest, then, though an uncommonly dirty one. Are you making a pilgrimage through all the pigsties for the love of St. Anthony?'

I decided the time had come to put an end to her impudence. I turned and coolly addressed the old man.

'Good man, are you the steward of this house?' His dress had already indicated he wasn't its master. 'If so, I should like to present myself in all courtesy to your master and beg leave of him to wash some of the filth from myself.'

He stared at me with rheumy eyes, his toothless mouth ajar. The woman behind me put her fork handle on the floor with a thump and said: 'Put some water to heat, Marie, and get out the tub. God knows, he does need a bath.'

'Yes, my lady.' The fat woman put the child down and waddled away toward the kitchen, while the child ran at once to hide its face in the younger woman's skirts.

'My lady?' I repeated with natural disbelief; though I'd heard Marie say it before, it hadn't seemed possible she was addressing this milkmaid.

She smiled sourly. 'Yes, priest. I'm Isabel de Trie, the mistress of this house. Never mind; we may all look like paupers, but we can still afford a guest a bath and some supper.' She gathered up the little girl tenderly, set her fork against the wall, and carried the child upstairs.

'I'll wash myself, woman, if you'll be so good as to leave me.' Marie had dragged out a tub until it was near the hearth and filled it with steaming water. Now she stood with a brush and towel, waiting. Her mistress hadn't returned from above, and the old man had tottered away out of sight.

'No man in a civilized house washes himself,' Marie said. 'That's woman's work. So, take off your nasty gown, Father, and climb in – unless you hold yourself so high you think only my lady should lather you.'

'I want no one to do it – it's indecent!'

She laughed hugely, enjoying my distress, and stood her ground. So did I. Then it came to me that when I had been a child at home, my mother had washed my father as well as any guest we ever had, at least their feet and legs. I turned my back to strip, on the opposite side of the tub from her, then backed into it and sat down quickly.

'Only two of them, like any other man, so it's all right,' she said, laughing. She took up a lump of greasy-looking black stuff and wallowed it on the brush before applying it to my back.

'What's that?' I cried, thinking it some witch's unguent.

'Why, it's soap, of course. Haven't you ever used any? It doesn't look like it.'

'Of course I have,' I replied haughtily. I had, but only once a year when the whole convent made a grand ablution in the spring. The rest of the year my baths, like everyone else's, consisted only of cold water and a stiff brush. Her soap was more pleasant-smelling stuff than ours of the abbey, which was concocted with an excess of lye. This was scented with herbs. I drew my knees up to my chest.

When she had scrubbed my head, back, arms, chest, and feet, she flung the brush and cloth to me and mercifully left me to finish the job alone. I was out of the tub and wrapped in a drying sheet when she returned with a bowl of steaming soup and part of a loaf of bread, which she set on the table for me. I was just sitting down to it when I saw her snatch up my discarded clothes. She dropped my gown and braies into the bathwater with a finicking gesture. I leaped to my feet and seized the cloak before she did the same with it.

She was astonished. 'Well, by good St Dismas and all his thieves, do you think I'm going to make off with your filthy cloak?' She held it up to examine it. 'Now, here's a thing! It's lined with vair, too good for the likes of you. Maybe it was you who stole it.'

'It belongs to my – to my lord. He commanded me to bring it to him.' I retreated guiltily at my own lie, but with cloak and letter budget safe in my hands. Alas, my sheet was slipping away, along with my dignity. Marie let me settle at the table again, then calmly took the cloak from me.

'I'll hang it to dry in the kitchen, then brush the mud from it in the morning.'

'I'll do that myself.'

But she took the cloak away and returned a moment later with a flagon of wine.

'You're a lucky man, to stumble into a house where honest women will take care of you. You've no right to behave as if we were thieves.'

I apologized meekly. She was right. No one could possibly covet the bishop's cloak in the state it was in. But she hadn't finished scolding.

'There're plenty in this world who might dream of coming home to a hot bath and supper such as you've had, but they can't – ever.

God grant there are good women to give charity to my lord where he is.'

I swallowed a hunk of bread. 'What do you mean? Is the master of this house gone on a pilgrimage?'

'More honor to him if he were, God pity him.'

'Is he a prisoner?'

'Say a prayer he isn't, Father.' She cut a piece from a wedge of cheese and shoved it in my direction.

'Then where is he, that he can't come home, woman?'

'Banished for treason.' The voice was that of her mistress. Isabel de Trie stood above us on the narrow gallery that ran across the far end of the hall. She came down the stairs, giving Marie a look that sent her trundling away to the kitchen. She had washed her face and plaited her hair, and put on her matron's veil, too, so she looked more the mistress of the house and less its milkmaid.

'That's a traitor's stool you're sitting on, Father. A traitor's bread you're eating. Are you a loyal subject of our duke? Perhaps you'd rather have your muddy gown back and leave us. It isn't wise to grow familiar with traitors.'

I stood up, clutching my sheet. 'Madam, I know nothing of your troubles, nor of the duke, but your charity is sweet to me. I wouldn't like to spend this night in the mud again.'

She nodded, gestured to me to sit and finish eating. While I did she sat at the far end of the table. She took a small measure of wine into her cup, but didn't drink it, only held it as she stared into the fire with a sad, proud face. If I moved my cup or made any noise with my spoon she would glance at me with a faint smile, then fall to her meditations again. What circumstances had made her husband a traitor and caused her to live in such solitude? I didn't know how to ask without risking offending her.

At last, wiping my mouth, I said: 'You take much comfort from the fire, my lady, and so do I. I thank you for giving me food and shelter.'

She half smiled again. 'I wasn't taking comfort from the fire, but from the sound of a man eating at my table. I was trying to believe you were my lord, come home again. It's the most comforting thing a woman can hear – her lord feeding at her table.'

I didn't know what to say to that. She was more fair in the firelight than before and younger than I first supposed; I couldn't guess her age, but it was nearer to mine than to Marie's.

'Another dream I was having – you'll laugh to hear it,' she said in a moment. 'I was thinking how good it would be if a woman were as free as a man to roam the world. If that were so, I'd go to Rouen, where I might hear some word of my lord.' She sighed. 'It's a wicked thought, I suppose.'

'I – I am going to Rouen, lady. Perhaps I could find out your news for you and send you a message.' I remembered I wasn't to talk of my business, but the offer seemed the least I could make, seeing her sorrow.

Her eyes flashed sideways at me. 'Beware, good Father. My servant began the tale of our woe for you and I have added the word *treason* to it. Are you not afraid? All my servants were; they've fled me, except my old bailiff, and Marie. My house – my barn – has been slighted by the duke's followers. Taking an interest in our doings could mark you as an accomplice in some men's eyes.'

She was right. I swallowed the brave retort in my mouth. 'What did your husband do, lady?'

Her chin lifted. 'He kept faith with his own liege lord, in a quarrel that was above him. But in these days even a true knight's fealty can be counted a crime.'

'I don't understand.'

She looked at me sternly. She had fine eyes, hazel, under delicate brows lighter than her hair.

'This manor is a knight's fee in the honor of Ralph de Tosny, Count of Conches. It was given to my father's father and to my father in turn. Now my husband holds it by right of marriage to me. Do you hear any news of the world where you come from? Do you know that William Bastard's son Robert Curthose has rebelled against his father for being refused the rule of this country, which his father promised him before he went to rule in England? Or that William Bastard even keeps the revenues of the county of Maine, the county he made Robert lord of – leaving his first son like a beggar without a sou?'

I shrugged. I had heard a little of it.

'Count Robert demanded his rights and rents many times and has been denied and humiliated as many times. At last he rebelled against an unjust father and is fled to his kinsmen in Flanders.' She looked at me for a moment as if I had had a hand in his disgrace. Then her shoulders slumped.

'There were many honest knights and young nobles who supported him, who had been made to swear fealty to him when his father presented him to them as their future duke. They were forced to ride with him when he fled, for the sake of their honor. Ralph of Conches is one of them. My husband is in his mesnie so he must ride with my lord Ralph. So, now they are all judged traitors. But if he had refused his true lord the service that was due him, he would still be a traitor, wouldn't he? There is no justice in these matters – none a woman can understand.' She rose and paced around the table.

'This is a family quarrel, after all. Is it right for other families to suffer for what divides one? William Bastard might forgive lesser men, who had no say in the matter, and bring them home to serve him. He might have done – but instead, he lets neighbors raid my manor, drive off my cattle, burn my tenants out of their cots. They've burned my barn roof. Who will repair it? My poor old bailiff – they struck him down when he tried to prevent them. He's in his dotage, but he alone offered to defend me.' She stopped, sighed, and held out her hands helplessly. Then she came swiftly to where I sat and bent over the table to me.

'Oh, Father, I may not understand all the ways of men, but I'm a knight's wife and a knight's daughter. I do know something about honor. If I could go to Rouen, I would beg Duke William to have mercy on my Amiot, who is in exile through no fault of his own. I would remind him how long this house has been in the keeping of men who have been loyal to him. And if the duke refused me, I would kneel at his lady's feet and plead with her as if she were the Blessed Virgin. She would hear me. She suffers from this as I do. It's her own son who is the head of those homeless men. I know she has a tender heart and would speak for me.'

She fell on her knees before me. 'Father – good young Father – will you take me to Rouen with you?'

My mouth opened and closed several times before I could speak. 'Oh, my – my lady, I cannot. I dare not. What would people say of you if you traveled all that way with a man who is neither your husband nor your kinsman? And I'm – only a priest. I couldn't protect you if it were necessary. And what would I say to Bishop O—' I stopped. How had I almost let that name slip through my lips?

'You are a priest of Odo's? Odo, who's the duke's brother?' Her long fingers gripped my knee, digging in.

'No, no, lady, only a courier from him to the court.' Oh, God, I'd done it again. 'Believe me, lady, I'm nothing, no one. If I were, I'd help you, but I'm no one.'

She stared at me with her falcon's eyes for another space of time, then let her head droop. 'Of course. I understand. It was uncivil of me to press my troubles on my guest. Forgive me.' She stood up. 'You're tired, I can see. Let me show you to your bed.' She poured a full measure into her wine cup, took it up, and gestured to me to follow her up the stairs.

'This was my own chamber, in the days before I was married to my lord,' she said, opening the door to a little room at the far end of the gallery. 'It's small, but the bed is good. I always took comfort from its being next to our little chapel.' She gestured to an alcove, where I saw a cresset burning above a prie-dieu. The only other upper chamber seemed to be at the far end of the gallery.

To my surprise and consternation she entered the bedchamber behind me, took a cresset from a hook on the wall, and went to fill and light it from that in the chapel. When she returned, with the lamplight making her eyes seem twice as beautiful and solemn, she said:

'We are poorer now than we were, but we still remember how to honor a guest. There is a shirt of my lord's on the bed for you to wear until your gown is dry. I will share the guest cup with you before I leave you to take your rest.'

She made sure I sat on the edge of the bed first. Since I wasn't gently born, as the other priests of her acquaintance probably were, I didn't know the ritual duties of a good Norman chatelaine and was both apprehensive and embarrassed by my ignorance. If there was a reply to be made to her courtesies, I was unaware of it and she would soon despise me.

But she only drank some of the wine, then offered the rest to me. When I had drained the cup, she set it aside, put her hands on my shoulders, and kissed me on either cheek and on the mouth.

'Good night, honored and holy guest. Sleep well and fear no harm. Our hearts are open, our doors are well barred, and our dogs are vigilant.' Taking up the cup, she left me.

I put on the shirt quickly and lay down on the bed, my head swimming. No woman other than my mother had ever touched me, let alone kissed me. I thought of the Rule about holding vain conversation with a woman. Was ours a vain converse? What was the punishment for letting a woman bathe me and another put her lips on mine? Had she noticed my agitation? Fatigue, as much as the memory of her hand on my thigh, caused my muscles to twitch now, like horseflesh. I balled myself up in the sheet, said my prayers, and began to argue in my mind what I should say to a confessor on the day's events. I couldn't even begin to frame an explanation, so I fell asleep.

I woke sometime in the night with a need to relieve myself, having slept like a dead man since before Vespers. I rose and groped my way downstairs, but found the door barred and a dog sleeping against it, which woke and growled. Marie and the bailiff were snoring on the floor near the hearth. I did the necessities against the kitchen hearth, then padded quietly back upstairs and was about to reenter my chamber when I heard a soft sound in the chapel alcove.

It was the Lady Isabel at her devotions. It must be Matins, I thought, shivering in my borrowed shirt, which was of a finer weave than I was accustomed to wear. I hesitated to join her for my own prayers because of my dress. I went to my bedside instead and knelt there, but as I began to bless myself the noise came again, soft and sorrowful. She was weeping. I flung the sheet around me and went to see about her.

She was kneeling at the prie-dieu, her white arms flung out over it, her face pressed between them. It was a most pitiable sight. I knelt beside her, not daring to touch her, but spoke a prayer for those in the unhappy house that harbored me, so that she could hear it. She lifted her head, folded her arms, and laid her cheek on them, gazing at me.

'You're kind to say a prayer for the duke's enemies, Father, but you'll need to repent of it when you reach Rouen.'

'Lady, I'm only a country priest, not one of the court chaplains. I doubt they'll be interested in my prayers in Rouen.'

'Oh, happy man, to be outside the interest of Rouen. Did I wake you? I'm sorry.'

'I'm used to waking in the middle of the night. You did me a service, to call me out of sleep for Matins. I might have slept through it otherwise.'

'I've often wondered how the religious could endure waking in the deep of night, as you do. Is it hard to learn?'

'It's a habit, like any other. But you do it, too, so where's the mystery?'

She sighed. 'There's a difference. I haven't been sleeping. But midnight is a good time for prayer, is it not? One feels that in the silence God must listen more carefully.'

I was uncomfortably silent; I rose to leave her, wrapping the sheet closer to my body. She reached out suddenly as I was going and took firm hold of my sheet.

'Hear my confession, sweet priest. I haven't heard a Mass or told my sins since my husband was judged a traitor.'

I stuttered in agitation. 'I – oh – I – I have no license to hear confession in this parish. I cannot offer the Holy Sacrament – my stole is wet with dirty water and must be cleansed – '

'Are you a priest or not?' she whispered fiercely. Her hands took hold of me. 'Hear me without absolving me, then, but hear me. I am in a state of mortal sin, because I continually hate my life and wish myself dead! I *would* kill myself if it weren't for my child, who would then be left helpless. I am alone here. Who will aid me if God refuses me? He has given me more than I can bear. Why? I have done no harm. Tell me, what shall I do when the duke drives me and my daughter from my house and gives it to one of his knights? How will I feed myself and my child without husband or property? Shall I become a whore?'

'Shh! You mustn't say such things to me or to yourself. This is no proper confession.'

'How else should I make one? I'm telling you the things that eat at my heart which I fear will damn my soul. Isn't that a confession? Tell me what I should say, then. Oh – sometimes I even hate my own husband – my good, loyal Amiot. I've wished he were dead and I knew of it. Then I would go to Duke William and say, "Give me a better husband, if you hated the one I had. This house will still be mine and loyal to you." '

I saw I couldn't escape her, so I looked about for a stool to sit on, to make the occasion more proper. It was decreed at the Synod of Rouen that a priest must not hear confession without his alb and stole, unless the matter was extreme. She made it seem extreme enough for a sheet. As I crouched on a stool, she crawled after me. I took her hands, made her fold them properly, and then tried to think of something to say to her grief. Her soft mouth pressed kisses on my hands.

'Father, I have stolen nothing, murdered no one, coveted nothing but peace and an honorable name. But I've still committed the unforgivable sins – to doubt the goodness of God and to wish myself dead. If these are unforgivable, as I've heard the priests say, you couldn't absolve me of them anyway, could you?'

'A priest may forgive what he believes is truly repented. But God knows your heart better than you do. It may be He knows you've never doubted Him or wanted death. Is this possible?'

She looked up at me, smiling very sweetly in spite of her tears. 'Every day I say to Him, "Send me the means and I will find the way." ' Is that what you mean?'

'Yes, if you hope still, you must still believe in God's goodness. In which case He will forgive you. For my part, I absolve you and bless you as much as it is in my power to do. For a penance, I say go to your daily prayers as before and hear Mass when you can. Leave it to God to settle your affairs with the duke. He will surely send you an answer.' I blessed her, thinking how wonderful it was that God had put the power of blessing and healing in my hands and the words on my lips when needed. Looking into her meekly upturned face, I was entranced with my own authority. It was my last coherent thought.

Struggling to rise, she was encumbered by the sheet I'd let trail on the floor between us. I took her elbows. In her distress I saw she had somehow loosened the laces of her gown. As she rose she snared her skirt underfoot and fell against me. I caught a glimpse by cresset light of the fairest breast I had ever tried to imagine, working from childhood memory and the furtive speculation of an adolescent on the chaste image of Our Lady.

I had attempted to stand to lift her just as she stumbled. The next moment we were both tumbling over the stool. Her hair poured over her shoulders into my face like a river of silk. I might still have kept my head, but as we fell our noses collided painfully and she gave a little cry:

'Oh!'

At that tiny note of alarm all my reason fled, carrying away with it those frail wardens of my soul – prudence, speech, and chastity – like so many drowsy infants snatched from a burning bed.

After the first thunderbolt had struck and left us stunned and gasping, we rose and stumbled to my bed. There we fell and lay entangled like kindred vines, too astonished for sleep. At least, I was so affected. My lady Isabel seemed in lively spirits. She nestled her head on my naked breast and prattled out all the history of her house, her father's deeds, and the superlative character of her lord, Amiot de Trie.

I lay listening, stroking her arm where it lay across my body. What had I done? I could scarcely believe myself. In the midst of my vanity I had been overwhelmed, thrown down, drowned, seduced by a little water from a woman's eye, a little breath out of her mouth, and the mere glimpse of her flesh.

I had always thought I knew what my temptations would be: I was ready for luxury; I was fair game for soft apparel and a secular office; I could bear accusation of greed for dainty food and sweet wines. But lust? To fall to raving hunger on a strange woman's body, like a swineherd on a stolen pie? My God, I could already smell the brimstone it would take to purge me for a thousand years!

Yet, when I opened my mouth to speak, instead of lamentations for my crime, I uttered lover's nonsense: 'The skin of your arm is like the smoothness of the night rail that leads me down to Matins-song. Sometimes, when my eyes are still half blind with sleep, I've felt it like this, a living thing.'

She lifted her head. 'I think you must be laughing at me. You aren't listening to me and you use very strange flattery.'

'Lady, I hear and adore you, but I lack better reference for flattery. I can offer you the wooing of King Solomon the Wise to the Queen of Sheba. His verses are the special study of our house: "I sleep, but my heart wakens. It is the voice of my beloved who calls me. Open to me, my sister, my love, my dove – my undefiled –" '

'Undefiled? Now I see you do mock me, when you've just ravished me!'

I broke off my rapture. 'What? I ravished you? Lady, it was you who did the ravishing. I wasn't the one on top.' I started to laugh at my own ready wit, but she punched me in the stomach with her hard little fist.

'Shh! You held me fast! You wouldn't let me go.'

'That is ridiculous,' I whispered earnestly now. 'While my head was still ringing from its knock on the floor, you – you made a fornicator of me. Now I know why that garment you women wear is called a shift. It shifted from your feet to your waist in half a moment.'

'Hey – it was your cock that made a fornicator out of you, boy! It knew its business. It's been to the hen yard before now, I think.'

'Lady, I swear on my – on my – I was a virgin until you fell on me. I scarcely knew what it was we were to do before we'd done it!'

She began to quiver in my arms, with rage I thought. 'Bewitched you? Have I done so? Spoiled you?' She lifted her face and I saw that she was laughing at me, laughing until the tears ran down her cheeks again, though she laughed without sound. She whispered: 'Oh, my poor, innocent, downy-checked, pretty boy, have I blunted the plow and stunned the ox? So he'll never plow again?'

She had set about deliberately to seduce me, and now she laughed at me. I gave a croak of outrage and seized her, but it was like laying hands on a shape shifter. She became at once all elbows, teeth, and nails, until the fierceness of her defense forced me to overpower her, as well as made me hot to have her again. When I had pitched myself over her, she turned all groans and sighs and boneless in my grasp.

I was too full of the heat of my victory to wonder at the ease of it.

Pinning her hands to the bed and her no longer thrashing legs beneath mine, I gasped:

'Now we'll see – how the ox can plow!'

He plowed marvelous well, for the little time he'd known the labor. I was hard put to keep him in harness. Her hands slipped from my grasp and gave a token push at my shoulders; then she surrendered entirely, lying like a lamb sacrificed.

When I was spent and my senses began to return, I felt a brute – a not altogether disagreeable sensation, I discovered. Still she lay meek and silent, sniffling a little; so, to make amends I began to kiss her, to blame myself, to tell her how I loved her. I begged her to let me prove myself by allowing me to take her with me to Rouen.

She turned and sighed, said we did wrong and it mustn't be, guided my hand to her breast without seeming aware of it, and had the pleasure of refusing me many times before she agreed at last to what she had determined I should do from the moment she set eyes on me.

9

I felt much less the bold harrower of women by dawn. I was sluggish, sober, and full of tardy wisdom like the boy who caught the bee.

Shamefaced before a smirking Marie, I was glad enough to pay for my breakfast by going to the barn in her place to milk their only cow. It was clear that Isabel had already made our plans clear to her servant – with neither blush nor stammer. In fact, from the looks that passed between them I began to understand that I was not so much the fellow architect of Isabel's design as merely a new figure added to an old draft.

'Your gown is washed and dried, Ranulph,' Isabel said when I returned from the barn. 'But wouldn't it be better if you put on some of my husband's clothes instead?'

'I am forbidden to travel in disguise,' I said grimly.

'You wouldn't be in disguise. You'd only be wearing a gambeson and hose, with the shirt you've already got on. It's a more practical guise for travel, surely, but not a disguise.' She leaned closer to me. 'Are you afraid someone will take us for husband and wife?'

'No, only that they'll wonder why a layman wears a tonsure.'

'Oh, but my lord left at home a fine velvet hood. I'll bring it down to you.' She started away nimbly.

'Get me my gown instead. I'll be your chaplain, lady.' I couldn't share her light mood with Marie leering at us from the hearthside. Isabel shrugged and went into the kitchen.

In all truth I was tempted to wear her husband's finery, just for the experience of appearing as a wellborn person. But I could hardly let her think she could rule me in her every whim. I thought she might be sulking, but she returned from the kitchen in the same gracious mood and offered me a pair of her husband's old boots in exchange for my mud-stiffened sandals. These I accepted.

When I was decently dressed – even the bishop's cloak had been brushed nearly clean of mud – I packed up Isabel's bundle of belongings and went out to the courtyard while she said good-bye to Marie and her little daughter. Old Carl, the bailiff, had been hobbling toward the barn earlier as I was leaving it. Now he came forth from it leading a somnolent horse of a strange tan color that I'd taken for dun when I fed him. While I looked on, wondering how such a swaybacked, thickbellied animal kept from breaking in two, Carl unfurled a piece of ragged saddle cloth, leaned back on one infirm leg, as if he were about to cast a javelin, and flogged the horse across its back.

A thick cloud of barn dust, hair, and particles of stable bedding flew into the air, almost obscuring both man and beast. When wind carried the cloud away, there stood revealed a placid, elderly *white* destrier, already browsing at a clump of grass, unstartled by the strange attack and his own transformation.

Carl saddled him; I tied Isabel's bundle and my own letter pouch to the saddle, then helped her to mount when she came running like a girl across the courtyard. I led them down the mud-rutted pathway to the high road, feeling like a fool in thrall to an elf woman.

By midday on the road I was drooping, while Isabel, perched on her destrier, was still gay as a thrush, entertaining herself with tales of her husband, who was a peerless knight, brave as Roland, handsome as Oliver, and distantly related to the Archbishop of Lisieux.

Her wifely pride was admirable. Her voice was agreeable, the day was fine in spite of much mud still underfoot, but all that moved me was how little sleep and how much exertion I had experienced in the two days past. I began to fall behind the destrier's head until he was leading me, jerking at my arm. Isabel at length noticed this and broke off her elegy.

'I think you must be getting lazy. Get up behind me and ride, then.'

'I've never mounted a horse.'

'It's simple. Put your foot in the stirrup and push up.'

This was inadequate advice. The horse didn't care for it any more than I did. He danced sideways, nearly putting us all in the ditch. Isabel dismounted, gave brisk instructions, waited until I was secure though uncomfortable in the saddle, then let me pull her up before me. She took the reins again and we proceeded most delightfully with my arms about her.

I discovered I no longer wanted to doze. There were too many distractions of her person to occupy my mind as we rocked together on the great beast's back. But neither my lips to her ear, nor my geometric fingers making computations of diameter and volume on her breasts, could stanch the flow of her speech on Amiot de Trie.

'By St. Michael and all his angels, lady,' I said in exasperation, 'how did you ever let this paragon escape you for a mere rebellion? Why not, at least, have made a golden image of him for your worship before he went?'

Now she was offended. 'Is it wrong for a wife to praise her husband?' She pushed my hands away.

'No, not at all, I suppose. But is it usual for her to praise him so warmly after putting horns on him, Madam? You must instruct me in this as you did in the horn setting.'

She jerked up the reins so suddenly that the destrier reared and I nearly pitched off over his rump. 'Isabel!'

'Get off. I see you've rested enough. Too much weight in the saddle will tire Charlemagne.' She gave me another jolt with her elbow, so it was dismount or sprawl. It was much the same thing in the end.

'I've a mind to gallop Charlemagne. It's a simple pleasure – *another* simple pleasure I haven't enjoyed for many a month.' She set off at a lunge. Charlemagne's hooves pelted me with pebbles and mud as he leaped away. I'd never have thought he had so much spirit left in him. By the time I'd taken ten steps, he had carried Isabel over a rise in the road and out of my sight. I was left angry and humiliated, until an appalling thought struck me.

'Wait! Come back! You've got my budget!' I ran after her, shouting until my breath gave out; worse, my boots took on so much mud that I was reduced to a heavy trot. She was nowhere in sight when I topped the rise. The road fell among lush meadows, then curved around a plot of woods. I floundered forward, reciting a litany of abuse.

'That stupid, proud, vain, conniving, lust-provoking woman has seduced and ruined me – oh, God, she has the bishop's letters! What if she opened them and understood them last night? Oh, God, what if they contain some secret she can sell to win back her wretched husband? What if she's thrown them away? Oh, God!'

I made an earnest appeal to Him and to Bishop Odo in my head, begging ignorance and youth, extenuating circumstances of an extreme nature worthy of their consideration before they condemned me. Failing forgiveness, I made a recommendation to the Almighty to strike me dead on the spot and save me the disagreeable duty of explaining to an unknown chaplain in Rouen how I had lost the bishop's letters.

I saw her at last, sitting under an ancient apple tree in a field by the road while her horse grazed nearby. I was pouring sweat and had the bishop's fine cloak wadded under my arm like a bundle of rags when I dropped down beside her and rolled flat on my back.

'Where – is my budget? Did you throw it away? I'll be flogged at least for losing it, if that gives you any pleasure.'

She was eating one of the freckled apples, but threw it away when she found a worm. 'I'd imagine you deserve a flogging, if not for that sin, then surely for some other.' But she took pity on my desperate groan. 'What's the matter with you, boy? Of course I didn't throw it away. You can see it on the saddle if you'd only look.'

I did, then let my head fall back to earth with a heartfelt sigh. 'What's in it?' she asked.

'I'm not allowed to say. Call it my life. Shall we go on, now that you've had your simple pleasure?' But I couldn't sit up, let alone rise.

'We'll go on when Charlemagne is rested and fed. He isn't as young as you, or as eager. How old are you, by the way, boy?'

I looked into the gnarled branches of the tree full of sour fruit, not yet ripe but already wormy. Like myself. 'I'm too old to be called a boy, except by way of an insult. I'm twenty and I'm a priest, by special dispensation of the bishop, however unworthy I may seem of that honor to you.'

She leaned over me indulgently, brushed something out of my hair, then wiped my sweating face with her hand.

'Twenty. Well, now. I beg your pardon for calling you a boy – and for frightening you so terribly.'

'I wasn't frightened, only concerned for my obligation to my superior,' I said priggishly.

'You were terrified.' She laughed. 'Oh, Ranulph, stop glaring into this tree and forgive me. It's your duty.' She bent and kissed me tenderly on the head.

I felt childish tears well up in my throat. 'Why did you choose me to make a fool of?'

She sat back and considered me gravely. 'I must go to Rouen. I can't go alone. I have no male relatives to take me there, except my cousin, who already lives there. He's married to the portreeve's daughter and should be able to get me a hearing before the duke or his lady. I told you I'd promised God that if He sent me the means, I'd find the way. He sent me you.'

I turned my face away from her so that she wouldn't see if I wept.

'There's another thing,' she said in a moment. 'I wanted a lover. You may have heard that women are weak vessels, filled with foolishness and desire for carnal pleasure? That's as a priest once explained womankind to me. Maybe it's true, though I never believed it before. But – I've been wed – and if my lord is dead, no doubt my cousin will see that I'm wed again. It's my duty to be wed and keep my land for my child.' She rolled a grass stem between her fingers. 'I love my husband, as I'm commanded to do, but I always wanted to know what it was like, just once, to – and you seemed to want loving.' She put the grass stem in her mouth.

I rolled over on my stomach and put my head on my arms so that I could watch Charlemagne grazing. I felt quite used and entirely pitiable. 'I've never been out of the abbey, except to go to the hay fields, or to Bayeux to take my orders.'

She said: 'I've never seen anything of the world, except my home and the convent of St. Mary in Lisieux, where I was sent after my mother died and where I stayed until I was married. My father brought Amiot to the convent and told me he'd be my husband. We signed the betrothal contract there with the abbess as the witness. A month later Amiot and my father came back and took me to the church, where we were bound together with the Sacrament, then we went home again. I was thirteen. Within the year I was kindled, but I lost the child. All my children have miscarried or died, except my Alice. I'm not so much older than you, but if my firstborn had lived, he'd be nearly fifteen now – almost a man. So, I feel nearly old enough to be' – she laughed – 'a little sorry for the way I've treated you. But I'm far too young to bear with your putting on priestly airs and asking me how I could love my husband, yet lie with you. You love God, yet you've lain with me. Do you hate Him now?'

'No. But He may hate me.'

'Yes, there is that to think of.' She fell silent.

I tried to find something to say to my own perplexity. But it was a warm day, the bees were humming over the dropped apples, and I was very tired.

When I opened my eyes, the sun was halfway down the western sky. I rolled over, expecting to find myself deserted, but Isabel was tightening the horse's girth strap. She led him toward me, stopping at the lowest branch of the apple tree to pick one of its fruits.

'May I comfort you with an apple?' she said lightly.

As I rose and took it from her, she slipped her arms about my waist and held me. It was an apt phrase that mocked my use of the Song of Songs to her the previous night – 'Comfort me with apples, for I am sick of love.' I was from that moment 'sick of love' for her. There seemed no remedy for it.

We mounted and rode again at a thoughtful pace until we came to Brionne, where we applied to the castle warden for hospitality and were admitted. There were half a dozen other travelers there to enjoy supper and a bed that night.

The meal was ample and the company congenial, several being pilgrims coming home after a summer of shrines, but by the time others were starting to yawn and search for a bedding spot on the hall floor, I'd lost my taste for the place. Sleep there would mean separation from Isabel, since all the women were collecting on the upper floor, while the men were spreading their cloaks in the servants' hall where we had supped.

My face must have reflected my concern. Isabel smiled at me and touched my hand secretly as we stood together. My heart pounded at her wise look and my face grew hot.

'Shameless boy,' she whispered. 'Aren't you weary yet, after such a night and day of labor?'

I shook my head dumbly, caught at her hand, and felt it squeeze my fingers in return. We made an excuse to the hall steward that we must be at Bec Abbey before their guesthouse gate was closed, to meet a companion who would be waiting for us there. We left the castle and rode only until we were out of sight of its walls. The warm sun and brisk winds of the season had sucked up most of the rain where the ground was grassy. We found a small crown of land above the fields that was sheltered by a rowan tree. There we spread Lord Odo's splendid cloak and lay together on its pelt, groaning in the throes of luxury and love until the night was half worn away.

I was lost; yet, from that night, though I was ever more in love with her, she was more distant with me. When we came to the famous Abbey of Bec, which I gladly would have passed, even at the risk of hunger before nightfall, she insisted that we stop.

'I must say a prayer for my lord and my daughter in the Virgin's chapel. I've heard it said that this shrine of Our Lady is famous for rewarding prayer,' she answered when I made objections.

I could hardly refuse to let her pray, but it made me uncomfortable to enter the place myself. I said my prayers quickly and apart from her, but felt no easier for it. I'd never yet left a shrine with quite so many heavy sins unrepented.

By way of partial penance, I avoided going to the guests' table later, where Isabel took a meal of bread and cider. I walked outside in the churchyard, fasting. It was there I first saw the famous teacher Anselm, the Italian prior of Bec.

He was already known throughout Normandy for being Lanfranc's personal choice to succeed him when that scholar left Bec to become Archbishop of Canterbury and William Bastard's closest adviser. Anselm was about five and forty then, I'd judge; like his old master, he was a tall, thin, aristocratic Italian with deep-set eyes and a Roman nose.

He was walking rather quickly into the churchyard, as if to get away from the flocks of pilgrims who always wanted to receive his blessing. It was believed he had such personal sanctity that only to have him near one would cure one of any ailment. He was sent for continually by the families of invalids, as if he were himself a holy relic.

I heard his name spoken in awe and turned to stare at him as he approached. He returned my stare with such intensity that I almost dropped on my knees to beg forgiveness for those sins he seemed to have inferred from one mystic glance.

But I was mistaken. He was shortsighted, even then. He didn't really see me until my heart was in my throat and we were no more than five paces from an ambulatory collision. Then he started a little, broke his stride, and nodded to me in an absent but friendly manner as he veered off on another course, followed by his admirers, leaving me shaken in his wake. I believe he was all but unaware that I was a human being and not a gatepost. I didn't see him again for fifteen years, when he had aged greatly, but once seen, he wasn't easily forgotten.

Isabel had fallen to gossiping with other pilgrims in the guesthouse, so we made a late start from the abbey. Our next shelter for the night, save some peasant's hut, was marked on my map as Elbeuf, a little town on the Seine.

The day was a long one for me, as I had forsworn food and was sweetly denied that recompense I might have had from Isabel when we stopped to rest old Charlemagne. She was benign, but adamant as a vestal virgin. I might not kiss her mouth, or embrace her, or lay her in the long grass, though I tried most valiantly to do all those things every time she dismounted. I was allowed to kiss her cheek and encouraged to kiss her hand instead, while I listened to her extol the beauty of Anselm's abbey.

I protested her niggardliness, almost weeping, but she only smiled at me like an indulgent parent.

'You should learn to kiss ladies' hands, dear love. It's the new fashion among lovers and I think it's charming. Here, let me show you how I was greeted when the Count of Conches came to pay us a visit two years ago.' She took my hand and lightly touched it with pursed lips, like a bird drinking from a puddle. 'They say – that is, Count Roger said – that if a man is a lady's lover, not just her admirer, he turns the hand and kisses the palm, like this.'

I took the opportunity to capture her chin in my fingers and kissed her soundly on the mouth instead. 'That is more pleasant to me.' I sighed, wrapping her in my arms. I would have kissed her so again, but she wriggled away, laughing.

'You're no lover, Ranulph. You're like a greedy babe who only wants to devour. You should learn to savor.'

'I do, but I know what's worth savoring. Your hand savors too much of Charlemagne, lady, but your mouth tastes sweet as honey, and there are spices in your breasts that I would sup on like a bee, if I could come to them.'

That pleased her mightily, almost persuaded her, I thought; but still she refused my desire. She rose to walk about as she gave me further instruction in the wooing of ladies by courtesy.

'Have you never heard the story of Sir Amiot and the Lady Eglantine?'

'Your husband's mistress?'

'No! It's a tale of love and chivalry I heard when we entertained Count Roger and his bride, whose name is the same as mine. Sir Amiot was a knight who loved a married lady who could never be his. But he drew his strength for battle from her, merely by saying her name. He was sorely wounded once, in a tournament, but recovered when she took pity and came to bend over his invalid's bed, to lay the tips of her fingers on his brow.'

'That sounds like a very silly and unlikely story to me, unless she boasted the healing powers of Anselm.'

Isabel was piqued. 'It isn't a silly story; it's a beautiful story, full of – delicacy. I fell in love with my husband because of it, simply because his name is Amiot.'

'You've been his wife since you were thirteen, yet you didn't fall in love with him until two years ago when you took a fancy to his name? That *is* an edifying tale, after all. I was named for St. Ranulph of Bayeux, who was much more delicate than Amiot's lady. He waited until he had been dead for three years before he healed a widow woman of the flux, which is how he came to be made a saint. Is there some hope you'll think better of me on that account hereafter?'

She pealed with laughter. 'Oh, Ranulph, you are such a vain thing after all. I'd almost forgotten how young men take everything to heart so fiercely. Amiot was like that when we were first married.'

'But he changed. I suppose you told him how it was you finally came to love him?'

She looked shocked. 'Merciful God, no! It wouldn't be decent to mention such a thing to him. After all, he's my husband, not a lover.'

I wanted to discomfort her as she had me. 'Did it ever occur to you that this tale of Sir Amiot and his highborn married love might be your own husband and Count Roger's lady? It was she who told you the tale, wasn't it?'

If spiteful looks could murder, I'd have been a corpse then. She gathered up her skirts and stalked away to catch Charlemagne. It was only with difficulty that I was allowed to help her mount. We proceeded toward Elbeuf in almost monastical silence. I was too rebuffed to offer her further conversation, while she rode above me with a face turned to stone.

As the day waned, the land we passed through became rougher, more densely wooded. The road wound about dark hills covered with black pines or tawny oaks. We began to think of thieves at the same moment, when I halted long enough to pick up a heavy branch to use as a club and she at last consented to speak to me:

'Perhaps you should ride now, too.'

I got up in front of her this time. Despite William Bastard's severe justice for such people, outlaws were not unknown. They risked mutilation or death at his decree for poaching game or robbing travelers, but still they poached and robbed. Isabel leaned more closely against my back as the day grew darker. A branch creaking in the wind made her startle. After a long spell of silence she tightened her embrace about my waist and whispered:

'I'll be sorry to see our journey end, Ranulph. Will you?'

But I was stolid: 'After these hills? No, my lady, I'm weary enough to sleep in a briar patch and hungry enough to take dinner in a tannery.'

'You'll be taking dinner with the Tanner's grandson tomorrow – at his expense, at least. I'll be with my cousin Beroald and his wife. Perhaps we'll never see each other again. It's very likely. Will you be glad for that, too, since I've wounded your pride?'

My stoicism crumbled. I pressed her hand where it lay against my heart now. 'Don't say such things. I can't bear to think it. I've promised I'll write you a petition to send to the king. Am I no longer worthy for even that service?'

'It may not be necessary. One of the women I spoke to at Bec told me that Count Robert and his men are now at a place just inside the French border called Gerberoy. She says the families of the rebels have asked the French king to make a peace between the Bastard and his son. King Philip is the Lady Matilda's kinsman; perhaps he'll do it. They're all his vassals in the end, aren't they? So it's his part to make them come to terms. I may be able to go to Gerberoy, if Beroald will help me. Have you ever heard of the place?'

I took up the reins again, feeling cold and defeated.

We found a deep incline between two cliffs that brought us to the river and into Elbeuf after sunset. It was a village of boatmen and fishermen, one of whom gave us directions to a merchant's house where we might find a bed for the night.

The merchant's wife, a red-cheeked, gregarious woman, gave us an ample dinner of grilled fish, cheese, barley cakes, and cider. She was very curious that a wellborn woman was traveling with a stubble-bearded young clerk whose cloak looked too rich for him. Isabel made up a tale to please her without the least difficulty, though it didn't please me at all.

'My husband is lying ill in Rouen. This is my brother, who has leave of his master, the Vicomte of Bayeux, to escort me to him.'

I saw the good woman had trouble believing Isabel and I were close kin, but the only expression of doubt she demonstrated was to see that our sleeping places on the floor of her house were separated by at least a dozen other people of her household.

I tried to get Isabel outside to speak to her privately one last time, pretending it was our custom to say our evening prayers together for her dear lord's recovery. But Isabel, who was already kneeling on her pallet, blessed herself like an angel and said, 'Brother, I beg your pardon for forgetting, but I've just said my prayers.'

So we went to rest. By and by the household fell to snoring. The fire fell into embers and the little mice and beetles came out of their holes to scuttle around us, gleaning the floor rushes for food scraps. I tossed and yearned. Isabel slept.

The next morning we boarded a barge that had stopped at the village to take on casks of pickled fish. Charlemagne was well tied and buttressed by heavy bales of hemp, but whickered nervously at the choppy river. The rough water and the prospects of parting from Isabel made me feel sick twice over.

She seemed unperturbed by either thoughts or blustery weather, but in a while she rose from the hemp bale she sat on and went to comfort Charlemagne. I followed. We stood together by the horse's head, out of earshot of the bargemen. She rubbed Charlemagne's nose and stroked his thick neck.

'You're kind to horses, but cruel to me,' I said in a low voice. 'Why did you waste our last night together? We might have slipped away to the stable and kept the horse company.'

She made a face of wry amusement. 'What a scandal that would have been to the goodwife, to have a pair of incestuous lovers in her stable.'

'Did you make up that ridiculous lie just to keep from being with me?'

'It wouldn't have mattered what else I said. She'd have been watching us anyway. Would you want the tale of your indiscretion to go downriver with you and maybe reach the ears of those you must meet at court? It would have done, you know.'

I closed my eyes and pressed my face against the horse's neck. 'What worse thing could happen to me than has already happened? I'm in Hell for you, Isabel, truly. Abstinence and silence won't answer for it.'

'Ranulph, please don't start practicing remorse on me again. It's very tiresome. Fornication is only a venial sin. Confess yourself tomorrow and avoid Hell.'

'This that I suffer is mortal.'

'Pah! Since when was itching without scratching a mortal sin?'

'What is mortal is that I love you. That's more serious than merely lying with you, or wanting to. It comes between me and repentance. I'll see your face when I should be feeling remorse. I'll die loving you – and then where will I be?'

She laughed a little three-note sound. 'Oh, Ranulph, surely you don't think you invented that sad tale. Why, King David must have used it to cozen Bathsheba.'

Nothing would persuade her I wasn't making stale lovers'

speeches. My sad face made her all the gayer, no doubt feeding her belief in those stupid love tales she'd lapped up in her ignorance. She never told me that their ritual required her to be the more cold to me, the more I appeared to suffer for her.

We docked at Rouen by mid-morning. She mounted Charlemagne, and after asking directions I escorted her through the narrow streets of town to her cousin's house, where she left me outside the door after thanking me for my aid and piously begging me to remember her in my prayers.

IO

William de St. Carileph, the king's chaplain and lord Odo's confidant, took my letter pouch, opened it and briefly examined the inscriptions and seals on the letters it contained. He was a heavy-cheeked man of middle age, with a bibulous nose and a slight cast in one eye.

'This seal is broken. Have you been browsing, Brother?' He asked it almost conversationally. But I was aghast.

'No, Father! I've never touched the letters since they were put in the budget, or even opened the bag, except once, to see if they – if they were still dry. If it's broken, it must have happened when I fell in the pig wallow.'

He lifted his sad, rheumy blue eyes to my face. 'I beg your pardon?'

I briefly explained my mishaps on the road. His loose face quivered; he snorted: 'God's Knees, I think I must believe you! Only a convent cub would foot it through a storm, or avoid a decent bed in Caen for a cradle in a ditch. Are you quite sane? Well, never mind. What else have you brought me?'

'Nothing, Reverend Father.'

'His Grace gave you nothing else to bring, or the pigs devoured it? Which?'

'He gave me nothing else – oh – he gave me his cloak to wear, since he couldn't spare me a horse, but that is all.'

He rested his jowls on one hand and studied me.

'Where is the cloak, good Brother?'

'I put it on a peg out in the hall. It's rather warm to wear indoors.'

'Go and get it,' he said with great patience, 'before someone with thinner blood or greater sense steals it.'

I hadn't considered that possibility, now I was in the ducal stronghold. I rushed out to retrieve my prize.

'This place is a thieves' den. Never forget it,' he said as he took the cloak from me and shook it out. 'If you have anything of value, keep it about you, or lock it up in one of our chests in the chancel. Even then I won't vouch for its safety if it can be sold.' He laid the cloak across his knees and began to stroke it carefully down the front edges. His warning made me the least bit apprehensive of his action.

'It's a wonderful garment,' I said. 'His Grace was very generous to give it to me.' Just so he wouldn't think he could make free with it.

'Yes, very thoughtful of him. You can't wear it here, you know, unless you tear out the lining. People of our profession aren't permitted to wear fine pelts.' He turned the cloak, sliding its hem between fingers and thumb. He stopped about a quarter of the way to the back seam and probed the fur gently. 'Ah, here it is.'

'What is it?' I could think nothing but that I'd injured the fur and would be fined for the damage.

'Come with me. This place is too open.'

I followed him in perplexity out of the chancel and up a narrow stair to a small chamber above. He gestured me to come in, then closed the door, threw the cloak on a table, and at once began to rip the hem from the lining.

'What are you doing?' I started to protest the ruin of my prize, then I stared: out of the inner parts of the vair St. Carileph loosened and brought forth a long, thin strip of white wool sewn into a tube. He caught one end of the wool between his teeth and ripped it, then began to squeeze and pull at what was inside it. One at a time, interspersed with plugs of lint, he extracted jewel after gleaming jewel from the cloak hem. Sapphires, rubies, moonstones, garnets, opals, bloodstones, lapis – every precious stone I could imagine existing. It took him several minutes to work them out, while I stood gaping, too astonished to speak. I had wallowed through the mire dragging that treasure at my heels. I had lain with Isabel upon it, never thinking I could put my fingers on anything more wonderful than the treasures in her flesh.

When St. Carileph had them all out, he counted the jewels swiftly, collected them in his palm, and poured them into a talc pot such as scriveners use to prepare their parchment. The pot was three-quarters full of glinting stones. He found another talc pot on a shelf and emptied enough of its contents into the first to cover the jewels, after which he briskly folded up my cloak and put it into a chest standing against the wall, which he locked. He picked up the talc pot and motioned me to follow him downstairs again, where he stowed it unconcernedly on the shelf under his own desk. He then chose one of Bishop Odo's letters, broke the seal, and read it; nodded, glanced at the rest again, and put them aside. He folded his hands on the desk.

'Now. Are you at all aware of what any of these letters contains?'

'No, Reverend Father.'

'Don't call me "Reverend Father." I may have been that once, but here I am only one of the many humble clerks in the service of our king and duke. By your leave, I will call you Ranulph and you may call me – Carileph. There are quite enough Williams and too many titles in this place without adding our own insignificant ones, don't you agree?'

I nodded, knowing nothing.

'Well then, Ranulph, since you don't know what's in my letter, I'll tell you. His Grace is pleased to recommend you to me as a courier who may be useful to our lady the queen, should she have occasion to need one. Now – you're fresh from the schoolroom, from the look of you. How's your memory?'

'Very good, I believe.'

'No, Ranulph, it is not. You have already forgotten that you brought me this budget and – the rest. Do you follow?'

'I – think so.'

'Good. Why have you come to Rouen?'

'Why, to bring you – '

'What? Bring me what? I see nothing.'

'I beg your pardon, I was mistaken. I came to Rouen to – I don't know why I came, Father.'

'Why, man, are you wandering in your wits? A priest doesn't just roam from place to place without purpose or leave. People will think he's a vagabond. I suspect you came to fill a vacancy left by the departure of one of my clerks, who went to Heaven, we trust. I'm certain that's why your abbot sent you. You can use the pen, can't you?'

'Yes, of course. Fa— Carileph, why can't you just tell me straight out what I'm to do? If the Lady Matilda needs a secret courier, I'm both willing and discreet.'

'No, you are most indiscreet. Who has mentioned the Lady Matilda here? Not I, I assure you. You say you can write? Then there's a place for you in the chancery. Since you're a priest, you'll also be counted as one of the tower chaplains while you're here.' He cleared his throat and recited:

'As such, you will earn double rations every day, feast or fast, for saying Mass, in addition to two wax candles on Wednesdays and Saturdays, for the services, and one for burning before relics. You will draw a gallon of sweet wine daily, for Mass, and one gallon of ordinary wine for your own purposes. What you don't consume you may sell back to the wine steward at a price of his own devising, which I regret to say will be infamous, but there's nothing to be done about it. He must have his profit or he'll carry tales to the chief steward about us.

'You will say Mass, or sing in the chapel according to your turn, then report to me promptly after first service to see if I have work for you. If I have none, perhaps one of the dispensers will. The rest of your time will be your own, for prayer or study, so long as you don't use it to make – yourself – famous here. Do you understand? Is that satisfactory?'

My mouth opened and closed wordlessly.

'Good, good. Then tell me about yourself. Have you ever been in Rouen before?'

'No, never.'

'Ever been presented to the king, his queen, or any of their children?'

'No.'

'What do you know about the Count of Maine?'

'Who?'

'His Excellency Count Robert, the first – son – of Normandy.' He had a way of drawing out his speech which was very distracting to me. But at last I could answer:

'You mean the one they call Curthose? I know he's rebelled against the king and fled to France, where he's now in possession of a place called Gerberoy, unless he's made peace with his father through the help of the King of France, who's their cousin.' He had been treating me like an idiot and I was pleased to show him I was no such thing.

He leaned forward. 'Dear Christ, Who bled for all our sins, where did you pick up all of that?'

'We – I heard some talk to that effect at Bec.'

'You stopped at Bec? Did you speak to Prior Anselm?'

'Good Lord, no! Do I look as if he'd speak to me?'

He grinned and pulled at his spongy nose. 'No, but then he's an odd fish. Whoever said the count has made peace with the king has misinformed you, however. He is an infamous prodigal and traitor; all who follow him are traitors. He isn't – mentioned – here.' He rose and put away the letters.

'Well, that seems to finish it. Oh – another thing about names and titles. While our great and noble master is in truth King of all England and enjoys hearing his title, his vassals here do not. It summons up for them an unpleasant vision of a man like themselves who's gotten above them. Here you will hear him spoken of as the duke. You would do best to speak of him as "His Grace." Also, his eldest son is not to be lightly named Curthose – even if he is a traitor and even if the name was bestowed by his own father in a fit of perception. You may hear it used in the court, I'll grant, but you will say Count Robert, or better still, not speak of him at all. His mother is quite fond of him and is pained by the *nom de jeste.*'

'I understand.'

'What a ready scholar you are! Come, are you hungry? I am, and thirsty, too. Let's go down to the hall.'

'But shouldn't we take His Grace's letters to the lady, rather than leave them here where someone might see them?'

He looked at me as if I had committed an indecency. 'No! Ranulph, there is nothing to take, and if there were, you know nothing of it. You have nothing to do with the lady, as you call her. If she should ever chance to look at you, you will make yourself vanish like a blown flame. If *I* ever chance to see you in her presence for the duration of time it takes to say *"mea culpa,"* your work here with me will be found unsatisfactory and you will be returned to your country abbey to cultivate cabbages and chant psalms until you fall from your stall in the utmost extremes of – senile – decay. Is that finally – and completely – understood?'

I bowed my head.

He sighed, gustily. 'Then for the love of God, let us go and have something to eat. I'm famished!'

So I became another mouth who fed among the countless other mouths at the table of Duke William, King of the English. I said my prayers, served my turn at the altar, lit candles, sang, and between times helped to make the constant inventory of the castle's goods and provisions.

The king-duke was not in residence when I came there, so the rule of the castle was divided between the Lady Matilda and her constable, Roger de Ivri. At first I could hardly tell whether I was more in a fortress preparing for a siege, or a greater house of religion than the one I had left. The lady, as I had been told, was indeed piously fond of priests; the halls of Rouen swarmed with them and with visiting nuns of gentle birth as well, who were granted leave from their convents to visit their patroness and assist her with her embroideries, made for altar cloths or liturgical vestments. She repeatedly gave some gift or other to this or that convent, most particularly to the abbey for women which she had founded at Caen.

I had been warned not to come near her, but it would have been difficult for me to do so, if I had so desired it, she was so well surrounded with solicitous clerks.

She was quite devout. She rose at dawn to hear Prime service, said her prayers again at Terce, heard the High Mass at midday with great devotion, and had a rector reading the Scriptures and works of holy men to her and her women as they sewed. Besides this, in the absence of her lord, she held court every day and heard the appeals of her people, making judgment as swiftly as her husband might have done, though she took counsel from two or three lords of Normandy who were named her advisers. When he was still in favor, her eldest son, Robert, had been her companion in judgment, though never her equal.

Now she sat alone in the ducal chair, looking like nothing so much as an aging child, for she was very small and only escaped seeming dwarfish by virtue of her slender bones. She had a face that had once been pretty, perhaps even beautiful, but was now somewhat overplump and spoiled by an expression of fretful melancholy. At her feet as she sat was the last chick of her brood, Prince Henry, a phlegmatic child of about eleven, with pasty cheeks and sulking mouth. He was old enough to be serving his time as a page in some other noblewoman's hall, but his mother had marked him for the Church instead of the battlefield and kept him with her, instructed by tutors until he was old enough to enter into his novitiate, presumably at St. Stephen's Abbey at Caen.

The next-oldest living son, William the Younger, hadn't been given his banished brother's duties at court, but followed his father everywhere – closer than his shadow, they said. Of the daughters I saw little. One was dead, one was in a nunnery, one was at the Convent of St. Leger-Preux, making ready to be a nun. The others, Constance, Adela, and Matilda, were kept safely out of sight in the lady's bower, which was only fitting treatment for three tender young virgins in a tower full of rude men.

All these things I learned in one manner or another while assisting the dispenser's clerk in taking inventories. I found, as always, that a clerk is as good a gossip as most women. My curiosity seemed to him as innocent as that of any bumpkin just in from the country, and it gave some credence to my furtive watch on the lady, which I made in spite of Carileph's dire warnings, because I hoped Isabel might appear before her some morning with her suit for Amiot. But as the days lengthened into weeks, she didn't come to court.

Nor could I roam the streets of the town looking for her. The ongoing inventory left me little time for anything but prayers, feeding, and reporting to Carileph. Theft was a constant concern in the castle, so everything must be counted over and over again, but that wasn't what I reported to my new superior. I was ashamed it was so, for it brought no honor to me, yet I could not help it: my true occupation was that of an informer for Carileph, in the interests of Bishop Odo. Why this should be necessary in the court of his own beloved brother I was not told.

Every evening after Vespers I presented myself to Carileph in his little room above the chancel to repeat everything I had heard or seen during my perambulations with the dispenser's clerk. Most of it was so trivial, I couldn't believe Carileph's patience in hearing it told, but in fact I did hear a great deal.

The inhabitants of the castle seemed to wander freely through the passages giving vent to their opinions, or those of their masters, on every conceivable subject. These people included family members, their servants, their squires, pages, churchmen, and attendants, lackeys, soldiers of the garrison, guests, petitioners, and merchants, in spite of the restrictions one would suppose would be imposed in the keep, if theft was so common.

Virtually no one spoke to me other than the dispenser's clerk, unless it was someone ordering me to stand aside if I was in the way. Otherwise I received no more attention than the packs of dogs that infested the hall at dinnertime, snatching at food scraps tossed aside by the diners. Clerks and hounds, alike common, alike invisible, unless they got underfoot.

Much of what I heard must have been stale news to Carileph, but he heard it all impassively, only occasionally requiring me to give a description of the man who'd said it or having me point him out the next day, if I could find him. The matter that attracted Carileph the most was any discussion that centered on the king's son, Count Robert, whether critical or sympathetic.

Of more interest to me was the chatter I absorbed at the clerks' table in the lower hall. There, any morsel of fact, fiction, or surmise was chewed over as vigorously as pig's knuckles or mutton ribs.

From that alert, malicious, and often merry company I learned that:

Duke William had been rejected by his lady when he first proposed marriage to her, because she said she wouldn't marry a bastard. This made him so furious that he rode to where she was, knocked her down with his fist as she came out of church, kicked her, and rolled her in the mud. When she recovered herself she accepted his suit, because she admired his daring.

Also: The Englishman Harold Godwinson had made his famous boat journey to Normandy, not by accident at the mercy of adverse winds, but to accept a bribe from our duke and become his man. There he swore on the famous casket of holy relics that he would serve our duke and promote his name as true heir to the English king. Harold made that journey because William Bastard had let him intercept a fraudulent correspondence between himself and the English Edward. This correspondence made it seem that Edward meant to placate both English and Norman factions on the matter of the succession by passing over his cousin William and letting the Atheling, who was his great-nephew, succeed to the throne and marry a daughter of our duke's. I have never found a confirmation of this tale anywhere, but it has an authentic sound.

More immediately I learned from my colleagues that this rebellion of Count Robert's might never have happened if his two younger brothers hadn't played him a boyish trick. More than a little jealous of his eminence and weary of his foolish vanity, William and Henry climbed to the gallery above where he sat one day, playing at dice with his worthless friends, and poured the contents of a well-filled chamber pot down on his head.

In a burst of justifiable rage, Robert flew up the stairs to revenge himself, intending to lay the flat of his sword against their backsides. But King William entered the hall at that moment, heard the shrieks and curses, saw the unsheathed sword, and thought murder was afoot. He drew his own sword, daring Robert to turn his weapon on him, rather than on defenceless children. Robert disarmed himself at once, but his father continued to abuse and insult him until his honor could no longer bear it. He and his friends quit the house, which was that of one of the duke's vassals, rode back to Rouen, and very foolishly tried to take the tower. Constable de Ivri wouldn't even let them through the gate. The citizenry pelted them with stones and filth, so they were forced to flee, and so languished abroad to this day, penniless, treacherous, but still defiant.

These tales were wonderful to me. I had no ideas about great men other than the enthusiasms put in my head by my abbot. That dukes might pummel their brides, or gently bred princes pour piss on their brother for a lark, seemed at once comical and reassuring to me. There was a strain of humanity even in kings.

The weeks rolled away for me in my tedious occupation, taking the last of summer with them, and still I had not seen Isabel at court. It seemed to me that I had only exchanged one prison for another and traded my fading adolescent melancholy for the sharper grief of being denied Isabel. At last I could bear our separation no longer, but grew brave enough to do what nearly all the other clerks did regularly, which was to shirk my duty and sneak away into the city streets in search of my love.

Feeling like a noonday thief, I attached myself to a group of clerks outward bound on some legitimate errand to the city. Once through the castle gate, I flew to where Isabel nested, quite forgetful of me. On approaching her cousin's house for the second time, I realized Beroald must be a man of some consequence: better than others on its street, the house was a full three stories high, brick below and timber above, with a porter at the door.

There was also a watchdog. The brute snuffled my aroma with misgivings rumbling in its throat while I waited for the porter to take my name up to the family. Now I was inside the house I had no notion what I was to say to Isabel that her cousin or his wife might hear with equanimity, but the echo of my heart rang in my ears like a blacksmith's hammer as I waited.

My first glimpse of her convinced me she was displeased to have me for a guest. Beyond rising to greet me and to present me to her cousin-in-law, the goodwife Arletta, who was nursing her latest babe, Isabel scarcely looked at me, but took her seat again by the hearth and devoted herself to her needlework.

Mistress Arletta was cordial enough – offered me cider and asked all manner of questions about my life in the castle and the present state of health of the Lady Matilda and all her brood. As she probed me verbally, her pale eyes took in every detail of my worn gown and battered sandals.

I was in torment, not knowing how many times I may have repeated my lame excuse for the visit – that I had only come to see if Isabel was well and to tell her I kept her and her loved ones in my prayers as she had directed me – to which she barely nodded her thanks. I had hoped, naturally, that she would take the lead in finding an excuse to put us alone together for a moment or two, but she offered nothing. A silence fell between Mistress Arletta and myself, broken only by the babe's fretting. I knew I must go.

Somewhat tardily, Isabel put away her embroidery hoops and said she would escort me to the door by way of courtesy. My heart began to swell again. I bade her cousin good-bye and followed Isabel down the dark stairs that led to the back of a narrow passage running from the kitchens to the porter's door.

She said not a word, but when we reached the bottom of the wainscoted stairs I took her arm; she paused, leaning against me, and I held her in the delicious agony of a silent kiss. For just an instant she was pliant to my lips and hands; then she pushed me away firmly and resumed her measured walk to the front door.

'I must see you alone. How can I see you?' I whispered, but she squeezed my fingers in warning as we approached the porter.

'Yes, it's a comfort to live so near to Our Lady's church,' she said as if in answer to my question. 'At home I could only go to hear Mass on the Sabbath, but here I may go every day, morning and evening, to pray for my lord.'

The porter held back his dog and opened the door.

'Good-bye, dear Father Ranulph,' Isabel said. 'Thank you for keeping me in your prayers.'

'God give you peace,' I muttered as I was gently thrust into the street. She lifted a white hand in farewell. The door was closed. I stumbled backward from it, almost tripping over a loose stone in the gutter. She had given me nothing, no word of hope for further meetings. The glimpse and taste I'd had of her would only make my nights a greater misery to me. I sagged against the wall of the house opposite and might have stayed there until the town's street wardens drove me away, but a cart driver wanted through and bellowed at me to move on. As I hurried to get out of the way, a great bell clanged above me, and I saw how the little street opened out onto the large square wherein the cathedral church of Notre Dame de Rouen was built. Its bell was striking the midday hour, calling its worshipers to hear God praised and served.

It jarred me awake. This was the Church of Our Lady, where Isabel went morning and night to pray for Amiot! She went there and so might I! I picked up my feet and ran across the square, up the steps, and into the church, slowing to a prudent walk only at the last moment.

I knelt in the slowly filling nave, dipped my head, blessed myself, then began to search the place with my eyes. Where, in all that cavern of stone, could Isabel and I find a place to be alone? My gaze followed the reach of one of those massive stone piers from its base to its top, to the arch that sprang from it, to the triforium arch above it. I rose and slipped over into the north aisle again, padding quietly eastward in it as the singers in the choir began their psalm. The north transept was deserted, as I had supposed, but I searched for and found what I was expecting: a door that hid a stair leading to the upper regions of the church.

I made sure I was unobserved, then quietly opened the door. In doing so I surprised a pair of bodies making the beast with two backs as lustily as cramped quarters on the stairs would allow.

The female of the two, her white legs twitching like a dying frog's, saw me over her partner's shoulder and gave a squeal of suppressed alarm in his ear. He took it for encouragement, I suppose, and bobbed away at her all the faster.

I stepped back in astonishment. The act certainly seemed less sublime viewed from that angle. The woman gave her rabbit's cry a second time and began beating her lover on the shoulders and head to get his attention, which only drove him on to more frantic exertions, until the deed was consummated. There was a groan from him and a sob of shame or fury from her. She tumbled him off her and hid her legs under her skirts in the same swift movement with which she hid her face from me.

He turned his head and gasped. I could do nothing but assume a thunderous frown to add to the foolishness of my open mouth.

'Oh, my God, Father – '

'Forgive us, good Father – '

'Out! Out! Out!' I whispered fiercely. 'Don't ever dare to come to this place again, or I'll have you up before the archbishop for a flogging! Shh! Not another word! Sacrilege! Shame! Be off, or it'll be the worse for both of you. Go!'

They fell over each other getting out of my sight and fled, staring and whey-faced, as if Hell already gaped for them, which indeed it did, desecrating as they had the very temple of God with their fumbling. I slipped inside the door when they were gone and leaned against the wall. The stairwell, narrow and steep, stank of their sweat and lust, which was as arousing as it was repelling. When my eyes grew used to the dark, I could see a dim light at the head of the steps. I went up them carefully, coming out in the gallery above the north aisle. There was another stair that led up to the space between the vault and the roof, but it would be too dark and cold. There in the triforium, where I could hear the sweet music rising over the choir walls and where I could just see my own hands before my face, I had found the place where I might be alone with Isabel. I slipped back down the stone steps and out the north door.

The next day I told the dispenser's clerk I was making a novena to Our Lady at her church and hurried away there. I lingered from Prime until nearly time for the next service, but Isabel didn't come. I risked Carileph's displeasure to make another journey there for Vespers, but she wasn't among the worshipers then, either.

The next day was the same, and the next. Each time I went, as I returned I paused across the street from her door, hoping to catch a glimpse of her at the upper window, but the only face I saw there was Beroald's, and he put me to instant flight with his adder's stare, as if he had been alerted to watch for me.

I was in despair. Isabel either would not come to meet me as she seemed to promise, preferring to torment me, or else she had been forbidden to come by her suspicious cousin. I made up a dozen plots, as I counted candles and bed linens the next few days, to get her out of that house, drag her out if necessary, and flee with her, but they were pitiful fancies. There was no place for two such as ourselves to flee, but to a foreign country or to her own house – neither would she choose.

'It looks as if the winter rains are about to set in,' said Carileph one evening, 'a bad prospect for travelers.' He had a nasty look as he said it, smiling and malicious. 'But there's no help for it. You must go.'

My heart sank. He'd been eyeing me sharply ever since my first unaccounted-for absence from Vespers in the castle chapel, though he'd asked for no explanation later. Now it was apparent to me that he knew all about me and about Isabel. He was sending me back to St. Vigor, as he had promised. There had been no further instructions for my use from Lord Odo, and it was certain that I had scarcely been worth my salt as an informer.

I tried to be a stoic: 'I'm ready to leave, when you're ready to send me.' My brief taste of freedom had been a disappointment, but so be it. I might as well be home again as so close to an indifferent and unattainable Isabel.

'I'm glad to find you so eager,' Carileph said. He beckoned me to his desk and held out a bit of parchment. 'Here's a guide for your journey, better than the last, I hope. We can't have you forever begging directions at the doors of pretty women, can we?'

So he did know about Isabel. He probably had spies to watch his spies. He had already assured me I did nothing out of the ordinary in being one of them. 'The king has spies in every hall of consequence in the land here – and, no doubt, in England, too. He expects to be spied on in return. Who wouldn't?'

I took the scrap he held and glanced at it. It didn't point the way back toward Bayeux as I'd thought. The road I was meant to follow led north and east. There were several names on the map, but only one jumped up to meet my eye:

Gerberoy.

I I

'You will leave tomorrow at first light. This time you'll have a mule and cart to carry you – and a few things besides. You'll take the road out through Apollonius's Gate and keep on it until you see the tower at Gournai. It's a day's journey with the wagon. When you see that tower, avoid it and cross the river there, just to the north. You will then be beyond our border, properly speaking. Continue on the most convenient path, turning east until you see the walls of another keep. Are you taking this in better than you seem to be?' Carileph said.

I glanced up from the map and saw his impatience. 'Yes, of course. The most convenient path to the east until – ' God, Who could not be persuaded to let me see Isabel again, was now going to let me go to Gerberoy and look at Amiot. Strange of Him.

'It may be that outriders from either castle will try to stop you. If those who do are from Gournai, you will tell them you are on your way to the Church of St. Quentin, at the command of your bishop, to present gifts to the saint's shrine and to beg a bone of him to take back to Bayeux. You will carry a reliquary in which to cherish that blessed fragment if it should be granted to you. You will also carry this letter from His Grace Bishop Odo, with his seal, for the priests of St. Quentin, which should satisfy your interrogators, if they don't merely wish to rob you.'

He smiled at my reaction. 'If, on the other hand, you escape that first party, you may expect to be taken by the second, that of Gerberoy. They will take you inside their walls when you refuse to answer their questions, and there you will present his mother's compliments to the master of that keep and give him the things she sends him. Is – that – clear?'

'Yes.' Christ, how his patronizing irritated me. A child of ten could do what he would have me do. 'Carileph, this is what I was meant to do all along, isn't it? His Grace wanted a courier no one here would know, so he sent me. Why have you kept me here so long? Did you doubt His Grace's choice of me?'

He breathed deeply through his swollen nose, then sighed. 'Do you really enjoy cautionary tales? I find them either boring or repugnant, but I'll tell you just this one.

'Once there was a clerk here named Samson, who was one of the lady's favorites. I knew him, myself, as we had many tastes in common. He was a hearty-souled man, with an eye for all the pleasant baubles of life – good food, a fat purse, an amiable woman.

'But the lady was greatly grieved and concerned for her dearest son, who had quarreled with his father and fled to Flanders with such speed after the quarrel that he was all but naked in his poverty and deeply in debt to his friends, whom he had carried into exile and disgrace with him. She heard such sad tales of him that she defied her lord, who forbade her to comfort her son, and secretly sent the good Samson out with a bundle of necessary garments and a few trinkets of gold and silver to cheer that poor exile in Bruges.'

'I don't think I want to hear this story.'

'I said it was cautionary, not horrible. Well, the lady's royal husband got wind of her deception, and he was very annoyed. He might have beaten her, or shut her up in one of his lesser keeps, but instead he sent a dozen of his knights out to apprehend Samson when he returned from abroad. He told them to slit the poor clerk's nose, put out his eyes, or, at the very least, deliver back into his hands those parts of Samson which he most prized and without which he would be unable to celebrate the Sacraments, if he ever took Holy Orders.'

'His hands.'

'You are too literal-minded, Ranulph. Remember your Leviticus. The priest must be whole and without blemish – '

'Oh, God.'

'Amen. However, Samson, though not as chaste as he should have been, was exceedingly strong and fleet of foot. Having heard some rumor of the king's intent even before he left Flanders, Samson traveled by night, slept under hedges, starved, and veered so far off his homeward course to avoid his enemies that, coming on the Abbey of St. Evroult far to the east, he bounded through its gate like a deer pursued by hounds and begged the good brothers there to take him into their community. He's still there, dining little, owning nothing, praying much, and straying – into sin – not – at all.'

He blessed himself as if he'd finished a prayer.

'Now, the king our duke has been visiting Gournai for the past two weeks, and that is why you have been delayed. Before that he was at Lyons-la-Forêt. He is making a tour of his duchy, you see, and was still somewhat too close for our comfort. But now we hear he has moved off to Aumale, to hunt with his brother-in-law. Still, you will take care as you go, won't you – dear – Brother?'

I wheeled my cart through the north gate as soon as the warden opened it next morning. The cart was loaded with two wicker hampers, bound and padlocked, and the reliquary, which was hidden in a sack along with bread and cheese for my dinner. I wasn't told what was in the hampers, nor did I care. Around my waist under my gown I had the bishop's jewels sewn into a belt.

It was a fine day, cold but brilliant. I had a keen eye for omens that day, and the first I saw when I came out of the castle was unfortunate: a sheep, skinned, drawn, and hung up for sale in the market. I began to say my service for the whole day when I saw it.

I passed Beroald's house and glanced up out of habit to its upper windows. In some bitterness I thought that if I stopped there now and left word with the porter of my destination, reclusive Isabel would come running through the streets after me in a moment, like a tinker's dog. The shameless, tormenting bitch would probably even offer to play the whore for me again just to be carried to where her virtuous husband was. What a good addition to Carileph's careful plan it would be, if I took her there and laid her on her back just as the noble Amiot came galloping out to take me prisoner.

I groaned for that vision, and for my folly in imagining it, because I knew I would take her there gladly if she went in sackcloth, with a penitent's candle in either hand, I was so desperate to see her. My brief tenure as her lover now seemed as ridiculous to me as it must always have seemed to her.

I had never driven a cart before. Luckily, the mule knew his business better than I did mine and needed no guidance on a firm-bedded, dry road. Our only difficulty with each other came when I stopped him in order to climb down and relieve myself. He pulled the cart off the road and began to graze among the nettles; it took me the better part of an hour to drag him from his feasting.

In spite of Carileph's disquieting warning and my own nervousness, my journey was without event otherwise, until I had identified and passed by Gournai. I was fording the river a little way ahead, holding the mule's head to assure him he wouldn't drown, when I saw four riders, helmed and enarmed, bearing down on me from the north.

They would be the men of Count Robert's Gerberoy. I pulled at my mule's head, eager to cross over to them before they reached me, but the mule balked, naturally, jerking up his great nose and pulling the reins out of my hands. I mounted the cart again to give him a taste of the whip. As I did, I glanced behind me and saw four other horsemen come out of the Gournai woods. The four from Gerberoy saw them, too, and pricked up their steeds to a canter, then a gallop. I laid the whip across the mule's back. He heaved his flanks and kicked back at the cart so hard that I thought it would splinter under me.

'Hold! Turn back!' cried a knight from behind me.

'Stand off! He's over your border! Our prisoner! Our prisoner!' bellowed one tearing forward toward me.

I lashed the poor, frantic mule while the converging warriors yelled threats and warning to each other. Those from Gournai were closer. The foremost of them plunged his horse into the water, churning it to a froth as he rode down on me. To my horror, I saw his sword raised naked in his hand as he cried: 'A Gournai! A Gournai!'

'A Normandy!'

I fell over the side of the cart to escape decapitation, as I thought. As I hit the muddy, swirling water I heard twin yells of defiance – 'A Gournai!' 'Normandy!' – and a tremendous clash of steel on steel as swords met, followed by splintering and a scream. I crawled out of the water as fast as I could because the mule, now taking fright from the slaughter so near him, suddenly broke the cart wheels loose from the riverbed and dragged it to shore, almost running over me.

I ran alongside the bucketing cart, trying to get in, as the combatants from either side of the river wheeled and plunged at each other. I caught the tail of the cart and dragged myself onto it, coughing out the water in my throat. There was a riderless horse careening past me, eyes wild and mouth foaming at the bit. Another rider came up behind him until he was even with me.

'Get in the seat! He's running away with you, you fool! Take him in hand!' He veered off to return to the battle, his face unrecognizable as human in his conical helm with the steel bar obscuring his nose. All I saw of him was the glint of his eyes.

I tried to climb over the hampers, but when I did I found the reins were out of my reach and I could do nothing but hold onto the seat for my life. Luckily the mule had chosen an uphill path, and as the noise of the battle fell behind us, the effort to climb began to tire him and he slowed. The rider, or another like him, overtook us again, bawled out cheerfully 'My prisoner!' and, bending from his saddle, snatched up the left rein, holding it loosely as he cantered by the mule's side until we reached the outer bailey gate of the fortress. The gate was up for us and we went straight in.

A half-dozen men ran up to catch the mule and soothe him, release him from the cart, and send him bucking and hinnying to the tether line. I still gripped the wagon seat, surrounded by flint-eyed stares. Nothing had worked out as I'd been told. The knight who had ridden in at the mule's head had now trotted off in the direction of the upper bailey, leaving no command behind to keep me either alive or in one piece. I had a very strong impulse to beg for mercy, but it didn't seem likely I'd find any there, so I sat frozen on the wagon seat while my footguard silently examined me and the hampers.

In a few minutes I saw the knight returning from the upper bailey with another man. They were both on foot. The second man was bareheaded, stout, and bandy-legged. He walked with that peculiar rolling gait one sees in sailors and dwarfs. He was dressed like a common soldier, covered with old mud stains up to the thighs. His voice when he spoke was ill-suited to his rugged appearance. It was high and querulous:

'Well, you thick-headed rascal, you've got one of my knights killed! Why didn't you move your damned cart out of the stream? If you'd gotten to the north bank in time, they wouldn't have challenged. We've agreed on it.'

I jumped off the cart and knelt to him, for he was surely Robert Curthose. 'Count Robert, I – '

'Duke Robert,' he said loudly. Then his heavy features softened into a sudden smile. 'This is the summer court of the Duke of Normandy, Father, in case its grandeur's escaped your notice. Who are you? What are you doing here? If you're bound for the Holy Land, you took a wrong turning somewhere.'

The men standing by the cart laughed at his jest, as he did.

'I'm from Bayeux, my lord, if it – '

'From my mother?' he asked eagerly.

'Yes, my lord. She sends you what my cart holds, as well as her – ' He held up his hand, his eyes squinting into the weltering sun. The gate was up again. Two of the knights from the river rode through it, followed by a third at some distance, who carried the body of the fourth over his saddle bow. Count Robert left me to amble toward them. I rose to see if they bore me a grudge, too. The dead man had fair hair, bloodied by the sword-cut that had been his death. Count Robert took him by the hair, turned his face to one side to view him, then let his head drop again, patted him on the back, and gestured to the rider to move on up to the castle. None of them as much as glanced at me. I had killed that man, Count Robert said. It was true, after a fashion, but why had they all converged on me when they didn't even know I had anything worth fighting for? What if my cart had nothing more valuable than myself? Would they have fought to the death to have me? Apparently so, since that was what had happened, as far as one of them was concerned.

Count Robert returned to me, tears in his eyes for the dead knight, but when he saw the hampers in my cart, once more his dull face underwent a transformation. He smiled, rubbed his hands, and clapped them. 'My mother, God bless her! She's outfoxed the old man again. Come, priest, let's take these sweet gifts into the hall and look at them.'

No one but he and I might do that, he said. 'These damned rascals about us could steal a hummingbird out of the air as he flies.' He heaved the hampers out of the cart bed one by one, dropping them to the ground, then took one up by its handles and hauled it away as if it were full of thistledown, though it had taken two men to pack it on the cart. I thought mine must be full of anvils. By the time I reached the upper hall with it, I was wheezing like a sunstruck pig.

Count Robert had gotten his shifted up to his shoulder by then and held it steady with one hand. 'On and up, Father. Up to my chamber.'

Under the curious stares of God knew how many armed men – the hall was crammed with them – I labored up the steps, stopping at every fourth or fifth to rest against the wall, while he climbed on, then kicked the bedchamber door open with his foot. I staggered into the little room, so winded that I let fall my hamper at the foot of the bed and sat down on it, entirely forgetful of my manners. He still had his hamper on his shoulder. I decided the queen must have sent him a goose-down bolster in it, but when he dropped it, it made a sound like a spade going into a gravel bed. He took the key I wore around my neck to open it.

Inside were chapel ornaments of silver and gold, wrapped in fine linen shirts to keep them from being scratched: cups, patens, candlesticks, plates, and, at the bottom, silver ingots and purses of coin. While he examined the contents of my hamper, which I saw contained rather more garments and less metal, I lifted up my gown and untied the cloth belt I had around my waist. Curthose turned his head from admiring his new wardrobe and saw me fumbling with the knot.

He gave an odd laugh. 'Well, now, did my good mother send me yet a sweeter treasure in you?'

I jerked the belt free and dropped my hem so quickly that he burst out laughing.

'It was a soldier's joke, boy. Your virtue's safe!'

I held out the belt, blushing. 'It was the best way to carry them, my lord.'

'What is it?'

'You'll have to cut them out. They're sewn in.'

He took the belt, laid it on the floor, and ripped it apart with his dagger.

'Holy Jesus!' He picked the jewels out of their ravaged nest and cupped them in his hand; he rose and took them to the slot of the single embrasure to examine them in the rapidly failing light.

'They are from your uncle, the Bishop of Bayeux. Here is a letter that goes with them.'

'Later.' He was bewitched by the jewels, turning them in his palm, probing them with a blunt finger so that they glistened faintly in the light. He drew a reverent breath.

'My uncle Odo. I never thought he cared for me. But he's a strange man – strange as my father.' He looked at me. 'Tell my uncle, I swear by the Holy Rood he may ask anything of me when I am back in Rouen, which will be soon, now. I'll give before he asks: I'll make him Archbishop of Rouen. Tell him that.'

As I bowed, I wondered if all Odo truly wanted was an archbishopric from his nephew. It seemed to me that he might as easily have had that prize from his brother the king and kept himself from treason.

For all his urge to secrecy with his gifts, Count Robert was never made to keep a secret. He boasted of his good luck to all in the hall that night, after a supper as heavy as any day-meal. He had dressed himself in some of his new finery: a tunic of scarlet velvet that made his face look like a burned brick, a woolen shirt, fine as linen, with English work at the neckband and wrists, supple boots of Spanish leather, and rings on every finger.

He was very gay and voluble, laughing at every jest, including his own, which, I will allow, were more witty than one would credit from his thick features and corpulent body. I had always imagined that wit went with a lean look, because of Cormac, I suppose.

But why was his uncle supporting him in his rebellion? He was addressed as 'Your Grace' and 'Excellence' by his friends of the high table, but even to my inexperienced ear they were only mocking him, for those titles fitted him less well than his clothes, which were stretched to cover his projecting belly. There was something in his face, too, that said he knew this was so. He looked out on the hall with the pleased but watchful face of a child who is gratified by the attention his elders give him, but suspects it will all end soon.

Perhaps this vulnerable air stirred the contempt of his men, even as they risked their lives and fortunes to defend his claim on the duchy. His claim was not without some foundation. His father had named him his heir three years before he made himself King of England. Five years after that, William Bastard had presented Robert to his Norman vassals as their duke and made all present swear fealty to him as if he were one, the same person, with his father.

Those who had sworn that double oath were now in some difficulty, whatever their motives. The elder barons had clung to the king, but their sons had fled with the son of the king, who would one day be duke and might later be king, too. How could they keep their honor intact, as well as their estates in hand, when this self-proclaimed two-headed power fell to quarreling with itself?

The highborn men who sat with Curthose were from the wealthiest families in the land: Robert of Bellesme, second son of Earl Roger de Montgomery and Mabel de Bellesme, for example. When he came into his inheritance, he would own a quarter of all Normandy and a good portion of England. He was no older than Curthose, but the difference in their bearing was striking: he made one want to cross himself if he happened to look one's way, which he did, often. Thin, dark, sallow, and with piercing eyes, he turned his head constantly, like a hawk in jesses, quickly scrutinizing every face, even if it were but that of a servant. He always sat in a corner or with his back to a wall, and no one who made a sudden movement, even to cut a piece of cheese, escaped his startled stare. Yet this was no sign of timidity. He was brave in the field, but so cruel to any enemy. that fell into his hands that he had ample reason to fear assassination. They said he impaled men from his own estates who were found guilty of no more than petty theft.

The others among the leaders were less terrible in reputation, but nearly as powerful in wealth and kinsmen: William of Breteuil, son of the Conqueror's sole intimate friend, William fitz Osbern; Roger fitz Richard, grandson of Gilbert of Brionne, the Bastard's guardian in infancy; Robert de Mowbray, nephew to Geoffrey, Bishop of Coutances, the king's chief advocate. These were no hungry free-lances, gambling their futures for a knight's fee or a rustic barony, they were the very heart of Normandy in rebellion against their elder lord.

At dinner I found myself at a table with the few other clerks in the rebel's camp. There was a Fleming, who was patently a spy put on Count Robert by his kinsman in Bruges (who had promised to support him in war with his father). The Fleming said very little one could believe. There were only two or three others, attached to the mesnies of Breteuil or fitz Richard. One, a clerk-surgeon named Goisbert, of the party of Ralph of Conches, seemed a decent sort of fellow. It was he who pointed out the various noblemen to me and told me something of their connections.

When he mentioned Ralph de Tosny, I remembered the name in Isabel's mouth and asked to have him identified. The rather sad, plump young lord he showed me didn't seem to be sharing the general merriment.

'Most of our lords are well-seasoned married men,' said Goisbert, 'or else accustomed to taking their women where they find them. It is to my lord Ralph's credit that he still behaves like a bridegroom, though he's been married several years. He misses his wife, but he hasn't had traffic with another woman the whole time we've been away from Conches.'

I said: 'I have a slight acquaintance with the wife of one of Lord Ralph's knights. Which one is Amiot de Trie, do you know?'

I was rather hoping he'd point out the knight who'd already fallen off his stool into the dirty rushes, overcome with wine, but Goisbert made a long face.

'You know his wife, but not the knight?'

'It's only the most chance acquaintance. I met her – in Rouen, where she's waiting at a kinsman's house to hear word of her husband. It would give her great comfort if I could say I'd seen him and that he is well.'

'But that's just the irony of it,' said Goisbert. 'He's the man who was killed this evening at the ford, rescuing you.'

I think my mouth must have opened, but no words came, because there was no thought in my head I might express.

'It's too bad,' said Goisbert. 'He was a good man. I had some acquaintance with him, as you've had with the wife. He and Lord Ralph had it in common that their wives both bore the name of Isabel and that they're both foolish-fond of them. Sir Amiot's loss is another reason for my lord Ralph's sad face tonight, I'd guess.'

'May I see him? Sir Amiot, I mean.' I don't know what made me ask. I hated him without even knowing him; I'd made him the object of my envy, for which he must needs be alive and full of sins, not dead and a hero for my sake. But Goisbert was pleased I'd asked. He took me away from the hall and up to the chapel, where Amiot de Trie's corpse was washed and laid out on a table, waiting for the carpenters to finish his coffin.

De Trie was a man in his prime, not corpulent or scrawny, but firm and trim. I couldn't judge his eyes, naturally, and his face was puffed and blue in death, but the lines about his eyes and mouth would seem to have made him a mild man. I could imagine he'd have been called handsome, too, before his slayer's sword cleaved his skull and cheekbones. He had fair hair, like that of his small daughter, which curled above his brow where it wasn't matted into the terrible wound.

I knelt beside Goisbert to say a prayer for him – and for myself. Isabel had declared she loved him; looking on him, I was forced to conclude she probably did. There he lay, the man she had been so desperate to regain that she'd been willing to make a strumpet of herself with the first fool who would lend her aid to come nearer him. She must be saying prayers of repentance twenty times a day now, to rid herself of the guilt.

Yet she'd been selfish as well as true. She'd been as concerned for her land as for her lord. I remembered how she said she wished him dead if he couldn't return. She'd said, too, that she'd always wanted a lover. There might be hope for me still.

Goisbert touched my arm. 'It occurs to me, friend, you should say the service for him when we bury him. I'm the only other priest to do it and I'd gladly give way to you, if you think it would comfort the widow.'

'What comfort would that bring her?'

'Why, that you're her friend.'

What could I say to that? I buried him that night in the castle yard, with Goisbert, Ralph de Tosny of Conches, and Count Robert as his dutiful mourners, along with his indifferent squire, who picked his nose through the whole affair.

The next morning I was wakened by a horn and sprang from my place on the floor, fearing an attack on the castle by the men of Gournai. But it was only Robert de Bellesme's way of keeping the garrison in battle readiness. All the knights and men-at-arms turned out of their blankets and rushed to the battlements and walls, arming themselves as they ran. When every soldier was at his post and a picked number of knights mounted to burst through the gate, the general drill was at an end. They returned to the hall to break their fast, then went to the cavalry yard, or to the outer bailey, to drill, first with the sword on foot, then to the lists to do mock battle with sword and javelin, mounted.

'Will it come to war between the king and Count Robert, Goisbert?' I asked as we stood among the soldiers at the lists, watching the affray.

He shrugged. 'It all depends: on whether the King of France makes good his pledge to support us here and give the duchy to Robert. In theory, he can take it from King William, who's his vassal, but in practice, someone's got to bleed for it. On the other hand, it is said that King William has sent a bribe to King Philip, to keep him from lending us any further aid and that King Philip is well satisfied to let us stew in our own broth here. One never knows which rumormonger to believe.'

'But hasn't there been any attempt to make peace between them? Civilized men choose men to come between them when they're angry, or so I've heard.'

Goisbert smiled. 'Yes, so I've heard, too, but it isn't so here. There've been attempts naturally. Earl Roger has spoken for peace, and so has old Hugh Grantmesnil, but it does no good. The king will not listen to any man who has a good word to say for his son, and Count Robert has been too often humiliated at his father's hands to risk another rebuff. I very much fear they will fight, yes. And soon. King William has never balked at a winter campaign, and he knows we have limited supplies to withstand a siege. The count is chafing for action, even now. If the king makes him wait much longer, he'll go roaring out that gate the first time he hears the trumpets blow – and it'll be all over with us, I fear.'

'Goisbert – why do you stay here? This isn't your quarrel and you don't owe anyone sword service. If you stay, and things go as you say they will, you could be killed.'

He nodded, then glanced at me with a resigned smile. 'True, I owe no military service, but I am the servant and friend of my lord, who is a good man and who says he needs my prayers for his soul's sake. I value his need for me and am bound by it. There are more ways to bind a man than with an oath.'

I stayed there for a week, because Count Robert didn't think to dismiss me, having all but forgotten me. During that time he gave away most of the treasure his mother and uncle had sent him, no doubt to pay his debts. He might have hired a mercenary army twice the size of the garrison he had, if he'd gone to Paris, or to the Flemish court, with the jewels alone, but he seemed satisfied with the disposal he made of them. I think he could have been happy to stay forever in Gerberoy, readying himself for a battle that he need never fight. He was a headlong fighter in the mock battles they held there every day.

Once he did remember me, he gave me a generous purse and had me write a letter to his father. It was interesting for its naiveté:

Robert, Duke of Normandy and Count of Maine, by acclamation and by the sacred promise of his parent, to the King of the English and his father, greeting:

My lord, you know right well that you confirmed me in my title when I was but a child and that not once, but twice, you had all the men of Normandy swear fealty to me as duke.

In the same manner, you made me Count of Maine, by treaty with the Count of Anjou at Blancheland this last year. Yet you deny me any part in the government of either place and most shamefully keep my rightful revenues from Maine, leaving me a pauper unable to maintain myself or even to pay my faithful servants.

You reward lesser men with lands, but give none to me, who am your firstborn and have never heard it whispered that I am bastard. All the men of my generation have greater honor from their fathers. Why, then, do you refuse me and keep me beggared?

As for the trouble at Laigle, where I offended you and you drove me out in the presence of my friends with gross insults no man of chivalry could bear without redress, it was unworthy of so much rebuke. My brothers played me an evil trick, and I drew my sword only to chasten them with the side of it. Do you believe that I, who am a knight, would draw my sword to murder mere boys? When you entered the room

I was very hot with wrath, but did I not throw down my sword at once and ask your pardon? If you had dealt as softly with me as with my brothers who shamed me, pouring slops on my head for sport, I would never have left your side. And let me say a thing about the affair at Rouen. I did not attempt to take the tower, as de Ivri supposed. I commanded him to open the gate to me as co-regent of the duchy, which was my right, but he treated me as you have done, as a man of no word, and refused.

If I had wanted to do you a mischief, I would have burned the town around the tower, or slaughtered its people, seeing I had near to three hundred men with me at the time. But I did not. I have complained of all this to King Philip, and he bears me out, but I would rather have justice at your hands than at his. Bid me be your son again and I will obey, since I desire nothing but my rightful revenues and to serve you in good faith.

He made his mark on the letter and sealed it. I promised to deliver it to the duke when I could, since he had not yet come to Rouen. But I knew very well I must deliver it to Carileph.

12

The whole castle was in an upheaval of packing and loading when I returned. The court of the Lady Matilda, still lacking her lord, was moving to Caen, having dwelt at its present location somewhat longer than the usual two months. The privies were overflowing, the larders all but empty, and the place was rapidly becoming unfit for occupation.

Carileph took Count Robert's letter from me and put it in his bosom. I'm certain it never reached the king.

He was in a cheerful mood. 'Let's take our leave of the wine pots here, since there's no more work to do,' he said as the porters were carrying out his desk. The chests, armoires, and hampers in which the writing room's rolls were kept had already gone to the wagons. All we had left were our pallets, which we would fling aboard a cart next morning.

Since he didn't seem eager to hear about my journey, I slipped away from him as soon as I could. I was frantic to see Isabel before we went. As soon as Carileph was well settled in a dispute with a colleague, I sped away out the gate and through the dark streets. This time when I banged on the door, Beroald's porter wasn't disposed to open it more than a crack.

'The master and his family have gone to Lyons.'

'I don't want to see them. Where's the Lady Isabel? Did she go with them?' Why hadn't she waited for me? In my haste I had forgotten she didn't know I'd gone to Gerberoy, didn't know I was being hauled away to Caen at dawn and might never see her again.

'Do you have leave to speak to her?' the porter asked suspiciously.

'What do you mean? Is she still here, then? Yes, of course I have leave, you fool!'

'From the master? He didn't say – '

'From her husband!' It was the only thing I could think of that might persuade him of my trustworthiness.

I heard Isabel's voice from above my head: 'You've seen Amiot? Where, Ranulph? When? Let him in, Rolf! Please! It will be all right, I promise.'

I burst into the passage. The porter's dog lunged to the length of his chain at me, but I was past him before he could snatch at more than the hem of my gown. My flight down the hall reanimated the suspicions of the porter, who pounded after me to the foot of the stairs, where he caught me. But Isabel was at the top of the flight, saying: 'Come up to the hall, please, Father. It's all right, Rolf. This is a trustworthy priest.' She said it in such a cool, imperious voice that he let me go, but with a sour look at her that I didn't like. I bounded up the steps and glanced around for other servants, but the hall was empty; truly empty, as Beroald had moved his furniture to Lyons, too.

Isabel stood back from me, her hands clenched at her waist. I reached for them, but she avoided me. She looked pale, but expectant. 'Shh!' She nodded toward a door. 'Come up there. This place has too many ears left in it.'

I followed her up another dark, closed staircase, to a narrower passage that led to the back of the house. The room she entered was like a servant's cell, hardly larger than an armoire. It held a bed and a small hamper, a stool; over the bed a window was shuttered.

'This is where I must stay, except for taking meals, until my sweet cousin decides what to do with me,' she said bitterly. 'He was glad enough to see me, until he found I wouldn't give him the farm of my estate – or let him put his bailiff there to keep it for me. Since then he's discovered I'd disgrace him before his friends, being the wife of a traitor.' She closed the door then and her face lost its petulance; she smiled at me. My heart turned over, but her words disabused me of thinking her smile was for me.

'Never mind Beroald. Tell me about Amiot! Oh, Ranulph, is he well? Is he here? Or in France, or Flanders? How did you see him?'

Now I was baffled: I hadn't come to tell her about Amiot. Let someone else do that. I'd only wanted to see her, to tell her of my own destination. Her eagerness made me want to embrace her. I reached for her again.

'Say something kind to me, first. I've missed you so much. Haven't you missed me even a little?' I tried to kiss her cheek, but she stiffened against me, her face changing. The light of the single cresset made her glance all the sharper.

'What is this? Good news doesn't wait to be told. What do you know about Amiot? Were you lying about him, just to get in here again?'

'No, no. Can't you put your arms around me just for a moment? I'd think you'd be a little ashamed of lying to me about how often you visited the church. I waited for you for days.' I was making things worse with every word, but I couldn't think how to make them better.

She shoved me away from her, anger and fear contending in her eyes. 'No! You know something. I can see it in your face. You came to tell me, but now you – what is it, for the love of Christ? I can't play at nonsense with you now!'

I sagged against the foot of her bed. Why had I come? Why had I persisted in believing she had the least interest in me, when she had made it so clear she'd only used me for a purpose? There was no way to avoid telling her the truth, no way to tell it decently. My eyes filled with tears. She seized my shoulders and shook me.

'Tell me!'

'He's dead.' I hid my face, not to see hers. I heard her take a deep breath and her fingers dug into my shoulders.

'Where?'

'At Gerberoy. I was sent there with a – with a letter for Count Robert.'

'You said you spoke to Amiot. When did you do that? When did he die? Why did he die?' She shook me again. 'Are they at war and we know nothing of it? Tell me!'

I thought perhaps if I told her the truth it would make her feel better. He had died in a chivalrous fashion, according to her thinking, which she might prefer to a tale of death by fever or disease. I began to stumble through the details, giving him a more prominent part than I believed he had, making him my chief rescuer from the men of Gournai. I let him slay several of them before he fell, and told her with truth of the high esteem in which he had been held by Count Ralph and Curthose. I told her that I had buried him decently and that the whole company of knights had wept for him.

When I dared to lift my face to her again, her sparrow-hawk's eyes were burning into mine, tearless and fierce. Her chin quivered. She let go my arm and drew herself up. Then she made a fist and hit me in the face. Before I could throw up an arm, she hit me again and again, fist over fist, until I fell backward onto the bed. She fell on top of me, pummeling me. We both rolled over the edge of the low bed onto the floor, I trying to catch her wrists and protect myself from her knees without hurting her. My nose was bloody and numb, as if broken; my ears rang with her insults, yelled in my face:

'Jakes-spawn! Stupid, sniveling – you went there! You caused his death! *You* did it, you peasant bastard! You!' She burst into sobs at last, collapsing on top of me, weeping into my shoulder, shuddering with grief.

My brain was as numb as my nose, but when I felt the rage go out of her I put my arms about her and rolled her off me, so that we lay side by side. I tried to comfort her, rocking her against me, kissing her limp hands. 'Isabel, Isabel, sweet – '

'It's God's judgment on me,' she said suddenly. 'He used you to bring Amiot's death, then He sent you back here, to tell me, so I'd know it was my sin that did it. My sin, my fault, my fault that I never repented. My sin I must pay for now. Oh, God!' She began to keen. I put my hand over her mouth, alarmed at the noise, but she thrashed until she was free, turning her head from side to side as she wept. I stroked her hair, kissed her hands and breast. In spite of all, my heart was still brimming fire for her. The only words that penetrated my thick wits were those, that she had never repented of loving me. I was trying to gather her up to hold her better when the passage outside thundered with running foot and claw; then the door was flung open. The porter was there with his dog on leash and another servant gawking over his shoulder. Isabel opened her eyes and saw them. She fought to rise, to push me away. She shrieked.

'He's forcing her, the bastard!' cried the servant, and the porter let slip the dog leash by a foot or so. Isabel yelled again at the sight of the dog. There was no help for me there. I scrambled over the bed and went out the window.

I fell headfirst, trying to turn onto my back. I'd have been killed for certain if the drop had been sheer, but there was another roof a few feet below the window, slanting out over the kitchen to the laundry yard. I slid sideways, carrying down a hail of roof tiles with me, plummeted from that roof to a smaller one lower down, then fell on my belly in the yard. The porter's dog was out on the higher roof by then, clawing and skidding down in my direction.

Without waiting to discover broken bones, I leaped up and fled through the dark, over a fence, through other washing yards and herb gardens, vaulted low walls, until I found myself in the street near the church square. I had left in my wake all the furious dogs, porters, householders, and servants that my flight had wakened.

I ran to the church and stayed there until I could begin to breathe and think again, and to examine my hurts. Much later I crept out to wash myself in a horse trough, then made a circuitous return to the castle, where I was relieved to find a late-returning group going in the gate. I followed them, head down, arms folded to shield my torn gown. By some miracle nobody paid particular attention to me. I scuttled into the lower hall, stepping carefully over the sleepers, found a cloak very carelessly hung on a peg outside the jakes, stole it, and slipped away to the bailey again to settle for the night.

I made Carileph a very thin excuse the next morning about the state of my face and my robe, at which he grinned.

'You'd have been safer to get drunk in the hall and try a kitchen wench. Don't let it happen again.'

'It will never happen again,' I muttered. I had my fill of women. My life would be blameless thereafter, I promised myself.

Two days after we arrived in Caen, I was embarked for England.

'His Grace will want to hear what you've seen,' Carileph said. 'Also, these letters are for him.' From the stuffed pouch he showed me, I realized Lord Odo had an extensive correspondence filtering through his brother's chaplain at his brother's court. I began to see I might play only a small part in his designs, whatever they were.

'How long will I be gone?' I asked.

'What's the matter? Afraid you'll miss me?' Carileph smirked. 'Never mind. You'll like England. I daresay His Grace will send you back before you're ready to return.'

'I've never heard it was such a paradise,' I said stolidly. My nose was very sore and one of my teeth seemed loose.

'The English are a mad, bad, greedy lot of savages who deserve to be ruled by us, since they can't do it for themselves, but in spite of their faults they have a few things to recommend them. They eat and drink like kings. Even the common folk eat white loaves on a feast day, else feel themselves very badly used. Their ale tastes a bit more like horse piss than ours, but it'll do. For an adventurous fellow like you, however, there is that fine old Roman diversion they still enjoy, which you can't find in Rouen.'

'They feed Christians to lions?'

He laughed. 'They might, if it was Norman Christians they could get hold of. No, I'm talking about the stews, the public baths they have in London. You should try one while you're there.'

'I don't need an Englishman to teach me how to bathe.'

'No Englishman will teach you, turnip-head. It's the whores who keep the baths going there. Try it. It's more discreet than whatever you were up to last night. For a penny the women will scrub you till you squeak, rub you till you're rosy, and teach you naughty tricks after. It's absolutely delightful, and if you use your manners, you won't get your nose bloodied.' I must have looked as disapproving as my new chastity dictated, because he snorted and said: 'It appears you're in need of a physic, but never mind. The voyage will take care of that.'

He was right in that prophecy. I made a poor seafarer, and it was a much purged and chastened ex-fornicator who stood before Lord Odo four days later, after a rough crossing to Portsmouth and a ride in an oxcart up to London.

When we creaked over the London bridge, I clung to the side of the cart, unaccustomed to such lengthy timber bridges, or such wide rivers. Compared to the little rivers of my home, the Thames looked almost as wide as the Channel.

The city of London was a wonder to me, too. I had expected a town similar to Rouen, if not so large, with a high wall all around and buildings of stone, brick, or tile. London had a wall of sorts, very old and in much need of repair, but its buildings made it look like an immense village. The English built even their finest houses out of timber, thatch, and wattle. An enemy sailing up the Thames could have fired the whole town without bothering to disembark.

There were many church bell towers showing above the walls and a great one on a hill to the left. There were two motte-and-bailey castles on the river at either end of the walls, too, with a smaller one showing its timber ramparts to the far west just behind one of the larger ones. I left the oxcart as soon as we reached the end of the bridge and was soon wandering in a maze of market stalls that lined the river wall and were the life's blood of the town.

'Where may I find Bishop Odo?' I asked several people along my way. I found my pronunciation of his name differed from the English one, but in time I made myself clear to someone, who directed me to the 'old palace' up beyond Watling Street and St. Paul's yard, to St. Giles's Gate.

St. Paul's was a decent enough church, though it didn't compare with Notre Dame in Rouen, but the old palace astonished me again. Made of timber like the rest of London, it looked more like a huge farmstead than a palace, even like a great mews, for there must have been a thousand ravens perched on its roof thatch and strutting about in its courtyard. I went in to present myself to the chamberlain.

'I have letters for His Grace – '

'He isn't here,' said the desiccated little man, who didn't even look up from his psaltery to answer me.

'If you could tell me where I might find him?'

'You may leave the letters here and they'll be given to him when he returns.'

'I beg your pardon, Brother, but I'm not at liberty to do that. I must give them myself.'

He looked up then and took in my worn costume and battered face carefully. 'Where're you from?'

'Bay – from Rouen. Well, from Caen, really. The court just moved there before I sailed.'

He smiled wryly. 'Who are your letters from?'

I was offended. 'How can I tell you that? I'm only their courier.'

'Haven't you looked at the seals?'

'Of course not! What do you take me for, Brother?'

Now he smiled openly. 'Extraordinary,' he said softly. 'Well, Brother, His Grace is hunting at Windsor, and he will return when it pleases him. You may wait for him here, or not, as you choose.'

'Thank you.' I turned heel to stalk away, where I couldn't imagine, and found a boy-faced clerk with frizzy pale hair, like lamb's wool, in my way. He smiled brilliantly, stepped aside with a flourish, then fell in step with me.

'You'll have a long wait for Uncle Odo. He's got other deer than the four-legged kind to hunt at Windsor, you know. And he won't come back to London so long as Lanfranc's here. They detest each other. Lanfranc, on the other hand, is so old he's in no hurry to move anywhere faster than a land tortoise, so you may wait for a month. What will you do until then? Do you have any money?'

I'd have wasted no time answering his impudent questions, but his use of the word *uncle* gave me pause. 'I'll manage. Who are you, Brother?'

'Robert Bloet, Brother. I'm from Rouen. My ears pricked up when you said you were from there – among other places. I'm still heartsick from leaving it. Tell me, is Moldy Maud still in good health?'

Now I was truly flummoxed. Uncle Odo? Moldy Maud? 'Are you referring to the Lady Matilda?' I asked in a properly iced voice.

It was his turn to look astonished; then he threw back his head and roared. 'Oh, Lord – you're not from the cathedral chapter, I can tell! The lady, Moldy Maud? Oh, Blessed – Moldy Maud had a bakeshop near Caux Gate when I was there. She had the whitest, fattest, most hospitable thighs in town, and she fancied young clerks. How in God's Name could you think I meant the queen?'

We were outside the palace now, walking back down toward town. I was hot with shame for my error, but Robert Bloet's laugh was infectious, not malicious, and it was still a fair day.

'You mentioned your uncle Odo and I thought you must be – '

'A member of the Family.' He cleared his throat portentously. 'Well, I am, if you count cousins to the ninth degree and don't mind a sprinkling of bastards. I call him Uncle Odo because of his manner. He really is the most avuncular old scoundrel you ever met. Have you met him, by the way?'

'I'm in his service.'

'Ah, then the chamberlain was right in his suspicion. I saw how he summed you up. You're one of Uncle's spies.'

'I am not!'

'Uncle has dozens of spies, and they all look very much like you, my friend – very callow and very serious, no offense intended. Don't let the word worry you. We have something else in common. I'm in his service, too. Not as a – you know what, mind you. I'm his choirmaster. He took a fancy to me in Rouen two years ago and brought me over here to make something of his chapel choir at Rochester. He's very fond of good music, good food, handsome clerks, if you'll pardon my saying it, pretty wenches, and a ring on every finger. That's our Uncle Odo, long may he flourish. What's your name?'

I told him and was relieved that he didn't inquire into my antecedents, but only said:

'I'll bet you're hungry, now you've got your land legs under you again. So am I. Where shall we go to take our dinner?'

'I was hoping to get mine at the bishop's table. I don't know London. In any case I haven't much money to buy meals.'

'Who said anything about buying? I spoke of *taking*. We'll save your money for better things.'

Less than an hour later we were sitting on the steps at St. Paul's, finishing a most delicious ill-gotten dinner. Robert was a consummate thief. He had taken me on a progress through the market above St. Paul's, greeting vendors, tousling children's hair, smiling at pretty girls not too well watched by their mothers. I didn't even see him take the chicken from the spit, until he thrust it on me, whispering to put it under my cloak. He tucked a couple of pears away in the same manner, then stopped at a bread stall to charm a young matron and to nip a cocket. I know she saw the loaf going, but she let herself be robbed because of his white smile and his fingers twining with hers.

When we'd thrown the chicken bones to the dogs, licked our fingers, and scrubbed our faces clean on our sleeves, we talked; or, rather, Robert Bloet did. I listened, thinking that England must not be such a dreadful place after all if I could make a friend so easily. Of course, it was he who had made a friend of me, though for what reason other than his own good nature I couldn't divine.

By the end of that day I had heard as much gossip, theory, and legend about the great men who ruled us as I might have hoped to hear in a month at Rouen:

'Our master feels himself ill used by the king, in spite of all his rewards, because he isn't first among his counselors,' he said. 'Lanfranc the archbishop is that. If you understand this much, you'll find little mystery in the things with which we occupy ourselves here. Odo hates Lanfranc, and the archbishop returns the feeling warmly. They share the rule of the realm when the king is away, but they try never to be in the same place at once. They share the county of Kent, too, and Kentishmen are kept busy trotting from Canterbury to Rochester with their petitions. But you've heard all this and more in Rouen, no doubt.'

I shrugged. 'I'm only a country mouse. I scarcely knew the world stretched ten miles past Bayeux until two months ago.'

'Ah.' His lively eyes came to rest on me for a moment, but he seemed too polite to ask the obvious question. 'Well, you'll learn quickly here.'

That gave me pause. 'Do you think he'll want to keep me here? I never thought about staying.'

'No need to think about it, since you'd have nothing to say in the matter in any event,' said Robin easily.

'But do you think he would? Keep me? What use could I be to him here?'

'An interesting question. What use were you there?'

I didn't answer. Robin shied a rock at a pack of dogs slinking up on us in search of more scraps.

'Uncle Odo has almost as many clerks in his house here as has the king, now, and more coming all the time. We all keep busy. I expect you will, too, if you stay. He has much business to conduct, here and in Kent. They don't care for him there. He's been too efficient at stealing them bare-boned, but he's popular here in London.' He laughed. 'We like to think that when the next rebellion comes, we'll all sit safely, because whatever happens to the rest of the country, London will belong to Uncle Odo.'

I had reason to remember that prediction in time, though it took years to bring it to mind.

Odo returned to London the following Saturday, with twenty men in his hunting party, fifty men in his guard, and sixteen rounceys carrying the carcasses of deer they'd slain. Two wagonloads of household goods, including his personal chair, his bronze braziers, his bed, plate, portable altar, and wardrobe, accompanied him to the hunting lodge and back again. He kept his state wherever he was, as if he were a king.

We heard his trumpets blare his arrival at Cripplegate (I should call it St. Giles, for him who helped cripples, but I early fell in with the English habit of botching their place names, so foreigners are left in the dark as to their whereabouts). The whole palace turned out to meet Odo, cheering him, as did the ragtag populace who heard his coming through the gate.

When he arrived I had just returned from a ramble about town with Robin Bloet, who'd taken me down to see the great foundations of the new keep that the king was building on the eastern reach of the river.

This new London Tower would be the first building made all of stone in the entire city, St. Paul's still having timber outbuildings. It was a marvel to the townsmen, who liked to gather and watch the masons working, when they could find them there. The building was going very slowly, though it was meant for the royal residence. The present royal residence, such as it was, lay outside the town walls at a distance of a mile or so, where Edward Confessor had preferred to live by his life's work, the church called the West Minster to distinguish it from the minster of St. Paul's. The king's house there was of little better quality than any English thane's hall. The wind blew through the chinks in its walls; rain seeped through the thatch.

London Tower was to be a replica of the tower in Rouen, which was of some significance to us; what it was for the English was harder to divine. It stood on a hill that had been an ancient, sacred place, according to Robin, where the head of one of their old kings or demigods had been buried. The spot was also a gathering place for revelers during the late-summer harvest feast they called Lammas-tide. It was known as the White Mound, though there was no hint of chalk under the earth or anything else white that I could see.

When we heard the trumpets bray, we were just coming up from St. Paul's yard; we broke into a run and reached the palace in time to see Lord Odo and his train enter the gates like an army coming home. Robert Bloet excused himself and trotted off in haste. I was left dangling for a moment; then I remembered my letters, which the hall steward had let me store in the chancel. I ran there at once to get them before he gave them to the bishop and made me seem a slackard. But the armoire he'd put them in was locked, and while I was trying the door one of the chancel clerks found me and thought I was stealing something.

Our struggle made such a noise that the bishop himself came to see about it, still dressed in the sweat-and-blood-soaked garments of a huntsman. As I seemed to be the aggressor in the struggle, having gotten my back against the armoire and my hands around the other clerk's throat, Lord Odo naturally took his clerk's side by giving me such a clout on the head that I sank to the floor like a dead man.

The next thing I knew I was lying on the floor with half a dozen of the household staff hovering over me, Robert included. He was grinning, but the Lord Odo wasn't, until Robert explained me to him. He stopped scowling then and gave out a ringing laugh.

'Well, Brother, I approve your zeal, but now you see how it is that zealots are so often martyred. Take yourself up and wait until you're called for. My letters are safe enough in my own cabinets.'

I slunk away to a bench with Robert's support, endured the laughter of the clerks who had come to know me, then began my wait to make my apologies to my lord. I was several days waiting, since he was consumed with the affairs of the king, holding a lengthy court every day to hear petitions or judge disputes. When at last I was sent in to him, it was after Compline, but he was still working. His room was both bedchamber and study combined, with a chimney hearth built into one wall. I had never seen such a fireplace in a private room and was much impressed with it, as with the furniture and the smell, which was one of incense and clean floors rather than mice and mildew – like most bedchambers in timber houses.

He was reading when I entered. Without his bishop's regalia he looked like any man of wealth in the middle years: portly, handsome, but plainly dressed in a brown tunic. I thought he had some difficulty reading by the firelight, and he breathed like a man who has been climbing turret stairs, though he sat at his ease. He finished his reading and put the roll aside, then folded his large hands on the desk.

'Well, Brother Zealot, I've read the letters you brought; now let me have your own report. Take a stool if you like and tell me how my nephew does.'

I was jerking with internal anxieties, but I began to speak, slowly, because I had expected no such general license. Soon his sharp question brought me around from general description to matters I would otherwise never have dared to mention, or to those I'd have sworn I knew nothing of until I heard myself answer. He was a masterful interrogator. When he had wrung me out, he knew enough about Gerberoy and its inhabitants to defend the keep himself, or to breach the walls of it. His questions seemed trivial at first, but they were all of a piece to reach full understanding.

As I spoke I gradually lost my fear of overstepping politeness and began to see the fortress and garrison in my mind again. I forgot to say 'Your Grace' at every breath, as his easy manner and intent interest seemed to dismiss the necessity of it. Only with Isabel had I ever spoken so at length and ease since I was a child with my mother. If, by intuition or secret knowledge, he had suddenly inquired of my own life, I suppose my whole tale of Isabel would have spouted from my lips. Therefore I was surprised when after a pause he said:

'You've done well. I've had good report about you from other sources. They say you don't talk too much in the ordinary way of things. That's good.'

I had to smile. 'Your Grace, I seem to have been talking the night away.'

'To me, yes, but not to others. There's no one here who can tell me anything about you beyond the fact that you're from Bayeux and my courier. You don't boast, then?'

'My lord, there's nothing to boast of.'

'The vices and trivialities of the court must bore you. I suppose you'd be glad if I sent you back to your abbey after this.'

'Oh, no, my lord! I – would prefer to serve you, if I might.'

His eyebrows lifted. 'Gratifying. But why? Is it the freedom to gad about the world you enjoy? Young men are apt to love adventuring for its own sake, which is a worthy thing in the wellborn, but not so in a clerk. Your vows must be precious to you. You put them in danger if you keep roving. Does this not trouble you?'

'My lord, I'm a good clerk but a poor monk, to my father's sorrow. I write a fair hand, can calculate numbers in my head, and would prefer to serve God by serving you.'

'You hope I will enrich you with a good post, then. You are ambitious rather than devout, yearn for power more than piety. Gold or silver will be more to your liking than wisdom and righteousness. Is this a fair judgment?'

'My lord, you have already enriched me. I never wore a warm cloak until you put yours on my shoulders, never held a coin until you put your purse in my hand, and never spoke to a man of consequence until you sent me to speak to your nephew. You are my spiritual father and may command me back to the cloister and I will go, but I would more gladly serve you in any other way, if it were possible.'

He studied me for a moment, then said: 'It's your face that will be your fortune someday, not your hand or your tongue. That was a perfect, toadish speech, but you've uttered it without the least semblance of guile. You may have cause to repent of it, but very well: report to the master of the writing room tomorrow and he'll find work for you. Tell him to fit you out in better clothes, too.' He dismissed me with a languid wave of his broad, jeweled hand.

13

If Odo had a purpose in keeping me, he kept it secret. I found myself folded into the daily business of his house doing the work of clerks in Holy Orders in such a place, which was whatever the master of the writing office directed. I said Mass, sang in chapel, penned letters, copied or proved them; I was a courier, an accountant, a loiterer; but at no time was I called again to speak to Lord Odo.

If no one had a use for me, I was free to roam the town with

Robert Bloet and his friends, or to sit and brood on the memory of Isabel. In spite of my resolutions, I couldn't excise her from my mind. I yearned for her. In my day visions I acquired a permanent post with Odo, with a good competence, and sent for her. In the dream she came, a repentant widow, having no one else to turn to. But I knew she wouldn't come. I couldn't embitter myself by thinking she'd forgotten my name, because she would have had much explaining to do to her cousin when he came home and heard the tale his porter had to tell him. What had Isabel told him concerning that? Had he believed her, or thrown her out? Was she in her own house again, or prostituting herself in alleyways? Even if I found her there, I – God, I didn't know what I'd do, but the chance haunted me almost every night.

The king sent word to his brother that he meant to knight his third son, William, at Christmas in Rouen. Illustrious sponsors were wanted for the occasion, since King William now looked on his third son as his heir. It was only fitting that young William's favorite uncle take an honorable part in the ceremony.

We were packing hampers for the journey when the news came that Robert Curthose and his friends had finally proved themselves to be more than mere sulking malcontents on the border. They broke the peace of the Advent season with pillage and stark murder, raiding Norman farms and vills, burning barns and sheepcotes, slaughtering stock and hapless peasants who failed to outrun their horses. It was a deliberate challenge flung in the king's face to come and deal with them. They took no booty, but merely created ruin that sent every baron on the northern border howling to the king for revenge.

Wondering if we would arrive in time to see the king arrayed for war, we set sail from London port in a Danish merchant vessel with all the speed and grace of a drowned cow and got buffeted and bumped across the Channel by the winds. At the mouth of the Seine, Odo and his chief followers took to horse for Rouen, while the rest of us went upriver on a barge, in charge of his vast cargo, which included two milk-white horses, a destrier and a palfrey, his sponsor's gift to young William.

By the time we reached Rouen, Odo was already established in the little Priory of St. Gervase, just outside the city's west wall. I was disheartened to think I might spend the whole of the Christmas season there without a glimpse of the king at his feasting. If there was no room for us in the castle, we could hardly be included in the feast,

I thought; but I underestimated Odo. He kept his estate like a king, as I've said, and it didn't please him to be squeezed into sleeping quarters with a half-dozen other guests.

The next morning, which was Christmas Eve, we were assembled for Terce service when he appeared garbed like a Byzantine icon in a gold-embroidered, green silk cope, white-and-gold miter, with a red silk chasuble and his gilt-wood staff. A litter was assembled and made ready for him. He entered it, his chamberlain formed up the rest of us behind it, and we went forth from St. Gervase to the Caux Gate, as if we were entering Jerusalem.

The weather had turned for the worse. The skies were leaden and there was a hint of sleet in the air, but as in the spring when rain clouds serve to make the new green leaf buds seem the brighter, so did the snow clouds of winter make our master's litter and vestments seem the more magnificent.

Coming through the town gates, we picked up a further following of townspeople, who cheered at the sight of Odo and followed us to the cathedral, where Odo paused to pay a filial call on his archbishop. The archbishop looked like a pauper beside him and was a little vexed by it, but Odo bent his knee on the church steps and kissed the archbishop's ring with splendid humility, drawing more cheers from the crowd. They went into the church together, leaving the rest of us in the square while they gave thanks for the king's forbearance in not revenging himself on his traitorous son during the holy season. They were in there more than half an hour, during which time the weather worsened and a slushy rain began to fall.

I was numb from nose to buttocks from the wet and the cold, but when bishop and archbishop reappeared and we took up our progress again, I saw we would go by the street that led past Beroald's house, and my heart lifted in spite of good sense, as I thought Isabel must peep from a window to see me march by in the train of the glorious Odo. I looked up as best I could for the sleet falling in my face in fat dollops, but the shutters of that house didn't open.

Every street was jammed with men of the mesnies of the lords who came to Christmas Court. Every house that had a spare corner was obliged to give room to them. Bread stalls and wine stalls were set up in the streets in peril of cart wheels, or the good men and enterprising wives of the town sold bread, sweetmeats, or baked meats to the hungering multitude from their own doorsteps or windows. Prudent fathers shut up their daughters in storerooms and cellars to protect their chastity from the merry guests.

The castle was no longer the sedate and sleepy lady's court I had left in October. It was crammed to the walls with all the wealth and pride of Normandy. Blue-jawed men with ruddy cheeks and noses kept forever pale by wearing of their helms, men with chopped hair and sharp eyes, stood pressed together like sheep in a fold, talking to their peers about those things closest to their hearts: rents and bloodletting.

There were foreigners there, too, easily identified: the French were better dressed and more aloof than our barons; the Bretons more sullen; the Flemish more countrified. A few English here and there were the most striking. The older men still wore their hair in long plaits, like women, but proclaimed their manhood most peculiarly by wearing huge growths of hair on their upper lips, mustaches that hung over their mouths to their chins, which they shaved bare. Their tunics were long, nearly to their ankles, and dyed with brighter colors. None of them wore gambesons or hauberks by custom, as the rest did, which made them seem more effete than our warriors, if it hadn't been for those bristling mustaches.

Our King William sat on a raised platform at the end of the presence hall, with his wife and children around him. Lord Odo went through the press of bodies like a knife through cheese to bow to his brother, then kiss his sister-in-law's hand. It was thus I first saw demonstrated that chivalrous custom that had so taken Isabel's fancy, and I saw too how the older men in the hall reacted to it.

But the Lady Matilda was as much a woman as my Isabel; she smiled at the conceit, then gave her brother-in-law a proper kiss of greeting on either cheek. The king inclined his head to his brother in token of Odo's Holy Orders and let his thin mouth extend itself to a brief, wintry smile. I slid through the crowd and pushed myself around the hall piers to come as close as I might, in order to see this great man.

He was tall, above the average in men by five or six inches, a long-thighed man with a gross belly that would have looked more at home on a woman about to be delivered of twins. His broad, sallow face was without expression, his eyes small and too nearly closed for me to see their color. There was still more dark than grey in his hair, but his pate was bald and domed. His huge hands hung over the ends of the chair arms, broad and coarse, unjeweled except for his royal ring.

His tiny wife looked like a child beside him. Her feet barely touched the stool below her seat, and she seemed no taller than her youngest cub, Prince Henry, the image of his father, I now saw. Henry bowed to Odo and kissed his ring, as did the older son, who I guessed must be young William.

I didn't think much of him at first examination. Like Curthose, he was shorter than the king, though he wasn't dwarfish in the legs, like Robert. Unlike Robert or Henry, he was fair in his mother's image, with limp, yellow hair the color of tow. As with most people of that cast, his face was changeable from maidenly white to sudden red with every thought that smote him, and he looked all too conscious of his blushes.

Because of that, he was called Will-Rou, or Rufus, by his family and nearest friends. I watched him blush when his uncle spoke to him, blush when he laughed, blush again when he met his father's cold eye. I passed him over quickly as the least interesting of the family and turned my attention to his sisters.

There were the three who had not yet married or been vowed to a contemplative life: Adela, Constance, and Matilda. They all looked as if they had been chastised just before coming into the hall. They sat together on one bench gloomily. Only Adela had any beauty to speak of, being blond like her brother, but slender and dainty of face. The others were sallow, dark-browed, and too plump.

I went to the lower hall when it was time to feast, like all the clerks but the best. It was a fast day, of course, but there was plenty of fish of every kind, pickled, baked, fried, and minced into pies with raisins and onions. Wine, cider, and perry flagons were set out on the tables and kept filled by sweating, muttering kitchen help, who could hardly move fast enough to assuage our thirst.

After dinner Robin Bloet and I sneaked back up into the hall to hear the singers and see the jugglers and tumblers who performed before the high table.

One of the faces that passed in the mill of bodies caught my eye and made my bowels turn to water. It was Beroald. I turned away from him so suddenly that I almost knocked the cup out of Robert Bloet's hand.

'What's the matter with you?' he asked. 'You're pale as an oyster.'

I shrugged. My stomach had turned queasy on a sudden. It was because Beroald had seen me, too, seen me and frowned. In a moment I risked turning my head, to see if he was coming toward me, but he was gone. I drew a sigh of relief. Still, I kept looking for him to come past me again, this time perhaps to speak to me. But what would he say, in front of so many people? He wouldn't accuse me of attacking his cousin, there, in the midst of the Christmas Court, surely. No, but he might accuse me to someone in private, and it would be best if I made myself scarce and so avoid identification. He might not have known me after all. He had only seen me twice and then for the briefest of moments.

After several moments of debate with myself on what to do I took up Robin's last remark and complained of the eel pie.

'I need fresh air. I'll just go and stick my head out of doors. No need for you to come; I'll be back soon.'

I left him and hurried to the stairs, thinking I'd be more comfortable in the servants' hall, but halfway down the steps I met Beroald, coming up. Where had he been? I passed him after a nervous glance, but he made no effort to stop me or speak to me. I was much relieved. It wasn't I in particular he looked at with adder's eyes. It was only his manner of looking at the world in general.

I went through the lower hall and out into the bailey, but found it as crowded as the servants' hall; nothing but boisterous, red-faced people, drinking, laughing, quarreling. As long as I was out of the merriment, I might as well be out of the crush, too, I thought, so I went into the streets.

The sleet had turned to snow as night fell. It came down in great, swirling, thick clumps, as if Heaven were molting. As often when the snow finally arrives, it brought milder air with it. The wind was stilled. I put my cowl up and felt fit for walking.

There were still people in the streets, though not so many. Two of them in a hurry to be somewhere were coming up quickly from behind me. I heard their boots ring on the street and prepared to give way to them, but they came up too soon. I found them on either side of me. My heart began to make a terrible lurching movement in my breast, but I kept my head down and continued to walk faster, while they matched my steps exactly.

'Why are you in such a hurry, priest? There's plenty of time to say your prayers.'

I said nothing.

'Hold your head up, Father. I think I know you, don't I? Aren't you the one we had to set the dog on once?'

I said: 'If you lay hands on me here, I'll make a noise. People will see you. My bishop will hear of it. He's Odo of Bayeux.'

'Don't be frightened, Father. If you're the one we think, we've come to do you a favor. She wants to see you.'

'I don't know what you mean. I have nothing to do with women.'

'She sent us to find you. You'd better come. She won't be here tomorrow,' he whispered.

I turned to look at him. He was the lout who'd come with the porter and his dog that night. He grinned.

'I thought it was you.' His arm moved against me; I felt something sharp in my side. 'Make a sound and I'll put this between your ribs. Yell, and we'll yell, too. They'll think we're drunk. We'll keep you on your feet between us.'

They took my arms. I saw Beroald's house ahead, thought of running, thought of dying clenched between them. I made my decision, but it was too late. They shoved me through the gate between them, and in a moment the knife was at my throat. One opened the door and the other shoved me through. I heard the dog snarl in the passageway. The porter came hobbling toward us. I decided I wouldn't die like a sheep, my throat cut without a struggle. I grabbed the old man and swung him around, thrusting him between me and the man with the knife, then swung my fist at the other one's face, but his fist caught me in the ribs with such force I felt one of them crack. The breath went out of me. I rammed my head into his face anyway and heard the crunch of his nose breaking. My hand was on the door latch when I got a blow on the back of the neck that sent me to my knees. My arms and legs were like boiled meat, the muscles ready to fall off the bones.

I felt myself being dragged along the passage. Another door was opened and I was thrust through it. I fell at full length, still half paralyzed by the neck blow. The door shut and a key squeaked in the lock.

There was a pain in my head that made me nauseated when I lifted it, violently sick when I got to my hands and knees. I crawled away from my vomit, toward the door, but it was as black as one of Hell's nostrils in that room. I butted my head on a wooden cask instead, finally found the door, and pulled myself up it. I could see nothing through the keyhole for the key. There was utter silence on the far side of the door. I couldn't even hear the dog panting.

'I am a chaplain of His Grace the Bishop of Bayeux! You'd better not detain me any longer, unless you're prepared to answer for my injuries to him, you bastards!'

The silence that greeted that empty threat made me sit down against the door, sick with dread. What if they now went to the bishop and told him they'd just caught me trying to break into their house to molest a widow? I wouldn't be able to put up much defense if they broke my jaw first. In any case, the mere accusation of such a crime would make me abhorrent to Odo, who liked quiet, inconspicuous servants.

I tried a more reasonable tone, informing whoever was listening that I had meant the Lady Isabel no harm and had given none, as she would testify if they would call her.

No answer.

I begged them to have pity on me and let me go, and I would give them all the coin I had. By then I had no illusion I was speaking to anyone. The house was empty. Not even the dog was there any longer. It was bitterly cold in the storeroom. The utter darkness first oppressed, then provoked strange visions to my mind. I dozed or fainted, heard voices, saw lights and faces blooming in the blackness, strange colors, though no one had opened the door to let in light. I groped my way to a place on the floor between two casks and sat, running my hands over their rough wood and iron bands, to keep myself in touch with something material; otherwise I could believe I floated in the void.

It was a thousand years before there was any sound, before the lock creaked and light shone like a slim angel as the door cracked open. I had said every prayer I knew by then.

Three men entered the room, one holding a lantern. I rose unsteadily. 'Why are you keeping me here? I've done no harm. Where is the master of this house? Let me speak to him.'

'I am the master of this house.' It was true; I could see his narrow eyes glint in the light. He motioned to have the lantern lifted so that he could see me. I tried not to look as terrified as I was.

'Good Master Beroald, you've made a mistake – ' He hit me across the face. He was about my height but twice my weight. I sat down on one of the casks.

'You've dishonored my house,' he said in a dead voice.

'I've done nothing against you. I brought your kinswoman to you safely, when she begged it of me. I brought her news of her husband's death when I heard of it, and I tried to comfort her when she was wild with grief. Your men mistook me that night, as they do now. Call her and ask her if this isn't all that I did.' I was ready to proclaim my innocence on *that* occasion to the world.

Beroald grabbed me by the cowl and jerked me to my feet. 'I've asked her, whoreson. I'll tell you what she said: that you came running at her with your gown between your teeth; that you had her on her back a dozen times. She said you forced her, but that I may not believe, though it makes no difference in the end. For what you've done, I ought to make a corpse of you, but it's a holy season, so I'm going to have you flogged and thrown into the river. God may teach you to swim this night. We all hear of miracles. But if you survive, if I ever see your face again, if you live and ever pass my door, if you continue to breathe and ever breathe my family's name, I'll have you for dog's meat. Do you believe me?' His voice was so low he might have been saying a novena.

'What have you done to Isabel?' I could hardly whisper for his knuckles against my throat as he twisted my cowl. My question made him twist it tighter and shake me in a fury.

'You impudent bastard, did you say her name? Better ask what you've done!' He drove his fist into my stomach and threw me on the floor. 'Strip him.'

His servants obeyed, then each seized one of my wrists as I lay on my face, and one put his boot on my head. I thought my arms would be wrenched from their sockets until I felt the first blow of Beroald's lash, then I forgot all other pain.

To be whipped with a cincture is painful; it leaves stripes that turn to bruises. To be whipped with a scourge of oiled leather is like being flayed alive. I tried to hide my face to save it, but wherever his wagoner's whip fell on me, my skin split like a broiled sausage, until I fainted.

I came to my senses as my head and arms were being stuffed into my gown again. I was hauled up and the garment pulled over my bleeding back.

Beroald said: 'Take him to the river. If he sinks, it proves his guilt. The duke himself couldn't ask for a better test. If he swims, it must prove God has a use for vermin.' He took my jaw between his fingers, holding his face close to mine.

'When your whore spawns, son of a bitch, you'd better pray it's before her time, if you still have a liking for her. Her new husband may not be such a fool as to think a full-term child has been early breeched, because she tells him so. Safer for her if she drops it before it can live, since he isn't the man of mercy I am. For my part, I hope it comes forth blind, lame, and ugly and splits her belly in the doing, as she deserves. Take him away!'

Before they did, one of them gagged me, then pulled my cowl down to hide my face. I had pain in one side that made it agony to lift my arms, let alone be hauled through the streets as quickly as I was taken. It was dark and unearthly quiet; the snow was several inches deep underfoot. Yet I knew when we passed the castle. I could hear the gate being cranked up or down. I tried to balk there, to attract attention, but one of my captors put his fist in my side again, and I scarcely knew what they did after that, until I was put into the boat.

The little boat's bobbing frightened me as much as all that had gone before. I would have thrown myself out of it at once, but I was held. We began to move out into the channel.

'We should have tied a stone around his feet. He'll float.'

'He'll float, but it'll be downstream. The current's strong here. Say your prayers, whoreson priest. You won't have breath for it in a minute.' I was pulled up by shoulders and knees and thrust over the side.

The death chill of the water worked by opposites to shock me back to life. I had the gag out in a moment and was fighting to reach the surface no more than I was plunged into the water, but a blow from one of their oars sank me again, deeper.

When I surfaced I was out of reach of the boat, which had moved away rapidly. I thrashed and fought the icy water, never having learned how to swim, indeed never having seen it done. My gown was heavy with water, my cowl clung to my face, and my side felt as if a wild animal's teeth were tearing at it. A black fear took possession of me. I couldn't think of death, or Hell, or repentance, only of sinking into the thick ooze of the river bottom, choking on water, being eaten by fishes. I flailed upward with a roaring in my ears that would be my last surge of life.

I heard voices; light bleared my watery eyes. Something thin and hard touched me. I fought it and sank again, driven into the murk by a hard body that crushed the last air from my lungs. I fought it as it grappled me. I thought some man-eating fish or unspeakable water demon had me in tow. A tentacle thick as a man's arm wrapped around my throat and pulled me to it in spite of myself.

It was a man holding me, swimming with me, being reached for by other men from the side of a low-riding boat, a floating box, the ferry barge, crossing from the far side of the river to make night harbor at the town quays.

We were taken up by saving hands, pulled agonizingly over the side and onto the deck, where someone tried to press the water out of my lungs and nearly finished me instead.

'Let him be. He's broken a rib, I think.'

I lay clutching the deck boards and whimpering with pain, then shuddering with cold, until the barge touched a pier and I was lifted carefully and carried away somewhere – a dry place beyond the wharves, where there were light and fire and a cot. A warm blanket was pressed over my rapidly stiffening gown, but nothing stopped my tremors, not even a wineskin put to my mouth that nearly choked me again.

There was light on my eyelids, a sudden sharp word of surprise, my name. A hand caught my head as it lolled on the cot and pulled it around. I opened my eyes, flinching at the light.

'Well, I'll be damned for a donkey. Ranulph! Is it you? Bring that lantern to this side. By God, it is!'

He gave a short, husky laugh. There was everything familiar about the laugh and voice, but I couldn't see his face until he took my head between his hands and thawed my frozen eyelids with the balls of his thumbs.

'Look at you! How many times must a man save your life before you learn anything? What have you done to be drowned for, you sprat?'

It was Cormac.

14

Beyond saying his name several times, I was incoherent. He and his companions got more wine down my throat, wrapped me in a blanket, and took me to the castle, where my brothers of the tonsure flocked around me, scandalized and curious to see my injuries. One who was skilled in infirmary work put an ointment on my back that rekindled its fires; then he bound up my ribs until I could hardly breathe.

My own account of my assault was necessarily vague, but that was no matter. My attackers were plainly enemies of the Church, probably servants of German merchants, whose proud emperor still contended with the Pope. Or they were: Bretons, Flemings, French; or part of the Montgomery faction – Robert de Bellesme's family – expressing their sympathy for the vile rebels by beating a helpless priest. I was astonished to find how many people wanted to murder me.

'The town's full of nithings this week,' said an English clerk scornfully. 'The king shouldn't let them wander at will here. In England he imposed a curfew, a half hour before Compline. You don't hear of drunken scum mauling our innocent people in London after sundown.'

'No, the damned dogs do it there, that you let run free,' growled a Norman.

I sat up from the table on which I'd been laid while I was doctored; someone pulled a clean shirt over my head. Cormac was still there at the end of the table, studying me. His harp sack reared itself behind one shoulder like a black wing. His lifted brow said plainly that he doubted anyone had been the cause of my trouble but myself. The look made me feel ten years old again.

I also saw he was no longer tonsured, and wore a common short brown mantle, hose, and green tunic, like a huntsman. In that room full of clerks he had as much to conceal as I. If they had a hint he was a renegade monk, they'd have bound him and sent him back to St. Vigor, riding backward on an ass. I therefore appreciated his lingering to make certain I was all right.

A voice drawled: 'Everyone knows what the rabble do in the streets at night. But what was our young brother doing there – alone – at such an hour?' It was Carileph, who came pushing his way slowly through the others to have a look at me.

'I was ill. I went out for fresh air. I went to the cathedral to hear Vespers.'

'Very commendable. But it is now past Compline. What detained you?' That was pure malice. He would never have asked if he'd thought I was out on some murky business for Odo.

'He was with me for a bit,' Cormac said. 'I'm obliged to admit the time might have run away from us. We were renewing an old acquaintance.'

'You, Irishman? I suppose you were in the church, too, praying devoutly?'

'Oh, most devoutly, Brother. It was the very frenzy of my devotions that got his attention and caused him to recognize me. Yes, you can hold me responsible. We stood in the church square for over an hour, discussing the Mystery of the Holy Trinity and such other such things as old friends pass the time with. Then I took him from his proper path and led him – *mea culpa* – straight into the way of those heathen wagoners, God forgive me!' He knocked his breast. He was being very Irish, and I wondered if Carileph knew him well enough to know he was being mocked.

'Wagoners?' someone repeated.

'Why, yes, them with the whips. They were contending to see which of them could skin more hair off a dog's back as it ran by them. My young friend was quite in the right to preach them a sermon on kindness to all God's creatures, but I fear his zeal was his undoing after I left him, Jesus love him.' His accent was truly abominable.

'Is that what happened?' Carileph asked me.

'Yes, they – they followed me and stopped me.' What else could I say?

'And beat you and threw you into the river, for preaching to them?'

'Yes.' It was too ridiculous, but my brain refused to help me to a more likely explanation. Nor did I feel quite so much gratitude toward Cormac, now I looked at him again. He hadn't been the one who jumped into the water to save me. His clothes were quite dry. He was obviously enjoying the corner he'd just put me in and was only staying to see how I wormed out of it. Carileph hadn't finished interrogating me.

'Why, then, if they beat you shortly after Vespers, have you been so long returning here? Surely you weren't in the water all this while.'

Cormac laughed. 'What a precious lot of Christians you clerks are. Who's on trial here? The corpse? Look at him! Did you ever know a clerk who was guilty of something who couldn't give a better account of his doings? It's plain as a cow pat; the boy's wits are scattered. They knocked him senseless, then took him off to torment him for a while.' He turned to his several companions, who had offered nothing to the dialogue but occasional laughs. 'Will you listen to me, lads? Did you ever think you'd hear me playing advocate to a shave-pate? I give over the argument. My testimony taints the client. Take him and hang him, Frenchmen. He must be guilty of something, being half dead.'

'That's enough idle talk,' said my physician suddenly. 'It's time for all decent people to think of their night prayers, and this young brother wants his rest.'

'A wise judgment, Brother Daniel. You're worthy of your name,' Cormac said civilly. He turned away without looking at me again, as if he were suddenly bored with the company of clerks.

I woke, sore and stiff, to creep out and find myself a celebrated person. The tale of my lecturing two wagoners on their sins, and being nearly drowned for it, was a tale made for Christmas and went all over the castle in half a day, the celerity not an unusual occurrence, as anything worth telling once in a court will be told by everyone who hears it.

Odo was informed when he came from St. Gervase to celebrate

Mass with the archbishop that morning. The king and his lady must have heard of it soon after, because I was sent for when they took their seats in the hall, to show my back. Odo complained of the lawlessness among the rabble in town, which he seemed to feel was an affront to him personally, rather than just a general nuisance.

I stood, miserable and mute, unable to follow the thread of his argument, but admiring the fashion in which he took advantage of my celebrity to register slights against his household in England. After a while I began to think that the archbishop of Canterbury had sent phantom wagoners to beat me, just to spite the bishop of Bayeux. Odo was a marvelous speaker. Several of the more potent lords and nearly all the clergy gathered there were in full vocal agreement with him in a matter of minutes. Only the king seemed unmoved. William Bastard's face kept both charity and impatience at bay for the duration of the harangue, but when it was over, he said:

'The men who have done this will be found and punished. What compensation will you have for your clerk's back, my lord?' It was plain he wished to hear no more of me.

Now Lord Odo looked amazed. 'Why, no compensation, Your Grace. What will silver do to lace up a broken back? I stand in need of no coin, and this fellow has abjured it. Yet, in the name of charity –'

'Yes?' The word fell soft from the lips but hard on the ear.

'Why, Your Grace, I was going to say – will you keep my poor clerk with you, until he's recovered? As you know, I must take my leave of you tomorrow to see my own diocese before I return to your realm on your business. This young brother is scarcely fit for travel. Indeed, as I speak, it strikes me I might do better to make a gift of him, to someone who surely needs him more than Your Grace does.'

He smiled and bowed to his nephew, William Rufus, who stood beside his father's seat looking bored by speeches.

'Will-Rou, you're about to become a most worthy knight, but you've already seen the principal gifts I've brought you. Accept one more, with your uncle's affectionate wishes: a priest, dear nephew, to hear your prayers and guide you in the ways of virtue. A clerk to write your letters, since you've no time to learn the skill yourself.'

There was a general murmur of laughter, and young Will's face turned crimson. He looked at me with loathing.

His mother said: 'I think your uncle does well, my son. You are a man now and will need a clerk, as well as a good young priest to comfort you.' She smiled at me very sweetly.

'They'll suit each other well, *Maman,*' the daughter named Adela said, winking at her brother. 'The priest is not strong now, so he won't tax our Will with his devotions, while Will is so famous for his brief devotions, he won't tax the strength of his priest.'

Even the king smiled faintly at her little jest; the rest of the company roared. I looked at the floor, and my new master made the best of things by trying to join in the merriment with a high, nervous braying laugh.

'Uncle, you've gi-given me two fi-fine horses for my knighting and a hound bitch for my name day. Isn't that enough of a men-nenagerie?'

But there the king put a rein on the frolic. 'Don't mock the office of a priest by likening him to an animal, my son. Take the priest and make good use of him.'

The rebuke couldn't have made young William like me more than I liked him at that moment, but we were saddled with each other. I went away to savor my defeat. Robin Bloet found me and was surprised at my gloom.

'But you'll be chaplain to one of the royal family. That's not such a bad life.'

'I've been parceled off to the family cretin, with less ceremony than those two horses. Did you see him? Have you heard him speak?'

Robin sat down by me and would have put his hand on my shoulder in commiseration, but I flinched.

'Sorry. Yes, I've heard and seen him. He was sent to school with Anselm at Bec for a time, while I was there.'

'At Bec? What could they possibly have done for him?'

'Put him in the Church. He was the third son, remember. He never liked the idea, and I think he bears the clergy little love for the experience. Not altogether reasonable from our viewpoint, of course, but it doesn't make him a cretin.'

'He blushes and stammers and brays like a jackass.'

'I grant the point, but he's only eighteen. He's lived his life ignored by everybody until this last year, when he's suddenly become the heir and hope of two countries. Can you blame him if he stutters?'

I sighed. 'I suppose not. It appears you like him. I'll try to learn to do so, for your sake. I'm going to miss your company, Robin.'

'And I'll miss yours. You're very free with your wine ration and your coin. But we'll see each other again. If the king doesn't take up

Curthose's challenge to a war, he'll be coming back to England soon, and Rufus follows him everywhere now.'

I saw William de St. Carileph coming our way and stood to receive him. He beckoned me away to his cubicle above the hall. I wasn't in the mood for his irony or any further inquiries about my adventures.

'We shall be seeing more of you at court, it seems.'

'Yes. Do I have you to thank for my dismissal? You might have let me speak to the bishop for myself, Carileph.'

'Oh, has His Grace dismissed you? I hadn't heard of it. Though it's true he likes quiet, obscure men to do his errands, not the sort who make their faces – not to mention their backsides – famous all in a night.'

'As long as I'm ruined, will it do me any further harm if I broke your nose for you?' I made a fist.

Carileph held up his hands in pretended horror. 'Please, Brother, peace! Especially if you still have the desire to be an intelligencer.'

'For whom? What do you mean?'

'Why, you have a new young master to serve, but you may still oblige the old – for a consideration.'

'You can't mean that. He wants me to spy on this *boy?*'

He cocked his head and smiled almost winsomely.

'But that's ridiculous! What's there to know about him? I might as well be set to watch his little brother pick his nose!'

'Oh, you're disappointed in your new position!' He clucked his tongue. 'Perhaps you'll come to appreciate his virtues – among which is that he's grown very close to his father this last year, which is a thing no other man in the world has been able to boast of for years. The king's inclined to keep his own counsel, which, if it were not so, we wouldn't be put to the trouble of making so many tedious inquiries, would we?'

'I hate being a spy.'

'Then return to your cloister and we'll find someone who likes it better.' He dropped his pretence of good humor.

I groaned. My back and side were clamoring for me to sit and rest. 'What am I supposed to learn?'

'Whether we're to be thrown into a war. Whether the king has been using Robert's rebellion as a means of drawing out his enemies in order to destroy them. Whether he's really bribed King Philip to desert the rebels at the crucial moment, or if the rumor's a ruse to see if others are eager to take the place of the French.'

'Why should he do that?'

'Wars are expensive pursuits. The king is not liberal with his money. If he spends, it's to good purpose. There are those who haven't his wealth, who would simply like to know if they're wasting more treasure than they can afford, opposing a man who's already bought the peace. Now, that's all the policy you're going to get from me. It isn't good for you. But there will be a purse for you, paid quarterly, if you can keep us reliably informed. Now the king is here, you won't come near me too often. Write your reports and put them in your desk. I'll see they're delivered.'

'Very well. But it's hard to believe that a man who doesn't confide in anyone else would tell his soul's secrets to a boy like that.'

'We shall see. One thing more: I don't believe your tale about last night, especially considering your chief witness. That Irishman's no friend of yours, or anybody's, unless it's the Devil's. I don't know what you were up to, but I remember another time you came home late and limping. You're quite a handsome young cockerel, in a sullen sort of way, and I expect you know it. If there's an aggrieved husband here in Rouen who's still looking for you – and that's the most innocent interpretation I can put on the matter – let it be that he's seen the last of you. There are safer outlets for high spirits than you may have found. I would suggest good wine and Roman verse, but if some other suggests itself to you, be more discreet.'

King William knighted his son on St. Stephen's Day in the castle hall after None service. It was a simple ceremony, compared with those that are becoming so notoriously elaborate today. At that time most men hoped to receive their accolades on the battlefield, having killed their man and earned his arms and horse; or in their lord's hall, with no particular fuss. There were no night-long vigils and wearisome pageants, as now.

In this case, the event was marked more by the king's desire to establish a new heir than to award a hero. Young Will had never known battle, though he'd been in his father's army at the siege of Dol, as squire to Earl Montgomery. He hadn't needed to win his equipage from a corpse, or had to marry for it. His family and sponsors supplied all, quietly: the sword, from his father; the helm and shield, from his uncles, Robert of Mortain and Odo of Champagne; the horses, from Odo of Bayeux; and the shirts, tunics, baldric, and other accessories, rather like a bride's gifts, from his mother and sisters.

Rufus – I had already begun to think of him as such, though I never let the name pass my lips in all the years I served him – Rufus received the gifts of dress on Christmas Day and put them on the following morning, except the armor, with the aid of his newly chosen squire. I was present at the robing, having already confessed him that morning for the first time.

He was nervously high-spirited and familiar with his servants, who brought him his washbasin, and with his squire, William de Alderi, who was only a year or two younger than his master. But he was cool to me.

I had seen my new lord face to face for the first time the previous night, when I went to his bedchamber to hear his prayer and to give him the night blessing. It was just as well Robin Bloet had warned me about his strange eyes, or I would have put myself in worse case with him by staring, and we hardly needed more reasons to be offended with each other.

They were very strange indeed, but, being forewarned, I didn't find them abhorrent, though they had a sort of power not in keeping with his still rather babyish face. They were of diverse colors, as Robin had said. One was blue, of the clearest tint, and seemed the larger for it, both for its color and because the brow above it was always raised at a higher level. The other iris was a sort of hazelnut, or golden brown, like a hound's eye. It seemed the more knowledgeable, sharp, and inquiring. The effect could be called disconcerting when he looked a man full in the face.

I'd never seen such a phenomenon in a human, though I'd once seen a horse with what is called a 'glass eye.' The stablemen at St. Vigor wouldn't let it in with the abbot's animals when its owner came to visit. He was forced to tether it to a tree, which vexed him. The abbot had laughed about it later.

So, I didn't flinch from Will-Rou's gaze when he turned it on me that first time, though I had the distinct feeling he meant me to. He stared me down with the kind of inquisitive anger that dared me to match him. I may have done so, since I was still smarting from being given to him, like a slave. My body ached, too. He had made me wait for nearly an hour after admitting me to his presence, while he finished a game of tables with his squire.

I slept outside his door that Christmas night – another kind of test, perhaps. Passageways are crafty places for sleeping; there's neither fire, brazier, nor, in my case, even another body near to make the station more agreeable than a tomb.

When I went to him on the morning of his knighting, I was as stiff as a corpse and only half as amiable, therefore.

He was letting himself be dressed, and it was clear he hadn't gotten used to such service. He fidgeted, made lame, stammering jests, and laughed at an irritating pitch. He kept glancing at me, as if I were the only fly in his broth.

When his shirt and hose were on, he reached for a wine cup, emptied it into his mouth, then suddenly pitched it to me.

'You look dry this morning. Pour yourself a measure.'

The cup hit the floor before I could catch it, but I wasn't meant to catch it; I was meant to bend my sore back and fractured rib cage to retrieve it while he watched to see the effect. I did so without wincing, though the inside of my cheek suffered biting for it. When I had it in hand, I refused his offer with thanks and put it aside. The look on his face changed to one of sobriety.

'I'm sorry,' he said. 'That was a bad toss. Your back must be hell for you. I saw the marks yesterday. Let me see them now.' I frowned, didn't move. 'Please,' he added.

I stripped off my gown. He urged his squire to help. 'There's blood on your shirt. You're stuck to it. Will, get the sponge.'

I didn't protest, but the sponge was of no use. The wool was firmly sealed to my welts with dried blood. They both worked at it and pulled the shirt away from my flesh, which started it bleeding again.

'Face of God! Will, get the horse salve. Bring some leg wrappings, too. You're in luck, Father. I just gave up horse tending, bu-but I still have my t-tack box. This will burn like Hell; it's got sulfur in it. But it's healing.'

'Brother Daniel put something on my back last night,' I said stolidly. It did burn like Hell. Tears came to my eyes in spite of all my blinking.

'Brother Daniel is better at making piss than p-poultices,' my lord said, 'though he's a good old man. But I am a very good sur-surgeon for leg slashes and shoulder wounds. You m-may ask Earl Roger's destrier if I'm not. This is n-no different.'

He and de Alderi wrapped the bandages around me snugly, then de Alderi held out my shirt and gown. The fire in the ointment was dying down a bit, and the pain, in any case, was less than when my shirt had been pulling at my flesh.

I stood up and said stiffly: 'My lord is very kind.'

'Well, we can't have you pulling up lame before you've even gotten into the field, can we?' Then he laughed. 'You called me "my lord." No one's done that before. Will, where's my gambeson? And throw this stuff back in the tack box.'

So, he tended me, but only as one of his several animals. I didn't like him for it.

The Archbishop of Rouen blessed the occasion; the king gave him the buffet; his uncles fastened on his spurs; and so Will-Rou became Sir William.

It is part of the tradition of making a knight now that the newly honored one should show off his horsemanship for his friends by vaulting into the saddle of his destrier without the aid of stirrup or squire. So it was then, too. After he had been cheered in the hall, everybody surged into the bailey to see him do it.

Rufus made it – barely. In a running jump he got in the saddle, then made the milk-white animal perform the levade, the capriole, and in fact the whole of the carousel formations which make a destrier such a terror to the infantry. It was a marvel of an exhibition and the bailey crowd cheered him, but plainly the horse had been trained to it by someone of Lord Odo's choosing, so I couldn't credit my master with more than the determination to keep his seat, in spite of his thick, short legs.

Later that day he met with other knights and fought a mock battle in the lists that were set out on the western edge of the town wall, in a frozen, marshy ground known as the Evil Swamp in the summer, for the stinging midges it bred.

There were prizes for valor: silver cups, daggers, even a sword for one of the victors. Hoots and jeers rewarded the losers who fell on their backs in the trampled, half-frozen mush. I had never seen a trial of arms before and took some interest in it, until the first man was carried off the field with blood streaming from his nose and ears from the crack made in his head when it hit the ground after his helm had flown off.

The ladies weren't offended. They looked down on the fray from the castle walls and waved and cheered the winners. The king and his male guests watched from the galleries, while the townsmen and all others crowded the town walls or clustered where they might.

I knew little of warriors' skills, but it seemed to me that although my lord was an eager contender, he wasn't yet a very skillful one. He was as wild as a boar at the charge, but lost his seat twice and won no prizes. He was crimson in the face, from either the cold or the humiliation, but he didn't lose his temper as several others did when they'd picked themselves up from a fall and heard the friendly jeers.

I was watching, hunched against the wind, at the north end of the lists when I felt a hand fall on my arm.

'I didn't know it was a royal chaplain I saved from the Seine,' said

Cormac cheerfully. His words were for me, but his eyes were on the field. He had a beard of several days' growth.

I still blamed him partly for losing me the goodwill of Lord Odo and getting me my present position, so I was short: 'I didn't see any water running off your nose. I think it was someone else who saved my life. Give him my thanks.'

He shifted his glance to me momentarily. 'Why, someone else did wet himself for you, but I saw your friends drop you overboard and I told the ferryman to pole for you. However, I'll convey your gratitude to Dick, who took the plunge.' His hand dropped from my shoulder.

I was instantly ashamed of my surliness. 'Cormac – wait. I – I'm glad to see you and I do thank you for saving me. If I sound ungracious, it's because I wish you'd left it at that. Why did you tell the king's chaplain all that other nonsense?'

'What would you have told him?' He was watching the lists again, keenly. Two riders came together in a bone-wrenching clash, and one was slammed off his saddle as the other sped past. Cormac's lips pulled back in a hiss of sympathy. Then he looked at me and grinned. 'Did you deserve drowning, Little Brother?'

'Possibly.'

'I see. Then that's why you're so grim to be still living. A different cast of mind from mine altogether. What was the nature of your crime? Some virgin's undoing? Or some bishop's doing?'

I was flustered by that near hit. 'Neither. I don't know what you mean. What bishop – virgin – would I know?' Very poor reply, but the roar of approval from the crowd for the winner of the last passage partly covered my chagrin.

'Ranulph, I've been loose on the world for a season or two now, and I've "seen Paris and heard of the oliphant," as the saying goes. Alas, I've known all your guilty looks since you had a shirt long enough to cover your arse. There's no mystery in it, as I can see: you're running for Carileph. Carileph pays people to sneak for him, and there's a bishop who pays Carileph. Am I warm?'

He was too warm. I turned my attention to the field, where the fallen rider was being helped to his feet. Two fresh contenders were already positioning themselves at either end of the center barricade for their run. Seeing the interest I pretended, Cormac said confidentially: 'That's Richer de Sourdeval at the far end, Jehan de Rennes down here. De Sourdeval's the better man. He'll take that fat Breton off; just watch.'

De Sourdeval did it, most painfully for the fat Breton.

'What are you doing here at Rouen, Cormac? I thought you'd be clear out of Normandy by now. What will you do if someone sees you and recognizes you – other than myself? You could still be tried if the abbot catches you.'

'No one's going to recognize me, Little Brother, and you'd be amazed at how little interest the world takes in misdemeanors such as mine. In any event, the abbot wouldn't want me brought back for trial – unless someone had been thoughtful enough to slit my tongue first.'

'But what do you do?'

'I'm the keeper of the Constable de Ivri's hounds. We Irish have a great way with dogs, you know.'

'Why not his clerk, if you don't fear recognition?'

'Well – I *like* dogs.' He smiled. 'And a man isn't wise to boast of competence in too many low professions.'

The insult didn't sting me personally, so much as it did for him. 'But you were – you were a scholar!'

He looked at me, and for a moment the irony left his eyes. 'Boy, you're – in our little world, I was whatever the abbot said I was. But in the rest of the scholar's kingdom, I'd be very much the journeyman scribbler. Open your eyes.' He knocked his fist against my arm and grinned. 'If you're worried about me, maybe you'll help me to a better place. When you're chancellor to the coming duke, you'll let me be your dog keeper.'

Out on the field Rufus was laughingly badgering the fallen Breton as he prepared to make another trial himself. My once feared and idolized master, whose fine penman's hands were now creased with dirt and chapped across the knuckles, turned his attention fully to him as he charged the lists with his blunted jousting lance and gave an inconclusive buffet to his opponent, who swayed but kept his seat. Nevertheless, Cormac nodded approval. Then, scratching at his bristled jaw, he said in an offhand way:

'If you think I need improving, you could recommend me to your unshelled duke for his servant. Would you do that?'

I saw he meant it. However casually he'd said it, he'd come looking for me just to ask it. I burned with shame for him. Whatever he now thought of his past reputation, it had seemed different to me. It was as if my own father had approached me to wheedle a favor. But I answered only as I could:

'I haven't yet recommended myself to him. If I manage to do that, I'll see what else is possible.'

15

I had more offices than I could fill. I was the chaplain of a young man who stinted his prayers and ignored me. I was a spy for Odo, with no intelligence to report. I was an advocate without influence for Cormac. I tried to make the best of things: Rufus folded his hands morning and night, while I said the prayers for him. I wrote a nonsensical letter for Carileph to send to Odo, outlining his nephew's character as if his uncle had never before clapped eyes on him. I thought it would show I was observant if not particularly useful. Young William might know every impulse and plan that coursed through his great father's brain, but if he did, he didn't prattle about them to me, or to anyone else, so far as I could tell.

For Cormac I did my unwilling best. I said very bluntly one morning:

'My lord, there is an Irishman in the service of the constable, a kenneler, who says he thinks he saw a spot of the mange on the liam bitch His Grace your uncle gave you. He begs leave to present you with some salve he's concocted for it.'

Rufus looked at me in surprise. It was the first time I had spoken to him on any subject other than the prospect for a good morning since he had salved and bandaged my back.

'What's this? Why do you take an interest in dog keepers? Do you owe him money?'

'No, my lord. I was speaking to him in the hall last night and he said it. I thought you might be interested in his opinion, since it's a valuable animal.'

He folded his rather short arms across his chest as de Alderi was lacing up his boots. 'That's the most unlikely thing I've heard before breakfast. There isn't a mark on the dog.'

I acknowledged it. 'I'm a poor courtier, my lord. The lie was mine.'

'What was the purpose of it?'

'The Irishman is the man who fished me out of the Seine. I owe him a favor. He said he'd like to serve you and would, if I recommended him and you agreed. I couldn't think of a better way to broach the subject. Forgive me.'

'Why should an Irishman want to serve me? Ralph de Ivri's no mean master.'

'I don't know, my lord. He didn't say. Perhaps it's because you are a prince, while my lord Ralph is only – '

'Only the Comte de Ivri; only Lord High Constable of Normandy; only standard bearer; o-only one of the richest men in the land. P-poor old Ralph! Your dog keeper must be ver-very particular, to prefer me. Look – my uncle sa-saddled me with you; is this d-dog man in his pay, too?'

'Oh, don't b-bother to look pained. I know my uncle. But I'm not my glo-glorious brother Robert, Father. I don't need a b-body of parasites hanging around me to m-make me happy. And I'm no prince, either. I've ha-had that all explained to me long ago. Henry's a prince. He was born after the crowning, you see? I'm only William, who's the son of the Duke of the Normans here, who got to be K-king of the English, too. Which is good enough, but s-soldiers need only honor and arms to s-serve them, not – not priests and ke-kennel k-keepers.'

I bowed my head at the rebuke and waited for him to dismiss me, but he said after a moment: 'What's your Irishman's name?'

'Cormac, my lord.'

He stood up and let de Alderi put his mantelet on his shoulders, then lace it at the throat. He was looking at me with a closed face, but didn't dismiss me.

'My lord, please forget I mentioned the man to you and don't hold my deceit against him. I felt grateful to him for saving my life. He seems a pleasant fellow, educated above his station, I think. He's fair-spoken – and he plays the harp. I hoped I might help him, that's all.'

Rufus motioned de Alderi aside and advanced on me with such a curious look, I couldn't tell what he meant by it, but when he got within range to cuff me, he stopped and smiled. He had a blunt, homely face, still not altogether free of adolescent blemishes, but his smile was swift and illuminating, like a child's.

'You're either a rogue, or the first honest priest I ever met in my life. I didn't think your breed knew anything about gratitude. They usually take anything offered them as their due, or a bit less. I'm going across the river to hunt w-with my f-father this afternoon. But you come and present your Irishman to me this evening. We'll see if he's got any ta-talents a plain man can use.'

I told Cormac that news and left him to mull it over. That evening when the tables were cleared and half the men in the hall were already drunk or gambling, I brought Cormac to the high table and then retreated to my own place.

The king had already left the presence hall for his council chamber in the company of the older lords. He was abstemious in the matter of drink and got no pleasure from watching others who were not; neither did he wager or dote on pleasant gossip.

Rufus and his few friends were left at the table. His best friend seemed to be Robert fitz Hamon, grandson of the old steward called Haimo of the Teeth – well named, and his descendant resembled him. And new, though he seemed old for much intimacy, was Edgar Atheling, the fallen English prince, who was an honorable hostage in King William's court. The others were of little consequence – the better sons of the duchy were apparently still not convinced Will-Rou would be the heir.

I thought Cormac ought to be a fitting addition to that company, if he exerted himself. They must have thought so, too. After a brief interview with Rufus, which I watched but couldn't hear, Cormac laughed and unslung his harp, uncased and tuned it, then played and sang something. The music, too, was lost to me through the rumble of talk, dice thumping, and bench scrapings. But I saw them applaud him when it was done.

He stayed with them the rest of the evening. Frankly, I was envious.

On the day after Epiphany a rider came at the gallop from Gournai, to tell us how the rebels of Gerberoy had made another raid across our border, with as great a butchery of men and cattle as before, and to as little purpose.

The king went into council with his barons, and in an hour the news was racing through the keep that the courier told of a French army massed not far from Gerberoy, ready to invade us in force at King Philip's signal.

It seemed to be true. At least this time the king said nothing about keeping peace for the holy season, as after the last outrage. An assembly in the lower hall could hear his high-pitched, nasal voice belling upstairs like a scent-crazed hound's, and his words concerning the perfidy of his sworn liege lord, Philip, would have made an admirable report for me to send to Lord Odo, but there was no need.

Every clerk in the castle was put to work penning summons of array for the lords of Normandy and all who owed their duke service. We could hardly scribble out the last of them before William Bastard was arraying himself and his own and was mounting his famous destrier with the aid of two squires.

My lord was a member of his father's mesnie and would now ride to his first battle. I watched him being arrayed by de Alderi. He was excited and stammered like a simpleton, but not from joy for battle.

'G-g-god damn Robin! If I c-c-could j-just talk to him! I'd let him pour s-s-slops over my-*my* head, gladly, if it would pu-put an end to this!' He looked at me thunderously. 'My da-damned tongue should ne-never try to talk. It's good only for licking fingers,' he whispered.

He ran his hands over his beautiful hauberk of silvered mail and surveyed himself from the chest downward. Under the shirt de Alderi had harnessed an iron plastron over his master's heart. Beneath that was the thick leather gambeson, which lay over a tunic and shirt of wool. He looked top-heavy. His unhelmed head was wet with sweat from being pushed through so many layers of garments, and his fair hair clung to his skull like a baby's. He glanced up at me from under his brows.

'Well, man, why are you standing there? Where's your cloak? Pull on your boots, for God's sake. They'll be waiting to load you up on the clerks' cart.'

'Me, m-my lord?'

Now he laughed at my stammer. 'Yes, you, you useless get! You're one-third of my f-following, aren't you? You go where I go – or you'll deeply disappoint my uncle.'

De Alderi gave him his helm and he fitted it on carefully. 'You can pray for my soul, while I'm f-fighting my damned brother, can't you? Yes. And if that's not enough to keep you busy, the marshals will find work for you – doling out f-fodder, or something.' He put his baldric over his head and strode out.

The Lady Matilda did not appear with her daughters to wish the king Godspeed on the venture. The promised clash between her husband and her firstborn was a great grief to her. Whether her next living son's participation in it took her the same way I never knew. Perhaps she told God about it.

The archbishop prayed for us; then the king put on his helm and strode out to mount, followed by all his knights and a crowlike flock of harried clerks, of which I must have been the most terrified.

There was no room on the clerks' cart for me. I marched behind it with a few other of the younger clerks who were not known to me. The foot soldiers passed us soon after we left the city gates; though we'd started well, we were quickly relegated to our proper place as baggage among the ox carts.

The roads were all muck and manure, following the cavalry. The wind was sharp and wet. Within a mile I was wheezing for the pain in my ribs. Our destination wasn't Gournai, but Aumale, where the king's sister-son waited to lend his castle and support. We had set out just after an early Prime. The king and his knights reached Aumale by midday, the foot soldiers by mid-afternoon, but the wagons and those of us who walked behind them weren't yet there by nightfall. Much of our time was spent watching the wagoners dig their wheels out of mud bogs, which afforded me some rest. Nevertheless, before we had gone a third of the way I was trailing the last ox cart. It was the driver of that cart and not any of my sympathetic brethren who finally allowed me to ride, which I believe saved my life.

Sitting still made me so cold that when I had rested I was willing to help with the digging, with bare hands if necessary, to speed up the journey, but one of the elder clerks who heard my rash pledge made me understand that this was unthinkable – not because of my injuries, but because it was better to freeze than to degrade myself by offering to aid such low persons in their appointed tasks.

I had supposed that when we reached Aumale the clergy would be housed inside its walls, but that was impossible. It was already packed with the Aumale garrison and the king's chief followers and was expecting more illustrious guests than its halls were prepared for. Even Rufus spent the night in a tent with three other knights and their squires. I was assigned to a tent full of clerks, where I spent the most miserable nights of my life – up to that point. I am as accustomed to cold as any other man, I think, and make no complaint of wind or weather if I can be dry and warm for a little while at the end of the day.

But on that campaign I first knew what it was to be poorly clad and have no prospects for change for many days. It has made me, I hope, more charitable to ragged men, and even beasts, on a January day, for the rest of my life.

We were at Aumale for three days, until the rest of the host summoned by the king had caught up to him; then we folded our tents and moved in a slow, grim tide down to Gournai.

During that walk I saw Cormac among the riders of horses, with his harp slung where others carried their shields. I was puzzled to know why Ralph de Ivri should bring his kenneler on campaign, but when we reached Gournai I saw Rufus hail Cormac and take him into his tent, where I had never been summoned since we took to the road.

At Gournai, councils were held by the king and his barons, while the sergeants drilled their troops in the fields and the knights banneret drilled theirs in the saddle. In the afternoons they had their mock battles, while waiting for the king's spies to make a survey of the country and say whether there really was a French army somewhere making ready for us.

Meanwhile, the camp quickly grew rank with horse dung, ox droppings, human ordure, and camp refuse. The crows and ravens hung over us as if we were already carrion and at last grew so bold as to light in our midst and examine our leavings.

The Lady Basile de Gournai departed in a little from the castle for another of her lord's estates, with a bag of pungent spices pressed to her nose as she passed us.

On St. Ita's Day, the ides of January, we were routed from our lice-infested blankets at first light and moved across the Brai, to lay siege to Gerberoy. That castle looked even bleaker than it had the last time I'd seen it, since all life had been erased from the earth around it, first by burning, to rid the ground of any cover that could hide an enemy, then by the falling of a mantle of snow. Everything was stark: grey skies, black walls, white ground.

The king set his own camp with its back to the trees that bordered the river. The other lords dispersed to either side of him. Our lines were laid down, our entrenchments dug, pickets driven, privies excavated, and every man now put in mind of the biblical injunction to cover his waste with the dirt left heaped beside the holes, an orthodox hope that had failed of its purpose up to then.

King William sent his herald out to cry before Gerberoy's bailey, but not before Rufus had begged earnestly to be allowed to go instead. His father refused him in a voice that carried over the camp:

'Your mouth was never made to frame speeches, my son. Your brother, like most fools, has the gift of easy argument. Rather than you bringing him to reason, I fear he'd pull you inside the walls by the ears with his speech. Let be. This fellow will make him understand me.'

It was the most humiliating rebuff imaginable for a young man like my master. He went white, then scarlet, but he bowed his head and stepped aside. I thought if that's what it was to be the most favored son of this king, it was little wonder that the least favorite stood armed to the teeth behind guarded walls.

The herald sprang to his horse and bolted off to deliver the message, which was that Count Robert was a vain and silly prodigal who had betrayed his most sacred bonds of blood and fealty on the advice of false friends who would soon betray him. If he ever had hope of pardon, either from God or from his lord father, he would come forth from his cowardly refuge and bend his neck to the king, or else do battle with him that day to the death.

We watched the herald ride across the field and up the hill to the outer bailey walls, where the bridge was let down and the gate lifted to let him enter. He returned within the hour.

'Did he hear you?' asked the king.

'Your Grace, he did, most courteously. When I had done, he let the inner gate be raised and sent me out a cup bearer with a draft of wine, which he commended to me after my lengthy speech – as he said.'

'And what did he answer?' Others within hearing may have smiled to hear this recognized gentility of Curthose's, but the king's mouth might have had a bridle bit in it.

The herald answered in his clear tenor: 'Your Grace, Count Robert commends himself to you, but begs you remember that this is French soil on which you stand now, which lies under the benevolent rule of your mutual lord, King Philip. He says that since King Philip has seen fit to bestow Gerberoy on himself, Robert, Duke of Normandy and Count of Maine, it is not himself but his revered father who is a rebel and a breaker of holy vows, if he invades this land and breaks its peace.'

They must have heard the king's roar up at Le Tréport on the coast.

'Let me be your herald now,' Rufus pleaded with his father afterward in his tent. (I didn't hear this directly, but got it from a reliable source.) 'It's Bellesme and his malice that's put Robin up to this. All the Talvas clan hate us and want us divided. You know my brother could never answer you like that, or even hold his anger in him for more than five minutes, unless he was forced to it. Let me go to him and bring him here under truce. Speak to him face to face and you'll get your terms.'

'I'll bring him to terms with an empty belly where he is now,' said the king. 'He's never been siege-fasted. Now he can choose either to eat horseflesh, or saddle it and fight me.'

'He doesn't like being where he is!'

'I like him where he is! By the Splendor of God, I think I like him better now than I have in years!'

All his captains agreed that there was no immediate prospect of honorable battle in view, so the king swathed himself in thick furs and went to hunt on the Gournai preserve beyond the river.

In mid-afternoon while the king was gone, Robert Curthose sent a young squire with badly mended yellow hose out on an exercise-starved horse to offer courteous challenge to any six knights of his father's camp for a passage of arms with any six knights of his own, for the purpose of honorable diversion.

The invitation was eagerly accepted, there being neither king nor constable to say no to the offer. Knights hate a siege. Their purpose in life is to fight, not to sit and wait. They were already bored with life on a leaguer, not being privileged to go hunting with their betters. Nearly the whole camp fell in behind the chosen six among them when they went out into the field for the trial, which had been appointed for only an hour thence.

We lined up at a safe distance from the battle, to watch, while Count Robert and his familiars stood on their walls. Our knights had drawn for the privilege of fighting. Rufus wasn't among the winners, but he was a hearty supporter of them from our sidelines. The event was a huge success. Only one of our men was unhorsed and wounded, while our side accounted for two of theirs going bloody from the field.

The wounded man's horse was forfeit, but he was given an escort back to our lines by the man who had vanquished him, and a second contest was affirmed for the next day. There was a struggle to keep the contestants down to eighteen on either side this time.

Spirits were high in our camp that night. There hadn't been a real campaign in which to blood the younger generation since many of them had been bare-arsed weanlings at their nurses' knees. The prospect of being struck off their saddles by something more deadly than a quintain arm, or a tournament lance, had them all smiling like merchants at a fair. I thought it strange then, and still do, that men should be so eager to be maimed.

Rufus was part of the second drawing and was the most jubilant. He would fight, in spite of the objections of the constable's lieutenant, who was starting to imagine what might happen to him if the king returned and found his son had gotten his brains knocked out in a passage of arms during his absence. But nothing he could say would deter Rufus from the trial next morning.

I went to his tent to shrive him before he went forth and saw him being arrayed by de Alderi – and Cormac. I felt it my duty to point out how his father might view his taking part in this contest. His temper flared at once.

'It's an honorable contest! Stick to what you know, priest, and let me tend to my own honor. Even if you weren't a priest, you wouldn't understand chivalry.'

That was true enough; the conceit of honor in warfare has puzzled me throughout life. I saw there was nothing I could do for him, and Cormac didn't behave as if he meant to stop him either. He even grinned when Rufus added:

'Besides, priest, this will give you something to report to my uncle, to make you worth your hire, won't it?'

I heard later from de Alderi of how Rufus in advance of the rest rode to the bailey wall, unhelmed himself so that his brother could recognize him, and called on Robert to come down and have single combat with him if it would assuage his pride for the dousing he'd gotten at Laigle.

'That's the whole cause for your being here, Robin, so come down and have your revenge that Father spoiled. Bring your chamber pot as well as your sword!'

'Curthose was so furious he left the walls,' said young de Alderi, but I doubted it. I remembered that tender-hearted drunkard who had shed tears for Isabel's Amiot at his grave, who had paid his foolish debts with the treasure that might have bought him a mercenary army. I couldn't believe he bore a grudge against his brother for a boy's trick. It was the father he blamed. But it did seem like him to play the trick he played on Rufus that day.

He let one of his knights go into the lists wearing his own helm and riding his own horse, to make Rufus think he was there. That knight, far more experienced than my master in horsemanship, rode circles around him until young William's milk-white destrier was ready to sink on its tail from so much curveting. At the end of the battle, when the winded Rufus had been kept from real harm, the knight took off his borrowed helm, saluted his astonished opponent, and rode away.

The victory was on Gerberoy's side that time, with two of our contenders knocked brainless with battle-axes and only one of theirs so wounded he was brought to our lines for a cautery to stop the blood flow. He was given wine and every courtesy by his captor and would have been escorted back to his companions, as our man had been, but before that could happen the king returned.

He came with a larger party than had set out. One of his companions wore an iron crown attached to his helm.

Philip of France. He looked exceedingly amiable for a lord who had been about to invade his vassal's territory and put a rebellious son on a father's throne.

So, there had been no hunting party, but a fishing expedition instead, and William Bastard had brought home the catch. When our king heard rumor of the jousts, he was angry and demanded to see the wounded knight, who came before him and fell on his knees.

'What's your name and who's your lord?' asked the king.

'I am Reynard de Bonmoulines, Your Grace. My lord is William de Moulines.'

'William de Moulines is the son of Walter of Falaise, who is my vassal. His son should serve me, as his honorable father has. Instead, he's chosen to be a traitor. All who follow him are traitors likewise, and the punishment for traitors is death and dismemberment.' He turned to Ralph de Ivri. 'Hang him up alive on the nearest tree.'

The knight went white and all but fainted at the king's feet. He cried: 'Have mercy on me, most merciful king. I am an honorable man. My father will pay my ransom.'

'I will grant you this much mercy, which is more than your ingratitude deserves. I will see you dead before you're split. Take him.'

The camp assembled to see him hanged. It was a slow business, as the fall didn't break his thick neck and he had to strangle. I didn't watch. Instead I looked at Rufus, with Robert fitz Hamon holding one of his arms and Cormac standing behind him, taking a placidly curious interest in the execution.

When he was cut down, Rufus said thickly, 'Must you maim him, my lord?'

The king replied in his speech-making voice: 'We must temper our manners to the times, my son. Treachery is more than a breach of courtesy, and war is more than its mockery in the lists.'

'The cuh-cuh-courtesy of arms is mo-more than – '

'The courtesy of arms is best spent on our friends,' the king said harshly. 'Courtesy to the enemy is none to the men we lead. Think of them! You expect them to follow you, give their blood or lives for you. Is it right that you release your enemy today, so he may do battle against you tomorrow and hack out the bowels of your brother-in-arms, or the man on foot who follows behind you? No! Crush your enemies; then be merciful to them if you choose. But be merciful to your own first.'

'They returned our wounded to us,' Rufus dared to say in a low voice.

'So they should. Ours was a true knight and they knew it. This was a traitor and they'll know it. If I did him full justice, I'd have his privy parts cut off and flung to the first dog who comes sniffing at his blood.'

My lord stared into his father's eyes, then looked about him to the grim and watchful faces of the king's vassals; to King Philip last of all, who stood with arms folded and a faint smile for the discussion at hand.

Rufus bowed his head. Then his fingers found his dagger and jerked it from the sheath. Without waiting for some lesser man to be appointed the task, he strode to the body, knelt by it, cut the hose laces, ripped apart the thin woolen braies, and emasculated de Bonmoulines as if he were gutting a hare. He gathered up the shriveled, purplish flesh he'd hacked and held it aloft as he stood. At that moment I made a bolt for the privy holes, but I heard him cry out:

'So let it be with all traitors to my father!' There was a shout of assent from the whole camp.

When I'd finished retching at last, I went to wash my face in a horse bucket. The royalty had gone into the royal tent; the rest of the camp was watching the corpse's quarters being packed on a saddle. I looked about, but didn't see Rufus. Cormac and Robert fitz Hamon were sitting in front of his tent. I approached it with the water bucket still in hand.

Cormac looked up from plaiting some strands of leathery grass and said quietly:

'Leave it. It's not the time.'

I nodded, but went in under the tent flap anyway.

Rufus was sitting on the ground by his rolled-up pallet. I knelt by him, put the pail down, and looked for a towel. A careless squire had left one, half frozen, on the ground. I soaked it in the water and wrung it out.

He sucked in a deep breath and turned his head, blinking at me as if he'd been asleep.

'What in Hell do you want?'

'To wash your hands, my lord. Let me have these first.' He still had the gruesome things in his fist.

He opened his hand and looked at them, then gave a cracked laugh. 'Why? Do they want shriving? They'll never s-sin again, for sure.'

I took them – they were soft and loose as the belly of an old brach bitch – and put them in the water pail, then washed their bloody ooze from his hand with the cloth.

'This is nothing,' he whispered.

'No, my lord. Only a little blood.'

'He was a traitor. Oaths should be kept, or what's it all for?'

'Yes, my lord. He was a traitor.'

His voice shook. 'I've never killed a man, yet, but now I've drawn first blood. I wish I c-c-could have killed this b-b-b – rather than b-been his damned co-cod cutter!'

I looked at the organs rocking gently in the bottom of the bucket and realized that something must be done with them; but what? I couldn't just throw them out with the water. I untied my purse from around my neck, slipped my last two deniers out of it, and put de Bonmoulines's genitals in, then pulled the neck of the purse shut over them with some difficulty.

Rufus watched me with a puzzled frown. 'Christ, but you're tidy!' Then his face worked, crumpled, and he bent over laughing. The grisly humor shot through me, too, and I laughed with him.

'My f-father – once had a man flayed – fo-for calling him – a tanner's grandson,' he gasped, clapping me on the ear with his wet hand. 'If you'd been there, you'd have rolled up the skin for parchment!'

The tent flap lifted and Robert fitz Hamon stared at us; doubled over, faces streaming with tears as we laughed. I got to my feet, suddenly sobered. Fitz Hamon's face disappeared. Rufus sighed, snorted, and was silent.

'My lord, may I help you rise?'

'No, by God, I've been womanish enough.' He dipped his hand into the pinkish water and rubbed his face, then heaved himself up, drying his cheeks on his sleeve. 'I've suffered a puke in the corner. Get de Alderi to clean it up.' He left the tent. I heard him speak to fitz Hamon as their boots creaked over the snow. I took the bucket, poured water over the vomit, lifting the tent's edge to let it flow away, then went out to dispose decently of what I'd put in my purse.

16

In the dim light of earliest morning when only the cooks and spit boys were stirring, the rebels of Gerberoy came out to avenge their mutilated dead.

We woke to massive confusion: tent poles cracking, the shrieks of men and horses, the bellowed war cries of the attackers. I ran out of the tent and fell over a stake, which sent me sprawling and saved my life. A rider swept past me, using his sword like a scythe. He missed me, but caught one of my tentmates under the chin just as he blundered out behind me. I saw the severed head go bouncing off, still gaping, while the man's body yet stood. I doubled up and rolled like a wood louse to save myself. Another rider vaulted over me, a brand in his hand, and suddenly our tent blossomed into flame. Tents were burning all over camp, and there was no closer shelter than the trees near the river.

Someone kicked me in the rump as I groveled.

'Get up and dress me! God damn his eyes, where's my squire?' Rufus stood in his gambeson and hose with a bare sword in his fist. 'William! God damn all cowards from here to Hell, coming at us this way! Arm me, priest, before they come again. William de Alderi!'

He ran back to his tent and I followed, hobbling on my stubbed toe. When I entered he was already pulling on his padded breeches. 'Bring the plastron – plastron, there!'

I struggled with it.

'Other way around. Cross the straps. Now the mail.'

I seized the shoulders of the heavy leather-and-steel shirt that hung below my knees, and turned it to open up the skirts.

'God damn them, this is a wolf's trick! Lift it higher!'

I got it on him somehow and tried to untangle the laces at the back while he bent for his boots, dancing on a leg to thrust a foot into one. Outside, the conflicting shouts of the bannerets calling their men rose in pitch with the tardy blasts of trumpets farther down the lines. My fingers were like warm butter. I couldn't tell if I had laced properly or just further snarled the thongs.

'My coif! Where's de Alderi? Did you see him? He'll muck the jakes for six months for this. Let be, now. No time for the chausses. Give me my helm.' He grabbed it and ran from the tent to saddle his destrier. Others whose squires hadn't rambled were already mounting, if they could catch their mounts. The raiders had cut the picket lines and scattered the horses to make havoc through the kitchen tents.

Rufus caught his and forced the bit between its grinding teeth, threw the reins over his head, and cried: 'Hold his nose down, or help me up!'

'There's no saddle!'

'There's not time!'

I seized the horse's noseband and swung my weight from it, my face only inches from the stallion's teeth. His rolling eyes terrified me; I danced away from his trampling hooves. Rufus sprang on his back and jerked his head back by the reins as he toed his feet under the animal's thick rib cage, like a carter's boy mounting a dray mare.

'Let him go!'

I fell backward, the white forelegs slashed out over my head, and he leaped me. I lay flat on the ground, arms over my face, until I was certain I was still alive.

Within a few minutes every rider who could catch his mount was up and gone, and we in the camp could hear their cries, taunting the fleeing enemy to turn and fight.

The rebels had broken through the lines farther down on their return sweep and were well on their way back to their bailey, but they turned to the challenge and fought with us on the frozen ground of that meadow, in a cold fog that hid them from our eyes until the sun came up and burned the mist away.

No one has made a song about the battle of Gerberoy, extolling either side, for shameful deeds were done there that few liked to remember. I found William de Alderi sitting dazed by the privy trench with a lump on his head. Beside him lay another squire, a kinsman of his, with his breeches still down and his brains smashed out. The blow that killed him had mangled him beyond recognition.

I trussed up his breeches and tied his shirt up around his ruined head, then lost my stomach for the second time in two days. We dragged him back to camp, de Alderi and I, where others were discovering their dead or binding up their wounded. Most of the casualties were boys, clerks, or foot soldiers who had just risen from their frost-stiffened blankets on the open ground when the attack came.

The king had ridden into battle. By good fortune, he was already up and dressed but, they say, at his prayers when he heard the alarm. King Philip stayed in the camp and watched the battle, without, I fear, much concern about who gained the victory. Some knights never caught their horses in time, some hung back from battle, some ran out on the field with the infantry to save honor; but whatever they did, the battle ended as swiftly as it had begun.

I could just begin to see the steel-gleaming figures milling their mounts, sword arms chopping, axes swinging, when a rider fled from the chaos, screaming:

'A horse! A horse for the king! The king is down!' The cry was taken up by several other voices, though some riders who broke from the battle were merely chasing unmounted horses loose on the field, which they meant to capture for themselves.

A young Englishman named Toki, who had only just caught and saddled his own horse, sprang to the saddle and rode out to answer the king's need. He was of the king's personal guard, an honored hostage or willing servant who was said to be of high rank among the Danes of the English north. We watched his bright, unhelmed head disappear into the mist and turmoil of steel-coiffed men.

The conflict had slowed, I thought, but now there were more shouts and it took fire again. All in our camp stood staring when someone cried: 'God Help!' It was the cry the Normans had raised at Senlac, where Duke William defeated Harold.

A hand grabbed my arm. It was Cormac, his face as pale as the mist. 'They've killed him. The king is down and dead.'

'No, unhorsed, they said.'

'Down and dead,' Cormac repeated with conviction. 'Listen!'

But there was nothing to hear. The riders milled; arms rose and fell. Then there was a high, wordless cry of command, echoed by a dozen voices. Horns sounded. The men on foot withdrew raggedly from the general mass and re-formed on its flanks. The riders fell back and parted to let something through. It was a close knot of men walking beside a mounted man. The others broke off into groups, turning to the left or the right, while the rebels fell back from them and formed a line for attack on the far side of the field. But they didn't move.

The horns continued to blow. Two riders pressed their way to the retreating group and thrust the men on foot aside, so that they could ride knee to knee with the other man, who slumped in his saddle.

It was the king, with Robert Curthose and Rufus riding at his stirrups. All in the camp rushed to meet them, until we were so tangled in arms and legs before them that they could hardly proceed. Count Robert, his head bare of helm, sprang down from his horse and helped his father to dismount.

'As God is my witness, Father, I didn't know it was you. I'd cut off my hand before I'd harm you.' He scarcely reached the king's shoulder, but the likeness of his pale face to his father's was striking, except that the king did not weep.

I thought he must be gravely wounded, but though he swayed a little when his feet were on the earth, he brushed past Robert as if he were a stranger and walked up to the camp without help. He was holding one arm doubled up against his chest, with his other hand encircling the wrist. Rufus remained on his destrier, silent, as if in a daze.

Gilbert Maminot, the Bishop of Lisieux, who was also the king's physician, rushed forth from his tent to give his master aid.

'It's nothing, I say,' the king growled when Gilbert tried to examine the wound. 'Form your lines again. This battle is not finished.' His voice wasn't weak, but there was no command in it to make his hearers obey him. Instead, they surged after him, craning their necks to see if he bled. Count Robert disappeared from my sight then, obscured by them.

'The battle is ended, Your Grace,' Ralph de Ivri told him when the king repeated his toneless command. 'We saw him kneel to you. Where is he now? My lord Robert, come forward. Clear the way for him! Clear off! Sir William, disperse this crowd! His Grace is only slightly wounded and we have the victory. Hear me! The king has triumphed!'

That caused a ragged shout, and the crowd began to thin a bit. Gilbert Maminot and the king went into his tent with Lord Ralph and King Philip after them.

I heard Cormac say, "Will you dismount, my lord?" He spoke to Rufus, who still sat his horse at the back of the mob. I recalled he might need me for a squire again, since de Alderi was still apt to be wit-scattered. I went after Cormac, who, reaching Rufus's side, said sharply: 'By the Blood!'

There *was* blood, much blood, soaking the quilted breeches Rufus wore without the protective chausses to cover them. It stained his thigh and knee, down to the boot cuff of his left leg. He took no notice of Cormac's alarm, but lifted off his helm with both hands and let it fall to the ground. I caught it up.

'Robin almost killed him. How could he not know him?'

'You're wounded, my lord. Let me help you to dismount.' Cormac took the reins from his hand, threw them over the horse's head for me to catch, then held up his arms for Rufus.

'Come down and be easy, boy. You've had your victory.'

Rufus stared down at him, his eyes dull, his face blackened with muddy spume thrown up from the field. 'He would have split his head if I hadn't stopped him. Can you believe it?'

'My lord, dismount.'

'He was sorry for it. Offered his own horse. Christ, if I'd done what he has, I'd offer my head. Where's my squire? I think I'm cut somewhere.'

He fainted and slipped from the stallion's lathered back. Cormac caught him; I dropped the reins and ran, yelling for Gilbert

Maminot, pushing my way rudely through the throng before the king's tent. Those in the tent stared at me aghast as I bawled at Gilbert to come with me at once.

Gilbert looked more offended by my insolence than concerned to hear the king's son might be dying.

The king raised his head and said: 'Go with him, Gilbert. This is no hurt.' But he kept his arm stretched out for Gilbert to finish bandaging, and the tedious old man completed the job before he would come with me. Before he moved, he must also give instructions to one of his clerks on how to treat such a wound should it suppurate, as if he were lecturing his students in the schoolroom.

I burst out: 'Bishop, a man has only so much blood in him, which even a fool like myself knows. If you don't come soon, it may be a corpse you lecture over next!'

There was a general gasp at that, and the haughty old crane straightened himself to his considerable height and gave me a deadly look. I could see my whole career in the court crumbling under that stare, but the king saved me.

'Go with him, Gilbert. It's my son he's offending you for. Is he badly hurt?' he asked me.

'Wounded in the thigh, Your Grace. Very badly, I think.'

'Will he die?' Someone I didn't see asked that. I stared around for him, but Gilbert Maminot gave me a rude push ahead of him through the tent flap. I heard another voice: 'If he dies, what choice, then, but Curthose?'

He spoke the general opinion, whoever he was. The leaguer of Gerberoy had dwindled to an end; a peace between the king and his son was necessary, before anarchy took hold on the land. Even Rufus begged his father to make peace before we had him carried to Gournai in a litter. The king went there, too, though he didn't find time to visit his 'favorite son' more than once. The wound in his hand fretted him too much to allow him to draw a bow, but he went out into the forests with the lord of Gournai every day, for his health's sake, as Gilbert said.

Peace was the desire of all the barons who had sons at Gerberoy. For a week they remained at Gournai, persuading the king he must send an envoy to Robert, who had retreated again to his keep, though half his supporters had already slipped away into the king's camp, and it was painfully clear to him he had no friend in Philip of France, who went home to Paris.

The king yielded to his advisers. An envoy was sent, a plan formed. Robert would come to Rouen in a little while and there would be reconciliation. The host was disbanded. It was agreed in advance that there would be a general amnesty for the rebels.

Now the lord of Gournai sent for his wife to come home again to tend to Rufus, who had contracted a fever and lay in delirium. Gilbert Maminot put the cause of it to my lord's choleric humor, but I thought it was apt to be caused by the vile concoctions the great physician invented for his treatment. The Bishop of Lisieux was well versed in physics, but he took little interest in the jagged wound in my lord's thigh, saying it was a surgeon's business to see to that, not a physician's. A rough fellow from Le Mans sewed the gash up when Cormac refused to let him use the cautery iron on it, because he said the scar that would result would keep Rufus from ever riding comfortably again.

Cormac and I tended Rufus and fed him, when he was able to be roused to eat. Since nobody else was concerned, and the Lady Basile was home again, the king was soon satisfied he could leave his son in her good hands, so he took his leave for home. His own wound was healing; he'd gotten only a cut across the heel of the palm when Curthose's blade jumped over the quillons of his own sword and struck him a glancing blow. He came once more to the bed of his son before he went but, finding Rufus sleeping, didn't wake him.

'You'd better go with them,' I said to Cormac when it became apparent that wasn't his plan. 'The constable is a better future for you now.'

'I've lost interest in dogs.'

'The constable won't lose interest in you, when he hears you've deserted without his leave.'

He shrugged. 'I'll be a renegade again. You needn't worry about me, Little Brother. Besides, you'll want some help, won't you, if you mean to look after him? His squire's still suffering the headache from that knock on the pate he got.'

A generous offer, but I didn't want Cormac to stay with us on any account. In truth, he made me uncomfortable. We were neither friends nor enemies, but I regretted recommending him to my lord; he had moved into his confidence all too easily and now treated me with indifference when we were together in the company of Rufus. His warmth toward me when we were alone only made me more wary of him.

But he stayed, and nobody in the castle questioned his presence as one of my lord's attendants. The castle was all but empty, Gerald de Gournai and his son having followed in the king's train.

When Rufus's fever abated, the Lady Basile put his recovery down to her own good broths and possets, as Gilbert might have given his poultices and fumigations the credit if he'd been there. I tended to the lady's side, myself.

'Be certain to tell the king it was that very wine possets your lady mother once gave me that did the work,' she told Rufus when he was strong enough to leave his bed. He was up soon, because when she saw he was somewhat better, she had begun to smother him with attention, coming into the chamber on every excuse with her two serving women to feel his brow or ply him with broth until he was sick. She was a large-breasted, motherly sort of woman, very comfortable I thought, but Cormac had a rude name for her and Rufus got scarlet with suppressed laughter and ill ease whenever she bent over the bed.

He fretted in his character of invalid and was eager to go after his father, but his torn thigh muscle still made it impossible for him to sit a horse or raise himself to the saddle even with the help of Cormac and de Alderi.

I knew he was eager to go to his family and bask in well-deserved praise for his first battle. He was anxious, too, for his father's injury, though I assured him I had seen it and it was well scabbed and gave the king little trouble.

When we had been at Gournai another week, he could bear the exile no longer. 'I'll ride ladywise, if I must, but we leave tomorrow!'

Dame Basile was relieved to hear the news, though she doted on her patient. Hers was a well-reasoned fear: what could happen if anything should go amiss with the king's son while he was in her care.

Cormac and I were equally concerned that we might be accused if Rufus took to bleeding on his way home. Cormac attempted to delay the journey and met with my lord's wrath:

'I am well, I tell you! I have a wound, yes, and it hurts me – by God's Face, yes, it does! But I'm used to a little pain and stiffness. I'll not swoon again, if that's what you're thinking. Don't fret me like a wet nurse.'

We were at our last dinner in Lady Basile's house. Rufus sat in the guest's seat by the lady, with Cormac and me graciously allowed to join them. Cormac had been asked to play his harp for Dame Basile, who smiled on him frequently. It surprised me that he, who had a demeanor he could adapt to any man, couldn't be smooth with her. He was courteous, but he had a manner exactly like that of a dog that's been commanded to let a guest examine him and detests it. He bowed, he smiled when she complimented his voice, but he never once looked at her.

'It seems to me, my lord, you have some trouble in turning your head. I only wondered if your neck has been injured, too, and you've said nothing of it?' Cormac said.

'It seems to me, harper, that you have trouble holding your tongue. Now forget your concern and give us music, rather than sermons on health.' Rufus was flushed with anger at being questioned in front of the lady, though he tried to laugh it away.

I smiled to hear Cormac rebuffed. I imagined the fate of any of his former students if they'd so much as sighed to hear his advice. He wasn't yet wholly resigned to his menial character. He couldn't forbear to say:

'My lord is better schooled than I at soldiering, but I have some little knowledge of – '

Which was a mistake. Rufus let his temper flare. 'By God, *will* you le-le-lecture me like a d-damned priest? Ge-g–!' There he stuck, as if his tongue had frozen to the floor of his mouth. His face flooded with blood, then darkened as if he were strangling. He pushed himself up from the table as if he'd sat on a brand, but instead of standing he fell backward over the stool, his back arching so that only his head and feet touched the floor. His face was terrible.

Lady Basile shrieked and shrank from him. 'What's the matter? What is it? Has he gone mad?'

Cormac laid his harp aside and vaulted over the table to kneel by him, as de Alderi and I ran to join him. The rest of the Gournai household, frozen by my lady's dread, stood but did nothing. Rufus's mouth began to stretch out into a ghastly parody of a grin, teeth clenched as he convulsed.

Cormac ran his fingers over the rigid jaw and neck. Where he probed the muscles, Rufus gave a cry of pain.

'What is it?' In the face of such an attack, Cormac's silence was as alarming to me as Rufus's agony.

'Be easy, my lord. It will pass,' he whispered to Rufus. He looked up. 'Get something hot: water, soup, wine, anything, quickly.'

Dame Basile ran out of the hall, screaming for the kitchen servants. I looked about wildly, saw the tureen of veal broth on the table, and lifted it, slopping some in my haste. 'But he can't swallow it. He'll choke!'

'No, he won't,' Cormac said in the same soothing voice. He snatched the lid from the tureen, took it by the handles, and poured the mess over my lord's distended throat and rigid shoulders. It was still hot, though not scalding. Rufus gave a great cry and collapsed, sobbing, his paroxysm broken. Cormac soothed him and issued orders in the same breath.

'Easy, easy now, my lord. Don't move. Bring a board from a table to carry him on. Tell them in the kitchen to heat water, tubs of it, and send them up to his bedchamber. We want blankets and all the towels they can find, too. Someone go build a fire in that room.'

'But there's no hearth there, only the brazier,' I said.

'Christ! Yes, well then, we must have him in a room with a hearth or keep him here.'

Dame Basile had returned at my lord's great cry, with the kitchen staff behind her. She was weeping pitifully.

'Is there a hearth in your chamber?' Cormac asked bluntly.

'Yes, yes, but what ails him?'

'We'll use your chamber then, by your leave.'

'My bower?' cried the lady. 'Oh, but where will I and my women sleep?'

Cormac turned his head and looked up at her silently. She fell back with her hand over her mouth, as I would have done myself.

Rufus had stopped sobbing, but gasped as if he had been wrestling a giant. 'What's wrong with me?' he whispered hoarsely. 'Is it poison?'

At that word, Basile became frantic. 'No! No! You can't say there was poison here! I tasted every dish! We're no murderers here, my lord! My husband won't endure that charge!'

'Be still.' Cormac's voice cut through her hysteria like a knife. She put her hand over her mouth again, her eyes wild.

We put him on a table board, de Alderi, Cormac, and I, and carried him up to the lady's bower. A fire was fed, hot water was brought up in tub after tub, and blankets and towels supplied. We bathed him, put him in a clean shirt supplied by Basile from her husband's armoire, and settled him in bed. I was just beginning to draw a breath of relief that it was done when he suffered another seizure, this time without provocation of words or anger.

It was fearful to see him convulse on the bed, as if someone had driven a dagger into his back from beneath. It was more terrible to know he was coherent during such a fit of seeming madness. Under Cormac's guidance I dipped towels in hot water, wrung them out, and laid them over Rufus's neck, shoulders, and stomach. As quickly as they cooled they were removed and dipped again. We half boiled him in the process. We lay upon him to keep him from convulsing until we were as wet and shivering on top of him as he was hot and trembling beneath us.

When the second seizure seemed to pass, Cormac made him drink as much wine as he could, and he fell asleep soon after, from its effects, and from exhaustion.

I was near to dropping. 'What's wrong with him?' I whispered when my heart had stopped its worst pounding.

Cormac sighed and slumped on a stool near the fire, shivering. 'There's a sickness I've seen once and heard about. It's like the dog-bite madness, but they say it can come from a wound of any kind, even a thorn prick.'

'But his wound is healing. There's no poison in it.'

'The poison – if that's what it is – works inward and doesn't show itself in the wound. It makes a stiffness in the muscles of the jaw and throat. I noticed, yesterday, how he had to turn his body from the waist to look to one side, rather than turning his head. I saw him put his hand to his throat and rub his neck several times, as if he had a cramp.'

'Yes, I saw that, too. Is it contagious?'

'No, not if that's what troubles him. Let be, now. We'll rest, while we can.' He stretched out on his stomach before the fire.

'While we can? You mean it'll happen again? Can he live through such a thing again? I thought he'd break his own spine this time.'

'Some do break their spines. Some bite their tongues off. Some die of a burst heart, so I've read.' His eyes were closed, his voice a thread, but I sat up as if I'd heard trumpets blow.

'Do you mean he's going to die? He can't die with only the two of us here with him! You heard that old woman screech when she heard the word *poison* mentioned. What will his family do, when he dies of no worse wound than he has and no fever? Cormac! We must find a physician. There's an abbey not far from here. The infirmarian will know what to do for him, better than we.'

'No.'

'No? You know who will be suspected here, if he dies? Not the Gournais. Us! Because we're hirelings.'

Cormac opened his eyes. 'You're the hireling. I'm only a simple renegade.' He yawned.

'Does that put you in a better light? You're an apostate, an excommunicated runaway, living by your wits – a foreigner: a fit person to take a bribe to kill a man, some people might say.'

He sat up slowly and got to one knee so that we were face to face. 'Who would say such things, Little Brother? You?'

I felt as if a lion had breathed in my face.

'I'm not accusing you, I'm telling you how it will be. The Gournais will accuse us. Everybody at court will scratch their heads to think where we came from, who we are. Somebody there will think of something. Carileph, for instance, who – '

'Who pays you to spy on this boy, yes.'

'That's no matter. He knows we're old acquaintances. He'll find out the rest with one letter to the abbot. Let me go to that abbey and bring someone here skilled in medicine.'

He shook his head. 'You'll get no one to come here, when they know who's dying. In case you haven't heard, the Bastard's family has a reputation for using poison to get rid of inconvenient friends and relatives – Odo, the king, even Curthose may have picked up the habit from his friend Bellesme. When *they* murder, others hang for it, just as you fear. So, no one's going to come running to share that honor with us.'

'Then I'll go to Rouen tomorrow to tell the king his son is dying here. It would be stupid to keep it a secret!'

Rufus moaned in his sleep and I turned to look at him. When I did, Cormac took me suddenly by the throat, pressing his thumb into my windpipe so that I couldn't cry out.

'Now, listen to me closely, Little Brother, and be still. We'll send for no one. No one will come near us. That cow is shaking in her fat skin downstairs at this moment. She won't be up here with her damned possets anymore. We will tend him alone. If he lives, he'll have us to thank for it, and so will his father. We'll have our reward. If he dies, we'll be out of here before his eyes set, and over the border into France. I have a friend in Paris.' He relaxed his hold and patted me on the cheek. 'But if he lives, we'll have a friend here indeed, because someday his father will make him king.'

I drew back from him to the foot of the bed, ready to kick him if he moved toward me again. 'A king! Why should he make him king now, when he's got Curthose back?'

'Did I hurt your throat? Your voice is cracked. He'll make him king, to revenge himself on Curthose for humiliating him. If he hasn't thought of it yet, he will. He's a vengeful man. We'll help him to his revenge and he'll thank us, later. So will this boy. Now, you go downstairs and tell that cow whatever she wants to hear. Tell her it's not poison. Tell her he has the falling sickness, or that he's gone mad, or any damned thing to keep her from sending word to Rouen that he's dying, *because telling them won't help either him or us.*'

At that moment Rufus muttered, then started, as if from an evil dream. The sudden movement sent him into a worse seizure than the two before.

17

For the next few days it seemed he would die each time he was stricken. I began to pray he would.

We forced a green stick the size of my thumb between his teeth, to keep him from biting through his tongue. He cracked the stick and one of his teeth. We swaddled him in near-scalding sheets, but though they seemed to loosen his rigid muscles for a short time, they added greatly to his pain and to the rage he couldn't express except by wordless bellowing.

When he was seized, in spite of the heat and the wine, we lay on top of him to hold him down and to invest him with our own body heat. Our efforts to sedate him with mere wine met with no success after the first time. Rather, we nearly drowned him; what was forced between his teeth came up through his nose, until I begged poppy juice from Dame Basile and dripped wine drugged with it into his mouth with the corner of a napkin. The poppy was one of the lady's most precious decoctions and was soon gone. When it was, she had nothing to offer but henbane, though she was loath to give it to me.

'It's very potent. It clouds the memory, and too much will kill him.'

'I know the drug, my lady, but if you have nothing else, we must use it.' I had persuaded her that it was an infection in his wound that gave him such pain and made him scream so. *Persuaded*, perhaps, was not the word, but I had convinced her it was something to do with the wound and not related to anything he'd eaten or drunk in her house.

'I won't have you sending for it from my stilling room without my knowing. I must measure what you give him,' she said, showing more spirit with me than she did with Cormac. 'I won't have you poison him with my own medicine, then blame me for it.'

I soothed her, blessed her for her wisdom in giving it to me so carefully, begged her to aid us with her prayers, kissed the hands that gave me the narcotic, and promised her I would praise her to the king above all ministering angels when my lord was recovered and we were back in Rouen.

Cormac, who had been listening in the doorway, sneered at me when I came up with the drug: 'That's very good. You may have to bed her to get the next drop. Do you think you can bring yourself to it?'

'Could you bring yourself to be civil to her? It may interest you to know she has a guard posted on us at the end of the passage and that she's got William de Alderi shut up for safekeeping. She's not just a cow and a fool; she's the chatelaine here. She may decide to send word to her husband any hour now, but even if she doesn't, she can have us hanged from her own walls and he'll praise her for it. Now, do you *really* know about henbane? Because I don't.'

'Then why don't you go down and cozen her into giving us some hot food?' He reached for the little pot in my hand.

'Cormac! Do you *know*?'

'I know! You forget, I spent ten years in thrall to a man who liked to swill at the trough of knowledge and spew out what he learned in treatises. Also, I was in Paris, in wiser company. But before that – never mind. Every shepherd and farmstead wife in the world knows about henbane; why shouldn't I?'

I lost track of the days and the times I woke from a snatched sleep to wrestle with that contorted body screaming on the bed. Day and night were all the same in that room, where the only light came from the fire and one lancet slit in the wall.

The seizures came night or day, with any movement Rufus might make in the drugged sleep we had induced. Every time I dripped wine between his lips I wondered if it would be the fatal dose. I could feel my exhaustion weighing down my reason; I could feel the very weight of the Gournai stones that would be heaped over me when I was put in some cell at the castle's roots, there to await trial and death.

One of the servants who brought up the tubs of hot water was a stableman. He came in time to see the last of one of the spasms and shook his head judiciously.

'It's no use working over him like that, priest. Give him his

Unction and let him die. They never live anyway, when they take the stretching sickness.'

Cormac was slumped over on the edge of the bed, head bowed. 'Sometimes they live. I've seen one,' he muttered.

'One, is it? Then he must have suffered from another kind of fit. I've seen three, and with the stretches they never live more than a week.'

I waited for an outburst from Cormac, who wouldn't suffer a real physician to come and dispute him, but he only lifted his head to appraise the man. 'Never beyond a week?' He smiled. 'This one's lasted five days. Give us another two; maybe you can say you've seen a miracle.'

The stableman frowned: 'You're killing yourself for *him*. What's the good of that?' He withdrew, shaking his head at our ignorance.

I began to worry Cormac would drop from fatigue and leave me to care for both of them. We slept by turns, and I was the very twin to a log. Cormac seemed to get no good from his sleep. He muttered and sighed, as if he were being persecuted in his dream. I couldn't tell what was the source of his trouble. His mumbling was incoherent but for one word, which I took for a name.

'Who is Mothumay?'

'What?' He stopped scrubbing his fist into his eye and blinked at me. 'When did you hear that? Say it again.'

'Mothumay; or is it MacToomey? You speak to him in your sleep so often, I feel I should know him. Is he your friend in Paris?'

His bleared look gave way to caution. 'Mothumay. God, your accent's terrible. *Maith dhom é*: forgive me.' He sighed and his mouth turned down. 'That's what it means, if I hear you right. MacToomey!' He laughed sharply, but didn't say what it was he wanted forgiving for in his dream, if he knew, or of whom he asked it.

There came an hour when Rufus's breathing changed; the rictus that had held his brows aloft and his mouth curled into a jester's grin left him. His mouth hung ajar, his eyes rolled up, and he lay in a swoon too deep to accept drugging. Then I was certain he was dying at last. I had given him his Unction as the stableman advised and slept beside him after his last paroxysm, exhausted. Cormac slept on his other side, and our arms were flung over him to warn us if he stirred. That we were able to do that assured me he was dying, since any touch was apt to send him into convulsion.

I woke sometime in that night, stiff and cold. The hearth fire was dying; the cresset was guttering in its bowl. I closed my eyes to pray for him, but slept again in the midst of my petition in spite of myself.

He woke me, groaning some word. Cormac's hand came up and gripped my shoulder and I clutched at him, prepared to force that tortured body down between us when it reared, but Rufus pulled his arm loose from his swaddling blanket and used it to lever himself to another position, a natural move he'd been incapable of making without provoking an agonized attack. 'Thirsty,' he whispered.

I fell backward off the bed to get water and a napkin to dip in it, but Cormac was first to seize a cup. He filled it, held it to Rufus's mouth, elevating his head from the bolster to receive it. Rufus swallowed several times, sighed, and slept again, drawing his knees and arms up for better comfort.

We stood by the bed, staring at him like two berserkers, red-eyed, haggard, filthy, with snarled hair and stubbled faces.

I croaked, 'He's better.'

'Yes.'

'He'll live?'

'He'll live. We've saved him, Little Brother. Just we two, alone.' He put his arm around my neck, hugged me roughly, whispered: 'Now he's ours.'

That morning Rufus took a little broth. I had been the one to feed him every drop of drugged wine, but now Cormac would suffer no one but himself to spoon in the broth. I was too tired to dispute for the honor, but took myself to a pallet before the fire and slept again.

The next time I woke it was to avoid the feet of women servants who were stripping the mattress. Cormac lifted Rufus bodily out of bed and held him like a child while the women put on fresh sheets. A hearth girl mended the fire, water was brought to wash the patient's face and hands, and a clean shirt was provided out of the lord of Gournai's wardrobe. Rufus lay back in bed again, quite exhausted, but laughing at the nonsense with which Cormac entertained him as he tended him.

I saw that Cormac had shaved and groomed himself while I slept, so he looked human again, while I was still a prodigy of stink and overgrown hair. Rufus laughed until the tears ran out of the corners of his eyes when he saw me.

'God's Face, what is it? I know you, but – what's your name?'

Cormac said soothingly, 'That's Ranulph, your chaplain, who's become an anchorite for your sake.'

Rufus rolled his head to look at me again. His face clouded. 'I know him, but I never had a chaplain in my life and never will.'

'You've been ill, my lord, from a wound you got in battle. The medicine we had to give you has clouded your mind, but it will clear.'

'A battle? Where? Where's my father? Does he know about this?'

'He knows it all, my lord. It was his victory and yours. Rest yourself now and don't fret your memory. You fought well; you were honorably wounded. Your father will praise you for your part in saving his life when you go home. Rest with that for now.' His voice welled with the old music. I excused myself and went down to the kitchen to find someone who could tonsure me.

That Rufus didn't remember my name hadn't surprised me; if he had ever used it I couldn't remember. He called me 'priest' when he thought to call me at all.

Cormac's inclusion of me in his exultation – 'Now he's ours' – did surprise me, and as the days of Rufus's convalescence passed, it further puzzled and discomforted me. Cormac meant to make himself indispensable to Rufus. He was at his side every moment, to serve, to amuse, as the occasion warranted. He didn't need me in his plan for any reason I could divine, unless it was as a shield of some sort. In my brief time of being abroad in the world I had been used for one purpose or another by several people – and in nothing to my advantage. I didn't care for Cormac's adding himself to the number. Yet it was hard to resist him when he hadn't made any demands of me, and harder still to give voice to my suspicion. There was still much of the master-pupil attitude between us. He gave me orders and I obeyed before I could frame a reason for refusal, promising myself after each time to be more watchful the next.

In the succeeding weeks the events of the recent past returned to my master, who spent long moments examining the still-angry scar on his thigh. He considered other things, too. One day, with evidence of embarrassment, he said abruptly:

'I've been forgetful of some things, but not of what the two of you have done for me. Even in my sickness, I could see your faces hanging over me.' He laughed nervously. 'I thought I w-was in Hell a-and you'd both turned devils, but you were better than the angels, keeping me alive.'

'It was your own strength that kept you alive, my lord,' I said. 'That and God's mercy, not us.'

Cormac gave me a very curious look for that, but the effect of my words on my master was more curious. He became very red and agitated, rolling his head back and forth on the pillow as if he would cry.

'No! God never shows me mercy – never! No. If it were s-so, H-he would have pu-put out one of m-my damned eyes! Or ma-made m-my cur-cursed tongue – ' He put his hand over his mouth and drew a steadying breath.

'Can you think what it's l-like to want to s-speak and only ga-gabble like a fool? Or t-to try to t-to look into the eyes of those you ah-honor and love and see them f-flinch? Even my own mother can't look me in the face for longer than it takes to count two. Only you have shown me that mercy, which I count as great as saving my life. I will remember that you are my friends when the day comes – if it ever does.'

He closed his eyes. The speech had robbed him of all strength for the moment. Cormac, sitting on the bedside, took up his broad, freckled hand and kissed it. I could only stand like a mourning ox and say nothing.

We went home to Rouen when he was able to ride, which was later by a week than he wished and earlier by two than I thought possible. He was still so weak that he trembled just to get into the saddle and couldn't stay there for more than two or three miles at a time. He had that puckered scar on the inside of the thigh that made him limp, too. The lameness infuriated him more than the weakness: 'God damn my stinking flesh! Do I need more infirmities?'

'It will pass when you're fully recovered,' said Cormac.

'Will it? Well, I won't go home hopping like a toad!'

Nor did he. When we dismounted at Rouen, he went up into the keep without a sign of the agony it must have cost him to climb those stairs. There were few people there to appreciate his homecoming. The court had moved, leaving the keep as bare as a peeled egg. There was a skeleton garrison and a knight-lieutenant of the tower acting for the constable. He sent into the town to find a mattress fit for Rufus to sleep on and had it carried up to the Lady Matilda's bower, where there was a small hearth. There was no bedstead to go with it.

When we went up to that room after a dinner of boiled mutton and a wine just this side of verjuice, I discovered the scar had broken open during our journey. My lord's braies had stuck to his flesh with the dried blood. He cursed me and the leg as I cleaned and bound it with strips of cloth torn from his other shirt. When I finished, Cormac put me aside and knelt by the mattress on the floor where Rufus sat rubbing his legs.

'You have the strength of two men, but you won't be able to walk tomorrow if you go to bed hot and well fed. Like your horse, you should be cooled out first.'

Rufus snorted. 'What would you like to do, walk me around the stable yard with a halter?'

'Nothing so tedious, my lord. Only lie back on your bed and be easy. I'll loosen your limbs for you.'

Rufus leaned on his elbows, with a not-too-friendly look. Cormac took one of his bare feet and began to knead it between his fingers from the arch to the ankle and up the back tendon.

'A hot bath will do as much and be less trouble,' I said.

But Rufus groaned and fell back on the mattress. 'Oh, God, that feels good! Send up a bath, but let him go on.'

'Yes, go and give orders for a bath, Ranulph.' Cormac was at work on the calf muscle.

I obeyed reluctantly. I sat waiting for the water to heat and drank hot spiced cider that a kitchen woman gave me. She gave me a ripe smile, too, I think, but I was busy trying not to let certain unpleasant thoughts take form in my mind and neglected to thank her for her trouble. The thoughts came anyway.

When the water began to steam, I urged the two spit boys to bring it up, with buckets of cool water to temper it, then ran ahead of them to announce the bath. When I threw open the door of the chamber, Rufus was sprawled on his back asleep, legs covered with a blanket. Cormac sat on the stool, warming his hands over the brazier. He appraised my face and smiled slightly.

'No need for the bath now.' He rose, stretched, working his shoulders to loosen them. 'De Alderi's already gone to find himself a warm wench to snuggle to. What are you going to do? The night's only just set in.'

'I'll sleep here in case he wakes and wants something.'

'Very commendable. In which case I'll take a night's liberty. I've been shut up in women's quarters too much of late; snug enough, but they leave the stench of their perfumes behind, don't they?' He went out, then opened the door again to put his head in. 'Ranulph – to ease your mind – he's still a virgin.' He grinned. The door closed.

I spread a blanket and lay down on it, with my cloak wrapped around me and my head on the edge of the mattress. I said my prayers in that position, then fell to brooding on how to limit Cormac's access to my master without giving offense to Rufus. I thought of writing a full report of my suspicions to Lord Odo, then decided that wouldn't help. Nothing about my commission from

Odo assured me that he would want to help his nephew avoid undesirable friends.

My reward for laxity in saying my Office was that I suffered abominable dreams and woke with a stiff neck.

My lord decided to remain at Rouen, until he had fully recovered his strength, rather than follow the court. I approved that choice, except that to achieve his end he rose early every day and took part in the garrison drill in the cavalry yard, then practiced at the butts or at the quintain for several hours. His determination not to be shown any special favor by the men of the garrison earned him their love, but the exercise took its toll of us all. By the end of the day his limp couldn't be hidden, and his temper increased along with his stammer, until it was nearly impossible for him to speak. By nightfall only Cormac and the lieutenant warden of the tower could say anything to him that didn't earn a grunt or a curse.

To make amends for that, and for our diversion, he and de Alderi would take Cormac and me out to practice at the butts with them. Now, my skill with a bow was nonexistent; I didn't even know how to notch the arrow to the string. My chagrin when I let the arrow fly cheered my lord considerably. I could send one arrow sailing above the butts at treetop height, then plow a furrow in the earth to its base with the next.

'Jesus! My sister Adela can hold a draw better than you, man! You're woefully slack in the arms. Pull it back to your ear. Now, hold it! Oh, Christ! Into the earth again. We're going to take you mole hunting next winter, we are!'

Cormac, on the other hand, showed evidence of early training, about which he was smugly mysterious.

'You must have been a busy man,' I said. 'Where did you learn to use the bow?'

'As a boy in Munster, before I – took to wandering.'

Rufus came up behind us as we were plucking Cormac's arrows from the target. No use to look for mine. 'We never forget early training,' he said. 'But there's more to it than just that. Cormac's got the instinct for the kill. It's in his stance, in his eyes. He wants this target butt to turn itself into a big, fat buck and meat on the table. While you – you suffer from the buck ague. You start to shake before you've ever seen the beast. But we'll teach him, won't we, Cormac?'

He took us riding with him, too, out beyond the marshy field where the tournament had been held on the day of his knighting, and where green shoots were beginning to appear among the dead stubble. In riding I showed more promise than Cormac, to my considerable consolation. 'Good knees,' Rufus said. Cormac excused his own loose seat in the saddle by saying that in Ireland people were accustomed to hunt and travel on foot, unless they were out stealing cattle. 'It's a sport we have in common with the Scots.'

Edgar Atheling, the Englishman, rode into Rouen from his estate a few miles away, found Rufus there alone, and invited him home for a hunt. Rufus accepted eagerly, then looked at us with honest regret. Plainly, he didn't want us with him, but he was loyal to his promise of friendship, so we were included.

It didn't take long for me to discover that Cormac disliked the English prince, which was odd, in a way. Physically they were much alike: long, lean, fine-boned. They were both well educated: the prince could read Latin and spoke five languages with some facility, though he'd had little use for his Hungarian or his German since his mother's death. She had been a German princess and cousin of the Hungarian king, Stephen, at whose court Edgar's exiled father met and married her.

'He's a parasite, like the mistletoe that hangs on the oak,' Cormac said. 'His father was called Edward the Wanderer. History should name *him* Edgar the Feckless. The king gives him the equal of a livre a day to keep him quiet here and cause no trouble. If he were worth worrying about, he'd have been shut up in a cell, like Earl Morkere, or Harold Godwinson's brother.'

I saw much of this was mere jealousy, because we were being shut out by our master's enthusiasm for the prince and his fine horses. Edgar did live in comfortable obscurity, something more than the king's hostage, something less than his kinsman and friend, but he had once been a source of trouble for the king when he was the rallying point for the rebellion at York.

Now he bred hounds and horses and heard Mass twice a day, for he was very religious, like all his family. His horses were for racing, rather than warfare. They were smaller than the usual palfreys, being the brood of Spanish horses that had mated with those of the Moorish heathen. He was said to have paid five thousand livres for the brood mare – which must be an exaggeration, since he would have done better to buy himself a province with such a fortune, as Prince Henry did.

My lord William Rufus was wild to try one of those little grey stallions. He would race every day against Prince Edgar, who was a superb rider; he seemed to be of one body with the animal, and he could run circles around Rufus when my master used his own palfrey. It was easy to see why my lord admired Prince Edgar. The

Englishman might appear to be too melancholy, and too fond of hearing Mass at dawn with the clerks, for the spirited Rufus, but Edgar could have been a champion in a melee, if it had been permitted for him to fight. But by the terms of the peace he had made with the Conqueror, he was forbidden to take part in any warlike activity, even a tournament.

Cormac and I were left alone to amuse ourselves as best we could while our betters delighted in horseflesh. I was content enough to try to make sense of that rare new game the prince generously allowed us to use, which he also played masterfully. It was the game of battle called *échecs*, which has now become more generally popular since some of our lords discovered it during the Holy Crusade and plundered the boards and pieces from the heathen.

I give Cormac credit: though he had shown a rather poor spirit to me where the prince was concerned, he didn't make life difficult for us by fretting or sulking because our master spent his days with Edgar once we were on the Englishman's own ground. He rather extended that charm of manner he had used on Rufus to include Edgar, who came quickly to admire him for his tales of holy Ireland, and for his songs of that land, some of which Cormac had translated into French. One in particular became Edgar's favorite. He asked for it almost every night:

> These are the arrows that murder sleep
> > Every hour the whole night through.
> Love all day is pain to me –
> > Hero of Roiny, where are you?

Though it spoke of arrows, murder, and heroes, it was no lay of battle such as young Rufus might have otherwise enjoyed, but a woman's lament for her lover who is dead. Its melody was strange, filled with quavers and broken notes in which the voice dropped suddenly, but because Cormac sang it with such a depth of sadness and passion – or because Prince Edgar listened with such intensity – my young master heard it courteously.

In the spring the king returned to Rouen, and our time of quiet ended. The Easter Court was swelled to half again its size at Christmas. Ambassadors came from Paris, Bruges, Rennes; the king called all men of good faith to witness his formal reconciliation with his son Robert.

On the day appointed, with the lords of Normandy, England, and

France assembled, Count Robert and his adherents came before King William and knelt for his forgiveness, which he granted them. Robert put his hands between those of his father and swore him service as if he were a new-made vassal. The king kissed him for it, the hall roared its approbation, the Lady Matilda wept, and the clerks of the chapel sang a *Te Deum*. So was the prodigal brought home again to feast on veal, and my lord, William the Younger, once more made obscure.

Rufus bore his brother no grudge for replacing him in his father's shadow, seemingly. Cormac was bitter about that:

'He rides with him, dices with him, laughs at his jokes – everything but sleeps at his feet at night, like a good hound!'

'I think he's glad to see peace made in the family, so he's willing to give way to his brother. He is fond of him, you know, Cormac,' I said, though I felt a little of his resentment on my lord's behalf, too.

'Give way? He's given up! What does he get for all this meekness? Who takes notice? Who even remembers that it was he, putting a sword between them, who kept Curthose from killing the old man? Who in this place even knows how badly he was wounded, or how close he came to dying for it?'

'Not to mention your part in saving his life?'

He looked at me sharply; then a slow smile twisted his mouth. 'Yes. That, too.'

In September, while we were following the king on a slow progress through his duchy, word came that Malcolm of Scotland had let his ancestral penchant for cattle theft so far overcome his fear of William Bastard that he raided extensively the English northern counties. Routing and burning from the Tweed to the Tees, slaying Frenchmen, English, and peasants' swine alike, he then turned home again, his swollen head no doubt bobbing joyfully to the murderous whine of his terrible pipers.

The Welsh caught the smell of blood and smoke clear up in their dark mountains and added to the havoc, attacking ill-guarded garrisons whose men had been marched off quickly to restore order in the north.

The young warriors about the king began to sharpen their swords and their appetite for battle, anticipating the Scottish and Welsh estates and titles the king might bestow on them when the season of war was done. But the king sent no summons of array, no command to raise the English army – the fyrd. As when Curthose had first raided him from Gerberoy, and to the same consternation among some of his followers, he did nothing.

Was he grown too old for battle? Did he now find the affairs of Normandy of more importance than a double assault on England? What more pressing affairs took his mind from avenging the burned fortresses of Hereford, the ransacked manor farms of Northumbria?

We had a wedding to prepare for and celebrate! Adela, his daughter, was to marry Count Stephen of Blois at Christmas. The king would linger to see that happy event, the first marriage of any of his children, the first opportunity to get a legitimate grandchild. Perhaps this *was* reason enough to hold back a season from war.

But Rufus went to him impulsively and said: 'Let me lead your host against the Scots. I'll dig Malcolm out of his lair and bring you b-back either his tribute or his s-skin.'

A brave speech, but green, and ill timed. He made it before his father's council, and the older men smiled at him as if he were twelve-year-old Henry asking for an army.

Even the king smiled. 'You've had the smell of only one battle. It's early days to be talking of catching a fox like Malcolm.' It was a stinging rebuke for a young man who hungered for his parent's approval as much as did Rufus.

He flushed, and his tongue at once began to betray him as he protested:

'There were men at Ger-Gerberoy who ha-had more experience in b-battle, but who di-died there, but I lived. Your Grace, the S-Scots are la-laughing at you – ju-just as you l-laugh at me now. Let me go against them, even under an-another c-captain. It's my *time!*'

At that the king's face hardened. 'No, my son. It's still my time. Will you now become as graceless and ambitious as your brother?' Curthose was quickly slipping out of favor again with his father, having taken up his old habits of drink and gambling once more. 'No,' said the king, 'I think you will not. You will bide your time in patience as befits a good son and soldier, until I require you – which is not now.'

There may have been affection in that as well as cruelty. Certainly, Rufus was only nineteen and scarcely tried in command or battle. But the chill affection couldn't lessen the humiliation. Rufus fled the court that afternoon and rode back to Edgar Atheling's estate with only Cormac for a companion. In going, he missed his brother Robert's reaction to the offer made:

'Well said! Good boy! Where is he? Call him in and we'll dedicate a cup to him: the New Alexander! The Conqueror of Scotland!'

I was dismayed to find I'd been forgotten in my lord's headlong departure, but his going gave me an opportunity to write my report to Lord Odo, which was long overdue. I was an unwilling spy, a more unwilling correspondent. The trouble was, I'd grown attached to the object of my surveillance, which a cautious Judas should beware of. I feared my negligence would get me removed from my post. Considering present prospects, that might well be for the best, but I didn't relish being impaled on Odo's hook and dropped into new, fishable waters. The homely, unreligious, and wholly honest young man I had been set to spy on had called me his friend – and I had as much need of a friend as he.

He returned from the Atheling's house within a week, but with a bleaker look than that with which he had set out. I couldn't discover why at once, but Rufus no longer sought the Englishman's company after that.

18

Now Rufus seemed almost demented in his energy. He went to the lists with anybody who would take his challenge. All winter he engaged them where he could, in the midst of a meal, in the midst of talk, in the midst of a church service. The final benediction seldom found him kneeling to receive it. He didn't wager; he simply fought to win. His endurance became something to wager on.

I thought that if his behavior was owing to pique over his rejection, it would pass in a month or two, but he swept the lists clean of contenders at the tournament held in honor of his sister's wedding. I don't mean he invariably won; far from it. Only that, if he lost, he would be back again, badgering the victor to meet with him again until he did win. That name which Curthose laughingly gave him – the New Alexander – was bawled out often enough with a laugh when he lay flat on his back in the cavalry yard with someone's foot on his chest, but there was something of Alexander about him. He was out to conquer everybody in sight if it killed him, which several times it seemed likely to do.

As spring came and others turned to more pleasant sports than knocking each other about, Rufus continued to match himself at spear throwing against even the foot soldiers, if he could find no one better, and I began looking for some other reason for his madness than injured pride.

'What is it?' I asked Cormac as we watched him slash and thrust one morning with Robert fitz Hamon, who was one of the few now who would willingly match with him without goading. 'It's almost like it was with his fever. He hardly seems to know himself when he comes away from this yard. Could it be that the fever still works in him and we don't know it?'

Cormac said dryly: 'Oh, he's got a fever, all right. But not that one.'

There was a bellow from fitz Hamon. His wooden buckler had split under the hammering of Rufus's sword. Rufus stopped, gasping and rocking on his toes; then his arm dropped, he laughed, and they examined the ruined shield together.

'What do you mean, not that one? What sort, then?' I was seriously expecting some sort of medical answer, since Cormac remained closer to Rufus physically than I. But Cormac looked at me scornfully and threw away the piece of straw he'd been flattening between his teeth.

'It's love fever, Ranulph. Don't you recognize the symptoms? Our lad's got a fever of the heart.' He didn't look happy to find the word in his mouth.

I could have laughed with relief, though I didn't let it show for Cormac's sake. Of course, such a distraction as love wouldn't please Cormac, who was still at work making himself indispensable to Rufus, but the diagnosis answered well enough for the extravagant and daring deeds my lord drove himself to.

I did risk a smile the next time I followed Cormac, trailing Rufus through the great hall with his alert but seemingly diffident patience, like a good hound waiting to be thrown a sop. A love affair, if it came to flower, would put a crimp in Cormac's plans. No more of those nightly rubdowns, with the little jokes, when Rufus had a wife to bed. And what if my lord set his harper to making love songs soon for his lady? I smiled the more to think how this infatuation must have grown up right under our noses, since our lad had scarcely been out of our sight for a year.

But who was she? There were scarcely any women at court who weren't either his close kin or some religious, even at Christmas, Easter, and Whitsuntide. No honorable man brought his virgin daughters or his comely young wife away from home, to be jostled, stared at, or spoken to by strange men. When we were occasionally guests in some baron's hall, the lady of the house greeted her husband's chief guests, then took herself off to dine apart with her daughters and tirewomen. The only women to be seen were the occasional laundresses, or a hearth girl, sweeping ashes; and no one fell madly in love with them.

My mind reverted to the religious who sometimes visited his mother, especially when we were at Caen. God forbid he'd conceived a passion for a nun! There were one or two I'd seen there who were so rosy and bright-eyed under their veils that they must make the Devil weep for their salvation, but I'd never seen my Rufus so much as glance at them, unless it was to stand out of their way if he met them on a stair.

Then what if she were already married? I decided that was even more unlikely than the nuns; I'd seen all the matrons who had given him greeting the past year, and a kiss on the cheek from most of them wouldn't stir an incubus. Robert of Bellesme was said to have a handsome wife, but he kept her in prison.

The only thing left was to suppose he had harbored this secret passion for more than a year and for a woman whom I had yet to see. I must wait to discover who it was, when Rufus had overcome his sense of unworthiness by enough victories over his peers to speak to his father on the subject of marriage. Then all would be arranged; or, if his love were unsuitable, he would work off his infatuation in time and another, more attainable female would be put in his way.

I pitied him a little, remembering my own grief in love. I thought he might be more comfortable if he could confide in someone, but though I was his confessor, I was not yet his confidant in matters of that sort. I, of course, couldn't tell him that my own experience in the field would make me his ideal soul searcher.

Once I did venture to suggest to him after confession that I believed there was a further matter weighing on his heart, which he might feel free to tell to me. I said it, I thought, with a confidence-inspiring and friendly smile. He looked at me for a moment, as if the invitation were tempting. I leaned forward eagerly and urged him: 'You do have some such burden, though perhaps not altogether an unpleasant one?'

He said: 'Father, I've got a burden, but it's in my bowels, not in my heart, and if you don't let me r-rise from this crouch to visit the jakes, I may b-be-shit myself.'

I let the matter rest.

In July, almost a year after Malcolm Canmore's raid on the English, after the Welsh had long since eaten the mutton they'd stolen from our marcher castle pens and washed from their hands the blood of ours they'd shed, William Bastard was at last ready to avenge himself on them both. He made sudden preparations to sail for England, where he first proposed to scour the heads of the Welsh himself. He left the rule of Normandy, as ever, to his good wife. Robert Curthose he chose to lead the host against the errant Scots.

This was a surprise to several parties. Curthose had been in a pet for several months, for lack of purse and occupation. When he heard he was to draw money from the Winchester treasury and hire such mercenaries as he saw fit to add to the host he would raise, he broke into a dance and a bellow of joy. He was congratulated by his favorites, who no doubt smelled their profit in his success. After a short counsel taken in private from his father, Curthose announced that Edgar Atheling would go with him as ambassador to Malcolm. He named the rest of his chosen captains on the spot. Rufus was not among them.

He looked so cast down by the neglect that even the king noticed and said, surely not at the wisest time, 'I have another task for you, my son.' He didn't say what it was, which made it plain to the rest that the assignment might lack something of distinction. But Rufus bowed his head, obedient as always, and kept still.

Baggage began to be packed, enough to take them all to the land of Punt from the look of it. Letters went out on the next ship, to Lanfranc, Odo, and William de Warenne, instructing them to prepare for their king's return with summons of array to all the men of the southern fyrd. Still, preparations went on in a leisurely manner. If the Scots and Welsh kept spies among us as we did among them, they would have had ample time to prepare their defences.

In the meantime, a calm of sorts fell over my lord. He ate, he drank, he attended the daily court, but his fire was extinguished. He no longer drilled or goaded friends into doing mock battle with him. He said very little, but looked defeated. I tried to cheer him; even Cormac attempted to rally him with such observations as:

'You're in luck! You'll get better sport fighting the Welsh, I can tell you. They're very close relatives of mine and would have been closer, only they couldn't learn how to swim when the rest of us decided to conquer Ireland. The Scots are only a poor pack of night raiders. They'll give up when your brother shows his army on the borders. They do that, then raid again when the army's gone home. The Welsh will give you a good fight.'

Rufus was only mildly scornful. 'The Welsh won't meet us in open battle. They're no different from the Scots, except they don't surrender. They'll just melt into their Black Mountains, like ice in a thaw. We'll be hunting them the rest of the year, while they burn our forts as fast as we build them.' But he looked slantwise at Cormac and smiled. 'You're a ridiculous man, harper. What do you know about war or the Welsh?'

Cormac said lightly, 'My father was a Welshman.'

I cocked an ear, but Rufus scoffed: 'There's another of your lies. You told me before that your father was the King of Munster. Now, how could he have a Welshman for a son?'

'No, my lord, the King of Munster was my grandsire, on my mother's side. The Welshman came into the family by accident, as it were.'

'And you, I suppose, were the accident?'

Cormac shrugged. 'Everything since the Creation may have been an accident, my lord. Or, if you believe some wise men, even that event.'

I was appalled. 'Cormac! That's heresy – blasphemy and – and God knows what else! You won't speak like that before my lord!'

Cormac held up both hands in surrender. 'I retract the remark. Much of what mankind does would *seem* to be accident, taking free will and ignorance into consideration.' He winked at Rufus. 'If your illustrious pirate ancestor hadn't chanced to fall on the French in a good year, he might have moved on farther south, my lord. Then you'd have been born a Spaniard, for example.'

Rufus laughed at his impudence. 'You rascal, you'd do better to commit heresy than say *that* to my f-father.'

They went on bantering nonsense for a little while, leaving me out of the game. My lord's spirits seemed to lighten, but when he was given a rest from Cormac's goading, he fell into silence again.

There was a parting feast for Count Robert and his followers, who were to sail ahead of the king. It was a mystery why the son should go before the father, when there was room on the ship for both. My opinion was that the king was simply eager to have Robert out of his sight. They had quarrelled with increasing ferocity of late, and Robert's boisterousness with friends since he learned he was to lead the royal host must have been especially exasperating to his father. The Lady Matilda was too distressed to come down and keep peace between them most days.

Besides the Atheling, Robert was taking with him many of the late rebels of Gerberoy, and while they caroused the king looked on them so coldly that one might have believed he had arranged for their arrest when they came to port in England, but of course this was not so.

The feasting and drinking lasted until near Compline before word came that all who were to depart must board the ships in order to sail on the night tide. There was a general chaos of leave-taking, in the halls and the inner bailey. Rufus, stare-eyed with all he'd drunk, went down to the ships with them to say good-bye, as did many of their kin. Cormac prepared to follow him, and I might have done the same, but my legs failed me as I tried to rise from the bench.

'Stay and rest yourself, Little Brother.' Cormac's hands pressed down on my shoulders; he kissed me lightly on the shaven pate. 'Give thanks to God you'll never make a good toper.' He had drunk far more than I, but he was steady on his feet.

'Don't let him go down there, Cormac,' I mumbled through half-paralyzed lips. 'Tell him – what's the good? It'll only make him feel – '

'Rest easy, soul keeper. Things will be more cheerful soon. We're going to war, we're going to win, and we're going to be rid of that monument to piety – may he fall in a Scottish bog and be molested by kelpies!'

I was confused. 'Who? Who do you mean? Curthose?'

Cormac snorted. 'Him? Christ, why would you think of him? I mean that quasi-sanctified piece of moldy English veal that Will's been sweating for since he was a sprat. Edgar! I thought you had eyes. Haven't you seen it?'

I'd never thought of it and couldn't then. My brain tried to engage the thought: Edgar? But it froze on the name. I turned to Cormac for clarification, but he had gone. I put my head on the table after a time and tried to sleep, but nausea was slowly creeping up my throat, until I had to rise and trot to the nearest jakes to relieve myself. Still sick, but more sober, I went out into the night air to walk myself well.

Edgar! What a fool I'd been, if it was true. I'd been watching to see who my lord let his eye dwell on, but forgot to notice who it was he turned away from too quickly, or sometimes couldn't look on at all. He'd been distant with the Atheling lately, but I'd supposed it was because Edgar had been too politic to take sides with him against the king. That he might have scoffed at the grievance, or even been bored by the telling of it – on second thinking, I saw that those reactions were unlike the prince. A sympathetic ear was what he had most to give. He was Curthose's friend, too.

He attracted the religious and the pious beggar almost as readily as did the Lady Matilda. His charities were to sigh and nod at a pitiable tale; to kiss the leper, as it were.

What had gone amiss, then? My master had formed an attachment for the prince from earliest manhood? He'd gone to him after his last humiliation, wanting the comfort and advice of someone who didn't despise him? They would have talked, perhaps ridden a pair of the Atheling's fine horses, dined and drunk, talked into the night. And then – why, they went to the same bed, as host and honored guest.

How, under the spell of infatuation, grief, or wine, had something occurred or been said to shame and hurt my lord further? Had he spoken and been rejected? Rejected only, or reproved too, perhaps? Repulsed? I flinched at the thought, almost as if I had received the shame; felt the disgust I would have felt for myself; loathed the memory of a time when I might have been so foolish or unwary as to be so shamed. I thanked God it had passed with me and could never come again, for man or woman. What a soul-stripping thing it was, to love!

Somewhere in the bailey I sat down to plot my lord's recovery from his grief and thought of the satisfaction I should feel in keeping word of it from his uncle. While I was thinking, I fell asleep. The Matins bell from the cathedral woke me. I was chilled, stiff, and had a bad head. I made my way sleepily back to the hall, but paused to look in on my lord's bedchamber before I slept. It was empty.

I went in, sat down on the bed, and waited for them to return. The Lauds bell sounded its one note and still they didn't come. I took a candle stub, lit it at the cresset, and went out to search the upper and lower halls for them. I found many of those who had gone to the ships to bid farewell and received curses and kicks for stumbling over them or waking them with my candle shine, but Rufus and Cormac weren't among them. De Alderi I found snoring in the arms of a kitchen wench. He was fuddled and didn't know where his master was, only that he hadn't sailed with Curthose.

My worry gave way to slow anger as I remembered Cormac's great good humor. That, at least, I could put a stop to. I went into the bailey ward again and searched near the stables where the hovels of the lesser servants and the men-at-arms were built against the inner wall.

'Cormac!' I yelled at the watchmen. 'Have you seen the Irishman? The harper?'

'Get down!'

'Shut up! Smother yourself, you bastard!' The cries came from the huts. The watch looked down on me in severe silence, believing me drunk.

I sat down by the gate to wait for them, but sometime before dawn I must have dozed. The changing of the watch on the walls brought me to myself. I rose and stumbled toward a pair of water barrels to relieve my desiccated throat and furred tongue. There was no dipper. The barrels were kept filled there to cleanse the castle steps of their daily accumulations of bird droppings and like filth. They were almost as high as my head. I was standing on my toes to lower a bucket into one for my drink when I heard a familiar voice coming from behind them. I let the bucket float and crept around the barrel carefully. Cormac was there and Rufus was with him. They were lying on straw, wrapped together in one cloak. My lord seemed still asleep, but Cormac murmured to him in a teasing whisper.

I stepped out of sight, let the bucket down into the water carefully, lifted it out, and waited a moment, then came around the barrel and emptied it on them both.

'Christ Jesus!' cried Rufus, rolling into a ball from the shock of the drenching.

Cormac, who had seen or heard me at the last moment, threw the sodden cloak aside and came off the ground like a wounded wolf. I hit him in the face with the side of the bucket, throwing him back against the wall, but he bounded off it with his fist ready and knocked me sprawling.

We battled, rolling in the mud and the dog turds, snarling like the hounds who came bounding to attack us, throttling each other, and waking the last sleepers in the bailey until Rufus dragged us apart and set himself between us.

His face was blotched, his eyes bloodshot, and his hair dripped dirty water. He snatched at my cowl and pulled me to him. 'What in Hell's name – are you gone mad?'

Cormac reached for me again, but was pushed back with an elbow to his ribs. Then, still staring me in the face, my lord loosened his grip on my cowl and gave me a little push. His sharp laugh alerted the dogs again.

'The next time you bastards play pranks on each other, make sure I'm not caught in the middle,' he said loudly, for we had two or three dozen auditors now. 'Here's no way to begin a morning. Take hands and be friends again.' He laid a firm hand on each of our arms.

'God help you when I get to you next,' Cormac muttered to me through his bloody mouth.

'God helps no one. Take hands, I say, and smile.' Rufus whispered, too, and the look he gave Cormac was as cold as any his father ever bestowed on an enemy.

I extended my hand as his fingers gripped me. Cormac took it. I smiled, or tried to; my stomach lurched to do it.

'There! Done and sweethearts again!'

The crowd laughed with Rufus, now it seemed safe to do so. Cormac showed his teeth, his fingers clenching mine so that I couldn't get away. His other hand was at his dagger hilt.

Rufus turned on his heel abruptly and strode away to the castle steps.

'Seven words from me and you'll be in the keep, waiting for —'

'You won't say three of them.' His dagger hand was beginning to move.

'Cormac!' Rufus was at the steps, waiting. Cormac let his hand fall, stepped back from me reluctantly, then swiftly turned and followed my lord up into the hall.

I went and had a wash in a horse trough, then got a stableboy to help me brush some of the filth from my gown. I was still trembling with rage and fear. I'd been a fool to threaten Cormac with exposure unless I meant to do it. Caution urged me to keep still. If I exposed myself to the king's notice a second time in some scandal, it would surely be the end of me in court, too. I savored the thought of giving Carileph the information. A renegade monk is as much a criminal as any serf who leaves his lord's land without permission. Carileph had some grounds for disliking Cormac; he would be happy to see him tried for running.

I rejected that thought, too. I had broken the king's peace in his own house. I, too, could be handed over to the court ecclesiastic for a whipping. My lord's advice was sound: we would all smile and say nothing, in public, though I meant to speak to him in private.

But Rufus avoided me, riding out with his father after the morning court and staying away all day. That afternoon I was informed by the clerk of the writing office that I must bring my gear down to the clerks' quarters, where I would sleep in the future.

Preparations were finished in a few days for the king to set sail with his followers for England. Hearing nothing to the contrary, I supposed I would be left behind. Carileph had said nothing to me, but gave me a graveyard smile when our eyes met. My heart sank.

Rufus or Cormac had told him some lie, which he would now report to Odo, and my own silence would work against me. I would be dispatched back to St. Vigor with a recommendation I be confined for brawling and God knew what else.

At the last moment of their going, I got my summons to join the other clerks who were attached to the king's company. We went down to the ship and lined up along the rail near the prow, to wait for our betters to follow. The trumpets blew from the castle walls, the town gates opened, and the king rode forth with his son and his captains in great splendor.

Their horses were boarded on another ship with their baggage. They came aboard ours. Cheers, drumbeats; the lines were cast loose, the anchors lifted; the rowers began to pull us out into the channel, where the tide could take us down to sea.

Once we were out through the mouth of the Seine, the sea winds turned rough. In spite of bright weather overhead, we wallowed across the water as if we sailed in a tub. It's heavy on the stomach, traveling in the prow of a ship like that, bounding up and down with every wave slap. We were a green lot.

Cormac passed near me several times during the voyage, on his way to the jakes at the ship's head. We exchanged evil looks. His mouth was bruised and swollen. I believed he would pitch me overboard if he caught me alone at night, so I took care to stay close to my brother clerks. I knew his intent, because I shared it. I would gladly have done the same to him. I loathed him now, for using his old power over me and betraying it. I loathed Rufus, too, for betraying himself, then punishing me for knowing it. I hated all the damned, long-nosed Normans on that ship. I was none of their kind. All my blood must have come from my mother. I had nothing in common with them, but I was bound to them forever. I hung over the rail, retching without gaining relief, and wished I could be swept overboard and heaved up like Jonah on a foreign shore.

At Winchester the king was met by his regents, Odo and William de Warenne, who turned back to him the rule of the realm. Odo, I thought, looked grander than any other in his earl's finery. He wore a tunic of crimson silk and a splendid mantelet of deep blue, clotted with English threadwork. He made even the well-robed king look like back-country gentry, garishly mantled over a grimy tunic and a travel-soiled shirt.

The king lost no time sending for his lords of the south to take counsel with him. Those who had already answered his summons of array were in the city. While they plotted the campaign, his knights began to harden themselves for war again in the drill fields or took to cavalry exercises in the New Forest. Rufus was part of that. Cormac lurked somewhere in the town.

I was in sore need of an occupation and had none. I dreaded my meeting with Odo when he had time for me. For the first time in my life I gave thought to running away. There were too many vagabond clerks loose in the world already, but I might find someone who could employ me for my head for figures and my pen – if I didn't starve first. I was contemplating my choices when I was sent for by Robert Marmion, the king's dispenser.

He was brisk: 'Earl Odo is returning to London tomorrow. You were a clerk of his before you were attached to this court. You will return to him now, as your duties here are ended. Here are two letters for you to give him, when he has leisure to receive them. You will notice they are unbound, so you may read them if curiosity overwhelms you, as they concern you. I am instructed to warn you, however, that you must trouble no one here at court with any questions concerning their content. Is that clear?'

I took them, feeling I held my doom in my hands. 'May I speak to William de St. Carileph before I go?'

He lifted his brows. 'Why should you need to do that? He's the king's chaplain. This is no affair of his. In any case, the answer is as I've said. That was made clear to me, if not to you.' It was clear to me that I had been returned to Odo without the thanks of his nephew, perhaps with his recriminations, and this small, wry-mouthed man knew the details.

I put the letters in my breast unread, an act of false pride. 'If these are for His Grace, of course I'll not read them.'

'Very well, then, you may go. His Grace takes his leave of us early in the morning. You'll find him preparing for it at Wolvesey Palace. You'd better try to join him there before curfew.'

Dismissed, I left the castle at once, repeating to myself several times 'glad to be gone.' Glad to be done with spying and false friends, with an occupation that was none at all. I would deliver myself to Odo, tell His Grace to do with me as he would, but I was finished with spying.

No doubt one of the letters I carried would make my wishes superfluous, but it didn't matter. Let him rake me over the coals, send me home, or lend me out to the meanest abbey in the hinterlands. My freedom from the cloister had earned me nothing but disappointment; multiplied my sorrows, not alleviated them.

As I left the gates and went into the broad High Street, I felt most miserably but righteously alone. That sensation was of short duration. There were footsteps somewhere behind me. I heard them but didn't give them thought until I came to the narrow lane that led to the cheap, when I paused to look back. The other walker stopped at the same time, but was nowhere in sight. My heart gave a lurch, but I reasoned I had nothing to fear here in the king's city. Still, I walked more quickly and couldn't help but shrink into the shadows when I heard the other's steps renewing their light echo on the cobbled street. The steps were quicker; he was running along the High Street. I fell against the wall for a moment of unwarranted relief, then sighed at myself for making too much of a common pedestrian. I would never have shrunk from footsteps in London or Rouen. I set out briskly for Wolvesey by way of the cheap and the churchyard – which was my mistake.

I'd no more than reached the cheap when I saw a blur of motion to my left in the upper road. I turned at once and ran back the way I'd come. He was stalking me; there was only one person I knew who would do it.

I was younger and might have outrun him, but my aging sandal strap tore loose and threw me just as I was up onto the High Street again. I fell, scrambled up, darted across the street to a narrow passage between houses.

He caught me at the mouth of the passage, thrust me into it, spun me around against the wall. His hand closed on my throat and I felt the tip of his knife blade touch me under the left ear.

'One squeal and I slit the vein, Little Brother. I can feel it here under my thumb. You'd be dead before you fell.'

I nodded and went limp. The knife was removed from my neck, but came to rest immediately in the hollow under my Adam's apple just as he took his other hand away from it. 'Now – I've *saved* your miserable life. Tell me why I shouldn't take it.'

'Why should you? I've done nothing.'

'Said nothing?'

'No!'

'You had a long talk with that hunchback the dispenser, the first time you've had three words with anybody since you crawled off the ship. What did you tell him?'

'Nothing! He gave me letters to carry to Odo.'

'Letters about what? About Will?'

'No. I mean – how should I know what they're about? I didn't write them. Listen, Cormac, if I meant to speak to anyone, why would I wait so long, then pick the dispenser?'

He ran his hands about my waist, looking for a knife, I suppose, then explored my chest and heard the crackle of parchment. His breath in my face was heavy with wine fumes. As he searched me, the point of his knife pressed less painfully into my throat. I tried to reason with him:

'Cormac, you've got nothing to fear from me and you know it – you made sure of it. I'm dismissed. That's what my talk with the dispenser was about. I'm sent back to Odo. You should be satisfied. Now you do as you like. I'm out of it.'

But he pushed with the knife again. 'And back to the bishop? You'll want something to impress him with, something he can use – and you've got it now – the sort of thing he pays you for – ' My throat was about to be cut.

'No! I'm not telling him anything. I'm not!'

'And lose his confidence? Why not? Not for love of me.'

'Not for love of you! For *him* – because he said I was his friend. *He* called me that; you, too. Is this how you'd thank him? This, and what you'll do to him? You said we'll serve a king! Is this the way he'll get his kingdom? No, it's the way to make him despised more even than Curthose, when people realize – ' I stopped as if my throat were already cut. The knife was burning into me like a hot coal. I grabbed at his wrist with both hands, closed my eyes, and shouted:

'Kill me if you will, but he'll know you did it! He won't thank you! He isn't like you in that way!'

A shutter banged open above us and a voice yelled in bad French: 'Kill him then, or swive him, God-damned Frenchman, but let honest men sleep! 'Ware the slops!'

Cormac jerked back at the first sound from above, and as he released me I darted away. A deluge of stinking filth fell spattering on the bricks and I heard Cormac curse. My sandal fell off me and I sprinted like a hare.

When I reached Wolvesey Palace, the gate porter heard my heaving breath and held up the lantern. His eyes took in my general appearance as I identified myself.

'Someone tried to rob me,' I panted, 'but I had nothing.'

He looked doubtful. 'There's blood on your neck. Shall I call out the watch?'

'That was a horse tick. I pulled it off.'

'Better tend to it. The head might still be in and then it'll fester.'

But I said I thought I'd pulled it all out.

19

I rode at the rear of Odo's train to London, to the old palace above St. Paul's, where I'd been before. As in the other time, too, I waited several days for an audience with him, though every day he passed by many times in the hall and nodded to me as if I were the most welcome and expected guest. When I was at last called to him, I found him in his chancel, writing letters in private. He already had the letters I'd brought, which I'd meekly turned over to his chancellor.

He looked up as I entered and bowed, but continued his signing, rolling, and sealing. It was perhaps something that wanted no witness that he wrote. When he put it aside, he folded his hands and smiled at me in his familiar manner, in which benevolence and a little sneer were intermingled.

'So, young man, you're with us again. My nephew says he won't want a chaplain, now he's going to war on the Welsh. Odd notion, considering the poor luck he had in his first campaign, don't you think? Or am I wrong? I've heard his adventures neither from him – nor from you. I may exaggerate his ill fortune.'

I took the point. 'Forgive my seeming laxity, Your Grace, but it was only that I had no time for writing when he was ill and near death – as he truly was. When he recovered his health, he kept me close to him at Rouen. The rest of the court had moved elsewhere. I had no means to get letters to you by safe hands. Also, to be frank, Your Grace, he knew from the first that you had set me to watch him. He gave me little to tell, but I believe there would have been little in any case. No man, perhaps not even our lord king, knew whether King Philip would desert Count Robert until he did it.'

'Stale news, now.'

'Yes, Your Grace.' Under his gaze I searched for something to say further, to placate him. 'As for my lord William, I think he gets little regard from the king his father, who treats him as if he were still a boy. Now he's no longer the heir, he has few friends. There's no guile in him, nor much ambition beyond his desire to serve his father. I think he'll be no trouble to – to anyone – henceforth.'

'And you're sorry for him and sorry to be cast off.'

'No, Your Grace, I'm glad. I've grown weary of – not of serving you, my lord, but of spying. As you have judged, I'm not very good at it.'

He was tapping the quill on the table, making a ruin of its nib. He said: 'I think you might be very good at it. What you're not very good at is telling me the truth of your former master. I give you a moment to reflect on that; then I mention the name of Edgar Atheling. Will you find me an answer?'

So he knew something of that. My reflection was brief: I was the servant of Odo. My loyalty to Rufus was unappreciated. My future was apt to be dim if Odo caught me in a lie. I said:

'My lord William was infatuated with Prince Edgar, or maybe with his horses. He wished to draw him into a closer friendship, but Prince Edgar wisely preferred the friendship of Count Robert. My lord William was disappointed in his hopes and now keeps clear of him. That is all. There was no plotting or treasons between them when I was near, if that's what Your Grace means.' How did he know about the Atheling?

'Infatuated? Is my nephew perverse?'

A very swift review of that morning I'd fought with Cormac went through my head. There were witnesses; were any of them in Carileph's pay as I was? Possibly not, but the tale of a brawl will always carry. I said:

'*Perverse is* a harsh word, Your Grace, if you'll forgive me. Your nephew is young, friendless, believes himself to be cursed. He makes an easy prey for – for those who might make him perverse. I myself thought there was cause for suspicion when we were still at Rouen. He has a servant, an Irishman, who follows him about now. I found them together in odd circumstances the morning after Count Robert set sail for England. I was alarmed for my lord's sake and struck the Irishman for what I thought might have taken place between them. We fought. My lord came between us. He was angry – which is why he has dismissed me, for breaking the peace of the house – but he was angry with us both and didn't behave like a guilty man. I own I didn't truly see anything of a criminal nature taking place. God forgive me if I was wrong to suspect it. God forgive him if he's guilty. But I may not accuse him on my suspicion, and in any event it was Cormac I suspected of entreating him.'

He examined the spoiled pen, then laid it aside. 'You suspected the very man you recommended to my nephew for a servant? Your motives are not quite clear, my son.'

Oh, God, he knew everything, somehow. 'Your Grace is correct. I did recommend Cormac. I'd known him in past years.'

'For what?'

'Cormac was a monk at St. Vigor.'

Odo's eyebrows knitted, as if in perplexity. 'Was? And now roams free to debauch my nephew? How is that, Brother?'

I drew breath. 'Cormac is a renegade. He fled the abbey after being accused of – having – unnatural intercourse with another brother, who proved their guilt by hanging himself later. But Cormac's nature was known to some even before that.'

'How so?'

'He was Abbot Robert's favorite – his lover.' My voice had dwindled to where even I could hardly hear it.

Odo leaned forward: 'And this was the man you recommended to your master for a servant? Did you consider it part of your duties as a priest to forgive this Irishman, or as among your duties as my spy, as you so charmingly put it, to ruin my nephew?'

'Oh, no, Your Grace. I only did it because he had been my teacher and I loved him once.' I thought if I didn't sit down soon, my knees would betray me.

Odo leaned back in his chair and studied me. 'There, now, didn't I say it? You do have it in you to be an intelligencer, and now, finally, you've told me something I didn't know.'

He sorted through some of the letters before him, found one, and held it up to read again. 'Well, my nephew seems not to bear you a grudge for sending him this evil friend. He's put you back to me with a benefice, to ease the burden of my feeding you, no doubt. Did you know that? By the king's grace and favor, you are named rector of Godalming. That's a royal estate in Surrey. The gift isn't a rich one, but you won't have to sell your wine ration to put money in your purse. That is, you won't have to when I've finished deducting from your fees what you've cost me in the last year. That's fair, isn't it? What do you say to that?'

I said nothing. He nodded.

'Just what I would have said in your place. Very well. In your new dignity as king's rector of Godalming, I trust you'll henceforth forgo brawling, drowning, and whatever else it is that sends you to me in rags each time. In return for that small favor, I grant you your wish: no further intelligence work.' He held out the letter. 'This is yours. I'll send for you if I should want you. Until then, report to the master of the chancel clerks.' His eyes dismissed me before his tongue stopped speaking.

'Thank you, Your Grace.'

I wandered through the palace, holding the letter loosely in my hand, until I came to the chapel. I'd been there often in the last few days, praying for guidance, but now I stood in the doorway rather than enter and kneel. The crucifix that hung above the altar was a gift to Odo from the Pope and was as fine a thing as any to be seen in the world, his chaplains told me. Its Christ didn't hang in naked agony, but He was both robed and crowned. He was the aspect of Christ Triumphant, a replica of the Holy Cross of Lucca, a relic said to have been carved by Nicodemus the Pharisee. It was fitting: even poor, bleeding Jesus must look prosperous if He would dwell with Odo.

'Behold, O Lord, Thy servant Ranulph, rector of Godalming, who need do no more spying, because he has now betrayed everything he knows – and everyone. Like Judas, I've been kissed for it, too, by the man I've betrayed; for I have betrayed him, with every careful word out of my mouth that seemed to defend him. But then, he's only a boy, with little hope of gaining any power I must respect.

'I'm a bent specimen, Lord, a broken reed, even among Egyptians. A great man need only knot his brows and look steadily on me and I'll fall away from any resolution, spew up any secret. No need to threaten me with words, when I have such a distaste for failing to please.

'Forgive me, Lord. I've troubled You too much with acts of contrition in the past when they were false. I know now that I don't fear the pains of Hell so much as the eyes of Odo; nor does offending Thee concern me so much as to keep him waiting for an answer.

'I've missed my vocation up to now, because I'm not meant to be a priest, or anyone's friend. I am the very perfect servant of such a man as Odo. Him I will never fail. I'll no longer ask You to take pity on my weakness, but only to teach me to love him as I should – as a dog loves the carrion that fattens it. Amen.'

My church had a vicar in residence, a tall, dour man with a seamed face, named Dunstan, who lived in my rectory with his wife, Blodwin. It was as well he did, because I had little time to spend in Godalming, and in any event, Dunstan and I were never destined to be friends. He naturally resented me as yet another French interloper on sacred English soil, while I put him down as the usual surly English priest who garbled his Latin and put his cassock on only when he was about to enter the sanctuary. Otherwise, one couldn't have told him from the peasants he ministered to. His wife was more eager to please me, at the same time effacing herself, as if every third country priest in the land didn't also have a wife or a 'housekeeper' to sweep his hearth.

I didn't go near them often because Odo kept me traveling as his courier and inspector of his widespread estates. Rather than visit them himself – he having no taste for rural company – he sent me with instructions for his bailiffs, which they took as unwillingly from me as Dunstan did. Odo had much business in other places, too. His correspondence with men of all sorts, of high rank and low, was prodigious. I was his courier for letters, too. I was seldom off a horse's back for more than three days at a time that whole year.

In Kent they called Odo the Tamer of the English, but meant no compliment by it. In his own county, and in the north where he had put down anarchy, he had wrung enough plunder from the English churches and monasteries to enrich his own in Bayeux and Rochester far beyond their merit. He was also called the Great Thief.

In truth, he was a man of several faces. He relished intrigue and took joy in war and plunder, but he loved music, too, and learning, and fine penwork. He rewarded the men who could please him with those arts. He was generous to the poor, when he wasn't robbing them. He kept a school for poor boys who wished to enter the Church; these he fed, clothed, and educated at his own expense, as he did my blood brothers.

He was especially magnanimous toward pilgrims to Rome. When I first began my travels as his overseer, I supposed his generosity was a means of making amends to the English for his earlier harshness. I was instructed to bring him the name of any man known to his parish priests or his bailiffs who wished to make a devout journey to the Holy City. Lord Odo would pay that pilgrim's way and make him a gift, too, if he would merely take with him some letter or token from Odo to lay before a shrine or give to some particular person.

Naturally, one expected a lot of people to begin hearing angelic voices directing them to Rome. But though the village priests sometimes found me a visionary or aspiring mystic among their flocks, the bailiffs seemed to turn up only slate-faced men of a distinct bearing, with pale noses and sunburned cheeks, which comes from wearing helms a great deal.

They took the purses I had for them, or the little caskets, which I never supposed held pennies to devote to saints. If I gave them letters, I had no fear they might read them. I couldn't tell what was the content of the letters, as they were all penned and sealed by Odo himself.

I mentioned this mystery to Robert Bloet once, when I was stopping for a few days in Rochester keep and we were walking out for a breath of air along the Medway, below the castle.

'And what do you think it all means?' Robin asked when I'd told him.

'I think it means Odo is buying up a little mercenary army for himself, of course; though I don't see the reason for it. Curthose has tempered the Scots for a while, and the king has chased the Welsh as far back into their mountains as anyone would want to chase them. It seems like a good season for peace.'

'Yes. Well, now, let me tell you a mystery. Last spring a ship put in here on its way out from London. It had an Italian captain and a crew you'd swear were heathen. I stood up on the battlements watching Odo's household guards load cargo on that ship, which was odd enough in itself for those lazy devils. They put aboard six large chests that four men staggered to carry. There were also a dozen barrels of the size to brew ale in, but they weren't rolled up the gangwalk, like ale; they were also carried by these same fine young louts, who wouldn't haul up the gate for themselves if the castle were on fire. There was a deal of cursing and sweating, I can tell you.

'Four of Uncle Odo's pilgrims went aboard with that cargo, wherever it was bound for, which I *don't* think was Bayeux.'

'But Rome? You think he's sending all these pilgrims to Rome, truly? Why?'

Robin shrugged. 'I only know there aren't as many pretty trophies of His Grace's northern campaign in his treasury this spring as there were the last. I know, because the warden has let me steal a peep on it from time to time – never crossing the threshold to do it, mind you!' He sighed. 'Call me frivolous, but I do love the sight of all that gilt and glimmer. It makes me feel like one of Solomon's Levites.'

'But all this about pilgrims and the Italian captain might just as easily be misdirection. There never was a man who liked complications as much as our master. Curthose is out of favor with his father again. They say he's in Germany now. Ships can put in at any port, no matter what race their captains. That makes better sense. Why would Odo be shipping off all he owns – and an army to boot – to Rome? No, he's still bound to make that dolt of a nephew duke before his time, if you ask me.'

'Well, I don't,' said Robin firmly. 'I don't know what it's all about and I don't care to. I love a good gossip, but I don't like intrigues. They usually end with moaning in the dungeon on the part of someone innocent, while the heads of the guilty perch rotting on the palisades. Ugh!'

We were agreed. Let Odo shift his fortune where he would. Let him connive and conspire with whom he would. I could have heated up and peeled off a letter seal at any time to discover the mystery of his correspondence, but I wouldn't. I was well clothed, well fed, well employed, and well out of all danger.

I had, in fact, begun to think England was almost as fair a spot as my homeland. I was grateful now that fortune had exempted me from the Welsh campaign. It had lasted until the winter snows without any real battles being fought or any real victories being gained, unless it was by the Welsh, who were left much as they'd been before. They are splendid fighters, the Welsh, but they take as much pleasure in swift raids and midnight arson as our folk do in thunderous leaguers. They had drawn the king into their wilderness, evaded him, taunted him, until he grew weary of them, declared himself the victor, and came home, leaving them to play wolf with the border-castle garrisons just as before.

I, on the other hand, had spent my autumn and winter making short rides to warm firesides, cloaked in the authority of my lord Odo of Kent. My welcome at his estates and vills might not have always been cordial, but it was invariably respectful. In his name I had license even to judge minor civil cases for him, a privilege that his tenants might have disputed, since I was in Holy Orders. But nobody disputed Odo's choices on Odo's land.

It was a slow business, hearing tenants' complaints. The little English I'd learned up to then was confined to ordering food, cursing a fellow who spat too close to my feet, or naming a pretty hearth girl *dyrling* when she smiled at me.

From the eyes of the men I received the message that I was a person of some little importance, which was pleasant; from the hearth girl – sometimes – it was that I was no monster for appearance, even if I were a Devil's spawn of a Frenchman. This was even more agreeable at the end of a long day, but I seldom got, or asked, more than a smile from them.

Why not? I often debated that with myself. To begin, they compared poorly with my memory of Isabel. I'd started my wooing of women on too high a plane for hearth girls and kitchen wenches to satisfy my mind. Also, if they were pretty, they also tended to be lousy, and I had a dislike of women who clawed their armpits while I kissed their lips.

Even if I found one that was both clean and comely, who didn't have a husband, father, or brother looking after her virtue, the sudden memory of my split back would get between me and my lust and cool the affair. So it was that even when I visited the stews in London, it was just to take a bath.

This second exile of Robert Curthose from his father's court might not have been the reason for Odo's secret doings, but it was fresh cause for the barons of England and Normandy to waver in their loyalties. In truth, it wasn't altogether fair the way poor Curthose was treated. He'd made a good victory up in Scotland, marched into it as far as Falkirk with such a vengeful pack of northerners at his heels that King Malcolm all but pissed himself trying to arrange a truce.

He greeted Count Robert as if he were the Conqueror himself, took him up to his foggy capital, Dunfermline, and there presented him to his English queen, Margaret, who was Edward Confessor's great-niece and Edgar Atheling's favorite sister. She honored the dazzled Curthose by sitting at meat with him and she caused Malcolm to present him with an oxcart full of rich gifts before he took his leave of them.

They say Curthose fell in love with the icy Margaret and might have stayed the winter, making songs to her pale beauty, but her husband was too jealous, and she too religious. So, having composed a final morning song to her, having stood as godfather to her firstborn female child, the lover came away sighing.

He did stop to build a strong fortress on the Tyne to stifle her husband's future ambitions for conquest. Altogether, he should have gotten an earldom for it, but got a scolding instead. His return rekindled in his father's brain all those old charges of prodigality and evil friends.

Robert had been rash enough to hold what amounted to a royal court at Newcastle, as his fortress was named. He was abetted in this effrontery by no less a person than my old spymaster, Carileph, who had just been rewarded for his *faithfulness* to the king with the northern bishopric of Durham. Carileph!

When the king berated Curthose for holding court, Count Robert was at first defensive, then insolent, then furious. He took ship to Normandy hoping to get comfort from his mother, but finding she could no longer pay his debts or suffer his whores and jugglers either, he went journeying again, along with his more enduring parasites. Edgar Atheling, who had gladly joined him on his high road, once more deserted him when they reached that fork which led to the lower one of poverty and exile. Edgar went home to his manor, his horses, and his dogs.

The king cursed his firstborn son in the presence of the court when he heard of his flight. The Lady Matilda shut herself up in her abbey for women to weep and to pray. She wrote letters to her lord which they said he wouldn't allow to be read to him. She wrote letters to her best-beloved brother-in-law, too.

It may be that Odo intrigued with the lady to lend aid to her favorite child. There were rumors he entreated the king on her behalf in private and was shouted down for it. For that, or for whatever reason, Odo suddenly gathered up his household while the king was in Normandy and removed himself and nearly five hundred men from Rochester to the Isle of Wight.

I was upcountry on some business at the time. When I returned to Rochester and found the place abandoned except for its warden, I took a day's rest then made my way to Southampton with no sense of urgency. I thought if the king had summoned Odo to come overseas and help do battle with the Angevins, or some such enemy, I could just as well stay behind. Fulk of Anjou was at that time fomenting trouble on our borders at home. Fulk was a miserable neighbor to Normandy, being a man of no honor whatsoever who stirred up rebellions among the inhabitants of Maine, so that they refused to let our king rule them. Fulk's evil disposition was also famous and, I believe, was owing in great part to his sufferings, which were divided in equal parts between his bunions and his insatiable lust for women not his wives. At one time he had three wives living at the same time, two incarcerated.

I wanted no campaigns that ended in negotiations with Fulk. I thought if I were too late for the sailing, I might take a holiday from my horse and rest myself in Godalming. So I rode south easily, enjoying the splendid weather, which brought with it the fear of famine, since it had scarcely rained the whole summer.

When I reached Winchester I saw the royal pennants flying from the tower, signifying that the king or his regent was in residence. Since Odo was the regent, I turned onto the east gate road, feeling disappointed of my holiday.

The town was unusually crowded with men, horses, and baggage carts. It wasn't a market day, I could see by the empty cheap, so what was the cause of the congestion? Between the church and the castle I saw a group of clerks and among them a familiar head, white and frizzed as the end of a new rope. I dismounted and called to him:

'Robin Bloet!'

He turned, grinned, and opened his arms to me. Another clerk was with him: Gerard le Gros, an amiable gourmand who was the nephew of the bishops of both Winchester and Ely. In spite of his holy antecedents, he had a lively interest in matters of the world and had been affable to me when I visited his chapter at St. Paul's.

'Here's another orphan, Gerard,' said Robin after he'd hugged me.

'What's this? Is the king here, or just Odo?'

'You haven't heard?' Robin put his arm around me. 'Look at him, Gerard; he hasn't heard. Look at the simple expression – ignorance is so touching. You tell him.'

'I think you must have found a widow with a wineshop. What have I missed?'

'Odo's been arrested,' Gerard said.

'What? What for? Who – '

'The king himself. No brushing aside that bailiff, eh?'

'On what charge?'

'Treason,' Gerard said. He nodded to a couple of passing clerks, whom I heard debating: '. . . try him . . . Lanfranc's in his rights . . . '

'I'm starving,' Gerard said, indifferent to debate. 'But I suppose we'll have to wait for our dinner today.'

There had been a soothsayer in Rome of late who desired of his demons to tell him who would sit on the throne of St. Peter when Pope Gregory died. It may be that he was incited to this curiosity by the gold of the German emperor; or by that of some Romans; or by that of any number of people who desired to look beyond Gregory's death to a brighter day. There were as many men in the world who hated the great Hillenbrand as there were who thought him the very savior of Holy Church. However it may have come about, this warlock convened his college of familiars with the proper smokes and incantations, until a preternatural voice informed him thus: the next Vicar of Christ would be a Frenchman named Odo.

Our own Odo was so impressed by this devilish annunciation that he began to bribe Roman senators and members of the Holy See to make certain of its fulfillment. Ever eager for the will of God to be done, he stuffed the scrips of pilgrims with petitions and gifts. He bought a palace in Rome, too, in which he planned to go and dwell while his election was pending. He arrayed an army from his own household, with many landless knights in addition, to take overseas with him. In this enterprise he got the support of some very consequential people. Hugh the Wolf, the great Earl of Chester, was one of them, and it was rumored that the King of France was another.

They say Odo made promises to the senators to assure his place: he would put his nephew Robert on the throne of England; he would induce Robert to renounce the English practice of choosing bishops and abbots in his realm. This was a thing demanded by Pope Gregory, which King William Bastard had refused him, in spite of the debt he owed the Holy See for helping him to his kingdom.

A wonderful plot, but what was it all for? Pope Gregory still lived. Did Odo plan to murder him, or was he merely thinking to be a counter-pope? If so, why did he later insist he'd raised his illegal army to offer it to Gregory, so that the Pope might free himself from the powerful Guiscards of Apulia, who had him under virtual house arrest at the time? It was all too fantastic, but who could defend the ever-conniving Odo of Bayeux from a charge that was merely fantastic?

As it turned out, there was no need to try, because when Odo was apprehended on the Isle of Wight with his embryo host, those were not the charges the king leveled against him.

William the Great was both judge and advocate for the Crown. Robert Bloet said he looked apoplectic. Considering the length of time involved between his discovery of his brother's doings and when he faced him, that rage must have been somewhat forced. There was a smell of entrapment about the trial.

Yet, there was no trial in the ordinary sense. Neither the king nor Odo would stop shouting at the other long enough for mere legality to enter into the dispute. The king made a lengthy accusation, which Odo repeatedly interrupted.

The king first attempted to review his own accomplishments, noting as he did all those people and occasions that had conspired to undo his great works. Odo reminded him forcefully that he, too, had fought at Hastings and that he had been the king's champion in upholding the peace. The king angrily persisted: he spoke of his ungrateful son and the young men who clung to him – rebels and now double traitors. Odo protested that when the earls had conspired to revolt in '75, he was one of the two who did *not* enter into their treachery.

The king lamented in his high, harsh voice that now his own brother, whom he had raised to the highest estates of the world and the Church, had spurned all his vows and turned traitor against him, too. He then launched into a recital of Odo's crimes: he had abused his power as justiciar, oppressed the English people, despoiled their churches, seduced the allegiance of knights brought hither by the king, and was conspiring to take his unlawful army out of the country now, which was an open act of treason in any kingdom and incapable of defense.

When William had exhausted himself with indictments, he said to his council: 'Consider these grievances, my lords, and tell me what I shall do with such a brother.'

The council sat mute to a man. They had no natural leader, Lanfranc being absent, Odo accused, and Hugh of Chester compromised. Not one among them was used to speaking without first determining the opinions of those three men, unless it was Geoffrey of Coutances. But Geoffrey, although a lifelong friend of Odo's, was not the stupidest man in the hall.

Odo stood with arms folded, glaring at his lord and brother. He smiled coldly.

'My lords, His Grace is in need of good counsel, but since none of you will be bold enough to give it to him, I must. It is this: this court has no authority to try me *on any charge*. This is a lay court. I am a clerk and the Lord's anointed priest, whom it is unlawful for any to bring to trial but a court ecclesiastical. We are missing two members here, who might have informed the king of that and saved us all the embarrassment. I speak of the archbishops of Canterbury and York, my lords. Where are they?

'I'll wager Lanfranc is at home in his minster, hiding his face from God in shame, because it was he who devised this tale against me, out of jealousy and malice. York is at home, too, not out of shame, but because he's too sensible to believe the senile dribblings of an old fool!' He had been addressing the hall at large as he spoke, like a good rhetorician. Now he swung about to face the king again.

'I'm surprised at you, my lord, that you who think yourself so well versed in Church law that you will dispute decrees with the Pope should be ignorant on this point. A bishop cannot be tried by any court, even an ecclesiastic one, without the consent of St. Peter's throne. I am the bishop of Bayeux! Bring in a papal legate, or send me to Rome, if you want justice done to me!'

There was a stir and murmur in the hall, and the heads of the listening clergy nodded like little flowers in a breeze to the words of Odo.

King William rose from his stool, his long arms moving as if he were limbering himself before casting a javelin. He strode forward from the dais, and the clerks who were perched on the edge of it nearly fell on their faces to give him room. Odo took a step backward, then held his ground.

The king advanced to him and roared in his face: 'I don't see a clerk here! Or a priest, or a bishop! I see the Earl of Kent that I made myself! By the splendor of God, if no one else has the courage to speak, or to lay hands on this man, I'll do *that* myself!' He caught Lord Odo by the nape of the neck with one hand and flung him forward to his knees.

Odo gave a great bellow of rage, a wordless yell, but as he cried out, the king grabbed him by the hair, pulled him upward, then flung him down again.

'Arrest the Earl of Kent, for malfeasance of his stewardship that I gave him in trust! I deseize him of his title and all his honors until he renders account to me. Take him, I say! And hold him fast.'

As if released from a spell, half the men of the council rushed forward to lay hands on Odo, sprawling in the rushes.

20

'What's to become of us?' The question would have had more pathos, except Robin Bloet spoke it while trying to chew a huge bite of mutton. 'We're poor, homeless scholars and wandering waifs now. The king's seized Uncle Odo's goods; what will he do with us chattels?'

We were feasting mightily at Gerard's expense, having discussed the disgrace of our master exhaustively without reaching any conclusions as to what it had really been about.

'I still like to think of Odo making himself Pope,' Gerard mused. 'It's a foolish tale, but I'm fond of it. Just imagine: you two reprobates might have become papal legates.'

'To hell with Odo, now! Think of me, will you?' I was getting morose with wine. 'He's my bishop. I'm bound to him, whatever the king does with him. Robin's only been his – his – '

'Humble preceptor – or passing fancy? Which term are you groping for, dear boy?' Robin wiped his mouth briskly. 'No matter; I'm not proud. Nor am I lame. As soon as I had a hint of what was in the wind, I applied straight to our good Gerard here, who's so influential I knew he couldn't fail to aid me. You tell him, Gerard, and put an end to his pathetic whining.'

Gerard said offhandedly: 'Maurice, the chancellor, for whom I work my fingers to the bone, has room for a few men who are quick and love drudgery. I've spoken to him about you.'

'Will he take me?' I asked.

'Of course he'll take you, Raf. He'll take us both, because I'm quick and you love drudgery. How can he refuse our anguished eyes? Besides, I'm related in some distant way, of which I shall never tire of reminding him. It's *so* good to have relatives. I'll urge you on him. It's time you got cured of your saddle sores and completed your education.'

He then launched into a ridiculous story for Gerard's sake, about how on our first encounter he took me to an English bathhouse.

'I introduced this virgin to the best bathhouse in London. You should have been there to see it. After two cups of wine and a little back scrubbing, during which he kept his eyes closed, he was ready to pay the wench and leave. When she told him what else she would consider doing for a penny, he thought it meant he'd have to marry her!'

'This is a shameless fabrication, Gerard.'

'It isn't. When he finally got the drift of it, there was simply no stopping him. He seemed to think he was Romulus, plowing the perimeters for the walls of Rome. Lud help her, the poor slut was so exhausted, I think she went off with a Danish sailor to get some relief – '

'This never happened. It's his own story he's telling you.'

'Hush. Now, let me tell you what he said about Moldy Maud of Caux Gate – ' He continued to rag me for another half hour, which even the best of natures might find trying, but it was his way to express friendship in those days. I took it gratefully, glad to have friends in my need, even if they seemed to cherish me only to laugh at.

We duly presented ourselves to Maurice, the royal chancellor, the next day, and to my immense relief we were promptly accepted. I made myself a promise that I would earn Maurice's approval on my own merits, such as they were. I did not love drudgery, as Robin said, but I wasn't fearful of work, either, and I was tired of being handed from master to master, like the least pup from a litter of hounds.

I liked Maurice at first meeting. He was about forty then, a wiry, sand-colored man with a freckled, balding pate. He was always in motion, so he never accumulated that belly which clerks and knights get from so much sitting. Even when he dictated letters he would be up and stalking the chancel, with two other writs in hand, getting the sense of them without losing his thread of thought. He was the most complete and devoted servant to his king I ever knew, but he was never too full of his affairs or office to forget his vocation.

He was truly pious, a fair master, a good teacher, a surrogate father to all in his chapter of St. Paul's who needed a parent sometimes as much as an instructor.

He wasn't dean of the chapter, but he did both dean and bishop's work there. Hugh de Orival, the bishop, was a leper in seclusion from the world. He had left an aged dean to do his pastoral work, but Maurice was his adjutant, which meant he often worked more hours in the day than a peasant.

I decided he was well worth my allegiance and gave it to him without reserve, which, in the eyes of some at St. Paul's, made me a toady. Perhaps I was, but my motive was the best: a good master deserves a good servant.

I began in the most subordinate post of minor clerk, despite my Holy Orders – priest-clerks were common at St. Paul's. But Maurice took note of my industry and soon made better use of it. He stopped by my desk one day and asked:

'Where were you trained, Brother?'

'At St. Vigor-le-Grand, near Bayeux, Chancellor.'

'Ah! Robert de Tombelene's house. A fine scholar. It's too bad about him. They say his house has fallen on hard times, now Bishop Odo is imprisoned. I understand Robert was obliged to give up his rule and go to Italy. Do you know anything about that?'

'No, Chancellor.' I'd heard something of his trials, but I couldn't pretend to be concerned with a man I despised.

'Well, God be good to a noble scholar.' He paused, then asked rather diffidently: 'Do you happen to know much of the English language?'

'A very little, Chancellor. I understand better than speak it – and not the more edifying parts, I fear. But it's hard to forget what they call you when you offend them, and one can offend them just by being French.'

He laughed. 'Yes, no doubt. It's an interesting tongue, but I've never been able to get onto it. I need an interpreter for some old writs I've been studying, with the help of Brother Eadwulf. He's one of our few English brothers left in the chapter and he's getting a bit thick-sighted now. I thought it might be good if one of our own young men took the time to be tutored by him, in his spare moments. The English put all their writs and dooms in the vernacular, you know. We're still obliged to do the same, if we want to make ourselves understood by them. Well, think about it. I don't want to press you if it would be too difficult for you, as it seems to be for so many here.'

I was appalled at the prospect. The English tongue was full of strange sounds I couldn't utter, let alone hope to recognize in script. I had little if any spare time to myself as it was, since Maurice had become my master. I failed to understand why he had chosen me for this task, since there were men in his chancery with greater experience of the English people and their speech. But, as I was eager to make my way with him, I took the hint and presented myself to Brother Eadwulf for instruction.

He was an old man, devoted to the doubtful beauty of his native tongue and delighted to have a pupil. We had permission to meet after chapter in the rolls room, where Eadwulf undertook my education, while my friends Robin and Gerard were refreshing themselves in the dean's parlor with other brothers who enjoyed good talk.

Well, a man who has no leisure to talk, drink, make profit, or be agreeable to women must be good for something. I found I was a readier pupil than I'd feared I'd be, or else Eadwulf was a better teacher. I was no orator in English by six months' time, but I could read it better than any other clerk in the chapter, save a few of the native-born, who had somehow not recommended themselves to Maurice.

My reward for this industry was that at the end of the year Maurice put me to work in the archives, searching out documents for translation long buried in the dust of years. King William had sworn to the English on the day of his crowning that he would govern them according to the best precepts of their ancient kings. It was Maurice's task to see that he knew where the difficulties might be.

It was mole's work, and I was pitied for it by Robin and Gerard, despised for it by others. Any of the English clerks might have done the job, they said, if I weren't such an accomplished lickspittle. But I knew what Maurice wanted, and it wasn't the dull comprehension of mere words, badly translated into bad French.

Before he may have known his true wish himself, or at least before he thought to voice it to me, I began to divide the English dooms into parts, according to their intent, translated them with the aid of

Eadwulf, then collated them to make a volume. It was the work of nearly two years, during which time I hardly saw the light of day outside that portion of it which streamed dustily through the window.

Robin Bloet was wholly exasperated with me:

'Why are you doing this? What will it earn you? Look at you! You're as sallow as an anchorite. This is the way clerks go blind and brain-cracked. You'll be howling at the moon next, if you ever chance to look up and see it!'

'What does it matter what I do? One occupation's as good as another, so long as it harms no one, isn't it?'

'You don't mean that. You're not an ass, to carry firewood. You know who you remind me of? Rufus, risking his neck in one mock massacre after another on the off chance that his father might notice him and give a little nod of approval. He's still at it, and he still hasn't a title, an arpent of land to stable his horse on, or a sou to bless himself with.

'King Alfred was the last monarch of this island to reward scholars, dear boy. If you haven't reached that part yet, let me tell you – he's dead. You have to go a long way past mortal endurance to impress King William Bastard, as your former nurseling shows us, or Rufus would be Earl of Kent in Odo's place. If you want to be appreciated here, show our king how to squeeze more money out of his tenants. Get Maurice to make you a justice in the assizes; learn to wring mites from widows' hands; then you'll blush for all the gratitude you get.'

'I'll think about it.'

'You'll think about it.' He reached out and took me by the back of the cowl. 'Come along out of your fusty den. Gerard's sponsoring a dinner at his own house tonight, for a friend who's down here from St. Cuthbert's in Durham. In case you've forgotten, that's where your dear old master Carileph is now lording it as bishop. Gerard thinks his friend will enjoy hearing you tell how Carileph recommended the London baths to you. Even up north they like something to grin at, now and again. Come on.'

I accepted gladly. My eyes were bleared, and also I had discovered something in the armoires of the rolls room that afternoon which had shaken me.

After Odo's arrest his effects were confiscated to the Crown. His jewels, fine robes, and furniture went into the dispenser's ledgers, to be distributed to others, or hoarded, as the king saw fit. His accounts, ledgers, letters, and such had been brought to St. Paul's for perusal and safekeeping, but apparently had been neglected, except for checking on his goods.

I had found them that day, all packed together in a musty hamper, and I took time from my doom collating to examine them. I was apprehensive that my own name might be mentioned in Odo's works, and was determined to smudge the evidence if it was. I found myself and more.

In a bound volume I found a sizable list of names with varying amounts of money written against them. The name Ranulph occurred with greater regularity than I had ever been paid, so I gathered I wasn't the only Ranulph in his employ. I scotched our name wherever I found it, with a spittle-moistened finger. Then I saw: 'Pay to the harper ten deniers.'

I turned the page and found: 'To the Irishman ten deniers.' A little farther down the name occurred: 'Cormac,' with an amount that made me blink. The entries continued under his name at intervals to the point where Odo's accounting had been interrupted by the king.

I put the book back into the hamper, then sat at my desk brooding on my discovery. How had I been necessary at all to the scheme? Had I been given to Rufus only to provide a more certain way to insinuate Cormac into his confidence? Rufus knew from the moment I was presented to him that I was his uncle's tool, dull as I was. But Cormac came to him without that taint and so deceived us both.

'We'll serve a king someday,' he'd said to me, but it wasn't a king he needed to make of Rufus; it was only a channel for spying on the king, who no longer fully confided in Odo, who favored Lanfranc, or who simply kept silent until he was ready to act. There could be no other use for me than as a diversion, and none other for poor, undistinguished Rufus, except to make him an object for his father's hatred, if that should be necessary. It probably would have been made known in time, if Odo's arrest hadn't intervened.

My shock at finding myself superfluous was mingled with relief. I hadn't been so effective a traitor to my friend as I'd believed. My transgressions were still on my own head, but now at least I knew why it was that nothing I told Odo in his chamber that evening had been real news to him, because Cormac was in his pay, too. I was more than ready for a little diversion that evening when Robin offered it.

When I'd finished my collation of the English law with much help from Eadwulf, I recalled the skills I'd been taught in the scriptorium of St. Vigor: I folded, cut, sewed, and pressed my pages into book covers and presented the volume to Maurice. He was highly pleased. Soon after, he made me his personal clerk and saw to it that the king rewarded me at the next court with a few hides of land near Winchester to add to my income.

'Well! Virtue is its own reward after all,' Robin said. He wasn't envious, but his tone wasn't so patronizingly affectionate as when he'd told Gerard about my rustic background. Gerard congratulated me, too, but there were those in the chapter who felt I had risen far too quickly in the chancellor's esteem for a man without recognizable family connections.

Compared with most of them, who, like Robin and Gerard, were sons of the gentry and not obliged to live entirely on the Church's bounty, I was still a pauper. But the added rents from my pastures and cots in Hampshire, together with my little stipend from Godalming, which I no longer had to share with Odo, made me feel quite wealthy, and I began to think how I might use my riches.

Robin had a house of his own on Watling Street, just below the church. Gerard enjoyed the use of his bishop-uncle's manor near Westminster and kept his mistress there, disguised as his cook. Not a few of the men of St. Paul's chapter had flourishing families of children. Gerard's concubine had given him a son and a daughter.

I had no plans for family life, but I wanted a place of my own to go to sometimes, even if it was only a room at the top of some ramshackle English townhouse, gone to seed. I went out with a fattened purse to find it and found the widow Hermantrude.

She was the relict of a Danish merchant who had built a house on Cornhill, near old St. Peter's. Her sons now had the running of their father's ship and stalls, but not of their mother, as I gathered. Gammer Trudy loved her family well, but couldn't endure that her daughters-in-law do anything about her house except at her direction, even to the stirring of a pot of broth. Three women at variance before one hearth had made for so much strife that the men built a second house for themselves and their families, but as yet had made no suitable agreement with their mother as to what should become of their portion of her house.

I got wind of this in the marketplace and, after a period of confused discussion and heated debate among them, I bought a half interest in the house, leaving Gammer Trudy with her portion intact until she might wish to sell it to me. She remained, to cook me a meal when I had the leisure to dine at home, and to wash my bedclothes when they required it. She and I were delighted with our bargain, though her sons still looked uncertain if they had made the best bargain. I went out to find a carpenter who would make me a bedstead, a table, and a few stools. Trudy agreed to supply me with a straw pallet, a feather mattress, even a tablecloth when I needed one, in exchange for a reasonable price and my remembrance of her name in my daily prayers.

It was delightful to anticipate my new freedom, while I waited for her sons to remove themselves to their new abode. My free moments from the chancel I spent in the marketplace like a thrifty wife, buying up household goods. I must have a basin to wash my face, a candlestick for my table when there were guests, a cresset bowl to give more economic light when I was alone. I bought cruets for oil and vinegar, a leather jack to bring home wine from the wineshop; my purse was growing slender, but I was as happy as a jackdaw.

When at last Trudy's sons had departed and my own things were in place at the top of the house, I discovered what I might have known before: I had no time to enjoy my solitude. The same devotion to Maurice, which made possible my purchase of luxuries, made impossible my idleness to enjoy them.

I habitually presented myself to him for instructions in the day's work just after Prime. The orders might be changed before Terce, doubled by Sext, or thrown to the winds if the king should come, if Lanfranc sent messages, or if some angry alderman should stride into the chancel demanding a hearing.

The king might make laws or abolish them, and Lanfranc might be his second self, but it was Maurice and his host of scurrying clerks who kept the realm from collapsing into confusion.

The moment of my release from toil usually wasn't offered until Compline, when I took Maurice's blessing, bade him good night, and retired. Then I would seize a heavy stick I kept in the writ room, with which to beat off the abominable dogs that roamed like wolves about St. Paul's, and I'd rush off to luxuriate in the spartan comforts of my solitary room and bed.

I would stand at my single window, shutters opened to savor the peace of a night without other snoring clerks. I'd look down from my vantage to the smoking chimney holes and warped rooftops below Cornhill to where the moon-glinting river lay, its quays crowded with shadowed ships. I often scanted sleep to savor the richness of my solitude.

Yet, there is a contradiction of the human mind that has provoked and puzzled me all my life. At the very moment when I am conscious of my delight in being alone, I always find myself wishing there was someone with whom to share my pleasure! Leaning from my window or resting on my bed, my heart wouldn't turn to those meditations that will improve the soul, but I would begin to consider how I was alone, had ever been, and would be until my death. Then I would begin to wonder if there was enough work in the world to keep me busy.

I was twenty-seven. I would never be a scholar. I had no capacity for the spiritual life my vocation demanded, though Maurice's influence had made me more dutiful to my Office. I would never win high office in the chancel, unless at the extreme of old age. On what could I set my eyes for my future?

It was disheartening to me then to know I had no great passion for anything in life but safety and peace, the security of labor, and the possession of a few domestic trinkets. When I was dead, would men say of me that I had valued nothing more than these and the approval of Maurice? It was disturbing to think it, but if I had died that year, as many did of the fever, that would have been my epitaph.

King William was a man one might have pitied. He had never had but one true friend, and he'd lost him years gone by. His eldest son was prodigal and fled him. His nearest kin by blood and wit, his brother Odo, he'd imprisoned for his treasons. His fruitful, pious wife, whom he'd made alien by family dissent, had died the year following Odo's fall. Men he had made powerful used their strength to plot against him.

One could well have pitied him if any of this had ever made him other than he was: cold, avaricious, and grim, more suspicious every year, and ever less apt to praise or reward those who remained true.

When he was in England, which was seldom, he divided his time between hunting, his only pleasure in the ordinary sense, and complaining to Lanfranc or Maurice about the growing burden of his household expenses, which in fact did grow with every year.

He had enough mouths to feed to beggar the Goddess of Plenty, what with the ever increasing number of landless knights he kept about him. He'd made no new barons, made no new Earl of Kent to succeed Odo, but kept the revenues of vacant earldoms as he had since the revolt of '75. Still, the revenues from those vast estates seemed to shrink, not grow, though cattle will multiply and not every year can be a bad one for crops.

It was with some reason he suspected his bailiffs of withholding the true value of his revenues from him. His sheriffs had made themselves rich at his expense, each with the help of the barons they taxed. There were sixty thousand knights' fees in his realm, but who could say what their lands were worth?

One day Maurice returned from enduring a long session on the problem and came to us in the writ room looking quite worn down.

'I sometimes wonder why I wouldn't stay in Lorraine and become an abbot's chancellor, as my father wanted,' he sighed. He accepted a cup of watered wine from Robin while I unlaced his sandals and rubbed his ankles, swollen from long hours of standing before the king.

'You wouldn't have fared better. It's the same work, with worse drink,' said Robin.

I said, not really thinking of the words, but like a goodwife commiserating with her lord: 'If the king's not satisfied with what his sheriffs farm for him, why doesn't he take an inventory of his lands and see what they really hold, as any knight would do of his farms and vills?'

Maurice hooted comically. 'Oho, oh, yes, I should think so! And whom would he get to do his counting? Me? No, thank you very much!'

'Well, he could trust you, at least. You'd want the help of a lot of clerks, but we don't lack for them.'

'Our clerks would get their heads bashed in if they went to count sheep and beehives and make thieves out of the king's officers, Ranulph. God help them, they haven't much brain, but do they deserve that?' said Robin.

'But it would be at the king's behest. They couldn't be refused. And what about sending along some of those free lances he keeps, to see they're safe?'

Both Maurice and Robin grinned at me, but I defended my green notion:

'The king wouldn't think it so difficult. He marshals ten thousand men to march on the Welsh. Why not an army of clerks to make his inventory?'

'The fyrd is different. There is a chain of allegiance, command, duty. Who would command the clerks to be obedient to the soldiers, or vice versa? Or who would command the mercenaries not to sell themselves to the sheriffs, and who would bear the expense for it? The king would. He'd be spending more coin than he could hope to discover was being kept from him. Impossible!'

Nevertheless, the debate continued for another half hour before we dropped it. They kept piling up difficulties in the way of my army of clerks; I kept making light of their points and offering rash confidence in a group of men I knew to be fully as venal as any layman, until I sounded foolish to myself.

However impossible and naive Maurice declared he found my notion, he didn't forget it. On the next day he brought it out again for criticism.

'You know what you suggested, don't you, Ranulph? You were suggesting a census. That's what really makes it impossible; *census is* a word of evil omen. Every landowner in the realm would be piously reminding us of what befell King David when the Devil put it into his head to number the Jews from Beersheba even unto Dan.'

'Oh, yes,' Robin added, laughing, 'and those who don't curl up with the plague will come to us with their prodigies: 'Please, *hlaford*, the king's men come and counted all our cows and now our Sukie's borned a two-headed bull calf. 'Tis a curse on th' work, I tell 'e, loike the Scriptures says.' And there will be strange things seen in the skies, and that filthy little spring up near Finchampstead will bubble up blood again.'

'Now, don't make fun of that spring,' Maurice said swiftly. 'I've seen it myself, and it does give up something very much like blood – dark, sticky, and with a foul smell. Don't make light of the Scriptures, either. For shame, Ranulph, for laughing at him! I only say, *census is* a bad word and that's what it would be. We'll think of something else now.'

But we didn't. My idea, unshaped as a bear's cubling, wouldn't die, so we licked it into better form. It was Maurice's doing for the most part, and I willingly give him credit for making it such that the king could accept it. More than that, he made it such that the king could take it for his own and did, so warmly that Maurice could never be blamed if it should go awry. Yet the Recording Angel knows that it was I who first imagined the taking of that Great Survey, or inquest of the realm, which to this day is so familiar and so cursed that I need describe it no further.

The king chose to call his census an inquiry, but the great vassals and churchmen who held temporal honors weren't deceived. They predicted the very preternatural wonders Robin had forecast. Geoffrey de Mowbray, lord of Northumberland and Bishop of Coutances, as well as the second man after Lanfranc in the king's court, was also first among the critics. The king dealt with him admirably: he made him chief inquisitor and left him to form his council and get the work done, which suited Geoffrey's temper well. He was a hard old man who lived like a Caesar in his own northern county, all but forgetting that he was a priest as well, unless it was when he looked at a clerk. He would never allow this enterprise to go astray and leave him to blame.

Maurice was to be congratulated.

'He'll make you archbishop of Canterbury for this, when Lanfranc's gone,' I said to him.

'Oh, I doubt that very much,' Maurice said hastily, but by all that's holy he blushed. The idea had occurred to him, too, and he wanted it more than he would allow.

'But then we'll want another easy chancellor to take your place over us,' Robin said, winking at me.

'I'll be chancellor, if you like,' Gerard offered, just coming into the room in time to hear of the vacancy.

'You! You'd be easy enough. You're so lazy, Ranulph and I would be doing all the work! No, I think we'll make you bishop of London. Poor old Hugh de Orival's proved we can get along without one. We'll make Ranulph chancellor; then none of us will have to work. He'd gladly carry the whole burden on his fine, strong back, wouldn't you, dear boy?'

'Poor Hugh, God be merciful to him,' Maurice said, suddenly sobered. 'I hear he's finally dying. What a dreadful thing it must be, to see your own flesh rot off your body while you still live! He and I were clerks together here under old Bishop William. I've meant to pray for him daily, but other matters have often made me forget. Let us pray for him, now, my brothers.' He sank to his knees and we followed.

God rest Hugh the Leper, Bishop of London, for he died not two weeks after that day when I gave him scant help with my prayers. I scarcely thought of him at all, because my mind was stunned by Robin's light suggestion that I might be made chancellor in Maurice's place. Maurice would certainly get a bishopric as reward for service to the king, as all his predecessors had. Someone would take his place, and who better fitted for it than I?

Of course I had no reason to believe it could happen, but I was startled to find how much I liked the idea. After all, there was some hunger left in me.

The king being away and Maurice with him, a lull fell on my activity. I took up the study of English laws again in a more practical manner, going as clerk to the dean of St. Paul's to the weekly hustings. The town courts were held on the high field behind St. Paul's and the west cheap. There the portreeve and a representative of the Church sat each week to hear the suits of the London townsmen, one against the other. The portreeve, as chief magistrate of the town, heard all the civil cases, and the dean, as representative of the vacant bishop's throne, was privileged (or cursed) to hear all the ecclesiastical ones. The dean, being a Norman and having all the understanding of the English that most Normans have, took me along as clerk and translator.

It wasn't an easy task. The English are a litigious race and a mixed race, too. It was a harsh gabble of bastard dialects, Saxon, Welsh, Angle, Jute, and Danish, that had amalgamated themselves into the London tongue. I thought if dogs could be taught speech, it was English that would be most agreeable to them.

Then how disagreeable it was for me, when I attempted to pronounce their barbaric syllables in a civilized manner the dean could comprehend, and saw the portreeve, the English aldermen, and even the frothing litigants relax their furrowed brows and smile at me as if I were a lisping simpleton!

It was after such a time that I was paying glum attention to a case of assault on a city officer, a civil case. The dean was already falling into a doze.

There had been a brawl over the sale of a stinking fish at a stall near Billingsgate. The alderman of that ward had been browsing nearby when, attracted by the riot, he came with all proper dignity to break up the fight between seller and buyer. The aldermen of London are creatures of much self-esteem, well gowned, with flowing mustaches and long, plaited hair. The Londoners give them so much respect that there is little need for them to go through the streets armed or protected, or to show more force then that of a raised voice. But this alderman was unfortunate.

The fish seller and his customer were locked in combat on the ground, with their partisans cheering, when he commanded them to desist and stand up. They heeded him not. He made to separate them, seizing each by the hair, like naughty boys, and one of them, the buyer of the spoiled hake, struck him in the face with the object of discussion. Seeing whom he had offended, the poor misguided wretch tried to escape, knocking over the alderman in the process and stepping on him. He was captured by the same friends who had lately been cheering him.

It is a grave offense to strike the officer of the peace, as the man knew the instant he'd done it. He pleaded innocence of intent, saying he'd thought it was the fish-seller's brother who'd laid hands on him, but this wasn't sufficient, nor was the testimony of his friends that he was a good enough man when he wasn't enraged or drunk.

So the portreeve judged him guilty. His punishment was that he was obliged to walk in penance from the place of judgment to the church of his parish, carrying the ax with which penalty would be imposed for striking an alderman: the loss of a hand.

His wife shrieked and fell on the ground: 'My man is a fusterer! How will he carve the wood with only one hand? How will he feed without his work? Bastard Frenchmen!' She sat up and pointed a finger at the alderman: 'Our lives will be on his head! May he eat stinking fish until he dies, the son of a slut!'

There was a communal cry of outrage – slut only just approaches what she really called his mother – and the portreeve's men snatched her up from the ground still cursing. The penalty for insulting an alderman is a fine or the cucking stool, so the distraught woman was hauled away to be tied to that humiliating device and swung aloft from a rope to the delight of the crowd. Her child remained standing before us, a thin, miserable little urchin with bare legs and a ragged tunic. No one else paid the least attention to him. That was the final case for the day; the court and its hearers began to disperse for the day meal.

It seemed to me that someone might give a thought for the boy, who seemed too dazed by his double tragedy even to weep. Trudy could be persuaded to give him a meal and shelter, until his mother was released from the cucking stool.

I stepped off the platform raised to hold the judges above the crowd and called to the boy, smiling to reassure him. At the sound of my voice and my sudden movement, he started out of his mournful daze, his upper body swinging halfway around as he frowned at me. As the slender form moved in its thin garment, I saw I'd made a mistake. It was a young female who stared at me with pale eyes out of a little wedge of a face. Her dark, dusty-looking hair was half torn from its short plaits by the gusting winds of early spring. She must have been shorn for some childhood fever, I thought, and my eyes went once again to the very slight hillocks her breasts made in her earth-colored tunic. I had stopped when she turned, but I started forward again.

'God-daeg, dohter – '

At the sound of my voice she made a muffled sound, like a mouse shriek, and fled from me. I ran after her, shouting 'Stopen!' and all the variations of the word I could think of, but she only ran faster. I was almost within grasp of one of her wildly pumping thin elbows when she flung me another look over her shoulder that made me break my pace as if she'd jabbed me in the stomach. She disappeared into the butcher's street while I stood, gasping: 'Go, then. You probably have fleas!' Yet those glass-green eyes haunted me for the rest of the day.

21

Men must build stout traps to catch even the weakest of God's creatures, but what a slender snare it takes to capture a man. I looked for those green eyes in every face, until I began to believe I must have been bewitched. They had been elf's eyes, so long they were, with such clear whites that flashed at me through the lusterless tangle of her hair.

On the Eve of May even gray, coin-snatching London lets its right hand forget its cunning for a night and goes flower gathering beyond its walls, dances in the mild air, sings foolish songs. In the old times they burned great fires all night on Ludgate Hill and on the White Mound, where the king's new castle was now built. Beltane fires, named for some green god, or bone fires, because old bones were burned in them as well as wood to disgust and banish the evil spirits that like to hover over the doings of Man.

The great fires are now forbidden inside the town walls for fear of a general holocaust, but no one stops the kindling of little fires in gardens, even in churchyards. The nuns of Barking Abbey still make theirs and leap over them, holding hands and laughing like farm girls on May Eve.

Maurice always diplomatically removed himself from town on the occasion of the old holidays, lest he should find cause to rebuke his clerks for making May-fools of themselves. His departure, and the dean's, was our release. While the older brothers went to nap and sun themselves in our chapter garden, we younger ones rushed off to join the Maying.

Robin, Gerard, and I went marketing for a private feast we meant to hold in my new quarters. We bought a lamb for Trudy to roast, spring greens for a porrey to lighten our winter blood, and plenty of wine to wash it all down with.

When the lamb was spitted, we left it to Trudy and went to watch the antics of the dancers around that old Roman item known as the London Stone, from which the procession would begin.

The dancers wore masks, foolish or fearful, depending on whether they were seen by sun or firelight. Now they were comical: cocks strutted, bulls pawed the ground, horses tossed their heads, crones hobbled, and goggle-eyed monsters preened themselves that were difficult to describe. There was one in the shape of a beaming giant, who wore a monstrous great pizzle, under which he held concealed a pig's bladder filled with ale – or was it cow's piss? To have him affect to piss on someone was a delight to the crowd and was held to be good luck for the person who was drenched.

When the masked dancers had wound their way several times around the London Stone, they trailed out along the streets leading east, not all going by the same route. We followed a stream of silly, joyous people down Langbourne to the east cheap, then to the tower mound, where they met the others who'd gone by the lower streets and joined in a very Babel of a serenade, crowing, bawling, neighing, and bleating derisively at the iron-capped members of the king's garrison there, before ambling toward Aldgate.

Along the east cheap street I heard a cry of 'Thief! Thief!' but no one paid heed. Theft is a kind of privilege at the time of that frolic, if it's in moderation, it being believed that an easy loss then is a portent of plenty in the summer to come.

A red-faced baker struggled briefly to get through the mob to a fleeting figure, then gave it up, bawling: 'The slut's done me again!' I gawked backward at him, the crowd parted slightly; then someone thudded hard into my chest; fingers clutched at my cowl, swinging me halfway around.

'Hide me! Hide me, till he goes by!'

The crowd closed around us. She lifted her head. It was the green-eyed girl, or else I was truly bewitched. Her face changed when she saw me. 'Oh, Lud, a priest. I only took a honey cake. See? I'll give you half.'

I caught her by the arms as she put half the cake into her mouth. 'Don't you know what happens to thieves yet, girl?'

'The same as happens to eggs – they get smashed!' She jerked a hand free, dropped the half cake down my cowl, and smacked it flat

227

to my chest. It was like having a large beetle crushed against my skin. I flinched; she was free and dodging through the other bodies, screaming with laughter.

Robin and Gerard had been swept somewhat apart from me, but not too distantly to see that. They nearly split their mouths with joy for my mishap, then led me to an ale shop near the gate to repair my dignity.

Spring ale is powerful stuff, having been long in the barrel. It will befuddle a man quicker than wine kept for the same length of time, which generally only turns to verjuice. A few cups of it and the loan of the housekeeper's sponge to wipe the sticky mess from my throat and chest, and I was in a better mood. We decided to forgo our dinner awhile longer and follow the revelers out into the swampy meadows.

By sundown we were well beyond the gate, and I was beyond anger for anyone. We had ambled for a mile or so toward higher ground where there was feasting. We were offered food and drink in plenty and had been spat upon many times for luck. Gerard had strayed from us, remaining behind with a plump matron who fed him food with her fingers, which he kissed in blessing after they poked each morsel into his mouth.

The dancers had long since vanished, their places being taken in a more engaging way by the women and younger men, who wore daisy garlands and clover chains. Robin joined a ring of them at some time just about twilight, his gown tucked up in his cincture to show off his fine brown hose and calf-high leather boots. His lamb's rump of a curly head bobbed out of my sight, and I fell down in the grass on my back to rest, stuffed with food, dizzy with the mixture of drinks I'd swilled. I closed my eyes and listened to the whispering around me.

The dancers being gone, those who were left soon fell to snoring or to love making. If they were shy of being seen near the firelight, they got up and ran past it into more amiable darkness. After a time I looked about without lifting my head and wondered lazily if those forms I saw flitting were really naked, or only smoke phantoms from the downwind fire.

Someone out of breath and happy fell down beside me, gasping. 'Did you like your honey cake?'

Her hair was wild and stuck through with little white flowers, as if she'd been newborn out of a rose briar, but that wasn't the least of it. The bodice of her rough gown was opened and let down about her waist. Her nymphlike arms and breasts were gleaming in the firelight as if anointed with oil. Her smile was drunken; her teeth gleamed like the white of her eyes.

When I attempted to sit up, she pushed me back to my elbows, then stripped off one or two of her flower chains and put them about my head.

'There, now, I've given you something else, so you needn't be angry still. Are you? Say you're not and I'll give you something better.' She laughed softly, like some elf woman who comes out of the ground to confound a traveler. I wanted to bless myself, but I wanted more to touch her. She reached into a bag she wore at her waist and took something out of it like another cake.

'You've been to the baker's again.'

'No, they gave this to me. Eat it. It's better than honey cake.'

I lay back, examined it briefly to make certain it wasn't a sheep fart, then popped it into my mouth. It was sweet at first, then bitter, but before I could rise and spit it out her mouth came down and fastened itself over mine, taking part of it back and forcing me to swallow the rest. My fear was somewhat allayed about its being foul, since she had eaten some. As she hung over me I touched, then fondled, the incredible texture of her breasts, which were at once soft and firm and sticky with the ointment. My palms felt icy where they cupped her, then peculiarly warm.

'What is this stuff you're smeared with?'

She lifted her head and giggled. 'I stole it from one of the dancers. It serves him right for not letting me in. They said I wasn't one of them, didn't have a partner. But you'll be my partner, won't you? And we'll laugh at them.'

I sat up, catching her firmly by both arms. 'You're no child to dance in a posy ring. I thought you were, but – what in the name of Hell *is* this stuff you're gummed with?'

'It's theirs, too. I stole it. I've got more, see?' She produced from her purse a little leaf-wrapped glob of it, like melted tallow. 'They say if you put it on, you can fly. Do you want some? We'll fly over them; it'll serve them right.'

'No man can fly, greased or otherwise. They've lied to you, *deorling*, which serves you right. Throw it away and lie down by me. You'll do better than fly, I promise.' I pulled her down and kissed her mouth and her throat, where there was more grease. While I did, she ran her hand up my sleeve and rubbed some of the filthy stuff into my armpit.

'Stop that!' My lips and chin had begun to tingle from being smeared with the grease. She giggled and rolled on her back. She was only a little whore from the stews after all.

We tumbled about for a bit, but no matter how I tried to master her, she laughed and squirmed away and streaked me on the head and throat with her vile unguent. After a time my head began humming as if a whole tribe of bees had swarmed in my skull, and my stomach gave an ominous lurch. I rolled onto my back, lest I be sick and spoil the lovemaking. The sky shifted above me and the earth seemed to tilt. I closed my eyes. The elf girl bent over me, touched my lips; then I felt her hand stroking up my thighs. She took my private members between her fingers and gently kneaded them until they, too, became ice, then fire.

A sudden fear shot through me, increasing my nausea; she wasn't fondling me; the filthy slut was busy poisoning me with her witch salve! Why? For love of evil, or revenge for her father? I was dying from her play.

I tried to shove her aside with arms that had suddenly grown heavy. I rolled over onto my stomach, retching, struggled to hands and knees. 'Christ, why – get away! Let me be!' I vomited mightily. I felt her leave me. She was on her feet, but still hovered near.

'It isn't supposed to make you sick! It's only for the dancing. They can leap so high – it didn't make me sick!'

I stumbled to my feet. She shrank back from me, her face a white blur in the light from the fire. I heard a buzz of other voices; my head swam; and the great heat she'd engendered made me think my skin might be peeling off. I lurched after her, it seemed on air. She faded away as I came forward; then she was running and I was running – or flying – after her. Though I knew my legs moved and I didn't rise above the trees, I thought I flew. My heart was pounding in my chest as though it would burst as I labored forward up a long, sloping hill with a thin crown of trees.

There was another fire among those trees and shapes moving about it. A terrible fear came over me that I was flying toward my death there, yet I couldn't stop. What shape it would take I couldn't imagine, but it would be dreadful beyond ordinary death.

She tripped in the dark and I ran into her. We both fell painfully and lay groaning together in the dark. There was laughter from nearby and singing from farther off. I reached out and found her bare back under my hand. The terrible ice and fire still contended with each other to freeze or burn me, but I was no longer sick or drunk. I felt for her arm and turned her over.

She was sobbing quietly as I bent over her, but the effect of her damned salve had worked into her blood, too. She threshed about in the cool grass for a little while, cried out something about 'not before the Blessing,' then lay gasping while I attended to the main business of the night.

I woke in my own bed, with no memory of how I'd gotten there. From where I lay I could see the ravaged remains of dinner on my table. Had I eaten it, or had Gerard and Robin come back before me? I couldn't tell. I fell over the edge of the bed to my feet and surveyed my nakedness, streaked with mud, blood, and something greenish, like grass stains. With a jolt, memory of the past night returned. Even worse was my apprehension of the present. Behind me on the bed there was another body. I could hear its light breathing.

I shrank away from the bed, though I was unable to see any more of the sleeper than a tuft of dark hair just above the covers. Quickly, I put on my shirt and gown, thrown on the floor. I slipped down the stairs, wishing to avoid Trudy, and went out into the street. It was a dazzling day, already a quarter gone by the look of the sun, which hurt my eyes. Bells were ringing near and far, to tell me the pious were at worship on this feast day of the good Apostles Philip and James, while the ungodly skulked about the streets with bad heads or remained in bed, sleeping off their folly.

Before I reached the Walbrook I realized I couldn't go up to St. Paul's in my present state, nor could I confess myself, or hear a service, looking as I did. I slowed my pace and at last stopped to loiter about the boundaries of the churchyard, which as yet was not filled with its daily mob of litigants and food hawkers.

There was an early-rising seller of holy medals. I purchased one from him, to his astonishment. Priests were never among his customers. I clutched it to my breast, rubbing it over my heart for protection, without even looking to see which saint it might represent. I was beginning to dread witch enchantment again.

What had I done? It was bad enough I had courted damnation, lying with a witch when I was drunk and half lunatic from the poison she'd smeared on me. But to bring her home with me, ravish her in my bed, as I probably had, then leave her there alone – where she could wake and lay spells on all I owned! If she got hold of some article belonging to me, even a nail paring, what torments would she fix on me hereafter?

How could I have deceived myself into thinking she was only a common girl? I should have been warned by that look she'd fixed on me the first time we met, which I couldn't rid my memory of. And there was the way she'd stood tearless while her parents were carried off to punishment; witches are unable to shed tears for anything. I began to wish I had bought yet more medals, because I would surely need them before I could face that room again.

Once I began to think of returning there, my feet turned me to the path against my will. I dragged and dawdled, but irresistibly approached the house on Cornhill. I thought of going to the priest of St. Peter's with my fears, but pride forbade it. I knew him too well. Or was it that I was already held in a spell that forbade me to confess myself?

By the time I reached my house I was drenched in sweat, but I went inside, passed a grave and accusing Trudy, and went upstairs. The room was unchanged; the creature was still invisible under the bedclothes. I hung over the bed, listening to her slight buzzing snore, wanting to see her face while she still slept, but doubtful about turning back the covers. What if she weren't human at all? What if the face I exposed to the light had a snout and tusks, or a goat's nose, or if there was a second fiendish face where her belly should be? Such monsters had been the terror of my childhood after hearing one of the brothers of St. Vigor expound on demons.

I closed my eyes, said a prayer, but my fingers reached out of their own accord and drew back the covers.

She rolled her head, frowned, and brushed at the air with one hand, but continued to sleep, her upper lip protruding, the lower one slightly tucked in. Her body's reek assailed me, but there was nothing horrid to mar the perfection of her flat little belly. I was about to discover whether she might still not have a cloven foot when the movement of the covers woke her.

She snatched them back up under her arms in a moment, looking most offended, but there was something in her manner that wasn't truly surprised, so I gathered I had been mistaken in supposing her asleep. I sat carefully on the side of the bed. Her eyes glanced at me, then at the ceiling and around the room. She yawned, scratched her head vigorously, sat up, still drawing the sheets after her, but not with any great determination.

I fetched a sigh for my soul, because there was such power in her spell. I was about to do what no sane man would, if he believed of her what I did. I put my hand on her arm, and drew her hand to me. She snatched it back, but I took it again and very slowly kissed it. She couldn't have looked more baffled if I'd kissed a hound's foot.

'What're you doing?'

'Don't you know?'

'I thought you were going to bite me,' she said in disgust. Her eyes turned toward the table. 'You've got a good bed. You eat well, too. You must be rich, priest.'

'I feel very rich at the moment. Will you make me richer?'

She gave a laugh of astonishment. 'How could I do that?'

We looked at each other in perplexity, she, as if she were nothing but the ignorant waif she pretended to be, and I, because it seemed to me I deserved something in addition to the use of her body in exchange for the ruin of my soul.

'Will you stay with me?' I kissed her grubby hand again.

'Huh!' There was a great hauteur in the sound, but she glanced at the table again. 'Will you feed me?'

'Of course I'll feed you. Are you hungry now?' What an odd request. 'What else would you want of me?'

'What else? Well – I'd want a good gown and a pair of shoes – not clogs – and a comb, and a chape, and – ' Her eyes cut back to me and she added indignantly: 'That's little enough, to let a Frenchman slobber on me.'

'Very little indeed.'

She drew her knees up and became quite crisp. 'Yes, even the baker offered me that much to keep his fire and sleep with him. If you lie with me in this bed, then I sleep the night here, too. It's plenty wide enough and I'm tired of the floor.'

She slid off the far side of the bed, taking the blanket for a robe, and went to the table, where she grabbed up a lamb's rib and stripped it. She held out the bone for my inspection. 'That's not too much, is it? I'm not a glutton.'

This was scarcely the sort of bargain I'd expected. Was she a very subtle witch, or only a selfish, lazy one? I thought it must be the latter and decided I'd better speak up while I still had the power to do so, as she was already making my head spin with the bold way she looked at me and the careless manner in which she covered her flanks with the blanket.

'It's very gracious of you to offer to be my hearth girl, but I can get one of those with no trouble. I want to be the king's chancellor.'

She stared at me for a long moment; then her hand went out carefully for another piece of lamb roast. 'What's that?'

'The king's chief clerk of the chancel. See here, if we're to have a bargain, this is one thing we must get settled. I'll take nothing less for my soul.'

She stuffed more lamb into her mouth, a huge gobbet that bulged one cheek, but even then it seemed she was about to agree. The corner of her mouth curled as she chewed.

'You think I'm a witch, don't you?'

'I never supposed you were the Blessed Virgin.'

She stuffed in more lamb. Her voice was necessarily muffled: 'That's what you want from me?'

'If you're capable. If not, we might as well say farewell.'

Very sternly she said: 'I could turn you into a donkey.' She extended one hand, making two fingers wiggle at me.

I experienced a little qualm, but I said bravely: 'As to that, I have friends who saw me with you. If they find a donkey inhabiting my quarters, they'll know whom to fling in the river to see if she floats.'

She swallowed, wiped her mouth with her hand, and nodded wisely. 'Well, it doesn't matter, since you're all going to Hell, you Normans. But if you're going to be the – whatever it is – you can afford to give me two gowns and a shift as well, or I won't lie with you, because the Devil may love you, but I hate Frenchmen!'

That truly alarmed me. I hastened to placate her. My efforts were so earnest, or so magically directed by her will, that in a little while I was permitted to ratify our contract by carrying her back to bed.

That summer a rumor came to us by way of some German merchants that King Canute of Denmark, a namesake of that Dane who had once ruled England, was assembling a war fleet on the Finnish coast to sail to England and reconquer it to his own glory.

King William was in Normandy again when the warning reached him. He didn't view it as an unlikely event, in spite of his own hold on the land. Canute was of the heroic mold. He was also the new-made son-in-law of Robert the Frisian, Count of Flanders, who was the Lady Matilda's brother and therefore King William's in-law. He was also, notoriously, his enemy. In the king's view it was Robert of Flanders who had stirred up young Canute to make war on us.

To prevent this, the king brought over to England the greatest army of mercenaries anyone had ever seen here, even in the days of William's conquest. They came from France, Maine, Brittany, even Italy, and he scattered them from the Scottish borders to the Wash. To prevent Canute's finding either aid or sustenance if he landed, they burned the fields and vills that hugged the coast.

These mercenaries were too great an expense even for the king to feed, so he billeted them in every castle and manor within two days' ride of the coast. There was an outcry from the people who were dispossessed and ruined, naturally, but the fear of the Dane was on them, too, so they bore it.

Summer waned and the autumn rains began. The fields that should have nourished the eastern counties lay stark, burned and fallow, and the people of those counties were hungry. It was time for the ancestral 'autumn viking,' but still the Danes didn't come. Meanwhile the mercenaries ravaged everywhere – worse than the Danes, some said.

The king had made a stern law forbidding pillage, but couldn't enforce it strictly. If too many of his paid knights were blinded, castrated, or maimed for theft and rapine, his bought army would disintegrate. So, some he fined and a few he sent overseas, but many he ignored.

I might have been more deeply concerned about these dangers, as Maurice and Lanfranc surely were, but my greatest difficulty was that when the king moved about the country, Maurice followed him, so I was obliged to follow Maurice, as he had given me the honor of keeping the great seal of William Bastard which he appended to his grants and charters when they were signed and witnessed.

The survey of the realm was just getting under way, too. It seemed the worst possible year in which to determine our wealth, but when the army of clerks returned from the hundred-courts with their information, all the clerks of our chancel were needed to read the figures, question, prove, and compare them with what was known before. I should have cared something for that, too, but all that occupied my mind was what was in my bed in London.

If we were within a day's ride of the town, I would make some excuse to Maurice and fly off for a night in my witch's arms. I wasn't able to do that very often, but when I wasn't with her I was dreaming about her. It was suicidal to my ambition, which I knew, even if my friends didn't remind me of it constantly.

'Why don't you just go stick your head in a furnace, or volunteer to be a bell ringer in some Cornish monastery where the abbot runs barefoot among his pigs?' Robin suggested. 'Because that's what this is going to earn you eventually.'

'My dear Ranulph,' Gerard said, 'if it's a woman you need, let me find you an amiable one here. It isn't my usual line of work, I hasten to say, but for a friend in need, I could produce a handsome widow who's very discreet.'

'It isn't your widow he wants, Gerard. He's in love. Don't you recognize the awful symptoms?'

'But who is she? Who could there be in London? The portreeve's wife? The abbess of Barking?' Gerard burbled with laughter at his own suggestion because the abbess of Barking was about a hundred and two and notoriously ugly.

'It isn't – I can't say anything about it. I'm not in love.' I had to leave it at that, since I could hardly admit I had been bewitched by my hearth girl, whether she was a witch or not, and about that I had begun to have serious doubts. 'It's probably something like the summer flux that will pass. I'll stay here, so you don't neglect your own work puzzling over me. Does that satisfy?'

It must suffice, because when we moved to Gloucester there was no possibility for a swift ride to London. I applied myself to work, rose early, took purges and cold baths, burned candles by the score to the Virgin, and made a guarded confession about being too much taken by the desires of the flesh. But it did no good. Though I doubled the penance imposed on me and wearied my confessor with my frailties, I couldn't get her out of my head.

Her name was Elfgiva. It's a name borne by full half the English women who aren't named Ethelburga, or Edith, I suppose. It's a ludicrous name for most of them, because it means 'elf gift' and they're too solid and earthly to bear it. But for her it was perfectly suited, both to her slender form and deviable mind, which I could no more fathom than if she had truly come out from under a magic hill.

She said she was an orphan, or that her father was a potent warlock, or that she'd lived by her enchantments since she was a babe, though with a common family. She disclaimed any memory of having seen me before, though I still believed her to be that saddletree carver's child who'd had his hand chopped.

She affected to be very haughty with me, refused to remember my name or to call me 'master.' She sneered at my accent when I spoke English, but was equally scornful of my attempts to teach her French, though in fact she remembered what words I taught her. Yet, in spite of all this belittlement, she didn't leave me or rob me. She brightened visibly when I came to interrupt her days with Trudy and, by certain delightful signs, gave me reason to think I pleased her in bed almost as much as she delighted me, though neither of us uttered a word on that matter.

Her age mystified me, as my interest in it baffled her: 'What do you care about that? I'm young. I've got all my teeth, see? When they start to fall out, then I'll be old.'

Trudy became very protective of her, which more than anything lessened my belief in Elfgiva's eldritch origins, for old Trudy was a pious but very shrewd woman, a merchant's wife accustomed to examining goods for defects. She'd looked pinch-mouthed at me the first day, but she soon took my girl under her authority and saw Elfgiva didn't lack for company or an occupation while I was absent.

Elfgiva's favorite occupation – besides eating, muttering against the Normans, and letting me lie with her – was emptying out my bathwater. I had some difficulty persuading her that my occasional baths were harmless and not a sign of dangerous insanity. It was harder still to get her to join me in them. The first time, in fact, was rather like trying to wash a bitch wolf, and she continued to scoff at my eccentricity even when she came to accept it.

But when the soaping and scrubbing were done, she was more than eager to grab a bucket to empty our tub. The game was to see if she could get to the window and find a victim before I cried' 'Ware the slops' to clear the street below. A scream of rage and anguish from some unwary wretch caught walking after dark would send her into a paroxysm of infantile joy, until I clapped a hand over her mouth and dragged her from the window to the bed, naked, wet, and slippery as a trout.

She was a sore trial to me, and I felt a fool for being enthralled with such an uncivilized chit, but nothing she did could have put me from her. The whole purpose of my life became to gaze upon, contend with, feed, fondle, and lie with Elfgiva. Her place was as secure as if she really had put a spell on me. I knew if I ever came home, even wearing the chancellor's chain of office I coveted, and found her gone, I would sicken and most likely die, as if she'd cursed me.

The Danes still not having shown their dragon ships on our horizons, we celebrated Christmas in Gloucester. There so many people came crowding into the court to complain of the king's mercenaries, or to present petitions for redress of their wrongs, that we clerks were pushed out of the tower entirely and had to be housed on the town and even in the nave of the church, where it was bitter cold.

It was a surly feast the king kept for Christ that year, though he displayed himself with more magnificence at his crown wearing than in any year before. Regrettably, his velvet tunic, silken mantle, and golden rings did little to disguise his grim face and his sunken, watchful eyes, or to hide the monstrously bloated belly he'd grown.

He sat alone on the dais in his splendor, none of his sons being with him, and received his guests and petitioners coldly.

The gifts they brought him were more welcome than their

laments. He examined the jewels, the furs, the rich armor and rare ornaments, with the most intense scrutiny, though he never smiled his thanks, but only nodded gravely as he fingered them. He had always had the Norman's love for treasures, but since his lady wife had died and he was alone, his avarice seemed to grow to shameful proportions and in all directions. He hunted as if the game would soon be extinct. He dined longer than he was wont to do before. He grasped at little fines and wore thick rings and chains for his adornment, which they say had never been his custom in his prime.

Now he heard the report of the commissioner of the inquest with the greatest interest. Lord Geoffrey de Mowbray pronounced the inventory of the realm to be proceeding satisfactorily. In fact, it was all but finished; it would never be complete. Certain portions of the country were to be neglected, by private agreement between the king and the powerful lords who dwelled there. London never was searched, because it was feared the Londoners would rebel at royal intrusion into their ancient, though unchartered, privileges. The king never loved the Londoners, but he had a regard for their loyalty, so he let them be. London's escape from tallying didn't sit well with other towns that felt the survey had all but dragged their entrails out for Lord Geoffrey's inspection.

Now it was time for the king to show his appreciation to Maurice. A synod followed the court, and there King William presented his chancellor to his bishops and urged them to elect him bishop of London, which they happily did.

When he was so named, we in the chancel cheered him as if he were the hero of a tournament – and were driven out of the hall for our rudeness. We waited then with eager ears to hear which of us would get his place as chancellor. It would be the king's decision, of course, but he would surely take Maurice's advice first. If that were so, I felt certain I would be the one recommended. In spite of my recent lapses from grace, he knew I was most capable of the work.

To my astonishment, the post went to William Giffard instead. He was from an exalted family, being the younger son of old Walter, Earl of Buckingham, who had fought at Hastings with the king and was a member of the inner council. William was a member of our chapter who'd never been marked for his keen intelligence. He was being rewarded, undoubtedly, to placate his father for bearing with the Great Inquest in silence.

Gerard, Robin, and I stood gaping at each other when his name was announced.

'Well,' sighed Robin, 'it's a happy family that can even get its half-wits a chain of office.'

Giffard made a modest speech on accepting the chancellorship. 'Friends and Brothers, I pray we may live and work in harmony. I know there are many among you more worthy to wear this honor than myself, but be patient of your fortunes, as I shall try to be deserving of mine.'

We were in for a season of repentance, and oh, dear Judas, but I'd looked forward to hating him, too.

22

When we returned to London, I expected to hear some word from Maurice about my future with him. I was quickly reconciled to the fact that the chancellorship should go to a great house in that year when the king must bestow more favors than usual. A post in Maurice's own chancery would have pleased me almost as well for the time being. It would be less harassing and could lead me to the dean's chair in a short time, since the old dean was in fragile health. The infirmarian gave him small chance of recovery from the cough that racked him night and day. I was doing his work, so I ventured to speak to Maurice:

'What's to be done about the dean, Your Grace?'

'What can be done, Ranulph? We must pray for him and, I fear, prepare to mourn him. He'll be missed here.'

'He's a worthy man. Your Grace, have I served you well these past three years?'

'You know the answer to that, my boy. No one could have been more careful of me, or closer to me, if he were my own son. I'll miss you at my elbow every morning, though I understand your constancy has earned you a by-name from the dispenser. What is it now?'

'Flambard, Your Grace.' I bit back a comment on the man who had given me that insulting name, but Maurice saw my opinion of it on my face and smiled.

'If I were you, I wouldn't give Robert Marmion the satisfaction of seeing me wince at his little joke. Bear the title with pride. Torch bearer! A man who gives light to others, lest they stumble in the dark. What's wrong with that? Our Blessed Lord is a torch bearer to those who follow His light.'

'I don't think Robert Marmion meant I was like Christ, Your Grace. But about the deanery?' I drew breath and plunged: 'Might I not have it? Then I would continue to be with you as before, working by your side and under your guidance, which would please us both. I know I would do well, though it may not become me to say so.'

'You are most capable.' He ruminated; his eyes avoided me. 'As you know, Ranulph, the election of the dean is a privilege held by the chapter as a whole. He is their head, would be their prior if they were regular clergy – '

'But you make recommendations, surely. It's understood you must approve. '

'I – will not make – recommendations at this time.'

I said, 'You mean you don't want me for the post.'

'I mean, dear Brother, that I won't begin my rule here by making the chapter think me a tyrant. I will not have them say I have ignored their ancient rights to force one of my favorites upon them. The diocese of London hasn't had a very happy history the last few years, but now we begin anew. I would be happy if they should choose you of their own accord, but – '

'But that's not very likely, is it, without your approval beforehand? Because I'm a peasant priest and the son of a peasant priest.'

'My dear friend, I can't listen to such a charge. There isn't a man in this chapter who wouldn't give full credit to your many excellent qualities.'

'And to my low birth. The first year I was here, not a week passed that some one of them didn't affect to forget I wasn't the son of the Count of the Bessin, or the nephew of the vicomte, or at least a grandson on the wrong side of the blanket to some illustrious Ranulph with an army at his back!'

'Brother Ranulph!'

His watery eyes turned as fierce as his myopia would allow. I bowed my head in submission. There was a brief silence; then he said in a very soft, almost pitiful way:

'There is not a man in the chapter who, knowing your excellent qualities, is yet ignorant of your irregular conduct.'

'What?'

'Brother, everyone in the chapter has been talking about you and your concubine, who they say is hardly more than a child and with whom you have been living in the most flagrant manner since last spring.'

'That's what you'd have me believe they'd hold against me? My unchastity? God, when a fourth of them have made the same arrangements with "widows" who're supposed to keep their houses, but are little more than whores? They overpopulate our schools with their bastards, those "widows" who keep the prebendaries' beds warm!'

Maurice drew his chin up and his mouth down. 'Those men shall not become dean of St. Paul's by my recommendation, either, Brother, if that comforts you. And, Brother, you may leave me now, until you've collected your temper.'

I promptly fell on one knee. 'Maurice, forgive me for seeming angry with you. I'm not. I only feel the injustice of such a charge.'

He waved his hand. 'Your speech to me is forgiven as soon as you ask, dear friend. Your anger at the truth about your deeds you must work out with yourself. Please – '

I left him, bowing at the door. I had lied; I was furious with him. Robin caught sight of me stalking through the church.

'Giffard wants to see us after the day-meal, in the chancel.'

'Hell take Giffard and the day-meal, too. I'm going home.'

'What's got up your nose?' He had to trot to keep abreast of me. 'Ranulph, really, he isn't that hard to bear.'

'Robin, for you nothing is hard to bear. All is sweet and amusing, or only a little tedious. I wish it were so with me. I must get away alone for a while. Tell Will Giffard I have the flux, or anything that amuses you.' I didn't look back to see how he took my rebuff.

A blast of wind and sleet hit me in the face like an icy mare's tail as I rushed out the door. One of St. Paul's damnable mongrels darted after me, enlivened by my speed to think I was a trespasser and nip me in the leg. I fetched him a kick that sent him howling.

The air was thick with sleet, the ground slushy and slick underfoot. I'd forgotten to snatch my cloak off the peg as I passed it, so by the time I reached my house my boots and gown were soaked and my ears half frozen.

'Well!' cried Trudy in astonishment as I slammed the door, but I ignored her and ran up the stairs. There was no charcoal in the brazier there, and the heat from the fire below couldn't warm that room with the wind banging at the shutters like a bawd.

'Giva! Get out of bed, you lazy slut, and help me dry myself.'

Elfgiva lifted her tousled head from where she lay tucked in like a mouse in a hayrick. Her look was sulky, but mine must have convinced her it was no time for impertinence. She rolled out of bed in time to catch my gown as I flung it. She hung it on a peg, then came to pull off my boots. She even toweled my feet and legs with an energy that brought some warmth back into them, but not even that unusual service could mollify me. I looked on her narrowly.

'You're as sorry an example of the Devil's ministry to be found above ground,' I said. 'My soul's my own, after all! I suppose I should give thanks for that, at least.'

She took the towel to my head and shoulders next. 'I see you came looking for a quarrel. You always start up with that *chūdan*. I'm no witch and you know it, or you wouldn't dare talk to me like that. I don't think you ever believed in witches at all.'

'I've certainly lost confidence in you!'

'What's to be so grim about? *Wōd* and *groulsom* as a wolf that's stepped on a *glede*. I'd think you'd had all the best of it this winter, following your fat king about and eating at his table. We've been having bean porrey, Trudy and me – and without the beans.'

'You don't look any the thinner for it. What did you do with the money I left for food? There was enough in that purse to feed twenty useless girls.'

'On black bread and water, maybe.'

'Oh, be quiet! Go down and get me something to eat – and hurry!' While she was gone I got into bed for warmth, then lay wondering why I should take out my spleen on the poor girl. Why be so mad to get back to her, if I put her to sulking the moment I arrived? Poor fool, she understood no more of my dilemma than a dog. Women were such hapless wretches; I could be glad I wasn't one of them, at least.

I recalled a man who'd been fined at one of the hustings for throwing rubbish into the Thames. He was looking for a safe way to vent his rage while the portreeve still frowned down on him.

'I'll go home to my woman and her meal now, Your Honor. If it's table-ready when I get there, I won't eat a bite! But if it's not, I'll raise up devils out of Hell on her, the bitch!'

I was laughing at that when Giva returned with a bit of roasted chicken on a bone no bigger than my least finger.

'Trudy sends you this. She says it was to be her supper, but you're welcome to it.' She watched me strip the bone with no compunction for Trudy, then throw it across the room, still laughing.

'Roaring one minute, happy as a flea the next, that's you. If I was to act like that you'd say I was crazy and a witch, I guess. The mice'll take that bone under the bed tonight and then you'll hear a racket.'

She picked it up and pitched it out the window, shuddering. 'Lud, it's cold!' as she closed the shutters again.

I lifted the covers to let her in, but when I tried to pull her gown up she demurred: 'No, Trudy will hear us, and besides, it's too cold.'

'Too cold, after a two-month absence? It'll get warmer in a moment. As for Trudy, if she doesn't know what we're doing, I'm ashamed for her. Even the Bishop of London knows what we do. I have it from his own lips that the whole chapter of St. Paul's is probably biting its collective finger for envy of me right now.'

She shuddered with the cold or with the news. 'They all know about me? Will they do something – to me?'

'No, no, of course not. Forget about them. Just hold me close and I'll hold you, until we're warm. We'll save Trudy's shame, if she has any.' I buried my face in her breast and felt her heart thump against my brow, her fingers clasp my neck.

'I'm not to be chancellor, it seems, and I'm not to be dean. Only saints, or highborn fools, are wanted for the jobs.'

'Oh.'

'But all's not lost. I can go on being a chancellor's toady as long as I like. Even longer. Or I can take you and go down to the country, to Godalming, and be a country priest if I like. Keep hens and a cow. Plow my own field. Be an ox six days a week and a lamb on the seventh. How would you like that?' I asked bitterly, never expecting the answer:

'Oh, could we do that?'

I lifted my head. Her face was just above mine, eager, bright, as though I'd just offered her a gift instead of the way to an early old age and miserable death. 'You wouldn't like it, Giva.'

'Oh, yes! We'd be rich, with a cow and some hens. We could get a little pig and I'd feed it and make it fat. We'd sell it then and buy two – '

'And be pig keepers? My God!'

'I'd do all the work! You wouldn't have to do it. I know how. My mother, my real mother that died, kept pigs and ducks before we came to London and he married *her*, the one who threw me out. I'd know how. I would!'

She had never said so much about herself, or revealed so much longing. I was appalled by the longing. I took her face in my hands and kissed her mouth to stop the words, but as soon as I released it she whispered:

'You wouldn't be ashamed of me. I'd work hard and have lots of babies, too.'

'My God, don't say that! You don't know anything about it. You're still a – you don't know! Your mother died young. What killed her? Babies? Hunger? My mother is still alive, I think. She might have been no older than you when my father took her, but now she looks as old as Lanfranc, and he must be eighty. She was beautiful, like you. I can remember. What do you talk about babies for?' I'd had her for nearly a year and she hadn't conceived in spite of all our lust. She must be barren, since Isabel's cousin had given me good reason to think I wasn't sterile, and I wasn't sorry if she was.

She looked a little frightened by my outburst. I tried to make amends, laughing and kissing her. 'Never mind, chuck, it'll all come right, somehow.'

'But I like babies, don't you?'

'Of course I do. Everyone likes babies, don't they? But you hardly need one at your breast this minute, when you've got me.' After which, one thing led to another, and Trudy, unless she stuffed her ears, was put to shame by the creaking of the bed ropes.

I saw Giva every day as long as we were in London, no matter what Will Giffard thought. But I was Giffard's man, so when he followed the king to Winchester after Candlemas, I went with him and didn't see Elfgiva for months.

I'd been in such a reckless mood after Maurice refused me, I thought I didn't care if Giffard expelled me from the chancery, but I did. In spite of all that common sense told me concerning the advancement of people like myself, I wanted Giffard's place and still meant to have it, though I had no plan for making myself either more useful or more noble to get it.

Giffard, as Robin had said, was not so bad a master. In fact, he was too indulgent. If I'd had a clerk who made himself absent without my leave, treated me to dark looks and slow answers, I'd have had him scraping parchments with his tongue instead of pumice. But Giffard was a different man from the one I have become. He let me resume all my former duties except that of carrying the seal for him before the king. Odo had used me carelessly and I had feared him. Rufus had cast me off and I had grieved for him. Maurice had worked me like an ox and I had loved him. Giffard had pity on me and I despised him.

Yet, by the time we left Winchester after the Easter Court, I had fitted myself so well to his habits that he was calling me *his* flambard, as if it were to my honor, and others openly used it for my name.

For those who've lived their lives apart from great towns, let me explain that byname which Robert the Dispenser bestowed on me.

The London streets are narrow and murky to walk through, even before the curfew bell has put the shutters to and the candles out a half hour before Compline. In the winter, Hell's own donjons couldn't be blacker, and the wretched dogs that roam the streets become more hungry and bold. If you have any business to be upon those streets at such an hour, you must feel your way with a stick, encumber yourself with a lantern, or call out:

'Ho, flambard! Je passe, flambard!'

As you shout, you hold a coin out, pinched between finger and thumb. A door somewhere will fly open and a filthy little urchin will dart from it, carrying a knotted wick of rope drenched in grease and set alight from his hearth. He'll snatch your coin and run off ahead of you. You trot briskly to keep in sight of his flambeau, yelling your destination and hoping he won't lead you into a dung heap or, having gotten your money, douse his torch in a puddle and run off, leaving you groping until another like him answers your cry.

That is the sort of creature Robert Marmion made me out to be for Maurice, in my eagerness to serve him and clear his thick-sighted way as he bustled through the halls: a smelly linkboy, hasty to serve, eager for reward, and by implication not to be trusted. The flambards will sometimes fight each other for a patron's farthing on a cold night. Most of them bear ugly scars on their faces or arms from being singed by a competitor.

I understood the dispenser's jibe well enough and hated him for it, but the name stuck, as the worst mud always will, until in time I grew indifferent to it.

That was a disastrous year for everyone. There was no rain when the fields wanted it, then rain, hail, lashing winds, and fearful lightnings in the summer, to beat down what crops had been brave enough to grow in spite of drought. Owls took up residence in the palace of Winchester, a very bad sign according to the old men, who said that owls had come there in Ethelred's day and he had no luck thereafter; Redeless Ethelred, who spurned advice, overtaxed the people, and also quarreled with a warrior son who defied him.

We came back to Westminster for Whitsunday, oppressed by the news of cattle fever and deaths everywhere. At that summer court the king made his youngest son a knight with twice the panoply he'd bestowed on Rufus; he might have been fitting him out to take Jerusalem from the heathen.

Henry was the image of his father in miniature: sallow-faced, cold-eyed, tight-mouthed, though there must have been hidden fires, even then. He was barely eighteen and had fathered two bastards. His scanty crop of lank black hair was already showing signs of baldness, which they say is a sign of virility. By the time he would be twenty, Nature would tonsure him. It gave our witty dispenser the opportunity to bestow another name in jest: he called him 'Beauclerk,' which some fools have lately taken to be a sign that Henry was truly learned.

Rufus came to put the spurs on Henry after the accolade. It was the first time I'd seen him in five years. His reputation had traveled to England if he had not. He was a formidable champion in the lists now; it was certain he had changed. But he was somehow the same. He wore finer clothes, but they still looked as if made for another man on his deep-cheated, thick body. His hair was worn below the ears now, in the French style, and burnished to a glint by some barber, but his sweating, flushed face still wore the good-natured apprehension of an honest soldier dressed up to play the Fool-King at Christmas.

He gave Henry a richly embroidered Spanish baldric for his sponsor's gift, which he had no doubt won himself in a swift contest over hard ground at the risk of his neck. Like Edgar Atheling, who was his friend again, he raced horses to his profit. He had a crowd about him wherever he stood because he was once more the heir apparent of Normandy, but he welcomed common soldiers to his friendship as readily as the knights who were his peers, and even let them speak familiarly to him, making jokes about his rare defeats, as if he were some village quarterstaff champion they knew.

He quite outshone Henry in the tournament that day, and Henry took it poorly. Certainly, Henry Atheling was no mean contender according to his age and experience in the lists.

When I saw Cormac, I determined to avoid him. It amazed me Rufus had kept him so long. That he had made me wonder who was the master and who the follower in that friendship. The Rufus I saw now seemed unlikely to be still pliable to Cormac's will, and Cormac had never been one long to endure opposition.

Still, he remained, and he wore the signs of his master's goodwill upon his back; he was dressed with an elegance that approached young Henry's. He had a dark velvet tunic and wine-colored fine linen shirt. His legs were encased in pale blue hose of a fit only the best money could buy. He shadowed his master's progress through the hall as if it were assured he had every right to be there, but few people other than Rufus seemed to speak to him.

In spite of all caution I came face to face with him on the gallery passage above the presence hall one evening. He was standing in the shadow of an arch, looking down on the games that always follow a good meal. He saw me about the same moment I was aware of him, and it seemed cowardly to avoid a greeting.

'Most reverend and holy Father, is it really you?'

'Cormac.'

'You're looking sleek. I hear you're the chancellor's indispensable man now. Do you give proper credit to early teaching, I wonder?'

His voice, I swear, could stir dead leaves at the bottom of a tarn. I felt a quite unreasonable heart-pounding of the sort that used to shake me when I knew I was about to be singled out for ridicule. I blurted out rudely:

'Cormac, you dress better than an earl. Your lord must love you. Does he still send you purses from his prison at Rouen? Or have you taken to general pandering?'

For a moment his face didn't change, as if he hadn't heard, or I hadn't spoken, though my own ears seemed to ring with my words as if I'd shouted. I couldn't believe myself! It had never been my intention to throw my knowledge of his indenture to Odo in his face. The memory of his knife point in my windpipe was still the subject of uneasy dreams.

The little dry smile he always wore curled more to one side. He sighed. 'Well, God, can you believe it? He still cares.' He stepped into my path when I would have walked on. Since there were other people walking along the gallery I didn't push him aside. 'Have you been saving up that morsel to give to Will? I'll save you the trouble: he knows. I told him long ago.'

I shook my head. 'Oh, no, you didn't. If you had, you wouldn't tell me. But I won't put your lie to the test. There won't be the occasion. Now, let me pass, or there'll be an accident up here that might hurt someone down below.' Sheer bluff and he knew it. He laughed nastily.

'You know, Ranulph, if you were a woman, you'd be the kind that bites.'

I drove my fist straight for his face, but as he'd provoked the blow he was expecting it, and his reactions were still quick. He caught my bunched knuckles in his hand to deflect them, though he staggered as his hand was driven back to his shoulder. His harp case slid down his arm. There was a sudden burst of conversation and movement behind me.

'Father, Father, peace! It was only a jest!' Cormac said as I glanced about to see a group of clerks coming along the gallery from the upper stair. At the head of them was William Giffard. I wrenched my fist free of Cormac's grasp and bowed to him.

'Chancellor. '

'Ranulph. What's this? Not disputing?'

'No, Chancellor. Just – discussing – '

'The swiftness of thought, my lord,' Cormac said, who bowed obsequiously to him as he passed. Giffard nodded. He'd only taken fractional notice of us after all. As I pushed by to join the clerks, Cormac said:

'He wants to see you.' He jerked his head in the direction of the lower hall to indicate Rufus.

I gave that some thought first. Considering my foolish disclosure to Cormac, I wasn't certain I could trust myself to face Rufus. What could he want with me, after all? He wouldn't still be angry with me. Considering the low estimation in which he held clerks, I'd be surprised if he really even remembered my name.

Still, I couldn't ignore a summons, if that's what it was. I duly presented myself to Rufus the next day when I found him without Cormac, walking from the stable yard with Edgar Atheling. His quick grin when he saw me was reassuring. He clapped me on the shoulder and said to Edgar:

'Here he is – our bursar-dispenser, if we can steal him from my f-father. Leave the provisioning to him and we'll get on with the recruiting.'

I was baffled. 'Is there to be a war after all, my lord? I'd thought that threat was ended.' Canute of the Danes had been assassinated as he prayed in church, murdered by the orders of his own envious brother, who had since seized his throne and disbanded his fleet, putting an end to the threatened invasion.

Rufus said: 'There's already a war – a splendid war – between the Guiscards in Italy and the heathen in Syracuse. Why are you staring? You approve of fighting heathens, don't you? Of course you do! We're going to offer our services to old Guiscard to help him fight the Moors, or some such rascals. To the glory of God and our se-several popes! Didn't Cormac explain it? I thought that's why you came looking so eager.'

'He only said you wanted to speak to me, my lord, which was good enough news to me. The Moors, my lord?'

Edgar said quietly: 'The count of Apulia has sent out a call for mercenaries. The new Pope, Victor, has preached a holy war on the heathen, which Count Robert Guiscard has vowed to pursue.'

'Ha! You mean Count Robert's persuaded the Pope to let him do as he wants! The old Pope was his prisoner; this one's his doorkeeper,' Rufus said. 'But I don't fault him. B-by the Face, I never thought I'd hear of a Pope I liked, but I'll k-kiss this one's holy foot when I see him, for offering me a campaign.'

'He hasn't offered it yet, Will. Nor has your father, who must give us his blessing, as well as some of his army.'

'Stop pouring cold water on me, friend. F-father will give us what we want. He'll be glad to find an excuse to be rid of some of these fellows who're picking him like crows. What about it, Ranulph? You've got a reputation for good sense, which I know to be the case. Will you be our paymaster and marshal our supplies? You'll be first chaplain, and you'll pick your own staff. I know only one other priest I could stand to have come and he's got one foot in the grave. He's Lanfranc. Besides which, I don't think he approves of our new Pope.' He fixed me with his disconcerting stare, in which the brown eye always seemed more acute and the blue one more affable.

'I – it would always be my pleasure to serve you again, my lord.'

'You hesitate. You h-have ties here you don't want to sever.'

I thought of Elfgiva. I thought of Italy. 'No, my lord. I stand ready to do your bidding, if – '

'If my father gives his consent. Don't worry, he will.'

But he did not. Rufus, remembering perhaps how it had been the last time he had made a bid for a campaign before witnesses, presented his plea in private, I do not even know on which occasion, since there were few. It may have been a brief discussion, or a shambles; I was never told. But the refusal must have been wounding. Rufus went about with a set mouth and lusterless eyes, dragging after the king as if he had a halter about his neck. It was Edgar Atheling who told me there would be no brave journey to Apulia, calling me aside to do it.

'I hope you will have said nothing about this matter to anyone here at court – that is, about your part in it.'

'No, my lord, I spoke to no one.' I hadn't had that much confidence in the enterprise, though for a few days its possibilities sparkled before my eyes, only to be dimmed by the thought of abandoning Elfgiva, whom I would probably never see again.

'That is well. You might have found some prejudice against you afterward if you had boasted.' Edgar sighed faintly. 'It's too bad.

Our friend is eager to try himself, and there is nowhere he can be tested. The king will have him near him and no place else; he loves him dearly, but – I shouldn't say it, nor must you repeat it, yet it may help you find comfort for him – he called him a boy. Twenty-six years old and a knight, to be called a boy. It's hard. I know.' As he did, being near to thirty-five and still confined to toying with horses and dogs for an occupation.

Rufus didn't call me to see him again.

We went to Salisbury at Lammastide. There, to the surprise of all, the king gave summons for a special court, outside the seasonal four. He called to him not only his barons, but all men who held land above a knight's fee – eight hides or more, that is. When they came, he made them swear homage to him, even if they were the sworn vassals of other lords. It was an amazing, I might say an outrageous, act, which no king had ever done before. The oath each man swore there would take precedence over any he had previously given to another man, whether baron, earl, or bishop.

The landholders came in multitudes from Lammas to the end of August. They were sworn in convenient groups, as if they were to be witnesses to a trial. When they had sworn, they went home again, trudging down the steep hill that bore up old Salisbury above its surrounding plain. The great holders of baronial fees stood by with their mouths clamped shut while their liege men were made direct vassals of the king. How they must have resented – no, how they must have hated him for it, even while their minds tried to grasp his reasons.

I can't say what prompted the king to the business. He had several cogent reasons: there was always the probability of treason in the breasts of such restless and powerful men as he had for barons. Unrest had been fanned to a new heat, first by the inquest, then by the threat of war and the thrusting of his many hirelings on them to feed and content.

To my mind, it was probably the last wise thing he did in his life.

When the Salisbury Oath was taken, the court disbanded and the king went overseas to Normandy again. He took a good part of his host with him, but couldn't maintain them there with any greater ease than he had here. He couldn't make his Norman counts yield to him in the same way either, so in time he did what he might have done earlier.

He gave Edgar Atheling leave to take two hundred knights out of Normandy and down to Italy, where they later joined Robert Guiscard in an assault on the African city of Tunis.

Whether Edgar found glory or shame in his part of that campaign, in which old crones, babes, and cripples were slain as readily as armed heathen, I never heard. It is for him to tell it, not I, and he has never done so. But in going, he lost the love of Rufus, who was made to stay behind.

Will Giffard went to Normandy with the king, but I was not included in his train, to my great relief. I hurried back to London and to Giva, whom I hadn't seen since April.

She and Trudy were sitting in the kitchen yard paring apples when I found them. Each wore a broad headcloth such as plowmen's wives wear when they work beside their men in the fields. Giva got up from her bench when I opened the kitchen door, putting aside her apple bowl. Her body was as heavy and misshapen as her headdress. There was no mistaking the cause: she was massively with child.

23

We stared at each other for a moment. She took off her headcloth and the little straw hat beneath that made it seem so broad. Her face was expectant, as if it might burst into light all at once, but I must have looked like a dolt. Certainly I spoke like one:

'When did this happen? God's Breath, but you're a dumpling! Have you been to the May frolic again?'

Trudy croaked some word of reproof. I didn't hear it, because Elfgiva, whose face had darkened, gave a yell of fury, snatched up her bowl, and threw the contents at me – cores, peelings, and fruit – then rushed past me and into the house, slammed the door, but continued to cry out incoherent abuse.

Trudy began to pick up the scattered fruit, scolding at the waste in her old woman's mutter. I was ashamed of myself for saying the first thing that had come to my mind, but I was angry, too. The little bitch, treating me to such insolence in the presence of another woman! For that reason I asked harshly:

'Well, had she been trotting out or not? I saw no signs of breeding the last time. I've a right to be curious, I think.'

Trudy rose, panting, her gnarled hands filled with dirty apple pieces, her faded eyes rheumy with anger.

'No! She's not been trotting out. Not to my knowing. But then, I'm not her keeper, am I? You are, more shame to you for it. A priest of God! Ay, you must be forgetful, or else you have a poor opinion of your manhood if you blame others for what's in her belly. The babe began to kick two months ago, master. Count backward on your fingers from five months and see if you can tell where you were then. If it wasn't you up there popping the bed ropes with your leman, I won't give you a farthing for your soul, because the Devil's made your double, to damn you!'

I backed away as she scolded. People in the houses on either side had their shutters open to see what the roaring was about. There was a further shriek from Giva in the house, but a cry in another mode, full of pain or fear. I turned and rushed inside and up the stairs. I could hear Trudy still reviling me hotly as she trailed behind. When I flung open our bedchamber door, Giva was standing by the window, sobbing. She held in her right hand the little paring knife she'd been using; her left arm was outstretched, thrust away from her in horror, because it dripped blood. She stared at me with a face as white as her shift, then reeled and fainted into my arms as I ran to catch her. She'd cut the delicate veins of her wrist, and her gown was already soaked with blood.

I carried her to the bed, tore off a strip of her shift hem, and used it to bind up her wrist, but the blood kept welling through the linen. Trudy burst into the room, wheezing.

'What's amiss? Oh, Christ Jesus, he's killed her, the poor little thing!'

'Shut up, you fool! She's done this to herself. It won't kill her. Get something – some cobwebs – for the blood.'

'I don't have cobwebs! I keep a clean house.'

'Then go and make some, spider-hag! For the love of God, go down to the cellar and find some, then. And bring up some wine. And more bandage!'

I tied the bandage tighter, then lifted Giva into my arms so that she could breathe easier. The pallor of her face only made her more beautiful. I was struck to the soul with remorse. I kissed her brow and began to chafe her breast to make her heart beat again.

She opened her eyes with a flutter, then lifted her head, saw the blood again, and began to whimper: 'It hurts! When will I die? Confess me, Ranulph.'

'You're not going to die, you goose! It's only a little cut, but you've bled some. Don't fret; it'll stop when Trudy brings some cobwebs.'

'It burns like fire.'

'I expect that's from the apple juice. Why did you do such a stupid thing, Giva? Why didn't you tell me this before?'

'I knew what you'd say, but Trudy said it'd make you glad. But, no, you said I was a witch at first, then you made me a whore – '

'I could cut my tongue out. Trudy!'

Trudy came back, gasping, with a jack of wine in one hand and a good length of blackened cobwebs wound about the other. Together we stopped the bleeding and poured wine into Giva until she threatened to be sick. Trudy saw she wasn't wanted anymore and let us be alone. I lay a little above Giva and held her close, smoothing her hair, kissing her fingers.

'You're not angry then, about this in my belly?'

'No, how could I be, when it's mine?'

'You said – '

'It was a stupid, brainless thought. You should have used your knife on me, not yourself. Will you stop weeping now?'

'You're the one who's doing that. I can feel it in my hair.'

She was right. I wiped my face, then hers, and kissed her. 'There, now neither of us is weeping, or will ever weep again if I can help it. What can I say to make you know I love you and will never doubt you again?'

She burrowed her face in my shoulder. The answer was quite obvious: I could marry her. I had to think for a bit before I framed an offer that was possible.

'I can't marry you, Giva. The Church forbids it, the king frowns on it, and I have ambitions that would be denied me if I owned a wife in the eyes of the Church. I still mean to be chancellor here one day, perhaps more than that, someday later.'

'Yes.' Her voice came muffled against me. 'You can do as you please until you're tired of it; then you can say you're sorry for it and you'll be safe. But I'll still be a whore and that's an end to it.'

'No.'

'Yes. Chancellors can have whores, can't they? And bastards? That's all right, but what about the babies and the whores? What happens to them when the priests are finished with them? They can go to Hell and the priests will pray for them, that's what.'

I sighed and held her closer. There was truth in what she said. No doubt Trudy had put it all in her head, but what was I to say to it, and to her? It was unthinkable to let her go on believing me such an unfeeling brute as I was.

'Give, take my hand,' I whispered. 'Now, hear me swear before God that as I hope for His mercy and my salvation, I pledge myself to you – to cleave to you only, to honor you – as my handfast wife, my true wife, than which I shall have no other so long as we both live. I give you this pledge, as my father gave it to my mother, and vow to honor it, as he did, with body, heart, and mind. Giva?' I turned her face out of my breast and held it. 'Do you hear me? Do you believe me?'

She sobbed.

'Will you have me for your husband on these terms?'

She made a bare assent. I kissed her damp brow.

'Then you must say the same words back to me, holding my hand in the very presence of God, Who sees and knows us.'

She did, in a wet whisper and with my prompting, then lay sobbing heavily against me. I felt the child in her womb move between us and said:

'There's our witness.'

The child was born in November. It was a female and was baptized with the name of an English martyr known to Trudy and Giva, but not to me: Osyth, popularly called St. Toosey. I had no part in the selection of the name or the baptism. I never saw my daughter. I was in Normandy at the time, with letters for the king from Giffard. By the time I was given leave to return, Osyth had died from one of those infant maladies that will forever decimate the newborn. I felt some disappointment in having a child come and slip away again from me so quickly, but Giva was prostrate with remorse and grief.

'Poor little baby. It was a punishment on us for what we've done between us,' she wept. 'Poor baby, that didn't even know about it.'

'God wouldn't punish the child, Giva. To think that is to believe He's an evil being, which is blasphemous, my love.'

'Oh, you're so wise and holy and know all about what God can do, aren't you? Well, maybe He knows more about you than you know about Him. That's what the priest of St. Peter's says, and even I can see it: you'd be grieving more if it had been a son. Then you'd have howled and said it was a punishment on me for taking a knife to myself, or something!'

She had a way of getting to the quick of the matter. I would have felt the loss of a son more. But though we quarreled, I pitied her and had come to love her in a way that was more comfortable and less compelling as she had grown quieter and better behaved during her pregnancy.

I have heard it said that it is wrong to coddle women who have lost a babe, that it gives them false ideas of their place and function in this world, which is to bear young and suffer, as the angel of the Lord told Eve. But I could do nothing else. I bought her green wool for a new gown, brought sweetmeats from bakers' stalls to tempt her appetite, which had dwindled so after Toosey's death that she was no more than a wraith.

In the spring I took her to Godalming for a change of air, as well as to get her away from the priest of St. Peter's, in whom I feared she was confiding all too much. She had never been farther from London than the fields and woods that grow around it, so she had a look of dread mixed with wonder when we crossed the bridge into Southwark. Once out into the country, she exclaimed over every tree and praised each simple vill our horse plodded through, as if it were Adam's second Eden. With her for company I found Godalming a pleasant place for the first time since I'd become its nominal rector. The weather was fair and warm. The villeins were already predicting it meant a bad year for crops to have it warm so early, but country people will always predict bad things coming out of seeming good and seldom see themselves confounded. The trees were flowering almost a month early.

The whole purpose for the existence of Godalming was that King Alfred, or some such king, had built a hunting tower there once long ago, and the village had grown up to cater to it. It was a great, ramshackle Saxon hall with a high loft that sat on the edge of a natural ridge north of the village. Its warden at the time was a scarred veteran of Hastings who was half deaf and wholly affable. He let me have the freedom of the hall, possibly because he believed I was still seal bearer to the king, possibly because I had once said a blessing over a chilblain he had and it had subsequently healed.

While the warden and his goodwife were clucking to their fat geese in the manor yard as if they were their children, Giva and I would climb to the top of the loft some evenings to look out on the sunset and on the steep hills that rise to the north and west, ornamented with grazing sheep and apple trees.

Giva was content to go there with me, or to visit the orchards, look into the fish ponds, or fondle the lambs, but she was strangely shy of being seen with me before the people and wouldn't come into the church when I said Mass.

She was shy with me in bed, too. Her new hesitance was both

baffling and gratifying. It at once spoiled my pleasure and made her seem more desirable as she was less accessible. Once or twice I found myself thinking of the Lady Isabel as I touched her. When I took her up into the loft, I praised her, where no one could hear us, calling her my lady and my secret princess.

My extravagance made her laugh again for the first time. 'I'm not your lady, priest, I'm a fusterer's daughter, which is all you deserve. What would you ever do with a lady?'

'Unlace your bodice and I'll demonstrate.'

So, by degrees of foolish talk and fond loving, I brought her back to some degree of relish for me. I took great care with the loving, for I meant to get her with child again if I could, since I believed that was what she yearned for.

In that enterprise I was luckier than the farmers who put their seed in the earth that year. A month after we returned to London, Giva confided to Trudy that she thought she was kindled again. She still hesitated to confide it first to me.

It was another dreadful year, worse even than predicted: first drought, then floods, and terrible winds, and lightnings. Ships were lost in the Channel, so many that the markets were all but bare of goods. Fever came in high summer, to both man and beast. The churchyards couldn't hold the dead, and many were buried like the beasts in trenches. In city and village the church bells tolled constantly, mourning the dead. Once again God seemed to be telling the people He abhorred the king's census, his burdensome taxes, and his long absences from the realm. We talked of nothing but calamities.

The king had outlawed hanging for ordinary crimes, saying he didn't wish to be the murderer of his own people, but the mutilations he imposed instead of death seemed to me more ghastly than a swift jerk of the rope. Handless men, eyeless men, men without feet or their manly parts, grew such a common thing that one might almost forget there could be whole men, unless they wore tonsures or bore Norman names. Ralph Baynard and William de Mandeville lopped off so many extremities for theft that even William de Warenne, governing in the king's name, called them butchers and begged them to show more lenience. But those who had their dwindling food and property stolen still clamored for blood.

I would have sent Giva back to Godalming until her time came, but she wouldn't be parted from Trudy, who treated her now as her own daughter. I feared for her health, yet in all truth the country was as deadly as the city in that year. If she had been willing to leave London, I would have suffered the more. Seeing her at the end of a dismal day was all that made my life bearable, and when, as sometimes happened, I was sent away for a few days to Winchester, or perhaps Canterbury, I was frantic to get home again, lest Giva fall sick and die, too, before I could come to her. But though she grew thinner, as we all did on watered soup and watered wine, with no better bread to eat than that unbolted loaf which the English call *treet* and feed to their dogs, the child in her belly continued to flourish.

Abroad in Normandy, King William's troubles were no easier, but of a different kind. While he had last been in England, his liege lord, Philip of France, had given license to some followers to raid Norman lands near Evreux. King William made certain demands for reparations to Philip, and the reply he received was first indifferent silence, then an insult.

The reparations demanded were in the form of lands to which Normandy had long laid claim – the Vexin – but which we had lost by stealth to Philip some ten years since. It was during that time that a quarrel with the Bretons left us unable to oppose the insidious absorption of the Vexin by the greedy French.

King Philip was a young monarch with a high opinion of himself that was ill matched by his rather paltry accomplishments. He bore our king a grudge for his successes and for the defeat and humiliations of his father, who long ago had beat such an ignominious retreat from Varaville. He may even have borne a coward's conscience for the memory of that bribe he'd taken from our king to keep him from aiding Curthose at Gerberoy – though I think he took it willingly at the time.

So, now, on hearing of King William's demand for the return of the French Vexin and his complaints about the Evreux raids, Philip not only refused him, but added a jest to his answer:

'I hear the King of England is having a lying-in at Rouen this year. No doubt there will be many candles burned at his churching when the babe is born. Let me know the sex of the child and perhaps I'll send it a baptismal gift.'

King William was in fact lying ill at Rouen when his ambassadors made their suit to the king. He had a constant pain in his swollen belly which the doctors had failed to cure with either purgatives or diet. He had been too weak to stir from his bed and in too great a pain to eat more than clear broth. But on hearing of Philip's silly reply from his envoys, he rose from his bed and gave vent to one of his uncommon rages.

'By the Resurrection and Splendor of God!' he cried when he'd thrown his bowl of physic across the room and sent his servants and hounds cringing to the walls. 'I'll have my *churching*, as he names it, at Notre Dame in Paris! And I'll bring a thousand lances for candles!' After which the doctors couldn't keep him confined. In July he invaded the Vexin with a great army, destroying every farm and vineyard in his path until he came to the town of Mantes.

By August in London all winds and rains had ceased, and a thick pall of smoke and haze enveloped the city, making it difficult to breathe, let alone move or think. Commerce in the marketplace and justice in the courts was at a stand, all the merchants and magistrates having departed the city for their distant homes in hope of relief. St. Paul's was idle except for holy services. Not even the most litigious attorney had the energy to try a case for the example of his students in our nave.

At home Giva lay on the bed most of the day, too listless even to want my company, so I spent my time within the walls of St. Paul's, rendering the accounts of royal estates, which I must give to Giffard soon, to take to the king. Even in the innermost confines of that great building the stench of London reached me, along with the heat.

'By all St. Anthony's pigs, it smells like a tannery's on fire out there,' I complained to Robin Bloet in disgust. 'Is there any town in the world that stinks like this one?'

'Paris does,' Robin said listlessly.

'York,' said Gerard. 'York's the worst. The shambles is just next to the cathedral there.' He yawned. 'My eyes are burning too much to read. Let's go out and scan the sky for a rain cloud – if we can see the sky.'

We did this several times a day lately, to no avail, but I was still glad for the diversion. We went out and took our stand at the west end, on the south side, where we could look both up and down the river.

'By God, there is something burning! Look down there.' Robin pointed in the direction of Dowgate at the mouth of the Wall Brook, where thick smoke was rolling up. A church bell in that vicinity was ringing with a broken voice.

'I know that bell,' I said. 'It's All Hallows below Watling Street. That's the hay wharf on fire.' Another bell began to clang, then another. 'Christ, all the river side will take fire from such a start as that! Someone should wake Maurice and tell him. You do it, Robin. I'll rouse our sexton, if he hasn't already heard it.'

We hurried away separately and found other clerks trotting out of the chapter to listen to those bells that were tolling the doom of London.

Each ward and soke had its own fire wardens, and we had ours. Though the flames were still at a distance, we prepared for our protection. Water was drawn from the well into all the tubs and buckets we possessed, and ladders were assembled. One of the wardens climbed to the top of the church roof and secured a rope to the tower by which to draw up water buckets. He had a broom with which to sweep away or beat out any bits of burning thatch that an improbable wind might blow against us, but we felt our roof was safe from that sort of debris, being tiled over the oak planks.

Prepared, we waited, crowded into the churchyard with that keen expectancy that borders on delight which one sees in any mass of people watching someone else's fire. We weren't alone. Soon townspeople, driven out of their homes by their wardens, began to swarm up from the lower streets, some carrying their beds on their backs, some hauling chests between them or pushing handcarts filled with children and kitchen pots, bedclothes, or their tools of trade. House dogs came running beside their masters, met the curs of St. Paul's yard, and there was a canine Armageddon.

I don't know how long I lingered, watching sudden tongues of flame shoot from ignited roofs as the pall of smoke crept over the lower town and obliterated all sight of the river, before I thought of my own property and of Giva. When I did, I gave a shout like that of a man who's been stabbed and started running.

I didn't run far. Watling Street was already choked with people and carts coming up from the lower streets, as well as by those more prosperous persons who lived on it and, having more goods to move, were trying to get their great wagons out onto the street to maneuver them toward Ludgate. I swam in a sea of prodding elbows and red, angry, fear-stricken faces.

It was all madness, I thought, striking back at those who struck me. Cornhill was as safe as St. Paul's yard, and I would do Giva more harm by letting her see me struggle in to her, half stripped of clothing, than by letting her fret for a few hours over my safety. The fire would exhaust itself when it reached Watling, where the rich townhouses were set farther apart and well back from the street, with courtyards and trees to protect them.

But when I had swum that human tide as far as the Wall Brook, I saw my hope was deluded. The fire had caught the wharves along that little water and was racing north into the upper town.

It must have taken me an hour to reach Cornhill. The Longbourne Ditch was teeming with people attempting to draw water out of its muddy bed. The poultry market was a devastation of overturned cages and dead birds. Squawking hens fluttered and hopped over the tables, pursued by people who took time out from fear to secure a future dinner. The street leading up from the Thames bridge now seemed on fire, and the east cheap was smoking, as was the south side of Longbourne.

I began to shout for Trudy and Giva as I struggled the last few steps to our house. The door was standing open. I ran through it and up the stairs. My chamber door was open and the room empty. Downstairs I saw that all the cupboards were gaping and the chests were ransacked. Trudy and Giva had taken what was valuable and fled, thank God; but where?

They weren't at St. Peter's, though it was filled with terrified penitents and howling children, who would soon be driven out by the suffocating smoke.

I ran into the streets again, yelling Giva's name and Trudy's, until my voice cracked with the strain and the smoke in my throat. Elfgivas and Trudys by the dozen turned their heads dazedly and shrieked back at me in fresh hope, but none of them was mine. One old crone of a Giva fell into my arms and clutched me so tightly I couldn't tear away from her, then made herself more of a nuisance by fainting in the street, where she was in danger of being trampled. I had to lift and carry her bodily, as no one else seemed to take notice of her.

My initial relief to find Giva safely out of the house with Trudy began to turn sour, as I failed to find any sign of them in the streets. Unreasoning anger shook me. How in the name of Hell did they dare to run out into the streets and endanger themselves further, without my leave and guidance? Trudy was a fool! Giva would be trampled, or pushed into the Longbourne and drowned by one of these bellowing, panic-struck cattle! I think if I'd come across either of them while I was in that state of fear madness, I'd have dropped my old woman and beaten the both of them senseless.

But I didn't find them, though I searched every street up to Bishopsgate. I left the old Giva I'd been dragging along with me at a church near that gate, then continued my hopeless search back along the Wall Brook to Cornhill again; but now Cornhill was cut off where it met Longbourne by the blazing grain market that gave our street its name. I retreated at last to the old palace that had been Odo's and fell into the yard of a small church near it, half dead with the smoke and with despair.

The fire stopped at Longbourne on the north, except for the market, but it spread up and down the river from the king's tower to Ludgate Stairs. The wind we had so longed for in our drought had vengefully sprung up from the sea at last, only to spread the flames. Rain came at its tail, but not in time to save us.

We were laid desolate. St. Paul's was burned, along with the bishop's palace. The greater part of all churches in the city were destroyed. Baynard's Keep was spared, though its bailey burned. The tower of Montfichet lost its roof. All the markets had vanished, their ramshackle roofs, tables, and wicker hampers making quick tinder. Most of the rich townhouses had been severely damaged or entirely destroyed, and the poor in their hovels, of course, suffered worst of all.

When I could stir from the churchyard, I went to St. Paul's, where I helped pass buckets up to the roof, until it was apparent there was no saving it. The clerks posted there to sweep away the flying embers had their brooms ignited and scrambled down the ladder in haste when a sudden gust of wind caused the flames to shoot up in their faces. We abandoned St. Paul's and retreated to the old palace.

Maurice looked so befuddled and tragic there, with his miter askew and his staff clutched in sooty fingers, that I fell on my knees before him, to beg his forgiveness for my ill feeling toward him since he'd refused me the deanship. He embraced me like a father, and, like a child for the moment, I wept and told him I'd lost Giva.

With Robin Bloet's help I got Maurice into the palace, but he wouldn't rest in spite of our pleas, so we took him up onto the roof where he could stand like a bereft shepherd, watching his city smolder and flame under a light rain. We stayed with him there until it was too dark to see anything but the flames and we were cold and drenched.

By morning there were still some scattered burnings, but most of the lower town was a charred ruin. Where were the people who had dwelt there? How many were dead, how many injured? Hundreds had taken refuge in the fields beyond, or fled to outlying villages. The rest roamed the streets all night, looking for food, shelter, or their kin.

The aggressive found food, the helpless began to flow back through the town gates at dawn, and we gave what comfort we could to them. Maurice and the portreeve had sent riders flying into the night to all the nearest estates to bring such food as they could spare. A wagonload of flour and four bakers rode up from Fulham in an oxcart at midnight and set to work in the palace kitchens baking bread. All the religious houses sent what aid they might, but there were still more wanting food than could be fed, and the coming night promised to be almost as miserable for the homeless as the preceding one.

I would have spent the day looking for Giva again, but Maurice claimed me, assuring me that if she lived she would come to us, as so many did. But when the day ended she hadn't, nor had anyone I asked known of her, or Trudy's, whereabouts.

I went out the gate meaning to search the night through, but Robin caught up with me and stopped me. It was just past Vespers, though it seemed unnatural with so few bells to ring it.

'There's a little food for us inside, Ranulph, and then Maurice wants to see the two of us. Ranulph?'

'She's dead, Robin. She must be. She'd have come here otherwise, as Maurice said. There aren't so many places to take refuge that she wouldn't have found me. She was carrying heavier than the last time. If she was pushed down by the mob, she could have had her pains before their time – had the child torn out of her – oh, Robin, I'll have her on my conscience for the rest of my life.'

He put his arm around me. 'She's safe, somewhere. You can believe it. She's young and bright; she wouldn't just run into the fire like a stupefied horse. St. Helen's and St. Ethelburga's are doling out food. So are St. Botolph's and St. Leonard's beyond the walls by Aldgate. That's the way she should have run, I think. If she and Trudy are with any of those, they'd have found it wiser to stay there, don't you think?'

'No. She'd have come to find me if she could. She would have been worried about me. Oh, Christ, why didn't I send her down to Godalming as I meant to?'

Robin gripped my arm and shook me. 'Now look! Strayed she may be, but dead, no! So far as we've heard, there hasn't been one body found yet. These London people know about fires. God knows they ought to. Your Giva's more clever than you. She didn't go running out into the thick of the rabble; she went out away from harm, like the thousands of other sensible folk. Now, come along with me and have some broth. When old Maurice is finished with us, we'll go to the churches and ask for her. You'll see if we don't find her.'

But we never did that. Maurice was marshaling his forces to bring all possible aid to his stricken city. He had already sent clerks flying to Winchester, to Canterbury, and to all the great houses of religion that lay more than a day's ride from London, to alert them to our many needs: timber, nails, carpenters, smiths, tents, or canvas with which to make them. William de Warenne must be alerted in his castle at Arundel.

'And the king must know, too,' Maurice said. 'There's a ship, a Danish *knörr*, lying off the pier below the king's tower, waiting for the next tide. I've sent word to it and its captain will take you, Robin, to the king as my emissary. Ranulph, you're the chancellor's clerk. If he were here, he would go in your place, but I'll undertake to anticipate his wishes and send you instead. You'll take the accounts of the king's rents with you, and when he hears of our afflictions, he may be moved to remit some part of them for our relief. God make it so! Tell him we need – everything.'

'Everything but more soldiers,' Robin muttered.

I wanted to refuse, to say I couldn't go now, but I was drained by despair. As we had our frugal meal, the first news of fatalities had come to us. Several bodies had been drawn from the Wall Brook, most of them women and children who must have been pushed through the rails of the footbridge in the panic. Their faces had been eaten by fishes, and one of them had been a woman with child. I hadn't the heart to go out and see if I could identify her. Instead, I bowed my knee to Maurice, then went with Robin to find that Danish ship.

24

We went ashore at Le Tréport, just inside the Norman border, where the fortress of Eu guards both port and coast. We walked up to the castle to ask of its governor two horses for the rest of our journey and some news of where the king might be by now in his campaign against the Vexin. The way was steep enough to silence Robin who had talked to me almost unceasingly throughout our sea voyage, in hopes of distracting me from grief for Giva.

It was unnecessary. I had already shut grief out of my mind by an act of will, for fear I would be a disgrace to myself in the presence of others. My silence was a struggle to that end. I had her name in my mouth, but would not speak it, her face before my eyes, her voice in my ear, but I wouldn't think on anything she had ever done or said that might make me begin to weep again. To some degree my efforts to banish her were successful, but they left me little else to speak or think, either.

When we reached the castle and were brought before its warden, Robin spoke for both of us:

'We are King William's clerks with messages of great importance for him. We must have a pair of fast horses and a little guidance, if you'll be so kind. Where will we find him now? Still at Mantes? Or is it Paris, with his thousand candles?' He laughed. 'We've heard that tale.'

The warden stared at him grimly. 'The king is in Rouen now. If your news is urgent, you'd better mount and ride without waiting for your supper. The word from there is that he's dying.'

Robin and I exchanged glances. 'How is this? Was there some battle since Mantes?'

'No. Is that the last you've heard? If so, it's stale. They say he fell from his horse and did himself some injury. Go to Rouen for the rest of the tale.'

He was very curt with us, and I could guess why. If the king died, so did the Duke of Normandy, and there would soon be anarchy in the duchy. Every lord would lift his bridge and let fall his gate to defend himself, or else go out looking for weaker prey to rob and seize while there was no government. The French, the Flemings, the Bretons, the Angevins, all of them, might soon array themselves against the headless Normans, who would be too busy letting blood among themselves to notice, until it was too late. Even such weak guests as ourselves might seem like potential enemies, spies for some faction or another in this knight's eyes; so why should he gossip on the matter of the king's illness with us?

We took his horses with thanks, along with his preferred road to Rouen: Envermeu to Longueville, to Tôtes, to Clères, to home. Each of us rode thinking the same thing, I suppose: if the king were dead when we came, to whom should we resort? Should we turn back and warn William de Warenne or Lanfranc that the king was ill and might die? Would the English rise up on hearing news of his death, if that should occur, and drive us from the land before his heir could come and claim the throne?

I had never loved William Bastard or much admired him, but as I rode, I prayed he would live awhile yet, because if he died, Robin's life and mine might end in a celebration of slaughter among those who judged themselves competent to take his place. Who it would be in the end – Curthose, Rufus, pale Henry, or some other – would not matter overmuch to me, otherwise.

We reached Rouen the next day about Vespers, though there were no bells ringing to celebrate that hour. We went into the town by the north gate, dismounted, and said a prayer of thanks to St. Apollonius for our safe journey.

The streets were as empty of people as a cloister garth at mealtime. Window shutters stood open above our heads, but no one looked out on us.

'Where are they all? It's like a tomb,' Robin said. As if in answer to his question, a soldier in gambeson and helm stepped out of a doorway near the shrine of Apollonius and stopped us.

'Where are you going? No horses or carts allowed beyond the market without the gate captain's pass.'

We identified ourselves and our destination. He held a debate with himself, then nodded.

'That's all right then. But walk your mounts and don't make unnecessary noise. Constable's orders.'

Straw covered the street leading past the castle walls; straw was littered thickly in the bailey. The gate porter spoke in an unnatural whisper. No one laughed or quarrelled or cursed; no dogs barked. Even the castle geese were out of sight and silent. We went up the steps to the great oak door that led to the hall.

Robin said: 'If there's somebody sitting at the high table we don't like the looks of, let's turn and run for a ship again and tell de Warenne to make ready for war. This place gives me a chill.'

But when we'd stood and looked about for a few moments, he said: 'There's nobody here I recognize. Let's go up to the chapel and ask a brother what's happened.'

I nodded and we slipped away up the stairs without exciting the least suspicion; as William de St. Carileph had once pointed out, clerks are invisible. Straw covered the stair and the passage above, too. I could hear the sibilant whisper of a priest in the chapel. The only light there was from a flambeau sputtering in a socket and from the candles burning before the chapel altar.

Some ten or a dozen leather-clad men knelt in the chapel. A man leaned against the wall near its door, in such a leisurely posture as to show he took no part in their worship but found it tolerably interesting to watch. He heard our footsteps and turned his head. I caught the glitter of his eye as he glanced over me; then he lifted a finger to his lips to signal silence. It was Cormac.

'Hush,' he whispered, 'we're at prayer here.'

I took him for drunk and passed him without comment. We knelt at the rear of the chapel and heard the last of the service. The worshipers rose, blessing themselves, and I saw Rufus and Prince Henry among them. Henry turned on his heel as soon as his thumb had touched his nether lip at the end of the blessing. He went out with the rest, striding briskly to the stairs, his expression amiable to his friends.

Rufus remained standing before the altar. The priest turned, saw him, made as if to speak to him, then glanced quickly aside and passed him hurriedly with his deacon behind him. Rufus sighed and turned slowly from his reflection on the image of Christ Crucified above the altar; I saw the look that had made the priest falter. His eye roamed over me, then took in Robin, and his rather ugly smile changed in an instant to one of recognition and delight. He lurched forward unsteadily with a laugh and threw his thick arms about us both, hugging us fiercely.

'Robin and Ra-Ranulph! My cousin and my conscience. By the Face, what brings you rogues here? You don't want to join the rest of the carrion eaters that hang over m-my – my f-father's bed, do you? You're not wearing your frocks! That's why I didn't rec-c-cognize you. What – did old Maurice unfrock the both of you? What terrible c-crimes have you done for it, eh?' He was most pitifully drunk.

'We've had a long ride from the coast, my lord,' I said, 'and clerks' gowns aren't made for the gallop. My lord, are you going to be sick?' His face had suddenly gone slack.

Cormac came, smiling perfunctorily at me as he slipped between us. He took his master's arm from my neck and put it about his own, saying coolly: 'Will you go down to the hall to make your puke, or up on the battlements? The fresh air might save you.'

Rufus tried to draw back from him. 'Damned old woman! You hear how he speaks to me? Like a wet nurse to her babe. Hands off and by your leave, nurse, we'll take our f-friends downstairs for some wine before they – oh, God – ' He swayed, closed his eyes. 'I'm sick, I'm sick.'

'There, I knew it. Come on, then; don't vomit in the chapel.' Cormac seized him and bore him away quickly to the nearest jakes, where he immediately lost his stomach in the waste channel, then stood shuddering, arms braced against the wall above it.

'Resolve it,' said Cormac, 'you'll never be the wine bucket your brother is.' He left the jakes and returned in a few minutes with a damp napkin, with which he wiped Rufus's face and nape until Rufus grabbed it from him and flung it into the waste trough. Cormac clucked his tongue as it settled into the vile contents of that place. 'And dipped in holy water, too.'

Rufus glared at him, then snorted with laughter. He turned and saw Robin and me in the door. 'He's ever the fool, but he's right about me. I've no more stomach for wine than a suckling calf.' He wiped his face with his hand. 'You've come with news, I suppose, or you wouldn't have come at all. Bad news? Of course. What else ever comes from that miserable island? Well, you can't tell it to my father – he's ill – but you can tell it to me. Come down to the hall. You'll drink and I'll listen.'

He warded off further assistance from Cormac with a warning hand, then led us down to the hall, where his friends immediately surrounded him. There were fewer of them than I expected if the king's life was in jeopardy, but I was more interested in the way Cormac faded back when we approached them. He affected to take up a conversation with someone else, but kept within hearing. I thought it might have more to do with the cold look which Robert fitz Hamon bent on him than it did with the almost casual rebuff of Rufus.

Robin told our news of the great fire, which made several at the table groan, as they or their families owned mansions in the town. They questioned Robin at length on which streets had most suffered and which markets would lose their tallage for the year. Rufus listened, turning an empty cup between his thick fingers.

'Calamity and fire,' he said in a dull voice. 'This is the year for fire. What comes next? They say the world will end with the century – a thousand years since John the Revealer told of it.' He grinned at me. 'Priests' talk, of course, to get more money from our t-trembling hands, but it's got to end sometime, hasn't it? If they preach doom and death for a thousand years – it's bound to come true at last.'

That put a pall on the talk. We all blessed ourselves.

Robert fitz Hamon said: 'I don't believe it yet, but there are signs enough to make a man wonder. Two popes we've got now, the Church split, heretics abounding. The heathen have the Holy City, and no one in the Christian world is bold enough to get it back from them.'

'Let it go, then. Let it end,' said Rufus. 'The world was a bad invention, wrong from the beginning. Maybe the heretics are right and it was the Devil who made it after all.'

'My lord – ' I began, thinking to admonish him before he got deeper into heresy, but he stood up, ignoring me.

'I want some air and exercise before I sleep. I want a brawl, but there's no place for it in this manger of a town. Will anyone ride with me?' A half-dozen voices gave eager assent and they went out, wading through the thick layer of sound-muffling straw.

'Strange, isn't it?' Cormac came and sat in Rufus's place when he was gone from the hall. He poured wine, tasted it. 'The king, dying, should leave my lord a powerful man at last, whatever part of the inheritance he gets. He never treated him to anything in his life more than an excellent indifference. Yet my lord is not impatient to see the old man die, as you, or I, or any sensible prospective heir would be. Look at young Henry, for instance. Grief fairly makes his eyes sparkle these days. He'd take an earldom, but he dreams of a kingdom, if Rufus gets Normandy. He's had all his friends calling him Atheling with every breath lately.'

'Is it certain the king will die, then?' Robin asked.

'As certain as taxes. His guts are rotting in him.'

Robin shook his head. 'I can't comprehend a world with no William Bastard in it.'

Cormac looked about the room. 'The rest here can. Look at them, pulling their long faces with boredom. They're mad with impatience inside. He'll scarcely have his hands folded before they rush home to throw his troops off their land and start hacking at each other.'

'But he'll name his successor. Rufus, Henry; even Curthose will command some respect, surely.'

'How? When did *he* ever let any of them earn respect from these, the world's most natural cutthroats? None of them ever had the command of so much as a watchtower in a fen while he lived. He must have it all! Yes, there'll be another duke here when he dies – for a time. Those who matter here want Curthose, drunk and merry, to lead by the nose. I hope they get him.'

'And the lords of England?'

'When did they ever want a king? They'll take young Harry, I think – a boy of twenty and a vain cockscomb. Another one fit to be led in a halter, since his only interest is dragging sluts to his bed.'

I said: 'You've changed your notions since I last heard them, Cormac. What about your master?'

Cormac sighed, then snorted. 'He has the Devil's Eye! He doesn't love to hear long Masses! He won't take a bribe to plead for favors in his father's ear. He won't do at all for king or duke. He doesn't care! He *grieves*. He says he'll follow Edgar Atheling to Italy when all's over here, or stay just long enough to see Curthose rightly settled when he comes for his dukedom. In a word, Little Brother, he's become a fool.'

There was a silence. I could see that Cormac had offended Robin with his cynicism, Robin not hearing the bitter grief that lay behind the hard words.

After a time I asked, 'How did the king get his mortal wound?'

'There was no wound. Haven't you heard the tale? He put the town of Mantes to the torch for failing to open to him joyfully, after he'd ripped up its vineyards and axed its orchards. We had a splendid slaughter there. I'm making a fitting song on it now.

'Half the town ran out of the gates when they were yielded, to cry for mercy. They got broken heads and slit throats. Why not? The bastards had delayed us on our way to Paris, which was a pity, because I rather wanted to see Paris again.

'We lobbed fireballs over the walls with the siege engines to set the roofs alight, then battered down the supplicants and sacked the town. It was wonderful to see helmed knights fighting for possession of a cooking pot, or running after a slut, with sausages hugged under their arms that they'd snatched from a butcher's stall. I have a token of the event myself.' He held up his hand, adorned with a thick silver ring with a bit of dark stone in it. 'The owner didn't offer me a fight. In fact, he was nowhere in sight, only his hand, which I found lying in a gutter.'

'Christ, man, what about the king?' Robin said in disgust.

'The king remained outside the walls until the burning, rape, and pillage were accomplished. The next day he rode in over the fallen bodies and made a survey of the ruin. His horse stumbled, trying to jump a smoking house beam. The lurch, and his weight, tore him and his saddle loose, and both crashed to the ground. They say he fell on the pommel, which was wedged tight under his stomach.

'He screamed and couldn't get up. Will and Henry made a litter from a charred door and had him carried outside the walls again. Gilbert Maminot said part of his entrails had been thrust through his belly wall. He tried to put the gut back in its place, but the king fainted. The great doctor was afraid he might have caused the king's death on the spot, so he grew very fierce and forbade anyone else to touch the injury, or even to come close enough to see it. They made a horse-drawn litter and walked him back to Rouen.

'As you see, we've made a manger of the whole town, because the noise of even an oiled cartwheel keeps the king from the stupor that gives him rest. Tomorrow they'll take him out to St. Gervase Priory where it's quieter. Everyone's been forbidden to sneeze, break wind, or even walk on the streets tomorrow until he's safely carried away, except my lord and his brother, who'll go with the litter bearers.' He scraped back the bench and rose. 'My lord William has promised to flay the bearer who stumbles with his burden if it makes the king so much as sigh. That adds a certain interest to the event for you, Ranulph; I've been nominated one of the bearers. You might want to have a peek from the battlements.'

King William was borne to the priory in safety and installed in a common cell, according to his own wish. There his sufferings continued without relief, while his vassals hovered and made open wagers on how his estate would be divided when he died.

The king grew weaker. His bowels no longer functioned. He vomited dark bile. His eyes were like those of a man who has fainted, and his skin was suffused with a greenish tint. He stank worse than seemed possible for a living man.

Someone, remembering his reputation with the sick, had sent for Anselm, the prior of Bec. His sanctity was so great that it was believed if he merely came and sat by an invalid's bed the man would improve.

But who is there to physic such a physician? Prior Anselm fell ill on his way to succor the king and lay abed himself until it was too late.

I found the days of waiting trying, lacking any occupation but daily prayers and waiting on some word about the king. No matter how I tried to deny her a place in my brain at that time, Elfgiva haunted me. In what pauper's grave or common trench did she lie now, with her little, curled mystery still in her womb? Poor wretch; I had used her wickedly. I could be absolved of it now, being truly sorry for the deed; but what about her, in the dark she dreaded so much? I said more prayers for her than for the king, and I made a promise to the Almighty that He had heard from my lips before: no more women for me.

I could pity Rufus, who now suffered the imminent loss of someone he, too, loved. He stood by the king every day, watched his agony in silence, then went out to ride his horse to a lather, or do sword practice in an open field with such fury that his opponents were driven back milk-faced from his rage.

'Christ! Why can't he die?' he cried out suddenly to me one day on leaving the cell. 'He should have been dead a week ago. How long can he be made to suffer?'

A monk of the priory who happened to pass by at that moment stopped and offered consolation: 'God's mercy is often inscrutable to Man, my lord. In prolonging a man's death Our Lord gives him ample time to repent of his sins and so make his way safe to Heaven. What seems cruel is truly merciful, and we should rather rejoice for our lord the king, for he is tendered such mercy that he may make good use of it.'

'You call that mercy? God keep His mercy from me, then!' Rufus countered savagely.

My brother of the tonsure was horrified. 'Oh, my lord, never say such a thing in anger. Repent of it at once, lest you be taken at your word!'

'I ask nothing better than to be taken at my word, let it be by God, Man, or the Devil, you canting fool! Who gave you leave to speak to me?'

The monk fled. Rufus turned and glared at me with red-shot eyes. 'Do you want to follow him, or do you want exercise? Let's go out of this damned charnel house and ride! Where's Cormac?'

So, I found myself his companion again, as if we had never been separated. That day I rode with him until I thought I should fall from my saddle with weariness, and he talked compulsively when we rested, falling over his words, getting them clogged in his throat, until some of the tension left him and the words flowed without hindrance. I believed he could do this with me, not because of any high regard in which he held me for having some part in saving his life once, but because he held me in no particular regard as a person. I didn't frighten him in any manner, never showed strain or impatience when he faltered, being, on that occasion at least, too stunned with my own misery to be stirred by a disability in his speech.

He told me things about his life he may never have uttered to another soul, though I am certain it wasn't my office as confessor he was seeking that day, but only my hearing as a person of no consequence to whom he felt somehow attached by circumstance.

The first recollection of his life was connected with his speech impediment. He had heard some servants gossiping about a dark event that had taken place at the ducal fortress at Falaise a short time before. Duke William had just achieved his invasion and conquest of the county of Maine, to which he claimed title on behalf of his son Robert. The Count and Countess of Maine, Walter of Pontoise and his wife, Biota, were taken captive and had been held under honorable restraint at Falaise until their sudden deaths, which followed close upon each other. The servants' gossip was that Duke William had poisoned them to relieve himself of worry about their future activity.

This news, that his father had made his houseguests to die, was absorbed and repeated by the four-year-old William to his mother, who, when she understood his meaning, took him by the hair and thrust him into an armoire, locking him into it for several hours by way of punishment. She was too great with child to beat him, she said, but his father would do so when he heard of it.

'I don't know if he ever heard of it,' said Rufus, after musing on the memory for several moments. 'He didn't come to us for several weeks, and when he did, I got no further punishment. But I lived, day and night, in a great fear of him, that he should despise me for having believed such an evil thing of him – though I believed it no more, nor do yet! My f-father was never the man who needed poi-poison to conquer his enemies. But I feared nothing so much from that time as that I might harm him, or dis-disgrace myself in his eyes, so he might remember that b-betrayal – and I think my tongue was faulty from that time, too.

'When I was six, he was gathering his fleet to make his war against the English, and my uncle Robert took me to where the *Mora* lay, which would be my father's own ship. It was a gift from my mother. It had a gilded figure on the masthead, a boy – a sort of cherub, maybe. He had a horn in his hand and his mouth was open, ready to blow it. I remember Uncle lifting me up so that I could see him. The woodcarver who made him hadn't given him a tongue, just a hole in his open mouth.

'I asked Uncle Robert who the boy was, and he laughed and said it must be me, because my father doted on his golden boy. That pleased me a great deal, though it was nonsense, of course. But for several years I believed it – and I thought my father might have made the woodcarver leave out that part of me which marred me more than – ' He didn't say his eyes, but that was what he meant.

I was sitting in the prior's garth at St. Gervase some afternoon after that, trying to make amends for a neglected Office, when I heard two voices coming through the hedge from the cloister side:

'. . . a menagerie to choose from, he said: a dancing bear, a red bull, and a little poisonous grass snake.'

A quick, nervous laugh answered that. 'He should know them best. They're his nephews. But why he should still have his heart set on the bear, I confess I can't quite grasp, having seen him.'

'His Grace puts it simply, thus: bears can be led, if they're shackled, but bulls must be altered before they're tame, and what can be done with snakes, except step on their heads and quickly, too?'

'Yes, well – but that bull won't be easy to dock, even for Odo.' The same laugh distorted the final word.

'Shh, Osbern, for God's sake, can't you say anything without braying? As for the bull, there's a halter made for him already and someone close to him to slip it over his horns. Then a grip of the hot pincers and he's tame enough . . . ' The two who spoke were passing beyond easy hearing, so I rose from my bench to follow them along the high hedge.

'. . . too far with a metaphor, Fulcher,' the laughing one said in reproof. His use of the second name made me pause for a moment; then I stepped through a separation in the hedge that brought me out just a few steps behind the two speakers, young clerks, elbow to elbow, their polished dark heads bent toward each other like a man and his reflection in a basin. I hadn't seen either of them since the younger was still breaking his voice on the odd syllable, but I had little trouble recognizing certain family attributes. They reached the corner of the garth and turned to retrace their steps, which brought them around to face me.

'Well, well, my clever brothers. Who let you in here to trample the grass?'

Their heads swiveled from me to each other and back.

'Ranulph? Ranulph!' Osbern laughed and flew to me, flung his arms around my neck, while Fulcher cut his eyes sideways at the hedge, already calculating what I might have heard.

'It's all right,' I said, beckoning to him. 'But you're lucky it was I who overheard you and not one of the king's own. You've lost your pustules. Come and kiss me.'

We had a modest reunion in the refectory, where Osbern told me all the news from home, which was that my parents still lived, but Father was very frail now.

'He talks of taking monk's vows, but if he did, what would we do with Mother? She won't be cloistered, but then I doubt that any house would take her, with her temper.'

'Good for Mother! Why can't the two of you keep her? You look prosperous.'

Osbern reddened and laughed. 'Not us, no. You don't have a roof to call your own when you're one of the good bishop's men.'

'The good bishop?' I glanced from Osbern to Fulcher, who hadn't said much. 'The good bishop Odo? What a splendid title! Did he invent it himself, or is he a martyr to his people in Bayeux these days?'

'To those who know the truth of things he is,' said Fulcher stiffly. 'No one like him has ever been more generous to the poor and to their churches. You ought to remember that, for Father's sake, if not your own. He's long been a friend to our family.'

'Ah, yes. I have him to thank for several things. Did Father send you to him? What is it you do as his clerks, since he's still a prisoner?'

Osbern started to reply to that, but Fulcher stopped him. He looked at me defiantly. 'Father had good cause to love His Grace in the old days, and unlike some, he didn't forget him in his hour of need. The church of St. Loup has silver altar vessels now, and Father has a fine embroidered chasuble, which His Grace gave him before he went to England and was betrayed. These were his own goods that he gave to our father.'

'I know all about Odo's goods and his many gifts to the churches of his diocese, Fulcher. I helped him steal them from the churches in England.'

'I knew you'd become his enemy.'

'I'm not his enemy. Only I'm no longer his man. Do you understand? Loyalty is not like a love affair; it is a matter of responsibility. I am the king's clerk now, but the king will soon die. Then I will be the man of the next king. Whoever he is, I will serve him. So, naturally I was interested to hear your talk in the cloister, because it seemed to me you knew better than I who my next master might be.'

'Of course we do. Anybody with an eye in his head – '

'Be still, Osbern,' said Fulcher. 'You say you don't know who your next master will be, but you seem to have chosen him. You go about all the time in the footsteps of Will-Rou.'

'The red bull? Yes, I heard that. But he was once my master, too, for a time, thanks to the good bishop. Is that the reason you distrust me, brother? Because I once served him and your bishop dislikes him? He set me on him for a spy. Did you know that?'

'Fulcher's afraid you might be a spy for the other side now,' said Osbern frankly. I smiled at him. Every time he spoke I liked him less and Fulcher more.

'Brothers, the doings of all these gentry are as far above us as the gates of Heaven. We are clerks and are made to serve the great, but if we're wise we don't partake of their loves and hatreds, for things change and one never knows whose hand will be on his neck tomorrow. Isn't that so?'

They studied me in silence.

'We are each other's flesh and blood, though we've been long parted,' I said solemnly. 'Our masters may be enemies and brothers, but should I betray my own brothers for one of them? Or they me, for another?'

They consulted with their eyes again; then Fulcher nodded and Osbern said eagerly:

'Robert Curthose will be your next king, brother, and ours, too. He will bind the two lands together under one crown, the Kingdom of England and Normandy. He has the privately secured blessings of the Holy Father to defeat the King of France if he opposes this union, so it may be that our future master will call himself King of England and France. Bishop Odo will be his chancellor and will be given a cardinalship when he has delivered the investiture of bishops back into the hands of the Church, where it belongs.'

'If it had been in their hands when he was fourteen, he'd never have been a bishop, since it was his brother who made him so,' I said, but I caught Fulcher's watchful eye and smiled. 'But that's choplogic. This is wonderful news! How has the bishop accomplished it? I thought he was cut off from the world in his prison cell.'

'Yes, as Earl of Kent he's in prison. But as Bishop of Bayeux he is still required to conduct God's business, and he does, though he's been allowed only one visitor a month since the Lady Matilda died. But we've been able to manage very well on that. Fulcher's just returned from Rome on his behalf.'

25

When I had heard enough, I sat back to look at them with pretended admiration. 'So, it's all settled! While the whole court still waits in doubt, you, my little brothers, have been in the heart of the doing. I congratulate you! Why, we'll be a family to be reckoned with yet. But does Count Robert know how close he is to a double crown? They say he still wanders in the Germanies.'

'He should know and be on his way home at this moment,' said Fulcher. 'Robert of Mortain has already petitioned the king for Odo's release from Rouen tower. The king refused, but when Count Robert gets here our bishop will be freed whether the king still lives or not, and no one can oppose him then. Robert's the rightful heir, whatever quarrels he may have had with the king in the past. Lord Odo will soon have more friends than enemies.'

'I have no doubt. Well, brothers, you amaze and delight me. To think I was worried about your futures and thought I might be the one to do some good for you.'

'What good did you have in mind?' asked Fulcher.

'Oh, I thought I might have to find you posts in the English court when you were ready, but as it stands, I may be your suitor for a position, instead. When you're the good Cardinal Odo's chief clerks, you won't forget your poor, outlander brother, will you? I've had some experience in a chancery, you know.'

Osbern was flattered and promised I shouldn't go wanting. Fulcher still looked at me with clear, cautious eyes, though he smiled now. I could have kissed him for his silence. I might one day have a use for him, or, if things turned out as 'the good bishop' planned, he might have a use for me, because we understood each other well.

In the next few days we were much together, and I heard more of Odo's secrets. I kept them, because there was no one I could divulge them to at that time who would benefit from the knowledge more than I. I heard Robert of Mortain had begged the king a second and third time for the release of their uterine brother, and each time King William refused, saying Odo was a natural traitor and a confirmed meddler who would never cease to trouble the peace of the realm if he were free. The last time he refused Mortain, Rufus and Henry had been persuaded to add their pleas to his for Odo's release.

Fulcher watched me pretty closely during that week and was satisfied I had kept his confidence.

'What will happen to Rufus and Henry when Odo is free?' I asked him. 'Will he have as much pity for them as they've shown for him, praying for his release?'

'Nothing will happen if they acknowledge their brother to be the rightful heir in both territories.'

'But if they don't?'

He looked at me warily. 'Why do you care for them, brother, seeing they're so far above us, as you said? They will be taken at the king's death and kept quietly, until they do accept, or they will be kept – quiet – if they don't. Would that pain you?'

'By the Mass, no, Brother! I'd rather live in a realm at peace than in one at war with superfluous princes.'

His brow cleared slightly. 'Yes, that's the sensible way to look at it.

You mustn't think me bloody-minded. I, too, hope the princes will come to no harm and look for peace.'

'There's only one thing that puzzles me, Fulcher. This whole worthy enterprise is predicated on one event: that King William will bestow both crown and coronet on Robert, because in the end he's the rightful heir. But the king professes to despise him. Can you think he'd reward the prodigal with all, leaving the sons who have clung to him with nothing? If he doesn't do it, there'll be anarchy in both countries. Odo won't get his cardinal's hat and the three of us won't get our peace.'

'Gilbert Maminot has promised Odo that the king will name Robert. He's his confessor and should know.'

'What, has Gilbert broken the seal of the confession?'

'Of course not! But he has great influence with the king and with the ecclesiastical council. Every bishop in Normandy will plead with the king to free Odo and to name his eldest son rightful heir for the sake of peace. How can he refuse?'

'How, indeed? Are they all so fond of Robert?'

'Brother, you amaze me sometimes with your innocence, truly you do. The bishops have urged the king for years to yield to the late Pope Gregory's command that investiture of bishops and abbots be left to the Church, but still he denies them. Why, since Gregory's death the king has not even acknowledged the new Pope's existence! One might almost think he even secretly favored the schismatical Clement whom the Germans have set up against the true Vicar of Christ, Victor!

'Bishop Odo has always been a true son of Rome. He swore himself to God under St. Leo, and he has kept faith with every rightly elected Pope ever since. He has promised Pope Victor that Curthose will yield to him on the point of lay investiture. The bishops therefore favor Curthose over these two younger sons, especially Red Will, who apes his father's opinions in every way. Now do you see?'

'By your lamp, Fulcher, I now see clearly.' I gave him a hug.

It was a plan most worthy of Uncle Odo, one that seemed designed to wreck us on the shoals of German policy. We would lose our trade, affront the King of France by taking away even our nominal allegiance to him, invite invasion of all our borders by his allies. While it was possible that strife with other nations might keep us from anarchy within for a time, I couldn't believe that Robert the Drunkard, backed by his enthusiastic uncle, could keep us whole for long. With Odo's past luck working for him, we would all be learning either Danish or German in a year or two.

The king was at last plainly dying. He felt no further pain in his abdomen, or any sensation from his breastbone to his feet. He was tremendously bloated and yellow, but his mind was still clear.

He spent the better part of his last day making his confession, recalling with great accuracy all the cruelties he had inflicted upon others, as well as the treacheries they had visited upon him. When he had exhausted both memory and the pen hands of two clerks who scribbled it all down for posterity, Gilbert Maminot, Bishop of Lisieux, gave him the last comforts of religion, and he lay in peace. His sons, vassals, and all who could crowd into the little room came to attend him one last time.

Robin Bloet and I were fortunate enough to squeeze ourselves into a corner of that airless cell before all the rest of our tonsured brethren came flocking and found they must stand in the passage. Fulcher and Osbern were among the tardy ones, having borne the news of the king's last refusal to release imprisoned Odo from the tower.

The king roused himself, let his lips be moistened with a damp towel, and began to tell of the gifts he would leave the Church. He was more than generous. I began to wonder if even the wealth of his English treasury would suffice to satisfy the benefits.

When that was done, several lords came forward to ask pardon for relatives who had been imprisoned or exiled for various offenses. The king forgave them all. He freed the English rebel, Earl Morcar, and the last living brother of King Harold, commanding that all the royal donjons be emptied of their prisoners upon their giving oath they would do no more wrong, but be faithful to their future king.

'What about our brother Odo?' asked Robert of Mortain tremulously. 'Must he alone remain while all the rest go free? Great King and good brother, he was your mother's son, who suckled the same paps as you.'

'Let him stay where he is, if you love peace,' whispered the king.

'Let him be free, if you love mercy, my brother. He fought for you at Senlac Field. He routed the Bretons when the earls revolted and you were here in Normandy. He was your champion once. Will you deny him mercy and still hope for it yourself?' Mortain spoke in a lowing, grieved voice, but too quickly, as if he had learned the words by heart. He glowered about him as if to draw response from the others. Geoffrey Mowbray came and bent his knee by the king's bed.

'Spare your brother, great King, as you hope for Heaven.'

Gilbert of Lisieux knelt and asked pardon for Odo, too. So did the Archbishop of Rouen, and the bishops of Avranches, Evreux, and Sees, just as Fulcher had predicted. Even Rufus and Henry entreated him again:

'Release our good uncle, Father, for our mother's sake, who loved him,' said Henry primly.

Rufus flushed as he spoke bluntly: 'Let Odo be free, Father. There's some good in him, seeing he's your b-brother.'

The king looked long at Rufus. 'Do you pity him for my judgment of him?'

'No, my lord. I honor him, b-because he's your brother and my uncle.'

'Very well. Let him be free. My forgiveness he cannot hope to have, but only my mercy. I don't want him set free until I'm dead. Is that understood?'

Mortain wept and the prelates looked satisfied. Then Gilbert Maminot leaned over the bed and said softly: 'The king shows his wisdom in mercy. Now, what of your eldest son, my gracious lord? Will you suffer him to continue to lead a vagabond's life? He, too, is your flesh and blood and hungers for your mercy.'

The king made a grimace and sighed. 'Robert, yes. It's time to speak of him – and others.' He looked at Rufus and Henry, who knelt almost as one beside his bed, bowing their heads to his will, whatever it might be.

'I granted the duchy of Normandy to my son Robert when he was still a child, before I fought against Harold at Senlac, because he was the elder son and I didn't mean to weaken my land with Salic divisions. He had a younger, wiser brother, whom God saw fit to take from me, and he had two yet younger, who are his peers in valor and his betters in judgment, as God knows. My firstborn is a foolish man who cannot learn from misfortune, or he wouldn't be an exile from his home a second time.'

Rufus and Henry had both lifted their heads and looked on the king with the same stone-lipped patience.

'I fear the country Robert would rule would be wretched, as if it were governed by the caprice of a child. But – he has already received the homage of nearly all the barons of the land, and the grant once made, I cannot annul it. So be it – Robert has Normandy.'

A small, communal sigh escaped the lips of Curthose's adherents.

'And the crown of England, Your Grace?' asked Gilbert.

'I cannot appoint an heir to the crown of England.'

There was a gasp from someone, and the king's heavy-lidded eyes opened slightly; he could still enjoy creating dismay with a word.

'I didn't receive the crown by hereditary right; I took it from a perjured king by force of arms. Having come to it by battle and the shedding of much blood, I dare not leave it to any but God alone.'

I blessed myself. Then it would be murder and ruin for England, I thought. Robert, Rufus, Henry, and any others who could lift a sword would slaughter for possession of all or part of it, as men had fought for it in the days before the Confessor. The Danes, the Scots, the Welsh, and God knew who else would contend for what was left, along with the wolves and ravens.

But the king spoke again: 'I pray that my son William, who has always been faithful to me from his earliest years and dutiful under all trials to the best of his powers, will lead a long and vigorous life. If it should please the Divine Will that he succeed me on the English throne, it would please me as well.'

There was silence. A belated murmur grew out of it and spread from the cell into the corridor. Prince Henry turned pale, his mouth fell open a fraction, but he closed it again. Rufus looked dismayed, as if he had just heard himself cut off from all inheritance rather than the reverse. But in one of its swift changes the bafflement vanished and his face shone joy like a child's as he grasped his father's hand and kissed it.

'I swear I wi-wi-will k-keep that realm a-a-as if I were your second self, F-father.'

'My second self.' The king's stark mouth softened. 'Yes, God grant that you will be that. You must *keep it – increase it –* as I would do, now, if I were to begin. Do you understand me?' He squeezed his son's hand with a fierce grip.

There was a perceptible shift of attention now, away from the king, as he called for a scribe to set down his hopes in a letter for Lanfranc. The eyes of the room were fixed on Rufus, who stood, still holding his father's hand in both his. Geoffrey Mowbray and his nephew, the bearlike Robert, stood just behind the new heir, frowning. Gilbert Maminot and the Archbishop of Rouen consulted each other mutely. When the letter was written, the king made his mark on it and it was sealed and given to Rufus, at the direction of his father.

'Now – draw my sword from under this bed, my son. It will be yours – my second self.'

Rufus obeyed. He held up the famous sword that had been

wielded over the English at Senlac, the same with which William Bastard had won his first victory at Val-ès-Dunes; he held it aloft, then kissed the quillons reverently. There was a little moaning sound from the room at that gesture, which seemed temporarily to affect even his enemies. Normans are more sentimental about their weapons than about their children, I sometimes think.

'Go, now,' whispered the king.

Rufus acted on the word, pushing his way at once through the press of bodies to the door. Robin moved to follow and I went after him, but as I eased myself forward, Prince Henry asked in a strangled voice:

'And what do you leave me, Father?'

I paused. The answer had better not be an earldom in England, or history would be repeating itself with a struggle between brothers.

'Eh? Ah, Harry – yes, for you I have five thousand livres in silver, to be paid from my treasury here. It is no little gift – '

'Five thousand in silver? What good will a fortune do me if I haven't any land?'

I reached the door.

'My son, you are yet young and not without wit. You will be – patient – and give way to your brothers. In time it may be you will have all. You're a good deal younger, so who knows, eh?' King William still spoke to him as to an importunate child.

Fulcher and Osbern were still in the passage.

'Take my place, brothers, if you can. You may find it still instructive. Odo will be free on the king's death.'

'But your Rufus gets the crown?'

'If he can keep it, brother, if he can keep it. Go in now. There may be more to hear. I must follow Robin Bloet, but we'll speak together later at the castle.' I gave Fulcher a push in earnest, and Osbern aided me by shoving himself between us. I smiled encouragement as Fulcher was thrust by Osbern through the doorway, but the moment his puzzled face was out of sight I fought my way through the rest of the crowd in the passage to find Rufus.

I surprised Robin by rushing past him to catch up with Rufus in the abbey yard that led to the prior's stable. I nearly slipped on the stones as I ran up to him, so he wheeled in surprise and caught me by the elbow to keep me from falling.

'My lord, will you trust in me? You are in danger. Make merry at my expense. Laugh at me, for I'm going to fall.'

'What? What foolery's this? Are you drunk, or what?'

I let my legs go out from under me, nearly pulling him over with me, so that I could whisper in his ear. He was quick.

'God's Life, if I can see how a toper gets to it, even in an abbey! Get to your feet, man. Here, Robin, help me.' Under his breath he said: 'Who's ready to take me? I think you must be drunk, after all, you damned – '

'No, my lord! It was my own brother who told me!'

There were several of the king's men-at-arms loitering outside the stable, waiting to be commanded as messengers, who saw our struggle and came forward. Robin Bloet was sorely embarrassed by me, got hold of my other arm, and hauled me erect.

'It's all right, Haimo,' Rufus said to the sergeant who advanced on us. 'Here's just a fellow who fell into a friendship with the cellarer and nearly drowned himself in a wine butt. I'll sober him; I'll ride him around the town walls until he spews or sobers. Damned useless, winesopping priest! Cormac!'

Cormac materialized out of the shadows of the stable, the last person I wanted to see, since I suspected him of being that 'someone' close to Rufus who would put the halter around his neck and lead him to Odo. But there was nothing I could do to rid us of him. Horses were brought and held for us to mount. Robin was still trying to get a private word with me. He came close enough to realize I wasn't drunk.

As we rode through the postern gate, Cormac surged past me, nudging my horse so that the beast nearly wiped me off the saddle on the gatepost. He went ahead with Rufus on the straight, dark road to Rouen. Robin rode beside me. He didn't speak until we'd fallen a little more behind the two. 'Have you really taken leave of your wits, or what?'

'We must get him away from here tonight, Robin, or they'll take him – maybe kill him.'

'Who will?'

'I don't know, exactly. Someone back there. They won't wait long – ' As I spoke I heard sounds in the dark behind us, voices and hoofbeats. I urged my horse with a cruel kick, plunged his unwilling nose between the rumps of those animals that carried Rufus and Cormac, until I was all but sitting on Rufus's knee. He cursed my second intrusion:

'By the Face, where're you headed now? Control your mount!'

'Turn off into that grove of trees. Quick, and be still!' I was desperate. 'Turn him, turn him, Cormac, unless you're one of them! They'll take him!'

Cormac seized the headband of Rufus's palfrey and forced him off the road. My own disgruntled mare tittupped sideways, snorting with wrath and farting with the power of all the grain she'd gobbled out of the prior's stores. She was ready to pitch me off, but I slapped her between the ears, then on the rump, and she leaped stiff-legged into the woods. Robin was close behind me.

'Don't let your harness jangle.'

Rufus had his sword drawn when we came up to him. Now we all could hear the approaching riders, their pace increasing as they entered the wood-shadowed strip of road we'd just left. Rufus leaned forward in the saddle to peer after them as they went by. I caught a fragment of speech as they passed:

'. . . reach the gate!' They fled into the dark.

Cormac slipped to the ground and made a soft approach to the road's edge, keeping under cover of the trees. We stood as before until he said quietly: 'No more coming at present.'

Rufus looked at me; at least his sword swung around as he seemed to. He tapped the point of it on my chest. 'Now. You tell us what this means. There were six of them. Who?'

'I don't know, but they mean to prevent you from leaving Normandy, until your brother comes, or your father dies and your uncle's set free. You weren't meant to get the English crown; Count Robert was. The rest expected that, but your uncle means to make sure of it.'

'Why? You're talking nonsense, priest. My uncle has been penned for five years, and closely, too. I know. How could he send men out to capture me? How could you know it, if he did? I think there's more to this and you're the one to be wary of. Priest, if you think you can hold me here, talking mysteries, until some scheme you're in comes together – ' His sword blade moved upward to my throat, snagging my gown. I flinched and slid off my saddle in haste to escape it.

'No!' Cormac said suddenly. 'Hold off, Will. He makes sense; listen to him.' As I scrambled to my feet to avoid being trodden by my own mare, Cormac added: 'You know your uncle is partial to your brother, and you should know he's never been so mewed up he couldn't plot. The tomb will scarcely secure him from that. Even your lady mother gave him leave to hold his little courts and send out his messages. Remember the one he sent me – and a purse with it.'

'But that was four years ago.'

'There've been two or three since. I didn't think to trouble you with them.'

'So you were the someone close to him who'd put the halter on him,' I said. Robin had leaned down to help me mount again, but I preferred keeping the horse between me and that sword, though it now wavered as Rufus said:

'Cormac, you took his bribes to work against me?'

'I took his bribes, nothing more. My lord, I told you of the first one, which proves me honest. If an old man is so free with his gold as to send me purses when he gets nothing for the coin, is that my fault? I would have told you if there had been anything further to tell. I have the coins still and can show them to you. But as for Ranulph' – and how smoothly he now shifted the attention to me – 'there's a pair of sweet country clerks who come and go between Rouen and Bayeux, on charitable business for His Grace, they say. One is plump and the other is thin, but they each bear likeness to our Ranulph, especially when they have their heads cocked to catch each other's speech, as I've seen them several times lately. What about it, Little Brother? Have I found your source of gossip?'

'Yes, they're my brothers. They're the bishop's clerks and they've been his couriers, but they're not in the plot, except as – devices. I wasn't going to keep my source a secret, my lord. Only you didn't give me time to tell you. I've been at some pains to milk it from them only to warn you.'

So I told all my tale, not in the fashion or the time I might have wished, but straight and brief, as Rufus would best accept it.

When I had finished, Robin said, 'This is infamous.'

'But practical,' Cormac answered. 'Which way shall we ride for a ship, my lord? Lillebonne, or Touques? The riders will return soon, not having found us in the town.'

'Touques,' Rufus said after a moment's thought. 'There's a ship that leaves Rouen tonight for Brittany. We'll meet it at Touques and put it off its course as far as Portsmouth.'

'If I may speak a word here, my lord,' Robin said in his lazy way, 'ports near at hand are easily reached by more than one set of pilgrims. If Ranulph is right about this scheme, those searching for you will also ride to the nearest coastal ports when they don't find you in Rouen. Forgive me, but you're not a king yet, and the king who is commanded you to take his letter to Archbishop Lanfranc. Lanfranc's in Canterbury, and the nearest port to that is a long ride north, but horses will carry us faster than ships, if the wind's not from the right quarter.'

'Good man, Robin Bloet! Yes, we should ride north' – Rufus laughed sharply – 'out of Normandy, in fact! We'll leave my one scheming uncle and take cover under the cloak tail of another – the Count of Flanders. There's Calais, Wissant, Boulogne – three ports in a row he owns. One of them should have a ship for us.' He sheathed his sword. 'Mount up, priest. Tighten your cincture and see if you can make that mare trot as your tongue can.'

'Why take these clerks with us?' Cormac asked as we crossed the road and went immediately into the northern arm of the woods. 'If we want speed, these stool riders can't make it. Two can move more swiftly and make less noise than four.'

'My lord, you must have us! You need witnesses to say the king named you his heir,' I said quickly.

'He has the letter – and the sword,' said Cormac.

'A sword he may have gotten, but the letter proves little. What if my lord Robert, or Henry, or both should come to Lanfranc next week with similar letters? Whom should the archbishop believe?'

'He's right,' said Rufus. 'I need a clerk the old man knows and can believe, like Robin.'

'Take Robin, then, and leave Ranulph.'

'Don't you trust him yet?'

'He never trusts anyone,' I said from behind.

Cormac turned in his saddle, his voice purling sarcasm: 'Who says I won't trust a man who's betrayed his own brothers? What sweeter proof of loyalty can there be? I'd trust him to do you another service, my lord. Let him stay behind and misdirect your enemies, as he's said he did before. Tell them we've ridden to Touques. Give us time to reach Fecamp and get better horses. You'll do that, won't you, Little Brother?'

Rufus twisted around, plainly waiting for my consent. I had a vision of myself in Rouen's donjon, having my fingernails torn out by Odo in person, but there was no other answer I could make:

'I'll stay and tell them you've gone to Touques. Change your destination again, if you still don't trust me. But tell me why my brother, who isn't an idiot, should believe it when I say you've confided your plans to me, but wouldn't take me with you?'

'Good point,' said Cormac. 'Ride on, my lord, with Robin. I'll linger a moment and help our friend work out some credible story.'

'We'd best ride,' said Robin. 'The men who passed us may be on their way back now, not finding you.'

Rufus said to me: 'I place my trust in you, Ranulph. If you meant to lead me into a trap, this was the long way to go about it. Ride to Fécamp as soon as you can. I'll leave word with them to provision and aid you.' Then he and Robin rode into the trees and were lost to my sight.

'Let's go back to the road for a bit,' said Cormac. 'These woods are too gloomy for a pair of innocents like us.' He led the way and I was glad to be out of that thicket, but not to be alone with him. What if he meant to kill me, to put me out of all danger of betraying him? I was still uncertain of his own loyalty, though Rufus seemed to take him at his word when he proclaimed it. He had acted readily enough in getting us off the road, and he affected a great suspicion of me, but what did that prove? I nudged my horse across the road to make a safe distance between us. He saw the action and laughed.

'No need for that. Here.' He took the knife from his belt and handed it to me, handle first. I took it gingerly. 'I've been giving you some thought,' he said, 'and I agree with Will. If you'd wanted to lead him to Odo, you could have done it an easier way. Your suspicion of me seems genuine, too, though I'd have thought you'd grow less simple with age. If I'd wanted a richer master, I could have found a dozen anytime in the last five years. You know that.'

I said nothing.

'You know, I'm not the mystery here; you are. Why did you put yourself to the trouble of this? It wouldn't matter to you who was king in England or duke here; you'd have a place just the same. You're the chancellor's man. I've been thinking on that and I believe I've solved the mystery. You want position, but you want to be cherished, too. It won't be enough for you if someday they say, "There goes the great man." You want them to say, too, "What should we ever do without him?" Eh? You want power but you crave gratitude, as a child craves honey.' He laughed. 'It explains a lot about you, even why you defended me in the chapter house so long ago. You were thinking of me – not free – but crouching in the abbey prison, sighing, "Ah, that Ranulph, the darlin' fellow, to be sidin' with the likes of me!" If there was a candle between us, I'd see you blushing now, wouldn't I?'

'Not for myself, I assure you.'

'You loved me then. I knew it.'

'Cormac, when, for the love of God, will you grow tired of that fantasy? I admired you, in my ignorance, as a boy will admire his elders.'

'You must have wondered why it wasn't you, instead of Baldwin Milk-Face. I wondered that myself, you know, because you were a handsomer lad than that poor sprat, even as a knob-kneed boy.'

'Your conceit is beyond belief! I don't want to hear any more of your pathetic reflections.'

'The hell you don't! You may have taken another path since then, but the satisfaction of an old curiosity is a morsel you won't refuse. I think I never took to you because I felt that hunger for gratitude in you, even then. You see, that was what old de Tombelene wanted of me, after he took me half drowned from the sea – not just my company, or my affection, or my body to sweat and slobber over, but my endless, undying, eternal gratitude and adulation for it all. That's a thing a man might get, but nothing a man can ask for – even when he deserves it – or it spoils the whole business.'

'I'll keep that in mind from now on.'

'No, you won't. You'll always have that bit of a fool in you that makes you want it, long after you've come to believe there's no such thing.' He dismounted and studied the road.

'I think it might be well if those riders found you about here, to tell your tale of our flight.'

'Is that your advice? That I just sit here waiting for them; cry out, "Rufus has ridden to Touques!" and they thank me and fly by? Not very convincing, I think.'

'Well – you shouldn't be just sitting here. Come down and I'll show you what I had in mind. No fear, now; I've told you I trust you like a babe, and I mean to help you become a hero.'

I dismounted cautiously. He was gazing at the sky. 'It's a fine, clear night, which is good, because you shouldn't cry out, and they won't ride you down. I think you should seem a bit – fuddled – ' His fist slammed into the side of my jaw. I fell on my back. Whatever stars there were at the zenith went out for a moment, but I heard Cormac say cheerfully, 'Make a good tale of it, lad. I think I hear the bastards coming.'

26

The riders barely missed trampling me. I had just crawled to the verge of the road, trying to find some rock or stump by which to raise myself. They mounted me behind one of them and took me back to the priory, where I told my tale as best I could for a loose tooth, a bitten tongue, and a semiparalyzed jaw.

The faces that frowned down on me weren't those of mere numbskull knights come to do someone else's bidding; they were the familiar adherents of Curthose's cause: William of Eu, Ralph of Conches, Ivo of Grantmesnil, and Robert Mowbray. Old Geoffrey Mowbray was there, too, along with Gilbert Maminot. At the back of the crowd my two brothers peeked at me, in company with the prior and his dean.

'I tried to detain him, my lords. I said it showed poor respect for his father to gallop for the nearest ship as soon as he heard himself named his heir. I was too bold with him, I allow, but only for his honor's sake, you understand. He became angry, said his father had bidden him go at once and so he should. He said I was no person to instruct him. When I tried to protest this, his man called me a fool and a drunkard and struck me off my horse. It was that Irishman, Cormac, who did it.'

'Which way did they go?' asked Robert Mowbray, his round, unblinking eyes fixed on my face as if to divine a lie in the least painful twitch of it.

'To the nearest port – was it Touques, or Lillebonne? My head still swims from the fall, my lord, or I could be certain. They argued on it.'

They ceased to glare at me so threateningly when I mentioned those ports, though they continued to question me as to how I had become one of the riding party, until the good prior of St. Gervase took pity on me and sent me to his infirmarian, who offered me a poultice for my toothache and a bed to rest on.

Fulcher came after me to the infirmary and sat, looking thoughtful, until the infirmarian withdrew. There were no other patients in those quarters at the moment. Fulcher's silence made me restless.

'I've done all I could for you, Brother. I tried to delay him, but he was too eager. Look, you see my gown front? He even drew his sword on me at one point. Even my friend Robert Bloet abused me and rode away with him. I'm probably ruined at court for this. What more could I have done?'

'I've been wondering that myself,' Fulcher said quietly. He tucked his hands into his sleeves, rose, and wished me good night.

I wrestled with my pillow for a time, cursing Cormac. I'd made a botch of it, surely. Why should I have been persuaded to stay and misdirect the enemy when they would naturally have searched the nearest ports for Rufus and his party anyway? I had let Cormac cow me and plow me down again, when I might have done the same for him. But my wrath with him was tempered by the memory of his words – 'a man who'd betray his own brothers' – and the vision of

Fulcher's face. If Rufus were taken, I would lose credit with everyone, and all for a ruse that hardly seemed necessary to me now.

The Prime bell woke me. It hadn't rung the whole time the king lay sick at the priory, because the noise would disturb his rest. Now it clamored remorselessly as I rose, put on my sandals, and opened the door of the infirmary. I expected to see the cloister garth filled with monks on their way to prayers, but the yard was empty.

It was only then I realized what the long ringing of that bell meant: it was the death knell of the king. I hurried out into the garth and heard booted feet clattering on stones beyond the walls and cries for aid from squires. The king was dead and his faithful were fleeing to their own houses – or to spread the news abroad.

The monks were still in their chapel. Pages, squires, knights, men-at-arms, and mighty lords – all had gone. I looked for Fulcher in the chapel, to the chagrin of the doorkeeper who kept bidding me come in, but he and Osbern were gone as well. I went to the priory hall, where the king lay, and saw his body servants just coming out of it, laden with bedclothes, harness, basins, and ewers, like so many pillagers. One was carrying away the king's boots. I hid behind a pillar of the cloister aisle and watched them quarreling over their stolen goods as they made their escape from the priory. The doorkeepers saw them, too, and gave chase too late.

'Thieves! Thieves! God strike you dead for your sins!'

I slipped into the cell and found the king's body lying naked on the floor, stripped even of his pall. The very bed he had died in was dismantled and taken. The room was bare of everything except its crucifix, and the bloated body, already blue and stiff with death.

'Christ have mercy on us! There's no law in the land today.' I turned at the sound of the voice and saw the prior and one of the door wardens staring at the corpse. I thought of the men who had set out for Touques the night before. They would return before noon, perhaps for me.

'Prior,' I said, 'you'd best bar your gates and bury your plate. You're right about the law in Normandy this day. There'll be a new king in england soon, who may revenge himself on those who committed this sacrilege and, I'm even more certain, reward you for helping this unworthy priest today, if you can. Do you think there's a horse left in the stables I might have? I can't pay for him now, but I will send something when I reach England, if God wills I live.'

'If there's one left, take it, and go.'

Wringing his hands, he fell to his knees beside the dreadful corpse of William Bastard and began to pray.

The prior's horse was fat from too many days in the stable and too few on the road. He wanted to trot, but I made him gallop, though he wheezed most pitifully for it and threatened to fall dead before we reached Fécamp.

There, as Rufus had promised, I was expected. Provisions were packed for me, and I was entreated to stop for the night, which had fallen before I reached their gates. But I dared not linger, for if the bishop's men had already searched the ports around the Seine, they wouldn't be too long in riding north. I took the food and the two horses offered me and was off again.

I was no hardened soldier used to following the king in war or the chase. I'd ridden nearly forty miles in a day and broken the wind of a stout horse. It was well past midnight when I left Fécamp, but I went a little way into the wilderness of night before I could ride no more. I tethered my horses, slept by them and near the road in a ditch, oblivious to snakes or wolves, but wary even in sleep to the shudder of hoofbeats on the road above.

At dawn I was almost too stiff to mount again. No doubt I'd still have been riding by Michaelmas if I'd not found an English cog in port at Dieppe. I was let aboard her after a lengthy scrutiny by its captain, who despite my gown and tonsure, evidently took me for a ruffian. He satisfied his suspicion at last by taking one of my horses for my passage – which he said he must sell before we sailed. I was too relieved to protest the boarding fee, which amounted to pure theft. We were an extra day in port, during which time I slept.

When we cast off we made such a slow chop up the coast to the neck of the Channel that I began to wonder if my master had outdistanced us and was already set down on English ground. My conflicting thought was that he might have been captured after all. More experienced riders than myself, with fresh mounts and plenty to give them aid, would be spreading the dire news of the Bastard's death all over Normandy. William of Eu could be in St. Valéry even now, looking for a haggard, scuttling clerk who'd deceived him. I stayed very low amidst the deck cargo as we put into that port.

We passed Boulogne, too, without a sight of Rufus. I began to think which Scottish monasteries might harbor me quietly. But then at Wissant, a little port between Boulogne and Calais, I saw them on the quay, slumped on bales of hemp, their horses standing near, almost knock-kneed with weariness. I began to wave and yell as we drew alongside, hailing them over the ship's rail until I nearly fell across it. Rufus stood up, pointed, then fell to laughing when he saw me clearly.

As soon as the landing plank was run out, I was caught up in his bearlike embrace which nearly lifted me off my feet. Robin, even Cormac, laughed and beat me on the back, until I remembered what I had to tell and withdrew from them to kneel at Rufus's feet. He sobered at once.

'Your Grace – '

'So, it's over then.'

'Yes, Your Grace.'

'Your Grace – that's a title I never thought to wear. When did he die?'

'On the morrow of the Virgin's Nativity, my lord, very early in the morning – only a few hours after you made your escape, very timely.'

'What, has my brother come home?'

'Not when I left Rouen, but his friends were eager to find you, even before the king died.'

He put two of his fingers under my chin to lift my head. 'Which of them gave you that buffet on the face? I'll repay it for you someday.'

I glanced at Cormac. 'I've forgotten, my lord,' I said. That was a debt I meant to repay in my own good time.

Rufus said solemnly: 'You have proved yourself my loving friend, putting yourself in jeopardy for my sake. I will requite it. No man shall ever strike or s-spurn Ranulph my chaplain again without answering to me for it.'

He spoke calmly, but with the new sense of power in him that made both Robin and Cormac remember their duty and bend the knee to him, to the great astonishment of the cog's captain, who stood gaping at us.

We reached Canterbury the next day, after a hard ride from Dover. Rufus had his meeting with the archbishop after Compline, with Robin and me in his company to give witness to the late king's letter.

Lanfranc seemed old and frail beyond belief, though I had never known him other than as an old man. He sat, staring as if blind, while Robin told of the bequests made to the Church and King William's voiced wish that God might see fit to let the crown pass to his son William. There was a constant tremor in Lanfranc's body that kept his head forever shaking a denial as he listened. I recognized it as one of the infirmities of old age, but the no-no sway of his head made me uneasy.

When Robin had finished, I stood forth and told of the king's death and the theft and abandonment that followed it. I had saved that tale until then, so Lanfranc saw its effect on Rufus as did I. If he had any doubt about the feelings of the son on leaving the father so abruptly, they must have been banished. Rufus nearly strangled on his rage:

'Wh-why didn't you tell me this? I-I-I would have gone back – I w-would have r-re-revenged myself on them a-all! God's Face! God's Death, Ranulph! G-god damn them all!' He looked at me as if I were the culprit and he might slay me on the spot, but then in his remorse and anger he wept. Lanfranc wept with him, and so I knew I had served him better than if I'd told him beforehand. We were dismissed, and the archbishop took counsel with the king for nearly an hour.

'That was a bit overblunt, wasn't it?' Robin asked when we were pacing the cool aisles of the cloister.

'No,' I said. 'It's as he said – he *would* have turned back. I know something of him, remember. After the first outburst of anger or grief he hides his feelings, because his stammer shames him. If he'd lived to come here at all, it would have been as a hard man. But if the succession depends on him alone – and it does, since he's got no army – the archbishop must believe he's been sent the right man to anoint, the son who loved the king as Lanfranc himself did. He has got the right man, of course – so I did nothing wrong, did I?'

Robin shook his head. 'No, only I wonder why it is that I keep thinking of you as an innocent, when I know you once served Odo. Don't be too clever, Ranulph. I know a little something of Will-Rou, too. He doesn't like the devious.'

'Who's devious? I intend to be the king's man, and knowing his nature, if I act contrarily to it for his own good, have I harmed him? No. I tell you something, Robin. We're in an enviable position at this moment. The king will have his chief counselors, and they'll no doubt be much the same ones his father had before him, but they're growing old, while he as well as we are still young. Who will come after them? Would it be so great a wrong if we who love him make sure it will be ourselves and not some incompetents like Will Giffard?'

Robin smiled. 'So you're already fitting yourself for a miter, are you? Well, there's something in the thought, but it's a long labor, friend.'

'So is bedding a woman, but the labor's not unpleasant.'

'There's an analogy! But there'll be other suitors. They won't be long making their way to pay court, with garlands on their heads and honey in their mouths – old Mowbray, St. Carileph, Giffard, Montgomery, and the rest.'

'Thank God, for the time being they'll have to speak to Lanfranc first. I think he's up to dealing with them.'

'What about that two-legged hound that follows Will even to the jakes – Cormac, I mean? He'll have notions of fame, too, now.'

'Yes, but you notice he was left cooling his heels in the archbishop's hall tonight. Cormac's time is passing. He's a well-worn shoe, but now it's time to put on finer boots. I believe he truly loves the king, so perhaps he'll see it and step aside, ask for a little manor, and retire to it.'

'He's the last man in the world to step aside from a good thing. He'll have to be pried out like a winkle, but who's to apply the prick? I elect you, dear boy.'

I had already elected myself, but didn't mention it.

When Lanfranc and Rufus came forth from their council, Lanfranc sent for one of the late king's stewards, Eudo of Rye, who was in the archbishop's palace at the time with a private suit. When he came, a stout-bodied old man in his middle forties, Lanfranc said to him in the presence of his household and ourselves:

'Eudo, you've heard the news from Normandy by now. The king is dead and all men must weep for him. But here is his successor, if God be willing.' He indicated Rufus, and Eudo bent his knee to him.

'God save King William the Younger.'

'Amen. King William rides to Winchester tomorrow, to claim the keys of his treasure house and bring out the English crown. He'll want an escort.'

'Then I shall give it to him, Archbishop, thanking you and His Grace for the honor. I've only a dozen men with me, but we'll gain followers along the road when the news is spread.'

'No, Eudo,' said Rufus. 'The archbishop has another ride in mind for you. Listen to him. He'll be my first adviser in all things, as he was my father's.'

'The lords of the coastal forts are still abroad in Normandy, or else on their way home,' said Lanfranc. 'The kingdom is divided from the duchy. Some men have a double allegiance now, to the king and to his brother, Duke Robert. Before any of them take up their honors with us again, we must have their oaths made fresh, before witnesses. Do you follow me, Eudo?'

'Archbishop?'

'You'll take your own knights and as many of mine as you think needful and ride to the keeps of Dover, Hastings, Pevensey, Lewes, Bramber, and Arundel. In the name of the king you will demand that their castellans give up their keys to you. Remind them of the oath they swore at Salisbury – that they are the king's men before any other's. On the sanctity of that oath you'll make your demand of them.'

I sighed with satisfaction. What had seemed to many at Salisbury to be a token of William Bastard's senile envy of his barons now seemed a miracle of wisdom, no doubt put in his mind by Lanfranc.

Lanfranc continued: 'Leave an officer of your own in command of each garrison, if you have the least doubt of its castellan. My clerks will write letters for you to hand over with your demands. But remember: it is in the *name of the king you* demand it. No further explanation is necessary or will be given.'

Wise old man. If the castellans thought William Bastard still living and the author of the demand, so much the better. If they knew him to be dead and their lords were not yet returned to make their own oaths, then let them think Rufus was already crowned.

We rode to Winchester in the company of four of Lanfranc's knights, but in haste and without panoply. No trumpets blew for us at the crossroads; we took no hospitality from any manor on the way, but slept on the ground when we were exhausted, then went on again.

When we reached Winchester, all but unnoticed among the merchants' carts and market-goers crowding through the gate, Rufus passed the palace and went straight to the house of Sir William Pont de L'Arche, the treasure warden. He was taking his day-meal, but rose, astonished to see Rufus, who refused his offer of refreshment and took him aside for speech. Cormac stood at his master's back during that exchange. I saw Sir William look astonished, then grim. He shook his head. Rufus drew a letter from his belt and showed it to him. Obviously he couldn't read it, but the great seal that dangled from it was enough, though there was a long enough pause after he saw it that Cormac's hand strayed to his dagger.

Sir William's hand shook slightly as he returned the letter to Rufus; then he unfastened the ring of keys at his belt and handed them over, too. The man who held those keys truly held the kingdom.

We rode to the palace with the warden for company. As Cormac, Robin, and I stood by, the treasury door opened under its true owner's hand and he went into the chamber. We peered through the door like children spying on a banquet.

It was wonderful to see. Gold and silver ingots were stacked like little honey cakes in a baker's stall. There were coffers upon coffers of coin, and the shelves that lined the room were filled with precious ornaments of chancel and banqueting hall: candlesticks, platters, heathen collars, arm rings, basins, ewers, patens, wine bowls.

Lying across a hamper was a shirt of mail sent to the late king as a gift, but surely one that had never fit him. It was black-enameled steel, overlaid with gold in the figure of a dragon. It shimmered in the torchlight like a forest pool under the moon. Rufus, breathing heavily, touched it tentatively, then lifted it and measured it against himself. Seeing the warden watching him, he gave one of his self-deprecating laughs.

'I feel like a thief! I've never seen – all this, you know. Never been allowed. My f-father was close with his possessions. But I remember this. The Welsh prince sent it to him while we were fighting them in 'eighty-one. He was hoping to be acknowledged as king there.' His smile faded. 'I'll have this if it fits me.'

'All that's here is Your Grace's to take, if you wish,' the warden said. 'You'll want a fresh inventory made, naturally. Will your clerks do it, or shall I call mine?'

'Yes. Later.' The king then took up two rings from a casket, examined them, and with an almost furtive look at the warden put them on his fingers and signified that the inspection was finished. The room was locked again, and we all went down to the hall, where a hastily assembled congregation of servants, knights, and townsmen hailed Rufus as king. The old bishop, Walkelin of Winchester, Gerard's uncle, came tottering into the hall, tears running in the seams of his face, and gave the king his blessing. It was a good beginning.

That night, however, Rufus slept ill, crying out in the middle of the night to frighten awake those of us who slept in the chamber with him. Cormac would have driven us all out and soothed him in private, but to the surprise of us both, as the squires shuffled out yawning, Rufus said:

'Ranulph, you stay. I want to speak to you, alone.'

Cormac lifted his brows at this, but bowed and retreated. I lent the king my hand to help him from the soft wallow of feather mattress.

'Your Grace, are you ill? Shall I bring a doctor? The bishop has a sound one.'

'No. Get me something to drink.' Rubbing his face, he went to the window embrasure and leaned against it.

I poured a cup of wine from the little flagon kept for rinsing his mouth in the morning and gave it to him. He swallowed it, examined the cup incuriously, then looked at me half sheepishly. 'I had a bad dream.'

I smiled. 'Not unusual, my lord, for a man who now has the cares of a kingdom to fret his mind. Tell your dream and dispel it; that's the way to rout them.'

'Can you interpret it, if I do?'

'Not I, Your Grace, any more than anyone else. It's forbidden to Christians to make readings of dreams, or to plot our future by the stars.'

'But you're a priest, you – never mind. It had no meaning. Only it g-gave me a horror. I was in the forest, somewhere, maybe the New Forest; the glade was familiar. I was in a stand, waiting for a deer. I waited a long time and there was no one near me, though I could hear voices. It began to grow dark, and I was cold and stiff with standing. Suddenly there was a cry from the hunters I couldn't see, and a stag broke cover just in front of me. It was a huge beast, and it snorted and pawed the ground like a destrier. I raised my bow and shot it – a clean shot just behind the shoulder. It reared and fell into the underbrush, and I ran to see if it was dead, yelling for the chief hunter to come and see the kill.

'No one came to my call, so I knelt and slit the belly to let out the guts, and as I p-put my hand in to search for the heart' – he gave a little bark of a cry – 'the beast changed its form and became my f-father! I had his blood on my hands and his intestines in my fingers when he opened his eyes and said to me, "You'll eat n-no more of me." Then I cried out and woke myself.'

My spine was chilled. I made haste to pour him more wine, to give myself time to think what to say. 'My lord, this is fearful at first telling, but I think it needs no prophet to make a case for it. You waited long years for your kingdom and now it's come to you. The deer was the symbol in your mind of your realm, on which you mean to fix your mark. But the king and his realm are one body, as some say. Your father was this body, and so, for you, the stag became him as you knelt to take its blood and substance.'

He looked doubtful. 'This is very fine stuff for a man who says the Church won't let him divine dreams. Some would say I envied my f-father his kingdom and longed for him to be dead, but not having the gall to k-kill him in life, I did it in a dream.'

'No, my lord, not if they consider all the elements of the dream. The stag didn't fly from you; you didn't pursue it, but waited alone until it came. It stopped before you and pawed the ground, inviting you to take aim at it. This is to say, your father came to you at last and delivered his power to you of his own will.'

'And what about the words he spoke to me?'

I drew breath for thought. This was quite beyond me. I had dreams enough to give the Oracle of Delphi fits, but I never believed them once my night sweat had cooled on me.

'He gave you himself in his kingdom, then showed himself plainly to you, so you'd know it. When he said you'd eat no more of him, it wasn't a threat, but a – a benediction. He meant that now you were truly his heir and would eat of your own bounty from this day, which you will. The realm is yours, the treasure is yours, the crown is yours. Remember, he said he couldn't give it to you, but he hoped God would do so. I believe God has sent you this dream as a sign that He approves your election.'

He sighed and reached out a hand to grip my shoulder. 'I'll keep you for a prophet, until I get a Samuel. I don't believe your nonsense, but you've soothed my mind. They call you Flambard here, don't they? I'll call you that, too, since even in my dreams you come running with your light of common sense. I owe you a penny.'

He returned to his bed without calling back the others, and I lay down on my pallet again. I heard him snoring before I slept.

We rode out for London the next morning, carrying with us on a rouncey a hamper packed with the robes King William had worn at his last Christmas Court and the crown of the English with its twelve great pearls. Lanfranc met us at Westminster, attended by all the bishops of the southern counties and as many lords as he had thought fit to send summons to. There, on the fifth day before the ides of October, the archbishop, with Maurice of London and Walkelin of Winchester, anointed and crowned my lord William the Second, King of the English.

When the acclamation was shouted, Lanfranc also handed to the new king a written document, which the king kissed and placed upon the high altar for the length of a prayer; then Maurice took it and read it aloud to those in the minster.

It was the customary coronation oath to the people from the king, which Lanfranc may have written afresh, but which was little different from the oath I had once read of old King Edgar's, given to his people a century and a half ago.

But the king's face flamed as Maurice read:

'In the Name of the Holy Trinity, I promise these things to the Christian people, my subjects: that God's Church and all Christian people shall enjoy true peace; that all ranks of men are forbidden robbery and wrongful deeds; that I command justice and mercy in all judgments, so the ever-living God Who reigns above may grant us His everlasting mercy in turn; and that I will take counsel of the Church and of Archbishop Lanfranc in all matters before I pass judgment on any man.'

When the ceremony was finished, the king retired to his palace to remove his heavy mantle and make ready for the feasting that would follow. Alone in his chamber for a moment with no one but Cormac and me, he gave vent to his irritation:

'I gave him my word as a knight that I would take his advice, as my f-father did before me. Did he have to p-proclaim it like a d-damned herald, as if it wanted witnesses?'

Cormac said: 'Now you're king, you must take up teaching old dogs new tricks. Make him know he'll consult you before he speaks, too.'

'Lanfranc meant you no discourtesy, my lord,' I said. 'It's the custom among the English to have their kings swear such things to them. From the time of St. Dunstan, who was archbishop in half-pagan times, and a man not unlike our own archbishop, as I've read – '

'Who cares for the customs of the English now?' asked Cormac. 'The old times are gone and this isn't some puffed-up thane they've elected from among themselves, or some Dane who still makes offerings to an oak tree. This king's above their customs, as he's above their muddled laws, you'd think.'

'The king is both law and custom, so he can be neither above nor outside them,' I said, feeling at the moment I answered that he was baiting me for some reason of his own. I said to the king: 'Your father gave such an oath at his crowning. Lanfranc should have told you of it, but he's an old man, for whom time passes quickly. He probably forgot that you were a child and not present at the occasion. No one would accuse your illustrious father of allowing hollow custom to rule him, but he was wise enough to know that bowing to such harmless practices makes for an easier rule. Be angry with me, if you will, Your Grace, since I have read enough of

English law and history to be aware of this oath, but forgot to mention it to you.'

Cormac laughed. 'By God, he'll have you consulting *him* even before you consult the old Italian!'

But Rufus didn't rise to the taunt. 'Let him be, Cormac, he's in the right. There are things I must learn here and I mean to do it, for my father's sake. I'll bend my ear to the archbishop, not for custom's sake, or because he made me swear it like an upstart, but because my father wanted it. And Ranulph will tell me where to look before I put out my foot, because I trust him and he loves me.'

I forbore giving Cormac the glance of triumph I might have.

27

Next morning, after a late feasting, we rode into London so that the king could survey the damage done by the fire. I dreaded the journey. The smell of charred wood still hung over the town; it even wafted out to greet us when we were still a half mile from Ludgate. Yet, when we came over the hill and through that gate, a sight met my eyes that seemed impossible to believe.

There were some low houses that backed on the marketplace by the river that had never known the fire. They belonged to the foreign merchants, whose stalls had been below there, and they'd been hastily thrown up in the same ramshackle timber, daub, and thatch that had invited the flames before, but they were *new-built*. All the churches that had been along the river were still desolate, and there were empty lots still heaped with rubble, but the quays and docks were under repair, and ships crowded thickly before them at the Hythe and at Dowgate. Above Fish Street St. Paul's still stood without roof and windows, its doorway gaping like an anguished mouth.

People came running into the streets from Baynard's Keep onward to see their new king and cheer him. He was a sight to make them glad; he rode without helm or mail, open and vulnerable to them, dressed in a tunic of green silk and a mantelet of darker green velvet, lined with yellow sendal. His pale hair caught the sunlight and was blown by a light wind into a rough halo around his plain red face, which beamed with gratification at their shouts:

'The king! The king!'

'God keep him, good Red Will!'

He couldn't understand the words, naturally, but their smiles and uplifted arms approved him. Beyond their enthusiasm they were a sad lot of beggars, however, to have such a golden idol. Thin-cheeked, dirty, even the better dressed among them seemed to be wearing the same soot-streaked garments left from their fighting the fire. In their faces one could see the real damage done by the holocaust. If the comfortable craftsman remained dingy, the real poor were reduced to gaunt-faced scarecrows who ran alongside our horses, their filthy, clawed hands outstretched for charity.

I had a purse of the king's from which to distribute largess to the needy during that progress. At first I tried dropping a coin into some individual palm, but the crush of poverty was too close; those who were out of reach began to shout and shove from behind, threatening to thrust those in front beneath our horses' feet, so I gave up the practice and flung out the rest of my purse over their heads, then held up the bag to show it was empty. It was empty too soon. The mob increased, and in the tumult I heard Ralph Baynard cry from behind: 'Ride on, Your Grace! I'll deal with this rabble!'

The king pricked up his palfrey and I found myself surrounded by Baynard's guard, iron helms glinting, swords already drawn.

'Ride on, priest! Ride, damn it!' one shouted, and I tried to obey as the swords swept down on the heads of the crowd. They used the flats of their blades to admonish, not to kill, but the effect was the same as if Baynard had ordered a massacre. Shrieks tore the air as men fell back under each other's feet, or under the horses. The knights surged forward around me, lifting their weapons as the mob fled.

We turned on the Bridge Road, rather than ride on to the royal tower. More people came running, but we were going too fast for them to trap us. At Langbourne the king wheeled again, lifting his arm to direct his cavalry onto that street, which led back toward St. Paul's. We were galloping and the faces were a blur, until we approached the bridge over the Wall Brook, which is narrower than the street. I pulled rein. There were a few women near the bridge with baskets in their hands, as if they'd just come up from doing a washing in the brook, as country women do. I saw them quail and stumble aside from the sudden onslaught of horsemen; then I was urged forward from behind again by an impatient rider and lunged for the bridge.

In that moment I saw Giva.

In the next moment I was past her, thundering over the planks of the bridge with twenty men behind me. I nearly fell from my horse in that recognition, but there was no time to call out. I thought she had seen me, too. Her mouth had been open, as if she were calling my name, and one of the other women was reaching for her arm, to pull her back to safety. They froze in my mind in those attitudes, as if they had been painted there; not dead, not burned, not faceless and rotting in an unmarked grave, but alive and the child still alive in her.

We turned up the street that led north from St. Paul's and rode into the yard of the old English palace, where Maurice waited to greet the king and present the aldermen of the town to him – along with their complaints and petitions. I wanted nothing as much as to jerk my horse's head around and ride straight back to Giva, but that was impossible. I dismounted, unaware how much the shock of seeing her might show in my face. I caught Robin Bloet by the sleeve, whispered, 'Robin, Robin,' and shook him. He stared at me, frowning.

'What ails you?' Cormac asked, coming over to us. 'You're as pale as a hermit's backside.' He looked at me with that perverse mixture of amusement and concern he sometimes visited on me, when he wasn't trying to damage me, that made him the more irritating. I brushed aside explanation and went to follow the king.

At his behest I stood behind his stool in the hall, and when some point of English law or London custom was in dispute, he lifted his finger for me to bend down and whisper what I knew about it, then leaned his ear in the other direction for Lanfranc's illumination. This got me a withering look of dislike from that old man and even a slight head-shaking from Maurice, but the king was my master and he would have it so.

For the next two weeks I was held to the king's side from the hour in which I greeted him with a morning prayer and benediction until I saw him bestowed in bed again near midnight, when I fell on my own pallet. He held court in his father's way every morning after first Mass, hearing any man who had a cause to bring before him and receiving those lords of the realm who had missed his crowning, but now came to attest their allegiance. All those who returned tardily from Normandy bent their knees to him: old Earl Montgomery; his son, Hugh; William of Eu; William de Breteuil; the Mowbrays, uncle and nephew; Henry de Ferrières; Richard of Clare and his mole-eyed sons. All came and most remained, though it was yet two months to the Christmas Court.

In the afternoons the king sat and listened to a recital of his estates and their worth by Will Giffard. I was amazed to hear Giffard refer to the late king's inquest of the land as 'the Doomsday Census.' Before I knew it, I had broken in on him:

'My lord Chancellor, surely you don't take that to heart, as the ignorant do who gave it that name. Next you'll be telling His Grace of the two-headed calves and other prodigies said by the foolish to have been born of it.'

'Ranulph, I only named it as many people do – ' began Giffard, taken by surprise at my rudeness.

'As if it were some celestial reckoning, my lord? Or rather, such a reckoning as the reckless make to tempt Heaven? No, Your Grace, I assure you, when your noble father ordered this account to be taken of the realm, he showed the greatest wisdom and the greatest care for his posterity. Let me explain . . . ' And I ventured to expound a bit on the increase of revenues he would enjoy as a result of that inquisition which had counted anew the flocks, herds, beehives, thriving ponds, and arable plowlands to which he was heir.

He endured me for a while before he began to fidget. In a short time he rose, called for the great seal to be given to him by Will Giffard, and placed it in my hands.

'In lieu of that penny I said I owed you, you'll be keeper of the seal again. Robin Bloet speaks true: drudgery does seem to suit you. You'll be glad to stay here and be good and industrious. I'm going up to Windsor, and no one's to come near me with a writ, a petition, a tallage, or any other embroilment, do you hear? Will Giffard will come with me' – he flashed a grin at Giffard, who still stood amazed at the loss of the great seal – 'because he must be as famished for fresh air and fresh venison as I am. If there's any difficulty it must come to you for a remedy – my *Flambard*.' He laughed and smacked my cheek lightly.

'Don't look so worried. Lanfranc will really be managing everything, as usual. But you will s-sit in court beside him and keep him in m-mind of *me*.'

All the lords who were still at Westminster joined him gladly for a week in the chase. The court room fell empty. Lanfranc looked on me every morning and dismissed me almost as soon as I showed my face. So, at last I was free to return to London and see Giva. I went, imagining her cry of joy when she saw me come through the door. I cautioned myself not to make my entrance too rudely or suddenly, for fear of causing her to miscarry. If she hadn't seen me at the bridge, she might well believe me to be dead, as I had believed of her.

I went to the house on Cornhill, expecting to find it burned, but meaning to ask of anyone in the street where Gammer Trudy's sons now lived, for surely that's where they'd taken refuge, though I'd never once thought of them before. But the house that was half mine still stood. The roof had been singed, but that was all. I tied my horse to a curb ring, hailed a boy loitering nearby and charged him with watching the animal, and went softly inside.

The smell of cooking assailed me, so I first went through to the kitchen to Trudy. It would be gentler if I sent her up to prepare Giva, rather than just throwing open the bedchamber door without warning.

But it was Giva I found in the kitchen, her hair bound up with a napkin, frying bean cakes and onions, like a cotter's wife. Her face was blotched with the heat of the fire, and the size of her belly was prodigious. She was six months gone and looked ready to bring forth.

'Elfgiva? *Dyrling?*' I said tenderly.

She turned her head. 'Oh, it's you. We were wondering if you'd pay us the honor of a visit. Trudy wins the wager; I said not. Do you want a bean cake, or is that too common for you now?'

It was hardly the greeting I'd dreamed of. I tried to embrace her, but she sidestepped me, muttering, 'Watch the skillet, it's hot,' as she swung around from the hearth to deposit her bean cakes on a wooden trencher. Trudy came in from outdoors, saw me, screeched, and threw her arms around me to give me a kiss. At her insistence, I took a seat at the table where the servants would have eaten, if there'd been any, and accepted a measure of cider from Trudy and a carelessly placed trencher of bean cakes from Giva. Rather than joining us, she went to the door and held it open, fanning her hot face with a kettle lifter, her back to me.

Trudy told me all about the fire and their escape from it.

'We took to our heels when we saw the fire coming across the Bourn. Who'd have thought it would cross water, even in August? But it was the Devil's own wind that blew it. We went to St. Ethelburga's by the Wall, ready to run out onto the moors if we must, but it was safe there. My sons found us next day and took us home, thanks be to the Fourteen Holy Helpers, where we found all sound but a little part of the roof.'

The account had made her weep. She wiped her eyes, then grinned her snag-toothed smile at me. 'Eat, eat! It's common stuff, but nourishing. We worried for you not coming for us, after.' She made eyes toward Giva's back.

'But I did come for you. I couldn't find you and I thought you must be dead. I thought the whole street was on fire when I came to the cattle market and found it blazing so I couldn't pass. I was near to mad with the sorrow of it, Gammer. I looked for you on every street that wasn't burning, from the market cross up to the Wall, until I was blind with the smoke.' On impulse I leaned over and kissed her hairy cheek.

'There, now, child, what did I tell you?' she said to Giva.

'If he thought we were dead, he might have come to bury us, at least dig us out of the ruins. Or he might have learned his mistake if he'd come the day after.' Her voice was heavy with assumed indifference.

'Give, I couldn't come! The church had burned; we had people looking to us for comfort and food. Then Maurice sent me – ' It came to me of a sudden: I did myself no good making excuses to a woman's back like a churl to a haughty mistress. I stood up, wiping my greasy lips.

'I came when I could. Now I must go again. We're kept very busy these days. I only wanted my other shirt and my cloak and boots. I'm glad to find you both well.'

I went up to our chamber, found it very clean, because every single item of mine that could be hidden away was stuffed in my chest, even my cup and candlestick. While I was changing my shirt, the door creaked open and Giva entered. She stood watching, her arms folded above her capacious belly, her chin puckering ominously, while I drew on my cassock again and tied up my cincture. I took up my purse, weighed it in my hand, then held it out to her.

'You'll want some money to repay Trudy. This is all I have at the moment.'

She came forward as if to take it, then with a sudden swing of her hand slapped it from my grasp.

'Do you think money and the sight of your smooth face make up for anything? Do you give a purse to all your whores when they get big bellies, then leave them to spawn your bastards alone? Pick it up! Take it back! I don't want it! I'll keep what you put inside me; that's all the remembrance I'll need from you! When it's born, I'll feed it. I'll go and be somebody else's whore, if I can't get a real husband, so you won't have to beggar yourself for us.' She swung her hand at my face, but I caught it and the other one, too.

'What do you mean, a real husband? You have a husband, though your manners don't warrant one – '

'No! No, I don't! I've got a man who beds me, who'd take me out of my winding sheet to plow me one more time, but no husband, no!'

I was half minded to box her ears for that libel when she suddenly grimaced and bent forward. Alarmed, I caught her, lifted her, and carried her to the bed. She gasped for breath.

'Now, if you've brought on your labor by this mad-catting, it's no fault of mine,' I said, but I was afraid for her. I felt her belly for contractions, then loosed the napkin from her head and wiped her face with it. In a moment she sighed and let her legs ease out straight. I half lay beside her, watching her face for pain.

But she sighed again and spoke breathlessly: 'A cramp. Nothing more. It's all right now.' She looked at me, tears falling out of the corners of her eyes and into her hair. 'I thought you were dead. I thought you'd been burnt in the church. I went there, but I was ashamed to tell them I knew you when they could see how it was with me. I thought they wouldn't bury you in the churchyard if they knew about our sins.'

'Giva – '

'Then Trudy went up a few days later and asked for you, and they said you'd gone overseas and they didn't know when you'd come again.' Her face crumpled.

'Shh, it was a sorry misunderstanding, but it's all right now.' I glanced at her belly, thinking to divert her from her grief, and laid a hand on the mound: 'What are we breeding here, a new Goliath?'

She blew her nose on the napkin, then lifted her head to look down. 'Twins, Trudy says. Sometimes I think she must be right, when the kicking starts.'

'Twins?' I explored her dimensions. 'Trudy may be right, indeed. But they're quiet now? Yes. Terrified of their mother's wrath, as I was.'

She sniffed. 'You, afraid of me? Oh, yes, I'll believe that!'

I smoothed the tendrils of hair that had escaped her severe combing and lay wetly curled on her brow. 'Believe it. There's an animal in the heathen world, a kind of forest lion, called a pard. They say its eyes cast a spell over its victims, so they can't move from its path as it stalks them. That's how those eyes of yours affected me just now. My bones all but turned to water, and I caught your hands to keep you from tearing out my throat. But now you're tamer and I'll dare do this.' I kissed her lightly on the mouth and on the brow.

When I drew away, her eyes were hard again; her mouth hadn't responded to my lips.

'Still angry.'

'When you were gone and no one knew if you'd come again, I began to think about my sins that I was passing on to my baby. I thought, "He'll repent of me, so I must repent of him, and make everything right with God."'

'So you confessed me and were given a penance of – what? Ten Paters, ten Credos, and a hundred Aves a day for a month? Bread and water four times a week and nothing stronger in meat than an egg, or a bit of fish, the rest? You're a little pagan, Giva, if you've never had a penance given you before.' I tried to speak lightly, but her eyes didn't waver from my face.

'I told the priest of St. Peter's my sins – Father Eoghan. He's an old Irishman, but he's been kind to me before. When Toosey' – her baby name for our dead Osyth – 'died I was only repenting the things we'd done before we were married, when I didn't know I could get a baby and love it and lose it.'

'Never mind. It's over now and you'll soon have another.'

'Father Eoghan asked me in which parish I'd married, since he didn't remember seeing me at his porch, and so I told him how we had done it and why – and he said it was a false marriage.'

She gazed up at me. I said nothing.

'I told him you were a priest and ought to know about such things, but he said – '

'Father Eoghan is a good, ignorant peasant priest who can scarcely say a prayer without garbling it and who couldn't read a psaltery if the Virgin herself came down and put her finger on the text to guide him. I've often wondered how he came to be in a church like St. Peter's.'

'He said you deceived me and that you know it.' She sat up.

'Giva, I am a lettered man who has studied under one of the most respected scholars in Europe. I'm the king's own chaplain, clerk to the royal chancellor, and better versed in English custom and common law than nine-tenths of the English themselves. Now, who do you suppose has a better grasp of what makes a binding marriage?'

'Father Eoghan says the Pope forbids all marriages not blessed by the Sacrament and that I'm only your whore and our child will be a bastard, no matter what I do.' Her nether lip trembled and she got up from the bed to stand over me, but I wouldn't be cowed by her little knowledge.

'Damn Father Eoghan!' I shouted. 'Damn the pope, too! Which one is he referring to, incidentally? The one who's just died, or the two who've replaced him? Did he tell you we rejoice in two popes at the moment, who spend their days writing bulls against each other? Did he tell you that neither our last king nor his Archbishop of Canterbury could bring themselves to make a choice between the two? Did he say how many popes, cardinals, and archbishops, not to mention abbots and even saints, have had wives, or how many never bothered to make their women any sort of vows, but bred their housekeepers and still managed to get a miter?'

'*Now* you're the man I remember from the *first*, always shouting when you know you're in the wrong!'

She started to run out the door, but I caught her and held her wrists. 'No, you're not going to run down to Trudy and hide in her skirts, like a spoiled child. You started this dialogue; now stay to hear the rest of it. If you think I'll bend to your will and take you to Father Eoghan for a wedding, you've got the wrong idea. I daresay your mother never saw the church porch before she bedded with your father, nor any of your grandmothers, either.'

'They've nothing to do with us!'

'Nor has your Irish priest! When I saw you first, you were running through the streets stealing things. When I met you again, you tried to poison me with some damned witch salve you'd stolen from the animal dancers. I went in terror for my soul for a week because of that. You seduced me, in fact – not the other way around, as you've probably made the priest believe. You came and hovered over me with your naked breasts smeared with witch poison and invited me to take you, then came home with me and lay in my bed and said I might do anything to you, if I'd feed you and not make you sleep on the floor. There wasn't much talk about sin then, though you were old enough to know what we were doing; so why does it worry you now, when I've sworn to keep you as long as we live?'

She was sobbing again.

'This is spite for my leaving you for a time, or else just the frenzy you get into when you're breeding.'

'Yes! Yes.'

'But why?' She shook her head in silence, but the answer was the same as before. She was afraid of dying in her travail, afraid of losing another child to Purgatory. I pitied her, looking at her contorted face and distorted body which at the moment it seemed impossible I could ever have lusted for. I pitied her, but I felt I must break her, knock impossible ideas out of her head, or she would tyrannize me for the rest of our lives. I took her by the shoulders and made her sit on the bed again.

'Now, listen to me. You're not going to die. You're strong and healthy and the child in you is strong. If God punished all the women who didn't get a church blessing before they bred, the world would be short of people. Perhaps it's the right way to be wed, but for us it's impossible now; especially now. I'm on the doorstep of real advancement, and I won't jeopardize it for a wedding. The king has a poor enough opinion of priests as it is. He'd scorn me, and I won't have it; not for you or for any child yet unborn.'

'Does he like you better because you're a priest who takes whores?'

'He doesn't – why do you keep harping on that word? Have I used it to you? Do you even know what you're talking about, labeling yourself and saying you'll take up the practice to spite me? God, have you ever really seen a whore – a real one? Have you ever walked past the stews and seen the hags who look out of there? Do you want to be really damned? Do you want strange men, outlanders, men with no love for you, to pull your legs open and shove themselves in you, ten, twelve, twenty of them a day, until you can't feel anything? Would that be just punishment for having me? Would that be better than living with me? Shall I take you down there and show you how they live? There's a place I know – and if it burned it's certain to be built new again – where I could take you and sell you like a calf and nobody would mind that you're big-bellied; they'd set you to work at once. Is that what you'd prefer to me?'

Giva's sobs rose to piercing shrieks. Trudy stood in the door, her eyes like coals.

'For the love of all the saints in Heaven, what are you doing to that child?'

'Teaching her! Go and tend your hearth, Gammer. This is no concern of yours. Be glad I beat her with words and not fists!'

'You'll mark the babe! It'll be a curse to you.'

'Get out, Trudy, and let me deal with my wife as I see fit!' I got up and thrust her out the door, slammed it, then returned to the bed, where Giva was keening like a mad woman, her hands clutching her belly, her knees drawn up. The old woman had put another foolish thought in her head now, worse than my threats – a marked child. I relented. My own anger had shaken me almost as much as Giva. I sat by her, touched her.

'I wouldn't do such a thing, no matter how you despise and accuse me, because I love you. Do you hear me?'

She didn't make any sign that she did, only lay as if she'd lost her wits, shivering and moaning. I leaned over her, gathered her up awkwardly, made her put her head on my shoulder, tried to soothe her with stroking.

'I never meant this. I love you. My life is empty when I'm not with you. I thought you were dead until two weeks ago, and during that time, if any man had offered to put a quick end to me with a sword, I'd have let him. They said there was a woman with child pulled from the water after the fire and her face was gone. I wept bitter tears for that woman, thinking she might be you, thinking the fishes might have eaten these sweet lips away.' I kissed them, felt their timid response. She let me kiss her cheeks, her throat, her fingertips, while she lay like a broken poppet in my arms. The effects of rage and her sweet defeat had roused me to great tenderness for her. If she hadn't been so swollen, I could have lain with her then and loved her all the better for it. But as I touched her breasts and kissed her, I had a sudden clear memory of Cormac, long ago, thrashing me all but senseless that first day at the monastery, then coming to me in the dorter and laying an unguent on my back with gentle hands, speaking to me in the same soothing voice I now used with Giva! Was I becoming like Cormac, to take pleasure in cruelty, then more pleasure in obliterating it? The thought chilled me on the instant.

I held her away from me. 'Giva, I'm sending you down to Godalming in the morning, where you'll have peace and good country air. Don't shake your head at me! There'll be a wagon at the door for you just after Prime, so pack up your things tonight and be ready. The court should move to Winchester in a month or so for the Christmas season, so I'll be better able to visit you there.'

'I want Trudy with me when my time comes.'

'No, I think part of our troubles are due to Trudy and her childbed horror tales. You'll see her again, but in the meantime my curate's wife will take good care of you and you'll have all the honey and apples you can eat. Your arms and cheeks are thin. I want them all rounded out when next I see you.'

She didn't protest again. Her eyes looked at me with such lack of illusion or hope that I was twice smitten with remorse and said a rash and foolish thing:

'I love you as much as my own life. If you love me, too, that should suffice us. But if, when I see you again, you still feel such little confidence in our vows and so great a fear of what God might do to us, I'll have my curate marry us quietly at Godalming before the child is born.'

Not even that made her smile.

The next morning I had a wagoner there, his cart made as soft as possible with straw and wool-stuffed pillows from Westminster Palace. Giva's parting with Trudy was painful on both sides. Trudy behaved as if I were abducting a child of hers, and Giva looked as if I were truly going to sell her into bondage. Her leave-taking from me was lifeless, though I urged her once again to believe my love for her and brought her a length of fine linen to make into clothes for the child.

I gave her a letter for Dunstan, which made clear to him with what honor she was to be treated on pain of his dismissal. I put her into the cart, and the last sight I had of her she was curled miserably in the corner, giving no evidence she understood the pain it cost me to see her go.

28

In my mind the first work of my Lord's reign should have been to make more certain of the loyalty of those subjects who had hovered over his father's deathbed, begging forgiveness for his brother, then lingered in Normandy to see Robert come ambling home at last to take the ducal chair. I would have had him make sure every fortified keep or town of theirs in his land had an equally well-prepared fortress of his nearby, to keep watch on their loyalty.

But such was not the view of the king, who welcomed back his tardy faithfuls with open arms, feasted them, took them to Windsor tower with him, and heard their advice as if they were, every one, his godfathers.

With Rufus, the first order of business after his week at Windsor Lodge was to have me mark out and distribute those monies and treasures which his father had willed to be given to the churches and abbeys for the repose of his soul.

Every minster in the land was to receive six marks of gold – some ten – besides gifts for their altars or for their priests to garb themselves in. Every little church of no bigger size than a henhouse received sixty pennies, and there seemed suddenly to be more churches than souls in England when I began to number them in the rolls of the Great Survey.

To the abbey founded by William Bastard on the site of his English victory went greater gifts than all beside – an emperor's ransom in vestments, books of Divine Service, vessels, jewels, and coin. The choicest gift of all was added to the Battle Abbey's hoard by Rufus, who sent them the great mantle worn first by the Conqueror, then by his son, at their crownings. It was packed for the journey in a chest made precious in itself by its silver bands and jewels. It was obvious Rufus already regarded it as a holy relic and so must the monks of Battle Abbey, if they knew what was good for them.

It was alarming to me to see how the wealth of that splendid little room in Winchester tower began to diminish. I spoke to the king about it:

'Wouldn't it be better to put off payment of some of the bequests until next summer, Your Grace, until your own revenues can replenish you? Some of these great minsters already have gold candlesticks enough to set Heaven on fire and could well wait for reinforcements, while you – '

'Am I a beggar? This is my father's gift to God, priest! You aren't suggesting that either of them would forgive us if we ignored them, are you? You're too much a priest for that, aren't you? We'd get thunderbolts, wouldn't we?' He laughed, but the divine emphasis he'd just laid on his father was quite clear. 'See to it and be done, man. We'll have coin enough to see us through the winter.'

'Coin enough in peacetime, maybe, Your Grace, but if there should be any trouble – '

'What trouble? Where's there a war brewing that I don't know about?'

'Nowhere – now. But what if His Grace your brother should decide to contest the inheritance with you, say in the spring, when our treasure will be very low?'

His differing eyes dwelt on me, the brown one seeming hard with malice, the blue one wide with astonishment.

'Why should he do that? He's got enough to do now, keeping his own hounds kenneled and fed across the Channel.'

'That was partly my thought, Your Grace: he has enough and maybe more than enough appetites to satisfy there.'

He stopped smiling. 'Now you sound like Lanfranc. He sees enemies everywhere. I swear by the Face, that old man would be a Caesar if he had his last hundred years to live over. But I say no,

Robin's got his duchy, his jugglers, and his whores to keep him happy. Even the Atheling's come creeping back from Italy to leech on him.' His mouth hardened at uttering Prince Edgar's title. 'And all who know Robin and me equally are gone to roost on one side or the other. My uncle Robert has made his choice. He's back in Pevensey, sends me his love, and will be at the Christmas Court. Even my uncle Odo, it seems, has thought better of his leanings and writes to me.'

'Your Grace, I've seen the letter, but surely you won't let him – '

'Won't let him what? Who says what I must do or not do? Not you, or Lanfranc! The old wars weren't mine. He's my uncle and he has more wits than the lot of you. Even Carileph chimes in against him, but, by God, I see myself in that man. He's sick of Robin and he wants to spend his old age with kinsmen he can trust. See here, priest, I won't argue family matters with you or any other man. See to your bequests and leave my relatives to me!'

I gave Cormac a hard look, thinking it must be his doing that Odo was suddenly so much in favor, but he answered me before the king:

'Don't look to me. My tongue's been shortened on that subject, too.'

'Exactly,' said Rufus, 'so, let it rest, the two of you. I mean to have peace in my court, with honor and no backbiting. Any man who makes an accusation against another before me, as I'm a true knight, he'd better back it up with proof or a sword.'

So I was silenced and found myself in uneasy alliance with Cormac again, though I still half suspected him of being in Odo's pay, and he, perhaps, suspected the same of me.

We didn't celebrate Christmas in Winchester as I'd thought, though that was its time-honored site. Wagons laden with the bequests to the churches, we trundled back to Westminster, because the king preferred its newer hall and grander minster for his mighty almsgiving. I had been so occupied I had missed my chance to ride to Godalming and see Giva before our child was born.

We traveled over rain-soaked roads in which the treasure wagons got mired every furlong and had to be dug out with spades. Even the tireless king grew impatient with the delays in pouring rain and rode on to London ahead of us, leaving Bishop Carileph and his considerable mesnie in charge of bringing in our train. I'd as soon have left St. Dismas the Thief in charge, before he was translated to Paradise, but it wasn't my affair.

All the arranging of the Christmas Court was in William de St.

Carileph's hands, too. He had in three months become the king's most constant companion and the chief voice in the court, Lanfranc having gone home to Canterbury in October.

A bishop's miter had made a new man of him. No more the careful clerk with ink on his fingers, tonsured and robed in fusty black, he had become princely in his demeanor. He wore silks, he hunted with the king, he led a mesnie of knights that might have put my old Count of the Bessin to shame; for in the county of Durham the bishop is all: earl de facto and justice of his own court.

Having already become the new king's close companion and foremost adviser, because he had been chaplain to the old king and his hunting companion, too, Carileph took on himself the guise of master of ceremonies for the Christmas Court as well. He spent freely of the king's purse to make sure that first court would be to the king's glory. No smoking torches or sputtering cressets lighted our hall that fine day, but wax candles the size of a man's arm and perfumed oil in the cressets instead of kitchen grease. New garments arrayed the backs and rumps of all the palace servants, new cloths were worked for all the tables, and we had food enough to glut a Roman legion just in from a twenty-mile walk.

The king delighted in it like a child. His urgent laugh belled out at the antics of every tumbler, juggler, or trained bear brought before him; his face, radiant with joy, smiled to see these tokens of his kingship. No use for me to drone to him on economy then.

Nor could he have been a disappointment to those who came to see him. His robes were of green and gold, with so much bright English work at their edges and hems, it was as if a whole race of hummingbirds had been hired to flit their wings about him. His pale hair, fine as any babe's, was so brushed and burnished that it gleamed like gold, like the rings on his several fingers. He had just recently begun to wear a beard and to let his hair grow until it now fell almost to the level of his chin in the French style. That stammering, uncertain boy I'd first known now looked strong, able, and as full of promise as a green field.

He took his throne in that banner-swathed hall on the morn of Christmas and there was a sudden hush. I thought of David, or young Solomon, coming into his kingdom. The chancel choir broke out into praise:

> *Christus vincit,*
> *Christus regnat,*
> *Christus imperat . . .*

Lanfranc took the Confessor's crown, which had passed through the hands of three other bishops, lifted it high, then set it on the king's head. Whereon, the plain, blunt face of William Secundus took on such an expression of exaltation that I felt the same lurch of the heart one sometimes feels at the moment of the transmuting of the Host, almost a sickness of awe. There were many in that hall who must have felt it. The man anointed and crowned thus, with the blessing and praise of the Church, was an image of Christ Himself in his enthronement. Between such occasions he had leave to be cruel, or kind; warlike, or pacific; his mother's son, his brother's enemy. But when he assumed that throne and the symbols of sanctified majesty, he was a God-kissed reflection of Our Lord, Who had approved him to rule over us; as blessed as a priest, holy as the most precious relic of a saint.

The choir fell silent. Then the hall rumbled with the cry: 'Life! Life to the king!'

I saw Cormac draw a breath and nod, as if he had received some part of the weight of that crown and the glory of that acclamation. When our eyes met, we smiled slightly, our minds united for the first time in years without a tinge of malice or envy.

We had, as I've said, become allies of a sort in more than one struggle. Carileph had made a strong attempt to banish us both to the back of the hall, well out of the eye of Rufus. I was naturally distasteful to him, being a reminder of days he must now wish to forget. Cormac was plainly marked by him as an interloper who had long overstayed his welcome in the king's company. He'd banished us to a table so far to the rear that we might not have heard that first *'Vivat rex'* until St Stephen's Day. But the king, possibly on Cormac's hint, took a last-moment interest in the seating arrangements and had us both moved forward to a respectable midway position.

Carileph protested that our low rank would offend those of better class placed below us. The king pointed to my slim chain of office, and when the bishop reminded him that Cormac had no office whatsoever, Rufus said:

'He's my physician, Carileph.'

'Physician, Your Grace? I never heard he was – versed – in that art.'

Rufus, who seemed to find Carileph's drawl amusing rather than irritating, grinned and answered: 'Oh, he's well versed. He sings me verses every day, to lighten my heart. Which improves my health. Which makes him a safer doctor than most, wouldn't you agree? Seat him at the table with the bishop of Rochester. Maybe he can cheer up old Gundulph the Weeper to the point he can finish my London tower, which my father set him to do *ten years ago.*'

So it was that Cormac was placed directly across from the learned architect and I was put beside him. It would have made weary company indeed, but that Gundulph mistook Cormac for one of the royal Scottish hostages and spent the meal trying to communicate his compliments to him in Gaelic.

When all ceremony was complete, the feeding commenced with such succulent meats as venison, goose, capon, and spitted boar. But hardly had we begun to grease our chins on the royal bounty when the hall marshal lifted our heads, pounding on the floor with his long staff. He stood at the far end of the hall, near the stairs.

'Your Grace, my lords, holy Fathers, and all noble guests, now comes an emissary from the duke of Normandy. His Illustrious Grace, Odo, Bishop of Bayeux!'

And up the stairs came Odo, sweeping out his silken mantle behind him; genial, noble, handsome; dressed in such liturgical splendor as might have made both Pope and counter-pope bite their fingers with Italian envy. He was followed by a pair of apple-rumped pages carrying a rich casket between them, and by a gaggle of clerks, among whom I recognized my brothers.

The diners rose, scraped back their benches, and gaped at his passage among them, like the Queen of Sheba swooping to surprise King Solomon. His gloved hands lifted to bestow greeting and blessing. The king stood, wiping his mouth on his napkin, made a brisk journey around the end of the high table, and came to a halt where his uncle made a grand obeisance. No man in the world could ever humble himself with such pride as Odo. The king came forward, lifted him, kissed the episcopal ring. They embraced, kissed cheeks. A certain claque of admirers bellowed approval; then the whole hall went up in a cheer, men stamping their feet or pounding their fists or knife handles on the tables. The yelling went on as the king led Odo up to the high table and stood there with him.

Robert Bloet sidled over and said in my ear: 'Hasn't anybody told my cousin what his uncle had in store for him, if he'd caught us last September?'

I looked at him askance. 'Oh, foolish man, of course we did. But we're living in new times now, full of honor and knightly trust. This is how we demonstrate our faith – by handling adders.'

That afternoon the king restored to Odo all his honors, his title of Earl of Kent, and his place as foremost counselor to the royal court, which made most people very happy again, except of course myself and Cormac – and Carileph, who had just begun to enjoy that honor before seeing it snatched from him. And Lanfranc, naturally.

The old Italian kept his opinions to himself during the high feast and the merriment that followed it. Every time Odo greeted him fulsomely and kissed his ring, one expected an outburst, and the king especially seemed to take pleasure in watching their courtesies to each other.

Lanfranc went home directly after the feast of Epiphany. He did speak briefly and to the point with the king before he departed:

'Put him out of the country, or lock him up again, as you very wisely did those two English rebels your father set free from his deathbed. My son, he's a natural Judas. He can do nothing but betray.'

Rufus scoffed gently: 'But, good Father Lanfranc, where's Christian charity then? My uncle's come and freely made his oath to me. I never called him and he needn't have done so, if he didn't mean to have peace. And he made his oath on Christmas Day, too. That should mean something.'

'To me, yes! To him, oaths are like pasty crusts, made to be broken.' His continual head-shaking gave grave emphasis to his denial. 'You made me an oath, that you'd take my advice in important matters before you acted. I've given it. If you won't heed it, I can't force you. There it is. I'm going home now. I'm too old for these broils. Perhaps I'll die soon. If I do, I'd hoped I'd die in peace, leaving you with a firm government, but there's little chance of that with him in the country.'

The king blushed a little, but put his arm around the old man's frail shoulders. There was affection in his voice: 'You won't die yet. You're hardier than any of us, like an old apple tree. You'll see, at the Spring Court. I'll be all worn down with care and you'll be flourishing anew. Go and have your winter's rest and leave worrying about my uncle to me. Remember, I've known him all my life. I'm versed in his ways. But he's my uncle, after all. If I lose him, where'll I get another half so clever? Uncle Robert's a bit of a fool, don't you agree?'

'A fool and a serving boy for Odo. Watch him, too. Do you want my blessing before I go?'

Rufus knelt at once, and Lanfranc put his thin white hands on the king's pale hair and prayed for him. Then he said:

'Remember, God anointed you for a king, not a nephew. And if you want some more good advice, shave off that beard and get your hair trimmed, too. The old kings of France gave long hair a bad name, and beards belong on he-goats and Jews. Get married as quickly as you can. Get a son or two. Earl Roger has a good-looking girl, Sybil, who's old enough for bedding now. I saw her once when she was a child. You should know her; you were his squire. Take her, or someone like her.'

Rufus got to his feet. 'I won't have time for courting a wife, Archbishop.'

'Pah! What time does it take? By the Holy Ghost! Speak to her father! Have him bring her to Easter Court. He can keep her safe at Romsey Abbey. I'll stay alive long enough to say the words over you. Courtship's a lot of modern nonsense, fostered by silly women and jongleurs. All there is to a good marriage is having a right understanding between the two families, the Sacrament, and two healthy people in bed together. Natural instinct takes care of the rest. See here – ' He broke off suddenly, wheeled, and glared at me. I took the hint and fell back a few paces, turning my head as if I were distracted by something in the galleries. I caught a few further words: '. . . tales about you . . . let them go on . . . your father . . . sons, sons, sons . . . fond of you . . . ' Then he went out of the hall with his patient clerks, shaking his perpetual 'no.'

The king had patched cheeks; he glanced around, saw me, shrugged, and grinned. His eyes glinted, but whether from tears of affection, or shame at the old man's rebuke, I couldn't tell. Later, I saw Cormac, who had been a much more distant witness, shaking his head and his finger under his master's nose, and Rufus laughed at him.

Soon after Lanfranc's departure the greater part of all who had come to court went their ways, and winter closed its hard fist on us. Only Hugh of Chester, Robert fitz Hamon, William de Warenne, and a handful of others were left to keep the king company. The lords Odo and William de St. Carileph remained, too, of course, each contending daily with the other to show himself the king's better angel.

The king, released from care until the next court, happily led us, his shrunken entourage, from royal lodge to castle to manor through the winter. The delight of realizing the extent of his possessions was still new with him. Every day he held a morning court to hear petitions or cases. As with his father, that court might be held in a presence hall, a bailey, a snug manor, or even an open field.

He took great interest in the arguments for a man so restless he could hardly sit on a stool long enough to ingest a meal. He liked it best when the law was indeterminate enough that justice depended on his own common sense and judgment.

The afternoons he devoted to such hunting as was, and at night we dined well; then the hunters sharpened their tales of prowess, cleaned their weapons, mended their bowstrings, or played rough games like schoolboys. Even fat Hugh the Wolf might join in a boisterous, table-leaping game of tag. Cormac might be invited to touch his harp later and chant them songs of Roland or William Longsword. Sometimes peasants brought in dogs or cocks to fight, or strong men wrestled.

Rufus was proud of his strength and his skill at wrestling. He could hardly bear to see three falls before he'd throw off his mantle, tunic, and shirt and offer to grapple with some hulk of a timber cutter, blacksmith, or cattle drover. He had prodigious strength in spite of his short stature and was difficult to throw. He always warned his opponents that they should yield him no ground because he was a king, on pain of getting no reward afterward, but it was really no contest with most of them. The wagers he won from his friends for his victories he gave to those he defeated, if he felt they had fought well. When there was talk at dinner and after, it was more often of venery than of the affairs of state.

Now and then we'd have some news out of Normandy that was worth a brief debate. Robert Curthose was in his duchy now, and in the hands of his 'friends,' the Bellesmes, de Tosnys, Beaumonts, and Grantmesnils, who were snatching cattle, farms, and manors from each other much as had been predicted.

But Lord Odo turned aside any deep discourse on that topic, saying heartily that as long as the Normans fought each other, they wouldn't find time to make trouble for us, which made me a little ill to hear him, but it was what the king wished to hear.

Cormac and I were thrown together in the afternoons of a necessity, being among those too ignoble for the hunt. The other people of low degree might gamble, fish, or go bird netting along the shore of some reedy lake, while the few other clerks such as myself read their psalteries or snored comfortably by the hearth.

In the Atheling's house we had once played table games to pass the time, while Edgar and Rufus rode all day. Now we walked the perimeters of some castle, the grounds of a country manor, the bounds of the nearest village. We trailed a pack of curious children or much offended dogs, baffled by our meandering. Sometimes we walked the whole time without offering each other more comment than some observation of the weather, but eventually we must come to discussion on that mutual thorn in our hand, Odo.

'He's writing letters again, as if he had fresh designs on the Holy See,' Cormac remarked on one such day, drawing a fresh titter from our parade of ragged infants who were taken by his incomprehensible speech – that is, we spoke together in French. Their dogs followed only after the smell of well-fed men, I suppose.

'What's he doing with all those letters? He's up at dawn writing, then takes to it again at night when the rest are snoring.'

'I can't say. I've not been invited to sand them.'

'But those are your brothers who come and carry them off, or fetch back answers. Don't they ever tell tales?'

I shrugged. 'My brothers and I aren't on the best terms since last September. Fulcher treats me like a leper.'

'Is that the sly one? The other – the plumper one – is more like you,' he teased. 'Open, ingenuous.' It was the lightest taunt; he didn't bait me to anger me as he used to, but I was still inclined to be stiff with him.

'Osbern's a fool. He can't know anything about it. He's like a sponge; anything he sops will leak out of him again. I don't think I'm quite so porous.'

'Ah, I've offended you again. When will we be able to call a truce to our war? I'm sorry I hit you out there on the abbey road. I told you, I was helping to make you a hero. Do you think the men who questioned you would have believed you were really trying to stop a noble from doing what he wanted, if you didn't show them a punch in the eye? Of course not! Will was impressed with it, too. Loves you all the better for it, doesn't he?'

'What about when you tried to cut my throat?'

'I thought you were sneaking to Odo, to tell him all about me and Will. You were on the way there, weren't you?'

'Not to tell him. I was dismissed, remember. And that's a wretched excuse, anyway. What makes you think he didn't know to begin with? He hired you. He knew you well enough. No, that tale won't do for excusing murder, Cormac.'

'I didn't murder you, or mean to, by God! Here you are to prove it. Little Brother, I plead honest motives – after my fashion.' He gave me one of his lupine grins. 'Look at it this way: if you'd had a cudgel in your hands instead of a water bucket, what would you have done to me that time in Rouen?'

'I'd have beaten your brains out.'

He laughed, making the children giggle and the dogs bay at him.

'So – you see? We've offered each other mischief, only to keep him clear of it. We're not natural enemies then, are we? Especially now, when we've got him on his throne and all's smooth at last?'

'I suppose not.' I glanced at him. He could be most ingratiating, and though it did occur to me once again that he might be working me for some purpose, in the pleasantly stultifying life we were leading, there was no reason to prolong our enmity.

'Very well; shall we say we've made a truce?' I said.

He ambled along, his chin cocked up for a while, then said: 'What about a peace treaty?' He offered his hand, and after a slight hesitation, I took it. We had stopped, surrounded by our audience. Cormac looked down at them, put his hand to his purse, and flung out an assortment of small coins, mostly penny bits. The children and dogs wheeled and scrambled for them, probably both thinking they were something to eat. We walked on.

'So, we're friends again. And of course you're not a sponge, Little Brother. Far from it. If you were the common loose-tongued sort of man, you'd have let it slip about that little leman you've got tucked away in Surrey. As it was, I had to learn about her from strangers.'

I came to a stop. He turned and clucked at me.

'Don't look so fey. I know you've been trying to keep it from Will. I won't spill your secret – if anything can be called a secret that's known to everybody at St. Paul's, not to mention the inhabitants of Cornhill.'

'I knew there had to be something behind all this sudden excess of brotherhood. What do you want from me?'

He sobered and said with dark intensity: 'You. Nothing but your fair body will requite me for my silence!'

I knew he was making fun of me, but I couldn't unfreeze my face or stop the sudden jolting of my heart. I could well imagine how he'd bring the subject up before the whole hunting party at the most opportune time.

He began to chuckle, then gave me a swift buffet on the arm. 'When will you ever learn? I said if the king ever hears you're not a eunuch, it won't be from me. But for God's sake, man, why do you think he'd care? What a hypocrite you are! You know all my vices – you think – yet you go all white about the mouth when we speak of yours, which you don't believe are vices at all, just indiscretions. But what odds, between us – between us fornicators – however we go to it?

'What if I said to you, "My sins aren't as black as yours, because yours usually have the result of making yet more sinners to populate a wicked world, whereas mine go to the grave without issue"?'

'Ridiculous.'

'How ridiculous? I'll make you a sermon: the cause of sin is Man. If you go sinning and make more men by it, then you've multiplied both the sin and the cause of sinning. I inflict no pain to mention with mine, as you might. I'll never put a woman in travail, or send a son to a cloister to do penance for being gotten by the likes of me. Therefore I say your sin is the worse.'

I said, somewhat churlishly: 'What about Baldwin de Fourneaux, who's dead because of you?'

He said in a hard voice: 'Baldwin's dead for hanging himself. I didn't put the rope around his neck. He might have lived and repented of me, if he'd had any use for life, but he didn't. He wanted to be out of it. He couldn't bear being in a cloister, or out of one.'

There was some truth to that, but he was too certain of it to suit me. 'What about the king, then? Shall he have to repent of you? Sad day for you, when he does.'

'I didn't harm him! Damn it, he's what Nature made him and so am I – and so are you! Ah – Christ, let's don't quarrel about that again. It's wearying to a man my age to hear sermons on corruption.' He shook his head, then cocked it to study me. 'Ranulph – friend – if there was any corrupting done to Will that wasn't done before he left his mother's womb – it was done by that – that long-shanked horse-breeder, that damned English parasite, God give him boils on his backside!'

'Edgar? Oh, no, now you contradict what you said once: that Edgar had rejected him. You even cursed him for being too sanctimonious to take pity on what you called a boy's infatu—'

'Yes, yes, yes, it was so, and Edgar refused him then, being stuffed with sanctity at the time, just having come from Mass. But he began it all, long before then, as a nasty bit of revenge on William Bastard. It was in 'seventy-two, when they were all up in Scotland to sign the peace treaty at Abernathy. *There's* a whole other tale I could tell, but it'd make you sick.

'One of the terms of that treaty was that King Malcolm had to throw Prince Edgar out of Scotland. Edgar, you mind, had been the boy to rally around for the York uprising, back in 'sixty-eight. Malcolm must have thought he could still find a use for him, but in the end he wasn't sorry to run him off. Edgar always had his sister, Margaret, hanging on his neck. She doted on him so much that a coarse-minded, jealous old devil like Malcolm might even have imagined that they – That aside, Edgar was in a bad way, but not being much of a gambler, he didn't have the gall to just pick up a dirk and put it between the Bastard's ribs.

'But he wasn't a candidate for sainthood either, then. So, he waited for the carousing to begin in the hall, then he went and took aside a little red-faced, wall-eyed squire that he'd seen stand by the king's side to put his mark on the parchment when the treaty was witnessed. He did his job of revenge out in the stables. It was easy work for him – a fair-faced, honey tongued prince of the old blood, with grand tales to tell about his first campaign at sixteen. And it didn't hurt that he'd brought along a jack of that Devil's piss the Scots brew out of barley-corn and moldy boots.'

Cormac laughed harshly. 'Oh, that was a sweet night's work altogether – on a boy of twelve, no more – who he could tell at a glance had never known anybody to flatter him or show him a wink of affection. He talked of war and brave deeds; then he spoke of the love that brave men bear for one another. Will says he mentioned David and Jonathan – Roland and Oliver – for all we know, Jesus and St. John might have been touched on, delicately! He goes on in that fashion, putting his arm around the sprat and feeding him up with *uisgebaugh,* until the poor boy is fair on to losing his wits from all the courting and the drink. With what result? Why, hey, presto, passe-passe! Love is born, the braies are down, and the little cock's being taught how to crow.'

'No more, please. You've made it abundantly clear.'

'Yes.' He paused. 'Well, it isn't like our lad to forget a hero like that. Will was sailed away home in a few days and Edgar had to slink off to France, though he was back in Scotland in a year. The French king offered him a fresh chance to get revenge on the Bastard – gave him a castle just above the Norman border to raid from – Montreuil. He jumped at the chance, but bungled it fine. The ship he sailed to France on went down in a storm just beyond the mouth of the Forth. He nearly drowned. All of his servants and most of his crew did drown.

'It was his near death that must have given him his marvelous new piety that he could later hold up in the face of the boy who still loved him. Also, by then he'd found Curthose, and they were soul mates from the moment they clapped eyes on each other.'

I said: 'But it was years since all that happened. Our friend was a child. I still believe, if you'd just have let him alone, he'd have survived Edgar's rebuff and come out right in the end.'

'Right? Right in the end? What's that? He'd have more than likely come out dead! No, I'm serious. He was desperate to be one of those who went up to Scotland and made names for themselves – heroes – or died with a smile on their lips. He was desperate, I say! The damned Englishman knew it, if the old king didn't. Will hadn't just stammered out to his idol that he wished they might take up their old love again; he went to *beg* Edgar to speak to Curthose on his behalf; to get him out of his father's shadow and up to Scotland with Robert, even if it was only as a common soldier – no favors, no privileges!

'He was doubly rejected, because Edgar refused him that, too. He said it would be a great wickedness for them to be thrown together and tempted, when one of them had gotten himself so right with God that his farts had begun to smell like roses – or something to that effect.

' "Free yourself from all carnal longings," he told him, "and then you may be ready to be a true knight." That, to a boy who'd have cut his own balls off to be a true knight, if anyone had told him it was the regulation – and from a man who's never lowered a lance in battle in his life!

'But we must go down to the ship and say farewell to him and to Curthose, no matter. When we got there, Curthose, who isn't altogether a bad sort for an idiot, made a friendly jibe at Will about keeping safe from Welshmen. To Will, it meant Edgar must have spilled himself to Robert, to set him on to mock him. He went off that ship white as death. I laid hold on him and dragged him to a wineshop. I was even considering taking him to a brothel, if you can believe it. I was for giving anything a try! But the wine made him sick and the shopkeeper's jest about his green customer sent him off down the street at a run. When I caught up to him, he hauled out his dagger and said he'd be rid of himself – or me – if I tried to stop him.'

'But you stopped him from mortal sin with a fine speech, is that it?'

He sighed. 'No. His stomach went against him again. While he was heaving, I took the knife.'

'After which?'

'After – which.'

'And this makes you a better man than Edgar?'

He considered. 'Will lived. He's won out over all of them. He's got his crown and his reputation – his honor. Yes – *yes*, by God, it makes me the better man! I've never harmed him.'

29

Lent came, and bit by bit our company began to disband. First Carileph returned to Westminster, where with his considerable number of attendants he would pack up the royal household for removal to Winchester in time for the Easter Court. Soon after, we received word through my brother Fulcher that there was unrest among the citizens of Rochester, Odo's earldom's seat. Odo himself went to pacify it, good lord that he was. He bade the king an affectionate good-bye and gave all the high company the kiss of peace – *sans* Cormac and me. We were to him, as Cormac had called us, shadows, not to be seen.

We moved from Wychwood to Bernwood; then Earl Hugh left us for Chester; and soon the de Warennes took their leave, until there was no companion to the king worthy to hunt with him but Robert fitz Hamon. The king's holiday from care was over.

Before he made for Westminster again, to end that time of peace which was almost the last he was ever to know, the king determined to reward his one friend from childhood, Robert fitz Hamon, with some token of his esteem. The late Queen Matilda had been seisined of many rich manors in England, in Buckinghamshire, Gloucester-shire, and Cornwall. Rufus wished to give some of them to his friend. So, it was his pleasure to go into Buckinghamshire with fitz Hamon, to show him one of those manors, and to go unencumbered with state, as one of two free knights, with no more train than his squire, his harper, and enough servants to make his fires and tend his horses.

Me, he dismissed for a time along with the rest of his band, saying cheerfully: 'Ranulph, you look lodge-bound. Why not go along to London, or where you will, for a few days? So you meet me in Winchester by Palm Sunday, I promise not to fall into any grievous sins behind your back. Go along.'

I heard that command with joy and fled to pack a saddlebag and mount a horse to take me to Godalming. Giva had borne her babe two months before, if she was right in her reckoning. I was eager to see what we'd spawned, almost as eager as I was for Giva.

When I came down out of the long, wooded ridges that wrinkle the earth to the north and west of my parish, the plowmen were already tilling up the winter stubble, and the fruit orchards were beginning to show plump grey velvet buds. I kicked my horse into a semblance of a trot and made for my house.

Giva and Blodwin, the curate's wife, were feeding a mixed flock of poultry in the vicarage yard, flinging out golden handfuls from the depths of their folded aprons. They wore rough hats of plaited oat straw, new ones of their winter's making that gleamed in the sun. As I came to the north bounds of the village, I saw the brims of those bonnets lift to let their wearers observe me, then dip again as they went on with their task. I dismounted at the church, stepped inside for a moment to see that all was well and to say a brief prayer for my journey, then went on foot toward my house. Blodwin gave me a nod as I came. She emptied out her apron and turned to the door. Giva followed her.

Didn't she recognize me, or was she still angry for our last encounter? I stood at the gate with my horse thrusting his impatient nose into my shoulder to urge me on to the smell of sweet grain. I watched Giva's retreating back. She stopped at the edge of the yard, shook out her apron, and seemed to examine its weave as if it were of great significance. Her hat brim trembled; of a sudden she spun around, tore off her bonnet, and came running to me. I caught her up in my arms, lifted her over the gate, and held her so that her toes swung clear of the ground.

When next I noticed anything but the taste of her mouth and the firmness of her body against me, my horse had nosed open the gate and was inside, greedily snuffling up the hen feed to the chagrin of the poultry. Dunstan, my curate, was staring at us from the doorstep. I put Giva on her feet, but kept her pinioned with one arm.

'You're stouter,' I said. 'How can this be, when country people get leaner in the winter?'

She laughed up at me. 'It's from all the ale I have to drink to make enough milk for them – Ranulph! There're two!'

'So I felt when I hugged you. I can't wait to kiss them properly.'

She smothered her laugh and blush in my shoulder. 'Don't speak so loud; Father can hear you. I can tell he's really watching us. I meant babies, of course.' She lifted her head again eagerly and gripped my arms. 'Don't you want to see them? Did you know about them?'

'Of course I want to see them. It's what I'm here for, isn't it?' In defiance of Dunstan I picked her up bodily and carried her through the gate. 'And of course there are two of them. We decided on that months ago, didn't we? What do they look like? Do they have your eyes? I'll disown them if they don't.'

'You can't disown them; they look exactly like you. Ranulph, please put me down. Father – '

I did so. Dunstan's sour face never twitched a muscle as I set her before him. 'Good day to you, Dunstan! Has the winter been kind to you?'

He frowned politely in thought. He always behaved as if my English were barely comprehensible to him, though in my opinion I now spoke it with a good accent. 'Ah – aye, Rector, though the church roof's in need of thatching and the narthex door won't stand to without a shove.' It was as much as I'd ever heard him utter outside the confines of Divine Service. Now he outdid himself: 'Daughter, pick up your hat and kerchief. I've said you're not to show yourself out here without it, for them that might look down on us from yon tower.'

Giva sobered instantly and ran to obey him, then fled into the house. I stayed for a moment, wanting to twist Dunstan's stubby nose, but curious about his remark.

'Who's up in the tower?' It was a royal manor by designation, and no one had the right to be there without royal leave.

'Some lord's men.'

'What lord's men?'

'Some from next county.' He never looked more obdurate or stupid.

I let it go, seeing I'd have to drag it from him, and went to see my children. They lay like twin mice in a box cradle by the hearth. Giva was hovering over them. She took one up and gave it to me, then carried the other to the bed, which was the only piece of furniture in the single room, other than a table and a rough press against the wall.

As I dandled my infant gingerly, she unswaddled hers, put out her hands for its brother, and exposed him, too. My sons. They kicked vigorously, waved their fists, and tried to roll over onto their bellies. I sat on one side of them to prevent their falling and touched their soft puffs of black hair. I marveled at their flat little ears, their active feet, and the triple buds of manhood each displayed shamelessly. 'Very substantial, those. Not meant for church property.'

'Shh!' she hissed, as Dunstan now entered the house. He cleared his throat portentously and addressed some complaint to his wife.

One of the babes began to fuss, knocking at his nose with a fist that was trying to escape being eaten by his mouth. Giva at once began to wrap up both boys in their swaddles again.

'Well!' I said. 'We must have them baptized at once. I've given some thought to names, and – '

'Oh, but they're already baptized, Ranulph.'

'What? When? Why did you do that without my knowing?'

'There's no baptizing in Lent, Rector,' Dunstan said without being asked. 'Except in extreme circumstances.'

Giva said hurriedly with a glance at him: 'They were so small and weak at first. What if something had happened to them? Father baptized them as soon as it was mild enough weather to take them to the font. I wanted him to do it.'

'So be it, then. What names did you give them? I would have had one be William and the other, if there was another, Maurice.'

She gathered them up at once, somehow, carried them back to their nest, and deposited them tenderly. 'In that case you should have said something to me before you sent me away. Or you should have sent word here. Now you'll have to be satisfied with Thomas and – '

'*Thomas?* In the name of all that's – who names a child Thomas? It's outlandish! What? Thomas the Doubter? Is that what you want people to think when they hear of him?'

She had her chin set now. 'Thomas was a disciple of Our Lord's.' It might have been Dunstan saying it.

'I know that, Elfgiva. I have some education, after all.'

'A disciple of Our Lord's, who was called "the Twin." There's a – a Greek word – '

'Didymus,' Dunstan supplied, his back to me.

'Didymus! Good Lord, you didn't name the other one that, did you? Giva – '

'No, of course not! I said he must be named for you.' She looked ready to do battle for her choice. At her feet the babes had begun to wail, having been disturbed to no good purpose in their logic.

I held up my hands for peace. 'Very well. So be it again. I'm outvoiced. Thomas and Ranulph it is and ever shall be forever – amen.'

Dunstan turned about and sprang to life then as if he'd only just remembered I was there. He urged me to come and see what repairs would be needed to the church interior before our light waned. We went and I inspected the building from roof beams to undercroft; then we met with a few of the village elders and discussed how the work might be effected and who would get what compensation for it, whether in coin, barter, or fee relief. By the time all was settled and I had heard, like a minor lord, additional community complaints about abuse by neighbors, broken hedges, trespassings, it was time for Vespers. Dunstan had kept me from Giva for several hours, as I suspected he meant to do.

We took holy service together. A large part of the village was in attendance, most likely to see if I had sprouted horns yet for my transgressions. The candles at the altar, half tallow, half wax, sputtered as if they took part in my old curate's sullen dislike of me.

We ate a frugal meal that night, only barley porridge with onions, washed down with water. Unnecessarily, Dunstan apologized for it, saying I must be used to daintier food, but reminding me once again that it was Lent. Giva alone drank a cup of ale from the supply sent down to her most generously by the tower warden's goodwife.

There was sparse conversation at the table, as might be expected. Dunstan remained massively incurious about anything happening outside Godalming, and to whatever question I might ask in the way of pleasantry, he answered with a bare 'aye,' 'nay,' or a shrug. Any remark of Blodwin's was squelched with a 'Woman, what do you know of it?'

At last I left my stool and stretched, yawning broadly to remind my curate that I'd had a long ride and was now once again the master of the only bed. Giva looked ashamed for me and went to tend her babes, while Blodwin quickly cleared the table, washed the horn spoons and wooden bowls, then climbed the ladder to the loft, where there was a pallet for extra sleepers. Dunstan, however, remained on his stool, staring into the fire as if it had bewitched him.

I regretted there were 'some lord's men' up in the hunting tower. I'd have preferred to take Giva and our babes up there to that old queen's bower where we'd started the making of our handsome twins. Next day I must go up and see just who those interlopers were. I felt a proprietary jealousy that anybody should make free with the king's property. Why were they there? It was early days to be on the way to the Easter Court.

When it seemed Dunstan might stay on his stool forever, I said with forced friendliness: 'Why Dunstan, I won't disturb you if your supper's not settled, but I confess I'm weary for my bed. I've not slept in a real one since last summer. This one looks like a royal couch to me, tonight.'

It looked like a pallet on legs, being no more than a bag stuffed with chopped straw and a thin mattress of poultry feathers laid over it that was flat with age, but it did have ragged furze curtains like a real bed.

He looked up as if I'd disrupted a particularly deep meditation. 'Weary are you, Rector? Aye, that's good. Lent's the season for fasting and watching until we're weary and chaste, ready for the feast of the Good Tidings to come.' That homily concluded, he went outdoors to relieve himself.

I turned to smile and wink at Giva, but she was prim-faced and busy changing breechclouts. Dunstan came in again, gave her an admonitory stare, which she received meekly, then at last went up the ladder with great deliberation of step.

I turned to Giva at last. I wanted to sweep her up, carry her to the bed, unwrap her as she unwrapped our babes, and rediscover with my lips and fingers all the warmth and sweetness of her. But she was sitting with a child in her lap now, unfastening her gown to give him suck. I had never yet seen her perform that wonder, so I sat down cross-legged by the baby cot to observe it.

The low fire made an icon of her, burnishing with a touch of copper the fine dark hairs that escaped her coif, deepening the shadows of her lashes and underlip, laying a patina of warm ivory on her cheek, brow, and breast where the shadows didn't fall. I heaved a sigh of content for so much loveliness that was mine.

'Madonna mia.'

She looked at me without lifting her head.

'That means "my lady" in Italian. It's what old Lanfranc calls the Blessed Virgin when he has need of an oath.'

She bit her lip and whispered: 'It isn't good to use one of the names of the Blessed Virgin to me. It's sacrilege.'

I could almost hear old Dunstan's ears cracking up in the loft as they strained to make out our whispers. I said: 'No, properly speaking, I think it might be blasphemy, but only if I took you for a goddess. Giva, *dyrling*, you show definite talent for being a church advocate. I've noticed it before. But for now, and because I love you, would you just be a lovely woman nursing her child and allow me to be your admirer? May I say you have – the most beautiful face and hands and breast this side of Lady Venus, who's only a mere heathen goddess it's perfectly correct to steal titles from?'

She smiled, but as if it pained her to do it. I began to realize my error in sending her down to live with Dunstan for so long a time. Obviously he'd been hard at work to make her feel even more sinned upon and sinful than the Irish priest in London. I had much ground to recover, but I remembered how she'd run to me, throwing her hat away in defiance of Dunstan. She loved me; she'd borne me two sons in joy. As soon as I had her in bed I'd make her forget the quarrels we'd had and all of Dunstan's preachings in the joy we'd take of each other.

I changed tactics, however. I lifted up the other babe, dipped my finger into the last drop of her ale nearby, and let him suck it to his passing satisfaction, as he'd begun mewling.

'Oh! He shouldn't taste that!' she said in a little squeak.

'Why, because of Lent? Which am I holding now, Thomas or Ranulph?'

'That's Ralph. He's got a little red spot by his ear.'

'Ralph? Is that how you trim it? My mother called me Raf and my father, sometimes, Raoul. How strong his jaws are! He's gnashing his gums for sweeter food. Which is your favorite?'

'Mothers don't have favorites,' she said firmly, but then she added: 'Tom's the stronger, but little Ralph's more tender – being the younger, I suppose.'

We exchanged babes. I tucked up Thomas for the night, then rose to my knees to see how she put Ralph to the breast. My namesake fed on her, his eyes closed in ecstasy, his mouth fairly encompassing her nipple and working so that his cheek dimpled with every pull on the pap.

'This must be why it's so difficult for men to be chaste.' I stroked his cheek with the back of my fingers. 'This hunger for woman is in them from the hour of their birth. Unless he's maimed by life, or sickened with himself for some false cause, he'll never be so happy again until he finds another breast so sweet.' I saw she'd caught her lip in her teeth again. I put a finger on it to make her release it, then stroked her other breast.

Her free hand came up at once to stop me as our little suckling all but choked on the sudden flow of milk. 'Don't! You mustn't – poor baby!' She gave me a push in the chest that settled me back on my heels. 'It isn't the season.'

I stood rebuked. 'Is he all right now?'

At her curt nod I got up and went outdoors for a few moments, not so much to let her regain her composure as to struggle with mine. Dunstan had done his work admirably, aided by Giva's fear that we'd been responsible for the first child's death because of our irregular handfasting. She'd protect these two now, if I had to be put off with talk of 'seasons' until either I made her a proper wife, or Dunstan succeeded in making her an anchorite. What should I do with her? I looked at the stars for an answer, but they were clustered so thick in their heavenly bed they could hardly wink at me.

I went in, stripped off my clothes, and lay down on the bed naked.

She had been crooning to the babies, but she got up and pulled the curtains on me; for shame of my nakedness, I thought, until I heard the ladder creaking. I came out of bed in an instant to take her by the waist before she disappeared into the loft.

'Where are you going now?'

'Up there. It would be better if I slept with them.'

'The Devil it would! Let go the ladder.'

'Hush! You'll wake them.'

'Let go the ladder, or I'll wake them by pulling it down.'

She let go. I lifted her down and led her to the bed, where she stood obediently with bowed head while I unlaced her, then loosened her plaits and ran my hands through her hair to spread it. She pulled off her gown and shoes, but went to the far side of the bed to get in, still wearing her shift. I drew the curtains and lay beside her, but didn't touch her. She was extraordinarily quiet about it, but I could tell she wept. I turned to speak in her ear, so that we wouldn't be heard:

'Am I a devil now? Is it sure damnation to lie with me?'

She sniffed wetly. 'It's a sin for people to – to know each other – during Lent and the other holy seasons. If they do – do it – they must pay a fine before they take Holy Communion. I thought it would be better if – if I went up.'

'It's a sin to sleep with me, but not with that old man up there?'

'I've slept with that old man for months! You know I was too big then to climb to the loft, so it's always been the three of us down here.'

'Who slept in the middle?'

'That's a nasty, wicked thing to ask!'

'I'm sorry. But he sleeps with Blodwin now. Why is it wrong for you to sleep with me?'

She snuffled and wiped her face with her hand. 'They aren't tempted as we are.'

'Yes, well, one can see why not.' I sighed and touched her shoulder, just fingering the velvet skin. 'Giva? I'll pay the fine.'

She snorted. 'That's what Father said you'd say.'

'He did? The old devil!'

'He isn't, really. He's been good to me, Ranulph, like my own father before he married again. He says he knows all about the temptations of the flesh, that he was young once, too. But he says we mustn't think we can just do anything because we're young and hot, then pay the fine and forget it. That's mocking the mercy of God, which is a worse sin than just – doing it.'

Perfectly memorized. But I wasn't going to let Dunstan have the last word in my own bed. She hadn't drawn away from my touch. I stroked her arm and clasped her hand. 'If we'd been mindful of the holy season rule last year, we wouldn't have two sons to be proud of today. Did you think of that? God must not have been so very incensed by our loving, else He'd not have opened your womb to me. Or, if He did, He could have let you miscarry during the fright of the fire. But He didn't.'

She only sighed.

'Giva, I greatly respect Dunstan's piety and his judgment in ordinary matters, believe me. He's been a parish priest and knows all the deceptions practiced by the human heart, while I've been a court priest, dealing with writs and tallages. But does he take into consideration that we've already kept a Lenten season of our own for eight months? Such a long time, surely, for the abstinence that true lovers must practice apart.' I brushed her breasts deliberately in reaching for her other arm to turn her to me.

'I love you. What must I do? I can't remain until Easter sets us free. I must go back to the king. Then, who knows how long it may be until I'm able to come again? What if it's not until Whitsuntide, which is equally a holy season? Or before Christmas? Will he tell you we should deny ourselves each time?'

I felt her breath on my face and could bear no more delays. I took her in my arms and fell to kissing her mouth, face, throat, and shoulder with all the greed and desperation of a starving man who finds a mutton shank in his hands. She sobbed and began to whisper something, but I was too delirious with the feel of her to listen to it.

'Take off that foolish shift.' I pulled at it, then rolled her over on her back to get it up in front. As I did, her muttering became more distinct – she was praying rapidly, just finishing a Pater Noster! As I put my hand between her thighs she began the Creed. Her whispering was now quite distinct.

'Is this another piece of Dunstan's advice? Did he say, "When he puts his fingers here, say this prayer, and when he puts them here, say that one'? He's ten times the lecher, then. He lies up there and hears what we do by your prayers, then does it with us in his head."

'No!' She panted for a moment, then began to say an Ave.

'Stop that!'

'I made a vow.'

'To him?'

'To God. To say my prayers every night. But you prevented me. To be good, for my babies' sake, until – until someone marries me.'

'So, that's it! All this piety's just a sham to force me to that. Now we've come to the nub of it.'

'No. To keep me strong for them, until – until – '

'Until I marry you.'

'Until I don't want you to anymore.' She began to say her prayers again on no breath; only the soft clicking of her lips and tongue gave it away.

I jerked her shift down over her thighs and turned on my back again. After a silence I asked: 'You just want someone to marry you, is that it? Not me in particular; just someone? Who or what did you have in mind? A plowman? A pig keeper? Not another priest, no. What other honest stench would you like to take to bed with you, made holy by matrimony?'

She said, 'I love you.'

'And I love you, though my demonstration of it must lack something. Perhaps you'd believe "love" better from some Sussex oat thrasher who'd thrash you too, on all the holidays.'

'You don't love me! You only want me now. When I've had more babies and I'm slack, and fat, and old, you won't be coming to me. You'll get some other whore to take to bed. And you can't frighten me or make me ashamed with your threats anymore. You've already offered to sell me to the stews; now you threaten me with farmers. But it doesn't matter. Say or do anything you like, so long as my babies don't suffer for it.'

In honor of that piece of eloquence there was nothing to do but turn my back on her. In a while she stopped weeping, slipped under the covers, and turned away from me, too.

I lay inventing more vile things to say to her. She was unwomanly. Like all the other English females I'd had knowledge of, her tongue ran on as freely as if she were a man. Even my mother, a tinker's daughter and of the strange race of the older Bretons, never answered back to my father when he told her a thing was so. By God, these Englishmen were made cowards from too much managing by their women. If they'd beaten their wives, they might have found the valor to beat off the Danes and Normans.

I slept, in some fashion. Only the tumult in my mind made my dreams so much like waking that I got no rest. About midnight I woke, shuddering and stiff as a corpse, because I'd lain above the covers. I woke Giva in trying to creep under them.

She turned and whispered: 'Are you sick? You're shivering. Is it a fever?' She touched me and felt the chill of my flesh. She came at once to lie against me to warm me. In my midnight desolation and in her swift tenderness I drowned my wrath and clung to her like a babe while she rubbed my arms and shoulders to bring the blood back to them.

'Never say I don't love you. Never say it.'

'You've taken a chill.'

'Only from your doubts – from your coldness, and – I had evil dreams. So cold – ' My own pathos began to affect me as she kissed and coddled me. I wept, not to move her, but she was softened by it and began to kiss my face and murmur comforting endearments. Who could say who had yielded to whom? At some moment between the kisses and the stroking I said:

'I'll marry you tomorrow.'

'Don't say that now. Say it when you mean it.'

'I do mean it. I promised before, didn't I? If you weren't satisfied? I'll marry you tomorrow, so you'll believe I love you. So you'll be safe – tomorrow. '

She denied it for a while, but with our flesh touching in the dark and with so many kisses, tears, and vows of mine whispered in her ear, her heart was shaken from its resolve by love and pity, and she took me to her at last. Whether Dunstan kept vigil for our loving through the night I never knew or cared.

At first light she left the bed at some little sound and came back presently with both babies, already writhing with hunger. She satisfied them both at once. Lying on her side, she supported one infant body across her own, while offering the bounty of her other breast to the one who lay on the bed.

It was a pagan posture. Her slim body arched to give both children suck, her dark hair was loose and wild about her face, which wore a look both grave and pleased. I felt a pang of pure jealousy, in spite of the full measure of her love already given me. Ashamed of the feeling, I made a joke about the feeding:

'Perhaps, considering the situation, we should have named them Romulus and Remus.'

She gave me an uncomprehending look.

There was a creaking of the ladder rungs. Dunstan was coming down, on his way to ring the Prime bell. Giva and I lay smiling at each other while he hawked and coughed, then shuffled about to scrape a dipper noisily in the water bucket. I smiled because she was so perfect in her naked motherhood and she was mine. She smiled, I suppose, because it was to be her wedding day.

When Dunstan had gone out, I rose quickly and put on my clothes before Blodwin came down. I threw Giva's gown and shift in through the bed curtains, then followed Dunstan out to the church.

We rang the bell and said Prime service between us, with only a handful of villagers in attendance. I was ineligible to say Mass later, but I felt in no way abashed to sing God's praises unshriven that morning. I felt blessed, rather than in a state of sin. I reasoned that God, beholding me for a lover of women, had led me to promise to marry one, in order that He might be happier with me in the future. If He had meant me to be cold and chaste, He would have made me like Dunstan, who had taken a wife in all probability only to keep from paying her as his housekeeper. The Almighty knew I had never wanted to be a priest, so He might have cooled me in a dozen ways, unless it was to His purpose that I be warm. I denied Cormac's assertion that my weakness only increased the number of sinners in the world. Who could tell but that I might have engendered saints instead? Even saints are bred of loving women.

When we came out of the church, I stopped to gaze up at the morning, which was going to be perfect, then at the tower on the hill, where that pennant fluttered on the top in a stiff breeze.

'Dunstan, who is that lord whose men are in the king's lodge? You said he was of another county. Which county?'

He shrugged and worked his mouth as if he had to prime it to speak to me. 'The warden says they're from the Kentish lands.' He spoke as if it were from beyond Jerusalem they'd come, which no doubt Kent seemed to him. He'd never been farther than to the hundred-court.

'Lord Odo's men? Or the archbishop's?' But that was no banner of Lanfranc's, I knew even as I said it. Odo's men. 'How long have they been here?'

'Near to a week. I know no more about it.'

'How many are they? Surely you noticed that when they rode up there. '

He started away from me. 'They came in the night. Warden says they're on their way south to someplace called Pay Vohnzay, if there is such a country.'

'Pevensey? Did he say Pevensey? That's a castle on the southern coast.'

He looked surly. 'How is that different from what I said? I know no more about it. You're a Frenchman; why don't you go up and ask them what they're doing there? I must milk the cow.'

I dismissed his insolence, because the thought of Odo's marching his knights such a roundabout way to Pevensey was more disturbing to me. With all Kent to lord it over, with a tumult to put down in Rochester, and with a straighter way to Pevensey to be found going through Sussex, why should he send them to Godalming? Were they on their way with some urgent message for the king, believing him to be already in Winchester? No. If that were the case, they wouldn't be taking a week's rest before delivering it. They were sent to Godalming, either to hold it or to wait for someone coming this way. Who? Robert of Mortain? The king?

Giva called to me and I tore my gaze away from that tower, where there was nothing to be seen but the pennant to give a sign there was anyone there at all, except the warden. They were probably the advance guard for some journey of Odo's to his brother's, now his trouble at home was settled, but he had lingered overlong in some manor along the way where the hunting was good. Great lords may linger as long as they please, while their attendants wait. But still, why in Godalming?

I went into the house, still trying to puzzle it out. I decided I would go up to pay my respects to the warden, as Dunstan had sarcastically suggested; then I might discover the mystery.

We wouldn't break our fast until after the Terce Mass, naturally, so I had shaved and was about to make my visit to the warden when Giva tugged at my sleeve and cast her eyes at Dunstan, just coming in with his pail of milk, which Blodwin would make into butter and cheese, half of which was due to the tower. I knew what she meant. In the very moment of her reminding me, I knew it was impossible. I had been a fool to make that promise in the dark. She must have seen my hesitation. Her eyes began to widen. I was fairly trapped; I had to say something. I spoke, all too abruptly, to Dunstan:

'Dunstan, Giva and I wish to be married. Will you do us the honor this morning at the door? I'll pay well for the Sacrament and the dispensing with the banns.' It was the best I could do, since he couldn't despise me any more than he already did. Or could he? The way he drew himself up and cut his eyes at Giva and his wife before he answered told me he got great pleasure in saying:

'You should have thought of that before now, Rector, or searched your memory for what they taught you in your fine school. There's no marrying to be done during the Lenten season, as you must know.'

I tried to look stricken, since Giva's gaze was now utterly damning, and I replied in all truth:

'I do know it, but I've promised Giva before and – and I'm with her so seldom – '

'With her enough to give her three babies, Rector,' said the impudent old rascal, thoroughly enjoying my plight.

'Be that as it may, you've married many a couple who brought their children to the wedding, I'll wager. As for our case, isn't it better to marry in spite of the season and pay our fine than not to marry and prolong the sin?' She should have appreciated that I was repentant enough even to acknowledge myself in the wrong in the eyes of the Church, but no such thing. She turned her back on me and began to gather up breechclouts for laundering, as if the conversation were of no further interest to her.

'There's no fine I'd take for breaking the law of the holy season,' Dunstan said righteously. 'That would take a dispensation from your bishop, Rector. Go to him for your hasty weddings. He's a worldly man to your liking. I'm only a poor English priest who lives in the fear of God.'

30

Damn him, damn him, and double damn him! As soon as I had time to attend to the matter, I'd have another curate, I swore to myself as I went out to make peace with Giva. In the night I had truly forgotten the Lenten marriage ban, though the other aspects had been well presented to me earlier. I had thought only of my coldness, to which she tendered such sweet relief, and to the love I bore her, which she wouldn't believe of me otherwise. A fool and a woman together will always make great sport for the Devil!

She was well ahead of me on the path that led to the river, carrying her washing basket on one hip and walking as if she meant never to stop. I caught up with her and made to take the basket from her, but she wouldn't release it.

'I did forget, I swear by all that's holy!'

'I don't know what you know about all that's holy – a fine, educated man with a famous teacher,' she said. The damned memory of woman will never let go of anything a man ever says that can be used against him at a later time. 'I should have known you'd find some way out of it. Even an ignorant woman should know when a man whispers lies in her ear.'

'Giva, by St. Michael and all his angels – '

'And by all the saints, and by the Blessed Mother, and all your other oaths! Swear them! Swear away! That's what you think of me, isn't it? That I'm just an ignorant English *peasant* – that's what you like to call us all, isn't it? We're just stupid peasants, to be used and made servants of, and to tell lies to, while all you fine, educated, bloody Normans do as you like with us.'

We had reached the river's edge, where she threw down her basket. I was as angry as she by then. My good intentions were set at naught and my race was to account for my perfidy, as it always had when she was vexed with me.

'Have it your way, then; you're a stupid woman, stupid not to see I meant to be fair with you. Why would I waste oaths on you otherwise? What could I gain by it? Tell me that.'

'Nothing! Nothing at all; so why are you still here? What else do you want of me? Are you still cold? Shall I strip and sprawl for you here in the bushes? Here I am, then – lay me down again. What's one swiving more or less to me?' She began to tear loose the lacing of her gown. 'Here, do it and be quick about it, so I can get on with my work.'

Her insolence raised up such a fury in me that without thinking I slapped her across the face. In another moment I might have begged her forgiveness for it, but I had no time to find remorse. She gave me a push in the chest with both hands that sent me stumbling backward over the edge of the riverbank and flat on my back into the water.

The Wey isn't deep there, but I felt the river close over my head. Ever since my near drowning in the Seine I'd had a horror of being submerged again. I flailed and sputtered as water rushed into my mouth and up my nose; then the gravel bed received me and I floundered to the surface, spewing like a fountain.

Giva was shrieking. I went under again, unable to get a purchase with hands or feet on the shifting bottom. When I rose for the second time I saw to my horror that the bank was farther away and that Giva was running up the path rather than finding some sort of stick or branch to hold out to me. I fell forward on my chin and, like a dog, began to churn water with my arms until I felt bottom again and clutched my way to the bank. My ears must have been stopped with river ooze, because I never heard the horseman, only saw him blearily as I climbed the slimy bank, my gown weighed down with water and my lungs on fire.

He dismounted and came to give me his hand, hauling me up to the grass where I coughed and gagged for a time before rolling over on my back. His face swam over me, with Giva's just above it.

'God's Breath, Ranulph, were you after mermaids?' It was Robin Bloet, dressed in a rough tunic and brown hose, with a hood pulled over his tonsure, so that he looked like a forester. I sat up, still coughing, while he squatted on his haunches and examined me, grinning. Giva bent to wipe my dripping head with her apron. She was weeping, as she damned well should have been, and her breasts were half exposed because of her unlaced gown.

Robin's eyes took her all in, his smile fading briefly before it came back more wicked than ever. 'Is that the cause of it? No wonder! I'm half blinded myself. But you must try to fall toward them next time, friend.'

Giva didn't catch the French, but the glance was enough, I'm sure. She snatched her apron up to cover herself, rising and turning her back to us. When she'd laced up she took her wash and hurried away downstream where the water wasn't so muddied.

I stripped off my gown and shirt, then sat down to tug at my soggy boots. Robin generously took my garments to hang up on a willow tree.

'God knows, Raf, I'm no pry, but what – '

'It's of no consequence. Why are you here?'

'I'm trying to find the king. I thought he'd be in Winchester by now, but as you're here, he must be. What are you going to say to him of your dousing? It'd better be quite original, or my version will efface it.'

'He isn't here. What's amiss?' I realized there must be something exceedingly wrong to bring lazy Robin out on a horse from London in disguise. I had a sudden premonition: 'Is it something to do with Odo?'

'No. What about Odo? It's Carileph I came to tell about. Where is the king, if he isn't with you?'

'We're at cross-purposes, Robin. He's in Buckinghamshire. What's there to tell him about Carileph?'

'Why, that he's gone mad, or something. Yesterday he came into London with his household troops behind him. He took a grand tour about town to get attention, then came into St. Paul's yard to make a speech – saying he was taking governance of the town, because we lacked a ruler and our peace was in danger. He claimed there was great unrest in all the realm, because people didn't know *who should rightfully be their king.*'

I let my boots drop. 'Where does he come by that notion?'

'Ah, that's what some of those who were listening to him wanted to know, too. When they asked, he got very hot, made a wrangle with one or two of them instead of answering the question, and in the end had about a dozen of them arrested.'

'My God!'

'Yes. Some of them were aldermen, too, as it turned out. There was the very devil of a roil for a little time. Everybody in the chapter house came running out to see about it. Carileph had his prisoners marched off to Baynard's Keep to be clapped in prison, but Lord Ralph wasn't there and his warden wouldn't open to Carileph. They bellowed at each other about it, but the warden outfoxed him. He opened the postern, let out some of his fellows to come around behind Carileph's, then snatched in the prisoners while the rest were standing each other off.

'I thought there'd be a fair battle then, but Carileph backed off, took his men up to Montfichet instead, and occupied it. There was no one there of higher rank than a sergeant, I think, or else Carileph had learned something from his defeat by Baynard's warden. He's holding Montfichet now and won't come out.'

'He *is* mad. But – this is treason! You're right; the king should hear it at once.' I got up, realized my nakedness anew, and looked around for Giva in despair.

Robin said a bit wearily, 'Why do you suppose I've been riding all night? I meant him to know. But where is he?'

'Giva! Get me some clothes! Anything! Now!'

Robin cackled. 'There's nothing more ridiculous than a naked man giving orders. Sit down, Ranulph, or you'll draw all your village down here to see what you're bellowing about. Bring him a cloak, Giva, *sweeting*, and take your time. Ranulph, for God's sake, where's the king? Please? And, if he isn't here, who's in the tower? I saw a standard.'

'I don't know, but I think it may be some of Odo's men. I was going up to see, but now – I think I can guess why they're here. There's more to this than Carileph going mad, Robin. They're doing it together, earlier than I expected. My God, the ingratitude! The king's given them everything. Why betray him? But they have, I know it.'

Robin shook his head. 'You've lost me. Odo and Carileph hate each other – don't they? They were always bickering.'

'They may hate each other, but they go together in this like a hand in a glove, I swear. I know – listen, Robin, you've come the long way about to find the king, but maybe it's just as well. You must be hungry and your horse will need a rest, by which time my damned clothes may be dry, and I'll take you to him. But now, tell me what else Carileph said about the people being disturbed and – where was Ralph Baynard during this? Where were all the other town officers – the portreeve, Maurice, even Giffard? Why is it you're the one to come out and not their men?'

'You've mentioned hunger – please, a little food and drink and I'll tell everything I heard.'

While Robin ate I dried my clothes before the hearth, turning them this way and that to prevent their scorching. Giva made one attempt to touch my arm and draw me aside for a consultation, but I was unwilling just then to hear either apologies or additional accusations. Only when I was dressed again did I speak to her.

'Stay in the house while I'm gone, do you hear? Stay in, unless it seems there's going to be – I mean, if any more soldiers should come, or those up in the tower should come down and begin – if they come down at all, go to the church with the children and get down into the crypt.'

'What is it? What's going to happen? Where are you going?'

'I can't explain now; just do as I say for a change and you'll be safe.' It was the wrong way to speak to her; I'd only frightened her. Robin came to cheer her, though because of his accent and her sudden fear, I doubt that she understood half of what he said:

'Nothing but a small rebellion, *sweeting*. Don't let it concern you. You know how we Normans like to play our war games.'

I said to Dunstan: 'If there's any change here, whether those in the tower go or more come, get word of it to William de Warenne, or go to the bishop of Winchester's constable up at Farnham and he will.'

Dunstan was badly shaken by what he comprehended of our talk, but still he had the instinct to balk at a request I made of him. 'How should I do that? I've got no man to send running off to constables.'

'Then go yourself! Borrow a mule, or a carter's horse, or walk. No, run!'

I had wanted to say good-bye to Giva before we left, but I wouldn't chance a rebuff in front of Robin. As we prepared to leave, Giva, Dunstan, and Blodwin stood together, staring at us, forlorn as cattle in a rainstorm. I kissed my sons instead, then went out to mount up.

Robin said, 'If you don't kiss her, man, I'll be obliged to.' But Giva, who had come to the door, turned away abruptly and closed it, so we both went away unkissed.

We found the king at his estate in Wycombe. Robin told him his news and I added my bit about Godalming's mysterious guests. He listened with sharp attention, yet with a calm that surprised me, seeing the gravity I put on the situation.

'Who sent you to tell me this, Robin?'

'I came on my own order, Your Grace. Bishop Maurice was at his manor at Fulham, the portreeve was at his to the south, and Chancellor Giffard forbade everyone to meddle with the affairs of the bishop of Durham. So, I came away softly, though I hoped Lord Ralph Baynard's warden might send one of his men to you.'

'Baynard himself was here to see me.' Rufus smiled. 'He came about news of a s-similar nature in Dover. He's in London again and may have matters well in hand by now, but we'll go down and see, eh? I've sent Cormac to bring a few good lads from our other manors hereabouts. We don't want to be taken for beggars.' He laughed sharply, but I felt he'd had more than rumor from Ralph Baynard and held himself in check, as he could do, given time to master his anger.

We left Wycombe in the late afternoon of the same day Robin and I had come, as soon as Cormac returned with about a dozen knights straggling in after him. The king ever had a fine disregard for time, or the weariness of others. In himself he would allow no weariness. So we rode through the night at a steady pace, resting for brief times and going forward at a mile-consuming steady trot. We came to London at Cripplegate just as it was being opened for the day. The watch on the gate recognized the king and sent up a cheer for him that brought a few people running to see who we were.

We went directly down to Baynard's Keep, where Lord Ralph met us in the ward and took the king indoors for private talk while the rest of us stretched our weary legs and begged a drink of water from his garrison.

Presently Rufus came forth looking thoughtful, remounted, and took us away to Montfichet. That small keep was the only one finished of those which the Conqueror designed to stand by each gate of the town. It lacked a palisade, and Lord Ralph could easily have broken into it if he'd wished, but he'd contented himself with merely mounting an extra guard of bowmen on his own wall to overlook it. As we approached the rough timber tower, the king called out to its watch to open to him. A voice from the battlements answered:

''Ware! 'Ware, or we pour down boiling water!'

Rufus squinted upward. The bald head of Carileph showed itself cautiously over the battlements.

'Will you seethe me, Bishop? And on a Friday in Lent? Come down and feed me instead. I've had nothing since yesterday and I'm starved down to the nether gut!'

There was a scuffling about up there, the bald head vanished, then appeared again, and Carileph asked with a cracked voice, 'Is it the king?'

Cormac mused: 'Is this a straight inquiry, or the prelude to a rhetoric?'

'Come down, Will Carileph. I'm waiting,' said Rufus.

Carileph's pate disappeared. There were shouts from above echoing downward to open to the king, which was done. We all went up into the tower, which made tight quarters there. Carileph came down the ladder, pushed through the press of men, and fell at the king's feet.

'Noble and merciful King, they all do me injustice here! My authority is flouted which you gave me. I appeal to you – '

'What's all this talk of treason, Carileph? This town's as still as Jesus' Tomb, so far as I can tell, but you've said my aldermen are plotting treason. Do get off your knees, man, or you'll be stiff for it tomorrow.'

Carileph struggled to rise and then began his defense. Yes, he had said some people in the countryside had expressed doubts about the king. Rumors of that sort had gone around for weeks which he felt obliged to stifle, for fear of offending his gracious lord. There had been an unrest at Dover and other places which he had dealt with quietly. Then he had come to London to see if its inhabitants shared that taint of doubt, because all men knew how the Londoners were devoted to Lord Odo and followed his precepts.

Carileph had wished only to put the Londoners' minds to rest on the matter, but he was taken up, cross-questioned most impertinently, and had been greatly misunderstood in the matter of the arrests. He hadn't known the men were aldermen. The tower warden was an ass. Ralph Baynard had been lax in his governing and was now only trying to cover it. London might look quiet, but it was as liable to riot as a kennel.

'Why were you so careful to keep these riots from me, my lord? Didn't you think I was competent to deal with my own subjects?' asked the king, cutting in on this speech.

'Yes, of course, Your Grace, but – but when would I have found a moment to speak to you in confidence since Christmas, when you've sat at meat, gamed, hunted, and slept with the very source of your riots?'

'You mean my uncle? You'd have me think that all these things have happened at the wi-will of my uncle? Lord Odo?'

'I see you won't believe me. Very well, I'm to blame. After all, I welcomed him too, when he came to us at Christmas. I made way for him, stepped aside for him, made myself silent in the council for him, and what has it brought me? That he is set above me. He is trusted, and I am blamed! Well, he's to fault! And he has friends, too, who work and plot with him.'

'Who are they? Name them.'

Carileph's eyes had flinched from the king's steady gaze repeatedly. He seemed to want to hold with it, but it was beyond him; a changed man, certainly, from the one who was such a relentless inquisitor of me. His brows drew together in sullen pride. 'I'd speak their names, but it would take me an hour. The better man to ask, as you doubt me, is your other uncle. He – Mortain – follows Bayeux in all his plots.'

'So – both my uncles are traitors. And all my barons, too? All who just came to me of their own will and swore me fealty? Why is this so, do you think? What would they have here, if not a k-king? Who would they put in my place, these deceitful men?'

'You know the answer to that: your brother Robert, who was firstborn among you.' Carileph said it somberly, as if he'd revealed a great mystery.

Rufus laughed suddenly. There was a savage note in it.

The bishop shouted: 'Men have been known to want a fool for a king before this time, my lord! There's advantage to it!'

Rufus bowed his head and made a short progress around the crowded hall, fists on hips, then turned back to Carileph. 'Well, my lord Bishop, you may be right in that. My uncles are no babes for appetite, and my brother would be like fat in their teeth, where I might prove gristle. And it may be there's no man left true to his oath in all the world but here in this keep. We shall see. But: the way to put down rebellions is with armies, not speeches. Where's my host, Bishop? If you were going to be king for me, why didn't you call up my fyrd? Or, coming back to the question: why didn't you tell me and let me call them?'

'I've said – ' Carileph faltered, then took on dignity: 'I am the king's true servant, but he suspects me when I've done no harm.'

'No such thing. You are the Caesar of the North, Bishop! Where's your own host? Did you put down rebels in Dover with these few men? Oh – did you call on Lanfranc and his mesnie to assist you?'

'No!'

'No? God's Face, is he a tra-traitor, too? That old man, gone in with my per-perfidious uncles?'

'The archbishop isn't in love with me, because he had no hand in choosing me for bishop. Besides, I thought it best to act at once and not wait for other men.'

'So it would seem, if even the king is too slow-witted to make your company.' Now at last the king was beginning to show his anger.

Carileph was as red as Rufus. 'Am I to understand that I am your hostage now, Your Grace?'

'Who said anything about hostages? Hostage for what? I thought you were my ally. You say we have a war budding. You have a sizable host up north. Will you lend it to me to fight my enemies?'

'Naturally, Your Grace. They're yours to command.'

'But they're yours to array. Send for them. Or shall I have Ranulph pen you a summons?'

'Send for them, Your Grace? Shouldn't I rather go there and lead them?'

'No, no. Send for them. Now! And you will afterward come to me at Westminster, where we'll have ample privacy to discuss our danger. But not as my hos-hostage, Bishop; I'll go now and you'll follow, so I won't shame you in the sight of these Londoners.' He turned, strode out, and climbed quickly down the thick plank steps to the yard with all of us hurrying behind him.

Fitz Hamon protested as we rode out through Ludgate: 'Was it wise to leave him to follow you? He's done one foolish thing. Who's to say he won't do some other that's worse?'

'He's made a fool of himself, to be sure,' I heard the king say. 'Let him redeem himself honorably. But when he comes, he'd better come with proof that my uncles are traitors. Priests are tricksters and connivers by their nature, but my uncle Robert is a true knight and an honest soldier. No one's ever put traitor to his name, or any other crime. If he's slandered by a damned priest, he can't have satisfaction of him in the proper way. But I may.' Of Odo he spoke nothing in extenuation.

'His whole tale reeks of deceit. You should have had him hauled out of Montfichet and turned him over to Ralph Baynard.'

'No. He was my father's favorite chaplain. He's a bishop, my first justice, and my friend. He must come to see me freely, if he puts va-value on that. He'll come.'

But Carileph did not. As soon as the king was gone from London, he fled back to his diocese with all his men and shut himself up in his castle at Durham, whose walls and gates he at once began to strengthen. The king was mortally offended by the news and fell into such a rage that he was all but incapable of speech: 'G-g-god damn a-all p-pr-priests!'

I pitied him for the disappointment. He'd tried to deal honorably with a dishonorable man and was made to look the fool for it. I felt some little shame for my own gullibility, as I had cause to believe Carileph on the matter of Odo. I still thought there might be more truth than lie in his story and made an attempt to persuade Rufus of it.

'He was afraid of you, that's all. Send him some assurance that you won't be too hard on him for this moment's panic and he'll come down again. There is something strange in the wind. We've all had a sniff of it.'

'Se-send him assurance? I'll s-send him assurance that he's fi-finished. I'll de-deseize him of all he has! Get your pen. Send su-summons of array to all in York and Lincoln. Tell m-my sheriffs there that – God damn him! – I want him here! By Lucca's Face, I'll ha-have him here!'

The sheriffs of York and Lincoln leaped at the chance to ruin Carileph. They fell first on certain lands he owned in their territories, then went over into Durham to drag him from his stronghold. But Carileph, whether fled from guilt or fear, had shut himself up well. His barons came to his defense, no doubt having heard an entirely different account of his troubles from him.

Command was sent to the other northern counties to join freely in the destruction of a traitor, or bring him to justice, but there was no immediate answer to the summons from either William de Eu or the powerful Mowbrays.

Rufus seemed utterly obsessed with the matter of Carileph, while I still urged him daily to call Lord Odo to him for some explanation of those riots in Dover and Rochester, which both he and his erstwhile employee, Carileph, had dealt with so considerately. But my repetitions were taken ill. Rufus would have Carileph first, and to that end a great deal of property was seized or trampled over in Durham, but without yielding up a bishop.

When the first storm of the king's wrath blew itself out, he removed to Winchester for the rapidly approaching Easter Court. We were no more there, however, than we heard fresh news from Carileph. The bishop had sent the king a haughty letter by way of a merchant ship. He said he would come and answer any questions the king might put to him, if he might do it before a synod, and if he might have a written safe-conduct.

The king's reply:

William, King of the English, to the Bishop of Durham:
'Take heed of me! I command you that you come to me as I bade you
before. You shall face me and give answer to me, in the place of my
choosing. Just men shall hear us both. No safe-conduct is necessary to a
man the king calls to him. It is not my honor, but yours, that is in
question. I will hear no more excuse on this matter.

William the King (his mark)
Witness: Giffard the Chancellor
by Ranulph the Chaplain (seal)

The king spoke to the clerk who was to deliver this:
'Tell him I say that on my honor as a true soldier, he may come
and go freely, if he only speaks to me honestly.'
But when the clerk returned, he brought with him, not a bishop,
but yet another letter with a longer list of complaints.

Your Grace has promised me safety, but when I sent to the sheriff of
Yorkshire to give me peaceful passage through his country, my messenger
was abused. His horse was killed; he was beaten and set on foot to
complete his journey. He returned to me instead.
Further, I hear you have already given certain of my lands in
Lincolnshire to those men who pillage them. This seems not to be the act
of a king who would hear my pleas with justice. I like not your term
'just men.' I am the king's loyal and faithful servant, but I am also the
Bishop of Durham. I may not be tried by any but a court of my peers.
Give me a written conduct to come and go; assemble a synod to hear me,
and I will come.

William de St. Carileph
Bishop of Durham (by his hand)

The king snatched the parchment from me when I read it to him
and tore it across, then threw it into the fire, where its wax seal made
a brief blossom of flame.
'Now he wants a trial! Now he wants to drag in all the damned
bishops in the country on his side. I suppose if I sent up a papal
legate to lay palms under his horse's feet, he'd fi-find some defect in
the damned p-palms!'
'Frightened men are often unreasonable, Your Grace.'
'Guilty men, you mean. Well, let him stay where he is. Let him
pray he's got a well in his guardroom that goes down to the very

heartsprings of the earth, or he'll be drinking his own piss! When the next court assembles, I'll have a new bishop. My f-father made him; I can unmake him.'

I asked Will Giffard later, 'Did he truly give away the bishop's lands so soon?'

Giffard's thin brows lifted at the question, but he answered: 'Yes, he did. I penned the grants. He said that loyalty should be rewarded as promptly as treason. That won't sit well with the lords of the realm.'

'No, I suppose it won't.'

'It's too bad Lord Odo isn't here to advise him, really. He already had an inkling of how we would fare under this king. He said from the start that this one's little finger might prove to be thicker than the old man's loins.'

I wondered when Will Giffard had been privy to such a remark from Odo, but of course I didn't ask that. Nor did I run to report it to the king, as it was privileged gossip of that clerkly sort which Giffard could say to me, though he knew I was the king's chaplain, and which Odo could say before him, or to someone like him. It wasn't something Odo was likely to put in one of his letters.

The wrangle with Carileph continued to Easter. When Rufus took his crown and seat in Winchester that spring, it was with all the pomp and grandeur his father had shown at his last court, but it was an ominously reduced court that cried, 'Life to the king!' Missing were Odo, Mortain, Robert of Eu, Earl Roger, Roger de Lacy of Berkshire and Shropshire, Hugh de Grantmesnil, Robert of Rhuddlan, Roger Bigod of Norfolk – all the old troublemakers and the old supporters of Curthose, in fact, along with dozens of lesser men who owed them allegiance.

The king gave orders for the gates of the city to be closed, then took counsel with those who remained. Now all the news that had been kept from him by caution and distance came tumbling forth from the lips of his faithful; all the suspicions, the private doubts, petty jealousies, the letters received, the bribes refused – and the preparations of the rebels.

Geoffrey Mowbray, who with his nephew Robert was among those missing, had gone to Normandy, where he offered the English crown to Duke Robert on the occasion of either the capture or the death of the king. Duke Robert had accepted. This information came from a surprising source: old Wulfstan, Bishop of Worcester, the Mowbrays' neighbor.

Rufus sat unmoving, his eyes going from one man's face to another's as he listened. 'This is hearsay. How has my brother accepted? What proof is there he agrees to my murder?'

'The proof is in the absence of so many men who are his vassals as well as yours, my lord King,' Wulfstan said.

'There's more than that,' said Lanfranc. 'I had a rumor that Eustace of Boulogne and Robert of Bellesme were missing from Duke Robert's side these many weeks. Since they've hedged him in ever since his homecoming, I didn't believe there could be any mischief that would take them far from him. But there is one; a campaign against you, my son. A certain clerk of mine says they are at Rochester even now, with Odo.'

The king rose and paced. 'Carileph's nonsense was no more than a feint, then, to distract us from them. Well – so it begins. I was addlepated to believe – ' He turned. 'But the broth is spilled. What are we to do? The enemy is top-heavy with captains, my lords: Odo, Roger, Montgomery, and now Robert of Bellesme. A man would be a fool not to recruit himself under their standards. We're in the minority here. Shall we fight, or shall I just offer up my throat to be cut at the nearest shambles, to save them time? Shall I swim to Flanders to see if my uncle there still has a taste for meddling in Norman affairs? What shall I do, eh?'

He stopped before me, though I doubt that he truly saw me. But because his eyes were on my face, I said: 'Call up your fyrd, Your Grace. You are King of the English.'

'The English won't fight for us,' said Hugh of Chester scornfully. 'They'll stay in their holes and laugh while one Norman slaughters another. What difference to them which wins?'

The king nodded slowly, but old Wulfstan spoke up: 'The English are no coward race, my lord of Chester. I am an Englishman and I will fight for this king, because God caused him to be anointed for my ruler. I see you smile, because I am an old man and the most humble member of this council, being the only Englishman in it. But I have those I can call to my service, as you have. This clerk speaks true. Call up your English fyrd, King of the English, and they will answer you. They hate the Norman lords who abuse them, but you belong to them. Call up your fyrd and destroy these traitors!'

Rufus looked to Lanfranc for a reply to this old relic of the Church, who was thought a living saint by his people in Worcester.

Lanfranc, who had been known to say slighting things about Wulfstan's mental acuity and who had once even tried to get him removed as bishop, rose with difficulty to his feet, his thin hands clutching his pastoral staff. He bowed very slowly and with reverence to Wulfstan.

'God, Who is ever on the side of the just, puts wisdom into the mouths of the simple and gives strength to the sinews of the frail. I, too, am an old man, older it may be even than my brother Wulfstan. But I will not lie at home like a lame dog if he puts on the arms of war. This may well be our last battle, my English brother in Christ, but we will fight it together. Call up your English fyrd, King William, and strike your enemies before they strike you.'

31

Hugh the Wolf grinned crookedly at the two old men who bowed ceremoniously to each other; then he heaved his great hulk off the bench he sat on.

'Well, it may be I'm wrong about some of the English. But if these are examples of your captains to lead 'em, I'd damned well better be one, too. My lord King, I'm yours to the last battle, but by your leave, I think I can serve you best by going home to see to my own defenses. I'll be surrounded by rebels. Even my own vassal, Hugh Grantmesnil, is one of them, it appears, damn him. But neither he nor the Mowbrays will come for you by way of my land, without getting a taste of me first. If I see any Rhuddlans or de Lacys on my way home, I'll chop 'em for you, but that's the most I can promise until I see if some of my own English will fight.'

The court was disbanded next day. Each man went his way home in some danger of capture before he reached it, as the rebels held territory in all parts of the country. Lanfranc was among the last to go.

'I may not see you again in this world,' he said to Rufus. 'No, I'm not giving way to despair for you, or for myself. But Canterbury lies too close to Rochester, and for all we know it may now be in Odo's hands. He hates me more than any other man alive for revealing his conspiracy and his thefts to your father. I don't think he hates you, or that he'd let you be murdered to satisfy his greed, but I doubt if he caught me he'd give me a dry donjon to die in.'

'Go home by way of London with fitz Hamon,' said Rufus. 'Ralph Baynard will see you get a barge and a proper escort down the

Thames to see how things stand in Canterbury. I'll follow behind you very quickly, but there's someone in the south I should speak to first.' He gave fitz Hamon additional guard from the city's garrison to protect Lanfranc, which he could hardly afford to spare. He climbed up on the city walls to see them out the north gate. Giffard, Cormac, and I followed.

'Now what do we do?' Cormac asked. 'How about sending me overseas to cut your dear brother's throat before he can come and cut yours? If I went as a juggler, he'd be bound to take me in.' He grinned, but I'm sure he meant it.

Rufus said after a final look out over the north downs: 'Robin isn't our game. But there's good game enough. I think we'll go hunting.'

'Is this the time for the chase?' Giffard seemed bewildered. I had begun to suspect him of some sympathy or connection with the rebels, though I had no proof. Yet his family was represented at the Easter Court. His father, Walter, Earl of Buckingham, had sat as always in the king's council chamber – where he had been all but dumb when others voiced their support.

'There's time for this chase. When my brother comes for my throne, where will he land? If you say Dover, of course we can do nothing about it. But if he comes straight up from Seine-mouth and makes for one of our southern ports – ?'

'Pevensey,' I said. 'Because your noble father did the same in 'sixty-six, before he went on to Hastings. His Grace would think it a good omen.'

'Or he'd think our uncle Mortain would welcome him? I read your thought. Yes, but Hastings would tempt him, too, wouldn't it? What shall we do then? I can't dislodge my uncle and still be sure Robin won't have gone another way. At Hastings he'd come in to Robert de Eu's port. I don't think de Eu will welcome him. I may be wrong, but old Robert always despised a sot. What else?'

'Arundel,' said Cormac. 'The Montgomery has it, and all three of his sons are in thick with your noble brother.'

Rufus sighed. 'Yes, Earl Roger was one of those who didn't come to me, but he did send word that he was unable, not that he wouldn't. I don't like to think that the man who taught me the sword and the lance would betray me in his old age; not unless I hear it from him, that is. So – we'll just go and ask him, I think.' He smiled at Cormac.

'Just go and ask him?' Cormac snorted in disbelief. 'He's got more to lose at your brother's hands than at yours. What if he just shuts his gate and holds you for your brother?'

'Well – that's where the sport comes into it, isn't it? He might do it. But that old man owes me something. I've eaten his bread and salt, and I've been his servant. That's almost as good as a blood tie. He owes me – an explanation.'

We rode boldly into Arundel's walls with no more protection than my lord's confidence in his old master's chivalry and in the six young knights, all of little repute and landless, who rode with us. I for one despaired of ever leaving. Roger de Montgomery was at the top of his castle stairs watching us, as he had no doubt watched when we were first called to his attention by his guard. Pot-bellied and shrunken in the hams with his years he might have been, but he still had a good measure of what he has passed on to his sons – an aura of power and danger.

Rufus dismounted, threw his helm and gloves to one of his squires, unbelted his sword, and gave it to another. At his silent communication with them his six knights disarmed, too, pressing their weapons into the arms of a castle steward.

This untoward action seemed to activate Earl Roger, who came nimbly down the stairs, crying: 'Your Grace has surprised me!' In truth, he did look a little winded.

'My friend and se-second father, you surprise me!' Rufus embraced him heartily. 'When you failed to come to our court I said, "He must be ill." I couldn't rest until I knew for ce-certain it wasn't serious. But here you are, hale as ever I saw you. What kept you from us?'

Earl Roger looked properly flummoxed to have his reasons demanded of him so forthrightly and in front of his servants. He said in a less-than-convincing voice: 'Nothing, Your Grace, but increasing age. I was rheumatic.'

'I can't believe it. You'll never seem old to me.' Rufus took his arm and walked with him up the stairs. 'I still remember the strength of your arm too well – as when you c-clouted me for not remembering to sand your armor. My lord, we're starving men. Can you feed us?'

We went up into the high hall. The steward who had all the swords came staggering past us, pressed his burden on a hall porter, then trotted ahead to hear the orders his lord would give for our disposal. Cormac nudged me and made eyes of wonder.

We dined sumptuously, then sat for hours after, listening to the king regale Earl Roger's household with tales of their master's chivalry. He railed at himself for his misdeeds as his squire, telling how the earl had once picked him up bodily and dumped him in a horse trough for coming before the Lady Mabel with uncombed hair and a grubby face.

'But you were fair, my lord. You s-said I might do the same to you if I ever caught you using foul ways in decent company. I watched him, friends. I prayed I might catch him someday, but it ne-never happened.' He took up his cup and held it to the earl in tribute. 'This man was like a f-father to me. More than that: he trained more good and honorable knights than any other man in Normandy. To my teacher!'

Dru de Carentan, one of our guard, took the king up on his toast: 'I've always heard him so praised, Your Grace, but never so well. If you're his example, it must be true.' He raised his cup, too; so did we all.

The earl smiled faintly, rubbing his brow. He understood the design. Now, unless he wished to proclaim himself to his own household as the greatest traitor since Judas, we were safe within his walls, even if Odo and Curthose together came and demanded our blood. The question was, would all the flattery in the world keep Earl Roger from welcoming his sons, or Curthose, with equal courtesy? I slept poorly on that debate.

Next morning, very early, Rufus and Earl Roger rode out together into the earl's vast deer park. They were gone for several hours. Our knights cracked their knuckles, waiting; Cormac paced; even Robin Bloet was out of trivial conversation. I thought of how many ways a man might meet death by accident in a forest, of men waiting there to drag king from earl and see he was never found again. While we –'

But then they returned alone as they'd gone out. The earl looked grim and thoughtful; Rufus looked flushed, but not with anger. We heard Terce, had a brief meal, then went again to our horses, when we discovered that Earl Roger would go with us to London.

What was said in that greenwood I never knew for certain, but it made a follower, though an unwilling one, of Roger for the duration of the rebellion.

When we reached London, we found Lanfranc had been busy. The first men to hear the summoning of the fyrd were already camped outside the London walls. Their numbers grew rapidly until all the bleak moors and swampy fields around were covered with them. Someone said there were thirty thousand; I never knew a census had been taken, but there were a fearful number.

Having been called, they must be put to use quickly, or they would devour their substance as well as London's, then fall to fighting among themselves. They owed the king forty days' service, and he meant to make good use of them.

With the coming of the fyrd we first began to hear what our other enemies were doing who weren't content with mere sitting, like Earl Roger, but like good Normans everywhere had begun to ravish the lands and towns about them.

Odo was ruining Lanfranc's estates with great pleasure, burning farm after fertile farm. He'd cut the archbishop off from returning home, which caused Lanfranc to take charge of our English in the king's absence. Lanfranc met with the reeves and hundred-men, promised in the king's name that all their wrongs would be redressed, forbade all unrighteous geld to be levied on them, granted back woods and hunting rights lost to them, and made such generous policy that I feared the king would be hard pressed to live up to it. He called this necessary, and Rufus hardly seemed to listen to all the promises made in his name, but I could see that with all the burnings of tithe barns and all the relieving of gelds, we might be poor next winter.

Still, these vain promises were what the English yearned most to hear. It was brilliant policy, because it looked as if we would have a long war of it, and the English are notorious for their fickleness in military service, no matter what Wulfstan said. A Sussex peasant cares little or nothing for the plight of a Kentish peasant whose enemy is flaying the skin off him. He'll lend him aid if he must, to the extent of his forty days' service. Then he'll go home to his own fields and byres. Many a King of the English has learned that to his sorrow, including the perjured usurper Harold, whom many of his fyrd deserted when he was marching toward Hastings, because it was harvest time.

The Mowbrays and William de Eu, and some of Earl Roger's northern vassals, had raped the countryside around Bristol and burned the ancient city of Bath. They attacked Gloucester, but there at least the English fought them, raging out of their wattle hovels to repulse the raiders with sticks, rocks, slings, and even their deadly sickles. William de Eu . . . whose father, Robert, despised him – retreated from Gloucester and burned the king's castle at Berkley instead.

That 'infamous Breton,' as Lanfranc always called Roger Bigod of Norfolk, seized all the royal lands in East Anglia, thus revenging himself, I suppose, for his all-too-temporary exile when he had been one of the rebels who conspired against William Bastard at the famous bridal feast in '75.

All Hertfordshire, Shropshire, Worcester, and Leicester were overrun with roving bands of lawless men: Norman free lances, Welsh adventurers, even some English, who looted and burned. But the reports were so confusing that it was impossible to tell whose side they were on, or who was winning.

The whole of the north looked lost beyond hope, with both the Mowbrays and Carileph ranged against us. Even with such a response to his call upon his English freemen, Rufus couldn't do battle with all his enemies at once.

He did the only sensible thing, therefore: turned his attention to Odo alone and resolved to strike at him before his reinforcements came from Curthose.

The first object of our campaign was to cut off Rochester from Pevensey, so that his uncles couldn't join their armies conveniently and make a sweep across the southern counties. The link between the two castles was a third, Tonbridge, held by Gilbert de Clare, who also had kept away from Easter Court. As a fortress, Tonbridge was no great threat. It was small, nothing more than an ancient English earthworks, fortified by a rude wooden tower and timber bailey that didn't entirely surround it, since it depended on its height overlooking a river for the rest of its security.

Trailing our rustic army of English who carried broad-axes and heavy spears rather than swords and lances, and who walked along singing gloomy canticles about their long-lost battles, we went down from London to Tonbridge. We must have looked as purposeful as the Israelites about halfway through their forty years' wandering in the wilderness.

Fitz Hamon cursed our army and its dirges: 'What in the name of all the devils in Hell are we doing with this ragged-arsed collection of women-haired yokels? Gilbert will fall off his wall laughing at us when he sees.'

'Then we'll have a quick victory!' Rufus answered with a laugh. 'It's a green pack of hounds to run, I admit, but we'll have them well trained before we s-slip 'em on Odo.'

He was in a ferociously good humor, talking almost constantly to someone, laughing at any jest or slight mishap among his knights. William de Warenne studied him with a slight frown, as if he thought he might be a little mad – and so I think he was, but mad only for the joy of being king and having a campaign to direct, with no one to say nay to him. He had bested Roger de Montgomery, and now he was going to put down Tonbridge and face Odo, no matter the odds.

When our standard was let out before Tonbridge, we weren't met with laughter as fitz Hamon had feared. Gilbert de Clare, always a fawning, sneaking sort of appendage to his great family, had gotten his defences bolstered by a good number of seasoned knights, possibly on loan from Rochester. A shower of arrows met our herald's cry. Their bowmen's range thus moderately established, we drew back, let out our lines, dug privies, and sat down to wait for further developments.

It was an easier sort of war for me than Gerberoy had been. I would have enjoyed my new privileges more if I hadn't had Giva and Godalming so much on my mind. I dreaded the news brought each day by courier, for fear it would be word of some minor skirmish that had ended in destruction of a village I knew. I had urged Rufus to send some knights to Godalming, to see if his own castle was still held against him, but he couldn't be concerned. He was set only on the thing at hand and supposed my concern was for my rents.

'Don't worry. If they burn it we'll build you a better church – and me a better manor.'

The English quickly grew impatient with waiting – a form of warfare still at odds with their nature. Some of them had the notion it was Odo we had besieged and cried out for him to show himself:

'Tamer of the English, are you? Come out and tame us then, coward!'

When he didn't, they crept up on the palisade at night, bellowed war cries, let out weird calls and animal screeches to frighten the horses within and keep the bailey watch running from post to post. I got no sleep for it, but Rufus seemed impervious to the noise or any disturbance and slept like a babe.

The next day we saw our siege engine assembled. I was awed, never having seen one. It hurled great balls of oil-soaked hemp over the walls to set fire to the stable sheds and make havoc with the animals, or just to create a foul reek when it missed. While it did that work, the English tried to chop a door into the palisade. About twenty of them died for it, but we shot a half-dozen bowmen off the walls, too.

On the third day the outer bailey was abandoned and our English took it, storming the place and tearing down half the palisade. That destruction panicked Lord Gilbert into a rash act. He opened his inner gate and let out his riders, thinking to rout us with a quick sweep of broadswords over English necks. But there were too few of his knights and too many Surrey and Essex axmen who could sling their weapons with as deadly a force as any bowmen. They aimed chiefly for the horses, but damaged a few men as well. We lost a heavy lot of infantry, but Gilbert lost more: the confidence of his mercenaries. That night the English feasted on horseflesh and sang their mournful songs by the cooking fires. Rufus went out and dined among them. It was hard to remember that both king and men were Christians.

On the fourth morning Rufus took the place of his own herald. He stood in the shambles of the outer bailey and yelled to those in the tower: 'I've better things to do than sit here all spring waiting for you! I'm leaving you to my friends! Come out or stay in, as you like! But when I go, you won't get the best terms from them! Think on it!' He turned to go, and a swarm of black arrows buzzed over the walls and plunged into the earth behind him. By the grace of God none hit him.

'This is lunatic,' I murmured. But Cormac was laughing as he went forward to greet him.

We waited an hour; two. 'Strike the tents,' said Rufus. 'The fool thinks I'm deceiving him.' The tents were struck and folded, packed onto the carts.

The inner bailey gate opened and Gilbert de Clare came out, leading his own troops with the mercenaries following separately, as if there had been a rupture in their alliance. They stood apart from him in our camp, readily yielded themselves to the king, and begged to serve him in lieu of prison with no prospects of ransom. They were accepted.

Gilbert had been slightly wounded, having led that unsuccessful excursion the day before. It wasn't too serious a gash, but the king permitted him to remain at his keep with a much reduced garrison and one of our knights for his new warden.

Now at last we could turn toward Rochester and Odo. We had scarcely finished striking camp and set ourselves on the road, however, when we met a courier from Gundulph of Rochester, sent from his manor at Malling. The bishop warned the king that Odo had suddenly left Rochester with a sizable body of knights, and it was believed he had gone to Pevensey, because some merchant-ship captain who had sailed up the Medway said Duke Robert's fleet was preparing to sail, and that Pevensey was their destination.

'How many ships?' asked Rufus.

'He didn't know, Your Grace, but he said it should be a great fleet, as the king your father's was before it.'

'They say, they say. Well, so be it. We go to Pevensey, instead.'

So we turned south along that road. For a time, a strange duplication of events took place: we were marching on the same road perjured Harold had taken when he went to meet William Bastard at Senlac. I mentioned this to Cormac, who took it straight to Rufus as a joke to be relished.

'Even more ironic if you should have to burn Pevensey: Harold's Avenger, you'd be forever after to these English clods.'

For a change, Rufus failed to find any amusement in one of Cormac's jokes. He gave him, in fact, such a look and such a blunt, barnyard reply, Cormac retired from him in a sulk. It was strange to me that Cormac never quite grasped how Rufus felt about his father. Pevensey was the first castle thrown up on English soil by William Bastard when he came to make his victory. Its timbers had been cut in Normandy and carried with him on his ships. Pevensey was in unfriendly hands at the moment, but it was sacred, and he took no pleasure in going against it. Nor would he be the avenger of a man he had been taught to believe a Judas – not even for a song.

There was another reason for the king's short temper. He knew that although his father's first landing had been at Pevensey – and this might well influence Curthose to emulate him – the main force of his fleet had been sent to Hastings. Curthose might be expected to remember that as well.

Robert fitz Hamon detached himself from our main force when we were still a little above Senlac Field and, with a good portion of our strength, went down to surround Hastings and defend the port and coast from invasion. To Count Robert de Eu, inside Hastings Keep, Rufus sent a brusque message:

'Aid me, or do not hinder me, on pain of being judged a traitor.'

Robert de Eu watched fitz Hamon take possession of his port and let out his lines along its shores, but never stirred from his keep through the whole war.

At Pevensey our herald once more went before enemy walls and cried to those within to open the gate to their true king, who would show them mercy. There was a brief exchange between him and the gate warden; then Lord Odo came to the top of the gate and answered loudly so that I could hear:

'We hold this place for the true King of the English, Robert fitz William, Duke of Normandy, firstborn and rightful heir to King

William! It is William the Younger who must give up his designs, which are false, as he is false, to the laws of this land and to the laws of God and His Holy Church!'

Our herald was taken aback. 'Most noble lord and Bishop, it is for the King of England I cry who was anointed and crowned here by God through His holy ministers.'

'A true King of the English cannot take the crown without the election of his council. This king was put in his place by the Archbishop of Canterbury alone, without consulting the Witan or the people. The king the people long for is Robert fitz William, who will unite England and Normandy once more, as it was in his father's day. In him they will find all the old virtues of kings – '

'Drunkenness and lechery,' murmured Cormac.

'Tell the English who follow this upstart younger son that they have been deceived: in William the Younger they will find only vice – the vices of Edwy and Hardacanute combined!'

This was officially relayed to Rufus, who had heard it well enough, but without the rage he might have felt if he'd known anything whatsoever about the two kings he was likened to. 'Who are those people he rants about?' he asked.

The knights about him shrugged. A clerk or two here and there looked thoughtful. I expect that not even the English who had the insult translated for them could have told to whom the names belonged, since neither was apt to have been the subject of song. Only my browsings through musty rolls when I was Maurice's clerk had made me even faintly aware of them.

I said to Rufus: 'Edwy and Hardacanute were kings long ago, Your Grace. They were both young – younger than you – and known for their rashness and liberality. Your uncle proves himself a scholar, but only in a silly and trifling way.'

'He's proved he's lost his reason. Or he thinks Robin's going to bring all Normandy here on ships to rescue him. Well, let 'em come, if they're coming. De Warenne's got two hundred men spread out along the shore below the castle, half of them bowmen. They'll pick off Robin's oarsmen before they can get clear of the ships. My uncles were both fools to put all their eggs in this basket. They can't come out to aid Robin make his landing – which he won't make in any case with this wind against him. But where is he? He's overdue for his crown.'

We sat down to wait again, with our main force spread about the old Roman fort that had been refortified by the Bastard, and our bowmen and axmen watching the peninsular coast that spreads flat between the two estuaries of the Brede and Bulverhythe rivers.

'Who were these kings of Odo's, and why did he compare Will to them?' Cormac asked me later. 'I smell scandal.'

I told their brief histories: 'Edwy was a lecher who once left his Witan sitting while he ran into his bedchamber to have intercourse with his cousin, whom he'd married in defiance of the Church. Hardacanute was the predecessor of Edward Confessor for a short time. He was said not to be a Christian. He was a drunkard and a glutton, with a fancy for boys. God struck him dead at his drink one night and everybody cheered. Do you begin to see what Odo was stuffing in his letters now? Do you still think you've done the king no harm, staying with him?'

For six weeks we fed off the country while those in Pevensey fed on short rations and hope. There was no nourishment in their hope, because Curthose didn't come. The weather grew hotter and the seas calm, but still there were no ships. From other parts of the country we now began to hear reports of those battles and burnings I've mentioned. One bit of good news came from Bishop Wulfstan's Worcester. Worcester, too, had been invaded massively by the combined forces of the Mowbrays, Roger de Lacy, and others, but the bishop's town was saved from burning and its attackers routed by no less a person than Wulfstan himself. The lamb had savaged the wolves!

They say he put a curse on the enemy that turned their limbs feeble and their eyes temporarily blind, so that not one man of his town was killed or injured in fighting them. I decline that miracle, having seen a few maimed men of Worcester, but it was certain that the frail old bishop had done as he said: lent his own knights to the battle, which roused the citizens to join them with such a will that the marauders retired and Worcester was saved.

We had a miracle of a kind, too. The long-expected Norman fleet at last came into view. We heard shouts from the battlements, yells of joy, when they sighted them. But the fleet had delayed so long that they found our own ships lying ready for them, which Rufus had called from Portsmouth, Southampton, and London.

Even with our fleet in view, Curthose's still tried for a landing, but it was a sorry travesty of the one made twenty-two years before by the Conqueror. The boats that put out for shore were overloaded for their size. Some of them capsized in a swell of the sea. Those who managed to get near land were targets for our bowmen, and those that actually achieved land were fallen upon and their occupants butchered by the axmen, who waded into the sea to hack and chop. A few prisoners were taken; some boats turned back in time; some discharged their cargo of men, who made a good fight on foot before they were taken.

When it was over, it seemed the great fleet had been no more than four or five ships and had been without a captain. Robert Curthose wasn't among them. He'd chosen not to come and claim in person the crown for which his advocates were risking their lives and wealth.

When Rufus heard Robert wasn't there, he didn't laugh; he fell into a rage against his brother: 'The fool! The lazy, drunken, sh-sh-shiftless fool! My brother! Ha! He couldn't be pried from his whores to come and get a c-crown! What a man – what a hero we've lost! Go and tell the ta-tale to my uncles. Yes, get me a crier with a voice of b-brass!'

Our news was duly bawled out to the ramparts of Pevensey. There was no answer. One could imagine the gloom and despair inside those walls. Still, they held out a few more days, perhaps hoping Curthose had changed his course when he saw our ships and had landed at Hastings. But it wasn't so. They sued for peace; there was nothing else for them to do. They came out thinner men than had gone in, for certain.

Old Robert of Mortain looked jaundiced and confused as he was brought along with Odo into the king's tent. He knelt and offered his baldric and sword, which Rufus took from him gravely, almost tenderly.

Not so Odo: 'I've lost, but I've taught you something of value, nephew. You owe me some consideration for the lesson. Without me, you'd still be wasting your days in a deer park.'

'You've taught me n-nothing, unless it's never to doubt my f-father's judgment of men again.'

'So. What will you do with me? Imprison me again? How tedious. They'll say you do it because you fear me, as he did. He did, you know: he feared and was envious of me, because I could command affection where he got only duty or fear – in the people, in your brother, even in your sweet, pious mother.'

'I'll t-tear your damned tongue out!' Rufus roared, and lunged at him.

'My lord, he baits you!' I cried at the same time, and tried to put myself between them. Even Odo's guards fell back a step in alarm, seeing the king's blood-choked face and mad eyes. Rufus pushed me to one side, but as his hands were about to close on Odo's throat, he shuddered and slowly pulled them back, rocking from his toes to his heels with the effort. Odo smiled thinly and still attempted to rouse him:

'Well, if you won't tear out my tongue, what will you do with me? Something fitting; let me see: you might put me in a cage and carry me about with you, like an untrained bear. But, like a bear, I might live long, and you'd grow weary of me.'

'Oblige him,' said Cormac. 'It's a choice bear for baiting.'

'Be still, catamite, your betters are speaking,' Odo said nastily, and they exchanged deadly looks, in which they were well matched.

But Rufus turned away in disgust and went to touch Mortain on the shoulder. 'Get up, Uncle. The difference between you almost makes me weep.' He took Count Robert's arm and helped him rise. Mortain's gaze was distant, but he peered at Rufus as the king asked: 'Do you, Robert de Mortain, give me your solemn pledge never to take up arms against me again?'

Mortain said in a choked voice: 'Yes, I swear, Will-Rou – I mean, Your Grace – '

'It's all right, then. Go back to your bed. I'll send a leech to you. No harm shall come to you for this, as I'm a true soldier.'

When Mortain was being led away by two of the king's knights, Lord Odo sank to his knees and clasped his hands.

'Forgive me, great and powerful King, that I didn't know how to address myself to you. Spare me, too, as I'm near as old and feeble as my brother.'

Rufus swung back to him sharply. 'Don't mock a good man!' He paused, looking down at Odo, then drew a deep breath and seemed to expel with it all his anger. 'Uncle, you said I might grow w-weary of you. By God, you're in the right.' He smiled briefly. 'In fact, I'd already decided to grant your p-plea before you asked me so p-prettily. I'll spare you. I'll even send you back to my brother. He deserves you – and you deserve him.'

There was a general grumble against that decision by all in the tent except Earl Roger, whose face expressed a revived hope for his sons. The king waved his hand to silence the muttering, his eyes still fixed on Odo. 'Now – how you g-go is your choice. I can send you off in a cage, or in chains, as you say. Or you might go up to Rochester disguised as a man.'

'Disguised?'

'Yes. You would ride into the town with an escort of my choice and inform those on your walls that you've made an alliance with me. Release Ro-rochester to me, and I give you free passage home.'

Again the mutter of 'No, no,' but Earl Roger whispered: 'Your Grace, my sons, too?'

Odo's head sank to his breast as if in thought; then he lifted it again. 'Robert de Bellesme holds my keep for me. He may not choose to surrender it just for my asking him.' He glanced at old Montgomery. 'You know his nature, I think?'

'I know it. You must make him a good speech.'

'And if he won't hear it?'

Rufus leaned toward him and whispered: 'Why, then, such b-being his nature, he'll take pleasure in seeing how I show you in the market square, before I put you on your ship – after which I'll starve him to the bone where he hides.'

'My lords, will it be my fault if I speak to the man and he doesn't listen? Did the speech of a prisoner ever open a portcullis? Is this justice?' He appealed to the company at large, his hands held out beseechingly.

Montgomery came forward and said to the king: 'Say you will spare my sons; then they will listen to him. Shall I kneel for that, too? I will.' He began to bend his knee, but the king caught him by the elbow and bore him up.

'You want something too much of m-mercy, and he wants something too little of ju-justice! But I'll satisfy both. Let him make your s-son open to me, and I'll give a-amnesty to all – s-so they get themselves out of m-my affairs and out of m-my lands!'

Now someone should have cried 'No!' but none did, and I, who felt it most, could best see the wisdom of the king's leniency.

32

Odo agreed to the terms with a sullenness that belied their generosity. The camp was struck and the fyrd dismissed. They had outstayed their time, in any event, and it might have been expected that some of them had already begun to defect quietly. Yet many remained and marched with us to see the end of Odo.

It had been the king's plan for Odo to be kept prisoner until we were just outside the walls of Rochester, but as we were about to take to the road, William de Warenne collapsed from a wound he had gotten during the defense of the shore when the 'invasion' was defeated. At the time of his wounding there seemed no reason to think it too serious. But in the next few days the wound had festered, as he hadn't bothered to have it cauterized, and now he was suddenly dying.

Rufus was deeply grieved for him and wouldn't proceed until he saw his most trustworthy vassal and friend packed onto a litter to be taken home. To this end he would remain and determined to let Lord Odo's escort take him on to Rochester, so as not to delay the end of rebellion there.

There was opposition to this from Robert fitz Hamon and a few others, but the king wouldn't be moved. William de Warenne in fact was a kind of brother-in-law to Rufus, or had been until his first wife's death three years before. It was a connection that no one has ever made quite clear, but the lady of de Warenne was one Gundrada, who was said to be a daughter of the Lady Matilda's by some marriage, regular or otherwise, before she had married William Bastard. She had a son as well. Both of them had been well treated by the Conqueror and led prosperous but quiet lives, which is nearly all I know about them.

An escort was chosen to take Odo away. It was heavy and well armed, but because I argued that Lord Odo could suborn the Angel Gabriel, given time to work, Rufus looked about to choose someone his uncle might be safer with – and chose Cormac!

'Ride with him. Sleep with him. Stand by him if he goes to piss against a tree. Let him speak to no one unless you hear what's said. And if he tries to escape you, bind him and let him walk the rest of the way at the end of a rope.'

Cormac smiled serenely. 'No fear. He'll be as safe with me as if he were in Heaven.'

I didn't like the sound of that, any more than I liked the idea of Cormac's being called incorruptible. I protested, but there was no debating the king once he was decided. His choice had been made with a touch of malice for Odo. It struck him as amusing to send his proud uncle off to a final defeat in the charge of his favorite – a man Odo knew as his own former spy, who had become his nephew's intimate. Perhaps he also gave Cormac the office to requite him for being called his catamite in front of witnesses. Rufus wouldn't neglect such an insult.

'You think my *harper* isn't worthy to be a bishop's warden, Ranulph? Is that it? Why, I'll raise him higher, then. Cormac! Come in here! Cormac of Munster, I name you – my chamberlain of the bedchamber! Keeper of the – of the royal footwear, or something.

We'll think of a title.' He went to the field cot in his tent, dragged from under it his household treasure chest, and probed its wealth until he found a suitable chain of gold.

'Come to me, Chamberlain!'

Cormac, with a smirk for me, bent his head and received the chain about his neck. The king laughed and slapped him on the shoulder. 'Now you're a proper officer of my court. See you behave yourself and deserve it.'

There was nothing anyone could say to that. But I found a later moment to say to Cormac alone:

'Just be careful you don't rub Odo's nose in the dirt so much that he gives you opportunity to send him to Heaven. Everyone will say the king meant you to kill him, no matter the provocation. You'll make the king a murderer.'

Cormac looked amazed. 'Who said anything about that? Not I. If anybody does him that service, it's more likely to be his friends at Rochester, don't you think? I'm only a humble servant of the royal will – '

'Not so humble, please!'

'Entirely, I assure you. Little Brother! I know Will doesn't want the old devil harmed. But what's that to Bellesme?'

'What do you mean?'

'Why, imagine you were Bellesme, who'd come to get a rich piece of this kingdom for himself, who'd gotten a strong castle from Odo and plenty of men to defend it. Then comes Odo to your gate and says, "Open up. I've made a bargain with Red Will behind your back. Give up your defense and come out. We're all sneaking home like curs." What would you do, if you were the best military head in Normandy and the most suspicious? Why, you'd have one of your bowmen put an arrow between Odo's ribs and redouble your guard. So would I – and so might Bellesme.'

'If you think that, why haven't you said it to the king? And why would you want to be the man sitting at Odo's knee if it happened?'

'What, and spoil a good end to a tale? Besides, one shot is all that's needed to make the point.'

It was bravado. He didn't think it. It was only the way he planned to taunt Odo on the journey, I decided.

Odo and Cormac left us next morning with a dozen knights. We lingered only a day before old de Warenne expressed his wish to die in his priory at Lewes, which he had founded. His son took him away in a litter. Rufus didn't follow, having no taste for witnessing prolonged death in the confines of a priory. So we were only a day behind Odo's escort when we came to Rochester.

As we neared town, a rider came out to meet us.

'I come from His Grace Gundulph of Rochester! My lord King, you are betrayed! The bishop begs you turn aside and meet with him at his manor before you enter the town. He's with Archbishop Lanfranc.'

The two old men were waiting for us when we let our host settle itself south of the town. Gundulph was pacing the presence hall and burst into his familiar tears when he saw the king. Lanfranc was sitting in the bishop's chair but rose, cold-faced, to greet us. He told the tale in brief:

'They came into town, your prisoner and his modest guard. Why did you send so few? Never mind. They came as you sent them, and without bothering to present themselves to Gundulph here, or allowing him to give them additional strength from his own mesnie, they went up before the castle. Your *harper* called on those inside to surrender, saying it was at the bidding of their lord, who would speak to them. He then, so I'm told, showed them Odo with his hands tied to his pommel like a thief's.

'I'm told that Odo addressed a speech to the walls, saying all within would have amnesty if they laid down their arms and opened to you when you came. But as he spoke while in bonds, and with your *harper* toying with a dagger beside him, the speech wasn't very convincing.'

The king was both angered and humiliated by Lanfranc's rebuke. 'Y-yes, of course, you're right. C-cormac's been a f-fool. I should have s-sent someone else, but – '

'Your enthusiasm for courtesy – '

'My enthusiasm, Archbishop, is now to find out what ha-happened next! I suppose s-someone opened the gate door and my uncle rushed in while my men were s-still gaping up at the walls. Well, where's Cormac, now? By God, he won't g-get off lightly for this, I promise you!'

'Cormac? Why, your harper and all the rest that aren't dead are inside the walls now, with Odo.'

Rufus looked at him for a long moment as if he hadn't heard, then repeated in a husky, dull voice: 'Inside. They went over to him? Betrayed me?'

Lanfranc shrugged. 'Bellesme raised the gate while Odo was still speaking. He rode out himself at the head of a dozen knights and put the townsmen to flight. There were bowmen on the walls who slaughtered as many as couldn't run fast enough. Several of your men fell at the same time. There was a brief skirmish with the rest, then they were forced in through the gate. The Lord Odo is in command of his tower once more.'

'Cormac?'

'I've not seen his body, so I presume he's a prisoner.' Lanfranc's voice could scarcely have been more cold if he had been pronouncing an excommunication: 'You must call up your host again and give them stronger terms than before. When the news goes out that you let your uncle escape you, being once in your hands – well, it will put new heart in the rebels. What it puts in the hearts of your followers I won't venture to guess.' He bowed his head curtly and left the chamber.

Rufus stood as before. I said: 'Your Grace, the archbishop is right about a summons. Shall I assemble your clerks?'

He looked at me. 'I should have killed my uncle as he knelt before me. Instead, I've killed my friend.'

William, King of the English by the grace of God, to all his men of an age to bear arms, French or English, from the ports or from the uplands: come with all speed to the royal muster at Rochester, if you would not be branded with the shameful name of nithing!

They came until the town would hold no more of them. The king erected two wooden towers to oppose Rochester Keep, the first outside the walls on Bowley Hill, the second inside them, between cathedral and castle. Gundulph's own tower was filled, and even the nave of his church was occupied with men, while bowmen stood on top of all the towers to see that no one escaped from Rochester, either by land or by river. So our third siege began.

It's strange what effect some simple, harmless-seeming words can have on certain men. I've heard Englishmen cheerfully name each other bastards, fools, Goddamns, whoresons, and get a laugh as often as a blow for it. But to call an Englishman a 'nithing' – a mere nothing, a worthless piece of trash – will shame and enrage him, make him rise to prove the word untrue, even if he's a slave. It is as dangerous as calling a gentleman 'unknightly,' or mentioning ancestral swine to a Jew. The 'nithing' touch was mine, I confess.

The walls of Rochester were bound around with an iron band of siege. Those within were desperate and those without more grim and fell than wolves around a byre. The summer air grew hot and fetid with our stink. The sun bore down unseasonably with no rain.

The rebels grew hungry and thirsty, but so did we. The whole country was being foraged by our army. The rats inside Rochester's walls helped the rebels to eat their grain; we needed no rats, having so many men. Flies hatched out of the ordure and became a plague; they sat on our faces and hands, buzzed in our ears, nipped our eyelids and nostrils like gnats, floated or swam dying in our wine, gravy, water. We spat out flies every time we took a bite, or else swallowed them with the scanty, rank meat and thought nothing of it.

Every day Rufus went before the tower with a herald, who cried to those inside: 'In the name of the king, surrender yourselves and be saved! Send out your hostages and yield to the right, as you hope for mercy!'

To which Odo's crier regularly replied: 'Let the king secure for the Earl of Kent and all his faithful followers those honors which they hold in his land, and they will give up resistance and serve him gladly!'

When he heard that, Rufus came away laughing. 'He wants better terms now than he got for betraying me the first time! God's Face! Another treachery and he'll want half my kingdom!' But his humor soured, and he stalked the hall of Gundulph's tower, running thick fingers through his hair until he looked as if he'd been pulled through a thicket.

'Let them stay and rot. I can sit longer than they can. I'll keep Chr-Christmas here, if it suits me!'

Earl Roger made a plea for the rebels: 'I hate treachery as much as you, my lord, but these are our kindred, yours and – '

'Yes,' said the king through his teeth. 'Treachery seems to run in our k-kindred's blood, doesn't it? But then, Cain was Abel's *hrother!*'

'Keep them confined and watched; keep them lean with hunger, yes. But offer them water at least! There's been no rain for a month. For the sake of your noble father's memory – '

'My father wouldn't have done such a thing, Roger! You damned well know it! I should throw water in the streets first. I should roast an ox in the ma-market and let the dogs eat it, before I gi-gi-give them anything!' Rufus went to a wine flagon and made as if to pour himself a cup, but his jaw knotted and his throat worked as if it sickened him. He slammed the cup on the table, then hung brooding over it for a while.

'I'll yield you this much, Montgomery. Let them show me m-my friends, *all of them*, on the walls, and I'll let them draw up as much water as will fill a tun. Every day they show me my me-men in good health, I'll let them draw so much. But I must see all standing without help, and all m-my friends must *speak* to me. Tell them that, if you like.'

I saw what he dreaded: that Cormac had been mutilated. The offer was made. It went without answer for a day.

'They think I'll poison the water,' Rufus said grimly. 'It's what Bellesme would do in li-like circumstance.'

But on the second day there was a cry for truce and the hostages were shown. Word was sent to the king, who came at once on horseback to the place where the water tun had been set the previous day with bowmen to guard it from theft.

He put his hand up to shade his eyes and brush the flies off as he scanned the wall, then called out: 'Bertram! Giles! Dru, Alain, Hugh, Robert! Speak and say if they've treated you ill!'

The knights answered variously that they had not been harmed. One, Dru de Carentan, begged the king's pardon for failing his duty to die before he lost his prisoner.

'By the Face, lad, it's I who should beg your pardon. Do they feed you with themselves, Dru?'

De Carentan grinned most gallantly at that. 'We dine on the best rats from the bishop's table, Your Grace.'

Rufus laughed. His eyes searched the walls. 'Cormac?'

Cormac was at the end of the line of men, and no doubt Rufus had spotted him first but kept him until last. Cormac looked down on his master, his hands behind his back as if they were tied. He didn't speak.

The king called roughly: 'Cormac?' Then he yelled: 'Bring me an ax! There'll be no water unless all can speak!' An ax was promptly put in his hand, and he urged his horse toward the water tun, while our bowmen drew their strings back to their ears, arrows aimed on those above. There was a little panic on the walls; two of the knights and one guard urged Cormac to speak. 'By the Face of Lucca, if you've harmed him, you'll parch for it!'

Cormac leaned his head back and laughed soundlessly.

'Cormac!'

'Your Grace?'

Rufus let the ax down slowly. 'Are you all right?'

'Now I see you, yes.'

The king grinned. He said hoarsely, 'You almost missed getting a drink.'

'Do you think they'll give us drink, Your Grace?'

'They'd God-damned well better do it – and from the first bucket drawn, or they'll see me spill the rest!'

And so it was done: they were given water, sparingly; then the rest of the tun was drawn out, bucket over bucket, when our friends were taken from the wall.

Drink in exchange for a brief daily glimpse and a word was the bargain for the next few days, during which time Odo tediously continued to demand amnesty and full restoration of all honors, which were refused.

'If I make terms with you, Uncle, it'll be for the worse, not the better. Come out and I'll let you live.'

Odo disappeared from negotiations for several days. Then one morning early he came again and demanded to speak to the king. Rufus rode down there at his leisure when he'd broken his fast with a cup of watered verjuice and a crust of bread. As always, I went silently with him, as did Earl Roger and fitz Hamon.

'Thirsty already? Uncle, the water wagon isn't up from the river yet. '

Odo stared down at us for a long moment in silence, then turned away. Eustace of Boulogne took his place, looking not like his usual peacock self, but rather like a beggar in a fine, dirty shirt. He croaked: 'Cousin, we've taken counsel for half the night. We understand your terms are that we may all go free if we take ship at once. Your promise to Odo – '

'My promise to my uncle was made before he betrayed his promise to me.'

'Grant what you promised, in the name of a merciful God!' Eustace shrieked. 'You've shown your strength; now show sense! What will it profit you if we all die here and you can find room in the earth to bury us? Every court in Europe will damn you!' He had begun to weep openly and covered his face with his hand like a woman.

Rufus stared up at him for a long while. 'You must renounce all claims to titles here.'

'Yes! Yes, so we do!'

'Your titles are vacant anyway. Your lands belong to me. But you must renounce them because you are all traitors.'

'Yes, we are traitors! We renounce them!'

'No!' cried Odo.

'You will come forth to me unarmed, on foot, without any display, or any manner of dress on your backs but a shirt. You will walk to the ships and let the people see you go, naked and not taking hidden wealth.' His tongue never faltered.

'No!' Odo bellowed again. 'We're soldiers, not antics! You mean to have us stoned!'

'No man will throw a stone at you on pain of death.'

'You mean to shame us with your drums and trumpets.'

Rufus yelled, 'You've shamed yourself!' Then he understood Odo's last cry and laughed. 'Why, you're a fool, Uncle! Would you stay and starve to keep from hearing my horns sound the retreat for you? It's an old tradition.'

Count Eustace said: 'It's Bellesme. He says he won't come out if you bray at us and let the townsmen pelt us with filth.'

'Then let him stay and starve with dignity. Uncle! I want you to give up the keys to my chamberlain, Cormac. Dru de Carentan will be warden of my tower until I make someone else a gift of it. And my lord Uncle – do my chamberlain honor when you yield to him. Don't throw things on the ground. One thing more: not for a thousand marks of gold – not if you showed the Stigmata – would I grant you honorable retreat. Nor Robert of Bellesme, either!'

So in a while they came out, and our drums rattled and our trumpets brayed for them like lovesick mules. People ran to see them. There was great joy among the townsmen. They yelled insults, flung pots of filth or horse dung, but no one threw a stone, as the king's command on that point had been well cried. The great leaders came out first and were led away by the king himself toward the river, followed by their knights. The lesser men of Odo's garrison were turned aside and taken into the custody of Robert fitz Hamon to be held at our siege tower and fed what could be spared to them. On their oaths that they had injured no king's man and their pledge to serve the king alone thenceforth, they would be released, as they weren't to be blamed for the actions of their masters.

I was sickened by the sight of so much filth and misery and gladly would have joined the king on his journey to the ships, but he gave me another task: 'Where are Cormac, Dru, and the rest? Tell them to put a guard on the weapons and come out. No need to stay in that pest hole when they can come and bid our friends a cheerful farewell.'

The stench of Rochester Keep was worse than that of any charnel house. I didn't much relish being a courier to Cormac, either, when his insolence had provoked this last agony. I imagined I'd find him sitting in the high seat of the upper hall, enjoying his tenure as lord of the keep.

As I came to the gate, I saw the last of the miserable garrison being taken away. There were two clerks following in the tail of the train, like the very skeletons of crows. They were my brothers. I told myself I must go and lay claim to them when I'd seen Cormac.

Two of the king's knights stood just beyond the gate to keep out the curious or light-fingered. It seemed unnecessary, as the whole town had gone down to see the last of Odo. I said as much to the knights by way of greeting.

One of them agreed, but said: 'No one can come in. Sir Dru's order, until the king comes.'

'But I'm the king's messenger, with a word for Sir Dru and the rest. Where's Cormac, the Irishman who's got the keys to this shambles? Call him out and he'll vouch for me.'

He gave me that blank, disconcerting stare which all good soldiers must practice to achieve. 'The Irishman? The one they say the king favors? He won't answer for anybody. The rest have gone to tell the king.'

I pushed past him and ran into the bailey. My tonsure surely saved me from being clubbed down. The second knight was after me with sword drawn, but when he caught me at the top of the castle stairs, he only shoved me against the door.

'You can't go in, priest!'

'Cormac!'

The door swung open. I could see into the guardroom and up the steps to the lower hall. I went up with the knight still holding onto me and cursing: 'Christ! Well, now you're in, don't touch anything. I won't be scoured for a damned priest.'

'Cormac!' The hall was littered with cast-off mail and weapons. 'Where is he? Up there?' I meant the upper hall.

'No, down below.' He led me to a trapdoor with a ladder that went to the storerooms at ground level. They held empty sacks, barrels, broken harness. There were signs the place had been used to butcher horses. Flies hung in the air, humming like hornets. I put my hand over my nose and mouth, but the smell was like a living presence.

To the rear of the ground level there was a door leading outside. A smithy was there; I could see the forge. Just inside there was a small room, a tack room or the smith's quarters. The guard indicated that door and I went in.

Cormac lay across a heavy table, naked except for a soldier's short mantle thrown over his back. His hands had been tied together with a leather thong, then lashed to one of the table legs. His legs were stretched, and I could see thongs around each ankle. He had strained at the bonds so hard that the leather was embedded in his wrists and soaked with blood, on which flies sat gorging. His face was half buried by one arm, but I saw an open eye. There was a rag in his mouth.

'Cut him free,' I whispered, and when the young knight still stood in the doorway, I yelled, 'Cut him free!'

He came and severed the stiffened leather with his dagger. I pulled the mantelet away meanwhile, expecting to see a back made raw with beating, but the flesh was unmarked. Carefully, in case he had broken bones, I got one arm under him and turned him over. There was no wound in his breast or belly, and his loins were intact. I pulled the gag out of his mouth.

His tongue was still there, but blood and vomit clotted the rag. I felt his flesh. It was cool, but not cold.

'Bring me some water from the smithy. He may still be alive.' I put my ear to his chest, but my own heart's pounding in my head made it impossible to hear his. I turned; the man still hadn't moved. 'Bring me some water, damn you to Hell! This is the king's friend.'

'There's no water and he's dead. Can't you see it?'

'No! He'd be stiff. Cormac? Cormac, can you hear me?' I lifted his head and turned his face, so his eyes looked into mine. 'I'm going to say an Act of Contrition for you. You must say it with me in your head, if you can't speak.' I bent over him. 'O, my God, I am heartily sorry for having offended You, and I detest all my sins, because I dread the loss of Heaven and the pains of Hell – '

'He's stark dead, you fool! Christ, look at him, won't you? Look at the blood on the floor. They ran a sword up through him from his arse to his brisket! It was Bellesme's sword, de Carentan said. He pulled it out when we came down and found the poor bastard. They spitted him like – ' He gagged and spat. 'God damn the bastard who did it. Dru said he knew the sword.'

' – and the pains of Hell, but most of all because I have offended You, my God, Who are all good and deserving of my love . . . ' I laid Cormac down again, forgetting whether I had said the rest; put my hand over his eyes to close them; touched the copper-freckled skin of his brow and temples.

There was a noise of booted feet overhead, then a clattering on the ladder, a confusion of voices.

'Christ, Who had mercy for the thief upon the Cross, take pity on this poor sinner, cut off – ' I turned my head. Rufus was in the door. I backed away as he came to the table. His mouth was set small and thin like his father's, his face as pale as Cormac's. He stood a long moment unmoving, then laid his hand on Cormac's breast, as if to test for life. His breath shuddered through his nostrils and he took his hand away suddenly.

'Bury him.'

'We might take him with us to London – '

'No. Do it now.' His throat began to work; he turned abruptly and strode out.

A pair of gravediggers were put to work in the castle ward, where there had been other recent burials; a pair of carpenters came with boards and hammered out a coffin. Gundulph sent his sacristan with a winding cloth, candles, and a servant with a basin and a bucket of water. All these things he did out of the goodness of his heart and for love of the king, since there could be no doubt in his mind whether Cormac deserved them.

I had already bound up Cormac's jaw with a strip of cloth torn from the mantelet. I washed his body, too, while Gundulph's servant held the basin and tried to keep his gorge from rising. I wanted no strangers to help me with that grisly task, though I couldn't have said why I was so determined. When it came to the shrouding, I lifted him alone while they put the cloth under him. He was so wasted that it needed little strength; but he had begun to stiffen.

I arranged his arms, folding them across his breast, and noticed his rings. I tried to remove them to give them back to the king, who must have been their donor, but his hands had swollen from being tied, and the only one I could wrest off was surely no gift of the king's. It was plain silver, maybe only gilt over a baser metal, with a flat, six-sided face unadorned with a stone. This I put on my own thumb for safekeeping, then wrapped him, all but his face.

I felt the sacristan looking at me. I seemed to be weeping. I didn't sob, or feel the clutch of grief at my throat. In truth, I would be much relieved to be rid of Cormac. My mind had already begun to turn on how the king would be improved now this man wouldn't shadow him everywhere and remind people of the purpose of his company. Rufus would be wiser now, see the foolishness of his infatuation, and never let himself be held in thrall to such as Cormac again. It was painful to him now, but in the end it was for the best.

Yet, no matter what I believed, or thought I believed, still my tears welled up, until I was forced to stop and wipe my face on my sleeve for the shame of it.

'Bring in the coffin, if it's finished.'

The servant went out to speak to the carpenter, while the sacristan stayed by me, still praying. I wanted him to go, too, but the only way I might have budged him was to tell him that the man he was about to bury with prayers and blessing was an excommunicate. It was my solemn duty to tell him that, but I didn't.

I looked on Cormac for the last time. His jaw had set, so I could remove the ragged binding from it which was a horror to me. I did so, then I thought suddenly that he now resembled a certain wall painting of the shrouded Christ which I had seen at St. Alban's Church, above London.

It was blasphemy to think it. I shook my head, but there it was: the red-gold hair, browned now with age; the level brows; the small beard he had recently begun to grow in imitation of the king's; the long, pale face with its perfect, high-rounded brow and narrow-bridged, long nose. The agony of death having been smoothed away, his features seemed as serene and fair to me as they had the first day I ever saw him, when I was tumbled at his feet a breechless cuckoo's child.

I gathered up the top of the shroud as the coffin was being brought in, and on an impulse I couldn't deny, no matter who might wonder at it, I kissed his face before I covered it.

33

A *Te Deum* was sung in Gundulph's church for the king's victory over his enemies. Lanfranc and Gundulph led it; Will Giffard and Robin Bloet were in the choir. The nave was full of worshipers, and Rufus gave the service his bodily presence at least. Afterward, there was a feast of sorts with wine brought in from London by one of the king's ships. The king sat at the high table between archbishop and bishop, among his lords and captains, surveying his faithful knights. He ate sparingly but drank each time the cup was filled for him.

The confiscated arms were brought into the hall and heaped on the floor between the central hearth and high table. Fitz Hamon invited all the captains and knights banneret to take their choice of the spoils, but he did so first. Scanning trophies, he picked out Odo's famous mace and Robert de Bellesme's equally famed sword, known by the great carbuncle let into its pommel. He brought them both and put them on the table before the king.

Rufus shook his head silently at the offer.

'But they're rightfully yours, Your Grace!'

My lord looked at them with a blank face, his hands spread out flat on the table; then he pushed himself to his feet, reached for Odo's mace, and hefted it. There was a cheer from the lower tables.

He raised the weapon above his head with a swift, savage motion that caused Gundulph nearly to fall off his stool to avoid it. He crashed the mace down on the grip of Bellesme's sword with such furious strength that the carbuncle was shattered to a powder. Fitz Hamon sprang back, amazed. There was a wordless shout from those in the hall, half of surprise, half of approval. Earl Roger stood up, ashen-faced, but before he could utter a protest the king slammed the mace again and again, crushing the quillions of the sword, ripping up the rich linen cloth under it, splintering the heavy oak boards of the table. The platters and cups leaped and spilled as he hammered with that spiked thunderbolt on the sword of Bellesme with such force that I thought the whole table must collapse under it. The sword blade broke, the tip flew off and just missed the staring face of Robert fitz Hamon.

Every man in the hall was on his feet by then. The king's last blow cracked the haft of the mace and embedded its iron head in the table as deep as the length of its spikes. Rufus let the remaining piece of the haft drop from his hand. Like a man coming out of a dark dream, he drew a deep breath and looked about him, frowning. There was a brief silence, then someone yelled: 'The king!'

All in the hall took up the cry: *Le roi! Le roi! Le roi! Le roi!* They barked it like the hounds of Hell crying on their watch.

Fitz Hamon turned and bellowed: 'The weapons of dishonorable men are unworthy trophies!' Which made them stamp and yell the more. The noise went on until those not already drunk on wine were so with the sound of their own voices. Other swords were snatched from the pile and broken amid berserker screams of triumph. If the king had called on them then to board ship with him, sail to Normandy, and sack their very ancestral homes, I think they would have done it. But he had already left the high table.

When I thought it safe to do so without attracting notice, I went to find him in the high chamber reserved for him alone. I found a guard at the top of the stairs, who warned:

'No one is permitted up here tonight, by the king's order.'

'I'm his chaplain.'

'No matter to me if you're his good angel. He said no one was to come up.'

'He didn't think to exclude me. He expects me.'

'He didn't say so.' When I persisted in coming closer, he drew his sword, making a nasty, raking sound that set my teeth on edge.

'Good soldier, are you a Christian? If so, you'd better put out the torch that burns on the wall behind you. Then you may say you didn't know you had murdered a priest when you thought you were doing your duty.' I kept advancing on him, but slowly.

He licked his lips and glanced at the heavy door on the other side of the landing. I drew even with him, then passed him carefully. 'I'll say I slipped by you when you were called by your officer,' I whispered. I dared to turn my back on him; in a moment I heard his feet going down the stairs and his curse, for me.

I went into the chamber. Rufus was sitting on a bench, his back against the wall, his legs spread out before him, a wine flagon cradled at his crotch. His eyes were closed. I paused, observing him and the state of the chamber, then went to the bed, turned back the cover, and shook up the bolster.

'You've murdered my guard, of course.'

I paused, my back to him. 'I spared him. He was the devil of a fighter, but I left him trussed and hanging from a ceiling beam.' I smoothed the pillow.

He snorted. 'God-damned priest, you'd do it, too, wouldn't you? Just to poke your nose in here and see to me?'

'Yes.' I turned and went to him. He rolled his head on the wall to squint up at me.

'What now? You've seen.'

'Shall I help you to bed, Your Grace?' I bent to him.

He raised a fist as if to hit me, but only jarred me on the arm slightly. 'Damn all priests and meddlers,' he sighed. Then his fingers caught my arm and dug into it. 'Dru told me what they did. Was it true?'

'Yes. He died hard.' I squatted before him to ease his pull at my arm.

'Hard? Oh, Christ, yes – hard! I once saw Bellesme s-spit a boar that way, when I was s-squire to old Roger. The boar was m-mauling one of his dogs. He dismounted and got behind it. He drove the spear in halfway up its shaft, then jumped back, laughing. Oh – it was comical! The boar took to running in circles, with the s-spear s-sticking out of him and s-slamming into trees! Then he went off straight through the forest with us running after him. We chased him for – oh, God – for half a mile, I think, before he dropped. When we s-split him, we could see how the spearhead had all but reached his heart. All his guts were burst by it. But how he'd run, how he'd run!'

He was weeping and laughing together. His fingers had nearly dug me to the bone as he told it, but now they fell away from my arm.

'Weep if you will, my lord. It eases the heart.'

His face hardened; he gave me a sudden push away from him. 'Weep? While he's laughing? Bellesme's laughing now, out there on the ship – and my uncle, too. They'll relish telling it when they get home. Like some downstairs.'

'There's no man here who could take pleasure in your grief, Your Grace. They'd rather hate those the more who did it to him.'

'Ah – liar!' He cuffed me on the side of the head softly. 'Don't fret. They'll not see me grieving. I won't give them – give them that pleasure. Help me up, priest. I drank too much.'

I got him to his feet. He went to the table that held basin and ewer, poured out some water and splashed it on his face, then bent and poured the rest of the contents of the ewer over his head. I brought a towel.

'Shall I help you to undress now?'

'What for? D'you think I'll sleep?' He looked at me over the towel, scrubbing at his beard the while. 'Will you?'

'No, my lord, I may not.'

He threw the towel away. 'Then why stay here? Le-let's go down again – no: let's go out and ride!'

'Where shall we ride, my lord?'

'Anywhere! Out of this stinking town. Out where the air doesn't smell like offal and dead men!'

'The gates will be closed. It's after curfew.'

'Well, we'll open them again, won't we? We'll let it slip that I'm the king!' He laughed at my excuse and threw open the door.

The unhappy guard was waiting at the bottom of the stairs. When he saw the king coming so precipitously down at him, his mouth fell open, but before he could frame his plea for mercy, Rufus swept him up with a hand on his shoulder. 'Come on! You come, too!' And the poor fellow ran after him as if his life depended on it.

We took horses from the stable, rode through the dark streets to the east gate, where they would have raised the alarm, but the king's voice stopped them. They must have thought he'd gone mad, or else that we'd had news of fresh disaster.

When the gate was opened we tore through it, out upon the high road that rises above where the Medway makes a great loop. We pelted through a silent village there, then plunged downhill toward the river and all but rode into it, before Rufus checked his headlong pace. Somewhere in that first wild bolt we lost our guard, who must either have fallen from his unaccustomed saddle or else turned back in despair of us. I'd thought I heard him bellow something once, but when I turned my head he was out of sight. Rufus appeared to have forgotten him almost instantly after laying claim to him.

There was a moist, cool wind blowing in from the estuary, or from the more distant sea. We paced our horses then to rest them, trotting along the sandy flats for a mile, until the king spurred his mount and set off again, turning inland. I clung to my seat like a beggar's louse trying to keep up with him, but though I'd imagined myself a horseman after my seasons in the saddle on Odo's behalf, I couldn't do better than trail Rufus by several lengths.

In time I got my own second wind and began to feel some portion of that joy in escape which must have propelled him. I lifted my head and most willingly fled both grief and care, left behind in the dark the memory of Cormac's twisted face, Elfgiva's reproachful eyes, and the starved look my brothers had worn when they passed me on the way to the siege tower and I'd been too full of my own affairs to speak to them. More relief than prayer to me was the wet smack of wind in my face, the chill of the night air, and the surging of a fine horse between my thighs. I gave up striving after the king and simply rode for the ecstasy of it, as if I were making love to a woman.

I couldn't tell how far we ran. It seemed we might have covered half the distance to Canterbury before I took notice of my whereabouts again. The Medway Water still gleamed to the left of me, and that swell of greater darkness beyond it must still be the isle of Sheppey, not Thanet. My horse was wheezing with fatigue and slick with lather when I saw the king draw rein and dismount on a rounded hill above me that was bare of trees. I pulled to a halt, fell from my saddle on numbed legs, and stumbled to where he stood, breathing deeply. My horse I let stray as he had his. The beasts were too winded to escape, having found sweet grass in plenty on the side of that hill.

There was a half moon for light and the stars burned clear, but there was no sign of human illumination: no shepherd's fire, no drift of smoke against the stars from some embered hearth. The world might have been uninhabited but for us.

'I feel better,' Rufus said after a time.

'I, too, my lord.'

He sat down cross-legged in the long grass, and I did the same. We let the effect of that solitude work in us for a while. I had never felt so free since I first left St. Vigor, or so at ease with another person near me. Expecting his grief and tears, I welcomed his calm silence. When he broke it, it was only to ask:

'Do you know the stars?'

I didn't; only what was known to the most ignorant farmer. 'I know the Bears and the Hunter, the Seven Sisters, and Venus, when she's in the treetops. All else is rumor to me, my lord.'

He said Earl Roger had taught him some of their names and Lanfranc some others, when he was a boy. He pointed out and named a few, faltering only when he mentioned the constellation at the peak of Heaven called the Lyre.

'The mystery is, they've all got heathen names. Now, why is that? You'd think the Church would have baptized them by now, wouldn't you? Our several popes might see to that and leave off quarreling with each other, and with us, eh?'

'True, my lord. It would keep them occupied for a lifetime.'

There was another silence; then he sighed. 'What – did they d-do with his harp? Did you s-see it there?'

'No. It must still be there. I'll send someone tomorrow to look for it.'

'No! No, it's no matter. No use to keep to-tokens of the dead.' His voice thickened. 'You saw him buried and the rest? It was we-well done?'

'Yes, my lord, very well done. He rests in Gundulph's churchyard. If you would like to see the place, I – '

'No, no, that's good enough. Le-let him be.' I think he must have wept then, but most quietly, while I sat with my head turned away, offering no unwelcome comfort. When he'd done with it, he returned to his discourse on the stars with a determined humor.

'There's a line of little stars up there by the Lesser Bear that God didn't kindle, if you believe an old stableman we once had at Falaise. You see 'em? A snaky sort of line? They're all that's left of one of my female ancestors from my grandsire's mother's line of reckoning.'

'You had an ancestor who was a demigoddess, my lord?'

'Better than that: a dragoness! She was a woman of the French fens that one of my great-grandsires took for a wife when he first came to the French king's lands from his pirate ship. He was so struck with the looks of her, he let himself be baptized just to ma-marry her. Him being a new-made Christian, it seemed odd to him that *she* wouldn't go in the church door to be wed, but must have her nuptials on the porch, like any peasant. But he wanted to impress her, so he built her a fine chapel next to his keep, for her to say her prayers in.

'Now – the strange thing was, every time he'd go to hear a service with her there she'd get a colic, or an ague, or some such thing, and leave the church before the s-service ended. He began to think she had a lo-lover she met, but there was no sign that she went anywhere from the chapel but to her own bed. So, he determined to find out what would happen if she e-ever stayed for the whole of the Mass. He made his stewards come and crowd in behind them the next day and c-commanded them to bar the door if she made to leave.

'So, it began as always and went on as always. No more did the priest begin to chant than the lady began to chafe and sigh and feel of her brow. Only this time when she made to leave, her husband laid hands on her and held her. They say she fought him with the strength of two men and shrieked until the priest almost fainted, but her lord made a sign that the worship should continue while he held his wife in his arms and made her look on the cross – until she began to *shift her shape*! Her hair became a mane, her skin grew scaly, her little hooked nose became a snout! She belched out smoke and flame, flew up into the rafters, where she set the roof on fire, and escaped through the burning thatch.

'They all ran out of the chapel in time to see her fly away lashing her tail, right up into that part of the sky, where she disappeared. But when night came, they say that those stars took shape that were never seen before – and so she hangs to this day. They say. What do you think, priest? Is this possible?'

I hardly knew what to answer to that old tale, which I'd heard from my mother as a child, too, but with a Breton to husband the dragoness. I suspected him of waiting for a careful explanation he could hoot at, so I answered:

'That was a hot wife to hold, my lord! But I perceive the truth in the tale. The lady's indifference to religion still runs deep in certain of her descendants. Was your grandsire a chaste man afterward? I'd think so. Bedding dragons would spoil a man for cooler wives.'

He appraised me in the dark, then blew out a sudden gust of

laughter and fell on his back in the grass. I was quiet until he'd stopped chuckling and asked:

'Why in God's Name did you ever enter the Church? You can't use Robin Bloet's excuse, that you're too lazy f-for another trade. Why did you?'

'My father made a vow in the year of the great comet.'

'Ah, a vow – for you to keep, yes. I was vowed to it, too, in a way. My m-mother wanted to make a priest of me. S-she must have thought that only G-god could stand to look me in the eyes. But I wasn't fit. My tutors gave me up in a year or two. Henry was supposed to take my place then, but he wouldn't abide it, either. In the end, we had to p-placate God with another sister.' He propped himself on an elbow and said earnestly: 'But – didn't you ever want to be out of it? You might have run off and become a s-soldier.'

That was a compliment, coming from him, and it was in a different voice that he uttered it, one he had never granted me a hearing until that night when he'd asked if I'd killed the guard. It was the intimate, slightly lower pitched voice he kept for his few friends – for Cormac.

'I have known the times when I'd have been glad for a change of profession, my lord. But events went against me. Now, I'm like a dray horse that's become used to plodding. It's a fine dream, but too late to make me a charger.'

'You're no dray horse, friend. You're too well made – you know it. You're not so humble as you might be, or so blind to yourself. You're a comely man.' A little pause, then a breath of laughter. 'A man for the women? Or don't you think of women?'

I sat with bowed head, taking heed of that small hesitation. I know I answered in good time, but thought is far swifter than words and my thought had outrun his little silence to weigh my answer against it. I could speak a word now and open the way to a place and a power over him that I had scarcely dreamed on before. I was neither surprised nor dismayed by the prospect that might open to me, if I allowed it. The temptation to say that one word was like the pull of a lodestone on my heart and mind, after such a day and such a night.

But I put the temptation from me. I could never take Cormac's place in his life. I meant to serve him better than Cormac had, and so serve my own dream of him; but not at the expense of his shame, or by making a mockery of the love I bore him. I said: 'My lord, you read me well. I confess, I have been frail to the love of women since the first week I came out of the cloister.'

The slightest silence, then he laughed, relieved it seemed. 'Frail to women! Well said!' He sat up.

'Have I offended you, my lord?'

'What? Me? God, no!' No, only now he would put me in with his estimation of all other priests but Lanfranc and one or two others, yet was too kind to say it? He got up and stretched. 'There's light in the east. We'd better catch our horses and go back, or the whole town will be out searching for us. They'll expect to find me eating grass and having fits, like the m-mad king of Babylon!'

He put his fingers in his mouth and whistled like a stableboy. His palfrey came presently in answer to that, with mine ambling behind it. When we'd mounted and turned toward Rochester again, I still felt somewhat uneasy in his silence, so I offered him something I'd been meaning to keep. I took off Cormac's ring and held it out, saying what it was.

He took it without comment, rubbed it over with his thumb, then set it on his hand without thanks. He wore it there for the rest of his life.

He led his host to Dover, where the last remnant of Odo's supporters made haste to open to him and surrender that keep from whose battlements one can see France on a fair day. Thus, all that had been Odo's in Kent was given back into the king's hand, where he prudently kept it.

We rested long enough to hear good news come from other places, enough to tell that the rebellion was withering. Wulfstan, Hugh the Wolf, and others had done good work, but it was the English and those Normans of small fee who chose to remember the Oath of Salisbury who made an end to the war. Only William de St. Carileph, terrified and resolute behind his castle walls, still held out against surrender.

We made ready to remove to Gloucester, where we would receive the vanquished and celebrate the Whitsun Court a little out of season. I still feared the king might begin to shun me then, either for my telling of my frailty, or for his coming so near the revealing of his. But just before he left Dover, he gave me the deanship of the college of canons at St. Martin's. Lanfranc was opposed to me, having some other candidate of his own in mind, but Rufus defied him, even went with me to the chapter to see me well accepted. After which he gave me another honor:

'Take yourself off to Winchester now, and bring my wardrobe up to Gloucester.' By which he meant the crown and coronation robes. 'While you're there, you might look in on the monks of Hyde. They're a contentious lot who need a new abbot. See if you think you could tame them.'

So I was made a man of substance.

My brothers were the first to hear my news after Robin Bloet, who'd gotten a hint he would be the next chancellor. I'd rescued Fulcher and Osbern before we left Rochester; told fitz Hamon of their kinship to me and gotten old Gundulph to make him release them to my custody. Fulcher didn't look altogether ready to thank me even for getting him out of confinement, but Osbern threw his arms about my neck when I said I had a use for a good pair of clerks that day in Dover:

'You're my flesh and blood after all, and the bad days between us are over. Remember, we talked once of who might need to provide for whom when the choosing of kings and dukes was done? Well, now it is, thank God, and I'm ready to keep my side of the bargain if you two are. There's advancement for you if you serve me half as well as you served Odo.'

'It's a fair offer, brother,' Osbern said wistfully when Fulcher didn't answer at once. My more cautious brother considered the matter and gave a nod.

'Good! It's settled then. Now, I'll tell you the other half of my plan. I mean to send for our parents to come over to us. There might not be a place for Father in St. Loup when Odo gets home, but there'll be one in Godalming. I've got a curate I mean to be rid of. I've already spoken to my bishop about him and his dismissal's signed. Father will have his place. And there's another thing – ' I relished the look they gave me and each other when I told them about Giva and my sons.

I chose Osbern to sail for home to bring back our parents. Fulcher I took with me. He seemed suitably impressed to hear we were to carry the royal regalia up to Gloucester, with a dozen of the bishop's guard at our command, as we did. It was an honor not often given to anyone less than a great officer of the court.

We rode together at an easy pace, full of amiable talk on our future, when we would all be reunited and he and Osbern risen high in the estimate of the chancellor. For myself, I was particularly pleased to be rid of Dunstan and his blighting effect on Elfgiva. From now on, I would surround her only with people who had reason to speak well of me. She could spend her energies learning to deal with my mother, instead of trying to confront and confound me whenever I came to her for a few hours of affection.

There were no pennants flying over the king's tower as we came into my village. The fields were unburned and the orchards unchopped. Our invaders had melted away to Pevensey without doing harm to so much as a blade of corn, for which I gave hearty thanks to God. Fulcher and I stopped at my church, where I showed him what repairs he might oversee in the near future. His first appointment seemed to cheer him; at least he gave me his faint smile and one or two practical comments about the work.

Elfgiva was waiting in the rectory yard when we came out of the church. I could have wished she'd run to meet me as she had once before, but she looked beautiful standing there, with our boys tumbling around her skirts like puppies. When we met I bent down for one of them, picked him up, and got a shriek from him for it, then handed him over to a startled Fulcher.

'Behold! Your first nephew, brother! Or he might be the second. It's hard to tell.' I would have taken up his twin, but Giva had already swooped and had him on her hip. I embraced her, kissed her brow and the baby's. Holding her slightly stiff shoulders I presented her to Fulcher. She held out her arm for the wailing boy in Fulcher's hands, got him to her bosom, and said:

'Well, it's plain to see you're brothers. God be with you. Come in and rest.' She smiled at Fulcher, but not at me. She was still piqued with me for disappointing her of marriage, but that would be forgotten when she heard all my news. We went into the house after her.

'Where's Dunstan? I've got something to tell him he might not like at first, but the joy of it will grow on him, as it has on me.'

'He's had your news. It outran you by a bishop's courier. He and Blodwin left yesterday to see their new place at Milford. As you say, he was glad of it. He said it was a better house.'

'What? He went off and left you and two infants unprotected? The fool! He might at least have sent you up to the tower.'

'I did well enough. I've learned to bake, to brew, to cook – I've gotten quite useful to myself.' She put the boys on the floor and went to get a loaf of bread from the hearth, wrapped in a towel to keep it soft. She cut it and set it before us on the table, where there was a pot of meat drippings to go with it. She brought two cups as well.

I sat down, glancing at Fulcher. He was smiling, no doubt because of the way in which she'd taken my news from my mouth. But I put by irritation and began to tell her the rest of my tidings. As I spoke of my new livings, Giva went out the back door and returned presently with a jar of buttermilk from its cool storage in the well shaft. She poured a cup for Fulcher, who stared after her as he dipped and ate his bread. I took up my tale again, patiently:

'We'll have a house in Winchester in time, near the abbey. And of course we'll keep what we share with Trudy in London. But we might as well start planning an extra room or two for this place in the meantime – with a bower for you, like the one you enjoyed in the tower. Will you like that?'

She was leaning over me, her breast against my shoulder, to pour buttermilk. She glanced down at me, her green eyes shaded to a hazel color with the light. My voice may have betrayed the response those eyes invoked in me: 'Well? Is any of that worthy of a kiss? If only for Fulcher's sake, so he doesn't think such things fall into a man's hands every year?'

She put down the milk jar and bent to kiss me on the mouth, her own lips so sedately compressed I could have no further doubt of her anger. It was more than the lack of a wedding, surely. She'd added Dunstan's going to her list of grievances against me. I resisted the urge to pull her onto my lap and put an end to her loftiness, but that, too, must wait until the proper time and place, which would be in our bed that night, when Fulcher was upstairs, listening or not. Meanwhile, no dissent before Fulcher.

She drew back from me, settling that damned smile on her mouth again, and asked of my brother: 'Will you have more bread or milk – uh – what shall I call your brother, *my good* lord? Not Father, since I'm soon to be surrounded by fathers. Brother-in-law? No, it takes a wife –'

'Giva – ' I spoke a soft warning.

'Fulcher – you must call me Fulcher – Giva,' said my brother in a fatuous voice, and when she turned her smile on him as she offered him another slice of bread, he actually blushed and fumbled it.

We departed next morning very early and made the rest of our way to Winchester with more speed and less speech. I met Sir William, the treasurer, at his house, and gave him my warrant from the king, then accepted his escort to the treasure chamber in the castle. With him as my watch outside in the corridor I went alone into that place of golden wonder, closing the door as soon as I had set my torch in a socket.

After so disastrous a year as it had known, that little room's holdings were seriously depleted. I fitted a key into the lock of an iron-bound chest in which the crown and robes of state were kept, just to make certain that all remained as it had been stored after the Easter Court.

It was so: folded in a length of soft wool to keep them from creases lay the gold-threaded red tunic and the rich blue mantle. Topping them, cushioned on a pillow, reposed the scepter of King Edward Confessor and the crown that William Bastard had a Greek artisan design for him in the last years of his reign. It was made in the image of one worn by the Holy Roman Emperors since the days of Otto the Great.

Few hands had touched that magnificence that hadn't been anointed to be either archbishop or king, but I lifted it then. It was heavy with the weight of its eight golden plates set close about a golden band. Each plate but the foremost was enameled with designs and symbols of a sacred nature and inlaid with precious stones of every cut and hue. The face plate which was set above the king's brow was adorned with the famous twelve great pearls of William Bastard's choice and surmounted by a golden cross.

This crown I would carry to see placed on my benefactor's head, on the day when his enemies came to bend their necks to him – my king, whom I would serve and whose friendship I now held as firmly as I held the crown. I lifted it higher to let the torch's light play on the radiance of its gems.

Ah, God, to lift such and put it on a king's head! Higher, before my own dazzled eyes I raised it, as if to be a king – as if to be a king.

I can still remember the serpents-cold and the weight of it on my brow.

COUNSEL TO THE WOLF

34

My lord the king met his enemies in Gloucester and made peace with most of them. A few of the lesser rebels had fled the country, fearing his wrath when they heard of the fall of Rochester; some, who had charges brought against them by the Church or faithful lay lords, he banished; a few he fined. To those of the English who had aided him, he remitted rents or gave some portion of those lands he had confiscated from the banished.

But the great lords, save one, all made their peace so nicely that within a week of their bending the knee to him, they were his companions in the hunt, as if they had never intrigued for his throne or burned his farms. The exception to their case was William de St. Carileph, who still refused to leave his castle and come to the king with reasons for his sudden flight.

Carileph's stubbornness got him small sympathy from his fellow bishops, who refused him a court ecclesiastical to hear his plea of innocence. He demanded the right to appeal to Rome. The council refused him. He, in turn, rebuffed the king's pledge of safe-conduct to and from the court unless it was put into writing. That demand insulted Rufus, who had been half sympathetic to his plight until then.

'Damn him, he behaves like a felon, then wants written oaths from me! Send him a writ! Tell him to haul himself down here as fast as a horse can carry him, or I'll burn his damned town and him in it!'

Carileph bowed to the inevitable at last. He came to the king, and there was a long and contentious argument between them which neither would allow to be called a trial. The council of lay and clerical lords alike were against him and not only out of fear of the king. He was banished from his diocese and from the king's protection, which meant he must go overseas, but his office wasn't taken from him, though the mercy of the court on that point was a wonder to me.

When he was banished, I was sent to take inventory of his goods and make an examination of his estates that were forfeit to the Crown. It was on that occasion that I first saw the beginnings of a work that has since become my own dream to complete. Carileph was building a church worthy to hold St. Cuthbert's shrine, a great cathedral meant to be the northern rival of Edward Confessor's minster in every respect of grandeur and beauty.

Murdered Walcher first conceived the idea of a new church, but Carileph had begun it with plans drawn up for him by an Italian in the service of Lord Odo. If God ever gives me release from this prison, which seems more unlikely with each grey day that passes, I shall finish that work. God, if He hears my prayers at all, must know I would give up anything and everything in exchange for the privilege of adorning that Lady of Stone. Can there be a truer repentance, or a better penance, than that, for such a man as myself? O Lord, make haste to deliver me!

At that same Whitsun assembly when the traitors were forgiven, William Giffard put off his chancellor's chain and the king bestowed it on Robin Bloet. Some people in the court have said I begrudged Robin this reward for his many and undoubted services to Rufus: he had taken on the whole ordering of the clerks that summer and reorganized the scriptorium while Will Giffard lingered behind at Winchester, fearing to be named a conspirator.

I never begrudged Robin any of his honors, nor did I even hint he was incapable of his office. Was I disappointed not to be recognized instead? Yes, very much. I was better fitted for the work than amiable Robin, and he knew it as well as I. But I never bore him malice, and the coolness that spoiled our friendship was more his doing than mine.

Why bear malice? I enjoyed the trust of the king more than any other man save Lanfranc. I sat by his chair when he held court; I walked by his side, rode with him if he made a progress through the town; and when his body servants had prepared him for the night, I alone, except for his squires, was privileged to remain with him, to talk over the events of the day, or to play a game to soothe his mind before he slept.

He was lonely, in spite of a crowded life. He missed Cormac, though he never spoke his name after that night when we rode together out of Rochester. If he valued me, it may have been because I, too, had mourned Cormac; or it might have been because William the Younger was a man who gave back loyalty where he found it.

Unfortunately, it quickly became believed that I had taken Cormac's place in more than one way. I heard this slander, but refused to dignify it with a denial, so of course it seemed confirmed and grew. Even Robin believed it to a degree, as I later discovered. It was this that spoiled our friendship, not my envy.

The week before we were set to leave Gloucester, Earl Roger Montgomery came to the king and said:

'Your Grace, there is a visitor to your court today, one whom I beg you to receive for love of me. He comes to you a supplicant, as I do now, on his behalf.' He made as if to get down on his age-stiffened knees, but Rufus quickly stopped him. The manner of his appeal was guaranteed to move the king.

'Whoever he is, even Beelzebub, let him come and be welcome for your sake, my lord.'

Roger smiled most piteously, then made a sign to one of the hall marshals, who went out and returned in a moment to cry:

'Now comes Henry, Count of Coutances; Robert, Count of Meulan; and Robert, Count of Bellesme!'

Rufus, who had just regained his seat, went white. His thick fingers curled about the armrests as if to keep him from springing to his feet again. He shot a look at me, at Robin, and at Earl Roger to confirm whether we were equals in a plot, but then a grim humor overcame him:

'Well – I said even Beelzebub, didn't I?'

Prince Henry led the procession. He wore mail and had his helm under his arm, but carried no weapon, nor did the others. When he reached his brother's feet he fell to one knee. The other two were swift to follow him.

In the silence that followed I moved closer to the king, wishing Lanfranc hadn't already departed for Canterbury, because if there had ever been a time for his cool strength it was then. Why had Henry and Robert de Meulan, the son of good Roger Beaumont, come to Rufus in the company of this flayer and impaler of men, this most monstrous murderer since Edric Streona, who had slain King Edmund Ironside as he had unwarily prepared to relieve himself in a latrine?

All in the hall stopped talking and stared. Those who were in other parts of the keep came to the doorways to look on the spectacle of Robert de Bellesme kneeling before Rufus.

The king rose stiffly from his seat as though he must remind his legs how to move again. He went down from the dais to his brother, who looked up, saw the king's hand bidding him rise, and obeyed to embrace him fervently. I heard Rufus clear his throat. Henry's embrace seemed to renew life in him. He clapped him on the back, then put him at arm's length, only to draw him back with real affection.

'Well, H-harry! By the F-face! I hear you've spent your pennies to good p-purpose. Coutances! By God, who but you would ever have thought to *buy* a country?' His glass-sharp laugh broke as if to cut his throat. He released Henry and turned his attention to the other men still kneeling. 'My lords – '

Robert de Meulan rose at that bare invitation and took a somewhat more perfunctory embrace. Bellesme still knelt, his head bowed, though I saw it make its falcon's dart to one side when de Meulan moved.

Earl Roger said in a tremulous voice: 'Noble and just king, see my son prostrate before you. Hear his speech with the same wisdom you showed to his peers these weeks past. He set himself in opposition to you and you have rightly chastised him, as I would have done myself if I'd been given the opportunity.'

I thought this highly unlikely, and so evidently did Rufus from the look he turned on the old earl.

Roger's mouth worked a moment in silence, then he blurted: 'He craves your pardon for his offense in all but one thing, my lord, and in that he has been foully wronged. But let him acquit himself.' He glared at Bellesme.

'I'd hoped he hadn't gone mute,' Rufus said. 'I never remembered him without a tongue.'

Bellesme lifted his vulpine face and said, 'I can speak for myself.'

'In truth he can, but by your leave, my lord, let me speak first!' Prince Henry said quickly. 'Because I can put the whole matter in a nutshell. My lord of Bellesme has been accused of murdering a certain man in your service while he was held prisoner at Rochester. He has declared himself to be innocent of this crime to me, and I have cause to believe him. The guilt for that foul murder lies, most unhappily, on the head of our uncle, Your Grace. It's as simple as that.'

Rufus held Henry's eye for a moment, then turned abruptly from him, went up to his chair, and sat. His face was like marble. I leaned toward him to whisper: 'If you like, Your Grace, I can have the hall cleared in a moment. I'll tell this lord to put his petition in writing.'

His belly jerked as he stifled a snort of laughter for my presumption. I was relieved. I could tell by the set of his jaw that without a diversion he would be incapable of speech.

He said to his enemy: 'Which of his several murders does the lord of Bellesme deny? He murdered more than one of my subjects, I think. No, Harry, let him speak for himself!'

Bellesme said from his knees in a cold voice: 'I never killed your harper. Your uncle had it done. He boasted of it on the ship.'

'You lent him your sword?' He didn't stammer.

'He took it! When I was disarmed of it!'

'How was that possible?' The effect of the king's voice, just above a whisper, had a disconcerting effect on Earl Roger if not on his son. The old man looked as if his heart might fail him.

Bellesme got to his feet, his head jerking at each of us, and answered in a voice subdued but warm with temper: 'He got my sword because you demanded we pile up our arms before we came out. He didn't do it, but he had one of his damned boot-lickers do it, and claimed the kill later. He wanted to spite me as much as you, because he blamed me for losing his stinking castle. He said if I'd come to terms with you earlier he could have worked you so you'd let him keep it for the paying of a fine – which he might just have done. You do know him as well as I, don't you, *my lord?*'

'This is true, Your Grace,' Robert de Meulan said. 'At least, the bishop was very outspoken in his anger for what he said was his unnecessary banishment when he came to Rouen. He particularly blamed Bellesme to the duke for losing him Kent – as he said – by his stubborn defiance. He blamed Your Grace, too, of course. Also, others beside Lord Robert have told since how Odo boasted he had fittingly served your – your servant.'

'Will-Rou, to be plain about it, Uncle's been on a crazed rampage ever since he came home. He blames damned near everybody but himself for his defeat, and he's trying to drive out of our brother's council anybody who might accuse him for the fool he is. I'm out of favor; so's de Meulan, which is why we've come over to you – as you might already have guessed.' He shrugged and smiled.

Henry was the handsomest of the three brothers and had a fair set of teeth, but smiling never came easy to him. 'Our brother and uncle sit together much these days, trying to think how they came to lose a kingdom, but they never credit the chief causes, which were their own stupidity and your valor. I bow to the "New Alexander" who's proved himself a king.' He did so, then half turned to address the hall:

'If my noble brother will have me for his subject, I will serve him gladly. As for my lord of Bellesme, so certain am I of his innocence that I offer myself as his champion if the king puts him to the test of ordeal by battle.'

It was a good speech. All the silent witnesses who had been like wary dogs now growled their approval of his gallant offer and began to edge closer to the dais. One by one, friends of Earl Roger came forward to plead for Bellesme, urging his innocence and Odo's guilt as if they had all been witnesses to the foul crime in Rochester keep.

Rufus glanced my way, hoping I might have a solution to the case they'd pressed on him, but there was little choice to be made. He had forgiven others so readily. His chivalry was being brazenly tested; he must accept the word of a brother and a fellow knight who swore to Bellesme's innocence. To accept that oath went against the grain of his good sense, but to refuse it was to give a buffet in the face to those ten or more other good knights who had now put their own honor in the balance for Robert the Devil.

He stood and held out his hands to Bellesme, who came and took them, kissed them, and after a head jerk in my direction to confirm I wasn't creeping up on him with a well-deserved dagger, he met the king's stiff embrace.

'I thank Your Grace for this mercy. I hope we may now put all our differences to rest.'

It was always a shock to hear what a soft, ineffectual voice Bellesme used in ordinary speech. It must have made his cruelties the more terrifying to his victims, when he visited them during their suffering – which I heard he invariably did.

So – all was put to rights, at least on the surface. Bellesme lost no time in gaining the king's promise that he would be his father's heir in England if his brother Hugh should die before him. If I had been Hugh of Montgomery, I would have lived with an armed man at my back thenceforth. His father despised him for his perversity and his brother was Robert de Bellesme.

They all dined with the king that day with great ceremony, Prince Henry sitting in Lanfranc's seat beside his brother. I listened to them lament the anarchy and dissent in Normandy as if they were not its makers as much as foolish Robert Curthose.

Before they parted company for the night, Bellesme lifted his wine cup and proposed they drink together as friends and brothers to the peace between Normandy and England. Rufus drank his cup to the heel, but left the hall immediately after, going straight up to his bedchamber, where he vomited up the wine.

I came in as he was retching and dismissed his servants, then closed the chamber door and offered him a towel wrung out in cold water from his ewer. He wiped his face with it slowly.

'What's Harry want with me, eh? What's so p-precious to him that he'd s-swear his honor away for that c-corpse-eating j-jackal?' He flung the towel onto the floor and glared at me. 'You don't believe that – that s-sewer oath, do you?'

'Since we must appear to accept it, my lord, we might as well try to believe it. The lord Odo isn't a man I'd think would make a crude boast of murder, but he was very angry for his humiliation. He *may* have sent one of his servants to do the work with Bellesme's sword, to have revenge on both of you.'

The king made a guttural noise. 'Maybe. But I'll never look that bone-faced bastard Bellesme in the face without feeling m-my gorge rise and my hands itch to kill him. What about de Meulan? I thought him as decent as his father! Old Beaumont was my f-father's right arm!'

'The same might have been said of Lord Odo, Your Grace.'

He shook his head. 'And Harry? Ready to be that bastard's *champion*? Christ! I had hopes for Harry. What am I to do?'

'Listen to them as you've already done, with patience and caution. Your noble father couldn't have shown more wisdom and cunning, my lord. You did well. They'll tell you what it is they want soon enough. Promise them much and give very little, especially if they've come to get support for a revolt against your brother – because you haven't the means to accomplish that just now, even if they were your true friends.'

He bridled at that. 'Haven't I?'

'No. You can't afford a good campaign without the coin to hire good mercenaries.'

'I've got my English.'

'Only here, my lord, in your own realm. You may not call them out to fight for you overseas without the consent of your council, and Lanfranc will keep the lords of the Church from agreeing to that. The lay lords are in as bad a case as yourself. They're beggared by this war they've just made against you. Victor and vanquished are beggared alike. If Robert Bloet hasn't had the chance to reveal your losses to you, call him in tomorrow and let him read to you the list of your estates that have been ruined for the year. Those enemies who never had the courage to face you in battle did you greater damage than you might think. Whatever it is that Prince Henry and de Mealan want of you, please God it isn't a thing that costs you in coin.'

This was hard for him to digest, I knew, but it was the daily meat I must set before him for a time and he must learn to chew it. I had been terrified to hear how many royal manors had been put to the torch in three short months. I was distressed to see how he lavished rewards of unburned lands on his supporters, lands he might have kept for himself. We had seen created more than two dozen new barons of the realm since the peace, who had been no more than free lances before. I had been losing sleep thinking how he might economize without seeming to do so, because such a measure would humiliate him.

We weren't long in discovering what it was Prince Henry craved. The next day he made his request in the hearing of the general court: he wanted his brother to grant him all those lands in England that had belonged to their mother in her life. He demanded them, in fact, as his right; he was a native-born prince of the realm.

Rufus had already promised to give those estates to Robert fitz Hamon – had given some, in fact. Once more he was caught on the horns of honor: he must make an ally and vassal of his younger brother, to use him as a weapon against Curthose in time, but he had given his oath to fitz Hamon.

Fitz Hamon showed himself a friend indeed: he saw the perplexity quickly and gave his assent to Harry's request, saying to the court:

'This is a fair and proper exchange, my lords; a few hides of land for a loving brother!'

The council readily gave their approval to the deed. Their consent wasn't really necessary to the king, but it gave him an insight into their hearts. They sympathized with young Henry, who hadn't gotten an arpent from his father for an inheritance, but had made himself a count within the year. They also preferred it that Henry split his loyalty between his brothers, as most of them were forced to do.

The grant was made, and Henry knelt to put his hands between those of Rufus to swear him fealty for lands that were almost as bare-burned as the king's. Rufus loaded him with presents, too – fine armor, rings, fur-lined mantles, boots of Spanish leather, gloves, and a splendid pair of horses – all of which the young prince seemed to need. He had come to court looking as frayed as a common soldier.

Robert de Meulan's desires were of another kind. It was clear he had lost authority, not property, in Rouen, and this was what he hoped to acquire again with Rufus. Like his father, old Beaumont, he preferred the guise of counselor, guiding a great man's wisdom as to whom to bribe, or whom to crush with oppression. That is a kind of wealth which, once lost, no amount of treasure will make up for.

De Menlan held long discourse with the king in their rides through the deer park, which Rufus commented on later:

'Stone one crow, and another soon comes to take his place, eh, priest? I'll never lack for guidance. This de Meulan wants to be my uncle, too, I think.' He laughed.

'What does he advise, my lord? That you come and take the French Vexin and leave him to hold it for you?'

I'd hit the mark. He looked evasive. 'Why would he want that?'

'Because he as good as owns the Norman Vexin already, and a man is always glad of elbow room. You mustn't listen to him yet.'

He sputtered: 'You d-damned r-rascal! Why not? You-you're just like him, you know, wanting to be my t-tutor. You're s-so damned sure s-somebody will get between us! You're jealous! He's a good man. He and his father were two of Robin's f-friends behind my f-father's back, but they never betrayed him! They never took up arms against him, and they never asked for much. Give 'em credit for that, at least.'

'Yes, my lord. If Count Robert is a loyal friend of your brother's and in need of no reward, why is he here and not in Rouen? He's an honest man, but does any man give counsel against his own best interest? Does Count Robert want to serve two masters, being salaried of but one? Or does he merely put himself to labor for the good of both your souls?'

He threw a towel at me, but he didn't tell me what de Meulan had proposed to him, and I was some time in discovering it for myself.

When our greedy guests at last took their leave, it was the ides of September and I was sent down to Winchester with the treasure of the royal regalia, to prepare the palace for the coming of the king, who meant to enjoy good hunting in the Hampshire forests before hard winter set in. I took the opportunity to stop at Godalming to see how my parents had settled into their new home.

I found my father in the hen yard, staring at the poultry as if the birds had just told him their venial sins. He gave a cry of joy when he saw me and hobbled forth to meet me. I embraced him and found him alarmingly frail. I feared that not all the butter and cream in Surrey would ever make him hardy again.

My mother rushed out of the house at the sound of our voices. Her empty eye socket quivering with emotion, she flung herself on me, and I swung her off her feet as she hung on my neck.

'Raf! My boy! My son!'

Over her head I saw Giva come to the door with a babe on either hip. I put Mother down and went to kiss her and my sons, who bleated with alarm at my stranger's face and buried their faces in their mother's neck, bawling: 'Mah! Mah!'

'When will these rascals be old enough to know me?'

'When will you come and stay long enough to be known?' She bit her lip after she said it.

I took her face in hand and warned my sons: 'Move aside, you two. I'm your Dah, and I want to give your Mah a token to prove it.' I kissed her with great deliberation, then made great smacking noises on her cheeks, nose, and chin, at which the weanlings railed and Giva laughed.

My mother took the babes from her and put them on the floor. 'They'll never learn to walk, child, if you carry them all day. Come, come, let your man through the door so we can feed him, eh?' She spoke this in French, naturally, with a heavy Breton accent that Giva couldn't hope to understand. They had a problem communicating, but with their ready tongues the problem might be a blessing until they learned each other's ways.

I sat at the table, took the cup of cider my mother brought, along with a slab of bread and honey, then heard from my parents in confusing concert about their sea sickness, their homesickness, their suspicions of the locals, and their wholehearted approval of Giva and their grandchildren. Giva was very quiet throughout, busying herself with various little tasks and smiling dutifully at me when I glanced at her.

'Where are Fulcher and Osbern?' I asked. 'They're supposed to be building a new room for us here. Are they loitering, or what?' I didn't mean to share a sleeping chamber with them in the company of my wife, though none of them would have found it strange to do so, with the possible exception of Fulcher.

'They've gone to speak to a thatcher,' said my father, giving the thatcher's name with such a novel twist I didn't recognize it for a moment.

'He lives in Guildford.'

'There are none here that Fulcher will trust with the roof. The people here are good, but not wise,' he said charitably. 'If a man has a son to apprentice to a craft, he sends him to another village.'

'They are as stupid as cattle, these English,' my mother said, jerking her chin at the village in general.

'It's a poor vill, I grant you, but we hope to make it better, don't we, you, Father, and my brothers?' I spoke without conviction; I'd already begun to lose interest in the place, having decided to build a better house in Winchester when I was properly installed as abbot of Hyde. My gaze followed Giva about the room. I wanted desperately to get her alone to myself. My parents' company had begun to weary me, though I was glad to find them happy and well.

I said: 'I must go up to the tower and speak to the warden, by your leave, Father. The old man will be eager to hear the news, and he'll want to give me his accounting for the king's preserves here. Giva, come with me. Leave the babes to Mother. The walk will do you good.'

I took her by the hand and fairly dragged her through the door before she could find some excuse to stay behind. I sensed she hadn't entirely forgiven me, but I meant to make amends for our last encounter, or rather to erase the memory of it altogether with my ardor, if I could.

When we had passed the church, I veered off into the field, seizing her hand and running through the tall grass and ranks of purple foxgloves that grew almost to our shoulders on that fallow ground. She clutched at her veil and laughed, nearly stumbled, but put on a burst of speed that sent her ahead of me. I took fresh hope from that. When we reached the waterside where she did her laundry under the swaying willows that were already beginning to drop their yellow leaves, I spread out my cloak on the grass, plucked off her veil, and took her hungrily into my arms.

'Do you like my family?'

We had lain together for some time in contented silence. She'd been adamant on the matter of removing her gown, but I'd prevailed over her laces, which I made her leave open so that I could put my face between her breasts and savor the fragrance of her flesh.

'I like your father very much. He's as kind as Father Dunstan.'

'And only half as sour.'

'You mustn't say that. We have trouble talking. Or we did, until Fulcher came.' Her voice took fresh enthusiasm. 'He's been teaching me French and I've been teaching your father some English. It's not easy. I tell Fulcher the English word and he tells it to his father; then he tells me the French word. It's like a game. Osbern didn't think to do it that way, though he's been very helpful otherwise. He's a good playmate for the babies, very funny and dear, even if I don't understand him. He's almost like a babe himself, in some ways.' She smiled.

'Yes, I've noticed that. What about Mother? Do you get on? It's still your house, you know. You mustn't let her rule you, though she can take a lot of labor from you, if you'll allow her.'

'Yes. She – she loves the children. I'm not certain what she thinks of me. It's hard to read her face. She won't take part in the lessons after the day-meal, but I think she listens. Fulcher told me to call her *Maman*, but when I do, she doesn't seem to understand me.'

She sighed and stretched, then put her arms behind her head. I rolled on my side to examine her with admiration. She had matured since the birth of the twins, but only so much as to make her more desirable, not matronly. She'd had need of some increase in flesh, but I hoped she'd never grow slack and flabby as women do when they've borne children. Her body was my dearest treasure. I bent my head to kiss her breast.

'And what about Fulcher? Is he as amusing as Osbern?'

'Not amusing, but very good and patient with us all; very kind to me. I like him best of all.' The warmth of that hatched a little green serpent of jealousy in me.

'I'm not surprised, seeing how he's madly in love with you. Just don't like him too much, will you? Or I'll start to worry.' I said it very pleasantly, but she shifted her gaze from the flutter of willow leaves to my face, and her eyes clouded with instant resentment.

'Why must you say things like that? Can't you even have some – some charity for your own brother? He doesn't love me! That's silly!'

'Who says I don't show him charity? I got him out of prison, along with Osbern. I'm feeding and keeping them both, and I'll find them both places at court. But I didn't mean to start a quarrel.'

'It sounded that way to me.'

'I stated a fact.'

'Your sort of fact, right out of your head, with no proof at all.'

'He is heels over ears in love with you, damn it! I saw it happen with my own eyes when I brought him here this summer.' I tried to laugh at the memory. 'I daresay my father and Osbern are in love with you, too, but Fulcher was so stricken he rode from here to Winchester in a perfect daze. I only mentioned it because I thought you must have noticed.'

She sat up and began to straighten her laces. 'And I suppose you're going to say next that I encouraged him?'

'No! Giva, don't do this! Stop that! Come here!'

I pulled her fingers from the laces and dragged her down across me to kiss her. 'Why do we always wrangle? I'm with you so seldom. When I am I wish we could both be struck dumb, so we'd have nothing to do but make love, like this.'

She pushed herself up from me, her cheeks flushed with righteous indignation. 'Yes! That's all you'd ever like to do with me, isn't it? Nuzzle me, plow me, and tell me what I've done wrong! Well, this is where you've done wrong: Fulcher isn't in love with me and I never thought about him, but since you don't trust either of us and you've put the thought in my head, maybe I'll give him another look!'

I'd asked for that, but a red tide of venom flooded my veins when she said it. She tried to rise, but I caught her arms and held her. 'Will you do that? Will you bring him down here for the examination, or take him up to the loft? Do the old folks sleep sound?'

She stopped struggling. Her eyes spilled tears that splashed on my throat like hot wax. I let her go, vexed with myself, furious with her. She brushed the dead leaves from her gown, snatched up her head veil, and left me.

Jealous wrath is a hungry babe to nurse. It drained me before I could put on my boots and go up to see the old tower warden. I stayed with him until dark.

When I returned to the house, Fulcher and Osbern were there, full of tales from Guildford. They kept me at the table until late, telling me all the trifling difficulties they had encountered trying to find material and workmen to build my room. Giva sat mutely by my side through the discussion, her eyes shielded from me.

Mother took the babes into bed with her and Father, leaving Giva and me to climb to the loft to be alone. Giva put off her gown and lay down in her shift, her back to me. I removed boots and cincture, but kept on my clothes, as the night was chilly with a light September rain. I didn't touch her. I thought of how Fulcher had talked to me for several hours with Giva beside me and never glanced at her once. It was unnatural. It must be very difficult for him to do that. When I was gone again, where would he rest his eyes? What would she do with her discontent? On that unworthy thought I tried to sleep.

When I reached Winchester the next evening, all the talk was of how, as soon as Prince Henry and Robert de Bellesme set foot in Normandy again, Lord Odo had met them with an armed force and arrested them as traitors to Duke Robert. They were shut up in separate prisons. Robert de Meulan he had let go free.

35

Lanfranc died the following spring. His death wasn't unexpected, for he was in the extremes of old age and had been unable to attend either the Christmas or Easter courts because of his failing health. The king was grieved, but he must have felt some relief, too, as he had chafed to be under that constant eye. Still, for all the old man's meddling in trivial matters – such as the new fashions in dress and length of hair and his harping on the king's single state – Lanfranc would be missed. Unlike some of the other lords ecclesiastical, he ever had the king's best interests at heart.

When the news reached us I went down to Canterbury to take inventory of the archbishop's effects and to render an account for the king, who would be warden of the see until another archbishop was chosen.

I will never cease to be amazed at the outrage this reckoning of mine caused at a later time because when I was there the whole of Canterbury seemed far more interested in expelling the abbot of St. Augustine's than in mourning Lanfranc. The abbot, a Norman named Guy and a protégé of Lanfranc's, had been locked in a bitter quarrel with his monks since the old Italian had thrust him up their noses without a proper election. They had so far rejected him as to appeal to the townsmen for support, which stirred up certain troublemakers to riot through the streets for a matter they didn't understand.

Abbot Guy, for his part played the true Norman, having a small military force of his own to call on. When I arrived, his knights had just met some townsmen in the street and begun a head-cracking that looked as if it must soon involve every malcontent in the county. The people of the town tried to batter in the abbey gate and were so near to capturing Guy that he forgot his dignity and escaped from a window of his lodge to fly to rival Christ Church, where the brothers charitably let him in.

I took it upon myself to pay one of the abbot's knights to leave off skewering the town's pigs and dogs and ride instead to London and inform the king of the abbot's plight. Rufus lost no time in sending Gundulph of Rochester and Walkelin of Winchester to Guy's rescue with their own mesnies. The townsmen fled indoors, Guy came creeping forth from Christ Church to make his charges, the monks sat sullenly in their chapter house, while Gundulph and Walkelin heard witnesses.

They were firm and brief: the monks were at fault, no matter what Guy's defects. They had broken their vows by rebelling against their spiritual lord. They were all to be whipped, but because feelings had taken on a somewhat racial nature, no man among them must be able to say he had felt a sharper lash because he was an Englishman – or a Norman. Two scourgers were selected, one of each race, and the scourging was done in private, so as not to stir up fresh sympathy for the sinners among the townsmen.

I left Canterbury before the two fierce old men had gotten around to hearing charges made by Guy against the townsmen, but I understood they wouldn't get off easily. The punishment for rebellion is mutilation, since William Bastard revoked the death penalty after his own excesses at York in '68.

I returned to the king with what I felt was cheering news. The archbishop's estates, if Rufus would only hold them for a little while – say, until Christmas – would do much to redeem royal fortunes, especially when paired with the vacant diocesan lands in Durham, now that William de St. Carileph was banished.

'Well, now perhaps you'll allow me to hold my head up and answer the needs of my friends, here and abroad,' he said.

I laughed. 'My lord, do I constrain you? Well, I won't play the part of the good Lanfranc now and tell you to be at peace with what you have, since you still have far to go before you count yourself a wealthy man again.'

'Oh?'

'Yes. Last year was a bad one because of the war. The year before was poor because of the drought. The one before that – '

'Yes, yes, yes. There's always something, isn't there? What about this one? Will we have the plague of locusts, or what?'

I blessed myself. 'God forbid that we have anything but fair weather and good crops. But this spring has been very cool and wet, and the countrymen say – ' I saw I was losing him and brought my prophecies to a swift end. 'The good news is that we have peace on both borders, so we might let a few of the free lances go. As a matter of fact, my lord, though it's only a small expense, I wondered if you feel it necessary to keep quite all the hostages of the Welsh and Scots whom your noble father took in his last years. It seems we might have about a quarter of the royal blood of both countries here being fed and clothed at your expense, which on account of their being princes comes to no small fortune.'

405

He gave a yell of exasperation: 'By the Face of God! How damned stingy can I get? Shall I starve them? Shall I make them beggars? They're princes!' He asked with sudden interest: 'Who in Hell are they? Do I ever see them? Where are they kept?'

I had thought he wouldn't know and had made a list, as I had never seen some of them myself. They were kept in various obscure manors under the watch of careful guardians, so that they couldn't conspire to make mischief.

'You have the sister of the Queen of Scotland. Her name is Christina, and she lives at Romsey Abbey. In fact, she's become a member of the house and is one of the few hostages not at your charge for food and shelter.' I stopped, considering a thing that hadn't occurred to me before, but the king was very sharp that day and seemed to see my thought while it was forming.

'No, I won't take her for a wife! What do you want me to do? Rob God of virgins? Besides, I do remember her from when we were children, and she's fat – and homely. Get on with your list.'

'You hold the son of the King of Scotland, a young man named Edgar, at Huntingdon.' I saw by his face he didn't like the mention of that name and hurried on: 'There's a natural daughter of King Malcolm's as well, a girl about twenty named – '

'How old is Edgar?'

'I think eighteen or nineteen, my lord.'

'He isn't the eldest, is he?'

'No, there's young Edward, who is still in Scotland. Then there are the Welsh princes of various clans – ' I began to attempt to name them, though their names were as unfamiliar to me as heathens' names and difficult to pronounce: 'Bleary ap – '

'Oh, good God, Ranulph, if you're so interested in them, why don't you have them all brought down to court and we'll take a look at them?' He grinned suddenly in that appealing, childish manner he kept in spite of his wicked beard. 'We'll choose the picks of the litters and throw back the runts, if you like, eh?'

'There is another matter, somewhat connected with this business of the young hostages. It has to do with the royal wards. You see, Your Grace, when a subject of yours dies and leaves an heir too young to do you service, or to manage his – or her – own affairs, the Crown takes wardship of them, until the boys reach their majority and the girls are old enough to be married. This is at your expense, too. I've been thinking, it's hardly fair to ask the king to take responsibility for a man's children and get nothing at all for it. Their rents are held in trust for them until they can pay their reliefs, but it would be more sensible if their rents – which hardly ever amount to more than is sufficient for their keep – came to the Crown instead, during their minority. I have a list of wards that will surprise you – '

'No, it won't, because I'm not going to listen to it! Do as you think best, with Bloet's assistance. I can't be told about every knight's orphan in the kingdom before I've had my dinner, so take them in charge and – Ranulph, be a good father to them.' He laughed and motioned me to leave him.

It was much the same in the matter of the royal justices. The king held court wherever he happened to be, and any man with a just claim that touched on the royal interests might come before him and make plea. But he couldn't hear all the injustices in the kingdom. No man could. Therefore, his sheriffs heard pleas for the Crown in their shires and collected the fines imposed on the culpable.

But who kept watch on the sheriffs? They were great lords and quickly were becoming the wealthiest and most powerful men in England by their very simple expedient of 'farming' the king's rents, fees, reliefs, and fines. That is to say, they got for the Crown what it demanded, but whatever else they could wring from folk in addition was their own business. Often enough, that sum was half again or even double what they presented to the king.

Why should this be? I asked myself. Why not install royal justices to sit in the king's courts over all the land, men who were well acquainted with the law, but were in no position of wealth or family power to oppose the power of the king? In other words, why not choose clerks of no consequence but some learning to render justice in the king's name? They would be salaried men, and a watch should be kept on them to see they didn't start to live above their means. Whatever they might collect in the way of fines, rents, and fees had better be shown in their account rolls, or the people they robbed would have no fear of complaining about them.

I presented an outline of this notion to Rufus, supposing it would delight him, but the thought that *he* might have to choose a horde of faceless clerks to go out and do Crown business for him appalled him, instead. He put the whole matter firmly back into my hands and those of Robin Bloet.

Robin and I contended and fell out at once on the proper method of choosing these Daniels. Robin wanted young, promising noble-men, like himself, the very sort of men whose breeding and aspirations would lead them one day to expect a bishopric or an abbey for their services. I wanted common clay.

'Drudges! What you want are drudges – like yourself!' shouted Robin in exasperation.

'Yes, exactly! Not stupid, but careful. Not dull, but dutiful. Men of some age, who never expected and never will expect a higher office than they get. Their loyalty can't be to their names or their families, but only to us!'

'To you, you mean!'

'To me, then! And to the king.'

'Well, choose them yourself. Let me out of it. I've better things to do. Send a goat to gather a herd of sheep such as you want. A bellwether, rather.'

'Thank you, Robin.' Our friendship felt cooler weather.

There was a matter on which I dared not approach the king, nor could I confide in Robin: the matter of his squires and servants. I'd begun to keep a careful watch on any of his attendants who might seem too lady-faced. I had to tread carefully, because he would have such people about him; he must, and he must choose them. The king must never suspect how carefully I weeded out the bad prospects.

I couldn't say I ever discovered that he greatly favored boys. Those he had in his service he treated much alike. He was by turns strict or lenient with them, as a fond older brother or uncle might be. He genuinely enjoyed and approved the young men who strived hard to please him. He often liked to visit the yard to see them practicing at the butts or the quintain; he shouted rough advice to the clumsy, teased the overconfident, and sometimes even plunged into their midst to show them how they should foin with a sword, set a lance, or draw a bow.

It was what the rest of his court might think of his affection for them that concerned me. Those men who despised him for his love of Cormac had recently learned to respect him for his shrewdness and valor. I meant to see that not even a suspicion of his dealings with boys should fall on him undeservedly in the mind of a Mowbray, a de Eu, or a Bigod. Nor did I mean to let any Cormacs flourish near him again.

Like Lanfranc, I desired to see him married and the father of a son as quickly as possible. I still believed he was less perverse than misdirected in his affections, because of his pitiful lack of self-esteem. Men more homely than Rufus were yet great lovers of women – the gross-bodied Earl of Chester, for example. My king had never learned in his youth to meet the eyes of a woman with confidence, but he could learn. I would teach him to value himself.

He wasn't effeminate, thank God, like Hugh de Montgomery, who was brave enough in the lists, but who talked like a French abbess and swung his hips like a wineshop slut's as he walked. No, my king was only waiting to be wakened to the love of a devoted, sensible woman – if I could persuade him to try her.

My first thought on the marriage naturally was that the proper consort for a king was a king's daughter.

'What? *Who?* The daughter of the King of France?' He was openly astonished at my first hint, so much so that he forgot to be offended by my presumption. 'Fat Philip's daughter out of Fat Bertha? God's Face! Or was it one of the yet unborn babes he might get from his second wife that you'd have me take a lease on?' He laughed. 'Maybe somebody's got to make Philip a grandsire, but it damned well isn't going to be me! Why don't you take your proposition to one of my b-brothers? Either one will be glad to do the job for you, as long as the girl's breathing when they get on her.'

'It would scarcely be to your interest if they did, my lord. Unless you mean to dower the union with all the bribes you'd have to pay King Philip to keep him from making war on you in his future son-in-law's behalf.'

That stopped the laughter.

'Her name is Constance,' I said hardily. 'She's still quite young, so she may not yet be very fat. The French merchants who've had a glimpse of her say she's fair to behold, laughs often, and seems intelligent.'

'Wonderful! Let one of them bed her.'

'This maid is still too young to be bedded. But she might be betrothed. It's a wonder she isn't already. The man who contracts to marry her won't have to send for her at once, but he will have secured King Philip for an ally.'

'For what that's worth.' He folded his arms and sat down on his war chest, which was stuffed with all the beloved vestments for which he had no present use, which he so longed to put on for some great enterprise. He was still half amused with me, but he said politically: 'Well, I'll give it some thought. What should I demand for her dowry? All the bribes returned that my f-father paid Philip, trying to make a good ally of him?'

'You could ask for the French Vexin to be returned to you.'

He drew in a long, exasperated breath. 'Christ, Ranulph, what a weaseling bargainer you are! That would set Robin and my uncle on their destriers, wouldn't it? If I want the Vexin, I can think of a better way to get it.' He waved off my next speech. 'Well, well – I'll think about it. I will! Now, for Sweet Jesus' sake, go away and let me have a rest from that brain of yours.'

I hadn't seen my family for nearly a year.

They weren't neglected or in need. Fulcher and Osbern were charged with giving me regular reports on my father's progress in learning English, enough to hear his flock when they made confession. He'd had to call on old Dunstan to come over once a week to do that for him. My mother I knew to be in good health and of growing reputation among the natives of Godalming for her herb lore. My sons were toddling about like drunken geese, said Osbern, and jabbering in a mixed patois of French and English. Fulcher said, when I inquired of him, that Giva seemed to be happy and well.

Fulcher and I were not intimate. I valued him above Osbern; we understood each other's meaning well, and he was a conscientious worker at any task I gave him. Truly, I didn't suspect him of having any success with Giva, or her of encouraging him. I was ashamed of my jealousy on that matter. Only, we couldn't seem to warm to each other except in the case of duty or general family welfare. I wasn't too surprised when he begged off from accompanying me to Godalming, saying he preferred to remain at St. Paul's to study. He and Osbern were members of the chapter now, thanks to me. Osbern was up in York at my behest, making himself unpleasant in a very amiable way to an unpleasant man: Ralph Paganel, the high sheriff. I went home at last, alone.

It had been a sorry year for orchards and fields, as I told the king it might be. Winds had shaken the fruit down still green. Rains had swept over the land unceasingly, far into the summer, and the weather remained cool and cloudy, so the grain not stunted by storms was slow to ripen. The fallow fields and pasturelands were rank with thick grass bred of those rains, yet it seemed to lack nourishment for the cattle that fed on it. They grew lean as they grazed, and the cows bawled in grief for calves so spindly they sank down dying even as they were pulling at the udder.

August came, with heat and choking dust, now the rains seemed exhausted. I reached Godalming on the afternoon of the feast of the Transfiguration to find my church decorated with garlands of wilting flowers and the fields empty of laborers.

The whole village was convened in the street and churchyard, watching or taking part in various frolics and games. I passed a pair of grunting wrestlers inside a ring of red-faced, shouting men, while in the middle of the cow path opposite the rectory the village children were holding a three-legged race, abetted by their yapping, running yellow dogs.

My mother was the only one at home when I entered the rectory. She rose from the settle where she was peeling some spotted, puny Lammas apples and threw her wasted arms about my neck. When we had done all our kissing and complaining about my absence, she got out food and drink for me, screeched at a child in the street to come and take my horse to pasture, then sat down to examine me with her one good eye.

'What's this Osbern's been saying to me about Father and a cloister?' I asked to divert her questions. 'I thought he was happy here.'

She made a face and drew up one shoulder. 'It's the same old tale. He wants to repent of me, if you can believe it. I think he made a vow once. Every day he gets older, it bothers him more he hasn't kept it. Why he should worry when there hasn't been anything to repent of for years, I can't tell you. The old fool! I repented of him long ago without having to be shut up in a cell to do it!' She cackled and smacked me on the arm. 'Oh, but when we were young, boy, it was true mortal sin and no mistake about it!'

'Would it bother you if he went? You wouldn't be alone, you know – if it gave him peace – '

'Let him do what he will. He always has!' She sniffed and looked away pensively, her chin drawn almost up to her nose with resignation. Then she shot me a look. 'Wouldn't be alone, would I? I would, if you were all I had to look to for company. What ails you? Why don't you come here and see your woman and your babes? What do you expect of this girl? She's young, with the blood still hot in her. She needs a man in her bed and more babes. Why don't you attend to that?'

'Mother, you know I'm not my own master. There are no women in the king's house, so I can't bring Giva to me. And he wants me by him, so I can't come here more often than I do.' Which was not altogether true. She knew it.

'Why hasn't he got a woman of his own? He's no boy, now. Is it true what they say in Bayeux that he only does with men? That's why our good Bishop Odo made war on him in the duke's name, they say. Not that Robin Shortshanks is so much nicer, mind you.

They say he doesn't care what kind of meat's served on his platter, so long as it's tender.' She waited in vain for my reply to that. 'I see. Raf, I could give you a good spell to put under his pillow and something to put in his drink that would make a man of him in an hour – or kill him with trying.'

'Mother, you must leave the old lore in the past, along with your lost cow. I don't want people hereabouts saying my mother is a witch.'

'Who says I'm a witch? I'm a good woman! A woman who knows a bit about the good medicines Our Lord put on this earth to help us in our need. That's all. Some men have too much lust and need cooling. For them I make a paste of mouse dung to rub on their testicles. Some have the dropsy. I give them a little juice of the foxglove, only a few drops to put in their drink, to draw the humors out of them. Your king has a malady that can be cured, just as other ailments are cured – and I was only making a joke with you when I said it would kill him. At the worst it could only make him queasy.'

I laughed and got up to stretch, ready to plead saddle weariness to escape her pressing that remedy for the king on me, but she pushed me back down on my stool and began to rub my shoulders as she continued:

'There was a young man, once, at St. Loup, who was like that. He was near to twenty years old and didn't know how to make himself pleasant to women. His mother came to me, weeping . . . ' She went on with the edifying tale until I broke free of her, insisting I must get an hour's sleep before the rest of the family came home.

'Where are they all, by the way?'

'Visiting that old fool Dunstan and his wife. If he wasn't so dried up, I'd say you had something to worry about. Giva dotes on him. So do her boys.'

I went into the new room, which I had never seen until then, and lay upon the bed. It was suffocatingly hot. My sleep, when it came, depressed rather than freshened me. I woke to hear voices in the other room and went in, yawning, to find Father, Giva, and the children with a bowl of blackberries Giva had picked at Dunstan's house. Giva was laughing at some event my father was describing to my mother when she turned and saw me. Her smile sickened. She bit her lip, looked irritated with herself, then came to kiss me dutifully. I squatted before the two boys, who stood leaning almost backward when I spoke to them. They put their fingers in their noses and cut their eyes up sadly at their mother, who urged them to acknowledge me. I kissed them each on the cheek and rose, sighing at the outdoor smell of them.

We talked politely, had a pleasant meal, after which I went to the church with Father to say Vespers. The sweating revelers came willingly to hear me, making the whole church smell like a pigsty. We returned to the house where, after a rather prolonged and embarrassing time of putting off bedtime, I said I would be getting on up to the warden's tower and would sleep there, rather than put too many people in one bed in such heat.

My mother was outraged. 'What for? Why should you do that? What will people say when they see you come here, then leave your wife to sleep at the tower? This is wicked! Thurstin? Say something, old man; say something to your stupid son!'

My father looked abashed and annoyed. 'What do I have to do with it, woman? Ranulph must do as he thinks best. He may have made some private vow you know nothing about. We must respect chastity when we find it. There isn't much of it to be seen.'

'Chastity? What nonsense is that? A chaste husband sleeps with his wife, not in some strange bed. People will say he doubts his *wife's* chastity if he does that, *that's* where chastity comes in! Raf, are you listening to me? You'll sleep here, properly, or give me reasons. Where's Giva? Why doesn't she come and say something to you? Because you've shamed her, that's why. Go to bed with your wife, like a proper man!' She came close and whispered in my face: 'You haven't taken up the ways of that king of yours, have you? I'll believe it, if you go.'

So, I stayed. Giva and I, made even more uncomfortable by the outburst, slept in the same bed without the boys, who had been taken, mewling, to bed with their grandparents. When Giva pinched out the cresset, we lay side by side in silence. I was humiliated to be in such a position. If she had turned over and laid a hand on me, I think I might have leaped out of bed like a startled virgin. I didn't want her, even after so long a time. It was too hot. She despised me. I had shamed myself by letting her see I could be jealous of her. She couldn't possibly bear me to touch her either. It would be a confirmation of all she had said about me before, that my only thought was to plow her, then quarrel. We'd have no quarrels this time.

Our days and nights continued in the same uneasy manner for the next several days. Before my parents we were proper with each other. Giva called me 'my lord,' which vexed me, while I called her Elfgiva and hated myself every time the name escaped my lips. I was

miserable, rose every morning determined to leave, then remembered my other fault was that I never stayed more than a day or two.
I kept as busy as possible, making small repairs to house and church,
saying my Office, hearing confessions, not to mention complaints,
from the villagers.

My father was the only person who seemed to think my behavior
natural. He confided to me his belief that he had few years left to
live. We talked at length about his entering a cloister. He had a
yearning to exercise his ability to read once more before he died. He
wanted a house with a good library. I recommended Canterbury,
which would put him near enough to London for me to reach him
when he was taken by his last illness. We agreed I would look into
the matter for him before winter came.

He tried to encourage what he saw as my new life of celibacy: 'It's
a good thing to have grandchildren, my son. It was a joy to me to
have you and your brothers. Children are a blessing to a man in his
old age. But you do right to live as you do now. Don't let your
mother shake your vows. Giva is a good young woman. She has the
love and fear of God in her heart. She understands what you must
do, I'm sure. But you must see she's provided for. A virtuous life
can't be had at the expense of another person's well-being.'

I agreed, dumbly, then said I'd always see that Giva and Mother
were well housed and cared for. 'I mean to put my sons in the school
at Hyde when they're old enough. Giva may come and live in
Winchester, if she likes, so she'll be near them while they're young.'

My own words made my heart sink. I knew I wasn't chaste. I had
only grown cold. Was I really finished with women? I was thirty
years old and a year more. My blood had cooled, it seemed, without
my knowing it. I had been a week in the same bed with a vigorous
young female body and never once desired it. In the whole year I
had been away from her, I hadn't gone to the stews and no hearth
girl or kitchen slut in any royal manor could say she carried a replica
of me in her belly.

That was all it was: I was simply growing older, as all men do, and
the lusts of the flesh meant less to me, now I had enough useful
occupation to fill my days and make me ready for a good night's
sleep. Immediately I thought of my age, I recalled that the king was
only two years younger. If I was going to get him married I had
better do it soon, before his already chilled blood became torpid as
my own.

I decided suddenly that to stay longer in Godalming would only depress me. I had done well: quarreled with no one, neglected no one; now I must go and be about my proper business. There was no reason to come there again. Fulcher or Osbern could take care of our family's needs as well as I, and when it came time for my father to go to his well-deserved rest in a cloister, I would have one of my brothers bring Mother and Giva to Winchester – if they wished to come. Otherwise, I wouldn't force them.

I must tell Giva this; then I would go. She must know I wasn't angry with her, held nothing against her, and that she would always have a safe home while I lived.

I found her outside, sweeping the step free of poultry dung.

'Come out and walk with me. I have something to say to you in private.'

She gave me an odd look, put her broom away, and removed the heavy smock she wore to keep her gown clean. I started walking before she was quite ready, so she had to catch me up outside the gate. It was a sullen, breathless day; the air was stagnant with village smells and barn smells. The sky had the greenish look one sometimes sees before a windstorm, but there were no heavy clouds, only that strange haze.

The village dogs were whining at nothing. I was surprised to see how active the cattle were as we entered the western pasture. On such a day they usually congregate under a convenient tree and sit like boulders, chewing their cuds. A flight of birds swooping low over the fields put them to bawling and kicking like yearling bulls. The horses that belonged to the tower caught the unrest and began to run and bite at each other's necks. Summer madness, I thought.

I'd already brought Giva out far enough to speak to her without being overheard, but I kept walking, feeling some of the animals' restlessness, and she paced silently behind me. In spite of the dust and the heat, the act of walking seemed to cool my brain – though I hadn't yet chosen exactly what I would say to her.

We were approaching the end of the pasture where the ground rises to a low ridge lined with trees. Beyond the ridge lay the road to Guildford, which led on to Winchester and Portsmouth in one direction, London in the other. Within an hour I would be on that road and a happier man for leaving.

I stopped, rather than climb the hill, caught up a piece of grass to worry in my fingers, and said gracelessly: 'I'm leaving today. I don't see any reason for me to come again, unless you have need of something that my father or brothers can't provide. You'll be relieved to be rid of me. When Father goes to his cloister, you may stay on here, or come away, if you don't think you can get on with Mother. I'll let you keep the boys until they're seven, then – '

I was feeling suddenly quite ill. The sweat that ran down my face seemed cold. I wiped my mouth with my hand. Giva was staring at me strangely. My head swam briefly. I thought: My mother's tried out one of her damned potions on me to put me in rut.

Giva said: 'What are you angry about now? I thought we were living peacefully this time.'

'I'm not angry! I hope – someday – you won't be angry with me, either. But I can't see the use of our being together here when – we – ' It wasn't that my head was spinning; it was as if my whole body were trembling very slightly, or as if the whole world were trembling while I remained still. I closed my eyes and felt Giva clutch at my arm.

'What is it? What's happening?' She stared around wildly, then up at the birds, which flew so near us as they made repeated attempts to settle in the trees on the ridge. Each time they tried they seemed to be frightened away again. The lowing of the cattle at the far end of the field had reached a terrified pitch.

Suddenly I lurched; Giva shrieked: 'Oh, God! Oh, Blessed Virgin!' and fell heavily against me. There was a tremendous slipping sensation, as if my soul had just left its mooring in my body; but it wasn't me, it was everything. The very turf beneath our feet seemed to give way and sink.

Giva screamed again. There was another dreadful shift and we fell to the ground. One of the largest trees on the ridge slowly bent until it toppled over and fell down the hill, its roots snapping with a sound like that of a great crossbow shooting a bolt. As it fell, it took away a large section of the earth beneath it. The birds swirled over us, squalling like demons from the Pit.

I tried to rise and saw the hunting tower jiggling like a cup on a table where men are playing rough games. The south part of the palisade snapped loose and leaned out over the edge of the motte, then fell, slashing through brush and young trees like a boning knife.

'Is it the end of the world? Oh, God – oh, Ranulph, the babies!'

I grabbed the back of her head and made her bury her face in my breast, so that she couldn't see the maddened cattle that were racing toward us, and might have trampled us, but the falling tree shifted a bit farther down the hill and frightened them into turning.

I lay on my back with Giva clutched to me, staring up at the sky.

Was it true, then? Would the heavens open and the archangel's trumpet sound to call the Blessed up from their graves? Were the dead hands pushing the dried earth aside from their faces this minute, getting ready to answer that awful summons?

The shaking stopped. We lay together as if lightning-struck, afraid to breathe or cry out for fear of being found by a vengeful God.

There was no sound, none. Giva might have been dead, except that her fingers were still piercing me with their sharp nails. I shifted painfully to put her by, then lifted my head to look around. I could see a dozen or more little people, no bigger than ants, running about at the edge of the bailey yard, trying to discover what had happened to their palisade. There were faint cries of wonder, shouts of amazement and shock, but no screams of agony, no dead voices raised in praise of God for the Resurrection. There was nothing very unusual at all, except that I seemed to be able to see with more clarity, smell with greater sharpness all the herbs and flowers of the meadow, see the colors of the earth and sky as if I had never seen color before.

'It was an earthquake,' I said in wonder, because I'd only just realized it. 'I've heard of such things, but never knew what the word really meant before this.'

'An earthquake? Oh, Ranulph, what about our house? And our babies? Oh, God – '

'Shh, shh! It's all right. Can't you tell? Everything's all safe – we're safe. Can't you feel it?'

I had no way of really knowing that, but I knew. Whatever it was God had meant to achieve with His earth-shaking, it had nothing to do with punishing us. I gazed down at Giva, struck by how lovely she was, as if I had never truly seen her before that moment. She was awesomely beautiful and alive. The rough weave of her gown was wondrously woven. I touched her face, her hair, the little pulse that beat at the base of her throat.

She put her hands to my face, too, then cupped my head and drew me down to her. We kissed and groaned and wept, and coupled like drunken revelers on a Lammas Eve in the long grass of the cow meadow.

No one in the vill or up at the tower had been injured by the earth's upheaval, though there was a good deal of damage to roof beams and well shafts. Our babies had slept through the whole event, their bellies filled with porridge and buttermilk. I stayed another week to help make repairs to the house roof and to mortar up the cracks that had opened in the wall of the church nave. With all the other men of the village I worked from dawn to sundown in a plowman's smock, my cassock put aside.

Every night until I left I lay with Giva in the thrall of a new passion, dying the little death between her moist thighs, kissing the sweat and eager tears from her face, and never knowing whether it was God's miracle that brought me back to loving her, or the working of one of my mother's potions.

36

Elfgiva bore our third son the following May, whom my father made haste to baptize with the name of Elias. My specific wish to have a male child baptized William went straight out of his head, when Fulcher brought him news that Duke Robert Curthose had wed his eldest bastard daughter to a splendid knight named Helias de Saint Saens. A loyal Norman, Father simply forgot where he was living and which of his former master's nephews he served with his flattery.

I had been with Giva as much as possible in the intervening months, but it seemed I was never destined to see a child of mine come into the world, or to have the least bit of influence on his Christian name.

That May I went to Normandy at the command of the king, who had delayed as long as he felt capable before taking a hand in the sorry affairs of Robert Curthose. Duke Robert had sanctioned the imprisonment of Prince Henry and Robert de Bellesme at Odo's behest, but this brief show of strength hadn't cowed his contentious subjects.

When the rebels of Maine began to defy him he suddenly needed the strength of Bellesme's border garrisons to march with him to Le Mans, but Bellesme, whose release from prison had been won from Duke Robert too easily by the threat of retaliation from Earl Roger Montgomery, preferred to stay at home instead and pillage his nearest neighbors.

Duke Robert's weakness in giving in to old Montgomery earned him the scorn of all his vassals, who were in a constant state of strife, uniting with one another this day to prey on some other, turning against each other soon after, to lay waste to that which they had pledged each other to defend.

For King William to have entered this melee directly might only have served to unite all Normandy against him – for a day. It seemed wiser if he ventured in a step at a time, acquiring a purchased friend here, making certain of a bought neutrality there, until he had a base of support in case it ever came to actual battle between him and Robert Curthose.

I began my peregrinations with letters from my king to certain men, reminding them of their debts to him, their sworn fealties, their ties of blood – whatever might move them. I went quietly with a little nonentity of a clerk named William Warelwast and my brother Fulcher, carrying baggage that would seem normal for three clerks on a quest. I had a hamper filled with blankets, a few extra shirts, and a rolls budget, all of which fit easily on the back of a mule and left him strength to carry one or the other of us at a time. Around my waist – and very wearisome it was to me – I carried several purses of coin of the purest silver: earnest money, I believe the merchants call it.

We paid our calls without exciting undue interest or suspicion. At Eu, Earl Robert's son William was made to understand that in exchange for being forgiven his treasons and rebellion in England, he now owed his king assurance in Normandy. He saw how it would be wise policy if King William aided him at Eu by enforcing his garrison with men of the king's choosing, indeed, by letting him replace the entire garrison with paid men of my king's – and his. This simple agreement cost the king nothing but the transporting of the men.

Rufus hadn't planned that. He thought it would take a great deal of coin to bribe such great men. But he would have appealed to their sense of pride, which often is expensive with such people. I appealed to their caution and, with just a hint of the priest in me, to that sense of sin which may yet be punishable here on earth.

When we finished matters in Eu, we moved to Aumale. Count Stephen, Rufus's cousin, was the nominal lord, but his mother, the Countess Adelaide, the Conqueror's sister, was the true authority. That old lady was more than disgusted with her nephew Duke Robert and her half brother, Odo. She would have taken in our entire English host, if it had been available, and made her own war against them. We had a most amicable agreement, and I got the promise of a future meeting, to discuss the port of St. Valéry, by which the king might bring in his reinforcements without putting himself to the trouble of seizing a port from Curthose.

All well and good. We went to Longueville to speak to that most ancient and honorable Norman, Roger Beaumont, who had been the Lady Matilda's counsel when the Bastard left her to make himself the master of England. Roger Beaumont had been too old to fight at Hastings twenty-four years before, but he was still in control of his faculties and he had no use for Curthose.

Old Beaumont was Earl of Warwick in England as well. His son Henry would be his heir there. His other son, Robert de Meulan, was his mother's heir for much of the Norman Vexin and stood to inherit the rest of old Roger's Norman estates. Between them they held vast territories that would be torn asunder if Normandy continued its decline. They had been faithful to the Conqueror and had tried to be true to Duke Robert, but I showed them how they might keep better faith with their honor through allegiance to his other son.

I'd thought to pay a call on the King of France, to sound him out on a marriage between his daughter Constance and my king. I hadn't received permission for such a conference, and King Philip was in a bad way for making contracts that involved the Sacraments, as he had just been excommunicated for putting away his first wife to marry the truant wife of the Count of Anjou. Poor, gullible, gluttonous king! Poor, lecherous, wry-mouthed Fulk of Anjou! Both had been hoist on the pole of ridicule by that woman, Bertrada de Montfort. Her family had forced her to marry Fulk, who was disgusting, and who already had three wives. She concluded that if a woman must be wife to a disgusting man, the man might as well be a king. So, she made eyes at King Philip when he chanced to be their guest one season; then she wrote to him afterward. She appealed to his vanity in some fashion, making him believe he had overwhelmed her heart with the mere appearance of his gross belly and tiny, squinting eyes, until he was convinced he was madly in love with her and must put his soul in the fire to have her.

So he took her from Fulk. Now, wherever he went it was forbidden to ring the church bells and he might not wear his crown or robes or celebrate any festival in royal state. In fact, all that was left for him to do was to eat hugely and lie abed with the steel-souled Bertrada – which condemnation seemed to suit him very well, except that it put him in danger of war with both Anjou and Frisia, the home of his betrayed and cast-off wife.

He needed a friend. I thought he might prefer that friend to be a son-in-law and my master, rather than Robert Curthose, who was proving of very little use to him.

But before I could arrange a meeting with King Philip, I heard of a civil war in the county of Evreux, on the eastern borders of Normandy, where William, Count of Evreux, was pillaging the lands of his kinsman and neighbor, Ralph of Conches. These men had been two of Curthose's strongest allies in the days of his quarrels with his father. Ralph of Conches was that very lord whose knight Amiot de Trie I had buried at Gerberoy.

Now these two warriors, Evreux and Conches, one much older than the other, were at each other's throats because of the jealousy of their wives. Innocent monks were being routed from their meditations and hapless peasants clubbed insensible, because two women had set their tongues to wagging against each other.

Evreux had done great damage to Conches's lands, but in doing so he had lost a beloved nephew. It didn't make their anger less, but only their grief the more, that this nephew was the twin brother of the lord of Conches's wife! These rages between people of the same blood are always of the cruelest kind.

I went to Conches alone, because the road there was through country decidedly unfriendly to my cause and a priest alone is as good as invisible. I sent Warelwast home to give the king report of our success, and Fulcher to see that Father was comfortably settled at Canterbury before he moved the rest of the family to Winchester.

The peninsular hill on which Conches is built rises sheer out of a low, swampy plain. There are other, distant hills beyond that plain and a thick, dark wood to the north which is a natural barrier between Conches lands and those of Evreux. Though the warring towns are no more than three leagues apart, they might as well be separated by a mountain range for all the difficulty of getting between them.

Above both Conches and its vill on the very crest of the hill is the Abbey of St. Peter's. It was an impressive little kingdom, that high hill, and its queen was Isabel de Montfort, lady of Conches, a woman to put one in mind of those female warriors whom the Greeks called Amazons.

She was waiting to receive me – a woman past her youth, but of what age I couldn't say. She was very tall for her sex, with blonde hair and clear, intelligent eyes under straight brows. She looked me over when I bowed to her as if she might presently require me to show her my teeth before she would purchase me.

But her speech was very sweet: 'You are welcome, good Father. Do you always travel alone? It's a dangerous business these days. What if someone discovered who you were? Come and walk with me in my herb garden for a while; then we will have our supper.' Smiling, she took my arm and drew me out to a little walled herbery with a pool and stone benches around it.

'I was dismayed when my steward told me you were to be my only guest. I hoped my plea would bring someone more warlike, if you'll forgive me. But you are Will-Rou's friend, I hear. His dear friend?'

'Madam, I am his chaplain, and he has entrusted me with the hearing of your husband's cause.'

'Hearing it only? It will take more than a confessor's ear to cure our troubles, Father. We are abused by our neighbor, and it's more to his shame that he's our uncle as well. We want soldiers, or soon we may need only a sexton to bury us.'

'Lady, if your noble husband gives me reason to believe a friendship can grow between this house and my master, you may have them. Or he may intercede for you in some other way. That is for them to discover. Is your lord at home?'

She had been gazing at me still with the keenest interest, and I saw a little spark jump into her eyes when I mentioned that there might be some form of aid short of war in the case. But she looked away to her flowers and let go my arm as if distracted by them.

'My husband is away to court again, to complain of our last intrusion, Father. You will speak to me, I think, or else wait a weary time.' She plucked up a stem of some fragrant plant and put it to her nose, then held it under mine suddenly.

'You're very outspoken for a priest and rather too good-looking. Is this a disguise you wear, perhaps, to get you safely through dangerous country?'

I took off my hood and showed her my tonsure. She smiled and touched the herb to her lips as if to savor it, then tossed it away.

'Ah, yes. Well, perhaps it's no mystery that in Will-Rou's court even his clerks should be fair-faced. Is he still as homely a man as he was a boy? I've noticed that an ugly man will often surround himself with pretty fellows, if he can, whereas a plain woman wants plain servants.'

I felt myself begin to stiffen. I hardly knew whether I was meant to take these remarks, which bordered on the insulting, as evidence of her stupidity or her displeasure that I hadn't brought an army at my back. She seemed to hold my master in contempt, yet expected miracles from him.

'Lady, my king is a man who values deeds, not appearance. I hope you will do the same. If I find ample reason here, I can bring you more substantial tokens of a king's regard than myself.'

'You can do this without consulting with him overseas? Or has he come to dwell in one of the castles you've invested for him now?'

I thought it time she answered questions for a change. Instead of answering I said: 'Lady, we run on so quickly, I begin to think you'd have me back on the roads again before I've caught my breath from my last ride. I didn't see any armies of enemies when I came to your gate. There's no smoke rising from ruins here. Your husband still has enough confidence in the duke to apply to him again for redress of his griefs. Perhaps you don't need my assistance at all. Are you cut off from any road you must travel? Do they burn your hayricks at night? Has your lord taken all his garrison with him and left you defenseless? Will your uncle come tonight and storm your gates? If so, we must make our petitions to the Almighty, because, only He and not my king could give you help in time – if it were so.'

She drew in her breath, then let it out in a laugh. 'Of course, you're right. I am pressing you too much and too soon. Forgive me, good Father! You must be parched. I'll have some wine brought out.' She clapped her hands, and a servant who had been lurking just inside the door made an appearance, heard her desire, and went to bring wine. Meanwhile, she invited me to sit on one of the benches and take my ease. She sat near me and began a recitation of the harms done by the Count of Evreux, after which she questioned me very intelligently on the affairs of England since my king had driven out his uncle. She was especially interested to hear about the earthquake, which had shaken all the southern part of the kingdom and made itself famous to those who took it for yet another sign that God was displeased with His Creation and meant soon to bring it to an end. 'Do you believe this, Father?'

I started to say something about how no man can hope to look into the mind of God and foretell His purpose, but she heard the gong sound to announce that the tables were laid for the evening meal and got up to bring me into the hall. I was relieved, because as we had spoken she had kept her eyes so constantly fixed on my face that I felt as if I had been singed. I caught myself thinking, If I'm not careful this woman will have me in her bed tonight, and eat me for her breakfast shortly after! Tavern wenches and hungry whores look men in the face like that, not great ladies.

As we went up to the high table, we were joined by her own chaplain, one or two elderly men I took for officers of her hall, and a young man, or tall boy, with a dreaming face, whom she called to her and fondly kissed.

'This is my son, young Roger. He had a most remarkable dream soon after we heard of your earthquake. Tell the priest your dream, my love.'

The child, who looked to be about twelve or thirteen, dropped his head and murmured that it was nothing. He was old enough to be serving in some other house as page or esquire, but he had the look of the tonsure on him and I suppose his parents had already seen it.

'He dreamed that Our Lord came to him, laid a hand on his head, and said, "Come to Me, beloved, and I will show you the joys of life." What do you think this can mean, Father?'

Looking at the boy, who was uncomfortable to the point of tears, I thought of Baldwin de Fourneaux, dreaming of Heaven, yet dreading to confine himself for the promise of it.

'Perhaps it means your son has a vocation to follow Christ in a holy life, my lady – rather than an intimation of the world's ending. Has he thought of taking Holy Orders?'

'He can't do that! He's our only son, who must rule here one day. I've told him I think it must mean he will make a pilgrimage when he's been made a knight, in which case I will go with him to the Holy Land. I've always had a curiosity about the heathen who rule there.'

The poor, whey-cheeked son of this Hippolyte smiled piteously when he met my eyes. We went to the table.

There were few people at the table that evening, the main body of male inhabitants having gone to Rouen with Count Roger. I was unaccustomed to taking a meal in the company of so many ladies, but it delighted me at first to hear the conversation between them and the younger men. It was inconsequential, but a pleasant change from the grimness I had endured of late in the halls of Eu and Aumale. The subjects of their talk were the coming marriage of one of the young men and his probable sexual prowess, which they gauged by the size of his nose; it was somewhat longer than average.

I rather expected the lady of Conches to put an end to this teasing, for the sake of her own dignity and that of the several clerks and elderly men, but she did no such thing. She smiled at the nonsense for a time, then broke in with an observation about the King of France, which she had no doubt gotten in confidence from her sister, his new queen, which made the whole hall roar.

After a time she turned to me and asked, 'What do you think of young Harry, your master's brother?'

'I think it a shame Duke Robert holds him in prison only for coming to visit us last year,' I said dutifully, having no intention of joining in a discussion of his carnal capacities.

She smiled faintly. 'Oh? Then you'll be pleased to hear he's out of prison now and all his properties have been returned to him.'

'That is good news.'

'And Robin Curthose has made him his chief adviser in the matter of how to prevent Will-Rou from getting a hold on the north country.'

I nodded gravely.

She laughed. 'You really knew nothing about that, did you? Yet you took it down like a honey posset. You're very good at smooth answers and wise looks. Is that how you must behave when you open your lord's bedchamber door and find him under the sheets with another man?'

Others had heard her speak; there were titters from the lower table and her young son stared at me, pinch-lipped.

I felt a flush of anger climbing up my neck, but I said very quietly, 'I have never done that.'

'Oh, really? Then perhaps you're the man between the sheets.' Now there was general laughter.

I put aside my napkin and rose from my stool. 'Madam, this talk ill becomes you, as it ill becomes me to hear it. I'll leave you now. I've come a long way today and must give thanks for a safe journey, if you have a chapel here. If you have anything further to say to me that bears on my visit, I will speak to you tomorrow.' I bowed to her and to the abashed boy by her side, then left the table and crossed the hall to a stairway, as I thought the chapel should be above us.

I half expected her to lose her temper and call me back for leaving without her permission. It would have been unthinkable to do it if her husband had been there. I heard whispers behind me, but no imperious commands.

When I reached the upper gallery, I walked along it until I found the chapel, dark except for the vigil light, as Vespers had been said. I went to the small altar, blessed myself, and said my prayers. I hardly know to which Aspect of the Deity I addressed myself, since I was still seething with anger for her unexpected insult. I heard soft footsteps coming along the gallery as I prayed, but was in no hurry to see who had followed me. It was probably her senile-looking chaplain come to tell me of his mistress's displeasure.

When I got to my feet and turned around, I saw it was a woman, standing just inside the chapel door. Her head was cocked to one side, her hands folded sedately at her waist. She wore a black veil, a mourning veil. I didn't recognize her from among those in the hall I had been nearest. I waited coldly to hear her message.

'You've hardly changed at all, except that you've put on some flesh that you had need of,' she said.

'Madam?'

'You don't know me. Oh, Ranulph, how ungallant! That must mean I've changed quite a lot – or a vast lot of other women have come between us in the meantime.' She came closer. 'The last time I saw you in a place like this you were dressed in nothing but my husband's shirt and a sheet.'

'Isabel? Isabel de Trie!' I peered at her in the dim light, astonished.

She laughed a little crestfallen sound and held her hands out to me. 'Yes. Twelve years do make a difference to a woman, no matter what her age before.' She took my hands and gave each a squeeze. 'Please don't look so horrified, my dear. I'm an old woman; I know it. But I hope I haven't turned into such a crone as to frighten you.'

'Isabel – no, you haven't changed that much. It's just that I never thought to see you again, let alone in this place. Is your new husband one of de Conches's vassals, too?'

'My new husband, as you call him, has been dead three years, my dear. And please don't say you're sorry to hear it, because I'm glad to be a widow again. He was a brute who'd had three wives already and thought he'd outlive the fourth – but God and I fooled him.' She glanced back in the direction of the gallery. 'I can't stay away too long, or she might suspect I came to see you. Ranulph, you must come down and speak to her again. I didn't hear all that was said, but whatever it was, you can't make her angry with you, even if you come from a king. She isn't like other ladies you may know in England, truly. You had better come and make your peace soon. Perhaps after that we can find a time to talk. Oh, if only you knew how glad I am to see you.' She lifted herself on tiptoe and kissed me quickly on the cheek, then hurried away.

'Wait! Isabel!'

She turned rather reluctantly and came back a step.

'What's the matter with her? If she wants my help, why did she insult me? Is she setting some trap for the king, or for her husband? She doesn't seem to think much of him.'

'Well, she's cuckolded him enough! I don't know what she wants of you, my dear. It may be she was only testing you, to see how you'd jump. She likes to do that. Please, I must go now.'

I remained in the chapel, thinking for a little time, then decided I might as well say my neglected Office before I went crawling to the lady of Conches. I might need the goodwill of Heaven. Before I finished I heard tables being scraped aside and the laughter and shouts that presaged some game to be played.

When I entered the hall again, the younger women and men were leaping and falling about in a game of Catch-Me, while the more sedate members of the household stood or sat along the walls, watching them. The lady of Conches was absent. I, too, stood watching the silliness, which was familiar to me, but which I was unaccustomed to seeing played by women. Their part in it changed the rules somewhat, so that the man who caught them didn't content himself with slapping them heartily on the back, enough to knock them over, but tried to catch them with both hands, so as to fondle them.

In a while everyone was breathless and the game turned to Hoodman Blind. As the blindfold was being put on a buxom girl already giggling with anticipation, one of the hall servants approached me and told me his mistress desired to speak with me in her bower. I followed him across the hall, just avoiding the clutch of the 'blinded' girl, who was puzzled by the whoop of laughter that went up when I shrank from her.

I found the lady sitting at a table in her little room, which boasted a real fireplace in the wall, in which scented wood was blazing. I had made up my mind in the meantime that I could pass the time pleasantly with her, no matter how she taunted me, because I should be gone from her house very soon, whether we reached an agreement or not.

I bowed. 'My lady, I hope you will forgive my brusque manner with you earlier. I was much wearied with my journey and eager to say my Office. If you permit me, in the morning I will make my apologies to any others in your household I might have offended, or they will take me for a very rustic sort of fellow, which indeed I am.'

'Father, it's I who should ask your forgiveness, as you perfectly well know, and so I do. Please come and sit down. I'm having wine and cold meats sent up to us, as I know you didn't have a very good supper. Please –' She indicated a stool on the other side of the table, on which there was a chessboard with the pieces laid out as if the game were in progress. 'Do you know this game? My sister sent it to me as a New Year's gift, but only one young man from Paris who was with us for a time this summer could give me any useful help in playing it. It's a pretty thing, isn't it?'

It was. The pieces were of ivory or bone, one side's set having been dipped in vermilion. The board was of inlaid woods, light and dark. The figures, unlike the heathen types I had seen more often, were images of a king and queen, two bishops, two knights, and two stout towers. The pawns were men-at-arms.

'I know a few good moves. Are you familiar with the moves of the individual pieces?' She was. We began to play the game, I going slowly until I was accustomed to the change in the figures. She soon revealed that she was more than a little skilled in the game. It had been my thought to let her win a game or two, but I soon found I could play her as if she were a man, and I put my mind rather to saving myself from disgrace. A servant came with the wine and food, but we ignored it for the length of half the game. From time to time she made some comment on my skill, which was flattering, or on her lack of it, which was unnecessary.

'Father Ranulph, you took offense when I mentioned the inclinations of Will-Rou, which I thought were common enough knowledge everywhere. I'm very sorry for it. I knew him when he was a boy. He used to come to my uncle's house, or to my father's, when the old duke was alive. My father and uncle weren't always of like mind with Duke William, so I was taught to suspect him and his sons as well. I've known Robin Curthose for many years, and I've had no reason to change my opinion of him. The youngest son I know little about, except that he's able to turn his coat inside out and back again in an hour. Robin Curthose is a fool who will listen to any other fool who advises him. If he changed his shirt as often as he changes his mind, he'd be a pleasanter companion at the dinner table, though he's an able enough lover of women, in spite of his stench – or so I've heard.'

She lifted her lambent eyes to my face for a moment, then moved a pawn to confront one of my knights. 'So, you must forgive me if I doubt your king has any sort of purposeful mind. Men such as he are often ruled by their favorites, in which case one must deal with the favorites – or else rise every morning not knowing what sort of weather to expect. Are you such a favorite? Don't think I'll condemn you for it, but I must know with whom I am really making a pact and how much I may have to pay for it.'

'No, my lady, I'm not such a man. There isn't such a person in the king's company now, and I believe there won't be again. He's not a man who likes to be ruled by another or made light of by his enemies. He's a true knight and a good soldier – '

'Oh, dear God, do you believe that nonsense, too? I thought a

428

priest and a woman might speak together without resorting to that phrase – "a true knight"! What is that, can you tell me? I've known knights and soldiers since I was off my leading strings, and I've never known a "true" one who wouldn't forget his *courtoisie* if there was a denier's advantage in the forgetting.'

Coming from such a woman, this was so surprising and so downright that I had to laugh. She smiled, then joined me in laughter as she reached for the wine flagon and poured us each a cup. It was heady stuff, very sweet and heavy with spices. She offered me meat, took a morsel herself, and tore it with her teeth, still laughing.

'Are you amused with me, Father – or at me?'

'A little of both, if you'll allow it, my lady. I must confess, the subject of *courtoisie* has often puzzled me. If it weren't for my master, I wouldn't be able to conceive of it at all, but he takes his vows much to heart. I've known him for many years now, and I've never known him to break his pledged word. Does that satisfy you?'

'Not entirely. Why are you laughing at me, too?' She poured more wine.

I sobered and said more politely: 'Not *at you*, my lady; rather, because of you. I've never spoken with a gentlewoman who asked such direct questions, gave such – honest opinions, or looked so straight into a man's eyes while she did. I hope I won't distress you' – I didn't think I would – 'if I say that the pleasure of speaking to you, once I got over the surprise, is the pleasure of speaking to an exceptionally intelligent man.'

Her eyes traveled slowly down my face as her half smile all but faded. 'Am I less the woman for that?'

'No, you are not.' I thought it time to return to the game board. I moved a piece, but she didn't respond.

She said: 'Perhaps that was only the answer you thought you must give. Perhaps you have heard that on more than one occasion I have taken the field with my husband's mesnie, clad in mail and enarmed. That is true.'

'I hadn't heard.'

'Yes. I've never yet shed blood, but I have seen it shed. I can pull a bowstring and send an arrow into a target and find the center as well as my husband. I can put on men's dress and ride astride as well as a man. I have held this castle for my husband during the years he was with Curthose in exile and no one took it from me, not even Duke William, who said it was forfeit because my husband was a traitor.'

'You are a most valiant lady. Your husband has cause to be proud of you.'

She held my eyes so long after that I drank my third cup of wine in too much haste and said, 'It's your move, my lady, and your queen is in danger.'

'My husband is a great fool,' she said huskily. 'He's allowed himself to be held up for a traitor, exiled, and shamed. He runs to court and bends his knee to Curthose and begs him to help him keep what I've kept for him all these years. He lets my uncle insult him and raid his fields; he lets that witch who's my uncle's wife say things about me, and about him, that he should cut her throat for saying, if he were really a "true knight," or even a man.' She stared at the chessboard with a sudden frown, as if the pieces offended her, then shoved them off their squares with an angry gesture.

'My husband is a weak fool and I'm bound to him for life! Who can blame my uncle for attacking him? And, when he's attacked, my lord doesn't give back double his injuries. He goes begging for help – to a man who can't help himself, let alone us!'

She got up to pace the narrow room, then turned again as I was rising from my stool in deference to her. She came and stood before me, tall enough to confront me eye to eye.

'If I had the rule of this place – I want my son to inherit, but he may not. Robert of Bellesme may gobble us all up. He may even be the next Duke of Normandy if your king is too slow driving out Curthose. Do you think Will-Rou knows that?' She grasped my arms. 'Priest, if I could have Will-Rou's aid, his men, his arms, I would drive my uncle out and make my son Count of Conches *and* Evreux. I would! I am a de Montfort and a woman who should have been a man. I would pledge myself to Will-Rou – if he will pledge with me – and some good might come of it. If you told him this, would he treat with me? Would his word be good to him, if he gave it to a woman?'

She saw my hesitation and let her arms fall to her sides. 'Ah – I've asked the wrong question, I see. You told me *you* could call on the king's host, if you heard good reasons, didn't you? And you haven't heard them. You've looked at me all evening with those dark eyes and you've been thinking, "Here's a woman who wants to be rid of her husband." I've kept you overlong. My chamberlain will show you where you may rest. Good night, good Father.'

37

I was lodged in a chamber high in the tower, with one lancet for light and ventilation. From it I could see the side of the hill that sloped up to the abbey. Without cresset or candle to keep me awake, I still lay thinking of the lady of Conches, who seemed to want me to grant her aid, not to chastise her enemies, but to drive out both her husband and her neighboring uncle, so that she could rule all Evreux in the name of her sickly-looking son.

She had answered her own question, as she said. I couldn't urge my king to make a military pact with a woman. He would lose the confidence of every baron I had bribed for him; every lord at home who had conspired against his life would accuse him of condoning the possible murder and certain overthrow of a peer by his wife. Nature itself must cry out on the unnatural yearnings of this she-wolf.

But, Christ! What a woman! I could still see her jewel-stone eyes shining at me from the recesses of my brain and hear her low, determined voice in my ear. God must have a special care of Ralph de Conches to have kept him safe in the bed of such a creature.

Isabel de Trie had said the lady put horns on her lord repeatedly. If his wife's estimate of him was correct, he was a poor fish and possibly deserved her disdain, but who were the men brave enough to be her lovers? She had given thought to using me for that purpose; even without Isabel's timely word, I had caught that in her face almost from the moment she saw me. She had discarded the idea of me, as a weapon unworthy of her sheath, for which I might thank my good angel, I supposed. But in a cold bed on a long night it was difficult not to meditate on what it would have been to lie with her. She was a Circe who now chafed at keeping pigs and wanted to suckle panthers.

On that thought I decided I had let myself drift into vain fancy and tried to get some sleep.

I woke chilled and found the floor wet with rain that had been driven through the lancet by the rapidly cooling winds of mid-September. I rose in haste and put on my boots, my gown, and my cloak. My beard craved a razor, but I had no water or basin, I had been set so precipitously in my guest chamber. I went to the heavy oak door to call for a servant to bring me aids for washing and found the door shut tight against me, bolted from the outside.

For a moment I thought it had been bolted by error, the act of a servant who didn't know I was within, but when my shouts brought no response, I knew for a certainty that I was confined on purpose. Further bellowing was of no use. I sat down on the bed to wait.

Shortly after Terce the door bolt squeaked back, and the door opened just enough to let in a page with a tray of food. I repressed the urge to rush the door and throw myself against whoever held it from the passage side, but I stood ready for another caller. There was none. The smooth-haired, dark-eyed boy put the tray on the table that should have held basin and ewer, gave me a swift, curious glance, and made for the door again.

'Wait! Boy, who's on the far side of that door? Am I a prisoner?' There was no answer from without. The boy paused, glancing at me over his shoulder. 'What's your name, my son?'

'Martin, Father.'

'Martin, since the person holding the door is too shy to speak, will you carry my message? Will you tell your mistress that I've given thought to her speech to me and would answer her?'

'She isn't here.'

'No, of course she isn't. She's in her hall, or her garden. But will you go and tell her that I may have a remedy for her troubles?'

He turned and appraised me with his somber child's eyes. 'I mean, she isn't in the castle. She's gone out riding with the men.'

'Ah! When she returns, then.'

He half shrugged and squeezed himself through the opening, which promptly shut behind him and was barred again. I sat down heavily. Patience was my only remedy. What would it profit her to keep me locked up, when her husband would soon return and hear rumor of me? Or would he? I reached for the beaker of wine and the half loaf of bread on the tray. At least she didn't mean to starve me to silence.

The same boy came again an hour past None, with my day-meal. Once again I stayed him, hoping to find him more communicative. 'Is the lady in the hall now, Martin?'

'No, Father.'

'She's gone hunting, I suppose. Is that it? Does she keep a merlin or a kestrel? They're both fine birds, aren't they? Which do you prefer? You're about old enough to start training a bird of your own, I'd think.' The stolid child refused to be drawn into a discussion on the topic dearest to the hearts of castle boys his age. We both glanced at the half-opened door, as if we were conspirators, but then he picked up my earlier tray and said in a low voice:

432

'She's ridden out with the soldiers, to see where – '

'Boy – tend your duty and come along,' said a male voice in the passage. Martin hastily backed away from me and ducked out.

So, she'd gone out with the men of the bailey to see about something, perhaps to investigate rumor of a fresh attack by the Count of Evreux. Or could she have ridden toward Rouen to meet her husband? If that were true, did she mean to tell him some tale of my insulting her, or threatening her, to explain my imprisonment, so that he wouldn't hear me when he came home? I began to think what she might invent and so far gave way to my agitation as to spend some five minutes beating on the door and yelling for release. Then I sat down to eat my dinner and think.

I moved the little table over until it was beneath the lancet window, which was somewhat wider than those cut farther down on the tower. It had an embrasure nearly four feet deep, into which I climbed and worked my way up by fingernails and boot toes until I got my head and one arm out the opening, but could go no further. All I could see was a misty sky and a sheer drop beneath me of some fifty or sixty feet to the stone-bodied hill. I hung there, wishing some idle soul at the abbey would look out from its walls and see me, or I might hail him.

But what good would that do me? The Abbey of St. Peter's was a foundation of the de Tosny family of Conches and depended on their goodwill for its maintenance. If their patroness put priests in prison, that was her affair and not one on which they would likely intrude.

When a light supper was brought to me after Vespers, I didn't speak to Martin at all. I had a denier in my palm, which I offered him in silence, which was also the way he took it.

The next morning I was ready with another coin. As he bent to put the tray on the floor before removing the previous one from its table, I whispered, 'Isabel de Trie.' He glanced up, startled, then grabbed the denier and fled.

At midday I repeated the gesture and the name. 'Do you know her?' He barely nodded. 'Tell her about me – please.'

I lay on my bed, waiting. I waited until after midnight before I heard a movement at the door. She must have oiled the bolt and the hinges as well. I sprang up. 'Isabel?'

'What have you done? What did you say to her? I told you to be careful.' She put out her hands to find me; I caught them, drew her close, and we clasped each other cheek to cheek, in order to speak in the faintest of whispers.

433

'I didn't do anything. I didn't refuse her anything, only she thinks I meant to. Isabel, where is she now?'

'There was a tithe barn burned at the manor near the wood. She took two knights and seven men to see about it. They should have been back yesterday night. Ranulph, I'm afraid she might have been killed!'

'I hope to God she has been!'

'No! If she's dead, the count's men will be here soon to murder all of us.'

'No, they won't. They might come and invest the keep, since there's no one here to defend it, but they wouldn't kill women and servants. How many men are left guarding the walls?'

'I don't know. Not many. Oh, God, what will we do? All the women are afraid we'll be murdered, or worse – and I think so, too!' She began to weep, and her voice rose to a treble. I pulled her farther from the door, but a loud sob burst out of her that no hushing would suffice, but one. I took her head in my hands and kissed her suffocatingly, felt her hands grip my wrists to pull herself free. I kept my hold, forcing her mouth open the better to stifle her tongue.

In a moment she loosed her hands and put them to my face, then sighed and let her head fall on my shoulder when I ventured to release her.

'Oh, Ranulph, you must be as frightened as I am, to do that. It's been a long time since anyone kissed me.'

She put her arms about my neck and I drew her to the bed, where we sat holding each other. She was no fool, but still too much a-tremble to hear any plan of mine that might put her in a moment's jeopardy.

'Nonsense,' I said in her ear. 'You're still as beautiful as you ever were – more so, in fact. Why hasn't somebody married you, now you're ripe as an Anjou peach?' I fondled and kissed her again. 'Do you remember how we were, on that hill outside Brionne? It was like this.' I sank her to the bed. If it took plowing her to get her goodwill I'd do it, though my lust was as cold as a beggar's hearth that moment. Her hands soothed my head and shoulders, drawing me down until I concluded I must do it, but then she groaned and pushed my face away from hers.

'Oh, Ranulph, you're *such* a whoreson liar, now! You used to be so sweet; I believed everything you said. What is it you think I can do for you that makes you willing to run up my skirts?'

'Get me out of here for a start! Find me a door that can be opened without waking the dogs. Get me to the postern gate and find me a hood to cover my tonsure. Isabel, you owe me something. Remember how I took leave of you last time? I'm not able to go sliding down rooftops now.'

She laughed silently, putting her hand to my mouth. 'You deserved that, you know, for what you'd just done to me. I told you you shouldn't try to see me there, and you were unkind to tell me about Amiot the way you did. But I was worried about you. I thought you'd break your legs and the dog would eat you.'

'Your cousin nearly ate me instead.'

'I know. I'm sorry. But it was funny, seeing the dog jump out the window and go slithering down after you! There was such a rain of tiles; we had to have a new roof!'

'Shh!' We listened for the sound of footsteps, but it was only one of the long-toed hounds that patrolled the keep at night. Isabel eased herself away and sat up.

'Well, it might just be possible to get you off, except for horses. I don't know how to get them.'

'I'll go on foot, gladly!'

'Yes, well, but I can't and Martin would tire too easily.'

'What are you talking about? I said nothing about taking you with me. Why should you want to go? This place is safe enough, even without a full garrison, if they keep the gate closed.'

'Then you can stay inside it with us and wait for the men of Evreux to come, because if you don't take me – and Martin – we have nothing to plan.' She said it in the calm, firm way one would warn a child.

'How can I do that? You might as well ask me to take the whole castle on my back and move it to a better place. Isabel, that bitch of a mistress of yours wants me to give her the means to do away with her husband – a plan she won't want repeated in her lord's ear. She tried to seduce me with wine and soft looks; then she saw her mistake, and now she thinks I'm dangerous to her. I have to be gone before she returns, or I won't leave at all.'

'Well, husbands can be a nuisance. I should know. But I'd almost as soon have my old wife beater back again as to stay here and be her servant the rest of my life. So, I have a sort of plan. I was just thinking – '

'While I was making love to you? You *haven't* changed.'

'Do you want my help or not?'

'Yes, but not your company, I'm sorry to say, or that of a knob-kneed boy. What's he got to do with it?'

'He's your son.'

'What?'

'Haven't you looked at him? Three or four more inches and he'd look just like the boy I picked out of my pig paddle.'

'This is no time for one of your infamous lies!'

'He's your son. I ought to know! My late husband wasn't in any doubt about it either. My cousin had the lack of foresight to sell me off to a man with fair hair and blue eyes when I was already three months gone. That boy cost me many a bruise, and he's the reason I didn't get my widow's portion from my husband's estate, because his children knew there was a cuckoo in the nest. So, you owe me a favor, too, don't you?'

I put my head in my hands, but in a moment said: 'Very well. How are we going to get out of here?'

Martin didn't want to go. I never knew just what his mother said to him, but he continued to sulk and give me bitter looks for several days. I couldn't blame him; he hadn't been mistreated by the lord and lady of Conches, and he hadn't contributed to the misunderstanding that sent us packing. He was pulled away from where he wore fine clothes and was fed on dainties, to skulk through the rains and autumn fogs with his rather disregarding mother and a suspicious-looking stranger, who had evidently offended the lady and deserved to be locked up. He never did thank me for those deniers I'd been pressing on him.

In the dead of night we crept downstairs, stole a couple of cloaks that had been carelessly hung on pegs, and passed through the back passage to the kitchen, where we made off with enough food for a day's journey, as well as some meat to throw to the dogs. We were shadowed through our stealthy movements by a brindled mastiff with hackles raised in distrust. At that hour of the night no one moved during his watch. Isabel threw him a chunk of gammon, which he swallowed more in surprise than in gluttony.

Led by Martin, we descended through a trapdoor in the larder to the ground floor, where great casks and hampers held food for the castle and there was a byre for two milk cows and several nanny goats that supplied the kitchens with fresh milk. A cattle boy was asleep near the drowsing beasts, too. We took our time passing him to get to the door to the bailey ward, which Martin unbolted.

It was raining heavily, which was a blessing, because those men-at-arms left behind who might have been sleeping on their pallets in the open air had taken refuge in the upper keep or in the low huts built against the inner bailey. Also, the noise of the downpour spattering from the water runnels and falling noisily into water barrels set to catch rain for the laundresses covered the sound of our footsteps to some degree.

Still, we slunk along past the stable, where we dared not steal horses, to the postern gate. We waited there for several minutes because the guard on the wall-walk above us had paused just above the gate. He was cursing the rain but, already soaked, stood in place for a while, as we stood under him, our backs to the wall. I couldn't see how we would be able to go out without attracting his attention. But in a few moments there was a call from the main gate and the man moved away to answer it.

The town dogs were barking, stirring up the castle dogs, which ran out from their various dens with upthrust tails. The lady of Conches and her escort were coming home in the middle of the night in that deluge, which bespoke a defeat of some sort on her. Curiosity on that point was never satisfied, because it was our moment to slip away.

I was turning toward the town side of the path, but Isabel caught my arm and said in my ear: 'No! The abbey.' She was right, of course. No townsman would have let us in, and few of them would have even let us take shelter under their poorest shed without advising the castle in the morning. The monks of St. Peter's were obliged to admit travelers, and if Martin kept silent, there was little reason for them to know how short a journey we had made to their door.

We rang the sanctuary bell and were let in by a compassionate porter, who gave us dry gowns to put on and allowed us to bed down in the nave of the church on straw pallets kept for the purpose. I told him we were from Damville and were on our way to Evreux with a petition for the bishop.

'When we told the men at the castle gate our destination, they refused to let us come in, because of some difference between the lord of their house and the lord of Evreux. Thank God we saw this holy place above us, or we surely would have drowned tonight.'

The porter didn't look too pleased to discover he had let in people refused at the castle, but I thought this tale might keep him from mentioning us to the abbot, who might take the news down the hill too soon. He gave us blankets and left us to return to his own sanctuary by the gate.

Isabel slipped away into the dark of the church to exchange her wet gown for the penitent's robe. I stripped where I was. Martin sat down on his pallet. He was weeping. I tried to comfort him:

437

'It's a brave thing you've done. There aren't many boys your age who'd have the wits to guide me so well. I thank you for it. When we come to the parting of our ways, I'll have another reward for you.'

I didn't know where I'd be able to rid myself of Isabel, but I hoped she'd be content with the first castle we found next day. Martin, wiping his runny nose, turned his back on me, until Isabel returned and commanded him to take off his wet clothes and go to bed properly.

I took my pallet and left them to their own corner of the nave. When the monk came to ring the Prime bell, I didn't want him to find anything to gossip about.

It took no Prime bell to wake me. I was up at the first hint of grey light coming through the windows. I went quietly to find my own clothes, which were still wet, having been left in a heap on the floor near where Isabel and Martin still slept. I meant to wring them out and see if I could hang them somewhere out in the wind, which had risen in the night to blow away the rain. As I bent to gather them, I happened to glance at Martin, who lay nearest them. It was possible to see him clearly by then, though the sun hadn't yet risen. I knelt for a moment by him to see if I could tell he was truly of my flesh.

In sleep, his face had lost the wary, or sullen, look that was all he had shown me until then. He was dark enough of hair to be mine, but his skin was fairer and his bones finer than those my ancestors had given me. His thick lashes lay like drifts of soot on his cheeks; his lips, slightly ajar with sleep, were well formed and colored with a tint of rose; his ears were shapely and close-set; and the hands that lay upon his breast were long and slim, like Isabel's.

I looked up to see her awake and watching me. She lifted her head and said softly, 'Well?'

The good abbot let us dry our clothes in his slype. He heard the faulty tale I had concocted about accompanying my sister to the bishop to seek a dispensation for her daughter to marry a fifth cousin. He invited us to take the day-meal at his table and must have wondered why we dawdled so long before taking leave of him. We didn't set forth until I judged the people in the castle were taking supper and wouldn't notice three foot travelers on the way to town.

If it had been possible to buy a horse I would have done so, as the sight of an obviously wellborn woman on foot was enough to create interest, if not suspicion.

There was no way for us but to walk the swampy fields, the oozing cattle paths, the rutted cart roads, until we found Beaumont-le-

Roger. We might have made the same journey in a couple of hours if we had ridden. Afoot, with Isabel in her soft shoes made for no rougher surface than a manor floor, we were traveling until nearly midnight. We hadn't gone half a league before she broke down and wept for weariness and pain, falling to the road on hands and knees.

I let her rest for a few moments, thinking the mud she was sinking in would disgust her more than her weakness. Martin bent over her, trying to lift her, but she shook her head dumbly.

'Come on, Isabel, get up,' I said. 'You would start this journey. Now you've no choice but to finish it.'

'Don't speak to my mother like that, you damned priest! As if she were a – a common woman! If it weren't for her, you'd still be locked up, where you deserve to be!'

I looked at his pale, wet face, streaked with dirt and blazing with indignation. 'I beg your pardon, young chevalier. My *gracious lady*, since you can't go on, I suggest you stay here until you're rested, then let your son take you back to Conches. You may tell your mistress I forced you to come with me.'

'No!' She lifted her head and one muddy hand. 'Martin, help me up!' He did, still glaring at me. He put his arm about her waist to steady her.

'We're ready, then. Come along.'

I was heartless – perhaps. I couldn't see the necessity for their fleeing Conches, where they seemed to have been quite comfortable, and I was eager to find a shelter somewhere and get the use of a horse. Also, as we had walked, I'd been recollecting how my lady had used me once, then left me when she had no further use of me. I had no desire to make a second venture to satisfy some whim of hers, and suffer for it at the end of the road. I would have difficulty explaining how I came to have her in tow, more difficulty finding a place to settle her. I wasn't about to go near her damned cousin again. It wasn't beneath her to tell him I'd abducted her, if it would save her the inconvenience of his anger.

She and Martin limped after me until her feet were bleeding and Martin cried out in a voice breaking with fatigue that she must rest or die. By then we had reached drier ground. Isabel crept to the grassy verge of the road and lay down, quite beyond moaning or making complaint. I examined her feet. Her shoes were in such tatters that they were doing her more harm than good. I removed them and threw them away.

'Martin – you don't object if I call you Martin, do you? Good. Your mother needs something to bind her feet. I have nothing to use, but you have a very fine shirt. I'd suggest you take it off and we'll tear it into strips to bind her up.'

'My shirt? But it's the only one I have!'

'That's true. Take it off.'

'But what will I do, when people see me and – '

'If we should happen to meet Duke Robert wallowing in the mud on the road ahead, I'll explain your plight. Now, take off that shirt at once, before I forget my holy gown and pitch you headfirst into the nearest ditch!'

I tore it and bandaged Isabel's swollen feet. 'Why did you insist on this? Why? You had everything you could want there, but you must ruin yourself and this boy – and me! If the lady's found out we're gone and sends her patrols looking for us – stupid – '

'I want to go home,' she said in a faint, petulant voice. 'I wanted to go home when Arnulph died, but they sent me to Conches. I want Marie and my own bedchamber again – and my own house.'

'Why wouldn't they let you go home?'

'Because my cousin holds the estate. He says – it's for my daughter, so she'll be sure to have a dower if she marries. He says he must keep my rents for a long time, to repay himself for all the trouble I've caused him, but that's not true. He'd never give them back.'

'Then how in the name of all the saints can you go home? If he knows you're there, what will he do? Marry you off again, or drive you out on the roads? He isn't likely to kiss and make up, is he? I remember him well.'

She groaned as I pulled her from the ground. 'I don't know. I don't care. If I can only get home, I'll stay there, somehow. I'll think of something to say to him.'

'And what about the boy? What future will there be for him? Have you thought of that? You should have left him at Conches.'

She swayed and I grabbed her arm, put it about my shoulder, and grasped her by the waist. It wouldn't do. I must carry her, or leave her on the roadside. I pulled both her arms over my shoulders so that her body rested against my back and her feet just cleared the ground.

The gatekeeper of Beaumont-le-Roger was doubtful I was the same man who had left him such a short time ago, or that the silent, mud-smeared creatures I had with me were truly a lady and her son. But the sight of Isabel's bleeding feet softened him to the point of admitting us into the bailey. I picked Isabel up bodily and carried her up into the castle, to the constable's hall, where his wife was aghast at my pitiful burden. She called for her ladies, and together they bore Isabel away to be bathed and cared for.

Martin and I were shown to the lavatory, where we washed ourselves as best we could. The castle chaplain very kindly lent me a gown so that my own could be washed and dried. Martin's shirt was more difficult to replace, as the constable's lady's page was a good deal younger and smaller. He had to make do with a shirt of one of the servants, much patched and not very clean.

He refused it coldly, turning his head away from the boy who had been urged to offer it.

I took the shirt and thanked the boy, then took Martin aside and said for his own private ear: 'You're a disgusting little peacock, and your life in a fine castle hasn't taught you enough manners to clean a privy with. This boy had two shirts to his name and now he has one, yet he gave you the other and you can't thank him. The lord of Conches is well rid of you, I think.'

He was Isabel's own child; faced with his faults, he looked astonished, then took refuge in tears very proudly shed. 'I'm a gentleman's son. I can't wear a dirty servant's shirt. I'd rather go naked,' he said.

I squatted before him. 'Boy, you may yet have a chance to go naked in this world. I'm a king's emissary, but I'm glad for the rags this house's chaplain lets me wear for a few hours. Do you suppose I'd do my king honor to go naked before decent people?'

He looked at me. His expression said it made no difference what I did, as I was no gentleman. I took the shirt and returned it to the servant boy, along with a coin for thanks. Then I got myself a straw pallet and lay down to sleep. Martin sat on his, knees drawn up under his chin, for to lie down on such a bed without covering for his arms would be like trying to nest in a briar bush. I closed my eyes and let him suffer it out.

When I woke at dawn, he was curled into a miserable ball, his hands clasped over his upper arms for warmth. I went to find my own gown, put it on, then brought back the chaplain's and laid it over the boy. Once more I bent over him to have a look at those features which were supposed to be mine. I concluded they were. Isabel's cousin Beroald had said that she was with child by me, when he finished lacing my back with those scars I still carried. God pity this poor scut! I could give him nothing he would accept, and his mother had given him nothing he could use against a harsh world but a useless pride and a false idea of his parentage.

I left him sleeping and went to make my apologies and farewells to the keeper of the tower, to whom I committed Isabel and my son until they were fit to travel again. I took the gift of a horse and set out on my long journey that would now take me home to Rufus with a report on my success in suborning the northern border to his cause.

I thought it unlikely that I should ever see Martin again.

38

When I reached London with my burden of family feuds, crooked alliances, pillage, betrayals, and cold murder done in Normandy, Ralph of Conches got his aid from the king by the next ship to sail. We heard tales from every incoming ship of further decay in the order of Curthose's duchy. Robert de Bellesme and the whole of the Grantmesnil family were at each other's throats over the castles Bellesme was building on every promontory, without license from anyone but himself. The Grantmesnils were related by marriage to virtually half of Normandy, so their sense of outrage was quickly spread, until it seemed Bellesme was at war with everybody but Curthose, who was too cautious, or too indolent, to take measures against him.

One heard all sorts of rumors about Duke Robert: that he was imbecile with drink; that he snored in his bedchamber until None and let Odo hold his courts for him; that he had quarreled with Odo and now got his advice from some monk named William d'Arques, or Edgar Atheling – or even from his barber!

Early in November we received a messenger from Gerard of Gournai that was more shameful than all the rest. The king paced the council chamber as the courier recited, giving the young man such baleful looks while delivering such savage curses that the poor fellow could hardly finish his report.

'Fool! Fool! Fool! The damned, s-sorry half-wit! Raf! Tell the chamberlain to call in the council – now! They deserve to hear this.

Yes, get all the damned priests who've been crying for every penny I've s-spent – e-es-especially old Turold of Peterborough.'

I obeyed. The lords of the council who were with us were hastily assembled, having been rushed from the chapel as they finished hearing a Mass, which the king nowadays had begun to miss with as much frequency as he attended it. Rufus watched them come in, smiling and nodding grimly in a manner that said, 'See? What have I told you?'

'Now, my lords,' he said when they'd taken their stools, 'this young lad has come to entertain you. Listen to his song.' He shot a hand out at the courier, who had begun to sweat, but who bravely began to repeat his story:

'My lords and venerable Fathers, I come to tell you of grave events in our – '

'Trim out the poetry, will you? This is what happened in Rouen last week. Now, say it!'

'There was a citizen of Rouen, a Breton named Conan, my lords, who kept an estate as if he were a count, though he was little more than a merchant – '

The king sighed heavily and the young man blanched, but continued: 'This Conan was discontent with the way of the duke's rule over the city, so he sent word to my lord Gerard of Gournai, with whom he was acquain—'

'He knew him, yes! What did he want of him, boy?' urged the king.

'He told my lord how things were in such a state of unrest in the city that if any host friendly to the English king should come to its gates, the citizens would let them in and aid them in taking the tower.'

'There! There, do you see what it is to live in Normandy these days?' Rufus interrupted. 'Go on, boy. Get to the meat of it – and try to make your master look good, will you?'

'My lord Count Gerard de Gournai tried to send word of this Breton's offer to Your Grace, through your chaplain, but couldn't find him, so he thought it best if he answered the city's cry for help without more delay.'

'Cry for help, yes – '

'He raised a host of some three hundred men to march on the city, which he had raised up – '

'Like Jesus raised up a banquet out of a fish basket, I guess. Where'd he get so many so soon, eh? Never mind, go on with it.'

'He – but – Duke Robert had also heard of this plot against him, and he sent summons of array to all his chief vassals. When the citizens who supported Conan heard of the duke's preparations, they were afraid they'd be overwhelmed before their own help came. So, they began their riot ahead of the time, ran through the streets throwing stones and yelling "Death to the Drunkard!" and overcame the guard at the Caux Gate. While they were at this – '

The king intruded again, impatiently: 'While they were at this rabble-rouse, friends, my brother Robin was hiding in his keep, afraid to show his face to his own garrison, for fear they'd cut his throat. But some of his levies began to arrive on the other side of the Seine, my little brother Harry among 'em. Harry – listen to this – Harry came over the river and through the gate with three knights behind him. Three! Why so many? The gates of that damned town might as well be turnstiles, you'd think! Go on, for God's sake, boy! Why do you keep s-stopping?'

'Yes, Your Grace. Ha— Count Henry had joined his levies to those of Count Gilbert de Laigle and Helias de – '

'What are we doing now, embroidering a tapestry? Let me te-tell it, then. Our good friend Gournai's miraculous army comes whistling through the north gate at about the same time Harry and de Laigle's levies come up from the river. They meet in the marketplace and start to cut each other into collops. Meanwhile, Harry has found brave Robin and slipped him out through the postern gate down to the river and put him in a boat. He has him rowed over the water and taken to some little cloister nearby – like a foundling babe! My f-father must be groaning in his g-grave!'

'Now – the town's turned into a shambles. Nobody knows friend from foe – so they just chop heads wherever they come to 'em. But Harry is the hero of the day. He comes back to the castle and finds that Breton bastard Conan, who started the melee, standing out in the bailey with a half-dozen piss-down-their-hose *citizens*, bawling out for the duke to come and save them from the soldiers!

'Harry takes him by the arm and asks him just what it is he wants from the duke, and the bastard says, "Justice." Justice! By the Holy Face! Well, he got it. Harry dragged him up through the tower to the battlements and pitched him off without giving him time to say his prayers. Then he had the body tied to a horse's tail and dragged through the town streets – which cleared the streets of horse droppings, but didn't stop the pillage. Yes, pillage! Everybody took to it, no matter which side they were on, and tore the town apart. Have I got the story straight, boy? Not left out any heroes?'

'No – yes, Your Grace!'

'Good! Give him some wine. He looks parched.' He slapped his hands together and surveyed his council. 'Have I said m-my brother's a fool?' He laughed in that shrill way that made the unwary jump. 'But what do we care for Robin's hard times, eh? God and my f-father gave him Rouen to rule, or ruin, so let him have it. You'd have to wonder: who'll he get to taste his meat and drink for him after this?' His eye fell on old Bishop Gundulph, who was quietly weeping for his native city. 'He's safe enough for the moment, so why should we weep? Why should *we* weep, or spend good English silver to s-s-stop these cousins of ours from rooting up our fathers' land, like hogs in a beech grove? What do we care what happens to those towns, or houses, or churches that our grandsires built and shed their blood for? Christ! It would be poor economy to take a few coins from you God-fearing servants of the Lord, to hire men to keep those holy houses you learned your prayers in from being burned by such scum as my brother has for subjects, wouldn't it?'

He blew out a sigh of disgust. One or two of the churchmen frowned at him, but most hung their heads. He noticed the abjection and nodded grimly. 'Yes. Well – I can call back my hirelings – though I can't call back the coin you prize so much that hired them. I can keep the rents and fees of Canterbury and Durham in trust for the next two bishops who take those sees. God forbid we spend a penny of *that* to set free the land that gave us our lives. Wars are un-Christian, aren't they?' He took his thumb and stuck it to his breast several times.

'But, though you won't grant me your purses freely, won't grant me the use of my own fyrd, won't lift up your eyes to look at me when I tell you how the fields that nourished you and the schools that made you holy men are being burned – I don't need your approval or permission to go overseas myself. By God, I'm so ashamed of my brother, I have it in me to be his mercenary and beat these scum back to their holes, if I can get no help from you! I can sail over there in a washbasin and ride bare-assed to my brother on a mule, if I must. But I'll lay you a wager that if I did, I could pick up an army on the way who would rather fall into H-hell tomorrow than face their fathers' spirits in H-heaven and tell them they let the whole of Nor-normandy go to ruin, because it's a s-sin to take Church money to fight an earthly war!' Here he mimicked the nasal accents of Prior Turgot of Durham Abbey, who continually rained letters on us protesting the seizure of Archbishop Carileph's ecclesiastical, as well as his personal, revenues to the Crown.

When the council left us half an hour later, the king looked at me grimly for a moment, then burst out in a shout of laughter, seized me, and hugged me. He'd gotten his promise of aid by unanimous consent. On the day after Candlemas we sailed out of Portsmouth with a great fleet to Le Tréport, then marched to Eu, where the king took up residence.

It wasn't necessary to fight a war. The king never laid a siege, struck a blow, or commanded a charge of horse against Curthose. He merely had to let out his royal standard there for men to begin to flock to him, some in search of revenge, some out of fear of their neighbors. They brought him gifts, hoping to be gifted in return and more generously, as they heard he now had a hoard to spend like that of no other prince in Europe.

If they came looking for glory in a king, they found it. They were dined, entertained with tournaments, serenaded with Welsh musicians, filled with wine until they rocked with it. Every morning Rufus kept court as if he were in his own realm. He awed those who came to gawk at him, whether they were Normans, French, Ponthoise, or Bretons; they goggled at the great standard above the battlements, which Pope Alexander II had sent to the Conqueror before he took ship for England: on a blue field it bore the Cross of St. Alban, worked in gold, with four golden orbs centered in each of its quarters, on which were worked the symbols of the four Evangelists. Below the standard was the king's own battle pennant, which he flew for the first time there: a red lion on a white field. Many who saw it first thought it was the red dragon of Wessex which King Harold had used for his royal standard, because the body and tail of the lion were so sinuous and the legs so short, to conform to the shape of the banner.

But it was William himself who was the most splendid sight, dressed in his English-work robes with their long, trailing sleeves, with his shoulder-length hair and curling beard like spun gold framing his broad red face. Those who remembered him as the mere shadow of his father and thought him unworthy to sit on a throne now saw a king revealed to them who put the father to sleep in his grave.

At the time of our coming to Normandy, Duke Robert was occupied with the shameful task of helping Robert de Bellesme lay siege to the castle of Courci, in Sées. It belonged to a kinsman of the Grantmesnils, that powerful family which has married itself to most of the blood of the duchy and whose son Hugh twice risked his honor and fortune to support Curthose in his quest for the ducal coronet. It was said that Duke Robert's heart was never in the business, but he couldn't deny his aid to Bellesme, to whom he owed much money. Curthose was sunk so low in public esteem by then that it would have been an act of charity to believe this was so.

At any event, when he heard Rufus had come overseas and was sitting at Eu, he broke off his part in the siege and rode away to Caen. We will set aside the rumor that old Hugh de Grantmesnil went to him and said: 'I've served your father and I've served you, in truth and honor. You stand between me and my enemy. I have a hundred livres in my purse for you now, if you'll withdraw from Courci to wherever it suits you best, for the length of so much as one day, so we Grantmesnils can fight our enemy without having it said we raised our swords against our lawful lord.'

However it was, Curthose was home in Caen no more than a day when he sent his courier up to Eu to speak to his brother thus:

'It gives me great joy to know that my beloved brother is once again in the land that gave him birth, as it gives me hope that he and I may now soon settle all our past differences and regain our former affections for each other. To that end, I invite His Grace, my most noble and royal brother William, to come to me in Caen, where we may speak to each other face to face and with the mediation of the most noble and illustrious King Philip of the French.'

When the young, fresh-faced courier had finished this noble speech, I bent to the king's ear and he nodded.

'Will there be room enough at the table?' he asked the boy good-humoredly.

'Your Grace?'

'How many – guests – is the F-french king bringing?'

The lad took his meaning. 'Oh, Your Grace, this is meant for a peaceful meeting. His Grace the duke has asked His Grace King Philip only to – '

'Leave off all these "graces," sir, or you'll never come to the meat.' He turned to me. 'Three Graces are enough to hold hands and have a dance, aren't they? To bewitch Hercules?

'Now, sir, what if I told you to tell my brother that I'm well satisfied where I am? If he wants to meet with me and bring King Philip, he must come up to me. I was ready to come to him once before, but he didn't keep the watch of his time and missed the appointment.'

There was a laugh for that from those in the hall who heard it. The young courier glanced about him, his cheeks patched with blushes. With the stiff pride of a man still half boy, he said:

'If that is the answer Your Grace sends, I will deliver it. His intent, I believe, is an honorable meeting, with no need for suspicion on anyone's part, but if he has another answer, he will send it to you by another courier.'

The king leaned forward. 'You have great care for his honor, then?'

'He is my lord.'

'You mean you are in his hire. What if I offered you twice your hire to speak for me instead?'

'My lord, I am not in his hire, since he can't pay me. But I may not take the wages of a second master, when I'm sworn to be the duke's man.'

Rufus drew a sigh and sat back. 'Tell my brother that I'll meet with him in Caen within the next ten days. If he can still command honor from you, I'll venture to trust him. But see here: it's on your word alone that I do. You'll answer for it, if he plays me false.' It was the manner of a man talking in mock earnest to a child to make him think himself a man, but the young man blushed with pleasure at it.

'Your Grace has no need to fear, then; my lord will be most glad to see you.'

When he had bowed himself out, Rufus sat back in his seat and laughed. 'What a green sprout he is. He reminds me of myself at that age – only I was never given such a charge to bear.' His smile faded.

I said, 'And what if King Philip has an army at his back when we arrive?'

'Philip? He wouldn't come down with an army unless he'd been paid. You heard the boy: Robin can't afford to pay *him*, let alone Rumble-Guts of Paris. No, Robin will be glad to see me, even at the expense of the loss of a few arpents of land. He knows I don't mean to take it all – or I'd be in Rouen by now.'

So, we rode down to Caen with a modest escort at our backs by way of the coast, which was friendly to the king, especially Fécamp. There, where he had spent some of his childhood while his mother took the sea air as a restorative after childbirth, he was welcomed as the king he was. Even the monks of the abbey climbed up on their walls to cheer him. We had begun to take on uninvited followers, almost from the moment we left Eu. By the time we approached the gates of Caen, our retinue of common folk had reached nearly one hundred. Many had to be refused entrance to the city because there was no room to house them and no authority to feed them. I was given a purse to dispense among them for their return home.

The king went straight from the city gate to the Abbey of St. Stephen's, where his father's body was entombed, still without a proper monument or even an epitaph beyond that of his name and his titles. Commanding the rest of us to stand back from him, Rufus went to it alone. After a moment, standing in thought before the tomb, he knelt and kissed the stone, then came away.

Duke Robert waited in his hall, which was empty of honor, as it was of men of any substance when we came to it. The lower tables of the presence hall were crowded with those who should have been downstairs among the servants: huntsmen, musicians, serving women who disported themselves like whores among the men. Robert sat at his high table with three or four others, among whom I recognized Edgar Atheling. They all stood when the king entered. Curthose lurched forward unsteadily to embrace his brother.

'Here he is! I knew he wouldn't fail me, friends.' He seized the king and hugged him, then burst into drunken tears on his shoulder. Rufus put his arm around him, said something to him privately, then made him release his grip, but gently. He was looking at Prince Edgar.

Curthose scrubbed his face with his hand, then clapped Rufus on the shoulder. 'Come up and wet your throat! Hey, someone! Bring wine for the King of England! We don't have any golden cups at the moment, brother. Will a silver one do?'

'Put a poker in it to heat it, and I'll drink it out of a boot,' the king said. 'It's damned cold in Caen.'

Robert laughed. 'Yes, damned cold! So it is! Mull that wine for my brother, steward!'

Robert fitz Hamon, who had walked at the king's back, now signaled for our knights to disperse along the walls, rather than sit at the tables. He and Hugh the Wolf took their stands at either end of the high table while the king and his brother went up to it. Prince Edgar and the others, one of them the monk William d'Arques, stood away from their stools to let the king pass. They bowed; Edgar went down on one knee. The king glanced back at him when he'd passed him.

'Edgar.' He took the stool next to the duke's chair.

'Your Grace.' Prince Edgar rose and remained standing, possibly hoping to be invited to sit again, but the king ignored him.

'Robin, you need a barber. Did you leave yours at Courci?' He took the steaming wine cup that was offered him, then looked up and saw it was Constable Ralph de Ivri who offered it. He rose and embraced him. 'Old friend. I'm glad to see not everyone's forgotten his service to my b-brother.'

Robert Curthose blinked rapidly and wiped at his face with his sleeve. He looked twenty years older than the man I'd seen first at Gerberoy. His drunkard's nose, which had already begun to redden then, was now knobbled and purpled with broken veins. His tunic was filthy with spilled food and wine. When the wine was brought, he clutched his cup as if he feared it might overset itself and spill a precious drop. He finished it and held it out for more before Rufus had set his to his lips.

Robert looked at his brother almost covertly: 'I was in bed late this morning, resting up for your visit. I broke off a campaign to welcome you, when I heard you were here.' The campaign was evidently with some whore.

Rufus answered him with a set smile that bore a resemblance to his father's. 'So I heard. I thought I'd be the first to entertain you a season or two back, but you didn't come. We had the tables laid for you.'

Robert laughed and twiddled his wine cup between thick fingers. 'Well, you know, it didn't seem the right weather for sailing. You weren't too disappointed in me, I hope.'

Rufus shook his head slowly. 'Not too much.' As Curthose's face fell a little, the king looked about the hall. 'Your house smells like a fish shop. Tell your marshals to clear out the whores' – he turned his head and glanced at Edgar – 'all of them. Then we'll talk. We have a lot to talk about.'

By morning the castle might have belonged to us. The king's knights directed the servants to clean it. Fresh rushes were spread on the floor of the hall after a collection of months-old filth and straw was removed. Our cooks invaded the kitchens; our knights stood guard at the top of the stairs when Philip of France arrived and heaved his gluttonous bulk up them. For a man under sentence of excommunication, Philip looked cheerful.

Summons were sent for all men of worth who were faithful to the duke to attend on him. The Archbishop of Rouen and all his bishops came, except the Bishop of Sées, who was dying, and Odo, who chose to remain in Bayeux. Old Roger of Beaumont, Roger of Montgomery, Hugh of Grantmesnil with his son Ivo, Robert de Meulan, Roger de Ivry, and William of Evreux came: the old lords who had clung to the Conqueror. Few of those younger who had once been Curthose's adherents were there. Meanwhile Rufus and

Robert rode out daily and made plans for the erection of a fitting monument to grace their father's tomb.

Robert was looking more sober and his dress was cleaner, but every day he looked more beaten in spirit. Robert de Bellesme didn't answer his summons, nor did Prince Henry. His strong supporters at Rouen – Gilbert de Laigle, William de Breteuil – came, but were cold to him and made themselves known as friends of the English king's.

When all who were likely to be present had arrived, the details of the treaty were hammered out in private council, with all but the high lords barred from the discussion. Several times I heard voices raised above me as I sat in the lower hall, playing dice with Gerard le Gros. Curthose's voice was notable among the many, but never the king's. He had little need to shout; he controlled the council.

On the fifth day the treaty was made, copied down by clerks in three languages – Latin, French, and English – then read aloud. I was called up from below to write the English translation and to read it when the moment came, though there were few who could understand my reading, except perhaps Edgar Atheling, but he was nowhere in sight.

The meat of the treaty was this:

That King William should pay to his brother a sum of money sufficient for the payment of his debts, to be established at a later time.

That King William's men were to be left unmolested in the castles where they were placed, and that the lords of those places were to be considered the king's men thenceforth, by which was meant Eu, Aumale, Gournai, and Conches.

That the port of Falaise was to be the king's, together with its castle, town, and abbey.

That the king was to have possession of such lands as the duke and his father had given to Edgar Atheling, an English subject, and of any other lands and estates granted to Englishmen in the duchy of Normandy.

That the king was to have possession of Mont St. Michel and Cherbourg, together with their castles, ports, and so on in the Cotentin. This was Prince Henry's county, of course. He wasn't present to protest.

In return for these grants, King William was to aid Duke Robert in recovering all those lands which his father had left to him, except for those which he now granted to the king. This meant Maine and the French Vexin, which didn't make King Philip very happy, but the lands weren't mentioned specifically, so he may have been too busy gourmandising to consider the possibilities.

All those men of the duke's who had lost their English estates as a result of the rebellion would be restored and forgiven, with the exception of Odo of Bayeux, also not present to protest.

The duke should have certain lands granted him in England, not mentioned but understood to be those lands which had formerly belonged to Odo. He must come overseas and do fealty for them and must live on them for a fourth part of every year, so that the people there would know him for their true lord by his care of them.

If the duke should die without a son of lawful issue, King William should be his heir for all of Normandy, with the King of France giving his assent.

If the King of England should likewise die without lawful male issue, Duke Robert should be his sole heir, the English Witan giving its consent.

When all this was read and signed by the two participants, the French mediator, and the twenty-four chosen witnesses, the bells rang out and a great feast was proclaimed. King Philip accepted a purse from the King of England to reward him for his wise counsel. All those in the city who wished to come in and see the three noble rulers in their glory were allowed to do so.

I had been quiet throughout most of these proceedings. Robert Bloet, William Giffard, and Maurice of London were the king's chief clerks for counsel, and only my knowledge of English brought me forth from the obscurity of the lower hall for most of a week. For a time I felt the slight and the tenuousness of my position. I was only one of the king's many chaplains. There was no room for me, either at the table or in the bedchamber. The castle was so crowded with men of the three rulers that not all could even find a place on the floor to sleep, so I was boarded out in the town, along with many others.

Therefore, it was with the sense of an outsider that I lounged against the pier of an arch in the gallery overlooking the great hall, when the castle was thrown open to visitors and petitioners the following days.

This practice had entertained the Conqueror when he had no graver matters to contend with: the trespassings, the misappropriated well, the dissatisfied customer complaining of a baker who used too much leavening, so that his loaves were large but not up to proper weight. Rufus looked bored by it in half an hour, as usual; Robert looked as if his head were paining him, and it no doubt was. King

Philip sat belching from the huge breakfast he had been at liberty to consume while the rest fasted until after Terce service. Being an excommunicate had its compensations with him. If he wished for anything, it was probably to get home quickly to his bed and the bride who had caused him to be cast out of the Church's mercy.

I saw a woman being ushered before them and recognized Isabel de Trie. Martin was with her. I broke off my conversation with Gerard le Gros to hear what she said.

Her complaint concerned her property, naturally. It seemed her snake-eyed cousin had been among those killed at Rouen during the rioting. His property was now forfeit to the duke, because he was suspected of being an adherent of Conan's. As he had been receiving the rents from Isabel's estate, it had gone into the duke's pot, along with the rest. She wanted it back.

She made a comely widow in her black veil and white gown. She looked half a nun. Duke Robert and King Philip alike had roused themselves in a moment when they looked at her. Robert was smiling at her and, I think, disrobing her in his mind, to see if her body matched the still-pretty face she turned to him.

Rufus took interest only when he heard her say she was the widow of two brave soldiers and now had a son to rear whom she hoped might emulate them in time. He looked at Martin, who remained obediently silent at her side.

'Who was the boy's father?' he asked. 'He has a face that reminds me of someone I know.'

'He was Amiot de Trie, Your Grace,' Isabel said quickly, 'a knight in the service of the Count of Conches. He died at Gerberoy.'

'Gerberoy?' Rufus looked at his brother. 'Do you recall him?' Robert shook his head, still entranced with Isabel. Rufus said to Martin: 'If your father died so long ago, you should be in someone's service now. Who's the lord you're squire to?'

Again Isabel answered for Martin: 'We were in the household of Ralph of Tosny, Your Grace, but we had the misfortune to be torn away from it, and now the lord and his lady no longer receive our petitions.'

'How's that, madam?' He glanced about the hall for Ralph, but couldn't seem to find him.

'Oh, Your Grace, it was the most terrible thing for us. There was a man in the castle who was being kept prisoner for Lord Ralph by his lady. He captured my son when he brought him food, and made him help him find a way out of prison. Martin brought him to me for a cloak to disguise him, but then the man forced us both go with him in the dead of night. By the grace of God, Who heard our prayers, we were able to escape from him and find refuge with friends, but the lord and lady bear us a grudge for the man's escape and won't allow us to return to them.' Isabel began to weep, as only she could, without reddening her eyes or causing her nose to run. She had immediately picked up the note of interest in the king's voice and now turned to extend her eloquent white hands to him, rather than to Curthose.

Robert shifted in his seat. 'Well, well, this is a sad tale. We must do something for the widow, eh, brother? Madam, I'll have my clerks look into your cousin's affairs and bring me word on who holds your land now. There may be some way to retrieve it, or there will be compensation, I promise you.' Isabel swung back to him, like a lodestone toward iron, but Rufus asked:

'Who was this man who carried you both off? Was he armed? Where were your wits, boy? Why didn't you raise the house?'

I leaned over the rail of the gallery to get a better look at the king. He knew I had been at Conches and had some difficulty with its lady, though I hadn't described my exact leave-taking to him. I half hoped, half feared, he had already seen Martin's resemblance to me in the boy's features. I wasn't eager to acknowledge any more bastards, but I resented Isabel's giving my son a false father – and for the sake of her damned property, again!

Gerard took hold of my arm. 'You're going to pitch over on your head in a moment. What's the matter?'

'Oh, Your Grace, I never knew who he was. He was a big man, with a terrible look in his eye, as if he might have been a murderer.'

'Was he a soldier? An outlaw? A poacher?'

'A soldier! Yes, I think he was one of the Count of Evreux's men that the lady's guard had captured,' Isabel said. Martin said nothing until then, but seeing the king was still interested in him, he blurted:

'I want to be a soldier like my father! I'd serve you, if you'd take me, my lord. I can be a page, or anything.'

Rufus smiled. 'A page? You're too old for that, aren't you? You should be an esquire by now. How old are you, thirteen?'

Isabel took Martin's arm and answered: 'Yes, Your Grace, that's his age exactly. Oh, if Your Grace would take my body – I mean, my boy – ' The whole court went up in a shout of laughter at her slip of tongue. Martin looked mortified and hung his head, while Isabel put her hands to her face and sank to her knees. I withdrew to the shadow of the pier, laughing. The king held his hand up for silence and got it.

'Madam, we take your meaning. I have a tongue that fa-falters now and then, too.' He looked at Martin. 'Don't hang your head if you want to serve me, boy. What's your name?'

Martin told him, lifting his chin in Isabel's way.

'Very well, Martin. Go and see my senior squire about your duties. Routrou – ' He snapped his fingers for the squire. 'Brother, I'll leave the rest of this widow's comforting to you.'

39

Robert Curthose lost no time pressing his treaty claims on his brother. He was delighted to give Rufus Cherbourg and Mont St. Michel, which were Prince Henry's, because he wanted the Cotentin returned and Rufus must take it back for him, if he wanted to get to his new possessions.

Henry got word of his danger within a day or two of the treaty signing and at once began to fortify those two places, as well as Avranches, for which Hugh the Wolf was his nominal vassal. Earl Hugh was more than eager to invest Avranches for the king and so dispense with one of three masters he then served. He took his mercenaries and his mesnie in that direction, while Rufus and Robert marched first on Cherbourg, but found it worthy to leave to underlings, as Henry had shut himself up in his island fortress of St. Michel with the main body of his host.

We spent the Lenten season making him sorry for that choice. Mont St. Michel has one means of access to the mainland, a broad causeway that is covered with seawater at high tide. If its inhabitants can't use that causeway to bring in food and water, they must rely on ships to carry their supplies to them. But the king took note of that and had his fleet standing guard on the seaward sides of the island, while he and Robert, with the hosts borrowed from Eu, Aumale, Gournai, Conches, and those men who still adhered to Duke Robert, stood watch on the mainland. All the trees were hacked down within a half mile of their camp to make firewood for their camps and to expose the countryside behind them, so that no tardy friend of Prince Henry's could come upon them unawares.

Such sitting wars make weary times for a man like Rufus, who would have been happier to be born in his great-grandsire's day, when the rule of war was open battle, attack or retreat. The king soon grew restless and took to hunting in the woods that bordered the Sélune River as far as Pontorson. If he didn't hunt, he made his mercenaries drill as if they were new recruits, dividing them into mock armies and waging bloodless melees along the sandy beaches of the sea inlet, within sight of the island castle's watch. While he amused himself in this exhausting fashion, his brother drank, gambled, or lay abed in his tent, listening to his *castrati* minstrels shrill him the deeds of his ancestors.

If he felt more energetic, he rose and rode around the bay to Avranches, which had quickly fallen to Hugh the Wolf, to visit the castle where he had Isabel de Trie installed as his current concubine. He no doubt would have brought her into camp for more convenient swiving, but Rufus forbade camp followers of female kind and enforced the rule by having several whores from Avranches flogged out of camp, fining the men who had entertained them.

'If you want exercise, take it on the beaches or at the archery butts,' he told his mercenaries. 'I'm not paying you to fornicate.'

Cherbourg fell to those who besieged it, and those in Henry's fee were paroled on their promise to swear fealty to Rufus. On giving their knightly promise to ride to him and offer him service, they were allowed to come away from Cherbourg. Some who were mercenaries must have made off for foreign ports at once, but a small band of knights did ride down the Cotentin to us and, having forded the Sélune, came upon Rufus with his men, making their mock charges.

Rufus saw them and, not knowing who they were, called to them to identify themselves. Neither they nor he bore any device to show who they were, so each faced enemies. The knights of Cherbourg quickly enarmed themselves as the king and four or five of his men did the same. They charged each other with mutual bellows, glad for a real fight at last. In the clash that followed, the king gave chase to one of the strangers, but was met by another, who put a lance squarely into the center of his shield and unhorsed him. He might have been dragged to his death by his spur, which had caught in his stirrup, but the man who overthrew him wheeled and captured his destrier's reins to claim him as a prize when he'd dealt with his rider.

The king was lying half conscious when his stirrup was loosed from his spur; the knight evidently thought him already dead. But he came to his senses and opened his eyes in time to see the man bending over him to pull off his helm, a dagger in his hand to give him the *coup de grâce* if he stirred.

'Hold, you damned rascal. I'm worth more alive. I'm the King of England.' He groaned. He raised himself and cast off his helm with both hands, then looked up fearlessly. The knight stood back from him, evidently saw the king's men rushing down on him to kill him before he murdered their master, and quickly threw away his dagger. He was surrounded in an instant, while the king was raised to his feet and examined for injury. Someone ran to the beach to scoop up water in his helm, which Rufus took and poured over his own head. Then he wiped his streaming face and looked around.

'Who unhorsed me?'

The knight was pressed forward, now unhelmed, too, and looking terrified, but he faced his victim and said honestly:

'I did, Your Grace, unknowing. I took you for a soldier, not a king.'

The king was pleased with that. 'Who are you? I know your face.'

'Walter of Poix, Your Grace. I was your father's squire once.'

'Wat Tirel is what they called you, wasn't it? You were good at the bow, I recall. What were you doing here in our woods? Are you in my brother's service?'

'In yours, now, if you'll have me, Your Grace. My friends and I are on our parole to come and surrender to you. We've been at Avranches, serving your brother Henry.' He was about the king's age, a wiry-thewed little man with hair curled like an Italian's. The king beheld him with pleasure.

'So, you took me for a soldier, did you? By the Face, I'll take you for one, too. You're mine from this day – on my rolls, do you hear?' He clapped him on the shoulder and shook it as Walter Tirel gasped in the heat of his recent exertions, hardly able to believe his good fortune.

It was his good fortune, better than he could ever have dreamed, though he didn't bring the same luck to the king, who instantly took him for a friend, in the manner he had of picking up friends in an instant on the strength of something they said or did that appealed to his chivalry.

I didn't witness this event, but heard about it in detail, as did everyone else in our camp.

In that time there were many tales growing up around the king that showed him to be the sort of liberal-handed knight, hard in war, soft in heart, who makes the subject of so many songs. Of late I've heard another one repeated in a manner that shows how these deeds may be interpreted by those who don't love the whims of chivalry. I'll tell it first as it's come to be known:

Nearing the end of the siege of Mont St. Michel, Prince Henry sent a man of his out on the causeway, bearing a white flag, to beg a favor from his brothers. The food supply inside those walls must have been all but exhausted by then. The man who bore the flag of truce came walking, though he was a knight, which signified that horseflesh was being eaten, if the beasts weren't already extinct within St. Michel.

He said for Prince Henry: 'Our cisterns are empty and there's fever among us. We can go without food, but give us water.'

It was a blunt plea. Henry was never a man to frame a gracious request. But Duke Robert was moved by the sight of the gaunt man who requested aid and gave orders for water barrels to be filled and hauled over the causeway before the tide rose again. Rufus heard this and came riding from his own camp to protest:

'You've got a fine notion of how to conduct a campaign. How will we ever subdue this dragon of a brother of ours if we let him eat and drink his fill of us? Shall we have him out and feast him for Easter, too?'

But Duke Robert for once remembered his own honor and answered: 'Would you suffer your own brother to die of thirst, when you were so generous with our uncle who betrayed you? Where shall we get another brother half so clever if we lose this one?'

At this remark the king was said to rail, but in the end he gave in and allowed Robert to send water to Henry.

But: Robert was quoting Rufus to himself, when he asked where they should get another brother half so clever, and Rufus didn't rail; he laughed and said: 'A man can't say a stupid thing once in his life, but it will be remembered ever after.' He then not only let the water barrels be filled and passed over the causeway, but sent another wagon after it, filled with the kill of three days' hunting.

Henry surrendered the island two days later, for a very good reason: the monks of St. Michel had run out of stores, the stores he and his men had forced them to share and which had been the sole reason he was able to hold out so long against his brothers. When he and his men came out over the causeway, it is true that only Henry had a horse left to ride, but because he knew from the first that he would get no assistance from the mainland, Henry had ordered all the horses save his own to be killed and salted immediately after the gates were closed. He had lived relatively well on Mont St. Michel during that siege, except for the lack of fresh water. He came out,

I'm certain, only because he was as bored and restless inside the walls as Rufus was outside them.

The king hoped for a reconciliation between himself and both brothers, but when Henry entered his tent the first thing he said was:

'You damned hypocrite! You promised me Mother's estates. Now I hear you've turned them all over to that beaver-toothed parasite, fitz Hamon, who's always at your heels. Where's your honor, now?'

'Harry, calm yourself and have a cup of wine. You know damned well you b-betrayed me as soon as you were let out of Bayeux's donjon – and you'd already told me a bald-faced lie about Bellesme's being innocent of mu-murdering my harper. One b-bad lie deserves another, doesn't it?'

'Your harper! Your cock-wife, you mean! And how the Hell should I know who killed him, anyway – or care? I'm your brother and you lied to me!' He pointed a finger to Duke Robert, who'd just ridden into camp and was ducking in under the tent flap. 'He's my brother, too, or he's supposed to be. But he's robbed me. I begin to think there must be some truth in what they say in Bayeux – that Uncle Odo got him on Mother while my father was fighting Geoffrey Martel. It's the only reason I can find that justifies Odo favoring him and Father hating him!'

Duke Robert blazed into anger, snatching his dagger out to stab Henry, but Rufus got between them.

'Robin, put it away! He only said it to make us quarrel.' He turned to Henry, seized him by the front of his tunic, and said: 'I won't kill you, but I ought to th-throw you in the privy for that, you little t-toad! You can say that about her, when she made you her p-pet – '

'Our mother already had two bastards before Father married her. Why not three? Or four?'

The king struck him across the face with the back of his hand, bloodying his mouth. Now everyone in the tent rushed to part them, Duke Robert first of all.

'Stop it, Will! Now he only says it for spite.'

'Do you want to challenge me? Do you?' yelled Rufus, shaking Henry. 'Do you have the belly to defend your dirty m-mouth?'

'Yes! Give me a sword and I'll show you how soft you've grown since you took to wearing women's robes, you fat sodomite!'

But he was dragged from the tent by two of the king's men, while Curthose pushed Rufus back to the tent pole and held him there until Henry was out of reach.

Later, there was an attempt to make peace. Henry came and

459

apologized for slurring their mother. Rufus was cool, yet offered to take him back to England and to make some compensation for his lost English estates, but Henry refused him: 'By your leave, I'd rather serve a stranger. It's better so. We aren't meant to be friends, the three of us. You'll find that out, if you haven't yet. What did you gain here, helping Robin run me out of the county I paid good money for? You went behind my back for your damned towns. Why didn't you come and deal with me, as you did with Roger Beaumont and de Tosny?'

'Why didn't you come to Caen and defend your rights?'

'What, and be thrown in prison again?' Henry sneered. 'But it will all come to the same thing, now, won't it? Well, do it, and be damned! You're so hungry for friends, you'll do Robin's dirty work for him. You'll even pretend to believe in Bellesme's innocence, just to keep Montgomery with you. Well, my royal brother, power doesn't have friends. I'm ten years your junior and I've learned that much. So, put me in prison and rob me. I'll outlast both of you and I'll have it all, some day. That's what Father told me, after you'd left him dying to run after your crown. And he was right! I can wait.'

The king let go of his tunic and said wearily: 'Go away, Harry. I don't want you for a prisoner.'

Prince Henry left our camp, with no more escort than a single knight, a clerk, and three squires. He went first into Brittany, later to the French Vexin, where he was said to have hired himself out as a free lance. Curthose was well pleased to see him go as a begger, but Rufus, though he was angry, felt some little regret, I think. He admired the kind of reckless courage that made Henry challenge a king when he hadn't a friend to stand beside him.

The king pretended to forget that slur Henry had made on their mother's name in his rage. The charge, however, must have struck some similar suspicion buried in his own brain, or echoed some old rumor he once heard. When I considered it, I remembered how Odo had infuriated him by suggesting that he had the love of the Lady Matilda above even that which she gave to her husband. Yet, Robert couldn't be a bastard; he was his father's image in all save height and intellect. If any of the three brothers could be said to bear even a remote resemblance to Lord Odo, a fair-haired, fresh-skinned man, it could only have been – well, enough of that.

I was sent home soon after to make a circuit of my courts and see how my carefully picked judges were dealing with the royal fines and fees. I stopped in Godalming for two days to see my family. My father was already cloistered at Canterbury. Fulcher had taken him there in the spring, when he felt himself too frail to wait longer for my return. Osbern had seen him since and reported him now much stronger and completely happy.

He could be happy, though my mother grieved for the loss of him. Still, she tried to reconcile herself. She devoted her days to her distillations and to spoiling her grandchildren.

The children were healthy, thriving – and still strangers to me. Once more they stood silently as Giva gently explained me; then they tried to tolerate my touching and embracing them. They felt nothing for me; how could they? I felt nothing for them but a mild curiosity to see how they'd changed each time I came to see them. Giva knew it and it hurt her, but I couldn't help myself any more than the twins could. Each time I looked at them, rolling in the dirt of the hen yard, running barefoot with wet noses to complain of each other to their mother, I found myself thinking of Martin, slender, self-possessed, in his fine new tunic and hose, holding a basin for the king to dip his fingers into after a meal. There was a growing hunger in my heart to acknowledge him, to proclaim him mine.

As I lay abed with Giva those nights, it was all I could do to keep silent about him. I rehearsed in my mind telling her: how the only flaw I found in him was that he was not the issue of her sweet body which I loved, rather than of that calculating whore's, Isabel de Trie; Isabel, who had once seduced me and who was now letting Robert Curthose leap her, to secure to herself again those few miserable arpents of worn-out land that she valued above everything else in the world.

But since I could say nothing of Martin without mentioning Isabel, I kept silent. Still, I had to speak of him to someone, so I confided my secret to Fulcher when I met him in London, to draw up the accounts of the royal estates, crown fees, and revenues before the king returned. Fulcher was proving every season a more responsible steward. Not only did he act on the king's business in my behalf during my absence, but he had collected my own rents and invested some of them in the purchase of a house in Winchester, to which we could move the family.

He heard my tale of a newfound son with disapproval: 'Revel in him if it pleases your vanity, brother, but don't lay claim to him. You have enough mouths to feed. I've already told Osbern, if he marries this girl he's got with child, he'll have to provide for them out of his own purse.'

'What? Osbern? He – when did this happen? Why haven't I heard about it before? The damned little pup! I saw him just last week and he said nothing about it. Who is she? Where is she?'

'She's still in York with her father, but you'll soon hear enough about her if you go up there. She's a butcher's daughter – so they won't starve – but the father's been threatening to lay a complaint before the archbishop.'

'Oh, Christ! The Archbishop of York already dislikes me enough. Her father won't be satisfied with compensation?'

'He'd take it, but I think he wants her off his hands as well.'

'Perhaps letting Osbern marry her might be the wisest thing after all. She could come down and live with Mother and Giva. After all – '

I was startled by the face Fulcher turned on me then. 'How much more burden are you going to put on Elfgiva, Raf? How much more can she bear?'

'I don't know what you mean. Where is her burden? She has a house and children, but she has a well-filled purse, too. She's fed and clothed and has Mother to help her with her work. What else is there she needs? Tell me and I'll provide it, though I scarcely think it's your place to tell me how to care for my own wife.'

He shook his head as if I amazed him. 'You see and hear everything that happens in the court, you run the king's justice as if you were driving oxen to a market, but you don't look at your own *wife* – 'if that's what you're pleased to call her – with any more understanding than that of a brothel keeper.'

'Now, see here, Fulcher, you're overstepping a brother's privilege. I love Giva and I've cared for her to the best of my ability. She understands me and I understand her, better than you can imagine.'

'Well, perhaps I understand her a little, too, since I see her a great deal more than you do lately.' He seemed to regret he'd said that. He turned away and took up his pen and counters again. 'She was ill after the baby came, last spring. She had milk fever. Did she tell you that?'

She hadn't, but I wouldn't give him the satisfaction of hearing me admit ignorance on the point. 'She said it was nothing. She seems fine now, and so does little Elias.'

'Yes, except for his foot.'

'What's the matter with his foot?'

'It turns in. He may be slightly lame when he learns to walk.' He turned on his stool again. 'You didn't notice? She didn't tell you?'

'It's nothing! Babies' feet! Who can tell if they're straight or not, swaddled up as they are?' It would profit me nothing to quarrel with him, or to defend myself against the look in his eyes. He was still infatuated with Giva, that's all it was, and it gave him a barren sort of pleasure to imagine he cared for her more than I. I should find him a place where he couldn't see her as much. It was inconsiderate of me to make him my steward, when he was so valuable to me otherwise. I found I had ruined my pen nib, meanwhile, worrying it with my fingers. I threw it away and began to cut another.

'I'll be going to Rochester on Tuesday, Fulcher, then to Dover, after. I want you to come with me. The king means to give Bishop Odo's estates to Duke Robert. We must make an inventory of the estates and see that all the rents have been collected to the Crown before he takes possession. That should go some way toward making up for what the king's had to give him to settle his gambling debts. We'll want to look in on Canterbury, too, while we're there. I don't understand these damned monks! They're supposed to be unconcerned with material things, but they carry on like a bunch of Spanish Jews if they think they've lost a penny. We'll go down together, and you may stay there for a month or two, to make certain the prior isn't trying to pad the bursar's accounts.'

'Even monks have to eat, Raf.'

'They eat! Have you looked at Prior Guy? They have clothes on their backs, plate on their altar, and plenty of coin in their treasure box. The pilgrims' gifts alone should keep them. The place has almost become a shrine to Lanfranc, since he died.'

'Is the king so poor we have to rob church boxes to keep him, then?'

I turned on him in anger. 'The king has spent as little money as possible since he got his crown, except for what his father willed away to enrich these churches. He's had me spend as little as possible to settle affairs in Normandy – and I assure you I am not a spendthrift – to make certain there's peace here for a time. That should be worth something to these abbeys and great lords of the Church. They certainly seemed to think so last year, when they voted him an aid to do it. You have no right to say we're robbing them, by God! Whose side are you on?'

'I'm only using the word you'll hear when you go there. The churchmen are beginning to complain that your exactions are too strict, considering there's no war that justifies their support now.'

'But that's just the thing! *There's no war!* And there isn't going to be one. Good God, we're going to have a little peace in this country for a change! Isn't that worth anything to them? The king is strong enough to prevent rebellion now. But he has to have their support and a little of their precious coin to keep himself ready for troublemakers. What short memories these people have! Their precious Edward Confessor, whom they're always harking back to, collected the Danegeld *every year*. We've never asked for it.'

'Raf, nobody alive now remembers the Danes – and there are no Danes, or anybody like them, threatening us now. That's the point.'

'Fulcher, it isn't oppressive to ask a little of these fat churchmen to make certain the king – the man who holds their lives in his hands – can raise an army to protect them if he needs to. And if you can't see that, maybe you'd better go back to the Bessin and see what it's like to live under the threat of war every day, because your incompetent duke can't curb his vassals or protect Church property. Maybe Odo will let you have Father's old parish to starve in.'

He bowed his head for a moment, then lifted it to favor me with his dry smile.

'You're quite right, of course. I only tell you these things to prepare you for what you'll hear when you make your visitations. If you don't want candor from me, just say so. I rather thought that's why you put up with me, not because you felt any great surge of affection.'

'That isn't true. I mean, I do feel affection for you, and I do want you to speak the truth to me, naturally. Oh, Christ, Fulcher, it isn't easy for me to be the king's tax collector, you know! I'm ready to take the slurs from anybody else. I just thought you would understand. Kings are expensive people to serve.'

'Yes. In more ways than one.' He was silent for a time, moving his counters and making notes. 'I think a lot of the discontent might be smoothed out if you would tell the king that it's time he appointed a new Archbishop of Canterbury, to take the bishops in charge. It's been a year and a half since the old Italian died, and even Maurice thinks the chair's kept vacant because you encourage the king to take its revenues. He'd like to be archbishop, you know – Maurice. Have you thought about that?'

'I don't make archbishops – not yet, at any event.'

He smiled. 'Perhaps you'd better start – if you have as much influence with the king as everybody thinks you do.'

When I finished my business in Kent, I went to Winchester to prepare the castle for the king's return. Robert Bloet should have performed that task, but he was still in Normandy with Rufus. I took Fulcher with me. Osbern caught up with us in Rochester and confessed his sins with the butcher's daughter of York. I told him he must bring the girl to Winchester without marrying her, if it were possible, but make the marriage a private one if there was no way to avoid it. He seemed delighted. He really was in love with his butcher's daughter, whose awful English name was Swanhilda, but whom he called *Peu Cygne,* a misnomer, if there ever was one: little she was not, nor swanlike, but a great, gawky girl with red hands and hair who looked as if she might give birth any instant. She was as tall as Osbern and as stupidly good-natured. They were an ideal pair.

While I was in Winchester, I inspected the house Fulcher had purchased for us, found it sound enough for an English dwelling, hired a carpenter to make more furniture for it and a glazier to install a glass window in the upper hall, which looked down on the High Street, then sent Osbern with two oxcarts to bring our family over from Godalming.

There was a great deal of interest in the window, which was the first of its kind in an ordinary residence there. As might be expected, the bishop envied it, and the townspeople soon identified my name with extravagance and luxury, though one or two of the richer merchants soon had a solar of their own for their fat wives to preen themselves over, and nobody accused them of extortions to pay for theirs.

When Osbern arrived with the women and children, my mother went straight out into the market to buy poultry to foul our new garden, while Giva went up and down through the entire house, opening doors and looking into the rooms, as if she expected to be ordered out of them. When we came to the upper hall, with the window, she looked at it for some time from the doorway before I could urge her in to examine it more closely. She touched it lightly, running her long fingers over the leading, then starting a little as a shaft of sunlight broke through to illuminate it and her hand. She sat down on the window seat to gaze at it.

'How could you pay for it? Oh, Ranulph, it belongs in a church, doesn't it? You haven't taken it from one, have you?'

'What sort of thought is that? No, I didn't pilfer it. I had it made for you and I can afford it, so don't worry.' I sat by her and took her hands, which I noticed were getting rough with labor. 'I'm going to hire a girl for the kitchen and one for the laundry. These hands were meant for needlework, not scrubbing baby clouts.' I kissed them each in turn.

'But I don't know how to do needlework. That's a lady's art and I'm not a lady.' She smiled, but I thought her face looked drawn and rather sad.

'Then you must learn to do it, because you won't do harsh work with these hands anymore. They're too beautiful. Tomorrow I'll give you money to go to the cloth merchants. You and Mother will want new gowns, I expect, and there should be new shirts and swaddles for the boys. They look like a tinker's get. What's wrong, Giva? Are you too tired from your journey to enjoy your new house? It's all for you, you know, because you deserve it and I can afford it – without pillaging churches.' I drew her forward to kiss her cheek. 'Because I love you very much. Now that the king has settled his affairs in Normandy, I hope I'll be able to see you more often – be with you more – love you more. I promise you, from now on our boys will know my name and face.'

I took her in my arms to kiss her more fully, but to my surprise and consternation she bowed her head and burst into tears against my breast. While I was soothing her and chiding her for her tears, Fulcher came to the chamber door but, seeing us so embraced, turned abruptly and left again.

I made her go to bed early, but when I came to join her and took her in my arms, she still complained of tiredness, though she was submissive to my loving and sighed when I fondled her. I discovered tears on her face again. I held her for a long time afterward, letting her weep silently while I stroked her hair. It was true; she must be ill, I thought, or very tired from caring for so many children. It would be better for us both if she had a rest from childbearing, but how could it be prevented when our every union was like a bridal, so far as I was concerned? My mother would know. I resolved to ask her about it.

40

A courier from London put an end to my hope for a season of peace with Elfgiva. Malcolm of Scotland had once again taken advantage of a lax guard in the north to overrun our borders, with a host greater than any other he had brought down on us since the Danes joined him in '68 to oppose the Conqueror.

Nor was he routed this time as he might have been, because of the harshness of Robert Mowbray's rule over the Northumbrians. His uncle Geoffrey having made Robert adjutant there, many of the people were glad to see Malcolm come burning Norman tithe barns and driving off Norman cattle. It was rumored that in Carlisle, in Cumbria, the governor of the castle received Malcolm as a ruling king.

Message had already been sent to King William by his justiciar, Walkelin of Winchester, so I kissed Giva good-bye, leaving her in the care of Osbern, took Fulcher with me, and hurried to London to await the coming of the king.

His ships must have passed the merchantman that carried our message, because no more than three days after I reached London the trumpets of the watch blew for Rufus, crossing over the newly repaired bridge from Southwark with a great following of lords, knights, and pack wagons. All the people turned out into the streets to cheer him and his brother Robert, who had come with him. We in St. Paul's chapter house turned out into the churchyard to welcome him, and I saw my son Martin proudly mounted in his train, and also, to my surprise and the titillation of the crowd, Isabel de Trie and two women who looked like her servants, riding in one of the wagons, where they might naturally be taken for the king's whores. All the litigants in the churchyard flocked to stare at them. I saw Isabel pull her veil modestly across her cheek, but the other two preened themselves and made cheerful answer to the crowd; a brace of whores, indeed.

The king dismounted to meet Walkelin and Maurice, kissed their rings each in turn, and embraced them, kissing them on either cheek respectfully. He smiled, but as soon as I saw his face, I knew he was in a temper. The reason was not hard to find; it lay in the presence of his brother, waving, and being cheered by the ragtag mob around him.

We went into the chapter house, where a table and maps were put before the king for him to see where the Scot had laid him waste. I sat in one of the stalls, not taking part in the council, as he heard report from several more couriers who had come to London with news since the first. Young William de Warenne, the younger Walter Giffard, Earl Hugh, and the other barons gathered around the table and made recommendations for action, frequently interrupted by Duke Robert's light voice, raised in a jest.

Robert was one of those men possessed of a kind of wry wit who can often set a company laughing in a grim moment, but who lack the capacity to know when to keep silent or be grave, as if they fear their friends might forget their wit if they neglect to remind them. There is something extraordinarily tedious about such men, and I saw the king's irritation increase with every comment, though he smiled at Robert's japes and pretended to tolerate them.

Still, Robert gave good advice about Malcolm, though he had blunted its effect:

'There's no need to do battle with him, Will. He'd come out at you with his pipers yelping like hell-hounds, but he'll run like the fox before he meets you in open battle. He's got to do it. He's got a brother on his back, with all the Highland clans behind him, so he's got to pretend he's a bloodletter to keep his own folk happy, or they'll maybe open his veins for him and put Donald Bane on the throne. Go up and bribe him with something; he'll kneel to you quickly enough.'

'And betray me again next year?'

Robert shrugged. 'They don't look on it as betraying up there – only as an opportunity too good to waste.' He grinned, somewhat painfully. I thought he must be suffering the hell of a headache from all the sweet wine he imbibed constantly. Even then he had a cup in his hand. 'I might have finished him off and spared you the trouble, when I was up there in 'eighty-one, but Father wouldn't have liked it. And the savage has such a handsome wife – it seemed hard to make her a widow when I couldn't stay to comfort her. But bribe him! He's sitting in Carlisle – give it to him. Marry his daughter! Make him an earl!'

Rufus laughed harshly. 'If I keep rewarding people who stab me in the back, I won't have a hide of land left to myself!' He turned back to his maps. 'Send summons of array to the northern levies,' he told Robert Bloet. 'We'll march on their heels and give this damned cattle thief a surprise he hasn't looked for yet.'

After the council disbanded, the king seemed to notice me for the first time. As his lords left the chapter house, he beckoned to me, then flung his arm about me in a rough embrace. 'I've missed you, priest! Sinning was never so much p-pleasure, without you there to ch-chide me for it!' He said in my ear: 'Get me some relief from my brother. The old palace – it has a bad roof or something, doesn't it?'

'My lord, where will you take up residence tonight? Not at Westminster, I hope! The spring rains have gotten through the thatch again, I fear, and the floorboards are mildewed and warping.'

Maurice turned to me in surprise, as Westminster was no worse than it had ever been, but the king looked vexed. 'Damn that old ruin! I'm going to have it torn down when I have the time – and the money. Well, where shall we put our heads, then? The London Keep is still in the building, I suppose. Old Gundulph –'

'His Grace the Bishop of Rochester has suspended building for lack of coin,' I said. It was true. 'My lord, I am ashamed to meet you so ill prepared, but I would suggest you put your noble brother in Lord Ralph Baynard's house, to save him and his company the weary miles, while you must go to Windsor to find ample quarters.'

'That isn't necessary, Your Grace,' Maurice said. 'My own palace has ample room —'

'No, no, we can't put you and your clerks out in the stables to house us,' Rufus said hurriedly, giving my shoulder a squeeze. 'Ranulph's right — damn all these moldy old English barns! Robin! You'll be housed at Baynard's, do you hear? You'll get your dinner quicker there, and there'll be better accommodation for your — lady. The rest of us will bed down like soldiers, where we must, but my brother needn't suffer.' He laughed happily.

Robert Curthose wasn't difficult to persuade. He wanted the nearest table and the softest bed, and it pleased him to think he would be promenading through London the next day, receiving the cheers of the townfolk, after a night spent in luxury with Isabel in his arms. I was sent to make certain they were comfortable before riding west with the king.

I walked beside Isabel's wagon to the keep on the river. She gave me a triumphant look, then affected not to notice me. If I could have gotten her alone somewhere for a moment, I'd have wrung her neck. I saw it was bedecked with a golden chain and cross that must have belonged to the Lady Matilda.

I went into the castle with her as Robert Curthose lingered in conversation with Baynard in the yard, and saw her hampers taken up to a small chamber at the top of the square tower, where there was a narrow cot and a pile of straw pallets. Her women, if that's what they were to be called, had fallen behind to make eyes at some of Baynard's knights, but Isabel came to the doorway as I was inspecting the chamber.

'It's not very well aired, but I don't suppose you'll spend much time here,' I said, standing to one side so that she could enter.

She glanced at the bare mattress, with bits of straw sticking out of its worn cover, then smirked at me. 'You don't look nearly so glad to see me as the last time we were alone in a little cell like this. Have you forgotten?'

'Not a thing. Is there anything else I can do for you, my lady, or may I go now?'

'I think you're jealous to see me happy! It pleased you better to leave me with sore feet in a stranger's house.'

I started to leave the room, but she caught my arm and leaned against me to look up at me. 'You've no cause to be angry. You might even be a little grateful, since I never told anyone it was you who left me there half dead and without a sou. My lord says he'd like to have the liver out of the man who was so unkind to me.'

I unwound her fingers from my sleeve and pushed her away. 'You've repaid me for the silence I kept when you told your lover my son belonged to your lord husband. He might not be so eager to defend you if he knew how easily you bed down with common folk.'

She put her head around the door as I went out into the passage. 'He's a good lover, Ranulph, better than any I ever had before. It's a pity I didn't find him sooner.'

The stupid, silly bitch thought that would wound me! As if she were still the woman I had waited for every day in the cold nave of Our Lady of Rouen when I was a green boy. I bowed to Duke Robert on the stairs, then hurried back to my king. She had done me one good turn and probably didn't realize it: she had put Martin where I could watch him and take pleasure in knowing he was mine.

We rode out of London within the week, gathering our host as we went north. At every town our trumpets called men to duty from their tithings – freemen from their huts, knights from their fees, and lords from their country manors – to join us. Meanwhile, the royal fleet was set to sail from London and the southern ports, crammed with mercenaries and arms, to fall on Malcolm's coast and harry it, while we drove him back from Cumbria and his stolen vills.

But when we reached as far north as the Roman wall that once had been a barrier to the painted ancestors of the Scots, we found the land empty of all save our own levies. Robert Curthose had predicted it: Malcolm fell back at first word of our approach into the Cheviot Hills and beyond, to his own wilder marches. Our great army, nearly doubled by the addition of the northern fyrd, moved slowly north and east, spreading into Scotland from Northumberland and Durham, burning all they came to – which wasn't much. There were no towns of any size in the lower reaches of Scotland, only farms and cattle byres surrounding mean and ancient churches.

We turned toward the Forth, scouring all in our path as the cold sea air blew stronger in our faces, until we reached Lothian and heard dreadful news of our fleet. A pitiful straggle of men came out of the rocks to hail our vanguard. They were all that remained of the fleet.

Beating up the coast by St. Abb's Head, the ships had run into a storm that drove them perilously close to the rock cliffs of Lothian. They might have saved themselves, though their masts were snapping in the wind like kindling, but the inhabitants of that coast, warned of them, had doused the signal fires on their hills that told sailors of their peril. Now the shattered hulls of the king's ships lay strewn on the sea floor from St. Abb's to the mouth of the firth. Only one ship had survived to sail into calmer waters, and it had been taken by the Danish pirates Malcolm hired for his fleet.

The few men who found us had somehow survived capture when their vessels foundered and had been living in a half-starved condition, trying to make their way inland and south to safety by night marches.

Rufus was grim about his loss. He turned to Duke Robert: 'The prayers and candle burnings we made for them seem wa-wasted on God, don't they? If we'd let them sail without the Mass, they might have outrun the storm and still be alive.'

Curthose's chaplain, William d'Arques, nearly swallowed his tongue to hear that sentiment. He rebuked the king: 'Prayers to the Almighty are never wasted, Your Grace.'

'Then where are my ships?'

'The ways of God can't be explained as indifference, whenever there's a calamity, my good lord. To blame Him for our misfortunes is to blaspheme like unknowing children, who blame the sky because it chooses to rain on their folly —'

'Exactly! Just as I've always said: God has nothing to do with it, one way or another! It's wasting breath to blame Him – or to beseech Him for our fortunes. Ride on, master! I'm not in the mind for tutoring today!'

These angry words soon spread through the ranks of clerks and pious men, who muttered at the king's offending God when we might need the goodwill of Heaven to see our campaign to its conclusion. But the king had no sooner said the words than he forgot them and turned to plotting his march again, now his fleet couldn't give him the other claw of the pincers in which he hoped to catch Malcolm.

We turned along the coast of the firth and rode until we came to that hill fort which the Scots still name Dun-Edin, but which the English call Edinburgh. We sat down before its crag, protected by ravines and small lochs, which acted as natural moats. It had a town of sorts running like a sore along its eastern ridges, which we might have burned, but it was too high up and too well overlooked by the walls of its fort. Siege engines seemed useless for such a place, but the king ordered timbers cut for the making of an onager.

But before such an engine could be constructed, the high gate opened and three riders came out, the one to the fore bearing a banner as if for a truce. As he picked his way down the steep pitch, the wet sea wind spread his flag and I could see it was borrowed from God; it was the Cross of St. Andrew, the Scots' patron, embroidered in gold on a white ground.

At sight of it the king and Duke Robert were called out of their pavilion, along with their lords and squires. It was a cruel, cold day for that time of the year – only a little after Michaelmas – but the leaden sky had the way of such a one in the spring, that it lights and brings forth all colors under it with peculiar freshness. Even from a distance I could see the rich red of the rider's tunic and the wind-ruffled coif of pale hair on his unhelmed head. There was a glint of gold on his breast, too; he came altogether unarmed, so he must want a truce.

'It's Edgar!' Curthose cried out suddenly. His smile was like a child's in his surprise and eagerness to see his friend. 'Let me go out to meet him and bring him in.' He gripped his brother's arm. 'See, they want a parley! I told you so!'

Rufus lowered his head, looking up through his brows like a vexed bull. 'That damned parasite! I thought I was rid of him.'

'But where else did you think he'd go when you drove him out of my lands?' Curthose laughed. 'Let me ride out to him, for courtesy's sake, Will. I'll be your ambassador.'

The king nodded, then turned abruptly and went back into the tent.

Curthose called for his destrier and hopped it like a toad, raising his elbows and giving a shout, as if he'd sighted game. He went pelting out toward the Atheling, who drew rein at his approach. They met and spoke together. I heard Curthose laugh. Then they turned their horses' heads and went up the ridge toward the gate of Edinburgh.

For three days they were inside the fort while we kept watch around it. At the king's command, Hugh the Wolf took the finishing of the missile engine to himself and his men, while the rest of the lords of the fyrd drilled on the uneven ground or sat gambling before their tents in the firelight of an evening. Rufus stayed in his tent, unless he was on horse, inspecting his lines. Every day he grew shorter of temper and more sullen.

'He's up there, swilling! By God, when my onager's ready to kick, I'll remind him of what he's there for!'

Yet when Hugh of Chester made much the same comment on

Robert's delay, the king said crisply: 'He's my envoy. Let him do his work and I'm satisfied.'

On the third day a banneret from our western flank came galloping to say an army was approaching from West Lothian. There was an immediate scramble for mail, helms, and arms; trumpets blew, destriers screamed, and our host was astride and away to meet the enemy, leaving only clerks, boys, and wagoners behind.

It was Malcolm, coming in along the upper firth from Dunfermline. He hadn't been dawdling those three days past in Dun-Edin; Edgar had been delaying us until he came. We who were left in camp strained our eyes to see when the battle would begin.

But there was no battle. As the vanguards of the hosts approached each other, the gates of the high fort opened and let out a small troop of horse at the head of which were two riders, each with a white pennant of truce tied to his lance. They rode between the opposing armies and halted them; then, at a signal from each, two heralds broke away from their escort and rode, one to each army, proclaiming a truce and offering the mediation of Edgar Atheling and Robert, Duke of Normandy, to make such terms as should be agreeable to either side.

All this I report only as a Spartan messenger: from afar. From where I stood I could see little but the rumps of our own cavalry, and Robert riding down with Edgar to stop their advance. There was a lengthy parley; then the armies broke apart again into their several camps. The two kings went up together to the castle with their envoys.

After a time, a young squire came down to inform us that the kings were in agreement there should be no war, and we should prepare to remove ourselves to Dunfermline across the water. For the main body of the host this meant a lengthy march up the narrowing shoals of the firth, then back again as far, since Dunfermline lay northwest across the firth from Edinburgh. Only the king's own household troops were to stay and be ferried across the water, along with his baggage and household servants, of which I was one.

We crossed the water and went up into Dunfermline, climbing innumerable stairs to the crest where the king's great house shambled off in all directions. Again, it was more like an English thane's wick than a Norman castle, this ancient capital of the southern Scots. Queen Margaret lived there the year long, unwilling to leave her life's work nearby, the building of her priory.

I expected the inside of Dunfermline to be as barbaric as its shell, with smoke-blackened rafters hung with antlers, smoked meats, and perhaps the head of the late King of the Scots, Macbeth macFindlech, whom Malcolm had slain in order to reach his throne. But when I came into the hall I smelled roasted mutton rather than rotting timbers and stale rushes. The rude walls were hung with bright woven work, the tables were laid with snowy cloths, and there must have been a hundred torches as well as candles to light the splendid gloom.

Rufus sat at the high table with his host and the queen. Malcolm was a little fellow, rather bandy-legged, but broad in the shoulders and deep in the chest as a man is who carries arms all his life. He had an inordinately large, egg-shaped head, thatched with curly hair that had been flame red in his youth, but was now subdued with gray. His hair was plaited at the ends and his beard was full, reaching halfway down his breast. He had long, light eyes under scanty brows; fox's eyes, which took in everything as quickly as Robert de Bellesme, but with amusement rather than suspicion. Two of his sons stood behind his stool, one already sprouting a russet beard, the other still only a slender boy.

Margaret, his queen, sat next to him, looking serenely over her hall, though from time to time she inclined her head in her lord's direction, showing she listened to the speech between him and Rufus. I came to the foot of the dais in my turn and bowed to her, then took the liberty of staring her in the face, as she had already become famous for her wisdom and piety.

She was one of the most striking women I have ever seen. She had the same long, melancholy face as her brother Edgar, but colder and almost preternaturally still. When she spoke her lips scarcely moved and her voice was so low that it was difficult to hear, even without the uproar of a packed hall. Her eyes were like ice crystals, set with pale sapphires and fringed with amber lashes. Her hair was a rich, golden color, smoothed and worked into two great plaits that hung over her breasts down to her waist. She merely nodded when the lords of my king's court presented themselves to her, but when our bishops came, followed by the rest of us in black robes, her faint, sweet smile brought a tinge of life to her face, and she rose courteously to come down and kiss Maurice's and Walkelin's rings, then took us aside to a little chamber behind the hall.

'Good Fathers, please make yourselves free of my private hall and all my own chambers above us, which you may reach by those little steps. Kings and soldiers pay small heed to the days of fast, but I remember this is the feast of St. Denis of Paris. For those of you under his guardianship, I offer a simple meal and a place to pray or meditate on his virtues. Sit, and my servants will bring you food.'

She was about to retire from the room, having uttered that speech, when old Walkelin stopped her. 'Lady, we thank you. But will you not join us here and speak to us on a subject dear to the hearts of good Christians of any race – the state of the Holy Church in Scotland?' Maurice murmured his approval of that suggestion, which was taken up by several other of the clergy, especially Robin Bloet, who had been staring at her like a smitten lover ever since she had spoken his name in greeting.

She glanced about at them; then her sad little smile came again. She bowed her head, folding her long hands together.

'I am not worthy to say what you wish to hear, good Fathers, but it would honor me to sit with you for a time and hear you speak.'

'Lady, there is no one in Scotland better informed on the matter than yourself. You are famed for your charities as well as for your learning,' Robin said, at which compliment she gracefully yielded and took her place at our table.

For the next two hours she talked about Scottish piety, liturgy, ritual; about the ancient Celtic order of monks, the Culdees, who had built a religious house on Dunfermline's hill before there was a castle there, or a Scot who called himself king. Under the encouragement of her hearers, she spoke of her early life, how she and her family had come from Hungary to England at the call of Edward Confessor, when that old, childless man at last remembered his half brother's exiled son, who was her father. She spoke of the Confessor and made old Walkelin, who remembered him, weep. Her pale face and hair wore a halo of candle shine; her long white hands made gestures that put me in mind of pictures of the Holy Virgin.

As she warmed to her subject, her smile came more readily, until there wasn't a man in the room, from Walkelin in his dotage to the youngest chancel clerk, who wasn't glowing with love for her. Robin, who was sitting next to me, sighed. 'She's an angel! How could God give her to a brute like Malcolm?'

'Whom would you have given her to?' I murmured.

He frowned. 'I'm not a marriage broker. I mean she – she seems too exquisite for any man's touch. She's like a goddess, all gold and white.' He sighed again and forgot me again in looking at her.

Perhaps she was all she seemed, but I looked at her with the knowledge that she had tamed the wily Malcolm, borne him six children, reformed the Scottish Church to her liking with imported Norman priests and liturgy, and had such a hold on her brother Edgar that he still ran to her as if he were a boy and she his nurse. That lady was no ivory saint too good for this world; she was a woman much like Isabel de Montfort – even stronger, perhaps, as she never needed to put on armor to impress her subjects and kin with her strength.

I also thought in my private mind that she must be a delight between the bed sheets. No one ever rumored Malcolm to have gotten any bastards or kept any concubines after he'd wed her. But this opinion, though I might once have shared it with Robin before he was beglamoured, I kept to myself.

The next morning when Mass was said in the chapel, I saw the two daughters of Margaret and thought again how I might urge marriage with one of them on the king. It would be better than his taking another son for a hostage. They were still children, but the elder, Edgyth, was ten and tall for her age, slender and blond like her mother, with the same fine bones and clear eyes. I decided it would do no harm to feel the matter out with someone I felt might approve the union. So, when Mass was concluded and all the rest of the company had finished the day-meal and were dispersed about the castle, or gone out to ride with the two kings, I went up into the queen's gallery. I found her at her needlework with the children and her women around her.

I bowed. She graciously offered me a stool by her, though she was plainly surprised to have me for a visitor and was at a loss to remember my name.

We talked about the altar cloth she was embroidering for her priory; then I said: 'Your Grace, will you think me light-minded if I tell you of a dream I had last night?'

'A dream, Father?'

'Yes. I hope it won't offend or distress you to hear it. I must confess, I have never had much confidence in dreams myself, as omens or messages – except for those dreamed by saints and other folk holier than myself. But – do you hold that such dreams which seem to foretell the future are sent to us by God, or are only the whimsies of our own minds?'

I could tell I had piqued her curiosity. She knew this dream of mine must have something to do with affairs between her husband

and my king, or I would never approach her with it. Her eyes flickered to her women and the little girls; then she ran her needle several times into the fabric she was embellishing and laid her work aside.

'It's a fair day abroad, I'm told, in spite of the chill. Will you come and walk with me to the priory, Father? We say prayers there every day at None for the souls of those in the royal family who died in their sins. Scotland has had a bloody history, I fear.'

'Are there so many of them, lady? Not that I fear long prayers, but haven't the kings of Scotland been in the Faith now for many years?'

'Oh, yes, in the Faith – and out of it, when it pleased them. My lord the king was very lax in his duty to Holy Church when I first came here. I wouldn't marry him until he promised to attend Mass every day. I found he had neglected it, because he'd had a blood debt to pay and couldn't yet repent the sin in his own heart. That was for slaying King Macbeth macFindlech.' She blessed herself.

'But this King Macbeth – he'd murdered your lord husband's father, hadn't he? It seems to me his death must have been deserved.'

'All our deaths are deserved in the end, aren't they? Yes, Macbeth took Duncan's life. He was his cousin. But Duncan had slain Macbeth's father and brother, too, they say. So, I pray for them all, but especially for the Lady Gruoch, who was King Macbeth's wife, because she took her life in madness, in her grief for what her lord had done.' She blessed herself again with a floating drift of white hand, which I found myself wanting to catch, to see if it felt like human flesh.

As we walked out into the sunlight, all the men of the castle yard momentarily stopped their speech or labor to look at her, but we might have been on the moon for all the notice she gave in return. She had folded those lovely hands against her breasts, as if she were already at prayer for the bloody dead of Malcolm's race. It was a characteristic pose I had already seen her assume, but it seemed false, somehow; there was premeditation in all that she said or did.

'You are the chaplain of the king, I know – the one they call Flambard? You must tell me, sometime, why they gave you such a name. But now you may tell me of this dream of yours – and why you feel you must reveal it to me, of all people. If you think it has some meaning, you should tell it to your king, shouldn't you?'

'Madam, when I tell it to you, I think you will see why I didn't take it first to my master. It may be nothing, only I felt this morning that you had inspired it last night.'

'I?' She looked up at me directly for the first time since I had spoken of my dream. Her eyes were very intelligent. 'How have I inspired you to dream? I hope this is no foolishness, Father.'

'Madam, last night you spoke of how you came to Scotland, when you were no more than a girl, and of how you first heard the king who is your husband declare his desire to marry you. You told him you had no desire to marry, but rather wished to serve God as His handmaid in a house of religion.'

'Yes. From my earliest days I wanted to be a nun.'

'But you put that desire away from you, because you felt God had directed you to the man, to redeem his soul from the sloth it had fallen into.'

'Yes,' she said softly, 'that is how it was.'

A race of clouds passed over the sun and shadowed her face as we walked along the path to the priory church. The wind was strong on that hilltop; I spread my cloak a little to shield her from its gusts. 'Have you lived to regret your sacrifice?'

She didn't answer, but pursed her mouth slightly to show her disapproval of my bold question. 'What was this dream?'

'Your Grace, last night I thought I saw my master on the brink of a deep ravine, a greater one than this that runs below us. His feet were on the very edge of it, but he didn't seem aware of his danger. I, and some others, were calling to him, begging him to take care. I would have run to him and pulled him away from the chasm, but, as it often is in such dreams, I was bound by some invisible power and couldn't move from my place. Now, the dream was the more distressing because I knew, with that power that's given to us in such dreams, that the pit he stood before was no pit of this world, but the very Pit of Hell. I could see the glow of the eternal flames and smell the stench of the brimstone, but still he stood ignorant of the danger.'

'That was a dreadful dream, indeed. How did it end?'

'Most wonderfully. All at once there was another person by him, a young maid, very young and fair. She took my king by the hand and led him away from the precipice, at which time he seemed to know the service she had done him. He bent his knee to her and kissed her hands. I heard him ask her who she was that had been his savior. And this was the strangest part of all – she said: 'I am the daughter of the Two Exiles, who will soon come home.' Then I saw she was decked as a bride, with a chaplet of flowers binding her hair, though I hadn't noticed such a thing before. The king looked on her with great tenderness – and then I woke.'

I had caught this fantasy out of the air the previous night. Queen

Margaret was the daughter of King Edmund Ironsides's son – a man called Edward the Wanderer – who had been exiled from infancy because of the Danish conquest. She herself spoke of her mother's flight to Scotland with her and her siblings, after King William's coming, as an exile. I thought that to add more would be too blatant, so I didn't tell her that the virgin of my 'dream' was her little Edgyth, but rather left her to work that out for herself, if she would.

She had her head bowed in thought as we approached the priory gate, but as I rang the bell for the porter, she looked at me with an almost forbidding frown.

'You are certain that this is the dream you had? You haven't changed anything, or added any part? Sometimes, when we dream, we wake to such a confusion that we try to work a thing into our dreaming, to fill a gap of reason in it. You haven't done this? Be truthful.'

'Your Grace, I said it to you as it came into my brain last night.' Which was perfectly true.

The porter opened the gate and bowed to her, but she went in ahead of me, shaking her head. 'It's very strange – the daughter of two exiles? Very strange – ' She went up into the church.

41

Did the queen believe my fiction of a dream? Who can say? Women will believe what they wish to believe, the same as men. She knew what I proposed, and the idea had its appeal for her. How many chances could she hope for, to marry one of her daughters to a throne? In a few years she must give them up to someone, probably one of the half-savage Scottish thanes to whom her husband owed consideration, or to a cloister.

Queen Margaret was a proud woman, proud of her own piety, proud of her influence with her husband, and, above all, proud of her lineage. Her father was the direct descendant of the old pagan idol Wodin, if one chooses to believe the English fabulists. Her mother was the daughter of Stephen of Hungary and a kinswoman of the German emperor, through her own mother.

According to Margaret's belief, her brother Edgar had been cheated of his rightful crown by the treachery of his chief barons,

Edwin and Morcar, who surrendered to the Conqueror just after they joined Stigand of Canterbury in proclaiming Edgar King of England.

So, it couldn't fail but she had thought of putting a child of her body on the throne of an English king as soon as there was one available who lacked a wife. If I'd had any doubts on that matter, she put them to rest in the next several days by graciously sending for me to continue our conversation.

She was avid to hear all there was to know about William the Younger, though she seemed indifferent to him when she was in his company at the table. She said it was for modesty's sake that she refrained from taking part in the parleys of Rufus and Malcolm, but I knew, as everyone else did, that she had the ear of her lord whenever she wished to speak to him.

I obliged her by telling her what she wished to hear about my master. His virtues of loyalty and modesty she took without comment; they scarcely seemed to interest her. It was such weaknesses as I discreetly revealed that piqued her soul; his halting tongue, his ready temper, even his occasional irreverence toward the Church drew her better.

Why should a pious mother find these qualities more intriguing than his strengths? Few ordinary mothers would look for them in the man to whom they might consider affiancing a beloved daughter. But Queen Margaret was no ordinary mother. She was a born warrior, deprived of the glory of physical contest by her sex, but who had battled for the mind and soul of just such a flawed man in her own youth, giving up her professed dream of life in a cloister in order to wield power over King Malcolm.

He was her creation; she had made him fear her piety, made him fear God, attend Holy Service with regularity, indulge in charity, which was foreign to his basic nature. He learned to smile when she rifled his treasure chests to enrich a religious house, or to clothe and feed a host of sycophantic clergy. Unable to read a psaltery, he fervently kissed hers when he saw her perusing it. He was her great work, more so than her new priory.

But it was an old conquest. There was no challenge left in him for her, nor could she take on the challenge of another lost soul in quite the same manner, being a loyal and dutiful wife. In William Rufus she divined one who might be the work of her daughter's life. What next best thing to the conquest of such a king could there be but to send the flesh of one's flesh to the enterprise?

So, we spoke several times of the king, how he should marry a

480

pure and noble woman, but we never discussed the possibility that his bride should be little Edgyth or Mary. Had I been rash enough to propose such a thing to her, she would have been amazed and would have rebuffed me. The proposal must come from herself.

Meanwhile, we amused each other by toying with the idea, and with words, as we exchanged pious homilies on duty, happiness, and marriage. It was very much like a courtship, or a game of some sort with a worthy opponent – which was precisely why I think she found me agreeable company in her visits to the new priory. She was, for all her wealth and success, a woman desperately bored with her good works and her too-familiar sycophants.

Robert Bloet was amazed by my popularity with her; envious, too:

'Damn you, Raf, I adore that woman! If she let me kiss her little finger I'd never wipe my lips again. Why doesn't she invite me to take walks with her? I can't imagine what your talents must be, but I'd think you'd be decent enough to reveal the secret and give me a chance to shine, for the sake of friendship. What is it you talk about?'

'Politics, religion, the sinful state of Man, the high wages that must be paid to get a good stone carver. All the topics you find so boring when we're at home.'

'Oh, come now, I'm capable of better talk than that! I'm a very charming fellow; everybody says so, including me, and I can talk on any subject fit for a lady's ears.'

'Like the last hearth girl you cornered in your lodgings?'

'Like song, poetry, and the mysteries of the universe, damn it! A gentleman doesn't discuss the salaries of stonecutters with a goddess.'

I laughed. 'I'll put in a word for you the next chance I find, Robin, but I think you've mistaken your woman. She does like music, however. I can tell her you used to be Odo's choirmaster, before you became a man of cares. She might ask you to rehearse her choristers, or something. '

'Thank you so much, you bastard.'

I did recommend him to the queen, who found him as charming as he was. I had done what I could with her and now felt I should turn my attention to the direction the parley was taking. The king was a touch ironic about my reappearance by his side:

'Is the q-queen having birth pains?'

'Why, no, my lord, not to my knowing. Is she breeding?'

'I haven't noticed. I just thought it might take something like that to get you back to me. They're not lackwits in this house when they can distract *you* from your duty.'

'My lord, my days of dalliance are ended, but they were innocent. What is it that King Malcolm will have of you, for the trouble of burning your tithe barns?'

He snorted. 'About half my kingdom might s-soothe his conscience, I think. Yesterday he said I might make one of his sons an earl, or some such thing, since I had plenty of vacant titles.'

We were going down from the bedchamber to the great hall, on a stair so narrow that no more than two could walk abreast. I may have offended Robert Curthose by attaching myself to the king's side which made him walk behind me. He was straining to hear our talk.

'Tell him, priest, that making young Edward an earl is cheaper than keeping him for a hostage.'

'Cheaper than keeping *him* for a brother, too,' Rufus muttered. 'God's Face, will he go home when we've finished here, do you think? His endless talk is driving me m-mad.'

We entered the hall to hear Malcolm making a keening speech of reproof to his servants for not having prepared the table for us beforehand. His Gaelic cadences were so like Cormac's in that high-raftered, dusty mead hall that Rufus stopped short in the doorway. He caught my eye and made a wry grin.

'Just for a mo-moment, I thought – '

'Yes, my lord, so did I.'

'It must be the reason I'm letting him take advantage of me the way he does. Pass by, Robin, pass by,' he said too heartily to his brother, who was trying to wedge himself between us. We stepped aside to let the rest of our procession through the door. The king drew me to him for a further whispered speech:

'Yesterday he had the impudence to tell me he can't pay for what his thieves stole from me, but he'll give money to the new minster at Durham, to honor another Scot who wandered too far south.' He laughed explosively. 'How's that for cheek?'

'Perhaps he hopes his charity will earn him a better reception at St. Cuthbert's the next time he comes on a raid.'

'Well, it won't. I'm calling Carileph back to his throne there as soon as I'm free of this place.'

I was silent. He looked at me shrewdly. 'You don't approve? I've pardoned everyone else. Why not someone who can be of use to me? He knows how to defend a position, as I found to my cost.'

'My lord, he does that. But you have the use of his rents and fees now. If you call him back, you'll be the poorer in purse for it.'

'You'll find some way to make up the difference, I hope.' He moved away from me toward the waiting Malcolm at the far end of the hall. 'You're jealous of him? Afraid he'll crowd you too much?'

'No, my lord. He's an able man. I'll welcome his coming home again.'

'Liar. But he's coming, so get used to it.'

That day was the last of the parleys, as it turned out. The differences of opinion concerning where the true boundaries lay between our countries had been settled as well as could be expected and still they were vague in certain areas. We left them so and turned to the means by which peace in that shadowy area might be maintained. King Malcolm really wanted an earldom, I believe, but he settled for the rule and revenue of twelve villages instead, including the one that surrounded Carlisle, where he had already boldly installed an underling of his, the son of an English traitor.

For his twelve vills he would become Rufus's 'man': do homage on his knees to him at the next Easter Court. Afterward, he would take responsibility for guarding our northern coasts, on both the Cumbrian and Lothian sides, against pirates and Danes – which some people might suppose to be the same, but the Irish were their rivals for the trade.

Malcolm must use his own ships and crews, but Rufus would give him a stipend of twelve marks in gold per year for their maintenance. These, and other minor agreements, were hammered out that last day, for the most part between Duke Robert and Edgar Atheling. I sat behind the king's stool, watching the two of them, and thought it odd how they, who had so little power to direct their own lives and fortunes, were thus made potent in the fortunes of others mightier than themselves.

But it is often just such men who best lend themselves to the art of compromise, who make worthy tools for kings. Edgar was redeeming himself in the eyes of one such king. The sarcasms of Rufus when Edgar first made his appearance at Edinburgh were gradually muted; his sharp laughter lessened into an occasional chuckle, and his eyes were on Edgar's earnest face more often than they turned toward Malcolm's.

To give him his due, Edgar had done his job well. He exhibited both patience and tenacity in his often interrupted arguments for peace. He was never made angry by Malcolm's digressions or the ironies of Rufus. He never let go a point until it was resolved. This earned him warm praise from Robert's adherents and even from some among the barons of our own court, who were well aware of how he had just been deprived of his beloved estates and horses by Rufus and was grudged more than temporary refuge at the court of Malcolm.

I began to wonder if this rekindling of a dangerous old affection would come to be an inconvenience to me. Edgar wasn't a man of Cormac's unique stamp. He could never make so deep a mark on my master's heart and character as once he had. I allowed that if my king must have an infatuation for a worthless man, it was more safely bestowed on someone like Edgar, who was cautious, pious, and seemingly without ambition. But one can never be certain what the taste of power will do to any man. If my hopes for the king's marriage should come to fruition, Edgar's influence as the little queen's uncle might make him something else altogether.

I was still musing on that when the last affirmation was made and the two kings rose from their stools to clasp hands, then embrace.

That evening there was a feast to celebrate the accord. All the lords of the southern Scots were in attendance, some still glowering at us in spite of having given oath to support the pact. Our barons of note – Hugh, Earl Robert Mowhray, Count William de Eu, Richard of Tonbridge, and the rest – wore their finest shirts and smiled like happy men who would soon be going home to their more interesting affairs. The queen consented to honor the high table with her presence, looking something like the Blessed Mother – no sacrilege intended – in a white robe, blue mantle, and blue veil of exquisite sendal.

She poured out wine for all at the high table with her own hands, and I thought old Walkelin would faint when she bent over his shoulder and gave him her gelid smile. I sat at the upper end of one of the lower tables, content to watch the show, but I was unprepared for the turn it would take. King Malcolm, without prelude, suddenly brought forth that little matter I had been playing at with his queen:

'Our peace is well-nigh perfect, my lords, but still it lacks somewhat of a thing to give it substance.'

'Twelve marks and twelve vills – aren't they substantial enough, my lord?' Rufus asked with an irritated laugh.

Malcolm looked at him with a merry light in his pale eyes, which beamed out from under his rusty brows like those of a fox secure in its own earth.

'How if I gave *you* a gift, man – better than vills and purses?'

Rufus laughed again. 'Why, I'd take it! The novelty of it would be too much to resist. What will you give me, my lord, that's better than marks?'

'A wife, laddie! A guid wife, as it says in the Holy Book, is better than rubies. How do you say to that?' He was smiling broadly now, showing his yellowed, wide-spaced teeth.

Rufus let his own smile slip a bit, then coughed out a laugh and drank from his cup. 'What's this you'd have me do, marry one of your girls? They're babes; I've heard you say so. You don't marry infants here in Scotland, do you?'

'Who says my girls are babes? Not I. They're out of their swaddles by many a year. Girls they are, but girls grow into women soon enough, man. I'll let you see 'em for yourself. Margaret, send for them to come down to us. They're not in their cradles yet, are they?'

There was a general murmur of interest at the high table, but those who spoke were unable to see the face of Rufus, who was hard put to keep the anger out of his voice as he said: 'Leave them where they are, my lord. This hall is no place for children.'

'They see it every day,' Malcolm said. 'Margaret, my love, go and fetch 'em down.'

The queen rose to obey, her eyes cast down, no expression other than submission on her smooth face. While she was gone, the general conversation was subdued to hear Malcolm extol his daughters: 'They're *bonne* girls, both of 'em, my lord. You'll see. The least one is shy and might not suit you, but the elder, Edgyth, is a fair copy of her mother – and no man could ask for better than that, by God! She's a douce bairn, but smart as a Tay badger. She can read, by God, and she's got all her prayers by heart. She'd do you proud before God, and if she's like her mother, she'll bear you a houseful of healthy bairns, what's more important.'

The men of the lower tables cheered him for that observation, then scraped back their stools to stand as the queen brought her daughters down from her bower. Little Mary, who was about eight, was rubbing her eyes and clinging to her mother's side, as if she had indeed just been pulled from her cradle, but Edgyth, whom I had seen before, walked wide-eyed and grave without so much as a touch of her mother's hand to urge her. I felt she had been prepared for this moment, as her sister had not.

Rufus stood up, though Malcolm had just given an impatient wave of his hand to signal that all the rest should sit. The queen stopped by her chair, bowed her head to speak a word to Mary, but couldn't budge her from her fixed place at her skirts. Edgyth might have been given a slight shove, though I didn't notice it. She went to Rufus and made a courtesy, her slender back very straight.

He was red and sweating, but her demeanor pleased him enough to make him smile at her in that sudden way which always seemed to make him better-looking than he was. He offered for her hand and she gave it to him; he kissed it, as if she were a grown woman.

'Well, now, have we spoiled your sleep, my lady? What's your name?'

She told him. Her head turned slightly to one side as she frankly studied him.

'That's a fair name, like the maid that bears it.' I noticed he didn't stammer with her, in spite of his vexation. 'Will you give me leave to sit again? That way you won't have to look so hard to see me.'

'Yes, my lord,' she said in a faint but sweet voice. 'Am I going to be your prisoner, like my brother?'

'By the – who told you that?'

'No one. I just wondered. I'm the next oldest. Davy's too young for a hostage.'

'So he is. No, sweetheart, I'm not going to take you away from your mother, nor any of your sibs. I've heard good things about you, and I daresay they're all true, if you'd take your brother's place in one of my donjons.'

She looked a bit worried for that, but accepted the compliment. Rufus gave her hand another quick salute, then let it fall. 'Go back to your nurse, now, and sleep well, E-eeg – ' The Saxon name defeated him.

The child supplied it: 'Edgyth. You're like my brother. He has to call me Edith. Why are your eyes different?'

Malcolm stirred and frowned; the queen quickly bent forward to admonish the girl; but to everyone's relief Rufus smiled.

'To be honest with you, sweetheart, I've w-wondered about that, myself. I think God played a little joke on me, don't you? Which of them do you like better?'

'The blue one. It's laughing. The other is sad.'

He sobered and bent to kiss her cheek, then turned her back to her mother, who took her and her sister away again. Rufus took up his cup and drained it, then nodded to Malcolm.

'She's a beauty, my lord. As you say, she'll rival her mother one day.'

'She likes you well. Take her, man, for she's almost ripe for the picking and then she'll have suitors clogging up my door. You'd do well to pledge for her ahead of her time. When they're young, you can train them up the way you want them to grow, like a grapevine, or a good pup. Think on it, my lord, and maybe we'll drink a cup of a different kind together before we part.'

He got no direct reply. Rufus turned to other matters for discussion, but meanwhile his eyes scanned the faces of his barons, his befuddled brother, Prince Edgar, and myself. When he got to me, I thought he lingered thoughtfully. I smiled and half lifted a shoulder, and he switched his gaze to Robin Bloet. I would be questioned later, I knew. Yet I was pleased with myself. The interview with the child had been unexpected, but altogether satisfactory. She didn't flinch from him, and he had approved of her. It was a fair start.

The next day we took our leave of Dunfermline, though not of Malcolm and his family. They gave us attendance all the way down to Durham, where we paused to witness the signing of a charter for the monks of St. Cuthbert's shrine whom William de St. Carileph had installed there after expelling the secular clergy just before his exile.

It was remarked on that the queen was showing an extraordinary courtesy to us by accompanying her husband on this journey; even more, she brought her children with her. She rode in a litter, but the children, even Mary and Edgyth, were allowed to ride their ponies in the train of the two kings. I thought this was a bit too obvious, myself, though the reason given was that our Scottish princes who were hostages would be allowed to reunite with their family briefly in Durham – and so it was. Yet the chief reason for the outing seemed to me to be to expose Rufus further to the charms of Edgyth.

When we parted ways and final gifts and good wishes were exchanged, Edgyth came to the king with a holy medal on a silver chain and, with his consent, hung it about his neck. This made a sweet sight that brought tears to the eyes of old Bishop Walkelin and got a cheer out of our knights. Rufus thanked her for her gift, then, after a moment's hesitation, removed a ring from his little finger and placed it on her thumb, where it dangled loosely. His face gave nothing away of what suspicions might be lodged in his heart. It was only when we rode away south at a pace little short of a battlefield charge that some might have suspected the impatience that had been growing in him over the past week.

With the northern levies dismissed, he led the remnant of his host on such a chase over the low hills that our wagons were far behind and our horses wheezing with fatigue before he called a halt. After a brief rest we went forward again as if devils were in pursuit of us, until we reached our first day's camp at a great bend in the Tees.

He called me aside as his tent was being pitched and made me walk along the river's edge with him until we were out of earshot from the rest. Then he turned on me with a dangerous light in his eye.

'I have something for you, chaplain.' He took me by the wrist and dropped into my hand the silver chain and medal.

'My lord, this is too precious a gift to bestow on me.'

'Somehow I think you earned it.' He was no longer smiling.

'Your Grace, I –'

'Don't start "Gracing" me! You never do that unless you've got some honey-and-horse-fart lie you want to shove down my throat. You've been busy behind my back, haven't you?'

'My lord, it wasn't my intention to lie to you.'

'Good! Then tell me how you've had your tongue in Margaret's ear for the past week, because I know you have. I have those w-who do t-tell me things. Who gave you leave to be my f-father and make promises of me t-to a child? You're disgusting and so is that little wench's mother, if she agreed to it! Don't tell me you weren't in it up to your teeth, because I've been watching you. I saw how you smirked with joy when that infant p-pr-prattled to me at the feast. You'll be selling Irish slave girls next, you – I'd have put a curb in your mouth right away, if there'd been any way to do it in private, but I didn't, because I seem to have more c-care for your honor than you have for mine.'

'My lord, as God is my witness, I never mentioned a marriage between you and the maid to the queen. It was her own inclination. I meant to speak to you about it beforehand, but she outstripped me. You did have other important matters to take your time. But in the end what harm has been done, my lord? You promised nothing. The King of Scots is happy imagining you might. While he thinks so, he may keep to his side of the border. And – if you think of it without heat – the child is an amiable possibility, isn't she?'

'You're pandering again!'

'I beg your indulgence, my lord, but I'm not! She's a child today, not ready for marriage, while you are a king with much yet to do before you have leisure to take a wife. But in five years she will be a woman grown, while you will be a king well settled in his rule and still in the prime of his life. Is it not possible to consider it thus, instead of charging me with vice for having made a – a distant inquiry?'

There seemed to be blood coming into his eye as well as to his cheeks. He said in a low, rough voice: 'Distant? No. That's not your way of asking. Priest, did you take anything for this business? A bribe? Is there fresh money in your purse now? Don't lie to me.'

I was so alarmed by his tone that I forgot myself and cried out angrily: 'No, by God, there isn't! No! Take my purse and see for yourself!' I heard the stridence in my voice; it might have carried clear back to camp. 'I – my lord forgive me. I never meant to defy you. What I did was done for love of you and for no other reason. But if I've lost your confidence for it, I've lost more than the whole tribe of Scotland could pay me.'

His eyes held mine, but then he drew breath and sighed, his anger seeming to go with the sound. 'Very well. I believe you. Why not? You're my friend, my most valuable servant. Where's the need for you to take a bribe, eh? You have the farm of my rents, my wards, my court fees. That should be enough to keep you loyal. We'll say no more about it. You're still my friend. There isn't a man I know whom I'd more hate to hang.'

42

I felt as if a scorching wind had swept over my head when he spoke of hanging, but I reasoned he hadn't rejected my argument concerning the little princess; he had only resented my too-obvious work on her behalf, which seemed to make a fool of him. I would be more careful in the future.

I wrote my first letter to Queen Margaret the evening we returned to London. We no sooner came to town than the king was surrounded by couriers, come to tell him how the Welsh had taken advantage of his absence to overrun the marcher garrisons again. He was in conference with his barons far into the night.

It was ill news, coming on the heels of the Scottish campaign, but the king didn't seem dismayed by it. He was glad for the excuse to put off Duke Robert once more. Robert had been demanding he make good his promise to come overseas again and help him to win back his lost territories in Maine and the Vexin. Now Robert had no choice but to return home alone or accompany his brother to the Welsh marches.

He went with him and so did Edgar Atheling. The difference between the two of them was the difference between a man going to glory in battle and a man going to a distant kinsman's bridal – and not a kinsman he had overmuch affection for. To add to Robert's disappointment, he had once again lost his dearest friend to Rufus.

Since we had left Durham, the Atheling and the king had ridden together, raced their horses for sport and wager, laughed together, and, in the final days, shared a tent. The last was as much a pain to me as to Curthose, who found himself abandoned in his pavilion, ostensibly because of a game of draughts that had gone on too long.

By the time we reached London it was certain the old affection had been fully reestablished, without a care for what Robert or anybody else might think. I found myself barred from the chamber until sent for. All the other favored squires, knights, or common soldiers who had enjoyed free access to the king were put aside. Robert Bloet raised his fine brows at me and shrugged when we presented ourselves to the king on the morrow after homecoming and discovered we must wait a full quarter of an hour to be admitted to the bedchamber, where it was my privilege to say a morning prayer for him, and Robin's to inform him of his day's activities in court.

I said nothing to Robin's little shrug. I kept my face from informing against me. But I noticed one who didn't hide his sulks, and that was my son Martin. He was waiting impatiently in the passage outside the bedchamber when Robin and I came away from its door.

I touched him on the arm and said: 'Come along, boy. It seems you're reprieved from your morning duties. Have you been to your mother since we came home? She'll be glad to see you and hear all about your journey.'

Isabel had been left in London, in the home of a Rouen merchant who was personally acquainted with the duke and honored to house his newest mistress.

'Come with me, Martin. We'll hear First Service, break our fast, then ride in to see her together.'

He shook off my hand. 'I'll wait here. My lord may want me.'

'Boy, he has two other squires to call to dress him. Let them, and we'll visit your mother.'

'Visit her yourself! I have my duty.'

I hadn't the least desire to visit Isabel myself, the whore, but the boy had a duty to her and I liked to think he was man enough to know it. 'Go and see your mother, today. You may not have another chance for a while.'

Martin gave me a rude stare. 'What do you care whether I see her or not? I'll stay here and attend to my duty.'

Robin was taking an interest in our exchange, obviously surprised I should mention Martin's mother to him, so I left the boy slumped against the wall and went down to the hall.

'A case of hurt pride,' I said by way of mitigation. 'He's just discovered the humbling one gets in service to the great. The neglect will be good for his character, which is a touch surly.'

Robin said: 'He's just discovering what it is to be an outworn favorite. His fellows among the esquires are probably waiting downstairs to tease him, I shouldn't wonder, seeing how he's been preening himself for the past two months.'

'What's that?'

Robin grinned. 'I'm surprised you haven't seen it, if you've noticed him enough to know who his mother is. He's been kept busy, trotting from the king to the duke, ever since he came to court overseas with that winsome old trollop who gave him birth. It's a wonder he still has the strength to stand. It must go hard, having to share an admirer with one's mother. What's the matter with you? You look pale. Here, take my arm before you pitch down the steps.'

I put my hand to the wall to steady myself. 'It's nothing; a moment of giddiness. Too much wine and too little sleep of late. I'm all right now. No, really, it was nothing.' He was looking truly concerned, and the whole subject of Martin was forgotten on the instant.

'You need some real food in your belly. See Maurice. He'll give you dispensation to break your fast. You're not saying a service this morning, are you?'

'No, but it's nothing, Robin, truly. A sign of age. If you have anything to send to Maurice, let me go. I want to see my brothers at St. Paul's in any event.'

'Then go and see them. Maurice will be here in an hour or so. I'll make your excuses. Go, get some fresh air – and have a bite before you do.'

I thanked him and hurried away to the brief ride into London. As I rode along the river, I felt my stomach still knotting painfully at the memory of Robin's offhand remark. My son – Martin – doing catamite service between Rufus and Curthose? No, it was impossible! I would have seen it. I would have heard something. I was in the king's presence every day, while Martin – when had he taken to frizzing his hair in that repellent fashion that was taking hold on the younger men nowadays? And his garments – where had he gotten such hose, such boots? Rufus was generous with his squires, but none of the rest wore anything quite so fine. Why hadn't I suspected something when I first saw him strutting in them?

If it had been any other boy in the court, I would have drawn the same conclusion as Robin, but this was my son. Martin went back and forth between the king and his famous mother who may have sold herself to Curthose, but he was still child enough to wish to see her. Then why had he rejected the chance of seeing her with me today? I was the blind one, not Robin. I wouldn't see what was there. He was his mother's child in everything but appearance.

I kicked my horse into a quicker gait, suddenly determined to see Isabel before my brothers. That bitch would get a sermon from me that would bring her back to herself, or else send her off to her damned rustic estate – and Martin with her!

A few words of direction from the gate warden at Ludgate brought me to the house where she was living. It was a new one, rebuilt after the fire, on lower Watling Street near the ruins of All Hallows, which were only now being cleared for restoration. I made the gate porter understand I was on business from Westminster and demanded to be taken straight to the lady who was his master's guest.

The merchant was somewhat rebuffed by my manner when he came to see who was at his door, but he bowed me in and gave me the use of his little hall, which aped its betters in having a high table and a low. His wife and children were hurried out of their seats and I stood alone by the hearth, waiting for Dame Isabel to make her appearance.

She came in smiling, prepared to hear a summons from her fat lover to hurry to Westminster, I suppose. The smile faded when she saw me, but she put it back on with a difference and stretched out her hands to greet me.

'Ranulph! What a surprise. I'm glad it's you and not William d'Arques. He's a solemn bore and I feel the need of good company. It's been quite tedious, being shut up here with these good people for so long a time, though you may tell His Grace they've shown me every courtesy they're capable of.' She got an inkling of my humor and withdrew the hand she was about to put on my arm. 'You look gloomy, as usual, though. When did you last greet me with enthusiasm? Was it when you were shut up in a cell? What's the matter?'

'What have you made my son do, to win your security?'

She sobered. 'Your son? How gratifying! I never thought I'd hear you call him that, after you left us at Beaumont like a brace of lepers. What about *my* son? What have I made him do that doesn't please you?' Then her face changed. 'What's the matter with Martin? What's he done? Is the king displeased with him?'

'If he is, you've still got Curthose to send him to, haven't you? Oh, you bitch! Is there anything you wouldn't do to promote yourself? He's a boy! He's not even old enough for squiring, but you lied about his age to get him his post, didn't you? No wonder he's begun to despise you.'

'I don't know what you're – talking about.' But she did; it was growing in her face, which was now pale and stiff. 'What did I do? It was your king who took him from me. What could I say to that? It was your king – has he – has he hurt Martin? Were you there with them all this time, and you let him hurt Martin? Where is he? If you stood by and let that man hurt Martin, Ranulph – well, say something to me, damn you! Don't just stand there staring! Where's my son now?' She gripped my arms and shook me, her nails driving into my flesh.

I pushed her away. 'Don't play the good mother to me. You know what you've done to him and you must know what would come out of it. You had him in your sight for more than a month before you came over here, and yet my friend says he was already doing double duty between the king and your greasy-handed lover, so you must have consented to it. Oh, God, I know you've sold yourself, over and over, but to encourage a child to do it for you – '

'I didn't! It isn't true! You're lying to me! You've made this up out of jealousy, you miserable peasant priest!' She burst into tears and turned away from me to fall on a bench and put her head in her arms against the table, weeping.

The hall door half opened, then shut again. We had auditors we didn't need, because of her sobs. I looked at her heaving shoulders and felt the taint of guilt in myself. It was true, as she had said: I had been there, but I had been blind to what was happening. At first I'd been too full of thoughts of Giva at our last meeting, then afterward, of plans for the Scottish bridal. My anger ebbed. I went to her reluctantly, sat beside her, and put my hand on her arm.

'Isabel. Leave that. Listen to me. Whatever passed between him and the king is over now and not likely to be taken up again. I'm sorry. I confess I saw nothing of it. I heard it from one who says he did. It may be that – that there was nothing. The king is an honorable man –'

'Honorable? He abuses boys and he's honorable? He's perverse and you defend him now? Is that your honor at work?' She lifted a tear-stained face to me, and I saw for the first time that she now used some cosmetic to darken her lashes; it was running down her cheeks with the tears. I studied the ruin of her still-considerable beauty and, without giving thought to the action, put my finger on the stains to wipe them away.

'I'm at fault, too, yes. I came here in anger, straight from first hearing the tale. It may be untrue.'

'You're saying that now because you've just thought what it means to have to accuse your precious king.'

'And Curthose, too.'

'That is ridiculous! Whoever said that about him has a spite for him! He's a man! I can witness to that, as you've already generously pointed out to me.'

'There are some men who bed women and still make use of boys. I've heard he was such, years ago –'

'You've heard! You've heard!' She whispered: 'You knew more than what *you'd heard* about Red Will, but you didn't watch out for your own son, and now you defend the man that you *never heard* took a woman to bed. Oh, Ranulph, you're such a hypocrite!'

We exchanged reproachful stares. She put her hands to work, cleaning her face of soot and tears, which only made it worse.

'Well – what's to be done now?' she asked.

'We must remove Martin from the court, get him away from – from both of them.'

'The duke never touched him.'

'You don't know that. He's had his boys. There was talk of that when he was in disgrace and people didn't mind what they said of him.'

'Then that was the reason they said it. It's the king who's to blame, if there's blame to put on anybody.'

'I've told you, if there was anything, I didn't see it and I'm with him every day. He may have – have courted him – '

'Oh, God, Ranulph!'

'No, I mean, he indulges his squires. He may have given him gifts, which led Ro— my friend to suppose there was more.'

'How you will defend him!'

I sighed. 'Yes, I suppose it must look like that. Nevertheless, we must get Martin away from court.'

'How will we do that? Just go to your king and say, "I don't want my son to serve you anymore; give him his release"? What will we answer when he asks why?'

'We won't ask and we won't petition. You must leave England and take Martin home with you.'

She looked at me scornfully. 'I see. You, of course, will stay and do nothing, while I take the blame and go home in disgrace. I can't do it. I won't do it. I'm a pauper without Robert.'

'I'll give you money. I'll send money to you regularly.'

'Oh? Enough to keep me in honor, when I've known a duke? Where will you get the money? Will you rob your master's treasure box? Or do you think I should go back and take a little room in Rouen, somewhere near the church, where I can be a pious widow and say my prayers every day? What will become of my son if I do that? Which great lord will take him to service from the hands of a cast-off whore of the duke's? Because that's what everyone will think I am! What will happen to my estate that Robert's having repaired and that he's remitted the taxes from, until it's earning something for me again?'

'Your estate! Your property! Your God-damned, infamous acres of earth are all that ever come into your mind! What about your soul? What about Martin's?'

'What about your own?' She bent her head, half covering her face with one hand. In a moment she asked: 'How do you think you know that no more harm will come to Martin through the king? You didn't tell me that. Is he fondling another child in open sight of his court?'

'He – has an old affection which seems to have been renewed. It isn't a child and I don't believe a child could divert him from it, now. It's an old – affection – and he's not promiscuous in his affections.' It was a bitter thing for me to say, because it meant I must be resigned to Prince Edgar.

She dropped the shielding hand and gave me a look of disgust. 'I could almost think you were talking about a saint, rather than a sodomite. Who is the man?'

'It doesn't matter.'

'I'll find out. Robert will tell me, if there's any truth to it. Now he's back, he'll be here to see me soon and I'll ask him.'

'You're very sure of yourself.'

'Yes, I am. He's in love with me – and he's told me things of that sort before. He told me about that Irishman who was his brother's "wife" for so many years, and about the young knight who almost killed the sodomite and was taken into his tent for his valor. I'll hear about this one, too.'

495

She would indeed, and with more bitterness than she imagined. I rose from the bench.

'If the duke's coming here, it will most likely be today, after which you may not see him for another long time. The Welsh have come over our borders. The king is having summons of array sent to his border lords today. Tomorrow, or the next day, he'll march again. I've already heard that Curthose means to go with him. This is the time for you to part company with a bad bargain, if you have the soul for it. But you must do as you will, my lady, as you've always done. I'll take my leave of you. I wouldn't want to be in the way when your great lover comes through the door unlacing his braies.'

She made no answer.

I said: 'Tell him you're ill and need your son to come and be with you. He can get the boy reprieved to you better than I.' I waited. 'If you want to send me any message, you can reach me through St. Paul's.'

She had put her head into her hands again. 'What have I ever done to make you despise me so, Ranulph? I loved you once. I must have. I never accused you of any of the sins we committed together. I bore the child you gave me. I never shamed you with a confession – which might have ruined you when you were so hot to find a place at court.'

'If you kept quiet, it was only because confession would have ruined you, too.'

There was a noise of horses and voices in the street.

She rose. 'I hear my lord coming now. You'd better go, unless you'd prefer throwing yourself out the window at the last moment, as you did once before.'

The chamber door opened and a female servant put her kerchiefed head in. 'My lady, it's the duke. The master wants to know if you'll come down and receive him, or wait up here.'

Isabel glanced at me with a sour smile. 'Thank you, Etta. I'll wait for him here. Will you show this good priest a quiet way to leave the house? Take him down through the kitchens and see that he has something to eat and drink before he goes.'

I bowed to her silently. As I went out into the upper passage I heard Curthose's thin, nasal voice: 'Eh, Bernard! Where's my sweet lady? Isabel? Isabel!'

She sent me no messages; she didn't speak to Curthose; she didn't send for Martin; and within two days they were on their way west, leaving us both behind. There was nothing I could do. In the intervening time I kept a watch on my son; he was called neither by the king, who was surrounded by his lords of battle now, nor by Duke Robert, who spent his time with Isabel.

I approached Martin once again, rather hoping that my offer of sympathy, and my capacity as a priest, might cause him to open himself to me, but it was a vain hope. When I said I would pray for him while he was away, he almost gave up his gloom for an instant's mirth in disbelief: 'Why would you pray for me, Master Ranulph?'

'Why shouldn't I pray for you? I'm your friend. You did me a good turn once.'

'And was sorry for it. I think you mean you're my mother's friend, priest. Better pray for her.' He moved away to mingle with the other squires waiting for their masters to come out of the council chamber.

I felt someone near me; a hand fell on my shoulder. I turned and looked into the face of William de St. Carileph, who had been received back into the king's grace only that morning. His little, wet, swine's eyes were screwed up in amusement as they shifted from my face to the retreating Martin.

'Have you changed your tastes to keep up with the fashion here at court, Ranulph? It's a pretty little rump, isn't it?'

I moved to get his hand off me. 'My lord Bishop mistakes me.'

'Of course. Who is the boy? He looks familiar.'

'Just one of the squires. They all look alike at that age.' I avoided him as Martin had avoided me. He would be up to his old habit of snooping into everyone's affairs again, now he was restored to his throne and his place in the royal council. His purple-veined nose would be sniffing for any tidbit of scandal or gossip he could turn to his own use. I would not go near Martin again while he was near to watch.

The king departed the old palace at Westminster with his household levies and his barons, leaving us in his wake to prepare for the Christmas Court. Because it would be held at Winchester that year, I had an opportunity to visit my family. I determined to put Martin out of mind, as I could do nothing for him. But putting a child out of mind is often easier said than done. As I rode with Robin and the chancel clerks, I scarcely noticed the fine weather or the harvesters in the fields, my mind was so occupied with unwholesome fantasies concerning my son, who didn't even know he was my son and would undoubtedly reject the proof if it were put to him.

I dragged myself from a dark study to find we were at the gates of Winchester. I broke off from the wagon train of clerks and servants as soon as we were inside the walls and made speed up to the High Street to my own house and to Giva, waiting for me with sons of mine that I had already determined should never know court life.

I found my mother in her herb garden, swept her off her feet and kissed her, avoided the watchdog chained by the door, and ran into the house calling Giva's name. There was the sound of an infant squalling in the kitchen and the noise of children jabbering above me. I climbed the stairs two at a time to the upper hall, where I flung open the door and found Giva seated with my brother Fulcher before the fire. My boys were tumbling on the floor, contesting for possession of some trifle.

Fulcher looked up from some book he was reading aloud to my wife; I'd heard the last syllables of a pious sentiment, but all I wanted to hear was Giva's voice, greeting me with surprise and joy.

She glanced at me as if she were coming out of a dream. I had almost reached her before she moved toward me. I caught her close, buried my face in the sanctuary between her neck and shoulder, then felt her arms go about me as I kissed her.

I heard Fulcher greet me; then everyone came running up to the hall – my mother, Osbern, his pink-checked Swanhilda with her newborn son in her arms – and we took turns hugging and kissing until I felt my heart revive in the presence of so much affection.

After they had pressed me to take some food, we sat together in the warmth of the hall, with the failing autumn daylight slanting through my fine solar window, and I told them all the tales of the Scottish court, with its odd manners and detestable drink; of Malcolm and his icy queen; her desire to have her daughter marry with our king. Elfgiva sat by me in the shelter of my arm, with our youngest boy on her knee, asleep. From time to time as I spoke I paused to look at her, to drop a kiss on her brow, and to savor the moment when we would be alone together in our bed. She was more beautiful to me each time I returned to her, and this time there would be no quarrels to mar our days.

It was only much later, when she was asleep in my arms and I was drowsily fondling her hand where it lay against my breast, that I remembered just how I had found her in the hall, how she had looked when she recognized me – and stood – releasing Fulcher's hand. Or had he been the one so tardy to release hers?

43

On the day following the ides of October a great wind arose from the bowels of the sea and raged over England from west to east. It didn't cease to blow, to terrify, or ruin in the course of two days. It was the longest storm in the memory of those who dwelt in this island. When it was over, London lay in ruin again. A half-dozen church towers newly built since the fire were toppled, ships were smashed against the newly built docks, and six hundred houses were destroyed. Of the loss of life we had no intelligence for some time; so many people had fled the city when the storm began and didn't return at once, for fear of yet more destruction.

Robin Bloet sent me to London to bring him what news of loss there was to the royal property and to offer such poor assistance to Maurice as I could, in marshaling relief for the victims with a purse from the clerks of Winchester. I had been with my family for only two weeks, but I was glad to go. I had kept silent until my jaws ached, watched until my eyes burned, brooded until my brain seemed to have corroded with the ugliness of my thoughts. But I had said nothing to Giva or to Fulcher to make them aware I knew they were deceiving me, so I was at least able to depart with some shreds of that commodity which the king called 'honor,' though he might deny its existence in such a common person as myself.

The memory, which had been so slow in registering itself on my mind, was carved with an engraving tool now: she had been holding his hand in her lap, lacing her fingers with his as he read to her – from Ambrose's treatise: 'Blessed Are the Pure in Heart'! He'd brought it with him from Maurice's library – rendered into French by Maurice himself at one time – in order to give my wife a lesson in purity – or French – and to get his palm tickled for his pains!

All hell could have glutted itself on the jealous rage that filled me when I realized his cunning and her frailty that first night, but by the coming of dawn I had somehow reached a resolve that I found the grace to adhere to: I would not confront either of them with their perfidy, but would wait patiently until they revealed themselves.

And then? I didn't know. From hour to hour I changed my resolution on that. Should I be cold and condemning, fly into a just rage, forgive them and try to forget, or what? My lack of sleep and its results weren't lost on Giva for long. She taxed me with them while I was breaking my fast:

'You look dreadful! Are you ill? Your eyes are all bloodshot and your face is so pale, isn't it, Mama?'

'He needs a purge,' said my mother between mouthfuls of barley gruel which she dribbled on her chin.

'I don't think you should have come straight down here after so long a journey, Raf,' said my brother Osbern, who momentarily gave up admiring his plump Swanhilda as she suckled young Osbert. 'You do look as if you could use a good rest.'

'I am entirely fit and I have duties to perform down here, unlike some, who can sit around reading philosophy.'

'What duties?' Giva demanded, putting a bowl of gruel before me which I pushed aside. 'Making ready for a Christmas Court that's six weeks in coming? You've got time to rest. You should eat your food and go straight back to bed, or you'll be sorry for it later.' She bent, took my face in her hand, and raised it as she would have done a child's. Her expression was one of amusement and tenderness that almost made me wince. 'You can rest today and do your duty tomorrow. Let me spoil you a little. I'll bake some honey cakes with a bit of senna in them, to give you a good purge, and by tomorrow – '

'I don't need a purge, damn it!'

She took away her hand. 'Then don't have one, Master Groulsam and Gram! But when your stomach turns on you in a day or two and your tongue goes white, don't say I didn't warn you.'

I rose, leaving my food untasted, and went out of the house, stalked the High Street to the castle, and stayed there until it was well past Compline, burying myself in the king's business. My head ached with too much wine and reason when I came home again, to find all in bed. I undressed and slipped in beside Giva, who was deep in sleep.

Unbidden, the thought came to me that Fulcher might have been in that bed with her already. I damned the thought, and myself for admitting it. I lay, listening to the soft sound of her breath, wanting to wake her, draw her into my arms, yet fearing to do so, lest she murmur some other name than mine.

I was in Hell, for certain. But where was Fulcher? Did he lie awake below us, listening for the creak of our bed ropes? Did he sleep any better than I these days? Had I really found it so amusing when I first realized he was affected with a longing for my wife? Even when I laughed at him, hadn't I felt the least tremor of apprehension, telling me I should suffer for my smug pride at some later day? He was younger than I by several years – nearer her own age – but was such a little difference so much to her? No, it was more important that he was with her, when I was not. Yet, she hadn't shrunk from me when I took her last night. I tried to think what she had done, or said, but all I could remember was how she had let go his hand when I came into the chamber.

Had she looked guilty? Had he? Memory lapsed. Minds weren't always to be trusted with keeping every useful fact, but there was some inconsequential section of entrail that would twist and tell a man more about what he thought than his brain could. Was that the organ that really housed the soul?

As for Fulcher, he behaved much the same as he ever did toward me: quiet, rather diffident in his manner, always at my service, always prepared in his work, never given to more speech than was necessary to convey obedience and good service. He had prepared an account of my rents and fees while I had been away, which he laid before me in the chancel next morning, then waited quietly while I read it.

'This is very good.'

'Yes, you're going to be a rich man in a few years, if it goes on like this.'

'Hardly that, when the expense of the new house comes off.'

'You needn't bear all that yourself. As abbot of Hyde, you'll be entitled to require the building from them, if you put it on convent ground. The furnishings I expect you'll have to pay for, though you might ask the chapter to let you use what's already there. Since they'll have to move in the near future to make way for the king's new – '

'Yes, yes, I see. You've done well. Thank you.' I put the account aside.

'Raf, are you angry with me for any reason?'

'What reason could I have to be angry with you, brother?'

'I don't know. It only seems you are.'

'Why does it seem so?'

'Perhaps I was mistaken. Is there something else that troubles you?'

'There's a great deal else that troubles me, since you ask. The king's trying to pauper himself with the feeding of mercenaries. He's spent too much of his treasure in the homeland campaign; he's got his brother hanging on his neck, begging him to spend more when this Welsh business is over; he's promised still more to King

Malcolm; and I've got to find the coin for it all. Isn't that trouble enough?'

'Yes. You have responsibilities I wouldn't welcome myself, even for the gold it brings you.'

'Yes. You have time to read philosophy – and teach my wife French, or whatever it is you're teaching her.'

He quietly took the ledger roll he had shown me and left me to my work. I put my head in my hands and tried to drive out one devil by admitting another – I tried to think about Martin. But at that moment Martin didn't seem to be very important to me.

The misery I found in London could hardly touch me, either. People were taking refuge in the churches for lack of homes, or else they sheltered themselves in the ruins of their houses as best they could, lacking roofs. There was an attempt to begin new building, but the autumn rains had begun, the straw for thatches was both wet and dear, so there seemed little hope of getting them properly repaired until another haying. There would be many deaths from cold and famine, unless God sent a mild winter. The numbers of the dead were being reckoned already in the hundreds, and the church bells tolled constantly. I went about the city with Maurice and was shown horrors and wonders: a roof beam that had been carried aloft in the wind, then driven half its length into the ground a hundred paces away. The owner knew it by the marks he had put on it when he built his house.

There was a farrier who had been blinded when the wind blew the fire of his forge into his face. His house and his shop were smashed around him, but though his wife and children were crushed in the fall of the roof and his own life was shattered, God hadn't seen fit to kill him with the rest. Across the street from him the houses still stood, undamaged, except for the loss of a little thatch, yet for all of a day no one who lived in those houses would come out to answer his cries for help, for fear of being blown away.

My own house on Cornhill still stood, for a wonder. It, too, lacked of some thatch, but the lower part was habitable. I gave the use of it over to the priest of St. Peter's, to fill with the homeless who jammed his nave. I gave him what purse I owned at the moment to buy them food for a few days.

I made a survey of the damage done to the still-unfinished royal tower and found nearly all the scaffolding would need to be replaced before work could proceed at the snail's pace to which Bishop

Gundulph had now accustomed his masons. Maurice excused his slowness:

'He's had other duties – and the money isn't always there, either, Ranulph.'

'Well, I see he's gotten his own tower built in the same time, and a church to go beside it. If I had the say in this, it would be finished next year.'

'Perhaps you'll soon have the say in it. Gundulph hasn't been well lately. You're very harsh with him, Ranulph, when the king doesn't seem to notice the delay. I think he takes no interest in the work, and that's why its budget goes empty so often. Is there something troubling you, besides all this waste?'

'Isn't waste enough? God doesn't seem to want London to exist, does He? What news do you hear from the Welsh campaign?'

'Nothing to celebrate, except that the king has driven the raiders into the mountains and repeopled the castles they took. The church at Winchcombe in Gloucester, where he stopped on the way, has had its steeple torn down by this storm. God be praised it happened after he left it, or we'd have real cause to mourn.'

I blessed myself. 'Amen to that. We must get him home again and married, somehow, Maurice; married and breeding sons, just as Father Lanfranc wanted.' Finding him with a ready ear for it, I told him of my design to marry Rufus to the little Scottish princess, then enlisted him in the work to see that the king accepted the notion before King Malcolm made his visit to the Easter Court. Maurice nodded and approved. We agreed to begin a survey of the ecclesiastic members of the royal council to inspire their support for the Scottish marriage when they met at Winchester.

I remembered Isabel only when I was ready to take my leave of London. The merchant's house where she had stayed had been blown away with the rest of the houses on Watling Street near the river. I found her at Westminster, living at ease in the royal hall, in spite of its being nearly emptied of staff now, except for those who were cleaning it up from the effects of the storm. The miserable old building wouldn't fall down like the rest of its age in the city, but crouched under its tattered roof and groaned with the wind, like a flatulent old man.

Isabel came into the hall while I was speaking to the under-steward. She smiled, waiting for me to finish a discourse to him on the wisdom of keeping a stricter account of the food he was dispensing to refugees and not imagine he could get away with selling what should be given in charity, or accounting for what was sold by saying it had been ruined by the storm. I left him a sober man, and I would have left Isabel with no more than a nod, but she came and put her hand on my arm.

'Aren't you going to tell me anything, Ranulph?'

'What should I tell you, madam?'

'Whether you've heard anything about Martin!'

'I've heard nothing. Why should I?'

'Don't you write to the king?'

'No. The chancellor sends messages to the king, but he doesn't trouble to inquire after the health of the king's squires.' Then I looked at her face and relented. 'He's in no danger, Isabel. My lord wouldn't take a babe into a pitched battle when he has more experienced squires. Martin's probably snug in some marcher castle, learning how to throw dice and swear for his losses.'

She studied me for a moment, accepted my silent apology, and smiled tremulously. 'Are you in such a hurry to be gone? Will you stay and talk to me for a few moments? I have a chamber of my own here. It has a window seat and I can send for wine. Will you come and sit with me?'

She was wearing a gown of dark blue wool with red and gold bindings at the neck and sleeves, and a girdle of English work that hung almost to her feet. Her head veil was of the purest and finest linen, so I could see her hair through it. She had been spending Curthose's money, which his brother had given him and I must now find the means to replace. I nodded and followed her up the stairs to her chamber, which was meant to house a bishop in the court season.

She poured wine for me when the scullery boy who brought it had departed, smirking. We sat beneath the window and watched rain fall like a mist beyond the casement. It was a mild day, even with the shutters open. There was smoke in the air, but of a pleasant sort, mixed with the smell of roasting meat coming from the kitchens. She leaned against the inner casement, neglecting her cup, and sighed. I drank mine, which was heady, as I'd forgotten to break my fast that morning.

'Did you ever think we'd sit together like this, in a palace?'

'I had an inkling you would, as soon as I saw you dip yourself before Curthose.'

'Oh, Ranulph, must you spoil every moment with some sarcasm

about Robert or me? You were a tiresome boy who's grown into a tiresome man when it comes to speaking to a woman.'

'No doubt. Would you rather I went away and let you contemplate your good fortune alone?'

'No.' She took away my cup and filled it again, put it in my grasp, but kept her hand over mine. 'I'm sorry. You're not a tiresome man; you're only a very unforgiving one. We were friends once. Can't we be so again, if only for Martin's sake? We made him together. That's a tie not easily broken, is it?'

I took my cup in the other hand to drink from. 'You didn't feel bound by that tie at the time, my lady. I wanted to marry you, but you let your cousin sell you – to a man you say beat you. Your husband called Martin a bastard – he obviously had the proof some way. But you still didn't appeal to me. You gave my son the name of your dead husband instead.'

'If I'd named you, that man would have thrown me into the road for a beggar, or worse. Would that have helped Martin?'

'No. But what is it you want of me now? Yes, I admit I see myself in Martin's face. What of it? Will you tell him the truth when he comes home?'

'That would scarcely benefit anyone now, would it?'

'No, and neither will our "friendship," unless there's something else you want of me that you haven't mentioned. Is it money you lack? I don't have any at the moment, but I can see that something is paid to you.' I tried to remove my hand from her grasp, but she held it tighter, and pressed it to her cheek, then to her lips. She was weeping, which made me irritable and uncomfortable. 'Madam, so much thanks isn't necessary, I assure you.'

'No! Not thanks! Oh, Ranulph, I do miss him so much, my beautiful boy! I'm alone here – no one speaks to me, beyond a "yes, my lady, no, my lady." Even the priests sneer at me for being the duke's whore. I want to go home! I've thought about what you said, and I want to take Martin and go home, but I can't do it. Our lives aren't our own to do with anymore. You must help us, help me. I can't bear it here!'

She slid toward me and put her head on my shoulder and, somehow, my hand to her breast as she wept most pathetically. Her veil, even her hair, was perfumed with spices. I brushed the strayed strands of it away from my face and felt her arms go about me as she pressed kisses on my shoulder and whispered:

'You're the only man who ever said "I love you" to me – the only one – but I was young and stupid and wouldn't listen to you then. Oh, Ranulph, you still want me, don't you? I know you do. You could have me. I'm not too old. I could still love you and comfort you – '

I pulled her arms from about my neck and stood up. 'By God, you are the complete whore, aren't you? You'd sell yourself to the Devil for an advantage. What do you want that you'd fasten yourself on me again?'

'Get Martin away from that sodomite! Get him free of him! Get him another place! That's all I want – Martin safe from harm!'

'Keep your voice down! Do you think I can make miracles? I can't tell the king to release him without spoiling your fable about his birth. Is that what you want? I doubt it. No, Isabel, you've worn out your charm for me, so dry your eyes. If you love Martin, get him free yourself. But you'll have to keep him away from Curthose, too, and I don't think you're mother enough for that sacrifice!'

'Oh, damn Curthose!' She stood up, wiping her face with her fingers, her veil askew. 'Damn you, damn all the men who ever lived! When was any of them of any use but for breeding? Get out of here! I never should have let you in my house that night. I should have let you drown in the pig paddle, in your filthy gown, with your filthy peasant mind that can think of nothing but lies and excuses to keep you safe!'

'Shut up! You're going to have everybody in the palace up here in a moment.'

'I don't care! Let them come! I'll tell them what their precious king is! I'll tell them what he's doing to my son!'

I took her by the head and shut her mouth with my own. She struggled for a moment; then her hands clutched me and her mouth caught at mine as she groaned and sobbed. I held her so until she was quiet, except for the hunger in her mouth that would have devoured me. When I drew away, she sighed and let her head fall on my shoulder. I continued to soothe and hold her as she wept quietly.

I was astounded by myself! Where was all the anger I had harbored against her? When I took her by the head, it had been with the intention of shaking it until her teeth chattered. Yet there I was, my nose buried in her veil, kissing that white neck curved beneath my lips, as if she'd never scorned me, made a fool of me, caused me to be whipped and all but drowned; as if Giva never existed and I was the same fool I'd been when I first set eyes on Isabel!

I heard her mutter: 'I'll bar the door.' She slipped away from me while I was staring at her narrow bed against the wall, not three steps from me. I didn't regain my reason until I heard the bolt creak.

'No, don't do that.' I slid the bolt back again and shook my head at her silent question. But she put her mouth up to mine and we leaned against the door, so sweetly fused that I had to take her by the jaw again to part us.

'Why not?' she whispered. 'You want it and so do I – ever since I found you up in the tower room at Conches. No one will come here.'

I put away her fingers, which were making teasing little scratches against my breast. 'Call it my peasant caution, if you like, but I've lived in these places for a good many years now, and somebody always comes to a closed door.'

'If you go away now, you're going to hate yourself for the rest of the day.'

'If I'm caught bumping bellies with the Duke of Normandy's favorite lady' – she began to laugh silently – 'hating myself will be the least of my pains.'

'No one would dare tell him.'

'Oh, wouldn't they? You'd probably tell him yourself, the next time you were vexed with me. You smell wonderful. What is it?'

'Cloves and roses. Will you come back later?'

'No.'

'Ranulph!'

'No, lady. Sleep in the bed you've made for yourself; it's a good couch. We can be – friends – as you said. I have Martin's interests at heart, too. When they come home, we'll devise something together, but neither of us will pauper ourselves for a quarter hour of foolishness, will we? No.'

Her face clouded at the rebuff. I took her hands, kissed the palms, put them together as if she prayed, and slid out the door.

Whereafter, I generally loathed myself for the rest of the day.

I returned to Winchester without seeing her again. Once I'd gotten the scent of cloves and roses out of my nostrils I began to think of how I might encourage the departure of Duke Robert when the Christmas Court was held. Let him take Isabel and go home to his lute boys and jugglers. I could look after Martin myself.

After the Christmas Court there would be Edgar Atheling to deal with, but Edgar was a man susceptible to the pangs of conscience. I would have the help of the whole body ecclesiastic to vanquish him.

This time when I came home Giva was at the door to meet me, flinging her arms about my neck, telling me about the latest tooth little Elias had cut, what mischief had sent the twins to sit in a corner, and other comforting nonsense. Osbert and his 'Cygne' showed me their pucker-faced son again, whom I had scarcely noticed before. My mother extravagantly slaughtered two hens and made an aromatic stew in honor of my homecoming, and my return to health, which she put down to an innocent little spell she had woven for me in my absence.

After dinner I examined my boys' ears, to see if fur was growing in them to make them deaf to their mother's commands, made them giggle, kissed them good night, then took Giva on my knees when she returned from their night prayers and asked belatedly:

'Where's Fulcher?'

Osbern said: 'He's left us for the clerks' quarters at the castle, now that Bishop Maurice is coming down to stay. I think the chancellor might have said something to him about not being in chapel for his turn at choir service, and he took it very much to heart.'

'And so he should, if he wants to get ahead in the chancel.' I looked at Giva to see if she regretted the loss of Fulcher. She was studying me in turn. She smiled and kissed me on the brow.

'You're looking much better than you were. I was afraid you were coming down with a fever from too much work.'

'Perhaps I was, but I'm all right now. I thought you might be coming down with a sort of fever, too. You were looking pale, but now you're rosy.' I spoke in a low voice and held her gaze for a moment before her lashes drooped and she leaned her head against mine, biting her lip.

'Tell us about London,' Osbern said. 'Was there much damage from the storm?'

With Giva curled in my lap, her face half hidden against me, I told them about the ruin of London. My mother worked her jaws and said it was the Devil's doing, while Osbern and Swanhilda looked round-eyed and shook their heads. I could feel Giva's tears on my neck and put my arm closer about her.

'Don't weep for the Londoners. They come out of every calamity better than before. Some day they'll learn to build proper houses, if they get enough practice. Then God help the rest of England.'

She wiped her nose with her hand like a baby. 'I was thinking of Trudy and our room at the top of her house. She'd hate to know it's ruined.' But her tears had begun to slip before I'd mentioned the house, and I thought I knew why.

I whispered: 'Don't cry. These things happen and then they're mended, sometimes for the better.' Aloud, I said I was dropping with exhaustion and ready for bed, if everyone else was. Osbern and his Swan were already mooning at each other in anticipation of being in bed, while my mother appeared to be enjoying one of her momentary drowses over little Osbert's cradle. I set Giva on her feet, took her by the hand, and led her up the stairs.

We undressed in the dark and lay close together under the feather-stuffed cover. There was a light rain, half sleet, tapping at the shutters and a cold little wind insinuating itself through their cracks.

'I sent Fulcher away,' Giva said in a small voice. 'Are you angry with me?'

'Why should I be angry with you?'

'Because you knew. I could tell, though you didn't say anything for once. There was never anything – I told you that. But I couldn't go on having him look at me like that – so –' She lifted herself a little, her head above mine on the bolster, her hair brushing my face. 'I do love him, Ranulph.'

My heart almost stopped, then gave a series of feeble lurches, but I kept silent. Her hair was swept away from me as she sniffed and wiped invisible tears.

'He's so kind to the children and he'd talk to me, or read to me when I was lonely for you. But I kept thinking he would have to say something someday and spoil everything.'

'Did he?' She loved him. She'd made him go, because she loved him.

'He – no, but he – wept – one day, soon after you left. He said he didn't know what would become of him, and I knew – I thought I knew what he would say next, so I pretended to be out of temper with him. I told him I didn't know what would become of him, either, if he spent all his time here, instead of tending to his proper work. It wasn't fair, because he does work, very hard. But I said he was more like a child than a man and it was time he learned to be a man – and that I was tired of his nonsense, pretending he wanted to teach me to read, when he only wanted the excuse to be idle – and I had too much to do –' She sobbed, turned her head away.

'You love him –'

'Yes – more than Osbern – or even than your father. I know you wanted us all to be together here, but I couldn't bear the pain – in his eyes. I'm sorry if you're angry with me for making him go.'

I pulled her closer and held her tightly. I had been a fool, leaving him so much with her. I'd nearly lost her.

'You did the right thing. Fulcher knows it as well as I do. Neither of us can be angry with you. Is it our fault that we love an angel when one smiles at us?'

She sniffed. 'An angel? I'm not an angel.'

That had been a bit extravagant. She wasn't, or I need never have worried. But I said: 'I think you must be, to bear with the lot of us, especially with me. Don't fret about Fulcher. He'll be all right. I'll see he has plenty to do to keep him from brooding. Perhaps I'll make him my dean of order at Dover.'

44

Dover should be far enough. I spoke to bishop Gundulph about the matter when he came, then sent a letter to the canons of St. Martin's informing them of their good luck. They wouldn't like it, any more than they liked having me for their dean whom they'd scarcely ever seen, but that was no matter. They were sailing on the wrong side of the wind those days and were lucky they hadn't been turned out of their fat benefits to be replaced by regular clergy, as had been happening with growing regularity to smug canons. Not that they would have to put up with Fulcher every day; he was too valuable to me as a steward to part with him entirely. But it would, as I had told Giva, keep him occupied – and reward him for his good work, too.

There was snow on the ground when Rufus came back from his Welsh campaign, the same snow that had driven him out of the Black Mountains unappeased by victory. He had taken a hill fort or two, repeopled a garrison, received a few hostages in lieu of a surrender, among whom was a young man of good family, half soldier, half poet, who had all but enlisted himself as a hostage in order to escape his rustic prospects. His name was Bledry ap Cadivor, and his father was the head of all the hosts in the ancient Dyfed, which we call Carmarthen. If one wished to please him, one called him Prince Bledry, but it is certain his father never wore a crown.

As soon as our clerks got a look at him, there were wagers he would soon replace Cormac in the king's favor, but that was only because he carried a harp and was handsome. I hadn't been five minutes in the presence of the king and Edgar Atheling before I knew I could meet those wagers and fatten my purse, if I had been foolish enough to take an open bet on such a delicate matter.

Robert Curthose's face would have told me all I needed to know, if that of the king hadn't been so transparent. Edgar and Rufus were united, heart over mind. Curthose had lost his friend and was fast losing his brother's goodwill. When they came to town, Duke Robert went to Wolvesey Palace instead of the royal hall, while Prince Edgar, with a strained look, went back and forth between the two places several times in a day, as if to make peace between the brothers.

I presented myself to the king and soon heard the gist of their quarrel:

'By God, he thinks I'm made of m-money! I've paid his debts; I've paid his soldiers. I'm keeping an army to watch over his su-subjects, so they don't steal him blind while he taggles after me. When he goes home – if he ever goes home – he'll be in better case than he's been since he got his coronet, but is that enough for him? Oh, no! He won't be happy until I come and make a war on Ph-Philip for the Vexin for him. He can't hold what he's got, he resents me holding it for him, but he wants me to ho-hold even more. Is that reasonable – or is it Ro-Robin?'

He had just enjoyed his first bath in a month and was being dried off by two stiff-faced bath attendants who could hardly wait to get downstairs and report what they were hearing. Martin and another squire were standing by, holding clean garments to put on him. I waited until the men with the towels had done their work, then made a gesture for the boys to leave the dressing of the king to me. Both of them glared at me, offended by my presumption, but Rufus caught the intent of it and dismissed them with a laugh.

'Here, throw me my braies, boy, and let Ranulph have the rest. He's an old hand at dressing me.'

They left, most relucantly, especially Martin, who gave me a look of bleak hatred. The king was pulling on his braies. 'A s-silly custom, anyway, having yourself dressed like a weanling. Who began it?' He motioned for me to bring him his shirt. 'Now – what is it you want? Something secret, you don't want talked about? What is it?'

I shook out the shirt, which smelled a bit of the clothes hamper it had been residing in. 'Your Grace, are you satisfied with the service of your latest squire?'

'Martin? He's been spoiled, but we're coming to terms. What about him?' He frowned at me when his head was through the neck of his shirt, which I laced for him.

'Nothing, my lord. But his mother is the – confidante – of your brother. It seemed to me –'

'That Martin might be carrying tales to him? No fear. Our Martin doesn't much like Robin. He doesn't much like his mother, if it comes to that. Is that all you wanted to say to me? That I should be wary of a wet-nosed boy?'

'It was only a passing thought, my lord. What I wanted to remind you of was that you did, in fact, sign an accord with your brother, in which you promised to help him regain his lost lands. It was witnessed by twenty-four lords of the realm and Normandy.'

Do you think I could forget it? They squeezed it out of me! Well, it ought to be as clear as ale piss to Robin by now that I don't feel myself bound by forced promises. Let him complain all he will.'

I knelt before him as he sat on the bed, to draw on his hose of purple wool. He pulled them up over his thighs, then hitched up his shirt to tie them to his breech girdle. He stood again, so that I could tie them behind.

I said: 'A new campaign would be an expense you could ill afford in the coming year, unless it gained you new revenues, which this is unlikely to do. You've suffered great loss to your own properties. The palace at Westminster is in ruinous –'

'A damned, drafty old barn. It ought to be pulled down.'

'Just what I was about to suggest, my lord. But the expense of building another –'

'Why build another? I'll use the London tower.'

'Which is still unfinished; even this one is unable to accommodate your court comfortably, without farming some of them out to Bishop Walkelin at Wolvesey Palace.' I stood up. He put out his arms for his tunic of blue sendal, which I slipped over him. He glanced down at the effect of it on his stocky body, then studied me, scratching his oddly curly beard, which was some shades darker in hue than his pale, lank hair.

'You want me to plead poverty to Robin, instead of just telling him to go home – or to Hell – because of those twenty-four witnesses, is that it?'

'It would be wiser, my lord. So long as you don't refuse your brother directly, you've not broken your pledge, only delayed the redeeming of it – and for good cause. The lords of your council will understand the nature of the delay, especially if it entails the preparation of a suitable residence for a future queen and such heirs of your body as will make the realm secure.'

He gave me an unsmiling look and spoke in flat, barnyard words.

'Your harp's lost all but two strings, Ranulph – money and marriage. It makes a dull tune.'

'But lasting music, for all that, my lord. Is there a better tune to play that would discomfort your enemies and soothe your friends than a wedding anthem?'

'No.'

'My lord?'

'I'm not going to marry that child.'

'My lord, I was about to say, the choice of the bride is by no means final. The child might not be a child by the time that choice is made. It is very much the same as in the game of *échecs*. A queen may forestall a knight, but a knight may stand in the way of a queen for a time, too. It's the nature of the game.' I reached for his mantelet, but he turned away to the table that held his jewel box and thoughtfully rummaged among its treasures for the rings he would wear.

When he had chosen them and polished them on his shirt-sleeve, he turned his glance on me again, and this time it was less adamant, almost amused.

'I never thought that when I became a king, I would live by the rules of an *échecs* board.' He slipped the rings on, studied them, then laughed softly. 'It would make Edgar my uncle. How would he like that?'

'It would do him great honor to be bound to you by the bond of blood as well as friendship, my lord. He should approve it – or so I would think. You must ask him for his answer.'

He took the mantelet from me, swung it around his shoulders, and left the chamber.

I couldn't tell if this last sowing of the matrimonial seed had again fallen on barren soil for the next several weeks. I couldn't press it further with him, for fear of undoing what might just have taken root. He hadn't rebuked me again, or shown me anger; neither did he take my advice and mention it to his brother. He did begin to speak of the disreputable state of the old palace of King Edward at Westminster from time to time in his councils, and whenever his eye fell on Bishop Gundulph, he couldn't help but be reminded of how long great buildings are in growing to completion.

On the feast of the Conception of the Virgin, the eve of the nones of December, Prince Henry suddenly appeared among us. I had an inkling Rufus had sent for him through Robin Bloet, as he came better clad and in considerably better humor than when I had last seen him. If Rufus called in Henry to provoke Curthose further, he succeeded very well. Robert's well-known popularity with people in the court had been put to a strain in the days since he came to Winchester and fell once more into his old, slothful habits, carousing late into the night and sleeping half the morning. Now he awoke one day to find a new rival and one who was welcomed by the people of the town as a native prince.

More was the wonder when Henry answered their cries of 'Atheling! Atheling!' with a speech in English! I don't know when he had had time to study the tongue, as he had spent less of his life in England than the king, but the effort it had cost him was well rewarded, and my own interest in him doubled. He had learned something more than a few phrases in a difficult tongue; he had learned how to school his feelings, to smile, to feign affection for Rufus, who was more than eager to receive that homage from any man.

Henry had come to do battle for his inheritance, both in England and in the Cotentin. He didn't mean to go away empty-handed. Every day that followed saw him drawn closer to Rufus, while Robert fell farther away. Robert appealed to Edgar for support, but Edgar was beyond reproaching the king for anything, especially breaking a much overwitnessed pledge of aid.

The crisis came on the Eve of Christmas, when all the court feasted on fish, besotted themselves with honey mead, and laughed at the antics of jugglers and dancing bears until the Matins bells proclaiming the Birth of Christ would send them all to worship, then drunkenly to bed.

Lord Robert was the drunkest man at the high table, though Hugh the Wolf might have contended with him if he hadn't already fallen asleep on his stool with his great blubbery, grizzled head among the wine pots. The king, Prince Henry, and Prince Edgar had joined in song for young Bledry the Welshman, to teach him a lay that ran:

> Rudolph of Burgundy, while he was king
> He spent all his treasure upon swiving . . .

Not an especially edifying cantus for the Eve of Christmas, I grant, but it caused no offense to any in the hall, except Duke Robert, who gave over drinking to listen with a scowl. When the choristers reached the next turn –

Rolf the Ganger gathered his host,
He made him a castle of a miln post.
On its stone he ground his steel,
Took the miller's sails for his mangonel . . .

– Robert stood up suddenly, knocking over his cup and the king's as well. 'Now, by God, you're not satisfied with mocking me, but you mock our noble forefather, who got us our place of honor in the world! Or *do* you mock me?'

All singing stopped; all stool creaking and dicing, too. Edgar stood up, suddenly grave, but Rufus twisted his head around to look up at his brother with merry astonishment.

'He's awake! What's this about mocking? You've been dreaming, Robin.'

'I say you mock me! I'm the man who must take a millpost for my fort, it's plain, since I'll get no help for my cause from you! By the Feet of God, I see it now – you're the king in the first of the rhyme, who spends his treasure on swiving when he hasn't any honor left for keeping a pledge!'

'My lords, my lords, remember the season!' Robin Bloet said quickly. He'd been laughing at the song, too, but he was sober now. Prince Edgar stepped around the king's chair and put his hand on Curthose's arm.

'Robin, it was only a foolish song you've heard before – '

The duke pulled free of him, almost falling against the Count of Eu behind him. 'Take your hand off me and remember your place! I'm the Duke of Normandy, not one of your pot boys to paw and call by name. I'm your sworn lord, or do you forget vows as quickly as your lover?'

The king stood up. There was a most profound hush in the hall now. A few of the more cautious clerics were quietly preparing to leave it. Edgar straightened, his face as pale as his shirt. His lips scarcely moved.

'My lord, forgive me. I didn't mean to offend you.'

Rufus put his arm out like a bar between them and waved Edgar back. His face was flaming and his voice nearly locked in his throat: 'You're d-drunk. G-go to b-bed, my lord.'

'I'll go to bed – in my own bed in Rouen! I won't be mocked anymore. All in the hall who are mine, on your feet! We leave this place tonight!'

'Don't be a fool, Robin. You're too drunk to sit a horse. Where's his squire? Come and take him to bed.'

'No! I'm too sober to stay and watch you debauch yourself with

515

him!' He stabbed a finger at Edgar. 'My noble brother, who likes to hear himself called the New Alexander, and my so-called friend and vassal, who's forgotten his vows to go a-whoring for him!'

The king struck him in the face. There was a general outcry; Edgar tried again to get between them, but they were already locked in combat, their hands on each other's throats. There was pandemonium in the hall. All the duke's men were on their feet in an instant, but the king's were there to face them, daggers drawn, while the marshal of the hall bellowed for his guards below the stairs. We might have had a slaughter, but Hugh the Wolf, roused from his nap, waddled forward to seize the king in his bearlike arms and drag him off his brother, whose head he was now beating on the table. Prince Edgar and Prince Henry hauled Curthose up and fastened themselves to his arms, though no one could stop his mouth.

'Satisfaction! Give me satisfaction, if you're still any part a man! Sodomite! Bastard! You're no son of my father!'

The king gave an animal's cry and tried to throw Hugh off him. I feared he might burst a blood vessel. Hugh bent over him.

'Will-Rou, it's the drink in him. He's crazed with it. Don't heed him.'

The king's eyes were bloodshot with the extremes of his rage and struggle. 'Get him out! Ge-get him out, or I'll kill him! Give him an escort to the near-nearest port, or he's a de-dead man tomorrow!'

Hugh saw that the worst of his fury was spent and released him. We helped him to his feet.

'Where's Edgar?'

I looked about, but Edgar and Henry had succeeded in carrying Duke Robert out of sight. 'My lord, he's with the duke. Shall I send for him presently to come to your chamber? You have a cut on your face that wants tending.'

'Gone with him? He's gone with him?'

'Only to calm him, my lord. I'll send someone for him.'

'He should kill him! That's the way to ca-calm him.' He steadied himself against the trestle boards and stared about the hall. 'You out there, who serve my brother! Put down your knives and leave the hall peaceably, or it'll be the w-worse for you. Your master wants to leave us. Attend him, and see that he does, if you love him.' He grabbed a silver cup and hurled it into the hall, where it cracked against a pier and bounced on the floor. 'Get out!' His head swiveled, looking for a man to enforce the order. 'Fitz Hamon! Ta-take them out! Take 'em to the coast, by God, and don't let 'em so m-much as stop to take a pi-piss until they're on a ship!'

He fell into his chair.

I went to look for Duke Robert and found him in his chamber, sobbing and pacing, while his squires frantically threw his belongings into hampers. Prince Henry sat on the foot of the bed, watching him as a cat might watch a caged bird flutter in confinement, while Prince Edgar stood against the wall, his hands behind his back. They both started when I came in. Curthose checked his stride to point a finger at me.

'Here's his toad now, coming with an apology when it's too late. Well, Flambard, snivel it out and be done – or did he send you to challenge me for him?'

I glanced at Edgar. 'No challenge, Your Grace, only the assurance of safety under the king's peace. You expressed a wish to be gone from the country. Count Robert fitz Hamon is waiting in the stable yard to give you safe escort to Southampton, according to the king's command.' I lifted my eyes to him. There were wine and food stains all over his splendid tunic, as if he'd been dumped with the slops. 'My gracious lord, this is a sorry quarrel, if I may say so – '

'You may say so at your peril, toad-priest! This is a just quarrel, at least on my side, as you know better than anybody else who kisses my brother's foot! He's got your tongue in his ear for all he does. You know he's a sodomite and a pledge breaker! You call yourself a priest? Will you shrive him of this, too?'

'My lord, I may not stay to hear such things said of my king. I only came to tell you what is prepared for you. Will these lords be going with you?'

Henry fell back on the bed, laughing. Curthose sneered at him. 'Not him. He thinks he's fallen into the fat broth here. He'll stay to lap it up.' He turned his reproachful gaze on Edgar. 'I don't answer for him anymore. He's forsworn me. Let him speak for himself.'

Edgar's throat worked.

'Your Grace, I've never forsworn either my vows or my friendship to you.'

My ears pricked at that. Henry raised himself on one elbow to listen, too. Curthose swung around on Edgar fiercely.

'Ah? Is it so? You've been in his bed, but not yet in his purse? Well, his purse has stout strings! But what do you do for gold, now I'm not paying you? Take it from your sister, as you used to do?' I saw that Duke Robert had much of his father in him that not even wine could dilute: he never forgot a thing. 'You remember how it was when my father was alive? You slunk around Rouen like a dog without a kennel, until I took you for a friend. I spoke to my mother, to make her receive you. I petitioned my father to give you an estate and a pension, when I might have spent my breath asking something for myself. I gave you the blow of knighthood!'

Edgar Atheling fell to his knees before his benefactor. Henry sat up, his mouth pursed wryly, as if to keep from laughing. Neither the duke nor the English prince paid any heed to him, or to me. Robert bent over Edgar.

'I thought when you first went to him it was for my sake, knowing I needed *your* help at last. I shut my eyes to what you were doing, but no more. Christ, man! *He* was the one who had me put you out! He hates you! He's only used you to show his contempt for you – and for me. But you're his dog now. Let him have you.'

'Robin – it isn't like that, truly, and I've never forgotten what you did for me, or the love and duty I owe you.' Edgar lifted his long, sad face to his liege lord, but before he could give voice to further maudlin account of his affection, I thought the time had come to remind him of the king.

'Prince Edgar, His Grace has asked to see you presently. Shall I tell him you'll come?' I had my hand on the door latch as if ready to go out, though wild boars couldn't have routed me from that chamber until I'd heard what I hoped to hear. Henry drew up one knee and rested his chin on it thoughtfully.

'What did you say?' Edgar looked dazed with the bludgeoning his sense of honor had taken since Curthose's first outburst.

'I said, my lord, that the king wishes to see you. He's waiting for you in his bedchamber. Shall I say you're coming?'

'Well?' demanded Curthose, who sensed the crisis as surely as I did and now inadvertently joined me in pressing for it. 'What are you waiting for? Your master's whistled for you! Run to him! I won't curb you. Go to him.'

Edgar got to his feet, clumsily. He shook his head.

'Oh? Now, what does that mean?' Curthose asked, and his wintry smile was the very replica of his father's.

'No. It means – no. Tell – tell His Grace he must speak to my lord Robert – to make amends to him for the blow he gave him, or – or, if he will not – '

'My lord, you know right well he will not,' I said promptly. 'It's a great pity the holy season must be marred with dissent, but you know His Grace isn't the man to make amends for a blow he feels was justly dealt – if Your Grace will forgive me for saying so. I don't condone the deed. The king feels himself to be the injured party here. Yet he tries to calm his wrath. He offers safe-conduct out of the country to his noble brother, along with all who serve him, with the same sense of justice. Shall I say you'll come to him presently, my lord Edgar, or what?'

Edgar looked at me coldly. He knew I was forcing him. 'Tell His Grace I cannot come to him, now or ever. I serve Duke Robert and must follow him. Tell him – tell him I can do nothing else, in honor.'

I left him to his reconciliation with Robert, who was already embracing him. When I was halfway down the stairs, I heard a light step behind and Prince Henry joined me.

'That was a bolt well shot, good Father. I must beware of you, if fortune ever puts a real bow in your hands.'

'My lord, you mystify me. I know nothing of hunting. I only said what I was bidden to say: the king wished to see him.'

'Ah, but the moment you chose to take aim! That was where the skill lay. Now that you're rid of him, tell me: was he really that much of a nuisance?'

'Again, my lord, with all respect, you confuse me. I've never found the noble Prince Edgar to be a nuisance. How should I? He's a good, religious man. One sees few of them in the court these days. I've always admired him.'

'Oh, true, true. He's a good man. What a pity it is to see the pious so afflicted by devils in the flesh, eh? Well, God give him joy in Rouen and crowns in Heaven.' He laughed. It was always unsettling to hear him laugh.

'Amen,' I said.

I went to the king, who was in his chamber surrounded by his knights, squires, and body servants who were preparing him for bed, until there was scarcely a square foot of room left for me. I nodded to Robert Bloet as he shouldered his way out, having assured himself that the king's rage was abated and no midnight massacres would take place to interrupt our sleep; then I stood out of the way in a corner until the business of disrobing and commiseration was concluded and all had left the chamber. The king, naked except for his braies, had wrapped himself in a fur-lined coverlet and was warming his hands over a brazier set by his bed.

I lighted the candle above the prie-dieu in the corner, then knelt and said a prayer. The king made his responses from where he sat on the bed.

'Well – has he calmed himself? I ha-half expected he'd be in here by now, either to cut my throat or to make an apology. Is he sober yet? The damned fool! This will make a sweet tale to blow around the world, won't it?' He looked at me, his mouth drawn down like that of a child who's about to weep.

Now it came to it, I didn't enjoy the prospect of telling him about Edgar. He had too few people to love him, or to love; but Edgar had to go, or there would never be a hope of that marriage I believed would be his greatest victory over his rapacious lords and brothers.

'What should I do, Ranulph? I can't forgive him! I can't fight him. I didn't mean to hit him in front of everybody, but I wanted to k-kill him for insulting Edgar – and our mother! Christ, hasn't he got any mind at all? She doted on him!'

I said nothing. He got up and paced the room, but the icy cold of the stone floor soon drove him back to the bed, where he drew his feet up and shuddered.

'Damn it, this is my repentance: he's my elder brother, fool that he is, and I'm heartily sorry I hit him! You're supposed to be my confessor. What's my penance? Shall I go up and tell him I'm sorry in private? I won't do it in the court.'

'Your Grace, I believe in your repentance, but I think an apology of that sort would be useless. He was still incensed when I spoke to him, but I can't say he was still drunk. He seemed very clear to me. He's readying to take his leave tonight.'

He blew out his cheeks with resignation and relief, huddling in his furs. 'Let him go, then – good riddance. Go home and sulk for a while! He can't do much else, can he, with an empty purse, and my soldiers garrisoned all around his borders? Oh, Christ, why is he always su-such a damned fool? He's like a w-woman: he can never wait, once he gets his mind set on a thing. If he'd only held his temper until spring, I'd be better pursed to do his fighting. He's never hired soldiers, you see. *He* always gets them for nothing!' He sighed. 'Where's Edgar? Still holding his hand?'

'He's with the duke, my lord – and means to stay.'

He looked at me with slow comprehension. 'What? Coddle him through the night, like a babe with a toothache? Jesu! Edgar's got the stuff of martyrs in him for sure.'

'Your Grace, I meant Prince Edgar is with the duke in his quarrel and means to leave us. He said to me that he must follow his true lord, that he could do nothing else in honor.'

His dark eye was obscured by shadow; only the blue eye seemed to catch the candle shine, and it might have been made of glass, or ice, it was so steadily fixed on me. I found I could not meet the stare.

He said, after a moment: 'Going with him – tonight? Without speaking to me first?'

'Yes, Your Grace, so he told me in the presence of Duke Robert. He seemed quite fixed in his determination. Shall I tell him again you wish to see him?'

'No. Leave me alone.' He said nothing more, only hunched the coverlet closer to his neck. He was still sitting, bent a little forward in that manner, when I bowed to him and left the chamber. I didn't relish the discomfort after so many years, but I sat down with my back to the door to make certain no one came near him that night without my seeing him first.

No one came.

45

The following year the king marched north to Carlisle with his levies and drove out Dolfin, great Earl Gospatric's son, whom King Malcolm Canmore had placed there to govern the castle. A poor ruler was Dolfin, who let his Scottish garrison run riot through the land, robbing and abusing the English who were in the minority there. We were besieged by unsatisfied claims from that area, until the king was forced to take action.

Dolfin wouldn't move easily; he had to be burned out. When he was gone, the king restored the town and rebuilt Carlisle Castle, then sent word to me to find out those English families in Hampshire that had been deprived of their lands by his father in order to make a more comfortable deer park of the New Forest. These he offered new lands in the north, to repeople Carlisle, so that the weight of Englishman against Scot should be more in balance.

This was a wise and just decision on his part, but he has been blamed for it since, though no man has been bold enough to explain to me just how he erred. Some might say he broke the treaty with King Malcolm that gave the Scots king the rule of Carlisle. But Malcolm had broken the treaty first. He had sworn to keep the peace there and had not.

Malcolm was furious, but not so lost to his rage that he'd risk a war for Carlisle with the king's men set in the garrison. He showed his bitterness by refusing to come to the Easter Court as he had promised. In doing that, he forswore his oath as the king's man. For this act of defiance he did risk war, but the king was merciful – or he was scornful of such a little man as Malcolm – and forgave the lapse of duty. An envoy was sent to Scotland to inquire if Malcolm were ill.

During all this business I stayed in London, or made myself a visitor to the sheriffs and justices, to see that the king's laws were promptly and properly administered. Before my time too many cases brought before the royal courts were left to lapse into vain argument, and in the end whether a verdict was found or a fine taken was difficult to discover, or, if discovered, it was difficult to lay hands on the fine. It was likely to be tucked into the treasure chest of the sheriff, with a part returned to the man fined, if he had made a prompt payment. I took some pains to amend this custom, with the result that the king's own treasury was comfortably increased.

There were many other things I took upon myself to do in the king's name, since Robin Bloet disliked doing them. Robin was proving to be the slack chancellor I had thought he would make when the honor was passed to him. He didn't like being responsible for unpopular decisions, any more than he liked the grinding work of constant attendance to the king's estates. He was no Maurice, he said at the beginning. Soon I heard that he was saying he was no Ranulph, either. He now spoke of leaving the office and taking a bishopric, if one could be spared to him from those vacancies I held for the king.

I thought that soon I should be chancellor.

In his headlong rush to be gone from his brother's court, Robert Curthose had left behind one treasure that he evidently didn't think enough of to claim when his anger cooled: Isabel de Trie. I confess, her plight didn't occur to me at once; didn't present itself, in fact, until I rode into Westminster the next spring to prepare for the Easter Court. I found her where I had left her, but in a far different mood. She was, to say the least of it, looking winter-worn, in a gown none too clean. She put herself in my way as soon as she saw me.

'I want to talk to you.' Her eyes darted about as if there might be an objection to her presence in the hall. 'Where can we go to be private?'

'My lady, I've only just come from a long and tiring ride. Can you wait until I've washed off the mud and had a chance to speak to the constable? What are you doing here? I thought you'd be back in Rouen with your good friend.'

'Don't mention my "good friend" to me! I've had enough of

hearing about him these last months. He left me without a denier! I didn't even know he was gone until after Epiphany. Ranulph – ' Her nervous glance fell on someone across the hall who made her turn her face aside suddenly. 'Where can we talk?'

'What's wrong with your own chamber here, lady? After I've seen the – '

'No! I – I don't have it anymore.' She hunched her shoulders and turned her head away more.

I saw the hall steward coming toward us, the frown on his brow not at the moment directed at me. 'My lady – '

Isabel walked away quickly. He made as if to follow her, then recalled himself to me with a barely civil smile. 'Foolish woman never keeps to her place; always wanting something. What did she say to you, Father? Not begging, was she?'

I was surprised. 'Begging, Sir Hugh? Does a lady of Isabel de Trie's quality need to beg for anything in the king's house? I should hope not, Sir Hugh. She's a royal guest. The king's honor doesn't permit a guest to be in want of anything. See to it, master, or you're like to answer to him for it when he comes. Where's the lord constable?'

Now he remembered one of the reasons he disliked me. 'The lady is a bloody nuisance, Chaplain, as you'd know if she'd been haranguing you all winter for luxuries no one expects in an empty house. Why, the stupid woman wanted to take a bath, no less, and in her own chamber, too, as if she were a duchess.' He broke off in disgust when I laughed.

I didn't see Isabel again for a couple of days, during which time I confess I hardly thought of her. But when I had the leisure to go into London to visit Maurice, I found her hurrying after me across the bailey before I could reach the gate.

'Take me with you!'

'What? My lady, I'm bound for St. Paul's. Do you mean to take a suit to one of its advocates, or what?' I was already on horseback, but she seized my stirrup and held on fast until we were beyond the gate. The guards were amused by my discomfort. I could hardly let her dangle from my foot like a beggar, so I reached down and pulled her into the saddle before me, where she gave a great sigh of triumph or relief and leaned against me as we went along the river road.

'What do you want in London, Isabel? To see your merchant of Rouen? You might have sent him a message to come to you. And you've no cloak to cover yourself when it looks as if we're in for rain.'

'I sold the cloak as soon as it was warm enough to go without it.

I've sold nearly everything to that dreadful man's wife – and for a pittance of what it was worth, too, the filthy woman!' She drew my arm close about her and groaned. 'Oh, Ranulph, it's been dreadful! Just dreadful! I'm in a sorry case.'

'Isabel, I've never known you when you weren't. Have you written to the duke?'

'Written to him? I wouldn't speak to him if he came and groveled at my feet. The humiliation he's caused me these last few months is something a man of your quality couldn't understand, but I'm an honorable woman and I'm not accustomed to being treated as a – a charity beggar, let alone a whore! That's what the man called me, and I shall complain of him to the king! I don't care if I'm thrown into the street for it!'

'But, Isabel – sweet lady – what else are you, when you sleep with a man who isn't your husband?'

If she hadn't been facing the wrong way, she'd have hit me, but all she could do was to pinch me painfully on the thigh before she burst into tears.

'Now, now! We must face up to facts as they are. You didn't mind what people thought of you while you were enjoying the duke's bed and his purse. They're gone; but the reputation will stick like a beggar's louse. Did you think I could change things with a word? I'll write to the duke for you, if that's the problem, or I can take you to the merchant's house, if he's still there, and let you make your own arrangements with him. What shall it be this time?'

Her breast was still heaving with grief and indignation, but in a moment she twisted around enough to put her head against my shoulder.

'I can't go to the merchant. I've already tried and he avoided me. I walked all the way into the town, but his porter wouldn't let me in the house when I gave my name. It was so – shameful! He closed the door in my face.'

'Ah, yes. It's distressing, even for us lowborns, when they do that.' I was half laughing, but it was pitiful in a way. The rain had begun to drizzle down on us. I pulled my cloak around her as far as possible. 'Well, then, what is it you want me to do this time? I can't go on rescuing you from places you don't like, you know. Some of us have to be grateful just to be in out of the weather, without considering whether we like being where we are. It comes to that, my lady, when one throws his fortunes into the laps of people better than himself.'

'I have a cramp in my hip from sitting this way. Can we stop for a moment?' What a broken voice it was that uttered the words. I let her down, then dismounted. She put her arms about my neck at once, but I pulled them away again.

'No, we're not going to have that again, Isabel. It's too wet for it, and besides, I'm like a man who's had the smallpox: you can lead me through a pesthouse, but I'll never take the spots again.'

She crossed her hands over her heart and turned away, very tragically. 'I see. You put me in the same breath with contamination – the mother of your son.'

'Oh, nonsense! It was a figure of speech. Don't jangle your bells at me. I only meant – '

'There! You've done it again! Now I have leper's bells.'

'Oh – Michael's Angels! I did no such thing.' I put my arm and cloak about her, and we walked in peace for about a hundred paces, until she complained that her shoes were getting soaked. I lifted her into the saddle and adjusted the one stirrup for her, so that she could ride properly, then took the reins to lead the horse. It was only a short distance to Ludgate and I'd been riding too much of late, in any event. The elevation worked wonders on her. In a few moments she needed my cloak, or she'd catch her death. It was provided and her spirits rose accordingly.

'What news of Martin? Has he forgotten his mother, too?'

'Martin is well enough. If you'd bothered to have him taught his letters, he might have sent you a message.'

'Oh, he knows his letters.'

'Does he? I'm amazed you'd let so much of my occupation taint him. He's spoiled in every other sense, however, so it won't harm him much. Look, there's Ludgate ahead. Now where do you want me to take you?'

'Some charitable house of holy women will do, if London has such a thing. Perhaps the good nuns will take me in, seeing I have no friends anymore.' For a moment I was seized by an urge to drag her from the saddle and beat her.

'The abbess of Barking is a bit out of my way. She keeps All Hallows by the Tower, but I doubt if you'll find the amenities more to your liking than Westminster Palace.'

In the end I took her to St. Paul's, which was being rebuilt as quickly as Maurice could find the money to pay the cost of stone and stonemasons. His own palace he couldn't afford to restore in the same manner, but a timber manse had been hastily thrown up that was now serving as both chancel office and residence. I put Isabel down before the cathedral, pointed out how the choir and sanctuary were finished enough to shelter her while she said her prayers, then went to find Maurice.

When I returned several hours later, I had already resigned myself to admitting her to my own house on Cornhill. The last time I'd seen it, it had been full of homeless beggars put there by the priest of St. Peter's. I thought a taste of their company would drive her to return to Westminster, or else to throw herself on the distant mercy of Curthose.

But when we reached my house, I found no more than seven or eight people still harboring in it, which Isabel naturally took for servants and treated accordingly. They in turn thought I had brought my leman home to care for them and abased themselves agreeably to her, hoping to earn her favor. It appeared things might work out nicely for all concerned. I gave her a glimpse of the house and showed her where she might sleep in my old chamber, except the bed seemed to have disappeared into the fireplace in the meantime and the mattress looked as if it had been used by a litter of incontinent hounds. I gave her money to buy materials to make a new mattress. Wood was still very costly after the fire and the destruction of the storm, but I gave instruction to the most intelligent-looking of my beggars to find a carpenter and see what might be done. I then interviewed his wife and made her mistress of my lady's kitchens, sending her to the market with some coins to buy food.

In the space of an afternoon I had acquired a second household, with cook, porter, bailiff, and an assortment of eager roof menders. I hadn't realized how much repair was necessary to the old house that had been fortunate enough to withstand two calamities. If not for Isabel, I might have sold the place and cut my losses. But then, without Isabel I might look for fewer crowns laid up for me in Heaven, when my days on Earth are accomplished. Surely, God will remit some of my sins when He considers what I've undertaken for that woman.

I didn't go near the place again for some time, being better occupied with the king's business, but I sent her a purse now and then and waited to hear she'd grown tired of the meanness of my dwelling and longed to return to her beloved manor in Normandy, or even her beloved prison at Westminster. No such word came. She seemed content, and I was content to leave her so. When I had an opportunity to speak to young Martin, I reminded him that he had a mother and told him where she could be found. He didn't take my hint, any more than he took any advice or instruction that came from me. It passed all reason why I should continue to feel anything for him, seeing he despised me as he knew me and would despise me the more if he came to know our true relationship.

His stiff-necked – and ill-founded – pride, along with his frequent negligence of duty, made him the most chastised of the king's servants, but the penalties imposed were never as harsh as they might have been. Rufus seemed to tolerate lapses in him that he would have thrashed out of another boy. He dressed him out of his own purse, too, seeing he was indigent, and this made Martin the brunt of coarse rumor, as it would have done even if he hadn't been an exceptionally handsome child.

By the end of the year I had begun to brood anew over the consequences of the king's affection for him. Few boys of Martin's years could escape being enamored of a master at once so forgiving and so generous. Few men afflicted with the king's weakness could long resist revealing themselves to such a receptive heart. Against my will, I gave ear to bad rumor and balanced it against my still-enduring trust in the honor of the king; but in the end I decided it was time to have a private talk with my mother.

I couldn't be open, even with her, so it followed that she must suppose the concoction I desired of her was to be for myself. This was extremely embarrassing for me, but at the same time it gave me hope that she would be more than ordinarily careful with her measurements. It was the king's ardor I wanted to quench, not his appetite, or his life.

She understood, or thought she did: Giva was breeding again and I was a man in his prime, who might be expected to feel the want of her comfort when he came home at night. My poor mother did her maternal duty and chastised me for needing the help of her art to overcome my baser human instincts; then she spoiled the lesson by remarking, after a baleful pause:

'It's my fault. You get it from me, not your father. God knows, if it had been left up to him, you'd have been the only child he got on me.'

'Mother – '

'It's true! He was never a very lusty lover, but still I'd all but die whenever he put his hand on me. That first time, in the stables – '

'I've heard about the stables, yes – '

'He always said I must have more than just Breton blood in me, to make me so hot.' She cackled, her toothless mouth agape as she surveyed her own withered breast. 'You'd never guess now, to look at me, would you? No. But, I'll tell you a thing: I could still have a good man, if I could find one. Not that I'm looking, as long as your sainted father's still alive. Still – who'd have me, eh? To want me, he'd have to look worse than I do; then I wouldn't want him!' She laughed, tossing back her head like a girl. 'That's the true curse of woman's flesh, boy – that in our hearts and another place, we still feel young. But the young lovers shy away from us, even in our dreams.'

I kissed her cheek, which was like a very old leather glove that has been left to dry in a corner while crumpled. 'You're the same woman you were when you used to dance for me, secretly.' A palpable lie, but she enjoyed it, though she scoffed at it. 'You'll have that remedy ready for me soon, won't you? It won't have a bitter taste, or anything unpleasant about it, will it? Nothing to spoil the appetite, I mean.'

'Rascal, it's made to spoil at least one appetite! But don't worry, I'll make it sweet for you. Just put a half-dozen drops or so in a cup of wine and you'll never suspect it's there.' She gave me a shrewd, almost malicious glance. 'Maybe I should have dosed Fulcher with it; then he wouldn't be a stranger to us now.'

I thanked her for the promise of a remedy and hurried back to the king.

So it was that I began to administer a certain cordial to my master's drink. This was no easy task, as he seemed to have more people about him at all times than ever before from his moment of waking until he slept again. Nor was it an easy matter to my conscience to do it, for whatever grounds of reason, health, or his soul's safety. To do so openly and be found in the wrong is the ruin of a reputation; to do so clandestinely and be found out in any case is death.

I trembled for the danger of discovery every time I dosed that flagon by his bedside with one of my mother's little clay-stoppered vials, imagining a throat being cleared behind me, a hand laid on my arm, someone who knew me and knew how I stood with the king staring me in the face and knowing my guilt. There would be a moment of facing Rufus, my friend, who would question my motives. What would I say that might save me? Nothing. Nothing that would aid me, that is. I would be dragged away to some hideous cell and tortured, perhaps, before I was turned over to a court for condemnation and death.

I was clearly a fool to risk such a fate, and I have repented of it in my heart a hundred times over, but as with so many other acts that I have now recorded, I did not look for absolution in confession, except in the most general and unsatisfactory way.

We moved about the country restlessly after Christmas. Rufus seemed unable to settle anywhere for more than a fortnight. His energies demanded an outlet that was denied him, by which I mean not lust but the business of a soldier. There were no rebellions, no incursions, unrests, or defiant enemies for him to conquer, and now perhaps he regretted refusing his brother that campaign against the Centomanian rebels, which might have brought him glory.

More tournaments were held in that year than ever before or since in this land. There were practical reasons for them, other than to divert the king. The mercenary knights he hired and kept about him were in need of occupation to keep them from restlessness, which quickly turns abusive in such men. Therefore there were games and rich prizes for them, idle amusement for the common folk who flocked to see them do their mock battles, and much to condemn for the clergy who disapproved such waste of money, spirit, and human life.

It was this dislike of seeing money wasted on awards for men who were not actively defending Church and king, as well as the seemingly frivolous life the king himself was leading, that led the great men of the court ecclesiastic to begin a growl of dissatisfaction with the state of Canterbury. The see had been vacant for more than two years. Now that Lord Remi of Lincoln had gone to his heavenly throne as well, two bishoprics were vacant, their revenues in the king's hands turned to such follies as rebuilding Carlisle, strengthening Dover, putting a new roof on ailing Westminster Palace, not to mention the salaries of mercenaries and their tournament prizes – or so the argument went.

As the Easter Court approached, some of the lay lords began to take part in the grumbling, because they had been made to pay fines for various breaches of the king's peace which they were accustomed to forgoing in lieu of bribing a sheriff. Now they had to deal with my justices, over whom I kept a close watch to make certain that all fines owed the Crown were paid to the Crown alone, rather than the half of it remitted to some 'good steward' in exchange for a delay of justice, or for his 'finding' for them.

Then there was the matter of court wardships. In the past, young heiresses whose estates were supposed to be in the safekeeping of the Crown often found themselves in the hands of their less careful uncles, or cousins, instead. These men had little reason to find them husbands to inherit the management of their fortunes; rather, they delayed nuptials, or prevented them forever, by placing their female dependents in houses of religion, forcing them to turn over to them all their fathers' properties, except such as were rightfully assigned elsewhere.

I remember a certain gentleman who came to complain of his niece's inheritance being inventoried the day following her father's funeral. It was my own writ ordering that action he shook in my face when I presented myself for his censure in place of the king, who was better occupied at the moment.

'What are you up to? What is it you think you can imply by this action? They tell me this is your name on this piece of trash, priest! What does it mean? That you think I'll rob my brother's house the minute he's in his grave? I am the rightful executor of his estates, not some shave-pate you send to do it!'

I put my hands in my sleeves and waited until he had blown out his first wrath in a long, self-justifying speech that favored himself and slandered the king's officers. Then I said:

'My lord, this is no affront to you, if you love justice as much as you pretend. The maid's fortunes will be well looked after, as if she were the king's own kin – as she is, in a sense.'

'Sense? What sense do you find in that, chaplain?'

'Why, my lord, that the king is every man's heir. If he is heir to the deceased, it follows that he should hold himself to be as kin to the orphan, whom he will shelter and nourish, as she is in his gift, until he finds her a husband to hold her fee for her.'

'What sort of jiggery-mummery talk is this? Who says the king is my brother's heir while I'm alive?'

'The king does, my lord. Will you dispute him? You yourself hold lands of him which you fee to some knight of yours, let us say. The knight dies and leaves a child and some little property. What do you do? Turn all that you've given him over to his brother, an untried man, or one in service to an enemy of yours? No, my lord. You take his fee back from him, distribute his goods to his widow and child, having taken your relief from it. If you feel so inclined, you find a good knight to marry the widow or the orphan and take on the burden of service laid down by your dead knight. That is right and proper with you – and so it is with the king, who is the rightful owner of all lands in this realm and, therefore, the heir of those who hold them of him.'

'This is nonsense!'

'This is the law, my lord. Dispute it in the courts of St. Paul's, if it pleases you, but I pray you, not with me. The girl will be well cared for and her property will not suffer.'

'Who will care for her? The king himself – or you?' He sneered. He had a face for sneering, this midlands baron.

'An officer of the court will be appointed to look after her, some honest man with a wife, to stand *in loco parentis*, seeing she's motherless as well as fatherless now. It may be you: it may well be you, my lord, if you take care not to offend the king with your unworthy suspicions of his motives. Or it may be some other kinsman, or some abbess of a good religious house, if the girl is that way inclined.'

'And who will choose this person? Someone with an itching palm, eh?' He put his hand behind him and pulled the strings of a wallet he had tied to his belt. He weighed the little leather pouch in one hand. 'Some considerations are worth their weight in silver, they say. What is this one worth?'

I glanced at the size of the purse and smiled. 'A commission of worthy men will take that decision, my lord. Will you bribe them all?'

He was greatly incensed to find he hadn't bought me all in a moment and left, muttering he would have justice of the king, which in time was granted him. The girl had no more than two or three manors, the best of which was worth no more than twenty-five pounds per annum. The king, following my advice, married her to one of his own knights in need of compensation for his services. Her uncle got the comfort of a new nephew who stood well with the king. The maid got a man in her bed and, in short time, a son to cherish.

In truth, not all cases were so quickly and felicitously settled. Some widows were found new lords who did not please them or their families; some sons chafed at waiting for their majority to inherit; they thought themselves full ready to take on authority when they were no more than seventeen or eighteen, especially when they saw that others, such as young William de Warenne, had been permitted to do so in spite of their youth. But there will always be complaints where there are restraints, as any mule driver will tell you. In the matter of wardships I have no uneasy conscience. They brought coin into the king's treasure box and prevented unworthy marriages between natural conspirators, such as had once led to the 'Bridal of Norwich' that ended in ruin, exile, and execution.

*

We were to hold the Easter Court at Gloucester, and I had been occupied with preparing the king's mind for the coming of Malcolm Canmore. In the interval between Christmas and the beginning of Lent, when I judged my lord's carnal spirits to be sufficiently quelled by my mother's drug, I spoke to him again and again about the wisdom of making a marriage while he was still young and vigorous. Perhaps it was because he wasn't so vigorous as before that my homily seemed to take root in his mind. At least he began to listen to me, rather than rail against consorting with children. In any case, young Edgyth was no longer an infant, but bordering on puberty, and the year or so it might be expected to take to complete the preparations for a wedding would see her into womanhood.

King Malcolm needed soothing. The king allowed as much, though he denied (as do I) that his relieving Carlisle of the Scots king's unworthy retainer should be an affront to a wise man. Dolfin had ruled like the Fool at a Christmas feast, by whim and gross humor. Malcolm must have seen some justice in his removal, or he wouldn't be coming to us now. I had been in correspondence with Queen Margaret from the time of the scouring of Carlisle and had her assurance that her lord was eager to reach a better understanding with King William. What better understanding could there be than a betrothal?

King William, in the meanwhile, found a moment when he felt so well disposed toward the idea that he made a joke about it at the dinner table, just after we had settled in at Gloucester. His remark, which was a rather coarse one, I'll let go unrecorded, but its effect on its hearers might be worthy of note. All the rest either looked at him askance, or burst out laughing at what they supposed to be an absurdity. Only Prince Henry took the remark to heart. He rose at once, cup in hand, to toast the union:

'But what's her name, brother? We can't have a proper toast without a name. If it's a good name, maybe your Welshman can make a rhyme on it. What about that, Bledry?'

'Around it, perhaps, my lord, but seldom on it. Your French names go hard in my rhymes.'

The king, seeing the keen interest his brother took in his bride's name, and perhaps wary of too blunt a jest, repented of his disclosure and shook his head.

'I spoke out of turn. It wasn't courteous. Let be, Harry. There's a way to go before we toast her here.' He flushed, then laughed nervously at Henry, who still leaned over him. 'Besides, you rascal, if

I told it to you, you'd want to get to her first – and that you shan't do, because she's nearer to the saints than to the wenches you like to chase up hayricks.'

Henry gazed down on him. 'Could I move her, Will-Rou, when she's had a glimpse of you?' He lifted his cup again. 'To my brother's saint – and to my saint-espousing brother – a warm bed and a long life!'

We cried assent to that. But in a week our cries had taken on a more doleful sound. The king lay at the point of death.

46

He fell ill at the royal house of Alvestone, or rather in the forest near it, and was carried there by his hunting companions: his brother, Robert fitz Hamon, Earl Hugh, Richard and Gilbert de Clare, along with some dozen other gentlemen. A courier came flying into Gloucester with the news, such as it was; there were no details of his illness in the man's head, only the dread tidings that he seemed near death.

I may not have been the first to rush through the door and take horse when I heard that terrible word, but I couldn't have lagged far behind. Without regard for precedence, clerks, lords, gentlemen routed their squires or grooms and made for Alvestone. My moment of weakness was caused only by the fear that it may have been my draft that had sickened him, but I put that thought aside almost at once, as I had given him nothing for the past several days, indeed not since the assembling of the Easter Court when it became impossible to come near the wine flask in private.

My next thought, not unnaturally, was that someone else had poisoned him. But when we came to the royal lodge we heard what the stupid courier should have said at once: that it was through an accidental injury while hunting across the narrows of the Bristol Channel in the Forest of Dean that the king had been brought near death.

There was little agreement on how it had happened. He was chasing a wild boar and had galloped ahead of his companions through a narrow gap in the ferny undergrowth when he fell or was thrown from his horse. He fell against the shaft of his own boar spear, or against the pommel of his saddle, which had been torn from its girth strap by the sudden shift of his weight, as if the horse had balked upon meeting the boar. When his brother and friends found him, he and the saddle were sprawled on the ground; the horse and boar had fled. He was unconscious, though he didn't remain so for long. When he woke he was in great pain and could not stand. They made a litter of spear shafts and blankets and carried him back to the Severn, where he was taken by water to the landing nearest Alvestone. He was in great pain the whole way, they said, but did not lose consciousness again. He was awake when I fought my way through the crowd that thronged his chamber and knelt by him.

'Your Grace, how is it with you?'

'Not good.' He had to clench his teeth to say it without groaning, and the grip he got on my hand was painful, but he made himself smile as he whispered: 'Clumsy and stupid. I've done for myself, I think. I took a young horse out – to meet a wise old boar. Damned brute balked. I might have – might have known it would. Happened before, without the boar.'

The mere effort of whispering made him break out in a sweat. His face had a greenish hue, all the more alarming in a man of his usual ruddy color. I raised his hand and kissed it.

'Rest easy, my lord. The physicians will heal you.'

He just barely breathed it, his face half turned into the pillow: ' – talk to you – alone – '

I said, 'Has Your Grace made confession?'

In an almost normal voice he answered: 'No. I was waiting for you.'

I got to my feet. 'Clear the room, my lords. The king wishes to confess himself.'

This caused some alarm and anxiety. At the back of the crowd it was taken to mean he was on the point of death. To those in front, among whom were many bishops of the land, there was evidence my command gave offense, seeing they had been there before me. They moved, reluctantly, and with Robin Bloet's help I soon had the chamber empty. I returned to the bedside and knelt by Rufus again, but now he lifted his head from the pillow and beckoned me to get him a cup of wine.

I hesitated. 'Your Grace, truly, it would be best if you confessed first.'

'You know all my sins by now, and if God's all He's said to be, He's one or two up on you. Get me s-some wine, for the love of

Christ, Raf. My throat's sore with thirst and I want to – want to tell you something else.' That exhausted him. He lay clutching his belly. I poured some of the wine and lifted his head so that he could swallow it. He sighed and rested for a moment, eyes closed, then looked up at me fiercely.

'Go down and find my saddle. Get the girth strap off it and bring it to me.'

'The girth strap, my lord? I understand it was broken with your fall –'

'It was cut!'

'My lord?'

'It was cut half through. I saw it myself, before I tried to get up and lost my s-senses.'

'Cut?'

'Yes, man, cut! By a knife! S-somebody tried to help me to Heaven, you see.' He began to laugh, but a pain seized him and he groaned instead. 'God damn them! Of all the ways to die, I l-least wanted to die like my father – of a burst gut.'

'You won't die. You've survived worse than this. You won't die,' I said fervently, and only then remembered that I had forgotten to say 'my lord.'

He made a faint smile. 'You're sure of that? You can work another miracle? Without Cormac?'

'There was no miracle worked then, my lord, except God's, in giving you the strength to last out the pain. He saved you then, as He'll save you now, because He means you to live and be a great king.'

He closed his eyes, still smiling. 'Strange. He never gave me any sign of His favor that way.'

'Your Grace, let me confess you now.'

But he had fallen asleep, or unconscious. I knelt by him and prayed fervently for his life; then, when I couldn't rouse him to more than a murmured protest, I gave him conditional absolution and went to find that saddle.

The saddle was safely put away in the stable, but the girth strap was missing. I caught Martin at the first opportunity and drew him aside, much against his will, to ask him about it.

'How should I know? It must have fallen off when they dragged it home.'

'Weren't you there? You're his squire. It's your business to see that his harness is in good condition.'

He looked sulky. 'I wasn't there.'

'Then where in the Devil's name were you, boy? You were supposed to be with him. Which squire did he take?'

'I don't know. I was set to cleaning boots and armor.'

'I see. You were being punished again. What did you do amiss this time?' I grabbed his arm and shook him when he didn't look at me. He pulled away.

'That's no business of yours, is it? It was nothing, only a little thing.'

I took him by the jaw and turned his face forcibly to mine. He winced, but he saw he'd better not pull away from me again. 'Listen to me, Martin. The king wants that girth strap found – and I want it found – quietly. Do you take my meaning? I want you to go to the forest and search every foot of ground from where the king fell until you find it. And say nothing to anyone about what you're looking for. That's the king's command for you this day, and you'd better obey it to the letter, or it'll be worse than cleaning boots for you.'

'How can I do that? I told you, I didn't go there. I don't know where he was when he fell!'

I released him in exasperation. 'Yes, because you didn't do as you should have, you can't be of any help to him now, can you?' I expected him to dart away as soon as he was freed, but he remained, scowling at his own ridiculous shoe tips, which were drawn out to points and curled up like a scorpion's tail in the style made after those of Fulk of Anjou, who suffered from the gout. 'Martin – do you love the king? He's a good master to you? Fair, even when he punishes you?'

He shrugged and sniffed.

'Well, do you or don't you love him, you turnip-head?'

'Yes! When he's in a good humor anyway.'

'Would you rather be back in Normandy, feeding pigs on your mother's estate?'

'You can't send me there, priest, so don't try to make me think it.'

'Oh, yes, I can. Believe it, boy. I can say one word and send you to pig keeping for the rest of your days. And I will, by God, unless you attend to me now and obey me. Look into my face and see if I lie.'

He did; his throat moved but he didn't speak.

'Now then,' I said, 'you'll find out who the squire was who attended the king – and who the men were who were with him – every man of them, down to the last kennel man. You'll tell me, in private, and no one else. No one else!'

He nodded; I stepped back from him, signing him to leave me. He darted away like a hare.

The squire was Hugh de Guiche. I led him to believe the king had lost a valuable ring when he fell and that a reward would belong to him if he could find it. He led me to the very spot in the woods the day after next, under guise of returning to Gloucester with me. There was no immediate danger of his telling anyone why we went off together, as a mark in gold was a prospect he didn't feel obliged to share.

I didn't find the saddle girth, though we combed the ground for two miles from the site of the accident to the boat landing, where his friends had put the king aboard on his litter. I looked at the Severn, sparkling under a brilliant sky; there was the place to drop a damning piece of evidence, and no man the wiser for it, as the rest of them would have been hovering over the king – unless they were co-conspirators. But that thought was too much for me. Robert fitz Hamon was one of them, Earl Hugh another, and the king's own brother was at his side throughout the hunt, according to young Hugh, until that moment when Rufus burst out ahead of them all in his eagerness for the boar.

No, there could be only one man in that party who wanted the king's life, or else they need not have brought him home half dead. But who was the man? A hireling of Curthose's? Someone with a secret grudge? Someone in the pay of the Scots or a party of the Welsh? It seemed unlikely – but who, then?

We returned to Alvestone. I gave Hugh his coin, despite his failure to find that ring which was never lost, but I bought a little further silence from him by warning him that if he boasted of his wealth, he'd likely wake tomorrow with a broken head and an empty purse. He was a shrewd boy and swore he'd keep silent. I went to see the king, passing two physicians on the way, and heard grim tidings:

' – fever in the bowels as a result of the insult they were offered by the fall.'

'Nonsense, brother, he's merely got the stone and he's shaken it loose. Fevers don't bring blood in the urine.'

'They may, if there's swelling enough to rupture the bladder, which is more likely than the stone to account for the distension of the stomach and the bleeding in this case, friend.'

'Oh, by the Mass! He's distended because he can't pass his water adequately. If his bladder were ruptured, he wouldn't be passing any at all. It'd be going out into the abdominal cavity.'

'By your leave, brother, it would not. I had a case – '

'By your leave, brother, if I could but put a knife tip between his scrotum and his anus, I'd have the proof of stone between my fingers in an instant.'

'Good God, masters! You aren't going to cut him, are you?' I cried in alarm, interrupting their discourse. They turned and looked at me with the same contempt and astonishment.

'I am not a surgeon, young brother; nor am I holding a seminar for the ignorant. Kindly go your way.' They resumed their conversation. I fled to find Robin Bloet.

'Well, it looks bad. He's in a great deal of pain, and the worst of it is that he thinks he may be dying the same way as his father, which is as good a diagnosis as I could make for him myself. Dear God, I hoped I'd never have to see a thing like that again – or smell it. How could he meet with such an accident? It's uncanny, you know; first his brother, Richard, then his father – '

'He says it was no accident. He says the girth strap was half cut in two. '

Robin looked at me in silence.

'He says he saw it, before he fainted. Robin, I've been trying to find that girth strap these past two days and it's gone, though every other item of the saddle and harness is here.'

'If it was broken, it was thrown away.'

'If it had torn loose from the saddle, it would have been mended. I questioned one or two of his squires on that point.'

'If it was cut, you'd better have a care whom you question.'

'I think I've taken care. But how will we take care for him?'

'We can't. If someone that close to him is determined to kill him and Will-Rou doesn't suspect him and take care for himself, no one can prevent the traitor from trying again. As for myself' – he glanced about to see if anyone was coming near – 'I'm going to ask for my bishopric and get out of the way, before it's too late.'

'Robin, is that any answer?'

'It is for me. It should be for you, too, if you're wise. If he dies – and he looks like a dying man to me – will Curthose keep either of us when he comes to rule? I don't think so. We'll be back in the writing office, or out in some rustic church, so far from advancement we'll never taste honey again. If you want your promotion, now's the time to ask for it, while he can still hear you – particularly you, Raf. You haven't made any friends since you took over the running of the royal courts. You won't find a patron among the high men of this court or the one in Rouen when Will-Rou is dead.'

I went in to the king.

This time he was ready to be confessed. He stank with fever, and his eyes revealed a fear I'd never seen in them since he convulsed at the lady of Gournai's table long ago. I lost no time in bringing him what comfort I could; then I told him of my search for the girth strap and how I supposed it buried in the river. He nodded.

'Your Grace, who could have done this thing? Do you have any suspicions? I'll find him for you and bring him to justice.'

'I don't know – don't have time for that now. Ranulph, is there a curse – on my f-family, do you think? I've often wondered. M-my grandsire p-poisoned his brother, you know – to get the title. My father – he tricked Harold into swearing over those old bones. It was the only – unworthy thing he ever did, I think.'

I could think of several unworthy things the Conqueror might have to answer for, but that was no matter now. I took the king's hand and pressed it.

'My lord, there's no avenger of Duke Richard or Harold Godwinson here to injure you, or any curse that would put your brother on your throne, except the curse of a bribe paid to some traitor to remove you, for his sake. That's my thought, however it seems to you. Is there anyone with you, now, who you think might be capable of acting for Duke Robert?'

He looked at me with glazed eyes. 'Robin? He wouldn't pay to have me killed – not unless he borrowed the gold from me to do it with. Robin's a fool, but he's not – what you say. Forget that and listen to me. Wulfstan was here to sit with me for a while. He's a good old man, even if he is an Englishman. He says I must send for Anselm; that he can cure a sick man just by sitting next to him.'

'Yes, my lord. I've heard that rumor. It may be true; he's a very holy and learned man.'

'He was coming to sit with my f-father, you remember. Only he fell ill.' His expression darkened. 'It couldn't have done any good in his case, though – or in mine, maybe.'

I thought any hope was better than darkness to him and hastened to amend my opinion of Anselm's powers with more enthusiasm. 'Shall I send for him, Your Grace? He's still in this country, I believe.' I was happy to receive a nod.

Anselm had come into England a few weeks before, ostensibly to pay a pastoral visit to churches here that the late king had put into the gift of Bec. But there was more to his coming than mere pastoral business; his age and his well-known aversion to leaving his beloved school would have made it probable that he send a surrogate.

His reception in the country had been such that one might have thought another Baptist had come to prepare the way for Christ, rather than an elderly Italian scholar who had spent the greater part of his life shut up in a Norman abbey. When he visited Canterbury there had been a tumult. Christ's Church and St. Augustine's had forgotten their differences to cheer him together. He had come west at the invitation of Hugh of Chester, who displayed a sudden wealth of piety in escorting him to the Lenten court at Gloucester.

There the king had risen to greet him with honor and affection. Anselm had been for a short time, as I have said, the tutor of the young prince when his parents placed him in the school of Bec with a view of making him a clerk. Their hopes had soon been disappointed, as not even an Anselm could inspire Rufus with a love of solitude, prayers, or letters.

While Anselm visited in Gloucester I heard he had been questioned about the vacancy at Canterbury and had spoken against the king for holding it. Whatever it was he had said, it didn't reach the king's ears, for when he mentioned Anselm he approved his wisdom and said he would be a fit man to hold Canterbury, or even the holy seat at Rome, seeing how other Italians were making such a poor job of it.

It was unusual of Rufus to mention Rome, or to praise a priest of any race, but I don't believe, as Robin Bloet did, that he said it merely to irritate William de St. Carileph, who had a hankering for Canterbury he could ill conceal. The king had a true regard for Anselm, which he continued to feel even when Anselm had ceased, in his eyes, to deserve it.

Whether the king's flattering remarks were repeated to the prior of Bec to keep him in the country a little longer I cannot say. Whether the king's 'accident' had any part in some determined plan to make certain of Anselm's appointment to Canterbury seems less certain and is, in the end, a matter of futile conjecture. Anselm was nearby. The king was now near death. The great healer was sent for and the rest followed as if naturally.

In the meanwhile, as Anselm was being brought to us, very tardily to court came Malcolm of Scotland. He rode down to Alvestone with his son Edward, who was our hostage and whom he had plucked from his refuge in Huntingdon. He came like a man much aggrieved by the additional few miles he had been made to travel and demanded to see the king at once.

Rufus was in a delirium half the time by then, but not so far gone that he couldn't despise an ungracious guest and miscreant vassal. I went instead to speak to Malcolm, to give him the sad news of the king's health and say in smoother words than Rufus had uttered that he could not see the king at the moment.

'We had hope of seeing you this time last year, Your Grace, and then again at the past Christmas. Now you surprise us by coming before the feast.' I said this as humbly as possible, but the essential accusation still seemed to offend him.

He waggled his great grizzled-and-rusted head at me and aped my tone: 'How is it ye think a king's got naught to do but ride to the ends of the airth for a wee bit of ceremony, man? I've things to do in my own land, too, such as kings do. As for my comin' early, I had ither business to attend here, as well. I put my gairls in with the holy women at Wilton.'

'Your gair— your daughters? In a cloister, my lord?' He could speak quite fluent English when he had a mind to. He'd spent years in the country, both before and after his father's murder, to become proficient in the tongue. Now his accent was worse than any Northumbrian's.

'Aye, I've set them there, until they're ripe to be wed, which may be sooner than you'll like, matchmaker priest. Tell your laird he's got a rival for my Edgyth, now, and it's no use having you scribble any more soft promises to my queen, unless he's ready to back 'em with a proper treaty – one he'll be afeard to break, as he did the last.' He glared at me from under his eyebrows, like a fox peering out at a hound from its earth.

'I see.' I wasn't certain I did. 'Who is this suitor for the Lady Edgyth, may I be privileged to know, my lord?'

'Red Alan of Richmond!' He laughed sharply at my surprise.

Alan Rufus, Count of Brittany and brother-in-law to the king until the death of his wife, Constance, some two years before, was a man in his sixth decade, and he would now wed a girl who was not yet thirteen? More, he was known to be deeply enamored of a certain Lady Gunhilda, the daughter of the usurper, Harold Godwinson, and that lady was a nun at Wilton! I could only imagine that Count Alan had urged Malcolm to take his daughters to that house and affected an interest in the child in order to provide a cover for his wooing of Gunhilda, for whom he had openly professed his love and who had already petitioned the king to let her forsake her vows and marry.

But whatever Red Alan's reasons for this entanglement, which would be ludicrous to his friends and anathema to the king, it was plain that Malcolm had really brought his daughter into England to dangle her before Rufus, then sell her for the best terms he could get. It amazed me that Malcolm could be so naive in his approach to Rufus, or that he could find any reason for hesitation between choosing a king for a son-in-law, rather than a mere count, who was twice a widower and was even suspected by some to have helped his Constance into the next world by the aid of a little poison.

Malcolm was plainly set against me, too, having found cause for jealousy in my harmless correspondence with his ambitious and learned wife, but that was of little consequence to me.

'Your Grace, I will take your news to the king, since he hasn't the strength to receive you now. I pray you, rest yourself here, or at Gloucester, and take patience for a virtue. That is, make no sudden disposals of your – of your regard – on any man, before you come to the king.'

That seemed to satisfy him for the moment, though there was no reason it should. Most likely he felt he had struck a great blow against me by putting the girl at Wilton where Red Alan might see her and had given alarm to the king, whom he thought he would soon see struggling from his bed to wed her for his friendship. I knew better. Though I would continue to hope for a safe marriage for the king, supposing he was spared to consummate one, I gave up hope of the little Scottish princess for his future queen. There was no manner in which I could present Malcolm's unsubtle devices to Rufus that wouldn't make him angry.

Malcolm continued to wait with growing impatience for his audience, though there were plenty of people about him to assure him the king really was in the gravest sickness. When he grew weary of waiting, he took himself off in high indignation, and without the courtesy of asking permission to withdraw from his liege lord's court. With his son Edward he rode away, snatched his two daughters from the cloister again, and made his way furiously back to Scotland. It was a fatal anger he had brewed up over the rather trivial matter of Carlisle, and he gave it rein in a tragic manner within two months.

Now Anselm came to Alvestone, like a silvered dream of sanctity, his snow-white hair still thick about his tonsure, his Italian skin paled to an old ivory by years within the schoolroom and the cloister, his great, dark eyes lighted with a pity that belied their nearsightedness and seemed to make them keen under their thin, drooping lids.

His hands were like withered lilies when he raised them in a blessing; his step could scarcely have been more reluctant than that of one on the path to Golgotha. To see him was to become an enthusiast for vigorous penance, if only for the moment. To hear him was to be enraptured by a voice at once melodious and entreating of one's pity, for he said everything as if he were under a burden; he spoke only for one's own insistence and would far rather have kept holy silence.

All the men in the king's bedchamber fled at word that he had entered our bailey yard – all, except myself. I leaned over the king to wake him from his drowse and tell him the saint was coming. At his whispered request I washed his face and hands, tried to smooth his tangled hair, and pushed another bolster behind his head so that he was half sitting.

There was a hiatus of some quarter of an hour or more before Anselm could make his way into the manor and up the stairs through the crowd of his idolators, during which time I stood by the king's bed and wondered if this might be the end of our close friendship, as I knew what his council had primed Rufus to ask when the old man came to him.

Then Anselm entered the door with the bishops: Carileph, who already envied him; Wulfram, tottering with age; Walkelin; Maurice; Gundulph; and Archbishop Thomas of York. In a moment the chamber was so full of holy men that the laity had to shuffle to find places in the corners. I knelt and bowed my head; I felt the brush of long fingers trailing over my tonsure as Anselm passed me. As I rose, shivering slightly at the sensation of his touch, he was reaching with both his hands to take those of the king. He pressed them, then sat on the bed beside him, silently praying, while Rufus watched him avidly. At length Anselm lifted his face to the clergymen who thronged the room.

'Help me, my brothers. Pray for this man, that Christ may be merciful to him, a sinner, and restore him to vigor – to life – to perform those acts of a righteous king that he was anointed to do.'

The whole company fell upon its collective knees, and a vast suspiration of sound filled the room like incense, driving out the breathable air – or so it seemed to me, because I found myself almost panting for want of breath. I was on my knees again, by Robin. I could look nowhere but on the face of Anselm as he prayed. He took the king's two hands in one of his, passed his other hand lightly over Rufus's face and down his breast, stroked his arms, then laid his hand on the swollen belly.

There was a rattling at the shutters, as if an angel knocked, or it may only have been a gust of rain-freshened spring air; but one of the shutters flew open, banging against the embrasure. Everyone started at the sound except Anselm, who had the king's hands clasped between his again.

Suddenly he released them. His head drooped as if he were exhausted. He opened his eyes and stared at the stricken Rufus, whose own face was as pale as the prior's.

'Let It come in, my son. Let It come in,' he murmured. Rufus breathed a sob for an answer and Anselm sighed. 'Yes. Even so, come, Lord Christ.' He gently folded the king's hands on his breast, then roused himself as if from a dream and turned to Archbishop Thomas, who stood directly across the bed from him. He smiled wearily.

'It is well. Well for him and for us all. God is merciful. The king will not die. His angel has spoken, praise be to the Holy Name. We must give thanks to Him.'

There was a shout of affirmation: 'God be praised! Christ be praised!'

I felt as if a thunderbolt had fallen near me, or as if I had endured another earthquake. There was a noise in my ears and a tingling in my flesh. I tried to rise and saw the dark, liquid eye of Anselm turning toward me. He frowned slightly; there was a rushing sound – and I lost my senses.

It was only for a moment. I felt Robin's hand under my arm; with his aid I got to my feet, apologizing for my lapse. Yet no one else seemed to have noticed but Anselm. He gave me another intense glance; then he was going out the door and everyone was struggling to go after him. I looked at the king, whose face was streaked with tears, but Robin pulled me away from the bed and into the passage.

'I think you need air. Come along.' He drew me along the passage to the far end where the chapel was, and there he threw open the window shutters and hooked them to the embrasure so that the brisk wind blew in upon us. I leaned against the embrasure and drew a deep breath.

'Are you better now?'

'Yes. My God, my God, that man!'

'Anselm? Yes, well, now you see why they're determined to have him for Canterbury – and they'll get him, I make no doubt. It's a good thing our ambitions never reached as high as that, isn't it? Poor old Carileph must be gnawing himself with disappointment now. Ha! He'd have to draw loaves and fishes out of the king's nose to equal that business in there. But I'll content myself with Lincoln and good, easy old Thomas for my archbishop.'

I turned to look at him curiously. He was often affected to wonder or tears by people and events that left me unmoved, yet he seemed not to have felt anything of the power I had felt shake me in that chamber. All of Anselm's charisma Robin put down to lack of fresh air. I braced myself against the window and looked out over the bailey yard. Perhaps lack of air was all it had been, after all.

'You've asked for the bishopric of Lincoln?'

'Why, yes. I thought I'd better, before someone else did. I've served my time in court, or as long as I care to, haven't you? What have you asked for?'

'Nothing. I suppose I'll have the chancery when you've gone.'

There was a note of surprise, almost of pity, in Robin's hesitant laugh; then he said: 'But, my dear boy! You should have spoken. I thought you must have. I recommended Gerard for the chancery, and I believe he's already been told it will be his. I thought you'd want something – better. Of course, you still have the deanery of St. Martin's and the Abbey of Hyde.'

'Yes.' I looked at his cherub's face under its lamb's locks that were beginning to deaden to gray. Was he really so contemptuous of me that he thought those posts enough? No, not contemptuous, but he naturally supposed Gerard would be the better choice to succeed him; Gerard, fat, amiable, untalented but for his gourmandising, nephew of two bishops, son of a noble family distantly related to the royal house: a gentleman.

I smiled at Robin's rather tardy look of commiseration. 'Never mind. It's no matter. I'm sure to have my work still to do here, as the king's dog.'

47

Yes, Anselm would have Canterbury. It seemed that everyone was agreed on this and accepted it but Anselm. He shook his head and murmured, 'No, no, no,' when it was first mentioned to him that evening in the presence hall, where Prince Henry honored him with his own seat at the high table – and made himself so bold as to sit in the king's chair instead.

Anselm's adherents wouldn't take his mild 'no's' for an answer. They urged him to consider what good he might do for Christ's

Church and the realm of England if he consented to the archbishopric. He still refused, in his hesitant, pathetic manner:

'My lords, I am no Lanfranc, but only a poor monk and teacher of monks. According to my vows, I must shut out the world, not welcome it into my arms with all its perils.'

Gundulph of Rochester said tremulously: 'But this world has great need of you, brother. You must feel it; you were sent here to us at just this time, to take command over us in our need. This is a world that smiles on you and welcomes you. All men here favor you, even the king.'

Anselm said sadly: 'That is the great temptation which is offered to us, and not only by men of the world, but often by those who should think themselves fortunate to be out of it. But it is dangerous: if the world smiles on you with its favors, do not smile in return. It does not smile that you may smile, in the end, but it mocks you with its Prince, that you with its Prince may mourn. Therefore, however it beckons, you must turn from it, so you may rejoice when the Mocker mourns.'

I felt a qualm; did he mean the king was the Mocker who would someday mourn, or did he speak of the Prince of Darkness as the Prince of the World? It was always difficult to tell his meaning, as he tended to speak in similes and parables.

The others continued to press him, but he smiled and shook his head, as if he scarcely understood their arguments. 'My lords, you would do ill in this yoking of me to the king. It would be as if you yoked a weak old ram with a strong young bull.'

That was a better simile than it first seemed to be, as I was soon to discover, for old rams, however weak, are strong-headed and difficult to move, even when yoked to whirlwinds.

The king, meanwhile, felt some slight relief from his pain and had been thoroughly counseled that it was the work of Anselm. He understood from all his spiritual advisers, save me, that only by naming Anselm to the throne of Canterbury could he hope to merit forgiveness in the next world for his unlawful keeping of Canterbury's revenues in his own hands, thereby depriving the kingdom of a spiritual father, during which time God's favor had been withdrawn from him and he had been stricken almost to the grave. It was strong argument. The king was in a weakened condition and terrified of death, as are all men when it looks them in the face. He sent for the holy prior of Bec and, in the presence of his chief ministers, offered him the throne and miter of the archbishopric.

Anselm refused it; drew back, as if horrified. But Rufus had been made aware of his earlier refusals and was prepared. Once decided on the matter, he meant to have no refusal A company of clerks had been sent to Canterbury to fetch Lanfranc's own staff, which should have been interred with him but hadn't been, at his dying request to be buried as a simple monk. The staff was now in the hands of Canterbury's prior, who stood by the king's bed. Once more Rufus entreated Anselm to accept it willingly:

'Master, they tell me I have no hope of seeing my father in Paradise, unless I fill the vacancy at Canterbury with a worthy man. I have found such a m-man, and he stands before me now. Will you take the staff from me?'

'No, my good lord, I cannot. I am not worthy.'

The king pushed himself upright a little more, his face bathed in a sheen of sweat. 'Prior, the wisest men in my kingdom say you are worthy – and I say it. Come and take the staff.' He put out his hand and the prior of Canterbury put the staff in it. He gripped it, heaving himself forward against it, painfully.

'Prior, you're a merciful m-man. You heard I was in sight of my grave and you came to p-pray for me, but now you harass me. Rather than be my salvation, you would b-be my death!'

'No, no, my gracious lord. I pray for your life and health, but this burden is not for me.' Anselm closed his eyes, his voice almost a whisper.

The king fell back on his pillow for a moment, his jaw set with pain. He wiped his mouth with his hand and said bitterly: 'You weren't s-so reluctant to take other honors from a hand in my family. Do you remember the friendship my f-father and m-my mother showed you in the past? Are they nothing to you, now they're dead? Will you let their son die, in soul as w-well as in body, for the lack of your f-friendship?'

Anselm wept, shaking his head. The king, regaining strength and with a grim smile, lifted himself again on the staff until he was half out of bed. 'Help me, then – help me, Father – take this office from me, of which they say I'm already confounded and fo-for which they say I may be forever confounded, if I die with it on my hands.' Still no submission. The king looked ready to burst into tears or a rage.

'Is there no one to reason with him but me, then, my lords? I cannot drive him to it from this bed.'

Now two of Anselm's own monks, Eadmer and Baldwin, seeing that their master might indeed be throwing away a pearl of great price, tried to persuade him:

'This is a solemn calling, Reverend Father Prior. As they've said, you must have been sent for this office. Take it, I beg you.'

'All the afflictions of a kingdom may lie at your door, Reverend Father Prior, if you turn away from this now.'

'I would rather it were God's will that I should die, than to take on me this burden!' cried Anselm, but Baldwin answered him swiftly:

'Yet, if it be the will of God, who are we to withstand it, my lord?' His words were followed by a flood of tears and a sudden gush of blood from his nose, which he made haste to wipe with his sleeve.

Anselm looked at him, half smiling, as if he had discovered a Judas at his table. 'How soon your staff is broken, my friend.'

The king said to his bishops: 'Lend me your aid, my lords. Persuade him to it.'

And all the bishops fell on their knees and loudly importuned the old man to take the shepherd's staff with its golden crook. He in turn fell on his knees and begged them not to torment him. I was fascinated, but at the same time heard myself sigh in exasperation. There was something too much of this. We should all be shrieking and rolling on the floor in an instant, and the king looked as if he had reached the limits of his endurance as well.

Evidently my thought was shared by Archbishop Thomas and Maurice, for they suddenly seized Anselm and dragged him without further ado to the king's bedside. Maurice grasped his right hand and stretched it forth toward the staff, which the king held, trembling. Anselm closed his fist and groaned; Maurice pried open his fingers, like those of a stubborn child; Anselm shrieked with pain. The prior of St. Augustine's came to their assistance, and by main strength the staff was fixed between the thumb and forefinger of the protesting Anselm.

A great shout of triumph rose from the throats of all Anselm's monks and the king's bishops. The king fell back on the bed.

'Long live Bishop Anselm! Long live the king! Praise be to God! *Te deum laudamus . . .* ' Men wept; they took hold of poor old Anselm roughly and dragged him out of the chamber as they hymned praise to God, carried him, still protesting and weeping, down the stairs and out of the manor to the little church that served both manor and vill of Alvestone. By his cries and theirs one might well have thought either a crowd of sane men were overwhelming a maniac, or a multitude of madmen were carrying off the only man sane in the world.

Now the chamber was empty, save for myself and the king. I went to him and lifted him onto his pillows again. He winced with the movement, but he was laughing as he wiped his face with both hands. 'Ah, God! What a rout! Damned, crazy men! All priests are crazy – except you, maybe. He wants the office; he must. He s-smelled it from clear across the Channel and came here to get it, but can he take it honestly? Stamp his feet and clap his hands when he's got it, like an honest winner? Oh, God, no! He has to m-make God think it's all too much for him, eh? And the rest of them, they'll be before me complaining about him in a few months, or writing me letters, as they've done about old Thomas, or even Lanfranc, because he's a ma-man who's been put over them, like the others. But now they've got to shout "Alleluia!" and *"Te Deum!"* and p-pretend he's a saint, or God won't think they know their business.'

He sighed. 'Oh, God, I'm spent!' He glanced at me, seeing I didn't reply to his estimate of Anselm. 'What do you suppose God thinks of all this, eh? Is He laughing? Or does He either: l-laugh or think? Don't answer that, even if you think you can. I'm blown with religion like a three-day corpse.' He smiled. 'I've offended you, haven't I? Yes, I have. You're as taken with that old man as the rest of them, only you don't like to show it for fear of me. Well, love him, if you like. I don't mind. He's harmless. There's only the one thing: I'll be out of purse for giving him Canterbury. You'll have to do something about that.'

In a quarter of an hour the court was back again, half carrying the new archbishop, who had terrified them by fainting in their arms as they were bearing him to the altar. Robin Bloet came to the bedchamber to report this; then Anselm himself appeared a few moments later, his face slack with exhaustion, his eyes reproachful. He leaned against the doorpost and said to the king:

'This was the madness of a moment. God will not hold you to it, nor will I.'

'It needs neither God nor you to hold me to my s-sworn word, my lord,' the king said. 'My honor suffices for that.'

Anselm gazed on him bleakly and left the doorway.

The king's health improved to the point where it now seemed certain that Anselm was a true prophet; he would not die after all. The passage of blood in his urine lessened, then disappeared; the swelling was reduced without the crisis of passing a stone. One might have supposed the doctors would be confounded, but it was not so; he who had put the cause to the stone merely said the stone must have been drawn back up into the bladder again by the strength of the body humors, while he who had put the cause of the malady merely to a fever in the bowels was vindicated without further proof.

But Rufus was still half invalid and the more ill-tempered for it as his convalescence wore on to the end of Lent. When he was well enough he was carried in a litter back to Gloucester, and this seemed to shame him, as his long-ago infirmity had done. But there was no help for him now. He couldn't sit a horse or even stand without great pain in his loins. A black humor took possession of him that had all men about him walking lightly and speaking carefully. He couldn't endure to be asked how he felt, or to have any hint of his frailty brought out in civil speech, and a syllable spoken in praise of the Almighty for having spared him brought him to an instant fury:

'Enough of that! Enough!' He cried out to old Anselm when he had made such a pious reflection one morning soon after we came to Gloucester. 'God doesn't earn my gratitude for taking away a bruise He inflicted on me! Nor do I tha-thank Him for the relief when it comes. I live because I'm still too s-strong to die.'

'My good lord, this is blasphemous,' whispered Anselm, but he recognized the pettishness that goes with convalescence in a man unused to much ill health. 'The fever still works on your mind, Your Grace, but never let the Devil make use of it, to ruin you. Remember the man you were when you believed yourself to be dying. That was the truer man, who made atonement for his sins and hoped for Heaven. These pains will pass, but you must take care that you do not drive your good angel away with them.'

The king favored him with a dark look, then turned his face away on the pillow, no doubt regretting he had spoken so roughly to the old man, who seemed genuinely grieved for him. I thought of what I had heard my lord say, long ago, when I had made a similar speech to him: 'God shall never see me a good man. I have suffered too much at His hands for that.'

Compared with some men who have suffered, of course, the king had escaped lightly and Anselm must think so. He couldn't know what blows to the spirit made Rufus believe himself the object of God's anger, nor could they have been explained to him. To a man of Anselm's sort, who believed the world and all its glories to be mere filth which mankind inappropriately desires, the king's yearning for physical perfection, for the love that was denied him, for glory in the eyes of other men, would seem base and trivial. I felt pity for both of them, but especially for old Anselm, who every day saw more evidence that he was ill matched with his yoke-fellow, as he had called him.

Easter came, and the king, in spite of his weakness, made his appearance before his court to be crowned and sceptered. He walked without aid through the hall and sat for several hours on his throne, smiling and greeting his barons and the ambassadors of other kings, while his fingers gripped the curled arms of his throne until his knuckles gleamed white.

King Malcolm neither came nor sent an envoy, but someone else did who made the king forget all others. Edgar Atheling came with the envoys from Rouen, who bowed before the king, then offered him a letter from his brother which outlined all his failures with respect to the treaty of mutual aid that had been signed between them. Rufus handed the letter to me to keep and I glanced at it, satisfying myself that he didn't yet know what it contained and there would be no breach of the peace in the hall until after the festivities.

Prince Edgar took no part in the speech-making of his fellow ambassadors, but kept behind them until the last, then went forward and made his obeisance to the king alone. He wasn't noticed more than any other man who had come to do the same service, except by myself and one other. I saw Prince Henry turn his fine head and glance our way, as Edgar lifted his face to the king's. He couldn't hear that sound which I heard coming from the king's throat, between a groan and a snarl:

'So, you're back – as his pleader.'

'No. I came with those who are, but I'm not one of them. Your Grace, I came – '

'To see me dead?'

'To pray you might live. I see you do.' He smiled faintly. 'I thank God for it. Now I may ask your pardon.'

'You came for that? You came late.'

'My lord, when the news told us of your illness, I left the duke's court at once, but he was in the Evreçin. When I reached the coast, the winds held me back from crossing for a week. When there was a ship, it was blown off course. We made landing at Dover, rather than at Portsmouth, but I've ridden hard since then.'

The king looked down on him still with a scowl, his fingers loosening and gripping at their rests. 'And you came to ask my pardon? For what? Leaving me without permission? Go home a happy man, then: you're pardoned. It will be my br-brother's pardon you'll need next.'

'Not – if I have yours, my lord.' A rare, unmelancholy smile brightened Edgar's sad face for an instant. 'I'm grateful, neverthe-less, only to see you well again.'

The king's face worked; he rose with difficulty from his seat. Edgar moved quickly and put his hands out to grasp him by the forearms when he swayed. The king took him by the arms, too, and they stood so, while the talk in the great hall diminished and the speakers stared at them. Then Rufus threw back his head with a laugh of triumph and fell on his friend, clasping him in his arms like a beloved champion met on the field of honor.

Thereafter he began to improve in strength and temper with almost miraculous speed. We remained at Gloucester until he could ride again, during which time he asked the great council for its formal affirmation of Anselm and of Robert Bloet, who would now be Bishop of Lincoln. This was granted joyfully, except in the case of Archbishop Thomas, who didn't much like the declaration that Anselm was to be 'Metropolitan of all England.' That was a battle he had once lost to Lanfranc, but which he foolishly supposed Anselm would be too unworldly to remember.

During this time, also, I was required to write a letter to King Malcolm, sternly commanding him to make his appearance at the Whitsun Court, else he be charged with being recreant in his duty as the sworn man of the king and in defiance of the king's peace. This letter was long in being answered.

Of greater importance at the moment was the news from Bernard de Neufmarché, the new lord of Brecknock in Wales, who reported an uprising of the terrorists of Glamorgan, under the command of Rhys ap Tewdwr, who called himself their king. Rhys had been killed in the affray that followed, which meant that his heirs and enemies would now fight like devils to succeed him and, no doubt, make necessary a new campaign for King William to subdue them. The prospect gave the king more pleasure than anything else, except the return of Edgar Atheling.

We removed to London for a short time; then the king and Prince Edgar took themselves off to hunt at Windsor with a small company of friends, leaving Prince Henry to rule the diminished daily business as he saw fit at Westminster. I took the opportunity to lay hands on my son Martin and haul him to his mother's arms in London, where they made a very pretty picture of filial and maternal devotion, the one sulking, the other scolding him for his neglect of her.

I was amazed at the change that Isabel had worked on my poor, storm-struck, and beggar-wrecked house, though I flinched at the news she had put me in debt some twenty marks or better for her improvements. She had made herself wholly the chatelaine of the manor there: planted an herb garden, taken on new servants other than those I had hired for her. They looked on me with as much friendliness as a porter's dog looking on a mendicant when I took her up on the cost of all this.

Martin glowered at me, too, as if I might next propose to throw his beloved mother into the streets, though he'd not thought where she might have been housed until I told him. I decided, for the sake of peace, to hold my tongue from further complaint. The house, after all, was mine and it was looking better than it had ever looked. Isabel would be a good guardian of my property, which I myself hadn't the time to see to, and there was no denying that it was pleasant to sit at my own table for a change and glance with covert pride at my son, who was gaining in grace and goodly looks, if not in manners, with every passing month.

My son would be a knight someday. He must be allowed his pride. When he was a little older, I foolishly believed, he would come to realize the affection I bore him and return it in some degree, even if he never fully understood the bond of blood between us that engendered it.

I had time then to think of visiting Elfgiva for a few days, as the king would be at Windsor for at least a fortnight. I was preparing for the journey when I received a summons from the new lord of Canterbury, who was living on one of his estates near Rochester while waiting for the time of his consecration. This consecration might have taken place immediately after his installation, but he had put up a new difficulty: he demanded of King William that he, Anselm, be allowed to make his submission to one of the two rivals for the throne of St. Peter. The pope he had chosen to submit to was Urban, formerly Odo of Ostia, for whom the Roman necromancer's prophecy had rung true, even as it sent the bishop of Bayeux to prison for believing himself to be the fated Odo.

This desire of old Anselm's to be the man of either pope, whether it be Urban or the German emperor's favorite, Clement, was a surprise to us who had no reason to believe the merits of one pope or another to be of any importance to the king or his archbishop. It had never been the custom of any of their predecessors to bend their knees to Rome, unless it was for a sound political reason. No other bishop in the council of the king saw the necessity to take sides in this dispute between the Italians and the German emperor. The king had better cause to stay entirely out of it, as whichever prelate he might favor would make him enemies in the other camp. There was the

German trade to think of, and the Italian kinsmen of many of our most illustrious Norman families.

It was a pious whim of Anselm's which must be put aside, now he was the shepherd of our realm. More important to the king was the matter of certain Canterbury estates that he had let go for knights' fees while he still held them during the vacancy. He had asked Anselm to honor the gifts as he honored the king, but the old man had proved unexpectedly obstinate about these few miserable hides of farmland and had demanded their return, saying he could let nothing go that was Canterbury's.

It was this trifling matter (or so I thought at the time) I believed he wished to sound me out on, in order to reach an agreement with the king before his consecration. I hurried to meet with him on that account, and because I was flattered to have him call for me, rather than our new chancellor, Gerard.

I was mistaken. When I presented myself to him in his summer garden, where I found him reading, he looked at me with brief distaste, then focused his gaze on some flowering bush in the middle distance as I knelt before him. In his slightly distracted manner of speech, he said:

'Brother in Christ, it is distressful to me to have to speak to you. You offend me, but I had a thousand times rather be chastised of another than to chastise any man.'

'Your Grace, how have I offended you?' I asked in astonishment.

'In the same manner as you have offended God and Holy Church: by the neglect of your vows and the scandalous manner of your life, which has been made known to me by one who knows it well and fears for your soul as well as the soul you tend, by which I mean the king's.'

'Your Grace – who is this person you speak of? Let me know his name and the charges he brings against me, so that I may defend myself, for I swear to you – '

'Do not swear to me! Your sins are well known to many good men of this realm, and they surely are known to you, since their nature doesn't allow of self-deception. They are grave. They would be so in any man, but most particularly in a man of your professed vocation, who has the keeping of a king's soul in his hands.' He frowned, but he still didn't look directly at me.

I was on my knees in the dust before him. My mouth had gone dry, but I said in as steady a voice as I might:

'Good and holy Father in Christ, I allow that I am not without sins; no man is, I think. But where the king is con—'

'Where the king is concerned you are *most* culpable, Brother, and I must join you in culpability if I neglect to check you. I am the king's spiritual guardian and counselor, above all others, both according to my conscience and according to that vow which he made at the moment of his coronation.'

'That, by your leave, Your Grace, was a vow he made to Archbishop Lanfranc at his father's request.'

'I have seen the document. It was a vow he made to the Archbishop of Canterbury, which now, unhappily, I am.' Then he did glance at me, barely, with a frown. 'You may stand, Brother, and tell me whether it is true that you dishonor your holy vows by keeping concubines.'

'Concubines? I own I have a wife, but there are many other priests who would have to say the same thing, as you know, Your Grace. A wife, not a concubine, and certainly not in the plural.'

'You cannot have a wife. It is forbidden by papal decree. Those men in Holy Orders who believe they have wives are sadly mistaken – no, criminally mistaken. In your case there is no record of a marriage of any sort to be found; therefore you will not dispute me when I name the women you harbor your concubines.'

'Women, Your Grace, no – '

'One in London and one in Winchester, I am told. And you have bastards as well, which you're at small pains to keep hidden.'

My astonishment was beginning to turn to anger. 'I have sons.'

'Yes,' he said. 'God help them. What will they be?'

'I don't know what you can mean by that, Your Grace. They will be men, in time. If God wills it, they'll be lettered men and no worse off than many others of that profession, who are sons of priests, as I am, myself.'

Suddenly I felt *a frisson* along my spine. Who had told him all this? I had thought some envious enemy of mine, but now I thought of my own father, safely harbored at St. Augustine's. Had he had an opportunity to speak to this old man, or to one of his clerks, and, in order to perfect his own sanctity, unburdened himself of my history? There was no use in asking, but the manner in which the archbishop avoided meeting my eyes made me suspect Thurstin. Yet my father could know nothing of Isabel in London – unless Fulcher or Osbern had told him, of course. But I had let my mind wander from my own defense, and Anselm was speaking again, more harshly:

'You have admitted to half my charge. What matters the rest of it – the woman you keep at London? And the bastard you got on her?

Confess to that as well and cleanse your heart, my son. Then we may speak further.'

'My lord, there is a woman in London who stays in a house of mine. I confess I am the father of her son, but she is not my concubine now, or ever was. Our alliance was very brief and has been repented of, at least by me, many times over. I keep her in charity now, for the sake of our son, and I beg you to remember that this I speak is in the nature of a true confession. Martin, my son, has no part in my sin. He needn't know anything about it.'

'You don't need to instruct me in my office, Brother. In all humility, I am better versed in it than you. Now, there is the matter of repentance. '

I felt relieved. If repentance was what he wanted, he should have it in full measure. I made ready to go on my knees again, but he stopped me.

'Repentance is easy, you think, but penance is hard. Do you repent?'

'My lord, I have repented these many years what was done in the heat of my youth, but –'

'The heat of your youth still burns. You have a child yet unborn in the womb of the woman you lightly call your wife.'

I went to my knees whether he allowed it or not. 'I have never lightly called her my wife, Your Grace. I have believed her to be so and have been faithful to her since the day we pledged our vows to each other.'

'You had no right to make such vows, no right to ask for hers. This is a worse thing you've done, Brother, to put a young woman's soul in jeopardy of eternal torment for the sake of your lust.' He paused, waiting for my answer.

There was no other possible: 'I acknowledge all this, Your Grace, and I have felt the pangs of conscience for it, but what is to be done now? She is dependent on me and has no one else – '

'She has someone else more worthy than you, Brother. She has her Creator, her Savior, and the Holy Spirit to uphold her, if she turns to Them.' Now, though I didn't look at him, I believed he may have set his gaze on me at last. He spoke after a moment in a kinder voice: 'Do you love her?'

'Yes, Your Grace, as I love my own life.'

'Then you must put her away.'

I lifted my eyes to his and shook my head dumbly.

'Yes, my son, it must be so. There is no other way. I will accept your word about the other woman, that you do nothing unlawful with her now. But this other, this so-called wife of yours, you must put away from you.'

'Your Grace – holy Father in Christ – this is very hard – '

'Hard, yes. It will go harder.' His voice became firm again. 'I pity you, as Christ pitied the woman taken in adultery, but I must offer you the same warning: go, and sin no more. Until I am satisfied that you have cleansed yourself and renewed your vows with the full intent of maintaining them, I cannot allow that you remain the chaplain to the king.'

'What? This – this isn't your province!'

'It is! It is my sacred duty, to you and to the king I have sworn to serve and guide. I may not further entrust his soul to the counsel of a man who willfully neglects his own. No! As your spiritual head, as well as his, I charge and command you, Ranulph, that you put away your concubine and amend your life before you may go near the king again. You will obey me. You know the consequences if you do not. It is to be stripped of your gown and to be denied the Holy Sacrament, even if you were on your deathbed!'

48

I went away from him, sat in the precincts of the church, and tried to think, but my brain was numb. How had this come about, that I must make a choice and no choice was thinkable? I returned to speak to him again:

'Your Grace, set me down from the priesthood. Let me be a clerk only; then I can both serve the king and cherish my wife.'

'That isn't possible. Your friendship to the king damages him. Your lust for the flesh damages this young woman as much as yourself. There are more things to think about than your own convenience.'

'Convenience? It's more than that, surely. Did Christ command Peter to put away his wife, since he had her? No, he said a man should cleave to his wife and the wife to her husband.'

'We'll not play choplogic with the Holy Scriptures, Brother. You have no true wife.'

'Father, I love this woman as my wife – as my life.'

'Life is nothing; a brief thing, soon used up. If you love her body as you love your life, you're a fool. If you love her soul as you do your own, you must put her away. And if you love the king as you are said to, you will obey me in order to serve him. There is no other answer, Brother, so you may not come to me again until you are ready to do as I command you. I pity you. I cannot comprehend you, but I pity you.'

I went. I took my horse and rode away, not thinking where I was bound, until I found myself in Dover. Then I knew I had come there to find Fulcher, my brother, whom I had distrusted and sent away. Now I needed him. There was no one else I might speak to and get anything but an echo of the archbishop's command. Only Fulcher would understand, because he was of my blood and because he loved Giva, too.

I found him at Vespers service when I reached St. Martin's. I slipped into the church and knelt alone in the nave until the closing prayer, then hurried up the aisle to Fulcher. My canons recognized me and greeted me with reserved politeness, but I couldn't speak to them, only to him. He saw my fear and took me at once to my own deanery, where I sat on a bench before a cold fireplace and wept.

I told him everything. When I finished he was quiet for so long a time that I began to regain my composure and even to reflect on his silence. Was he rejoicing in my despair? Did it please him that I, who had driven him away from Giva, was now in danger of losing her, too?

'Well?' I said with surly impatience born of suspicion. 'What shall I do? Say something! I didn't come all this way to hear you breathe.'

'You didn't expect that I could tell you what to do, did you? You know what you must do.'

'Oh, and what's that?'

'You must provide for her and – give her up.'

'Must I? Out of all the hundreds, the thousands of priests who've taken wives, I must be the one to give mine up! Why should I lead the way? Let Bishop Robin Bloet give up his! Let the Archbishop of York give up his! Let Herbert Losinga – '

'Perhaps they'll have to, in time. But you must do it now.'

'Why?'

'Raf, you know why. He told you. Excommunication.'

'It doesn't seem to have harmed the King of France.'

'But it will destroy you! You'll lose your place with the king. No one will employ you. The chapter won't be allowed to receive you. No one, anywhere, will – '

'Yes, yes, you've made your point.' But my head was shaking no, no, at the same time. 'Oh, God, I can't do it, Fulcher. I can't face her with it.'

'Do you want me to go with you?'

'No! No. That isn't why I came. I don't know why I came.'

He touched my shoulder. 'It's terrible. It will be terrible for a while, but then it will be less so. You'll have your work and she'll have the children. After all, there've been weeks, even months, when you haven't seen each other. That must give it some kind of ease.'

I said angrily, 'What, do you think if I'm not in bed with her I don't think of her at all?'

He bowed his head prudently, but the answer was plain: he did. And it was true in good measure, I realized, though the knowledge didn't lessen my anger toward him. I rose stiffly and started for the door. 'Thank you for your sage advice, brother. I'll be going now. It's a long ride.'

'You won't stay the night, or even have a bite of supper? Shall I come with you?'

'No. Why should you? It takes only one tongue to tell the tale.'

He stopped me at the door. 'Listen, it isn't as if you must turn her out of doors to starve, or never see her. You can simply leave her where she is, with Mother and Osbern and the children. Provide for her, but don't –'

'Don't sleep with her, yes. Thank you very much. I'd already decided on that part of it. That part was easy. Good-bye, Fulcher.'

When I reached home in three days, I found Giva in the yard hanging up linens to dry. She turned with two clothes pegs in her mouth and came waddling toward me, so ridiculously gravid that I could have laughed for delight if I hadn't been so perilously close to tears. I caught her to me and buried my face in her neck to breathe the odor of fresh sweat and clean laundry that emanated from her skin. There were dark rings under her eyes, as if she hadn't slept well of late, but she was laughing with the pleasure of seeing me.

'It's like trying to embrace a cabbage,' I said, putting a hand to her belly. 'What is it we've got here, another boy?'

'A girl, your mother says, from the way I'm carrying it. To tell the truth, I can't tell the difference, except this one seems to lie heavier and kick less. A lazy girl, if it is one.'

I held her close again, causing her to cry out in surprise; then I kissed her as if I would never have the chance again, which alarmed her. She pulled back from me.

'What is it? Is there some bad news? What?'

'Nothing, nothing we can't talk about later. Where are the boys?

Let's go in. I'm famished. Is there anything to eat?' I smiled at her. We went in. I greeted Mother, Swan, Osbern, all the children. I fulfilled my duty as gossip-monger while bread, cheese, and cold pork were cut and thrust upon me, as if I were a miraculous beggar. I made myself sound as normal as possible, but all the time I rambled through the doings of the court Giva watched me. Having begun my deception, I found no way to broach the subject until we were alone together in our chamber at the end of the day. She sat on the bed beside me and said calmly:

'Now, what is it? I've been trying to guess all day. It can't be bad news about your father, or Fulcher, or you'd have told Osbern first. It isn't about the king, or you'd have told us all. So, it must only be about you, and you don't want them to know.'

'You've grown into a wise woman, Giva.'

'Are you dismissed from the king's service?'

I looked at her in surprise that this should be her first thought. 'No – I may be – but that doesn't matter. It's something else.' Her clear, green eyes dwelt on my face with concern; her nose and cheeks had begun to parade their summer's crop of freckles over her rose-flushed cheeks. I took her head between my hands.

'I love you, Giva. Remember that. Oh, God, I wish you weren't so close to your time. I want to make love to you. It's been so long.'

'Ranulph, you're scaring me witless! Tell me what's wrong!'

I told her. I blurted it out without the saving grace of those many phrases I had constructed and rehearsed as I rode to tell her. I might have been dictating a writ to my clerk for a person who was a stranger to me: twenty or thirty words, and I was finished.

She let her gaze drop slowly from mine to observe how our hands lay clasped between us. In a voice without color she said:

'I knew it would come, someday. I just didn't think it would be so soon. When you wanted to be a bishop – *then, I* thought – '

'You don't think I want this now, do you? Do you?'

She didn't answer. With a groan I tried to embrace her, but she made a sudden motion and warded me off, then lay her hands carefully over her belly.

'Giva – '

'What happens to this? What do I do now? Where should I go?'

'You'll have it, as you had the others, and you're not going anywhere.'

She shook her head slowly. 'I can't stay here.'

'What's that supposed to mean, for the love of God? Do you think

I'm going to throw you out in the streets, or put you in an anchorite's cell?'

'What can you do with me?'

'I'm not going to do anything with you. I'm going to appeal to the king, for a start. I don't think he'll like it much that his new archbishop is interfering with his personal staff. I've been with him too long; he's loyal to people who are loyal to him. He won't let this happen.'

'Oh? Can the king keep the archbishop from unfrocking you? Can he keep you for his chaplain when you aren't a priest anymore? That'll be news to God, I'd think. Now you know how I felt when it first came into my mind that it was wrong – ' She looked at me with new acuteness. 'What's the part that bothers you most: having to do without me, or losing your place with the king?'

Suddenly I wanted to box her ears. I shouted: 'Don't be stupid and female now, damn it! Try to understand what's at stake here. Is the king your rival for my love, do you think?'

'I have thought it, sometimes. But it doesn't matter now, does it, as you're about to lose us both.'

'Thank you for your confidence in me!' But that wasn't what I wanted to say, or what I wanted to hear from her. I needed the comfort of her love, even of her tears, not this sad, cold finality. I put my hands on her shoulders and said more entreatingly:

'Giva, listen to me. I haven't been able to think it all out yet; my mind's been chasing itself since I left that pious old fool. But I don't mean to lose *you* or see you in want of anything! I'm going to find a way out of this, but first I mean to make you secure. I'll sign over the deed to this house to you. I'll give you money, through Osbern. I'll take Mother and Osbern out of here, so it won't seem as if there's any connection left between us – and I won't be able to see you, for a while – but I love you and I won't – '

'Oh, Ranulph! You're such a clever man in some things, but you've never wanted to think about this, and I've thought and thought about it ever since our first baby died. I've prayed every day since then that God wouldn't punish us by taking another child, and at least He hasn't done that.'

'We go through this every time you breed, Giva. God doesn't murder babies to make people sorry for their sins.'

'Oh? Then what about those Egyptians – '

'Damn Fulcher and his *sermons*!'

'Abraham and Isaac – '

'*He didn't kill him!*'

We stood glaring at each other. Then she wept, hanging her head. I put my arms about her and hugged her to me as closely as the child would allow. I saw that neither of us could bear a whole night of this. I said at last:

'Maybe they *should* cast me out of Holy Orders. I'm sorry, Giva, sorry. You, Fulcher, and Anselm – you're all so certain you know what is in God's mind. I've never been quite sure that He cared, one way or another, whether I slept with you, if I loved you and did you no injury. But that may be just the thing here. I'll go, tonight, and sleep at the castle. I love you. I'll take care of you, somehow. We'll work this out so no one's too badly hurt.'

'Don't say things like that about God. I know you're angry and don't mean it, but you might say it to the wrong people now, and you're in enough danger as it is.'

She didn't beg me to stay, which I would have preferred at the moment to her good advice. I kissed her again. 'I'll see you tomorrow.'

She clung to me for a moment. 'Good-bye, God keep you. God keep you.'

I went downstairs and out into the street after pausing to look into the hall where my mother was sleeping. Had she heard us? I'd have to speak to her and Osbern, tomorrow, to explain my future absence and to make certain they wouldn't turn against Giva when they heard my tale.

There was rain on the street and a heavy, wet mist in the air. No lanterns flickered, and the clouds had covered the moon. It was a good night for thieves. But if there were any such persons lurking where I passed along the High Street, they saw in me a man who had nothing left to be stolen.

The next morning I spent some time in the scriptorium, writing out a transference of deed to my house to favor Giva. I took it and a sum of money to Hyde Abbey, where I gave both to my prior, instructing him to see that the deed was kept safe and the money was portioned out to her in equal measure through the next few months. Osbern came to the abbey looking for me. I told him briefly what had happened and made him promise to take care of Giva on pain of my displeasure. He was pale at my news. No doubt he saw himself being torn from the arms of his fecund Swanhilda, who had just been delivered of their second son, which they had agreed to name for me. I gave him some money for the child's baptism and Swan's churching. Then it seemed to me I had done all I could for the moment. There was little to be gained by seeing Giva again, even to tell her she was now safely independent of me. Osbern could do that.

It was one of those clouded days, with shafts of piercing sunlight that one sees in April, when the air is fresh and gusty and the newborn green of the trees seems vivid for its contrast with a sullen sky. I rode to find the king.

I meant to tell him in full of Anselm's determination to take the place of Lanfranc in all things: advising him, forestalling – yes, denying him – when he chose. Choosing who should serve him and who not. Rufus wouldn't like that news. He'd already begun to have second thoughts about his famous saint. It might be when he heard me that there wouldn't be a consecration at Christ's Church after all. There was still time.

Against all my other rivals – Cormac, Edgar, Prince Henry, Carileph – I had thought harm but done none. Anselm would be another matter. This fragile, gentle, implacable old monk whom I might have worshiped as devoutly as did the rest of his followers – this man had become my enemy, more to be feared than Cormac. I would turn his dreaming mind to matters that would drive out the memory of my small misdeed, or else be rid of him altogether. I could forgo Elfgiva for the little time it took to accomplish that task.

I found the king now recovered from his illness at Westminster. There was no immediate opportunity to talk to him about my affairs, his being the more pressing. Summons of array were being penned furiously for all the southern levies. The death of Rhys ap Tewdwr had caused the Welsh to fly at each other's throats. War was brewing in Glamorgan, and the king meant to take advantage of the strife to secure his own claim on the land.

Anselm arrived in a few days, seeming all but insensible to the excitement that surrounded him. He wished to speak to the king again on making his submission to Pope Urban. The king was impatient, but not adamant. He wished to speak to Anselm on the matter of those estates he had given to loyal knights while the see was vacant. Anselm sternly opposed the gifts as before, on the grounds that it was unlawful for him to allow anything of substance that had been granted to the service of the Almighty to be taken away for the benefit of men.

One or two other bishops chimed in to support Anselm, no doubt thinking their own fat possessions might one day be in jeopardy. The king looked doubtful. One of Anselm's defenders then was Carileph.

I leaned toward the king's ear from my place just behind him and said: 'This is a worthy argument, my lord, but a poor time to hear it.

If you take back lands from men who owe you knight service, where will you find your levies when you want them?'

He nodded. They wrangled some more. Anselm seemed surprised that his good arguments didn't get the reverent hearing and immediate agreement they were accustomed to receive in the schoolroom. The matter was delayed until the king should return from his campaign.

Before Anselm departed for home again, I asked for a hearing. I told him I had put aside my wife, with just compensation for her protection and that of my sons. I abased myself and begged his forgiveness. If it was possible my troubles could be mitigated by humility, I was willing to humble myself to the dust. But the firm old fool said he could not yet absolve me.

'We must see how well you can maintain your new chastity.'

I protested: 'A true repentance is worthy of true absolution!'

'A priest is not compelled to absolve when he questions the strength of the penitent's resolve, my son. You know that. Come to me in a month or so. Tell me what meditation and prayer, fasting and self-chastisement have worked in you. Remember, pride is a worse affliction and harder to uproot than the most virulent lust.'

The king rode away to his war. Carileph was made justiciar. I occupied myself with visitations on my judges and with drawing up plans for the rebuilding of the Westminster Palace, which had proved to be beyond mending.

Because I felt I might be watched by some minion or spy of Anselm's, or of whoever it was that had revealed to him my history, I took special care to abide by his commands. My fasting, prayers, and piety were remarked on and, in some regions, jeered at, but they weren't entirely a sham, though they may have begun that way.

I earnestly petitioned God to help me find some way to keep Giva near me. I beseeched Immortal Love to soften the heart of pope or antipope – whichever of the two He regarded as the true Keeper of Keys – to allow priests to follow the dictum of sensible St. Paul and marry if they might otherwise burn.

I contended with Him that it was recognized by His Holy Church how priests might sometimes become drunkards, yet wine was not forbidden to them. They might incline to gluttony, but not all meat was denied them. They might be vain of their persons, yet when they were in the sanctuary their raiment was allowed to be noble and, in the cases of bishops and cardinals, even gorgeous.

The hunger born in man for the love, grace, and comfort of a woman was surely no more deadly than these lusts! Why, then, must their bodies be totally proscribed? Or, if carnal love were really such a dark crime, let me offer my mitigating virtues to help my case: I had loved Elfgiva unlawfully, true! Very well: but I had loved her faithfully, since I first took her home to my bed. No other woman had cause to complain of me, or ever would have cause to name me her seducer. Never did I go to Giva like the drunkard to his wine pot, or the gourmand to his meat. I was kept from her embrace as often by prudence as by the press of my own duties. Prudence I had need of, for God knew, it took little more than the hanging of my cassock over the bedpost to make her breed, which was as much the doing of the Almighty as my own!

A pious man will say I found no grace in my prayers because I never prayed Heaven to teach me how I might live without Giva, but only how I might keep her. I couldn't ask to be deprived without exposing myself as a fawning hypocrite to my Creator. He knew me too well. Besides, as I'd told Giva, I wasn't convinced that the Maker of all things visible and invisible took such acute interest in my piety that He could be bribed by a transparent lie.

The summer wore on. The king was still in Wales, and Anselm was still denying me absolution and demanding the return of his estates, all the while complaining to his followers that the rank and power of an archbishop were beyond his means, that he was spiritually fit to be only a teacher and a prior. Carileph was in London, lording it over the realm like a petty Odo. I kept out of his path. I satisfied my need for work as I have described and my need for coin by taking the wardship of several orphans, by which action I was permitted to keep the revenues of their estates in exchange for my stewardship.

I sent the orphans, who were both female and too young for marriage, to Isabel. I thought it was time she earned her keep, but I let her earn it without my supervision; I never went near her. I might yet lose my office, as Giva was near her time and I longed to be with her for the birth of the child, but I would not let myself be damned for drawing breath under the same roof with Isabel, whose incessant demands for luxuries kept me in a constant state of anger. Now she must have the hire of a great, muscular lout to escort her to church and home again every day, as she had no husband and no son to do it. This was for the sake of her safety on the rough streets of London – and with St. Peter's no more than a hundred steps away! To her petition I answered: 'Beware, footpads and cutpurses of London! Isabel de Trie is among you. Take to your holes until she passes.' But she so harassed me with verbal messages sent by servants, whom I must feed and provision for the return to her, that I gave in and let the bitch have her footman.

The king and his host came out of Wales, not so much flushed with victory as sated with the futility of chasing the elusive Welsh, who were sanguine enough to battle both him and among themselves without any great change in temper. I began at once to make preparations for a court in Winchester to take the place of the Whitsun Court, which had been delayed by his campaign in Glamorgan. I hoped to present him with a statement of his treasury that would both please and surprise him. I had been working as hard to increase it as he had in lavishing it on his mercenaries.

Giva was approaching her time. My determination to avoid her while Anselm might already be in residence to observe me faded as I drew near the old east gate of the city. I must make certain she was well with my own eyes, not the familiar ones of Osbern. I could neither do my duty to the king nor steel myself for the battle I meant to do with Anselm unless I knew our babe was safely delivered.

I sent my brief escort ahead of me into town, saying I wished to ride around to the north gate to examine a piece of land where I might build a larger house. The land was that upon which the new Abbey of Hyde must be established, now the old cloister was in imminent danger of demolishment to make way for Walkelin's new cathedral. The translation of the monks might be a while in coming, but I proposed to make certain of their territory by building my house on it at once, before it was cluttered with ramshackle hovels such as continually spring up outside the walls of towns.

I rode in the direction of the north gate, but when my escort was out of sight, I went in through the new east gate instead and made my way quickly to my house. I found my mother tending her flourishing herb garden and carping at a congregation of infants – my sons – who were plucking the blossoms or trampling the medicinal foliage. I brought my horse in and put him to stable before I returned to embrace her. She was surprised to see me.

'What are you doing here so soon? Can Osbern fly now?'

'What do you mean? I've taken the usual time. What about Osbern?'

'He's gone to fetch you. You must have passed him.'

'What's he – is it Giva? Has the babe come?' Mother's look gave me a lurch in the pit of the stomach. 'Is something amiss? Oh, Christ, where is she? In bed?'

I ran for the door with Mother squawking behind me. Swanhilda came out of the kitchen with a spit fork in her hand as I leaped up the stairs. I was at the top before my mother's words reached my brain:

'She's gone, Raf! That's what he went to tell you.'

'Gone? Dead?' I flew to the bedchamber, threw open the door, and found the bed neatly made and unoccupied. I returned to the landing on suddenly infirm legs.

'What – where is she? What do you mean, gone? If it's dead, then say so, woman!'

'Gone's what I said and gone's what she is,' Mother said grimly, snapping her mouth so that her chin tapped at her nose. 'She's left us – left all her babes for me to tend to. Went out straying like a ewe that's lost its lamb, the fool.'

I descended a few steps uncertainly. 'Lost a lamb? Did she lose the babe? Tell me, for God's sake, Mother, without all the pauses. Where is she?'

Swan came to grasp the newel post with a greasy hand, her cow's eyes turned up at me mournfully. 'She's run away, Raf. Osbern said she must have gone in the night, but I thought I heard her stir just before dawn. It was two days ago, just after we heard the criers say the king was coming.'

I felt myself grow cold. My voice had all but sunk into my belly with fear and anger. 'Didn't my fool of a brother have the sense to go after her? Where did she go? In the name of the seven thousand devils that afflict the English – come on, you stupid bitch, I know you can speak! Where is she?'

Swan's face stiffened in shock. She drew back as I descended on her. 'Osbern looked for her, he did! He asked everyone – and he found her, only she won't come back and it isn't his fault! She wouldn't even talk to him. Oh!'

'She'll talk to me, then. *Where is she?*'

'At a cloister house out away from the town. I don't know its name!' She flinched as if I might hit her, which I was very near to doing. 'He was all day going there and coming back. I don't know the name. He says it's for the *athelingas*.'

'Romsey. Did he say it was Romsey? Did he say the name? Answer me, you ignorant cow!'

'Yes! Yes! That was the name – I think – Romsey.' With a sob she fled heavily into the garden to comfort herself among the children, leaving her own weanling to shriek on the floor as he felt her skirts torn from his clinging hands.

I came down the rest of the steps like a man in a stupor. I felt my mother touch my arm, almost apologetically. 'Let me fix you a posset before you take a fit and fall dead. It's how my father died, from too much choler.'

'Why did she go? I gave her this house. I told her – '

'She didn't take any of us into her secret. *Raoul, mon fil, mon pauvre fil–*'

I shook off her hand and ran out the door, snatched my amazed horse from his fodder, and rode away toward Romsey Abbey.

It is a ride of seven miles or more. It was nearly Vespers when I reached the walls, during which time I can't recollect having one coherent thought but that Giva had done this to spite me. How had she gotten all that way in her condition? Had she walked? Had she exposed herself and her babe to some half-wild wagoner, some mindless yokel with an oxcart, on his way home drunk from market? Like a common strumpet? What tale did she tell of me to the holy women of Romsey to gain her entrance? Romsey was a spinster's paradise of a cloister, where only the best-born of female gentry could hope to abide, where they treasured up their unwanted virginity and did fine needlework to pass the time between puberty and the tomb. When Giva saw me, she'd fall on her face with shame for what she'd told about us and beg me to take her back home again, or I'd drag her out by the hair!

I fell from my saddle at the gate and seized the bell rope, to ring it as if the fields were on fire. In a few moments the door grille opened and the porteress looked out at me with her pale, lashless eyes.

'Look at me well, Sister. I am Ranulph Flambard, the king's chaplain, and I have business with someone inside your walls. I think you know who she is. Let me in, then fetch her out. I want to speak to her.'

'That is not possible.'

'All things are possible, Sister, even that I break down this door. Let me come in!'

'This is a cloister for holy women that no man may enter but the priest who says Mass for us. I'll call the Reverend Mother Chamberlain to speak to you.' She shut the grille.

I shouted, 'You may call the abbess, or the Blessed Virgin, but you'll open this door to me in the end!'

There was no reply, naturally enough. She left me to cool my rage for a considerable time, during which I yelled for Giva, beat on the oaken door, kicked it, and considered whether I might mount on foot to my horse's back and so climb over the wall. The horse gave me warning he would stand for no such bravery. There were no vines stout enough to bear my weight on the wall.

I heard a scuffling sound and some wheezing, as if someone were moving a heavy object against the door. The grille opened and another pair of eyes looked out on me coldly. The voice that spoke matched their gaze to perfection.

'I am Mother Christina, Father. What can I do for you?'

I leaned on the door. Her voice had an indefinable accent, neither French nor English. In a moment I had placed her. I said as civilly as I could: 'Reverend Mother, I am Ranulph, abbot of Hyde, dean of St. Martin's in Dover, and the king's chaplain – '

'I know who you are. You're the king's tax gatherer. Your people have made you quite familiar to us of late – as has the young woman you wish to see.'

'Then at least, Reverend Mother, you know I'm no threat to the peace of your house. I know you, too, through your noble brother, Prince Edgar. Please allow me to come in to speak to Elfgiva.'

'You may not enter here.'

'Then send for her. Let her come to the grille and speak to me.'

'She has asked for sanctuary until her child is born. This the Reverend Mother Abbess has granted her. There is no more to be said.' The grille began to close.

'Wait! For the love of God! She's my wife! Don't shut me out like a nameless thief!'

There was a pause; then the cool voice said: 'You are worse than a thief, Ranulph Flambard. You are a priest who has forsaken his vows.' The grille closed. The heavy bench or table they had ready on the other side was shoved against the door.

49

Further shouting and beating on the door did nothing but stir up the doves on the chapel roof to another flight after they'd just settled in the wake of the Vespers bell. My horse was skittish when I approached him; I had to trot after him until I'd caught his dragging reins. I rode back to town too angry, too grieved to realize why it was my brother Fulcher should meet me at the gate with such a pale look.

'Christ's Blood! Where have you been? We thought you'd been murdered. It's been hours since – Raf? Raf!'

'I've been to Romsey. She won't talk to me. Breeding's turned her wits upside down. She's in there hiding from me as if I'd beaten her, for God's sake!'

Fulcher took my arm. 'They'll sound the curfew in a few minutes. Let's go home. You're exhausted.'

'I don't want to go home. If I do, I might – I don't know – do something to frighten everyone.'

He took my horse in charge and put his free hand on my arm. 'Let's go together. Nothing will happen.'

Mother was waiting at the gate with a lantern when we came to the house. Fulcher gave me over to her and went to put my horse away. I followed her into the house, which was unnaturally silent. I was like a man who has been wounded and suffers great loss of blood, but yet must keep to his feet for fear he'll never rise again if once he sits. She forced me to a stool by the table.

Fulcher entered and spoke to Mother in an undertone that sent her out of the room. He set cups and a flagon of wine before me, nudging my arm to make me take notice. I shook my head, but he poured a cup. I swallowed it without being able to say whether it was malmsey or verjuice. He immediately poured me another, then filled his own cup sparingly and sat opposite me.

'She's left you for your own sake. She's been wiser about this than you from the beginning, if you can make yourself see it.'

'I can see I'll be the chief source of amusement to everyone down to my stableboy, when it gets about that my wife has shut herself up in a cloister eight months gone with child.'

'Don't be stupid. Don't you suppose that by now all your friends have heard what the archbishop commanded of you and begin to wonder what they'll do with their women when he notices them? I hardly think they'll find your case amusing.'

'They don't equate me with themselves. They despise me.'

'Then forget about them. Think of Giva. This isn't the worst thing that could have happened. She's safe, you know where she is, she'll give birth to the child – '

'Yes, and then what? Stay there and rear it in that tomb for desperate virgins?'

'Would you rather have her hidden away in some country place where you'd never be sure of her safety?'

'No! I'd rather have her here where she belongs! Tomorrow I'm going back to that damned sepulcher and put a warrant from the king through the grille. If that doesn't open the door, I'll take an ax to it!'

'Don't be childish. How will you get Rufus to sign a warrant when he isn't here?'

'I'll sign it myself and seal it, too.'

'And be in the castle prison when he hears of it. What would it accomplish? And if you get into Romsey, what will you do? Drag Giva out by the hair? Beat her? Murder all the nuns?'

'Don't be ridiculous – although the part about beating her appeals at the moment.'

'If you go near that abbey again, you're apt to be unfrocked even without the help of Anselm, and there won't be a man in your chapter who'll be able to plead for you.'

'You can forget about the archbishop. There won't be an Archbishop of Canterbury in six months' time, I promise you.'

Fulcher stood up. 'There's no point talking to you when you're raving. Drink your wine and go to bed. Tomorrow you'll see things as they are.'

'I see things as they will be. I say there'll be no archbishop in Canterbury in half a year, because I'm going to rid the king of him. And the archbishop's going to help me to do it – he's just the sort who will. If you think I'm raving, watch Anselm work with me to send himself home to Bec.'

'You're no match for him, Ranulph. Good God, why can't you see it? He's right and you're wrong! Giva could see it. She's made a wonderful sacrifice for you, to keep you from ruining yourself the way you seem to want to do. It was an act of love beyond anything you could have hoped for. Don't spoil the sacrifice with your foolish pride.'

I loathed him in that moment, standing over me, his face stiff with pity.

'An act of love? That's something you aren't well instructed in, is it, Fulcher? Or am I wrong? Did you get something besides Giva's pity here last winter? Is that why she's run away from me now?'

His face went hard. 'I won't listen to this.' He turned to go, but I sprang up and caught his arm. The next moment I was sprawling across the table and he was shouting: 'Don't ever accuse her again – or me! I'll kill you for it, if God doesn't!'

I was unable to answer. I'd struck my side on the corner of the table. I sank to the floor, gasping with the sudden pain in my ribs. I heard Fulcher mutter: 'You'll heal. I'll see you in the morning.'

The house door slammed after him, setting our watchdog barking. After a few moments my mother and pale-faced Swanhilda came creeping in to help me to my feet.

*

I had a cracked rib. Mother bound me with strips of linen torn from old infant swaddles, so that I could breathe without too much pain. I went to the castle and gave myself over to preparing for the king's coming. My anger had congealed into something that felt like a lump of cold lead under my breastbone. It killed my appetite for anything but work.

I made inventory of the whole castle, to the great irritation and inconvenience of the household officers, who let me know I was intruding on their ground. I scoured them for their laziness, invoked the king's name, and put an end to grumbling, if not resentment. Their wrath with me they cast on the backs of their understewards, who passed it like a whip across the lazy arses of the scullions and clerks, until the whole castle was in a froth of rage and activity.

The result was that labor that might have taken a week was accomplished within three days. The floors were swept clean of filth, sanded, scrubbed, strewn with fresh rushes. The larders were filled, the platters and ewers polished, the candles counted, the royal bedchamber aired, and the castle burnished as I hadn't seen it since the first year of the king's reign.

On the third day I went into the script room and looked at the inquest roll that included Romsey Abbey. I searched all the abbey holdings, grants, reliefs, fees, and gifts for some irregularity worthy of inquiry. I found nothing except an abandoned dispute concerning half interest in a mill that formerly belonged entirely to an Englishman. His widow had laid a claim for the return of the half interest, but let the suit drop. While I was still reading, Fulcher came in. Without glancing at what I read he said:

'You won't find anything. I looked.'

I rolled the parchment and thrust it back into the bin. 'What would you have done if you'd found something? Scrape out the evidence?'

'I'd have shown it to you.'

'Oh! What miraculous wind is it that wafts you back to my side?'

'You're my brother. I owe you duty and service.' His voice fell. 'It wasn't my place to contend with you.'

'Nor mine, to accuse you. I'm sorry, Fulcher.' I put out my hand and he took it in both of his. There was something in his manner of doing so – a coil of dread began to wind itself in my bowels. He wasn't looking at me. 'Well, what is it now?'

'There's been a boy here from the village near Romsey. He was sent on horseback – '

'A village boy on horseback? Wonderful! With a message for the king? Am I charged with riot or – oh, God, it's Giva, isn't it? Her labor's started? What then? She wants to come home?' I was caught between hope and that spasm of dread that still tightened.

Fulcher said, 'She's had her child, Raf. It didn't live. She wants to see you now.'

It struck me then what his careful voice meant. I pushed past him and ran for the stairs. I heard him running after me, but with no words of reassurance for my fear. Heads were turned as we raced through the hall, down more steps, and out the door, down the great stairs to the bailey. Somewhere between there and the stables I collided with Osbern, who sprang back with a laugh and tried to grasp at me.

'Wait! There's no need to run, brother. He's still a few miles distant.'

'Who? Let me pass!'

'Why, the king, of course. You don't need to hurry.'

I thrust him away, fled to the stables, and found a horse. Fulcher mounted, too, while Osbern was still trying to discover the reason for our urgency. I was praying as I turned the horse through the castle gate and kicked him into a run for the city wall. I was offering the Almighty everything that might placate Him: I would abase myself before Anselm, kiss his feet, give up my office, anything, so long as He didn't take His revenge on me through Giva.

We galloped all the way to Romsey. It was broad day, but I might have passed armies unseen on that road. I remembered a thousand words I wished I'd never said to her, things I wished I'd never done; then words and deeds went from my mind and I was only riding, as I'd ridden on the night when the king fled his grief.

We reached Romsey. I fell from my saddle and let stray my horse, lathered and foaming like a mad dog. Fulcher was already at the bell rope when I began to beat on the door. The grille opened. Fulcher identified us. The door bolt was withdrawn. I pushed against the door, nearly throwing the porteress to the ground.

'Where's the infirmary?'

She pointed the way. I sped across the cloister garth, still green and filled with the sweet herbs that delight virgins who live in such places. The sister infirmarian was just coming out the door when we rushed upon her.

'Elfgiva – the woman with child – where is she?' I gave it up and threw myself on the infirmary door as the woman cried out in a voice like a peacock.

I thought the bare whitewashed room was empty at first. Rows of pallets lay sheetless on the floor, their rough tickings bristled with protruding shafts of straw. Fulcher murmured a word behind me and I saw a shape in the far corner, kneeling by one of the pallets. It was the old priest from the vill who said Mass for the nuns. He twisted his scrawny neck to stare at us, then struggled to his feet. Giva lay on the pallet before him, her eyes closed, a wooden cross in her hands.

The old man whined: 'There was no need to send for you, Brothers. I've given her Unction.'

'Get out of the way!'

He was astonished. 'Good Brother in Christ'!'

'Get out!'

Fulcher or Osbern took him away. I knelt by Giva, took up one of her hands, and thanked God it was still warm. I chafed it, then thought to feel her brow and found it hot. She was wearing an ugly veil bound snugly about her brow which would distress her in her fever. I pulled it off to discover they had cut her beautiful hair, very roughly. It was scarcely longer than mine. They had tonsured her.

'Giva, *dyrling*, what have they done to you? Giva!'

She opened her eyes. I put my arm under her to lift her; she groaned before she recognized me, then gave a little sigh. 'Ranulph. I wanted to see you – '

'Yes. Thank God you did. Don't weep, my love. It will be all right now. You have a little fever, but Mother can heal you, once we get you home. I love you, Giva. No one is going to separate us. Can you just put your arm about my neck now, so I can lift you better?'

'Ranulph – the baby died. I was afraid it had when it didn't kick anymore. There was something – something – caught around its neck. A cord – '

'Yes. Don't talk now, love. Don't tire yourself. Just put your arms about my neck and we'll go home.'

'I can't – '

'Never mind, then. I'll lift you. Just be still.'

'I can't go home. I made a vow – '

'They'll make you free of it.'

I gathered her up. As I staggered to my feet, I saw the abbess come in with Fulcher just behind her. Her puffed face was quivering with anger.

'What are you doing here? You should have come to me first! Put her down at once! This is – indecent. She's been confessed and given the Blessed Sacrament. Let her die in a state of grace, if there's any goodness left in you!'

'Woman, if you have any goodness left in you, shut your mouth about dying. She isn't going to die! Do you hear that, Giva? You're not going to die. Stand out of the way, Reverend Mother Abbess!' As I shifted Giva higher in my arms to get a better grip of her, her head drooped over my shoulder; her arms slid from my neck.

The abbess said coldly: 'This young person has thrown herself on the mercy of Christ and asked to become one of us as a token of her repentance. She has nothing more to do with the world, or with you. It was a grievous mistake for me to allow you to be sent for. I thought you might wish to pray for her, or else rejoice with her for her salvation.'

'I'll rejoice when I get her home.'

'Leave this place at once, or I'll ring the bell for men of the village to come to our aid and put you out. I shall complain to the king – '

'You may complain to the Devil! Fulcher, make her stand aside!'

'Ranulph – '

I pushed past them. 'Osbern, bring a blanket!'

Out in the garth the holy women were gathered with mouths ajar, their embroidery and distaffs drooping from their hands. I could hear Fulcher speaking to the abbess in a low, hurried voice and her sharp reply:

'I shall complain to the king!'

The porteress stood nervously before the gate as I ran out. Osbern leaped ahead of me to persuade her to unbar the door, which she did with nervous haste. As I went through it she quavered at me:

'Oh, Father, this is a sin. You'll be punished for it.'

'I've been punished already, Sister. God keep you.'

Osbern caught the reins of our horses from the bush where we'd tethered them. As Fulcher came running out, I put Giva in his arms so that I could mount. I got my feet in the stirrups, then bent down.

'Lift her up to me.'

But he still held her, looking down into her face. Above us the chapel bell began to ring as fast as a pair of urgent hands could pull its rope. Fulcher turned away to the cloister gate.

'Fulcher, no!'

Osbern let go the reins to follow after him as I slid from the saddle. 'What are you doing? Bring her to me!' I rushed on him and jerked him around by the cowl. Osbern pulled me back and held my arms, as Fulcher carried Giva back into the garth and laid her on a bench. The bell stopped ringing.

Hands were pulling at me from all sides. I heard someone give a cry that must have nearly torn his throat out. I remember nothing after that.

I woke in a place I didn't know. It was a narrow cell and I was on a cot, tied to it at wrists and shoulders. There were voices nearby, hollow and deep, as if someone were speaking from a well shaft. A monk came into the cell. I didn't know him. He bent over me as I shouted to be let free, but he went away as if he were both blind and deaf to my struggle. I yelled until I was hoarse and my throat so dry that I lost my voice.

When I woke again I was still tied, but someone was kneeling by my side, a white-haired old monk who looked like Anselm. I cursed him and he lifted his mournful face to gaze at me in silence. Again I raged and wept until I was exhausted. I cannot tell how many times I came to myself in the same condition to fight against the ropes, but each time it was with greater terror and less strength, and more than once I saw the old monk. I decided he was only a vision of Anselm that the Devil had sent to torment me.

One day I opened my eyes to a silent room. A shaft of sunlight fell on the floor from a circular opening in the opposite wall. I was too weak to strain at my bindings, too languid to shout, too hopeless even to curse. I heard a voice beyond the door, high-pitched, uneven; there was a murmured answer to it; then the door opened with a scraping sound. Sunlight caught at the gold chain on his breast and at his pale, burnished hair. He bent to examine me, frowned when I gazed at him mutely. His thick, calloused hand rubbed my brow and cheek, then took my head and shook it a little.

'Your eyes are open. Do you see me? Know me?'

'I know you, Your Grace.'

'Good!' He laughed in embarrassment. 'Well, no n-need to weep for the sight, man.' He bent to stare into my eyes curiously. 'They say you've been stark mad for a fortnight. Are your wits returned now?'

'I think so. Yes.'

'Then we can do without these cords, I think.' He pulled out his dagger and set me free. Two monks came into the cell to warn him softly of freeing me, but he scoffed at them. In the most gentle and natural way he took me in his arms as I struggled up from the cot, hugged me to him, buried my face in his breast, and kissed the top of my head.

'I thought I'd lost you, man. If I did, where would I get another like you, eh?'

I began to weep like a woman as I tried to excuse my lapse, but he wouldn't hear me.

'I know all about it. They told me – your brothers. It's hard, I know. I know – remember? But the cure isn't weeping, it's work.' His hand scrubbed at my head and nape, grasped my shoulder painfully. 'I can g-give you plenty of work, if you can take it.'

'I want it! Just let me out of here and I'm ready to serve you, Your Grace.'

'Now? God! No, I don't think so.' He released me and stood up. 'You'd better get your strength back first, because there are some people who think you ought to be whipped for what you've done, and it's out of my hands if they take you to trial. Church business, you know.'

I fell back on the cot. My head was swimming. 'I probably deserve the whip, my lord. I won't deny it.'

'Your brothers have already taken their stripes.'

'They didn't deserve it. They acted out of love and duty to me.'

'No excuse, that. Not in *their* eyes.' He tipped his head to indicate the monks who had withdrawn into the corridor.

'Yes, my lord.'

'Well – it may not come to a whipping. Old Anselm's been of two minds about it. Still, the next time you go out to break into a cloister and insult nuns, try not to pick one with an English princess in it, will you?'

He hated sickrooms. He turned away suddenly without a farewell and left me to my convalescence.

Three days later I tottered out of my cell in the Abbey of Hyde and presented myself to my own prior in the chapter house. I took a scourge from the hands of the prior of order and presented it myself to the prior, who gave it to a strapping great monk with an apprehensive face. I stripped my gown in the presence of the whole chapter and knelt before the prior, made my confession, and begged him to see to my fit punishment. As I bent forward with my hands over my face, the scourge descended on my back. The chief purpose of the punishment was humiliation, so the whip wasn't laid on with undue vigor. Yet by the end of it I could have thought a dragon had clawed me with iron talons.

A vinegar sponge was applied to my back to wash the blood away; my shirt and cassock were restored to me. I took a candle in hand and, accompanied by my monks, walked to the castle barefoot, where Archbishop Anselm and the whole ecclesiastic body gathered for the court waited to behold my abject repentance.

I abased myself before Anselm, kissed his feet, and begged his forgiveness, beseeching him to pray for me. He absolved me, warned me against further sins of the flesh and the spirit, and bade me rise. The king looked on, frowning. I went out from the great hall to the vestry room of the chapel, pinched out the flame of my candle, and threw the stub in a basket. Fulcher and Osbern helped me to dress after Osbern laid an unguent to my back.

Fulcher said in a low voice that trembled with pity: 'Now it's over. Forget it and live again.'

'Now it isn't over. It's over when he's gone.'

'He? Anselm had nothing to do with her death, Raf.'

'Then call it my death I'll avenge.'

Anselm left for Canterbury the next day, but not before he'd heard of a certain matter from the king. Rufus charged him with sending such a miserable contingent of knights to the Welsh campaign that they were all but useless to him – ill clad, ill bred, unprovisioned, and riding worse horses even than the Welsh, who mounted themselves on shaggy ponies scarce big enough to bear them.

The archbishop might have been expected to blush, hearing how the king had been put to the trouble and expense of accoutring them himself before they could be led into battle. But this just complaint against him, their lord, was met with either stupid contempt or ignorant disregard. Anselm put aside all such mundane matters as proper knight service to a king in order to lament for his see's 'misappropriated' estates once more.

'Mi-misap-misappropriated, my lord? That's not the w-word to use on me! The m-manors were in my keeping. I gave them to men who had served me well; useful men, who came to my call when I n-needed them, ready to fight!'

'The estates were in the royal keeping, Your Grace, but they were not in the royal gift. They were Canterbury's, and you were their warden only until an archbishop was named.'

The king's face changed color dangerously. 'And who gave them to Canterbury in the f-first place, eh?'

Anselm looked irritated, for this was to his thinking beside the point and he liked an orderly dispute. 'I haven't had the leisure to study their histories, Your Grace. Some former king, no doubt, who had the good of his soul and of his kingdom in mind.'

'Exactly so, Archbishop! Some King of England gave them to some archbishop. And when the see lay vacant, some King of

England took them back – and gave them again – according to his right.'

'How do you judge this to be your right, my lord, when the lands were donated to God, from Whom one takes back gifts at his peril?'

Now, I must say, Anselm didn't utter these words in a quarrelsome manner. Dispute and argument were meat and drink to him. But his was the dispute of the schoolroom where the master expects to win over the eager student in the end. It was not so in the dispute of chivalry which the king understood. The archbishop never learned that distinction.

Eyeing each other, they argued the meaning of possession, as a German might contend with an Irishman, neither understanding the mind of the other. The king's color increased alarmingly, along with his bafflement and impatience.

'By the Face, Archbishop, the lands you speak of are in the realm of England, which belongs to me! Would you ask me to go back from my sworn word to these faithful men? Take away from them what I gave in good faith, without a cause?'

'The "cause" is good, my lord, because it is God's, not mine. I would never ask for an arpent for myself, not so much as a man might be buried in.'

'But you want the revenues from it, don't you? I think it must be you who wants them, as God – *Who is my tenant!* – has yet to appear at a hundred-court to dispute His claim.'

Anselm looked deeply grieved. Those churchmen in attendance were shocked. Hugh of Chester whispered to Rufus to be lenient with this good old man. The matter was put off for another day and the archbishop departed. The king looked to me as the court dispersed.

'What are you doing here? You're white as a w-weanling's arse. Go home and go to bed.'

'I'm better on my feet than on my back, my lord.'

He grunted in sympathy for my still-torn flesh. 'What do you think of this business? Was I wrong? Remember, you counseled me in the first of it.'

'You are in the right, my lord. All lands of the realm must belong to the king, or there's no kingdom, but anarchy. The King of France must wish his ancestors had seen things as you see them now. He might be more the king and less the suitor in his own court, where his vassals are greater than he.'

'You're right. The old monk knows how to c-cling to his point, though, doesn't he?' He grinned.

'He means to rule you, as he said to me: to be your spiritual father, as Lanfranc was, your chief counselor, your mentor. If he can't accomplish that with reason and cunning, it seems he may attempt it with sighs and tears. You see how he moved the Earl of Chester just now.'

'Well, he won't move me! Not on this. It's a matter of honor.' Yet I thought he had been moved somewhat.

I said: 'The great scholar of Bec not only knows how to cling to a point; he knows how to deflect one.'

'How's that?'

'He warded off your just complaint that he failed to give good knight service to you according to his pledge, when he took from you the lay tenant's responsibilities for Canterbury. He owes you recompense, my lord, but I believe he doesn't intend to pay you.'

I didn't mean to do battle with Anselm directly, when I had a king for my good warrior.

In Canterbury the preparations for installing the new archbishop were advancing day by day. In Winchester the king prepared to take himself and a few friends hunting in the Hampshire Forest for a full month before he removed to London. In the meantime he received envoys from his brother Robert, who charged once more that the treaty between the two of them was broken by the king's neglect of his promise. Curthose demanded the removal of the English garrisons from Norman soil, or else that his royal brother submit to the judgment of those twenty-four witnesses who had signed their mutual treaty. Since the greater part of them had holdings in Normandy and one among them was the King of France, they would doubtless judge Rufus to be derelict in his vows.

'Robin must be in his cups again, to think he can f-frighten me' was the only comment he made. Laughing, he looked at Edgar Atheling, who kept silent on the subject, as befitted a man who had twice betrayed a trusted friend, yet hadn't the stomach to renounce his former keeper openly.

What Rufus saw in Edgar was a thing I understood less as I saw the man more. It was certain, however, that he had become the very center of the king's life. They slept in one bed, ate from one dish, knelt together in the chapel, and rode knee to knee in the chase.

There were other men of the royal following to whom Rufus gave affection and gifts: Bledry, his poet; Wat Tirel, who had unhorsed him at Mont St. Michel; Prince Henry. He still made a pet of my son, treating him more like a godchild than a servant.

But it was Edgar alone he loved, God help him. In the Old City the people were openly calling the Atheling the king's bearded wife, and those English who once had been Edgar's vocal supporters if he so much as stepped out on the street, now merely stared at him. Their silent contempt was no secret to him or to any other man at court but Rufus, who, if he had noticed, might have punished a few gossips with the lash or the cucking stool.

Yet it would have been only for the sake of Edgar's honor that he would have done it. As for himself, why, he was a prince who loved a prince, as David had loved Jonathan: 'Wonderful was thy love to me, passing the love of women.' The opinions of the rabble were nothing to him.

Love of any person was far from me, however. I could put off despair only with the tedium of labor. Fulcher came to me a few days after the king had ridden toward Lyndhurst and asked:

'When are you coming home again? Mother keeps asking.'

'I don't know. I'm busy at the moment. Does she need money? Take some from my chest and give it to her – with my love.'

'It's a short walk to do that yourself. You look as if you haven't slept for a week. Why not come home and rest in your own bed?'

'I can't come now. Tell Mother she may hire another servant, if she needs help with the children.'

He said in a low, angry voice: 'Do you think you're the only one who can mourn? And what about your children? They've lost a mother and no one's told them. Must they lose a father, too, and be none the wiser?'

'Fulcher –' I found I'd broken my pen. I put it down with care and forced myself to speak quietly, as there were other clerks in the room who had long ears: 'Fulcher, let me be. I'll come when I can – when I can – do you understand me? Let me just finish this letter; then we'll go down and have some wine together.'

'Don't you feel pity for anyone but yourself?'

'No! No. Since you ask, without her they're nothing to me. Is that too hard for you? Don't waste breath telling me. I've already let God know He could have had all three of them and welcome, in exchange for her life. I'm sorry. The paternal instinct in me seems to have dried up. They won't starve or be ill treated, I promise you that, but I don't want to see them. Now, let me alone to do my work.'

I took up a fresh quill and the penknife without looking at him. He sighed in resignation and left me to finish the draft of the writ I meant to have served against Anselm in the king's name.

50

I was much blamed for that. The critics have their point of view. I condemn myself; not for bringing suit against Anselm the saint, as being in default of a debt he rightly owed the king. It was a petty thing, but in the sight of the law I was in the right and Anselm was to blame.

But to serve him in the manner in which I did was a folly and I am rightly castigated, for I was drunk and fit for no duty to my king, but only for self-ruin and gross folly.

The truth was, I hadn't been sober since the day I took my whipping and was made to bow to Anselm's feet in the presence of the king and my friends. I didn't reel, or babble incoherently, nor was I incapable of my work in the chancel; but I kept myself safely numbed, until Fulcher came to crack my self-containment and let ooze forth all the corrosion that had been eating at my heart.

When I finished my writ, I went down to the hall and took my day-meal from a cup, then relieved a servant of his wine jack, took a horse from the stables, and rode to Romsey. It was late afternoon when I arrived. I didn't approach the gate, for it would only have caused another complaint to be lodged against me, and in any event my goal was the burial ground which was outside the convent walls.

When I found Giva's grave I meant quite simply to put an end to myself on top of it. That was a resolve which had grown slowly out of my sleepless nights and besotted days. How well my intent accorded with my courage I cannot now say. It may be that I would only have wept there for a while, then gone home again, imagining I had her forgiveness. But I was kept from discovering either my cowardice or my death by the most common of all certainties – death had gone ahead of me. Where there should have been but one new grave still heaped with raw earth and trailing dying grass, I found two. In the brief period since Giva's death, or else sometime just before it, another member of Romsey's convent had died. I must choose between two mournful piles of clay for the place in which to damn myself for all eternity.

The choice was too much for my suicide's impulse to sustain. If I slew myself on the wrong mound, some desiccated English virgin might howl for all eternity that I had dripped my detestable Norman blood on her sanctified bones. To enter Hell a sorrowing and defiant lover is one thing; to enter it a laughing stock for the damned is quite another. I sat down with my back to the cloister wall, cursed, wept, drained the contents of the wine flask, and fell asleep.

When I woke it was dark. I found my horse drowsing where I'd at least had the wits to tether him. I mounted him and returned slowly to Winchester. The gates of the city were closed. I waited with a few pilgrims to St. Swithin's shrine until they opened at dawn. A wineshop near the gate gave me heart to return to the castle, retrieve my writ, and attach the royal seal to it, thanks to the generosity of Gerard, who had made me its keeper. I tucked it into a budget, avoided my brothers who were now assembling for Prime, and took my leave of the castle, carrying with me several well-filled traveler's flasks.

From Winchester to Canterbury is a sufficiently long journey for a normal man to reconsider the wisdom of making war on an archbishop, alone. But I was in Godalming before I finished the last of my flasks, and the sight of my former home, now the dwelling of a new, fawning curate, was painful enough to drive me straight to the church's cellar to refill my flasks with wine meant for Holy Communion.

Poor Einhard, my curate, was horrified to see me so wild. It gave me pleasure to bully and intimidate him when he was charitably disposed to offer me my own bed again for the night. I escaped him, or let him escape me, and went on to Canterbury.

I reached Lanfranc's great church at mid-morning, in time to make an entrance that is now mercifully obscure to me, though it is undeniably engraved forever in the memories of a hundred other people who were present at the time. I must rely on their subsequent allegations for what I did there.

I came just as the monks were leading their venerable new shepherd into the sanctuary. I pronounced my business loudly enough to hush the choir from song and send them into raptures of indignation a few moments later. There was a protest from Anselm, and from Thomas of York, who was there to install him. I presented my writ and demanded compensation for the king before any further sanctification of a recreant vassal took place. They all replied at once that I was out of my mind, a bastard, and fit only for excommunication. When they scolded, I shouted; some of them offered to lay violent hands on me, but were prevented by Thomas, who had his archdeacons and all the doorkeepers struggling to come to my aid, or so he said.

I remember a deafening roar, then near suffocation, after which I found myself in the vestry, surrounded by critics while I vomited.

After that I don't remember anything, until I woke in a bed, flat on my back, with people who seemed vaguely familiar staring down at me. I didn't like their expressions, so I turned on my face and went to sleep once more.

When I woke again to that same bed and room, I recognized it for my old chamber in my London house. There was sunlight on the whitewashed walls, the sheets smelled of herbs, and Fulcher was sitting by the window reading a psaltery. He turned his head at my stir, then got up and came to me. He examined me as if I were some sort of marvel brought to town for sale from the farther corner of the earth.

'Are you awake now?'

'Apparently. I see you. Are you really there?'

'How do you feel?'

I considered that. I felt wretched; weak, hollow as the shell of a dead beetle. My mouth was dry and my stomach quivered when I thought of wine to moisten it. 'How long have I been here? How did I get here?'

'Good questions, both. According to the Lady Isabel, you came in raving last week, the day before Michaelmas, which was three days after you made a fool of yourself in Canterbury and the first time anyone seems to have seen you since then. You were drunk there, but you may have induced a brain fever with your raving. In any event if I were you, that's what I'd claim. The king's at the Tower now. He's heard all the other side of your affair with the archbishop. He wants to hear from you, when you can rise and speak.'

'I can rise and speak now,' I said in a surly voice. But I couldn't; when I attempted to stand, my head swam and I fell on the bed. Fulcher put me back under the covers, then bent over me and demanded: 'Why did you do it? You bloody fool, you've set the whole Church and court against you! What purpose did it serve?'

'I don't know. I don't know anything, or want to. Let me sleep.' I turned away from his accusing eyes, but the door opened just then and Isabel came in with a bowl of broth that must have been meant for Fulcher. Seeing me awake, she gave a little cry of joy and immediately sat down on the bed to spoon it into me. I took it, gratefully, as my throat had seemed ready to crack from the effort of speech.

Fulcher snorted at Isabel's ministration and left the room. She smiled at me indulgently, and when she'd finished ladling her soup into me, she touched my mouth first with a napkin, then with her lips.

'It's all right. I think he's left the house. What a fierce young man he is! He quite reminded me of you in former times. How do you feel now? I was afraid someone would think your fever was my fault.' With that she ran her fingers down my cheek lovingly, which alarmed me almost as much as her words and the smug, triumphant look in her peregrine's eyes.

I flinched. 'How could it have been your fault?'

'Well – I might have been partly to blame, even if you were already bloodshot and drunk as a tinker when you got here. But you were so – so desperate! I couldn't go on refusing you, could I? I remembered how it was with me, when my poor Amiot died and I was so cruel to you. I couldn't be so cruel again, could I, even if you were behaving more like my second husband than that sweet boy I once knew in Rouen.'

I stared at her, half in disbelief, half in horror. Something dreadful, some black stirring in my brain not distinct enough to be called a memory, gave me cause to shudder.

'Oh, no – oh, Christ, no – don't tell me that. Tell me I murdered someone, but don't tell me that.' I squeezed my eyes shut, unable to meet her gloating look.

She laid her cool hand on my shoulder, which gave me my first inkling that I was naked under the covers. 'What do you mean, don't tell you? Don't say you don't remember!' Then she laughed. 'Oh, I see! You're ashamed. Well, so you should be. After all, there were those two little girls you've put in here to live with me. I hardly knew how to explain it to them, later, especially when you wouldn't let me leave this room for the better part of a day!'

She hit me on the breast with her fist, laughing with fresh enthusiasm. 'Oh, Ranulph! Really, I was joking. They were asleep when you came, and I only had to explain who you were, since they've never seen you for all they're your wards.' Her fingers touched my chin to turn my face to her again, and her voice grew warmer. 'Truly, it wasn't so terrible. Not as if we'd been strangers. I'll whisper something in your ear to make you feel better about it, shall I? You're much better at it than Duke Robert. He'd be sorry to hear that because he's so proud of his virility, but there it is – and I didn't really mind a bit. So there.'

She was going to kiss me, but I bellowed: 'Get out of here! Out! Get out, before I strangle you, you damned whore!'

'Whore? Whore!'

'Whore! Hag! Vixen! Bitch! Out! Get out!' I snatched the soup bowl from her hand and flung it at the window. It sailed straight between the open shutters and down into the street. A shriek of alarm and a stream of English curses came back for it. Isabel took flight. I rolled over into the pillow to smother the howl of rage and self-disgust that tore from me.

When I came tottering downstairs awhile later, Isabel and her gape-mouthed servants were standing by the hearth in a clump, like cattle, eyeing me as if they expected me to foam at the mouth and bite them. The two little royal wards were in their midst, being protected from me. I had all I could do to walk, or I might have been tempted to rout them into the street. Instead, I staggered there myself and made my way with growing trepidation to the Tower, where I must face the king. It wasn't the thought of his anger that frightened me then; I frightened myself.

Rufus was playing at draughts with Edgar Atheling, in this same room where I am now held prisoner. He'd been laughing at some small victory on the board, but when I made my appearance in the doorway he sobered as if I were a gravedigger. His color heightened; he pushed the game board toward Edgar and rose. I stood just inside the door, forgetting to bow or greet him respectfully. He walked toward me, his eyes frozen on my face as if he might strike me, but when he came within range to do it, he stopped.

'You s-stupid, ba-bastard. What you've done amounts to treason. You know that, don't you?'

I said nothing.

'Well?' shouted the king. 'Are you still drunk? Still in a daze? Answer me! Do you know what you've done? You've ma-made a writ, signed it, and sealed it with my seal without my command! You've brought the whole damned herd of bishops in the realm down on me like a s-s-swarm of hornets – and all for something I n-never meant to pursue. God damn you, Ranulph! Say something to me, or I'll throw you to them, like offal to the dogs!' He came a step nearer, raising one fist.

I swallowed, not from fear, but because my throat had dried up again. 'Perhaps you should throw me to them, Your Grace.'

'Don't try me with humility now, priest. I've got no patience for boot-licking answers. Answer me straight. I want to know h-how' – his voice dropped to a near whisper – 'you were capable of betraying me.'

'Apparently, I'm capable of anything, Your Grace. It would be better not to trust me.' I was thinking of Isabel and I involuntarily shuddered.

He struck me across the face open-handed, not a very heavy blow. 'Don't do that! You're not drunk now and I doubt you were ever crazy, so tell me – now – or God help you, f-for I won't.'

I opened my eyes. 'I did it for you, seeing you were too preoccupied to command it – my lord. I did it because I serve you and have a care for your honor. Others may love you, but they take you away from honor, not toward it.' I glanced at Edgar when I said that. I saw he was paying attention.

'Now, just what does that signify, priest?' asked Rufus in much too quiet a manner.

'Why, my lord, I thought you meant to be king here alone, as you once told me, and not the boy of an archbishop.'

'Eh? Ah, I see. So you thought I'd be your boy instead, is that it? You'd take my seal, give my commands, to make me more the king!' He gave a short, furious bark of a laugh, swinging around to look at Edgar, who kept his eyes on me.

'No, my lord,' I said evenly. 'It is the archbishop who defies you, not I. I am at fault, but I face you, submit to your will, as all your good subjects must. The archbishop thinks himself above you. He defies you – in a small thing, if you call it so – that of rendering proper knight service for the wealth of land you gave him. He put his hands between yours and swore for it, just as my lords of Chester, or Norfolk, or Huntingdon have done. Now he says it doesn't please him to send you soldiers to fight your wars, that it isn't his business as a godly man, or an archbishop, to accouter warriors. What would you answer to that, if Earl Hugh, or even my lord Prince Edgar, answered your need with indifference? That it was too small a matter for your honor to pursue? I think not, Your Grace. I think – and I thought – that you would call him to account for it. Therefore, I risked your displeasure, even my ruin, to act in your best interest.'

He gave a sort of growl between his teeth.

'I am in the wrong in the matter, it seems, so it would be best if you dismissed me. But what will you do about the archbishop in the future, my lord? Say you command him to give you aid again, or even to come to court, and he refuses you for such good reasons as he can find in his heart to give. Will you forgive him again, if he should send not ill-equipped men, but none at all? Or if he is too weary to come to you, will you be good enough to go to him instead?'

'He'd never dare it.'

'He has dared this; why not some other thing? I tell you this, my lord: he's an old man and weak, but he's clever. It wasn't carelessness, or senility, or sanctity that made him abuse your trust. He has said he will rule over you as Lanfranc did. He says he has that right. Men will be waiting to see how well he succeeds in his boast. I tried to call him to account for his neglect before pride took root in him. I was wrong to go about it as I did; I was wrong to make use of my office to use your seal – but I wasn't wrong to think it should be done.

'I tell you something else, my lord, and then you may send me off to the poorest church in the kingdom, or have me flogged for it: you must deal with your archbishop very soon. Because every man who owes you service will be waiting to see which of you is to be the master in this kingdom, and if you hesitate, they'll take heart from him. The next time you need an army, you must be sure to hire mercenaries in plenty – because you may be short of levies.'

He stared at me for a long moment, then turned to commune silently with Prince Edgar. That man's face could say much without the need of words; he granted me the absolution of a nod. The reluctance with which he seemed to give it made it the more telling.

I said: 'Shall I leave you now, Your Grace, to better counsel? I have said all I know.'

'No. You stay.'

He said of me later – and proudly – that I didn't care whose hatred I invoked, so long as I pleased him.

The king gave notice he meant to be both firm and just. He must have his due, small though it may be, but he would concede certain things to Anselm. Did the archbishop think him unjust in the matter of the Canterbury estates? He would restore those lands to Canterbury, provided the archbishop took the men for his own vassals and let them keep what they had honorably earned.

Anselm didn't answer to this directly, but then he never answered directly. He said he could not see lands of Canterbury's that had been given to the service of the Church turned over for the use and enrichment of warlike men – as if he thought angels had heretofore occupied those vills and manors. When even his friend Gundulph urged him to a compromise, he spoke of his aversion to strife, to earthly ambition, to beards, long gowns, and frizzled hair – anything but to the purpose. It was like arguing with a lunatic, or a child. The king alternately forbade the mention of his name, or else laughed at him, but he couldn't put him out of mind.

At last, with the persuasion of Gundulph, Thomas, and even Robert de Meulan and Hugh the Wolf, the archbishop was made to accept the return of that for which he had lamented the loss, and to promise to make some small restitution for his poor knight service. He took the estates back, but never made the restitution. All that, however, was thrust out of mind by his next demand, which he made by letter: he wished to proclaim his allegiance publicly to Pope Urban, which was the same as to say submit the realm to the cause of that Frenchman who had the backing of the Italians and the hatred of the German emperor.

The king's denial of that request might have been heard in the precincts of St. Augustine's without exhausting a courier.

'No! By the Face of Lucca, my father saw no reason to bend his knee to the Germans' pope, whatever his name is, or to that other puppet who was put up against him by the Guiscards. I won't meddle in Rome's business and I'll thank them not to meddle in mine!'

That might have silenced any other man, but Anselm only replied that he had already given his devotion to His Holiness Pope Urban the Second when he, Anselm, was still only prior to Bec. He couldn't withhold his allegiance, now he was Archbishop of Canterbury and Urban's vicar for all the kingdoms of Angles, Britons, and Saxons in the Isles of the Northern Sea.

Rufus flew into such a rage he was all but incapable of speech. So were the main body of his clergy in the Great Council. I had prepared him with argument for them, to the effect that it was an English king and not a pope who had made the first Archbishop of Canterbury, and it was an English king who had made the see wealthy beyond the dreams of most archbishoprics in Normandy. The whole of the original benefice had come out of the largess of the English Crown, and in the event we should ever have to dispense with that see, we had still another in the north to sustain us, one with a claim as ancient, if Thomas of York was to be believed, and more honorable. No Archbishop of York had ever been thrust from office, as had Lanfranc's predecessor, Stigand, for treason and unlawful practice.

I'll allow there were refinements to that argument which I believed too delicate to bring to the king's attention, but then no one else did, either, especially Thomas of York, or that lawyer *par excellence*, William de St. Carileph, who was buzzing in the king's ear every day about his rights. Carileph had a yearning to try the climate of Canterbury after enduring the winters in Durham.

Christmas was approaching, and I was preparing to move to Gloucester as Anselm's couriers continued to cross words with the king's, when another piece of news came to us out of the north which put all popes, regular or otherwise, out of mind: Malcolm Canmore had invaded Northumbria again. A courier from Tynemouth brought us the tale with such tardy speed that Malcolm himself might have been knocking at our gates if he had lived to make the journey.

He was dead, slain by a young man who had grown up in his own court, a hostage held in exchange for one of his lesser kinsmen, Morel de Mowbray. This was the way of it:

Malcolm rode in through the Cheviot Hills with a strong band of pilferers, including his eldest son by Queen Margaret, young Edward, whom he was pleased to call his heir, though he had an elder son by his first wife: Duncan, who had grown up a hostage in our court.

The raiders cut a swath of ruin from the Cheviots to the seacoast, coming to rest at last at a vill called Alnwick, which made it seem as if their destination must have been Durham, rather than Robert Mowbray's castles at Tynemouth or Bamburgh. No word of Malcolm's coming reached Earl Robert until then, which seems strange, as news of a raid often outruns the swiftest horse. But when he heard of his enemy butchering his flocks and burning his vills, Earl Robert sent his young nephew Morel, who was steward of Bamburgh, to chase the Scot, or lay siege to him if he were already behind walls.

In some manner Morel managed to set an ambush for Malcolm, surrounded him, and personally slew him in battle. The young Prince Edward was badly wounded in the fight, but cut his way through Morel's cavalry and fled home with a squire and two knights. All the north country was in a state of jubilation. Their oldest enemy was dead, slain in the commission of his last crime.

Rufus was like a man stunned by a blow in the dark. As the courier delivered his story, the king kept shaking his head slowly. All those in the hall who might otherwise have shouted for joy at such a brave defense and righteous slaughter kept their peace, uncertain whether they would offend him. When the tale was ended he looked to Prince Edgar, who was likewise stricken.

'The fool! The c-crazed, bloody fool! But it makes no sense! How could he let himself be gotten around and taken by a boy who's never fought a battle in his life? Morel – why, he's no more than two and twenty, is he? Malcolm must have gone running mad for something.'

'It's that Devil's piss they brew and drink up there, Your Grace,' said Walter Tirel cheerfully. 'I've tried it. It'd put a lion's heart in a hare, let alone a crazy dotard.'

The king looked at him sharply. 'Hold your tongue, rascal. Malcolm was no dotard.' Tirel choked on his laughter and blushed deeply for the rebuke. Rufus returned his attention to Prince Edgar. 'You wanted to say something, my friend? What shall we make of this? Shall we call up our levies now, or let them quarrel among themselves for a while? There'll be the Hell of a broil up there, I'd think, but you know them better than I.'

Edgar seemed to come swiftly out of a dark dream. His face tightened; his voice rose stronger and more grim than I had ever heard it: 'Your Grace, there'll be murder done on all sides until there's a king there again. If you love me, let me go there now. Let me lead your levies. '

Rufus frowned, then smiled as if in reproach. 'You know I love you well, my friend, but if there's a host to lead, we'll lead it together.'

'No, my lord, I say: if you love me, let me go there now. I was wrong to mention the levies. I should go alone and quickly, too. I'm thinking of my sister and her children. I must reach them as soon as possible. Give me leave to go today.'

There was fresh muttering in the hall as this was considered, but the king silenced it with a lifted hand. 'She'll be safe, surely, my friend. Malcolm is a traitor to us, if this tale we've heard is true, but to the Scots he'll be a martyr. They'll not harm his widow.'

'My lord, as you've said, I know them better than you. They'll have a king again, but they don't love kings, and there are too many contenders for the crown at the moment. My sister may have more enemies than you think. I fear she may have one already who wouldn't hesitate to – give me leave to go, Your Grace. I've never asked you for anything before. Grant me this.'

To such an appeal Rufus could make but one answer: 'Granted. Gerard, send summons of array to Mowbray, though I doubt he'll need the warning. But tell him to be ready to follow Prince Edgar and obey him as he would me. He'll meet with him at – where was that place? Alnwick, yes. I want you to look at the ground, Edgar, and tell me how a man with your brother-in-law's cunning could let himself be ambushed and beaten by a wet-nose like Morel. I smell something in this tale more than honor. Question Morel and his friends – an enemy, too, if you can find one. I won't have it said that kings can be murdered in my land, even if they come stealing.' He looked over the assembly grimly. 'The person of a prince is sacred, or there's no use anointing him.' He rose, clapped Edgar on both shoulders, and shook him fondly.

'Go and see to your sister, though I believe she'll be safe. Put a son of hers on the throne if you can. Then come home safely to your friend.'

Though there were few in the hall by then who weren't privy to their affection, how many realized what it must have cost the king to let Edgar go campaigning alone? He was a changed man from the hour of Edgar's departure, more impatient with his servants, more suspicious of suits brought before him, less temperate at the table. Like his father and brother, he was already inclining to stoutness in the stomach, which Edgar's fastidiousness made him try to curb. But now he felt the sharpness of one hunger and assuaged another, in its stead. We sat late in the hall; the jugglers and bear keepers came back, along with the rash challenges to young wrestlers, the impromptu jousts in the tilting yard. Christmas came to us at Gloucester, and again we heard the challenge of Robert Curthose's envoy, to give him that aid he had long looked for against Maine and the Vexin, or else wage bloody war for those castles now held by English garrisons.

I cautioned against a hasty reply, but there was scant moderation left in the heart of Rufus, who declared that Robert should have his wish! He would go to Normandy and soon, but his brother should repent of having invited him. I had little love for Prince Edgar, but I realized that had he been in court there would have been a softer answer returned to Rouen and much coin saved for the treasury.

Edgar returned before the feast of Christmas was over. He brought with him the younger sons of Margaret – David and Alexander – and the two girls, Edgyth and Mary. They stood, travel-weary and apprehensive, in the spurting light of a hundred torches as Edgar said:

'My sister is dead, Your Grace. I bring you her orphans. Will they be safe here?'

'If they were our own blood they couldn't be safer,' answered the king, though he scarcely glanced at them. 'We share your s-sorrow for your sister, my lord. How did she come to die?'

'Of grief, Your Grace, and it will be the grief of my own life, however long that lasts, that she died alone except for her confessor.

'Prince Edward died of his wound three days after he was brought home, but she didn't hear of it until it was too late to comfort him. She'd been ill for nearly a year, but no one had seen fit to tell me.

She'd scarcely left her bed since spring. When young Edward was carried dying into Edinburgh, his brother who's my namesake hid him, then went to their mother and assured her that all was well with Malcolm. She didn't believe him. Yet, when he was forced to speak the truth at last, her heart failed her. She asked to be carried to her chapel, where she made confession and took the Holy Sacrament. She died the next day. The priest who confessed her said she willed herself to die. She couldn't even be buried properly, because so many people of the town had turned to supporting Donald Bane and were shouting for his return from the north. He was almost at the gates when I reached Edinburgh. I doubt if I could have gotten inside, except for being disguised as a priest.

'Your Grace, forgive me that I've failed you. I never took your levies into Scotland. When I reached Durham the news of Margaret's death put everything but her out of my mind and I rode straight on to Edinburgh in that disguise which the prior of St. Cuthbert's lent me.

'Now, I think there's little use to send levies into Scotland. Donald has the country with him and he's turning out all the foreign-born – English, Normans, French, even the Danes who've lived among them peaceably for generations. The cry of the people is "Scotland for itself and Donald for Scotland!" '

'Not so, Your Grace! Give me leave to speak!' The young man who cried out was Duncan, Malcolm's son by his first wife. He had been a hostage in England since his childhood. He was the English king's sworn man and had come to the Christmas Court to remind the king of his own claim to Scotland, though he hadn't yet impressed anyone with his ardor. Now he said:

'My uncle Donald has seized the throne unlawfully in a land that's still half savage, Your Grace. No one opposes him, because I am kept hostage here out of their sight, and they fall back into their old ways where a man's brother, or his sister-son, is his heir. Give me your levies and I'll know better how to use them!'

The king let his eye glance from Edgar to young Duncan and back again, as he absently rubbed his thigh. He couldn't approve the slur on Edgar's valor which Duncan's words implied, but it was a bitter thing to him that Edgar had made so little use of his chance to win himself glory. He spoke roughly to Duncan: 'The Scots have heirs of Malcolm enough up there, if they want them. I don't see your brothers Edmund or Edgar here. Where are they?'

'My half-brothers must wait their turns. I am the heir! I'm not a boy, Your Grace. I've fought – for you – in the Black Mountains.

I've served you in Kent. Let me win my crown and you may put it on my head at Scone!'

Edgar Atheling said coldly: 'Your Grace, there is one son of Malcolm's who's already fighting for that honor – my namesake.'

'Your Grace,' said Duncan urgently, 'give me leave to claim my right. If you won't give me an army, give me leave to find one for myself.'

'That's a fair offer. Granted,' said Rufus. 'Get your volunteers where you can. I won't deny you.'

Edgar Atheling took his sister's children from the English court and did not appear in it himself for some long time.

51

The king's baffled pride wouldn't let him recall Edgar to court. What had he done to merit such a silent rebuke? He had felt an instinct about young Duncan and had acted upon it with his usual swiftness. His act had been justified: Duncan quickly found his volunteers, marched into Scotland, and put his uncle Donald to rout. Edinburgh proclaimed him king no sooner than Donald had fled its walls.

It had all been accomplished with very little shedding of English or Norman blood, and Scotland had a king agreeable to the English throne. It had been right, therefore, to send Duncan; Edgar should be soldier enough to see it. That he didn't wounded Rufus almost as much as his absence, but rather than contend with him on their difference, the king used his own frustration and disappointment to spur himself toward another objective – a war against his brother, Robert Curthose.

Curthose's envoy had made certain of that when he spoke thus in his master's name to the king:

'My honest lord the Duke of Normandy sends you this word, King William of the English: that he despises and renounces all treaty made with you, unless you perform for him what you promised and set down in both words of writing and sacred oath before witnesses.

'If you will not, he declares you forsworn and truthless, dishonored of your knightly word and recreant of deed.

'Give him that aid you vowed him, or else come to the place where the sacred pact was made and, before those same witnesses, clear yourself of the charge of faithlessness by good and cogent reasons for your delay.'

Such a message was hardly wise of Curthose. Its language had the savor of Odo in it too much. But even if it had been less arrogantly expressed, the threat of Curthose's scorn was no way to make Rufus humble himself before Normans, or bend him to act as Robert would have him.

That envoy must have thanked his saints the king had a higher regard for couriers than he had for his brother, or he could have found himself languishing in a cell for his speech. As it was, he was in a sweat when he concluded, though there was a winter's chill in the hall. He stayed in Gloucester no longer than was necessary to receive the king's first blast of anger before he fled to his ship again.

The Christmas festivities were at an end; the synod that Anselm had asked the king to invoke was forgotten; the rope dancers, jugglers, wrestlers, and bear tenders were cleared from the hall and a war council gathered. The great men of the land, many of whom were Curthose's vassals as well, shared the king's outrage and approved his determination to put his brother in his place. The anarchy in their homeland since Robert's crowning had dealt harshly with their revenues, while the illconsidered revolt of '88 had made them respect the king's wrath. Even those among them, such as Robert Mowbray and William de Eu, who had been Curthose's allies, now offered rich gifts to the king to equip his host. William de Eu told Rufus he would be duke in Normandy before the coming summer waned, which Rufus was particularly pleased to hear, coming from the man who had taunted him with the title the 'New Alexander' in his first days of knighthood.

'If they'd been caught on the other side of the water when this happened, they'd be offering the same gifts to Curthose,' said Fulcher somewhat bitterly under his breath as we listened to the speeches. He had never entirely reconciled himself to his losses overseas.

'Yes, they would,' I replied. 'Therefore, we must give thanks they happened to be on our side of the water when the duke chose to make a fool of himself. But cheer up, brother. Did you want a ministry in Normandy so much? When the king is master there, perhaps I'll get you one.'

Anselm was in that council for the first time in his archbishop's cope. He was now the head of its ecclesiastical side. He said little when the council was debating, not, I think, for fear of offending the king with his moderation, but because he was offended by the loss of

595

his synod. The king had welcomed him to court with all courtesy, being of a mind to put aside what he felt was a minor difference between them now: the recognition of a Pope. Rufus hadn't yet recognized the tenacity of the old man.

When the barons and churchmen began vying with one another in the richness of their gifts to the royal war chest, the archbishop and his clerks murmured to each other and bent their ears to the other's advice. I could hear the tenor of their discourse almost as well as if they were spilling it into my own ear, so well did whisperings carry in that hall. The king must have caught a snatch of their speech, too. He glanced at them, then at me, and winked.

William de St. Carileph had just offered three hundred pounds in silver from the treasure of Durham, and Archbishop Thomas of York had felt it incumbent upon him to double that with six hundred. The hissings and mutters from the Canterbury corner became more animated. Anselm's face was as long as his sleeves when he cleared his throat and spoke:

'Canterbury will give in aid to the king the sum of five hundred pounds in silver, with the prayer that war may somehow yet be averted. We give, wishing only to show our love to the king, and so to be able to address ourselves once again to the spiritual duties of our office with a clear mind.'

The king scratched his ear and accepted the offer with a bemused nod. I saw he thought he'd gotten a victory of sorts over the old man who had previously refused to outfit a handful of soldiers for royal service, or else that he was unwilling to break the temporary peace by inquiring into the exact meaning of the archbishop's strange speech.

When the council was broken to allow the servants to set up tables for the day-meal and I was alone with the king for a moment, Rufus gave a short laugh and said:

'He's coming around to good sense! But did you see his face when he made the offer? Jesu! He looked as if he might want to give his silver Last Rites before he lets it go to us.' He laughed again.

I said, 'If the five hundred contents you, my lord, there's better cause for him to rejoice than mourn.'

'Eh? What's that mean?'

'Why, only that it's overmodest, when York gives six hundred and even Durham gives three.' Then I laughed, too. 'But we must take it and sing his praise, since we might have gotten a sermon instead.'

Rufus gave me a search from his darker eye. 'It's paltry, you think?' He lacked true appreciation of the value of coin. Until he gained so much with the crown, he'd had so little that he couldn't tell what a shilling would buy.

'Paltry, my lord? It depends on the giver. Five hundred is great riches to one such as myself. To a London beggar, a mark in silver is wealth beyond belief. But to Canterbury – well, it's a great house, isn't it? Greater than York, by Lanfranc's definition, and indeed by all men's. Yet he says he hopes his gift will buy not only soldiers, but your love into the bargain. Some bargain!' I caught his sour look at me and added:

'Pay me no heed, Your Grace. I'm always the critic, as you've told me so many times, while my lord Anselm is – an Italian. They're the best of bargainers. It's in their blood, as nobility and generosity are in yours. Take his gift. Maybe next time he'll have caught some of the Norman spirit and be more generous.'

He brooded on the matter for a moment, then asked, 'How much should he have given?'

When the archbishop requested a private audience with the king on the following day, I was ushered out of their presence along with everyone else, but placed myself on a bench on the gallery that ran above the east end of the hall, where I might hear.

'Your Grace, I am perplexed and astonished! My dispenser tells me you've now refused the aid from us which you accepted yesterday. I could hardly believe he knew what he said when he told me you thought our gift unworthy of you. Tell me this was a false rumor or some garbled message of a misinformed clerk.'

'He was misinformed, Archbishop. What I said was that the gift was unworthy of *you*.'

'I don't understand, Your Grace.'

'Don't you? Think on it. You're a scholar and a wise man, they tell me.'

'You're still angry with me.'

'*Disappointed* would be the better word, if you'd take the adv-vice of an unlettered man,' said the king with a bark of laughter.

'I see. You think the sum I've offered is too small.'

'I do.'

'Five hundred pounds in silver is a dear gift by any measure I know, my lord, especially when it comes freely and with love from one who has been harshly used by your tax collector.'

'By the Face of Lucca, Anselm, I've made you richer, not poorer, than you were! Is this to be your excuse t-to the rest of your k-kind, now? That I've beggared you, s-so you must g-give me the widow's mite, while others less than you offer su-sub-substance? Do you think me a fool, you and your damned, ch-cheese-paring monks? I know what you're worth!'

Anselm said in a quieter voice: 'I am justly rebuked for offering poverty as a reason, my lord. But take my apology, along with my coin – and the words of the poet who said, "A great love goes here with a little gift." '

Now I could tell the difference between the king's real anger and the harsh voice he sometimes used to bolster his own uncertainty. His stammer scarcely increased, but his voice grew rough and loud. He was a little confounded by the apology and the reference to Theocritus, whom he didn't know.

Gerard came out of the chapel and glanced at me with surprise. 'What are they fighting about now?' he whispered. I held up a hand to warn him of what he should know, that whispers carry down as well as up in the cavern of that hall.

Anselm said in answer to something of the king's rebuke: 'My offering is less than York's because my treasury *has* suffered more than his, under the management of the *bailiff* you gave it during the vacancy, Your Grace!'

Gerard cocked his head at me.

'But what was pledged was pledged from our hearts, not from our memories, or our just sense of caution. Think again before you refuse it. Caution counseled that for the sake of your honor and my own I should give less, or some men would say I had bought my office from you.'

'Archbishop!'

'Yes, I feared the charge of simony more than I feared ingratitude, my lord, which I thought unworthy of you! This is the first aid I offer you, not the last – or the best, if you will accept it. My earnest counsel – '

'Oh, damn your counsel! Ke-keep your j-jaw and your money to yourself, by God! Ge-get out of m-my s-sight! Your counsel give to your monks, n-not to me! N-never think you can rule me, priest! No one will rule over me! Get out!'

Gerard came close and breathed in my ear: 'This is all very sudden, isn't it? He seemed content yesterday.'

I shrugged.

'Yes,' he said, sitting on the bench by me and taking me in with a long, shrewd look. 'Sudden enough, I got no wind of it. How is it you don't look surprised?'

Anselm returned to his see, and soon it became known he had given to the poor that gift which the king had refused of him. It was said he rejoiced in the refusal, saying no one could now accuse him of having bought his office in the unlawful manner of some who held high places. Yet, he made one more attempt to persuade the king to accept his five hundred pounds before it went to charity. Rufus refused again.

He might have accepted then; even I advised him to do it. But his temper had become more violent since he learned that Edgar Atheling had taken ship for Normandy without permission to leave the realm.

'He runs away behind my back? Why? Have I become a tyrant to him, that he's afraid to face me? Did he think I'd refuse him leave to go? What have I done to merit this, can anybody tell me?'

It wasn't a question that begged an answer, but I said: 'Some men might ask, what has he done that would offend you, my lord, to make him take his leave of you in this manner?'

He turned on me instantly, ready to defend the man who had offended him. 'What's that? What are you hinting?'

'He goes to your brother, my lord, when you are at odds with your brother. Some men would call that an offense – a treasonable offense.'

'Treasonable? Who says that? Name them! Or is it just your opinion? One of those things you say, then try to make me believe you never said.'

'My lord, I protest; I didn't say it. I only tell you what a dozen or more men have said openly since the prince left us. Ask Walter Tirel, or Bledry – or even Earl Hugh – if you doubt me.'

'And what have they said? In so many words: their words, not damned clerks' talk!'

'My lord, I've offended you by mentioning this. Let me make amends. There are men in court who are the prince's friends. Let me call them to speak to you. Some one of them may know better than I why he's gone and where. The supposition may be wrong that says he's gone to Rouen to try to reclaim those estates from the duke which you had him deseized of. The reasoning is that he needs the revenues now he's got a family of nieces and nephews to care for.'

'Then why didn't he come to me? I made his kin welcome. Everyone heard me do it. Have I ever refused him anything, or any other friend who's asked of me?'

'My lord, you are the most generous prince in Christ's kingdom; everyone knows that. And I am your unworthy servant to grieve you with these rumors. I repent of it. No man can say why Prince Edgar has left us but the man himself. He *is* a prince and a proud man, but when you go overseas you're certain to hear his reasons, and your friendship, I hope, will be mended.'

He made a sudden gesture of rejection. 'No! No, he's made his choice. Let him go where he will. After all, what does it matter? Attend to your business. Pen me a writ to the sheriff of Worcester – '

Fulcher said to me later, when the writing was done and the king departed to see a new litter his favorite bitch had whelped:

'Well, that was neatly done, but aren't you getting too clever for yourself?'

'What do you mean?'

'Only that if you keep irritating him in order to get rid of the people about him that you don't like, you're in danger of getting dismissed yourself.'

'I'm in no danger of that, Fulcher; none at all.'

'Really? There are so few certainties in life, brother; how fortunate you are to be in possession of one of them. What's your assurance?'

'I'm the only man he has about him who tells him the truth.'

He laughed, a rare thing in him. 'Ah, the truth! You do have a talent for that! You can turn it inside out and still present it with seams invisible. But the others about him – Maurice, Anselm, Gerard, Bloet, fitz Hamon, and the rest – they're only flatterers, I take it?'

'To a degree, yes. I tell him the things he already knows but doesn't like to admit to.'

' "You are the most generous prince in Christ's kingdom" – '

'Shut up, Fulcher! He *is* the most generous prince you're ever likely to meet. You don't know him as well as I do. He may shout at me and pretend to suspect me, but he knows I speak only in his interest. He's got eyes, and a brain, and a heart, but he doesn't know how to use them with people who might harm him. Rather, he knows, but he likes for someone else to say to him what he knows. Then he shouts. But in the end, he knows what he must do.'

'Which is – ?'

'Learn to do without them. A king can have no friends. He can't afford them, no matter how much gold he has hoarded in his treasure house. A king has servants, vassals, and enemies. When he is content with that, he's safe.'

'Ranulph, lately you've begun to terrify me.'

'Your irony isn't always amusing, Fulcher.'

'No, truly. You've changed in the last few weeks, more than you seem to realize. You've become the king's own shadow – you're anathema to his friends, who can't come near him without brushing against you –'

'By his wish, I'm there.'

'That may be, but these men you've begun to think so little of are no shadows. They've got real swords and long arms. Take care you don't feel them, especially as you've begun to invent so many campaigns against them without telling them they're at war.'

'I'm afraid you've become too mystical for me now. What is it you do mean? That I've become a more efficient servant of the king than he's been paying before now? If so, I admit the charge.'

'I mean, you're turning into somebody you used to detest for the same reasons, someone I knew only well enough to say good riddance to when he was gone.'

I laughed. 'Your loving patron Odo? You flatter me.'

'I don't. I mean Cormac.' He turned on his heel and left me, no doubt satisfied that he'd dealt me a hard blow.

'What an imagination you have, brother!' I cried after him. 'You should compose a bestiary!'

We were still in the dead of winter, but directly after Candlemas the king was eager to begin gathering his host at Hastings for his campaign against his brother. To make certain Robert understood him well, Rufus had returned the Cotentin to Prince Henry and given him leave to go there immediately after Christmas to begin the strengthening of its garrisons and some preliminary raiding across its borders on Robert's vills and fields.

The whole court was called to assemble at Hastings, where their council would stand for the Easter Court that must needs be neglected. It was an occasion that even Anselm thought fit to attend and bless, having for the moment given over a quarrel he was making with Maurice of London about a certain church in Maurice's diocese that he had consecrated without remembering to invite Maurice's attendance.

We reached Hastings to feel a wind blowing in our faces. That meant the delay of the sailing until it changed. The king tried to make the best of the delay, which was costing him silver for the feeding of so large a host. The great Abbey of St. Martin's of the Place of Battle that the Conqueror had commanded to be built on the hill where Harold had fallen was now completed. Rufus declared that it be consecrated while he and all the realm's bishops were present, to do his father's memory the greatest honor.

Anselm was the chief celebrant, but the king served at the altar by his side, as was perfectly proper, though the old Italian seemed distressed by it. Every bishop took his turn in blessing and sprinkling; we were half the day adorning the sacred precincts, but it was a glorious occasion, one not seen in the land since my lord's coronation. It lifted our spirits to behold the majesty and might assembled there.

A few days later, the wind still not having abated, we had another ceremony, this time in the chapel of Hastings Keep. Robert Bloet was sanctified Bishop of Lincoln. The delay in his consecration had lasted nearly a year, because of a quarrel between York and Canterbury too tedious to relate. Dear Robin, what a cherub he looked that day! His cheeks had been getting rounder every year with his good living, while his flaxen curls had grown thinner and were now streaked with equal portions of yellow and gray. He was no longer the man to win over a wineshop wench to pass him a cup for a smile, but he was nearly a boy again in his exultation.

When the ceremony was finished and he was receiving his friends in the great hall, I bent my knee to him and kissed his ring. He forgot the coolness that had sprung up between us of late and embraced me.

'Thank God, it's over at last!' he confided in my ear. 'I'm wet to the skin with terror under all this finery.' He spread his arms and gazed down at himself, frankly admiring his beautiful green cope with its golden embroidery, then smiled at me. 'It will be your turn, soon, dear boy. Then you'll know how it feels, because I can't possibly describe it.' His voice roughened with the wonder of it.

'You needn't describe anything, Robin. It's all in your face. But I don't expect to wear a miter – not anymore. No, I'm serious; nor do I want one now. I'm a bursar at heart and always have been, remember? Ranulph the Drudge. But you' – I approved him with open arms – 'Your Grace! You'll do honor to your robes.'

'I mean to, Raf. I mean to.' Being still in danger of tears, he cuffed me fondly. 'Look at me, for the love of Heaven! It's hard to believe I was only a subdeacon two days ago, isn't it?'

I laughed. It was true. In spite of his nomination to the bishopric of Lincoln, Robin hadn't taken priestly orders until he was dead certain of his office. He had lived in the meantime with his young mistress, who had recently rewarded him with a son, Simon. Now that he was under the cope, she would find it dull being quietly installed in one of his country houses.

I went adrift for a moment, remembering how I, too, had taken my deaconate on one day and my priesthood on another; lain at Odo's feet, envying him his green shoes! I'd imagined then that I would someday hold high office, wear rich vestments, bless others as I was being blessed.

I had denied Giva peace of soul to gain that dream. Now that she was no further hindrance to it, the dream was dead. Anselm would never allow me to be installed on a bishop's throne while he was archbishop, nor was I wealthy enough to buy a place, as Robin had eventually been obliged to buy his, in spite of an archbishop's objections.

But it was more than that. My loathing of Anselm was as great as his of me and made me now prefer my place at the king's elbow, knowing how it grieved the old man to see me there. Not even for the throne of York would I leave that place, to kiss the floor before Anselm's feet!

I heard Robin's voice: 'Raf, I haven't said anything before, as there never seemed to be the moment, but you must know how I grieve for your loss. Giva – '

'Yes, Robin, thank you, but it's all right. I'm reconciled. At least now there are no distractions from my work, such as caused you to rebuke me before. I try not to think of her. Your Grace, I've taken too much of your time. There are others waiting to commend you. Give me your blessing. I'll be leaving here tomorrow, if this infamous wind slackens. I don't want to ride back to London in the company of Carileph.'

I knelt and felt his gloved hand touch my head.

But the wind blew on until Ash Wednesday and beyond. The host grew restless with inactivity; the countryside, poor with feeding them. Tempers sharpened all around. Fines imposed for breaches of the law did little to keep up spirits. Anselm took to preaching against the vanity and license of the knights, which bored them mightily, as he seemed most to inveigh against such trivialities as their wide sleeves and velvet shoes, their perfumed beards and long hair, rather than their brawling with the townsmen. He might as profitably have preached against the damned south wind.

Flowing locks and hanging sleeves were no devices of the Devil, or an example set by the king to make women of men, as Anselm was strong to hint. They were only a return to the splendor that Frenchmen and Englishmen alike were accustomed to enjoy in times of peace. Both races, like Samson, had once gloried in long hair as a sign of virtue and manliness.

But it was no use to point this out, even to Maurice, who scolded almost as much as Anselm on the subject:

'They look like goats, that's what! How can they bear it, blowing in their faces and choking their mouths when they eat? Then they get food in it, wine dribbles – they stink like cesspools – fah!'

'But when they wash the beards and put on perfume, you complain they're effeminate,' I said, laughing. 'Maurice, it's a thing of youth. It will pass, like pustules.'

'Will it? Look at that one, scarcely dry behind the ears, but he's twitching his buttocks like a bathhouse bawd and shaking his curls like a satyr. Evil little whelp! Are you telling me he'll grow out of what he's learning from his betters?'

The boy he pointed out was my son Martin, with whom I'd been meaning to have a word on the subject of civility since he learned I was now again in residence at the house that he thought to be his mother's. I could bear with his opinion of me, but when Isabel had come to Westminster to see him, he scorned to sit by her at table and reduced her to tears by his remark that if she kept a house for clerks, she should be licensed for it. I was about to leave Maurice to speak to Martin when I saw the king was going out of the hall and Anselm was in his train. I forgot Martin to follow them.

The archbishop had requested an audience with the king before he returned to Canterbury. One might have thought the matter of the audience would be of some consequence to the realm, such as securing the coastal ports that were in Anselm's keeping while Rufus was abroad, but no, the whole tenor of his lament was still the corruption of men. The king heard him out with wonderful patience, I thought, then asked:

'But what has this to do with me, Archbishop? Is it the duty of a king to tell his subjects when they must shave?'

'Your Grace, you go forth to war against your brother, it may be with just cause. You have asked the blessing of Heaven on your enterprise – the blessing of Christ. But how can you hope for success in this or any other venture if you neglect to check the evils that are uprooting the religion of Christ in your kingdom?'

The king smiled. 'My lord, I've seen the image of God, or so I've been told, and He wears both hair and beard. Hair and beard He gave alike to all mankind, so how can they be evil?'

'It is written in the Holy Scriptures that it is an abomination to a man if he makes himself to look like a woman – '

'Ah, I see. Then it's the s-sleeves you take exception to. Well, I see what you mean there. They're a nuisance, but they'll be shed before we do battle, I assure you. And to give you s-such other assurance as I can, I promise you that tomorrow each man that serves me shall take an inch from his beard and two inches from his hair in t-token of penance. Will that content you?'

Anselm looked grave as usual. 'Your Grace, it's a beginning, but now open your heart to the rest of my counsel. Since you were given to rule over this land there has been no synod held at your courts. While you are gone, allow me to call the bishops and the rulers of houses of religion together, so we may consult freely and speak to those evils that offend your good justice.'

I said under my breath, for the king alone to hear, 'The holding of synods is yours, not his.'

The king answered without glancing at me: 'Archbishop, the holding of synods is mine, not yours. I will see to this matter – when I think best. Understand me: as my fa-father was king, so must I be. He called synods, or not, as he chose. I will act according to my pleasure then, not yours.' Then he smiled again. 'When you get your synod, what will you talk about? Beards and long s-sleeves?'

Anselm said solemnly, as if he were pronouncing a curse, 'I would speak of the corruption of men, corruption of both flesh and soul, my lord.'

'Fornication, too? But the fornicators have been with us since Eden, my lord, a-and they'll be here when we're all turned to worm's food. S-so long as there are women, there'll be men who – '

'I didn't speak of fornication, or of women, but of the evil that men do with men. It is no new thing, either, that evil which brought destruction to Sodom and will surely bring destruction to any great city – or kingdom – if it is let to grow. I pray God daily that you have purged yourself. Now purge those who are beneath you. I speak – '

The blood had drained from the king's face, only to rush back in a scarlet flood. 'You speak of a great many things, priest! I'm amazed to hear what fi-fills your mind! What is this to you?'

'To me, nothing,' said Anselm serenely. 'To God and to you, I hope, much.'

The king dismissed him. He didn't lose grip on his anger until the old man was out of the chamber. As I ushered Anselm out, I saw Martin dawdling outside the door and jerked my head at him to be off. When I returned to the chamber the king was laughing, though there was a film of tears in his eyes.

'He's in his dotage! I thought I'd make peace with him before I went, but' – he grabbed up a goblet set by his elbow and hurled it across the room – 'there's no making peace with a fool! God damn him! God – !' He looked for something else to seize, didn't find it, braced himself against the table, and blew out his cheeks. 'A synod! He wants me to give him le-leave to hold a synod – against *me*! And I was going to name him ju-jus-justiciar, along with Carileph! Well, by God, I know better now! I've a better man for that.'

I sighed. So, we would have Carileph alone to rule us, as I'd suspected from the moment I knew that fitz Hamon, Earl Hugh, and de Meulan were all to go abroad with the king. I would have to take myself to Dover, or Winchester, and occupy myself as best I could with some building I'd planned.

But when the wind at last swung around to swell the sails of the royal fleet, I was the man the king named to rule for him in his absence.

52

The king reached Normandy, met with his brother at Caen, but found him unchanged in his willfulness. They parted with harsh accusations on both sides. The duke took up his quarters at Rouen again, but with less ease, as Rufus made his place at Eu and immediately sent out word to the free lances of the world that they should be well paid to fight for him.

My part was to go to Westminster and begin the razing of the old English palace, which would give way to a splendid new hall. While I endured reproof from my architect, and the April rains delayed my workmen, King William marched against Curthose, took the castle and vill of Bures, dispersed its troops, and peopled it with his own.

Duke Robert appealed to the French king to give him aid. Prince Henry meanwhile moved against the border fortress of Argentan and won it handily. King Philip, moved to valor by Curthose's silver, joined Curthose to lay siege to Argentan. So great was their combined strength that Argentan's castellan surrendered before they finished laying their lines.

It was a noble victory and might have signaled the beginning of a season of real struggle, but King Philip found even such easy campaigning too strenuous for his enormous bulk and hauled his carcass back to Paris, leaving Duke Robert to attack another of Prince Henry's conquests, La Houlme, alone. Wonderfully, he was successful; the castle surrendered, and its eight hundred men became the prize – and the burden – of the duke.

These men were held for ransom. The greater part of the garrison were rabble, naturally, but there were also a good number of knights to be saved from dishonor at great expense to their families, or to King William. Rufus didn't like paying for what was his to begin with, but what else could he do? His honor lay in their safe return. He sent to me for money.

The events in Normandy that year were all costly, both to the treasury at Winchester and to the landowners of the realm. I bore the brunt of the barons' displeasure. I was forced to lay a geld on the land for the first time since Rufus was crowned, less of a geld than the Conqueror had required of them when the Danes seemed to threaten. But one would have thought I was asking for the very bread out of their mouths or their children's patrimony, according to the complaints they brought to court – the same men who themselves greatly taxed their vassals for their own ends.

Those who could not come to rail at me in person sent writs by their clerks, which Fulcher read to me while I brooded over the plans for the delayed palace.

'My lord of Canterbury says he cannot oppress his own people to add to your comfort. There's a hint here that he thinks you're subverting the coin to your own use, seeing how you're building a house at Winchester and renewing the roof of the deanery at Dover. Shall you answer this?'

'Yes: Ranulph to His Grace, Anselm of Canterbury: I beg my lord to come and ask my builders why they still wear fustian instead of velvet, if I am so profligate with money.'

'You can't send him that.'

'Then I can send him nothing to his comfort. Let him complain to the king and not to me. That's where his money's being spent!' I put my finger toward the window, where the ruins of Westminster Palace now stood like a featherless crow in the rain. 'Damned, miserable place! Why should it take them so long to tear it down, seeing it was about to fall down anyway? My God, how I hate it! *And* the one that's supposed to be taking its place. I never hope to live so long that I see the stones rise above the seventh course in its walls. I'd sell my soul for a thunderbolt that would blow it all away at one stroke –'

'Ranulph, someone will hear you – '

' – but pilfer from the king's levy funds to build it, or any other damned building? God forbid! Let them hear! What difference does it make? They think I'm damned anyway, don't they?'

'You needn't antagonize them further then,' he said with a lopsided smile. 'For your clerks, be the cool devil.'

'The cool devil!' I laughed, pushed aside the drawings, and rubbed my face to wake myself. I'd slept ill since the king departed. 'Yes, I've got that name, too, along with Flambard the Toad. I am a cool devil. I'm using the royal courts to make myself rich, too, you know. I make a man pay a fine for his misdemeanors, rather than improve his soul with a flogging or sending him to the axman to have his hand lopped off in the good old way. That's mercy, you'd think, but these merciful priests think ill of such mercy. Ah, God, I wish Rufus had let Carileph have the fining and chopping part of it. He's gone back to Durham to build his choir, never comes down from his scaffold unless there's a widow to defend, or a baby to bless. He's getting ready for Heaven, is Carileph, while I'm up to my arse in Hell.'

'I know you're overworked, but you'd get along with the lot of them better if you didn't take on the king's habit of glaring and shouting at them. And the sheriffs might like you better if you made a show of consulting with them before you imposed your fines.'

'They wouldn't like me any better if I came in sackcloth and ashes, so long as I take money from them. I'm an upstart. You're one, too, so don't bother with their feelings. In fact, don't even talk about them; say something pleasant. How's mother? How're the children?'

'Well, but they miss you. Look, Raf, why don't you bring them up here to be with you? They need you and I think you need them as well.'

'I'd have no time to spend with them and the city's pestilent in the summer.'

'It's no worse here in the summer than it is in Winchester, and you'd have as much time to spend with them as you spend with that whore you keep on Cornhill.'

'Fulcher, please don't be my conscience this morning, will you? I haven't the leisure for remorse. I'm glad to hear the boys are well. I'll do what I can for them, if they need anything, but I can't – I can't look at them yet.'

'They'll grow up and never know you as a father.'

'Then they'll be fortunate. With the reputation I rejoice in, they'll be glad to say later that they never knew me. Let it be, for God's sake!'

In the late summer I went overseas to the king, to take him gold and hear his complaints about my tardiness. King Philip, having rested, was showing signs of wanting to become a warrior again, or else required a rich bribe to keep him passive. I sat in the daily councils at Eu and heard all the petty bickering that took place there. I saw that little or nothing had been accomplished with the money I had so painfully earned for the campaign, but to accustom fools and parasites to getting it from the king. There had been little warfare, save the taking or burning of a great number of miserable villages that were of no use to anyone on earth but the hapless creatures who dwelt in them. I spoke to the king about ending the war:

'Why not give the duke what he craves, the name of lord of the Vexin? It would be cheaper in the end to take your army there, scare out the French, and turn it over to your brother, nominally, than to do all this ransoming of each other's captives. You'd garrison the castles and keep half the revenues; he'd get the title and the trouble of placating Philip. It would cost him, but better him than you, my lord, and he couldn't complain you'd stinted your promises.'

He looked at me as if I'd suggested he break off his spurs and send them to Curthose as a token of surrender.

'Win him the Vexin? I'll see him in Hell first! If I win it – and I will – it will be mine. Let him whistle for his treaty, then. He *would* have me come over. Here I am – and I'll stay – to his sorrow.'

'My lord, if you take the Vexin to yourself, you'll be obliged to fight for it the rest of your life. Where's the money to come from? Can England buy up France? That's what it will come to.'

He was incensed. 'Now, w-when did you become a g-general? Haven't I got enough of those here, without you coming out of your counting room to add to the number?'

'My lord knows I speak only for his own ear and to his own welfare. At home they're complaining of the geld – '

'Let them! Let them roar for it. It's the first I ever asked of them, but if my brother h-had gotten his foot set in their door in 'eighty-eight, they'd have paid geld enough to him! By the Face, they'd have vomited pennies and p-pissed shillings, the God-damned vermin! They're s-snug at home and they complain for a little gold? Let them come over here and eat dust on the road with me, then!' He stopped to consider that, a smile splitting his face like that of a child who sees a butterfly.

'Maybe I should bring them over here. Then they'd have that to complain of. Yes.' He grinned at me, half in contempt, half in forgiveness. 'You want to play at being a general, Raf? Call up my southern levies for me.'

'Oh, Your Grace, what use could they possibly be to you that would outweigh their trouble? It's their lords who complain, who'll complain to me – ' I was appalled at what I'd have to contend with. 'They'll be nothing but a burden, lumps of terror from crossing the sea, more mouths to feed when you get them.'

He laughed at my discomfort. 'Go home and call them up, or get me the money to replace them. Marshal them to Hastings. I'll send ships. But before you take on your legions, you'll dine with me again and see this fellow who's been sent to amuse me. You'll never guess who sent him.'

We went into the great hall where knights, squires, clerks, and common soldiers stood like sheep waiting to be fed. It was as if Pharaoh had welcomed in the hordes of locusts God sent him and put them to his table gladly. In that crowd of faces I saw one I hadn't thought to see, since no mention had been made of him.

'I didn't realize Prince Edgar had made his peace with you again, Your Grace.'

He answered coolly: 'Oh, yes. Robin and I didn't exchange much ground, but that he ceded me.' He didn't glance in Edgar's direction as he spoke, which troubled me more than if he'd gone and kissed him.

'My lord, is it wise? He's given you grief enough. Should you – keep him?'

He sighed, then looked at me as if I'd made some amusing comment. 'He's no more grief to me. And a purse keeps him quiet, like any other man. I'd rather have him close than have him wander. Enough. Here's young Martin. Boy, we've a special guest today. Go and find that miserable sot who calls himself my juggler and see if he can amuse us.'

I was taken to the high table and placed at the king's left hand to the annoyance of William of Eu, who'd been prepared to take that stool. Our meal was served roughly and the meat was coarse, compared to what the king had been accustomed in his own halls, but there was plenty of it and he seemed to relish it: boiled mutton, hare pies, great slabs of cheese, and common loaves of brown bread, though fresh from the ovens. A soldier's meal, quite agreeable to the host in the hall who gorged on it.

I was surveying them with a measure of disgust and envy for their simple lot when someone came into the hall who surprised me more than the sight of Prince Edgar: once seen, he couldn't be missed, even from afar. His great beak of a nose jabbed itself this way and that like a falcon's; his elbows flailed at the air as he hobbled on his cruelly deformed feet toward the high table. It was Fulk le Rechin, Count of Anjou, eternal enemy of the Conqueror, constant harasser of Robert Curthose, and certainly no ally of my lord's. Or was he?

I must have gaped openly at the sight of him; even more, when I saw the reception he got from the men in the hall. Rather than rise to their feet in his presence, they hooted and laughed when he passed. He laughed, or cursed, scratched the lice in his frowsy grey head, and lurched forward.

The king didn't bother to rise in his presence either, but threw a mutton rib that landed almost at his feet, which were encased in those ridiculous velvet slippers with the long, pointed toes that his bunions had made famous. Rufus spoke:

'Well, my lord, I see you weren't too drunk to hear the dinner gong. Where've you been lately? Off harrying the French?'

'I've been looking for my wife, that's what. I think she's betrayed me.'

That brought a roar of laughter, as his wife had betrayed him most royally with Philip of France and he'd brayed it to the world.

'You should get another.'

'Yes, I mean to, but she'll need a good dowry.' He swung around to the hall. 'Who'll sell me his daughter? I want a virgin, mind you, not above sixteen, though a widow will do, if she's plump enough.' His voice was like a rusted hinge. A fresh shout of merriment and some ribaldry greeted his request.

I was staring hard. I knew Fulk was as famous for his eccentricities as he was for his lechery, but he must have gone mad to come to the king's court in search of a wife, though it was true that after his third wife cuckolded him with fat Philip, he'd gone through the Norman courts inquiring for a new bride.

'I almost had one this morning,' he croaked, leaning toward one of the lower tables for a moment like a bilious goatherd. 'She'd have been a good one – but she ran off with the count's pig keeper. I went after 'em, but' – he did a sudden shuffle and hop to lean the other way – 'they had an ass to ride away on, and I had one to carry.'

The hall roared. I sat back on my stool. This wasn't Fulk, though he had the gait, the nose, and the voice. As he shambled nearer I could see that the grey hair was dusted with flour and the nose made of glazier's putty. As he came toward the dais, Rufus pitched him another rib, this one with meat on it. The jester caught it, flourished it, and crammed the fat end into his mouth.

'He can do Philip of France to the life,' Rufus said, still laughing. 'The way he stuffs himself, you'd think he was truly made of suet, like that h-hog in velvet. Come forward, fool, and wipe your chin. Raf, this is Robert Cornard. Philip himself sent him to me!'

The fool bounded forward to the table's edge. With a bloodcurdling smile and a matron's voice, he cooed: 'And who is this pretty priest?' He fluttered his lashes at me like a bawd.

'Down, wench, this one's mine. Go and rob a cloister.'

I felt a flush suffuse my face at the king's careless remark. The fool's grin closed into a long, thin smile, unpleasant to a degree impossible to describe. Under the flour and putty he was young and possibly handsome. I thought King Philip might not be so stupid as report would have him. As I stared into Cornard's half-closed eyes with growing hatred, he straightened, did a quick turn, put his fingers to his chin and pate to imitate wattles and comb, and strutted away like a rooster.

The king laughed, cast his last bone to the dogs, and wiped his greasy fingers on his thighs, which showed the effects on their dirty hose of other such applications. The silken raiment was put aside; his hair had been cropped to just below his ears. He wore the thick grey gambeson of a common bowman. Of his former luxury only his beard remained, and – I thought of Maurice – there were grease gobbets and piecrust crumbs in it.

He had turned aside to hear something said by Robert de Meulan on his right hand. Throughout the evening he alternately exchanged crude jests with the men of the lower tables, foolishness with Cornard, and brief, sober dialogues *sotto voce* with one or the other of his captains. He gave me a merry, malicious look from time to time, but otherwise ignored me. I thought: He's in his proper place at last and, like a naughty boy, defies me as he would his tutor. How was I to speak to him of economy in this mood? I looked about for Prince Edgar. At the moment I would have welcomed an exchange with him, but he had departed the hall after dining at the farthest end of the high table.

When I left the king on the following day, he said again: 'Money and soldiers, that's all you need worry about. Get me money. Put a tax on the foreigners. Put a tax on pissing in the streets, or whatever likes you best. But before the snow flies, Philip will be out again and I'll need money.'

'Will you ransom the hostages of La Houlme, my lord?' I knew he hadn't done it, though I'd sent the ransom.

'The hostages? Christ, no! Why should I? They'll burden Robin as prisoners, and they'll never fight for him when they learn he doesn't pay. Let them get La Houlme back for me and I'll give them reward enough, but to pay gold for men who sat on their arses and let Robin take them? Never!'

And there was another change in him.

I came home to London and gave thought to what he wanted of me. He demanded the fyrd, but he had little use for it. He demanded money and, God knew, must have need of it if he meant to buy up all the Vexin, as it seemed he would. I sent out summons of array and said a few fervent prayers. The troops were to muster at Hastings. I went there to wait for them. If my thought was true, he would be delighted with my ploy; if not, he might dismiss me, or let Anselm unfrock me. Under the burden of the justiciarship, it didn't seem to me to be so terrible a fate to be dismissed, while his delight would be measured in gold that I could put to use in finishing my house at Winchester.

Each common man who is called upon to serve the king at his need is given ten shillings by his shire for his necessaries during the forty days of his service. The forty days of service by a country bumpkin were of little use to the king. His ten shillings were another matter.

I had my clerks waiting to collect the money from each group of men as their hundreds sent them in to Hastings. I kept them all marshaled as if for boarding ship, but when the requirements for each shire were tallied, I released them to go home again.

Twenty thousand men came to Hastings for that mustering who went home safe again, never to feel the chill of a winter campaign. It cost me a bit to feed them, but I put nearly eight thousand livres into the king's war chest and sent it overseas on one of his ships, with Fulcher to guard it. It arrived in good time: Philip of the French had joined once more with Curthose to march against the king. Their combined armies had advanced as far as Longueville, a day's easy march from Eu, when Rufus sent into the French encampment an envoy with a special argument for peace lashed across the rump of a pack horse.

King Philip was always in search of ways to make peace without honor. When Duke Robert awoke the next morning, he was no doubt dismayed to find his royal friend had vanished from the field like the Assyrian host from before the walls of old Jerusalem.

I bore the brunt of the expected outrage at home as I expected to do. The combined forces of town and tonsure came to damn me;

petitions were drawn up to send to the king, demanding my arrest, my defrocking, even my beheading, I think. That sneak of a papal spy whom Urban had sent to comfort Anselm – his good clerk Eadmer – came and threatened me with excommunication again.

I heard them all, then showed them the dispatches from Normandy, such of them as could read. To the rest I said:

'His Grace is well pleased. The southern fyrd has met the enemy and defeated them. They are heroes. And the wonder of it is, they fought so nobly, without suffering the loss of a *single man*. The king commends them for their valor!'

That sort of levity didn't go down well with Master Eadmer, or with some of the sheriffs and hundred-men who came to bawl at me. They would have preferred to hear of ten thousand English slaughtered at Longueville, I suppose, than to know they'd been deprived of ten shillings a head. But among the old soldiers who did their castle duty at London Tower I didn't see many who looked as if they hankered for the battlefield – and in the countryside, according to Osbern, my little trick won me a laugh and a toast in muddy ale at some hearthsides. For all that, I was now Flambard the Thief.

Still, the king pressed me for money. I traveled to Gloucester, to York, to Durham, and back to Winchester, all in two months' time by the end of that summer, trying to pry further aids and gifts out of fat religious houses, to keep from having to levy another geld the following year. Most of those places were exempt from the king's taxes and rich in worldly goods. They could afford me. Further, my reputation as a robber had now gone all around the kingdom, so I had no further fear of shaming myself; I was relentless in my search for gifts.

Where coin was not given freely – and in many places it was – I freely took it. For the most part this was from dioceses and abbeys left vacant by death or dismissal. The dismissal was a singular case: the Bishop of Thetford had lost his privilege for going to Rome for his pallium without leave of the king. Rufus had broken Bishop Herbert's staff before he set sail for Normandy.

These vacancies, however they occurred, left Church property in the king's hands, which I guarded for him. I took care that the priors, deacons, archdeacons, or whoever knew what a close estimate I could make of their worth. It was their part to be generous to me. If they were not, it was my part to see that they returned to their sacred vows of poverty without delay.

Not many abbeys were reduced to beans and ale for their day-meal by my measures, but if they were, should I not have gotten a commendation for it from Archbishop Anselm? Such simple fare was approved by his own philosophy!

But never mind; I take the charges laid at my door gladly. Once one has laid aside all hope of ever being thought a good man, it is almost a pleasure to strive for the opposite reputation. I was now a famous lecher, tippler, spy, cheat, and squeezer of coin from the fists of the poor and the chaste. Someone had even remembered I had something to do with the Great Survey and therefore with the famines, droughts, floods, earthquakes, and monster breedings that came as its result. I just missed being named as candidate for Anti-Christ, but only because the honor was soon to go to a nameless pack of infidels in a far corner of the world, who had never known me.

Shortly before Christmas, word was brought to me that Prince Henry had come to England in a ship, along with Hugh of Chester. There was no word that the king had accompanied them or planned to follow them. They landed at Southampton on the eve of the feast of All Souls, but neither made themselves known in Winchester or came to London.

I was seriously concerned. Why were they here without the king? Was there some dissent between the brothers that I didn't know of, and were they now plotting rebellion in comfort at the royal lodge in Southampton? I badly needed someone to consult with on the question, but there was no one I could turn to who had the means to oppose them, if my suspicions were borne out. Carileph was said to be ill and remained in the north; Robert de Meulan, William de Warenne, and Robert fitz Hamon were all abroad with the king. Ralph Baynard was in London with his troops, but they were insufficient to resist a rebellion, if that was what was about to stir.

I took a boat to Fulham to speak to the only man I knew who still had some regard for me: Maurice of London. Age and failing eyesight had made him less active in the life of the court, but his mind was still agile and he loved the king.

He met me in his pleasant garden with its fruit trees and herb beds to hear my tale. When I finished, he thought awhile, then spread his hands and said:

'But what does it come to? Prince Henry has come to England, which is his native land. The king has never denied him return, so far as I'm aware, and he has certain estates to see to here, if he chooses to concern himself with them. I don't see – '

'If he's here to some purpose, why hasn't he declared it? Why not go to Winchester, or to one of his estates? Why is he still at Southampton, and why is Earl Hugh with him?'

'You suspect the earl, as well as the prince? Hugh the Wolf was loyal to the king in his time of trouble, more than any other man.'

'Yes, but he was part of the would-be conspiracy with Bishop Odo in the old king's time, too. No man is above suspicion if he's a Norman, Maurice. Hugh's county of Avranches is next neighbor to the Cotentin. Who knows what he and Henry might have plotted on those long summer nights, now it seems they won't have easy victory over Duke Robert? They're impatient men, our lords and masters.'

Maurice smiled rather sadly.

'My dear friend, I see your point, but they've done nothing that men of their class may not do. I believe you're principally concerned because they've not seen fit to give you, or some other of our kind, notice of their presence. That's negligent, of course, seeing you're regent for the king. But I don't think they quite realize your importance, if you'll forgive my saying so. Men of their class seldom consider men of ours to be of any importance. It's distressing, but there it is.'

I bit my thumb, considering. 'No, there's something wrong. Old Hugh may forget me, but Henry likes all the ceremony he can get. If he were here for an innocent purpose, I think he'd have had me down to Winchester, scraping and bowing to him from Prime to curfew. At least he'd have taken up residence in the castle, where he could play the prince to his heart's content.'

'Well, how do you know he hasn't? You had your message how long ago? Three days? It's only a day's slow ride from the port to the city.'

'Maybe. But he hasn't moved in the last two days, or I'd have heard of it.'

'Ranulph, you're spying on the king's own brother?'

'Spying is hardly the word, and kings' brothers have caused their share of trouble before now, Maurice. Blame me if you will, but I can't get it out of my mind how easy it would be to raise a revolt here right now. There's only one thing that gives me ease: he hasn't had any visitors yet.'

'Visitors?'

'Let's say Gilbert de Clare went calling on him, or Robert of Eu, or Robert de Mowbray. Then what would you suppose?'

He was shocked. 'You think I should suppose treason? If I did, then anywhere two great men met together I should have to suppose it. Ranulph, I think you should send a message to the king, if you're really serious about your fears.'

'I've already sent my message, but the same wind that brought Henry here may be keeping my ship from getting out of the Thames estuary. You think I'm demented, don't you, or that I'm just getting above myself? I haven't been enjoying the duties the king gave me. I'm up to my chin with what he's heaped on me, but I mean to keep afloat, if I can. I won't see the country go off on another rebellion, but what can I do if it does? The fyrd won't answer my summons again. I have no mesnie, no friends but you and perhaps Robin Bloet. What should I do, remembering the year of 'eighty-eight?'

He bowed his head for a moment. 'In such case, you may only send word to the king – and pray.'

In a few days I sent a rider to discover from my watcher whether there had been any movement to or from Southampton. His news on return was that my observer there wasn't to be found, but that Prince Henry still kept quarters in the lodge. Gilbert de Clare had ridden to see him and remained, but Earl Hugh had ridden away on hearing that the Welsh had invaded his lands and burned some of his manors.

What happened to my clerk? I never found out. He was gone forever, either stolen away to some easier life, bribed to silence by Henry, or – could he be floating in the Solent?

I sent another courier to the king, begging him to come home by Christmas. As there had yet been no action, I felt it might wait on that auspicious day. I could imagine Henry relishing laying claim to the throne of England by acclamation on Christmas Day, as his father had done before him. News of the Welsh raids were some relief to me. With Earl Hugh occupied, surely Henry would do nothing rash or sudden.

Early in December, when I'd still had no reply from the king, Henry came to London with a modest escort that included Count Gilbert de Clare and his brother. Garbed in amiability, Henry greeted me as if I were his dearest friend from childhood. His gracious genuflections to Maurice and to the other clergy who had already begun to gather for the winter court put Maurice's mind to rest, I could see, if I had ever disturbed it with my fears at all. The people of London were shortly advised that 'their' atheling was with them, and a demonstration of affection was arranged the next day outside the Tower.

Carileph came in from Durham shortly thereafter, bringing his usual guard of honor, which was something slightly ostentatious in anyone of less rank than an archbishop, but I was glad to see it. I was tempted to speak to him, seeing that Robert Mowbray had now joined us and become one of the constant companions and whisperers about the prince, but Carileph's affectionate greeting to Henry made me hesitate and remember how it had been with him in 'eighty-eight.

At last I had word from the king, delivered by no less a courier than Martin. He would come soon, but must first have another conference with Curthose. Meanwhile, writs and pleas, most of them directed against me, were piling up in the script room waiting for the king to hear them. Prince Henry was the focus of every eye that came to court. He arranged a small tournament for the amusement of his friends while they awaited his noble brother. The prizes were his to bestow and they were rich.

I found there was nothing left for me to do. If I had a conspiracy to contend with, I was powerless to prevent it. I resolved that if God let me live another season to see the king go abroad, I should not be powerless thereafter.

I went home to my house on Cornhill, embraced a surprised Isabel, and told her that her son was home; told her she was prettier than the last time I'd seen her, which was about two weeks before; ordered supper to be held until I was ready to partake of it; and took that still pleasantly confused lady up to bed, though it still lacked something of None.

'I'll never understand the turns of your mind,' she said. I was half drowsing in the comfort and perfume of her flesh and hair. 'It wasn't a month ago that you called me a hag.'

'Did I say so? I was too brief. You're a very pretty hag. No one could guess your age within a decade.'

She pushed my face away. 'Is that supposed to be a compliment? Manners in lovemaking certainly have changed with you, too. When you first knew me, you recited from the Songs of King Solomon.'

'You're right, absolutely. What was it? "Thou art beautiful, my love, as Tirzah, comely as Jerusalem, and terrible as an army with banners"?'

'I don't recall that it was.'

' "Turn away shine eyes from me, for they have overcome me. Thy hair is as a flock of goats" '

'Never mind! I'm sorry I brought it up. Next you'll be saying,

"Thou art withered, my love, as a Lammas apple in the springtime," or something equally dreadful.'

'That's very apt. Apples at winter's end are a bit soft in the flesh, but very sweet to the taste.' I kissed her mouth. 'Let's rejoice in our mellowness. We're getting wrinkled, but we've survived the worms of youth.'

'I think you may be a little out of your wits, my friend.'

'I think you may be right, but the times invite witlessness.' I buried my face in her throat again. 'I don't like Martin neglecting you. I don't like him in service to the king any longer. I don't like his hair, or his strut, or his manners. What do you say we tell him he's a bastard and be done with it? Do you think it'll improve him?'

She sighed and stroked me. 'Do you really want him to know?'

'I don't know. Sometimes I want it. Lie closer to me.'

The king returned three days after Christmas, banners floating under a sky that spat wet snow. He greeted his court in the Tower yard, embraced his brother, heard his excuse that he had been on his way to answer the summons he had sent him, but had been blown off course by an evil wind and so came to England. He was forgiven. Whatever difference had been between them for the king to summon him was forgotten. The whisperings and meetings between Henry and his friends ceased, and all was merry until Epiphany. My suspicions of what might have been taking place would have been declared unworthy of me, so I kept them to myself. But I still suspected the smiling prince.

53

Edgar Atheling had returned with Rufus, but there were differences in their friendship. The king had surrounded himself with lesser men: the fool, Cornard, whom I despised; the Welsh singer, Bledry, who was the best of a doubtful lot; the handsome young Count of Poix, Wat Tirel, who had been away from us for a time, seeing to his inheritance, but was now wed to Alice, daughter of Richard de Clare Bienfaite, whose wife was a Giffard. Tirel's elevation to son-in-law in that illustrious family made him the ranking gentleman of that group, if one didn't count de Clare's son Gilbert, the traitor of

Tonbridge, who was trying to ingratiate himself anew. The rest were an assortment of new-made knights and squires, common bowmen, huntsmen, and soldiers of no rank whatsoever who had impressed the king with some personal trait of strength, ready wit, or physical charm. To my growing distaste, Martin was still among them and becoming more impertinent, spoiled, and depraved every day.

These, and his wrestlers, bear keepers, and kennel men, composed the companionship of the king. With him they made long evenings in the hall, jesting, drinking, gambling, and imitating a garrison of ruffians in a border outpost. I had never seen the king so happy, never heard him laugh so much, but he was restless with all of it, too, more than before.

As soon as Epiphany was past, he raised his levies and went into the west to give aid to Earl Hugh in his fight with the Welsh, saying that he would drive them all into the Irish Sea before he made peace with them again. But God must have put Himself on the side of the Cymri that winter, in spite of their thievishness, because the royal host no sooner reached Gloucester than heavy snows blocked the roads, putting a stop to all battles. The king came away, deprived of the glory he desired.

Now he talked of taking up his war with Curthose again. He sent Prince Henry back to the Cotentin with a huge treasure to buy up mercenaries and harass Duke Robert. He would follow in the spring and make himself master of Rouen. His noble advisers, William of Eu and Robert de Meulan, urged every bloody measure on him when that victory should be complete. He took their advice – their flattery, I thought – and promised they would each have great estates of him when Normandy was in his grip. Those who opposed further warfare made their speeches, but it meant little to the king. For my part, I was silent.

Robert Bloet, now among the peacemakers, chided me for my silence: 'Can't you make him see he can't go on calling up the levies every year, pressing for another geld when there isn't a real need for it? Curthose has gotten his comeuppance. He's no further threat to any here, and many people on the council have interests to protect over there. He can't ask them to go on working against themselves for little reason but a private quarrel between himself and Robert.' Robin himself had several estates in Normandy to think of now, inherited from his mother, so I wasn't astonished to hear him speak of caution, but I said:

'Why do you suppose I'd be able to turn him away from his destiny, Robin? That's what he calls it, you know. He knows his father meant him to take Normandy from Robert. He as much as told him so on his deathbed. Even if I had the influence with him that you think I do, I couldn't win out – over destiny.'

'Have you tried? You're closer to him than any of these – ' He left that unfinished. 'Closer than anyone except the Atheling since – '

'Since Cormac? I think I shall grow tired of that comparison one day, Robin. I am the king's confessor. I am his tax collector. I humbly believe myself to be his friend, but I'm not his confidant in matters military. He's told me so.'

'Yet you're the only person who's ever with him entirely alone, in bedchamber or chancel – no, don't walk away from me like that!'

I stopped. 'Your Grace?'

'I'm sorry, Raf. You know I didn't mean that as – as it sounded. I'd never accuse you, God knows, of what there are plenty of others to do for him. But there are men in this court who think you have special consideration of him and hate you for it. You could win friends for yourself if you used your influence with him to better ends.'

'What, should I prove nasty suspicion by compromising myself for them? You make me laugh! Let these upright fellows make their own pleas. What I say to the king on the matter of war and taxes is "Yes, Your Grace. I hear and obey, Your Grace." On matters of fact I may give him opinions, but on matters of *his* opinions I hold my tongue.' I made him a bow and left him. The coldness between us had returned and would remain, as far as I was concerned. I was shaking with anger. He was no friend of mine who could accuse me – and he had meant to accuse me – of what I made the most strenuous efforts to keep myself apart from.

In February we were at Gillingham in Dorset, where the air was milder and the snow had not fallen. Prince Henry had just departed for Southampton with his treasure chest, that treasure so hard-won by me, wrested from disgruntled and reluctant folk to strengthen the king's hand. Anselm came to us while we were at Gillingham. It was strange to see him there among the huntsmen and kennelers with the blood of animals smeared and dried on their tunics, and the king looking no cleaner than they.

Anselm looked unusually agitated. He had come with a reasonably small retinue, among whom was the ubiquitous Eadmer, his whey-faced shadow, and detestable Baldwin, that domineering Fleming who was head of Anselm's household and, I thought, the chief instigator of his opposition to the king.

Rufus greeted them civilly, called for a tunic to cover his nasty gambeson, and heard with patience the archbishop's speech. Anselm had come to the king out of season, he said, because of two vacancies of bishoprics in the land. One was Thetford, which the king took from Herbert Losinga for going to Rome without his leave. The second was Worcester. Old Wulfstan the Englishman had died in sanctity the month before. Anselm could only just have heard the news before he set out at his old man's pace to find the king and chide him for the vacancy.

Professing surprise for Anselm's haste, Rufus said: 'Have you come all this distance, my lord, only to ask me this? I wish you'd had better care for your health and my wisdom. It still lacks a month of the Easter Court, where such matters must be attended to, and – if you'll forgive me, F-father Anselm – they m-must be attended to by me.'

'They are matters pertaining to the Church, Your Grace. Surely it has something to say to you, especially about delay. Thetford has lain vacant for nearly a year now.'

'It has been in good hands, my lord,' said the king, meaning his own, or rather mine.

Baldwin said: 'The Church can ill afford to overlook the loss of even one of her bishops in this realm, Your Grace. Now there are two missing, which is what concerns His Grace of Canterbury.'

Rufus nodded. 'I understand you, Brother. Now you understand me as well: you must leave this matter to me, as God has s-seen fit to do.' He was watching Anselm, not Baldwin, as he spoke. The old man had dropped his head nearly to his chest, as if in deep thought. Then he lifted it and took us all by surprise by saying:

'Your Grace, I must take leave of you.'

The king laughed. 'What, my lord? But you're hale and stout as a beech tree, to come through snowdrifts to see me on such a trifling matter. You'll not follow old Wulfstan for a score of years.'

Anselm shook his head. 'I mean I must take my leave of your realm. I must go to Rome.'

'To Rome. Now you surprise me even more. Why to Rome?'

'I must go and receive my pallium from His Holiness, Your Grace. Another trifling matter, you'd say, but not so to me, or to Rome. I must have it within a year of my installation, or I may be deprived of my office, as you know, my lord. The year will soon be at an end.'

Rufus sucked at a tooth. 'His Holiness the Pope. Which Holiness did you have it in mind to go to?'

Anselm frowned at the offhand tone. 'Why, to the true Pope, the one acknowledged in every Christian realm but this one and the German kingdoms. I mean Pope Urban the Second.'

'You prefer him to this other – what's his name – Clement?' The king still wore a half smile.

Anselm said: 'God preferred him, my lord. He elected him. The Germans elected Clement.' His chin came up, in the manner of thick-sighted people who cannot seem to see straight on. I could see this would end in a bitter quarrel in a moment, which didn't concern me for Anselm's sake, but I was concerned for what the king might say in haste. No pope had been acknowledged in England since the days of Gregory. I didn't want anger to force a hasty choice on the king now.

'My lord of Canterbury,' I said, 'you are no less an archbishop for the lack of a woolen band to lay across your shoulders, but if want of one distresses you, we can have a pallium made for you before the Easter Court.'

'And I'll invest you with it myself,' said the king, looking the least bit relieved.

'No!' cried Anselm. 'You know right well that would be irregular, Your Grace. I must have it of the Pope – the true, elected Pope – who is the only one who may bestow it upon an archbishop!'

I said: 'Your Grace, with all respect, only a Pope may bestow such a vestment, *unless* it is the custom that a king may do so in his place, which is the custom of this island.'

Baldwin put in his opinion: 'A custom not much honored, I think, Brother.'

'It may not be always observed, Brother, but it is nonetheless honored, and it would seem to be prudent to observe it now, as there are the two popes and the king has been wise enough to reserve judgment on their election until now. My lord of Canterbury believes he knows which is the true one, but only God in His wisdom could really tell us that, perhaps by striking one of them down. Is that not so, Brother?'

Anselm turned to me angrily. 'No, that is not so, Ranulph Flambard, nor are you the man to dispute on it if it were! Your Grace, I am not deceived by this pretended argument of your sycophant. I know why you hesitate to recognize Urban, but that is neither here nor there to my purpose. I have fasted and prayed over this matter and consulted with others who are wiser than myself. You have made me an archbishop when I never wanted to be one. But now I am one, and I must do my duty. That duty must begin with acknowledging the spiritual sovereign who stands vicar to

Christ Himself for all men on Earth, which is Pope Urban. If I may not perform my first duty, how shall I perform the rest? What am I, then, but a monk out of his cloister?'

The king had grown severe. 'What are you, my lord? I s-say, you are the Archbishop of Canterbury of the Kingdom of the English, and I am your sovereign, and theirs. Let me show some truth to you, my lord: in my f-father's t-time, no man might so much as name another man "pope" without he wished it, let alone run over the sea to k-kiss his feet! My father was a religious man, but he kept this p-privilege s-sacred to himself, that the rule of his kingdom not be divided between p-popes and kings. Now I am king and I must rule. If I let you take my privilege from me, to do as you like, I'm no king. It's the same as if you took my crown. Do you understand me, my lord?'

'I understand you. You are a young man in the power of his pride. But even kings must take counsel when it is good, and even strong men must yield to reason. Listen to my reason, my lord. Let me serve my conscience in this matter, that I may the better serve yours. I went to Urban when he was first elected and acknowledged him. I ask only to do what I have done before. I need this good and holy man; I need his wisdom, his comfort, his advice. My spirit needs him, calls for him, thirsts for him. If I must have his counsel, I cannot deny his rule.'

I said: 'But, my lord, you can, easily. It's simple: when you first submitted to your friend, you were your own man, so far as any man ever is. Now you're the king's man.'

Anselm tore his gaze from the king to regard me with burning eyes and compressed mouth. He stretched forth his hand, trembling, and said: 'I warn you, it will cost you dear if you speak to me again without my leave, no matter who your master is. Think on it and be silent!'

His clerks smirked with satisfaction. The king looked at me slantwise, as if to see whether I would defy the warning. I kept silent, having said all I deemed necessary to inform the king of how best to answer. Anselm might delight in humiliating me, as I would in ruining him, if it were in my power to do so. He had the power to do worse, and not even a king could gainsay him.

Rufus, having surveyed my face and smiled slightly at my silence, turned to Anselm.

'Archbishop, you must pardon my priest's zeal. He's paid to keep me in mind of the laws by which I rule. Though what he says offends you, it's common knowledge – even to me.' He cast his eye at me briefly once more. 'Anselm, did you come to me last year to be invested? Did you kneel before me, put your hands between mine, and pledge yourself to me? Or was that a dream?'

'Yes, I pledged myself, but as a man – '

'Yes! *But* as a *man*! Are you anything more? I'm a king, and I'm not. I keep my vows; do you? How many masters will you have, my lord? Or is it that you'd have none, now your staff is in your hand? Is this your famous humility? Before you swore to me, you swore a like vow to my brother, I think. He released you from it, to come to me. Now my brother is my enemy. Will you tell me he's your friend? This Pope is a stranger to me; will you make him your gossip?'

'My lord – '

'How many vows do you have in your heart, eh? What will any man believe of you if you make them and break them so easily? Where's the honor in such vowing, when it can be set aside between a priest and his king? Is honor known to you, priest? I hear you came of a good family. Do they speak of honor in Italy?'

Anselm stared at him. They locked stares, the king breathing heavily, the archbishop grim and pale. Anselm said in a husky voice: 'We speak of honor, my lord. To have it is to keep the soul clean. King William, if I may not go to Rome with your blessing and in my office, I must go without either. I will give up my staff and ring and depart from your realm a private man.'

Rufus leaped out of his chair and yelled: 'You will do no such thing without my leave, by the Face! Try it, and see how far you go!'

Another silence, but a brief one. Anselm drew himself up and folded his arms. 'If I may not go, I must have counsel. This you will not deny me again. Call your wise men, King of the English, and set them between us to hear which is right.'

'Call them, then, by God!' cried the king. 'Call whomever you like. Do you think I'm afraid to hear 'em? Your philosophy won't help you with them, Anselm, because they know who rules them and who keeps them, even if you don't. Call all the saints out of their graves and you won't find an advocate!'

Anselm bowed his head, then turned away. When he was out of the hall, the king grabbed up his cup and threw it against the wall. 'God damn all priests to Hell!'

When he was calmer, I spoke to him in the privacy of his bedchamber when his servants had left us alone:

'May I say a thing to you that you won't like but must consider?'

He said sourly: 'Has your tongue come back to you? I thought it had gone on a pilgrimage down your throat. Say on, then. I won't bite.'

'He's got you in a forked stick. When he's had his council, no matter how they see the argument, he'll have forced you to a choice between Urban and Clement.'

'How do you see that?'

'Because he means to make that one of the chief arguments, not merely the matter of whether he may go to Rome. In the end you will have chosen, or seem to have chosen, simply by rebutting him. Would you choose with the Germans, if you must make a choice?'

He snorted. 'I wouldn't make it. The Devil himself could wear the triple crown for all I care. I wish my uncle Odo had gotten his wish and won it, by God. No, I don't mean to choose the German's puppet. Why should I?'

'Exactly, my lord. All France and Normandy, too, have chosen Urban. Now you mean to win Normandy from your brother. When you do, it would be troublesome for you to deny Urban on one side of your realm and deal with him on the other. There are some of your subjects here, and some soon to be on the other side of the water, who might make unwise alliances if you denied them their Pope whom they've already chosen. The logical thing, then, is to choose Urban of your own accord, if a choice is to be made.'

'Then Anselm wins without a fight! Whose advocate are you, anyway?' But I could see he was thinking about it.

'Not his, believe me, Your Grace. If I had my wish he'd go out of England tomorrow and spend the rest of his life begging to get back in. But I am your advocate in this, and for you I would kiss him on both cheeks. What I say is that you must take the making of a choice from him. Send to Urban and tell him you're prepared to acknowledge him if he sends the archbishop's pallium to you, to put on Anselm's shoulders. You'll have to send money with the offer, naturally, but only so much as Peter's Pence for the year, and that I can get without any trouble to you, from the Church, which owes it. Peter's Pence should be worth a pallium – and owning to a Pope who's far away would be a small price to pay for defeating this archbishop who wants to rule you.'

He considered it, scratching his ear. It smelled of defeat to him.

I said: 'It's as when you sacrifice a pawn to take a larger piece on the game board.' I waited. 'If you don't like that sacrifice, you might say to Urban that you'll acknowledge him if he takes Anselm off his throne. He can afford that. He has more archbishops than he can count, even dividing them up with Clement. He can find some irregularity in the installation. If he can't, I can supply one: Anselm refused to open his hand when you offered him the staff. It was forced on him. No priest may be ordained against his conscience, and certainly no archbishop may be elected without his consent. Anselm himself has said he is not fit for the office, and God may well believe him. Tell Urban your terms and you'll be free to choose a man more to your liking. You may say this one was thrust on you when you were near death. Your consent was no more freely given than his. Your conscience has troubled you that you took him ever since.'

He nodded slowly. 'Yes, by God. It was, and it has.' He slapped his thigh in decision. 'Yes, do it! Pick your envoys and send them. We'll have this council he wants and say nothing about the sending. Let him make his speeches as he likes, because I'm in the right there, and I'm going to make him know it. Meantime' – he laughed suddenly – 'Carileph would like to know about this, wouldn't he? He'd walk over his own grave to get to Canterbury. He'll be my advocate for this fight, and if he does well by me, he may get his wish. Pick your men and send them to Rome!'

Victory is always something of a mixed blessing. Would I be the man who would rid him of Anselm, yet he would reward Carileph for it? Well, I had tried serving Carileph before, and I could, if I must, do it again. He had learned caution from his own disgrace and exile, though I felt he was at heart the same old spying rascal I had known in Rouen. But if a man must grovel before another, as it seemed I always must, I preferred a rascal to the Holy Fool.

The council met at Rockingham on the borders of Northampton-shire, a fortnight before Easter. Rufus had chosen the place, partly because it was one of his father's favored hunting towers which he was having strengthened into a proper castle and had not had the leisure to inspect recently; partly because it was secluded, at the edge of the great forest that bears its name, and only the royal troops would be allowed to garrison it or come near it. The king's mind in these matters was of a more defensive kind since before he went into Normandy. Now and after, he secured himself prudently when he met with his barons.

Rockingham is no equal to other royal towers for size. It barely contained the men who came to it then. The king and his chief counselors sat apart from the rest in the castle chapel, while the multitude crowded into the hall below. Anselm addressed both groups from the gallery that ran outside the chapel and above the hall, but those below could hear little of what he said, as he spoke in his usual low, half-distracted way without regard to his hearers and often had to be asked to repeat some phrase. Those below couldn't hope to hear the argument, though they were informed of the main tenets of the dispute at the outset: Anselm had asked leave of the king to go to Rome and personally acknowledge Pope Urban in return for his pallium. The king had denied him this, saying it was the same as if he took his crown from him. The king's argument was that Anselm could not swear faith and obedience to him and to a foreign master at once. It was on this point in particular that the assembly had convened to give judgment.

Anselm put it another way: could he not keep his plighted faith to the king and his obedience to the Pope without a breach of either? It was a good question for rhetorical debate, but a poor one to put to royal council.

He seemed to have some sense of this, but he tried to get around it by inviting the bishops and abbots to be his advocates, to give him advice on how to act in this matter. They were not such fools as to do that. They knew where their own interests lay, even if Carileph weren't there to remind them.

I had been content to leave the gallery to Anselm and Carileph and go down into the hall where I could mingle with the multitude. I didn't need to tell such men as Thomas of York what to think. He was pleased to see Canterbury in a struggle with the Crown. So was Maurice, and so were many of the bishops of the southern see whom Anselm had reprimanded for their worldliness. Even his best friend, Gundulph, refused to aid him openly in defying the king.

When it came time for them to speak, the churchmen of England told the archbishop it was his first duty to throw himself wholly on the king's will and mercy; then they would give him their advice. If he made reservations in his loyalty, if he pleaded any call on behalf of God to do anything against the king's will, they could give him no help at all. They, too, sought to obey the will of God, but the will of God in England was that the king should be obeyed. Good, sensible Normans, all.

Anselm then made the same speech he had made to the king. If they could not give him the answer he desired, he would take himself to Rome.

'I gladly render unto Caesar that which Christ bade me, but I must also render unto the Throne of Peter that which Christ bade me.' The hall was quiet for a moment.

Carileph said quickly: 'My lord Archbishop, the question here is not whether you should render obedience to God before you render it to the king, but whether you should render it to this man named Urban.'

I could have laughed aloud to hear him say that, who six years before had stood before just such a council wih a similar plea to go to Rome over the king's head for his judgment. Odo had made the same plea. If Anselm had been blessed with any common sense, he could have made the whole council laugh at Carileph for remembrance of his folly. But he hadn't that sense, or he was too unworldly to make use of it. Like the weak old ram he had once called himself, he stubbornly insisted that his brothers of the Church must give him advice on how to serve two unreconciled masters, while they refused to be drawn into his troubles.

They would not aid him, yet they would hear more argument. They heard much more; for four days the battle raged, swaying now toward the king and his advocate, Carileph, who cried out like an aggrieved fishwife:

'Hear the complaint of the king against you! He says that, so far as lies in your power, you have robbed him of his dignity by making Odo, Bishop of Ostia, Pope in his England without his bidding! Now you devise arguments to prove that that robbery was just.' He bellowed this so fiercely that there was a little ripple of laughter from those who both saw and heard him. His purple wattles shook as he shouted; even Anselm ventured a dry smile. Carileph glared at him.

'Do not think that all this is a mere joke, my lord! We are driven on by the pricks of a heavy grievance. For that which your lord and ours claims is the chief thing in his dominion, in which it is allowed that he surpasses all other kings, that you take away from him, insofar as it is in your power, and by taking it away you throw scorn upon the oath by which you have sworn – fealty – to him.'

The king frowned at this, I was told, and asked under his breath: 'What in all the Devil's names is he talking about? Why can't he say it straight?'

Anselm answered: 'If there is any man who wishes to prove that because I will not give up my obedience toward the chief Pontiff of the Holy Roman Church, I thereby break the faith I owe to my earthly king, let him stand forth and he will find me ready to answer him as I ought.'

Rufus burst out: 'By God, there's enough of talk! Let the council do its business. I leave you to it, and s-so you won't mistake me, I tell you this: I withdraw all protection from the archbishop which he earns from his vows to me. Let him be free of me and I will be f-free of him!' He rose, pushed his way through the close-packed lords, and went up to the battlements.

I found him there a half hour later, pacing like an impatient sergeant.

'Well, what are they saying now?' he asked with a sharp laugh, seeing me.

'You've given them a fright. They think you mean to declare war on the archbishop.'

'And so I would, if the old fool knew how to fight. It would be w-wonderful, wouldn't it, if we could end all this with a melee down in the yard?' He stopped to lean over the battlements. 'Can't you see it? All the shave-pates on one side with their staves and crooks and me on the other, with a sword. Something sent you up here.'

'A truce is mentioned, until the Octave of Pentecost.'

'A truce? With hostages on both sides?'

I smiled. 'My people will have returned from Rome by then, with the pallium – or a bull for his dismissal.'

'I'll stifle if I have to sit in that chapel another day. It begins to smell like a whore's crotch. What does Anselm say?'

'He's still trying to get someone to tell him what to do, but I think he'll agree to it, if you restore your protection.'

He snorted. 'I'll restore it – to *him*. Not to that Flemish cock-robin – that Baldwin. I want him out of my country in ten days. I may have to put up with the old f-fool for the sake of an oath, but I don't have to put up with that officious bastard.'

Baldwin was sent out of the country, along with two of his clerks. This gave Anselm grief, because Baldwin was the mainstay of his household, but he seemed relieved for the truce and went home to Canterbury, though still lamenting he must go to Rome. Like a child who is denied what it cries for, he could only repeat:

'The king has power over me. He says what he pleases. But if he refuses me now, he may agree at a later time. I will go on asking.'

He didn't come to the Easter Court to ask again, however, nor would the answer have been different. My envoys to Rome were not yet returned, but I had confidence their mission would succeed, because of the men they were. Gerard le Gros and my own clerk, William Warelwast, were the men. Should it seem strange that I chose Gerard to go, when he was the chancellor and my nominal master? Not so strange.

There was no man in England better fitted for a mission to Rome. Gerard had great patience for waiting, a courteous and facile tongue when he was allowed to use it, and a vast hunger for the beauties and antiquities of Rome. My prudent clerk Warelwast was in charge of their purse, to see that Gerard didn't spend on rare books and relics what I had so quickly and painfully (to some) amassed for gentle bribery.

Robert Mowbray, Earl of Northumbria, though he had presented himself at the council of Rockingham, chose to be absent from the Easter Court. He sent no excuse, no deputy, no coin. I began to dream of treachery again. The king was grim and sent command he must come to the Whitsun Court at Gloucester with good reason for his truancy, or risk the loss of royal favor and protection, which would mean a war of swords and battles, not of mere words.

There was a fall of stars just after Easter when we were still at Winchester. They fell not by ones and twos as in past seasons, but in such quick succession that they could not be counted. The watch roused us from sleep half in terror to witness them. I was at my house that night, for the first time since Giva's death. We put on our clothes and went out into the street to stare at the marvel.

Like cold-fire struck from a smith's anvil, the stars appeared where before they were not, flamed, and fell swiftly into darkness out of a silent sky until it seemed all Heaven must be emptied.

Swan sobbed against Osbern's breast, asking: 'Is it the end of the world? Are they angels?'

'Shut up, you stupid girl,' said my mother. 'You'll frighten the children.' She gathered my twin sons to her, as they were whimpering. 'There are better signs than this for God's Coming. This is a sign for the king, that he'll have his victory over his enemies.' She said it for my benefit, as she knew little of the king and even less of his enemies, my loyal mother. Yet she was right. He had his victory, but in a way he hadn't dreamed.

54

'Does that whore's bastard Mowbray think he's dealing with my brother?' asked the king in a voice of brass. 'Does he think I'll sit and pick my nose while he defies me? B-by the Face! I'm the injured party here, and yet he wants hostages!'

He turned an angry eye about the council chamber, letting it dwell on each man in turn until he came to Bishop William de St. Carileph.

'By God, Will Carileph, he puts me in mind of you in 'eighty-eight, with his demands and wishes. What is it about the air in the north that makes you all so bold? What's he about? Eh?'

Carileph twitched and wiped at his veined nose nervously. 'Your Grace, I – I – cannot say. Earl Robert isn't in my – I mean, I'm not in his confidence. He's always been a rash man.'

'Rash?' The king brayed an angry laugh. 'Enough to take your counsel before he did this thing?'

'Your Grace, never mine! I assure you!'

'No? I've got a man in the hall today who says he saw Mowbray in your town after you left Rockingham. What was he doing there?'

'We were companions on the road home, nothing more.'

'He was your guest for three days in that fi-fine castle you once fortified against me when I sent for you and you wouldn't come except I s-sent hostages, Bishop.'

'My lord, he rested with me for a little time, because the rains had made the roads so bad. But we took no counsel of each other for any reason. We scarcely even spoke, save at meals, and then only of his hounds and his hunting. He was never a talker, you know, my lord.'

Poor Carileph! If he'd had a tail, he'd have wagged it. My heart rejoiced to see him squirm. He cast about for some support from his peers, but the bishops were silent; none was his friend. The lay lords of the council sat as if they were about to pronounce judgment on him. Suddenly he blurted:

'My lord the Count of Eu can testify that we plotted nothing together. He was at my hall, too. He rode with Earl Robert from Rockingham.'

William of Eu crossed his legs and smoothed his richly embroidered tunic over his thigh, smiling slightly as the king turned to regard him.

'It's true, I rode with Mowbray as far as Durham. I had some goods to collect from a ship at Tynemouth: Norwegian furs for my lady wife.' He smiled at Earl Hugh of Chester, who was his brother-in-law. 'I stayed the night at Durham and heard no treason spoke. I don't think Mowbray is a traitor, Your Grace. He's done a stupid thing, but it's his pride that's made him defy you. Have patience with him, send to him again; no doubt he'll come down to you. He's only just taken a wife. Why should he want to brew up a battle now?'

So he soothed the king, this golden-bearded cousin of his, this cock among the hens who was said to have three mistresses at a time to cool his lust, in spite of a docile and loving wife. Yet he spoke as a traitor, though he had been the innermost friend and adviser of the king for the year past. As soon as the Whitsun Court was done, he went home and fortified himself and made ready to betray the king. So did his friends and allies in old treacheries, Gilbert of Clare, Roger de Lacy, and others. These were the men who had been forgiven after the revolt of 'eighty-eight, who now planned King William's undoing again.

There was another of them I suspected, though he made no overt moves, but neither did he lend aid to the king as he had in 'eighty-eight. The Earl of Chester, Hugh the Wolf, who had come to England so mysteriously with Prince Henry, took himself off after Whitsuntide and didn't answer the king's call later in the year, pretending he had troubles with the Welsh.

For the moment, Rufus grudgingly took heed of William de Eu and sent another message to Robert Mowbray, requiring his presence without exchange of hostages or assurances beyond the king's sworn word that he could come and go in safety. Mowbray's scorn of his word offended Rufus more than his defiance, but he restrained himself from vengeance and sent one more letter of command.

Meanwhile, my couriers to Pope Urban had returned. Gerard never got to see Rome after all, it seemed. Urban had only the most tenuous grasp on that ancient city. He met Gerard and Warelwast at a place in the north of Italy called Piacenza, where he had called a council to condemn the heresy of Berengar of Tours, who denied the Real Presence in the Holy Sacrament.

He heard Gerard's plea and seemed to accede to it, even without the offer of a bribe. The blessed pallium should be sent home to England with them, but in the care of a papal legate, one Walter of Albano.

Cardinal Walter came through Canterbury with Gerard and Warelwast without stopping to speak to Anselm so much as a word. I sent him rich gifts in the king's name, which he did not refuse. He came to Gloucester, meek and full of smiles, to speak to the king – or rather to speak before the king. Being an Italian, he couldn't speak directly to him, but through me, and in Latin.

Much flattery was exchanged on both sides before we got down to business. Did the king wish to acknowledge Pope Urban as the true Vicar of Christ and his spiritual father? I translated this for the king, who said:

'Tell him I'll call him Pope, or anything else he likes, so long as he lets me be. Did he bring the damned pallium?'

'His Grace rejoices,' I put into Latin, 'to acknowledge Pope Urban as the True Shepherd of all Christians, but he must have assurance His Holiness remembers the ancient rights of the anointed kings of the English to be the stewards for Christ and His Church in this land, since the days of Augustine.'

'Did he say so much? It's an economic tongue,' said Walter, affecting surprise.

I smiled. 'He has already indicated his chief concerns to me beforehand, my lord Cardinal.'

He nodded. 'I believe I understand his concerns, my – I don't know your title, brother in Christ.'

'I am the king's chaplain.'

'Only that?'

'Only that, my lord.'

'I see. Well, my son, you may tell the king that the English kings have never been looked on in Rome as having legatine powers, but I can assure His Grace that no legate of His Holiness will ever be sent to England but at his choice. Now, there should be some proclamation made to the people that the king has acknowledged His Holiness as the true Pope. And after that I had hoped we might discuss the matter of the Romescot, or Peter's Pence, as your courier has called the revenues your king and his late father have so long withheld from the Holy See.'

'Has he got it with him – the pallium – or not?' Rufus asked again. 'Let's be done with this Latin jabber, can't we?'

'His Grace has expressed a desire to see the pallium before we go into the matter of the Romescot.'

'The pallium is in my baggage, which is being guarded by two of my own clerks. Have no fear for it; it is quite safe. Is Archbishop Anselm here? I had hoped to speak to him in the presence of the king, to reconcile them, if I may, before I bestow the Pope's gift on his worthy archbishop.'

'What's he saying now?' asked the king.

'He says he's the one who's going to put the pallium on Anselm. My lord, this may be a long wrangle. May I call for wine and some stools?'

He gave assent, I gave orders, and in a few minutes we sat down to it. It was a long wrangle, and the infamous Italian proved to be a master of deception. He had no French, and I no Italian, but when it pleased him to do so, he would suddenly find difficulty understanding my Latin as well. However he was pressed to consent to the king's presenting the pallium to Anselm, he managed to avoid it, giving instead yet another assurance that the king should find no difficulty with Rome on the matter of legatine visits. Again and again he returned to the proclamation we should draft, affirming the king's acceptance of Urban as Pope.

After several hours of this, the king angrily called for parchment and ink, and at Cardinal Walter's dictation, with a confusing number of counter-demands from the king, I wrote the proclamation. It was witnessed and sealed, then sent to be copied by my clerks. We all retired for the night, relieved and glad to be finished with one another for a while.

In the morning the cardinal seemed extraordinarily cheerful, having gotten a copy of the proclamation in his grasp. But when I once again attempted to take up the subject of the bestowal of the pallium by the king, he turned adamant. Under no circumstances might the king, a mere layman, put the blessed vestment over Anselm's shoulders. Only a Pope might do that for an archbishop, a Pope, or his appointed legate.

I could have strangled the man. He had come with his hand stretched out for our favors, taken them freely, smiled and nodded at every suggestion, and now he would not allow that very act for which he had been so generously endowed.

I hammered away at him until I was tongue-weary. Gerard, who did speak some little Italian, was called in to make certain he understood the king's demand and the reasons for it, but all to no avail. He smiled coldly and shook his head.

Rufus had long since left his chair to pace the chamber as we contended with each other, but at last he stopped in front of the cardinal, who made as if to rise from his stool but was prevented by one of the king's hands on his shoulder.

'Tell him this and let him chew on it: it'll be a cold night in Hell before he sees Italy again, unless he gives me my desire.' He turned and stalked out of the room.

I relayed the message faithfully to Walter, who started to smile until the full force of the threat crept upon him, then frowned, rose, and left me, beckoning his clerks to follow him.

He came at me an hour later when I went into the chapel for first service. The king was not present; he had gone hawking.

'Your master neglects his prayers, but he is more honest than you. How do you dare to come here to pray when you have threatened a servant of God and His Holiness?'

'You mistake me, Excellence. I was merely the interpreter. Nor did my king threaten you. He told you a simple truth. There'll be no going forth from here until you've rightly finished the business you've so badly begun, which is to make a friend of Urban's out of the King of the English.'

'My business is to receive the homage due to His Holiness from the King of the English and to bestow a pallium on a worthy servant.'

'I beg your pardon, my lord Cardinal, but were you not sent to bring home Peter's Pence as well? It hasn't been paid for several years now; it would amount to a good deal for a Pope who's barely got a roof over his head, let alone his foot in the door of St. Peter's. Well, you won't get the Romescot, my illustrious lord, and I doubt that you'd like to go home without it, so give over your notions that the king has threatened you. You will simply stay with us until we're all in accord – and the king will never be in accord with such miserable terms as you've given him. He would better like it if you'd done as he first asked of your Pope: dethrone Anselm and allow him to name a candidate more to his liking. You've heard how he was forced to choose him when he was out of his head with pain. What profit to him now, if you set this arrogant old man beyond his reach, after all he's offered you?'

'His profit is that he is reconciled to God and His Church again, after his wrongful neglect. That should be enough!'

'That would be a very foolish thing to say to King William of the English, if you'll take my advice for it. Let us go into the chapel now and pray that you think of something better.'

He wished to speak to Anselm. One could not deny him this, or imprison him. He was sent to Canterbury with an honorable guard, and the king, I regret to say, forgot about him almost on the instant of his leaving, so enraptured was he by the smell of revolt in the north.

Anselm fell on Cardinal Walter's neck when he arrived, I'm told, but their love didn't flourish much beyond the greetings. Anselm has never been free with his affections, except to those sycophants who pretend to his own severity, and the cardinal, whatever his personal chastity, was a worldly man. No doubt he tried my reasons on the archbishop, or some he had thought of along the way. But Anselm would never accept the pallium from the king, even at the insistence of the cardinal legate. He said he would rather give up his office and go abroad to a cloister again. There, at last, was a point on which my enemy and I were in complete agreement.

At last it came to this: the king would take part in the ceremony of the pallium, but he would not personally present the garment to Anselm. He received it from Walter of Albano in privacy, laid it in a silver casket, then returned it to him, in the full view of his chief councilors. The cardinal took it to Christ Church and laid it upon the altar, from which the archbishop took it with his own hands and put it on himself, with no aid but that of his suffragans.

Anselm had previously refused a reasonable request (from me) that he show his gratitude to the king for the trouble he had endured to bring the pallium overseas by paying a trifling sum for the privilege. He refused, saying:

'I will not dishonor the friendship of my lord and king by treating it as if it might be something that could be bought – or sold.'

He was riding high indeed. My enemies must have rejoiced to see me defeated. Only a miracle could rid me of him now. I had little to take heart in but a certain bitter omen, which was in the reading of the Gospel on the day of Anselm's triumph. Those who were in Christ's Church that day heard the tale told by St. Matthew of the king who made a marriage for his son and sent forth his servants to invite guests to the feast. But those who were invited made light of the summons, even dishonored the servants who had been sent to them.

Therefore the king sent again of his servants, to the highways and byways, to find such guests as they might, both bad and good. And when he came in to see his guests and found a man who would not wear a wedding garment, he had him cast out for his ingratitude, for many may be called (to the friendship of a king), but few are chosen.

I returned to London with the king, who was now of a mind to call up his levies and deal justly with the defiant Mowbray. He had spread his feast of peace in the realm, but his ungrateful subjects made excuse and betrayed him. Earl Hugh lingered at home and delayed to come to him; Gilbert of Clare came, pale and nervous, but with little heart for battle; Roger de Lacy spoke of yet more temperance and patience with the surly Mowbray. All in the barons' council were of such kind, except Robert fitz Hamon and Robert de Meulan. Even William de Eu, who had urged the king to do battle with his own brother for Normandy, now seemed mild in his speech.

When I ventured to uphold the king's honor in the hall, I was told I was urging him to act against his better nature.

'That is ridiculous,' I said to the man who made the observation, who was Gilbert of Clare. 'The king's better nature has been abused – and by men who have betrayed and abused him before and received pardon when they should have been sent into exile, or to the headsman, like Earl Waltheof when he betrayed another William who had befriended him. Now, *there* was a good lesson in headings, which His Grace would do well to remember.'

That was a rash speech for a man of my station to make to a man of Gilbert's. He was one of those former traitors who had been absolved. 'No doubt you will remind him of it.'

'No doubt I will, if he needs the remembrance,' I said, which may have led to what followed shortly thereafter, or so I have always believed.

I was at Westminster, goading my stonemasons to make better use of the fair weather, in order to please the king with their progress when he came to inspect it the following week. Rufus was at Windsor hunting and there had been little enough of fair weather that year. Dismal rains had swept us; high winds shook the fruit from the trees and broke the stalks of grain, making dangerous the work of my masons on their scaffolds. There was certainty of another famine if the sun didn't come to our rescue soon. All things in the whim of man and the power of Nature seemed to conspire to make my life difficult in that season. Not the least of my irritations on that particular day was that the king had left Martin with me to be my courier to him if there was need, and Martin was sulking grandly for it.

As we left the foundations of the new palace and walked toward the old queen's dower house where I was staying, I took the opportunity to chide him with neglect of his mother, a charge that he had heard too often and was becoming hardened to.

He shrugged at my suggestion he visit her that day, saying: 'Why should I go to her? She doesn't lack for company.' By which he meant me.

'She's your mother. She loves you, which is a continuing astonishment to those who know you, but there it is. Go and spend a quarter of an hour with her. The angels will noise it all over Heaven and I'll give you a shilling for the deed.' I thought he'd want the shilling. The king kept him well clothed but penurious, like all his squires, as he himself had been kept.

To my surprise, Martin took fire at the suggestion of the silver. 'A shilling! You'd throw that to a beggar! I've seen you do it. If she wants to see me, let her pay for it.'

'What, pay for a duty she's entitled to? You *are* an ungrateful son. She's done all she can for you, getting you a place at court.'

'She didn't do that and you know it, Master Flambard! She only got herself there, for a time. She's keeping my inheritance for herself and pretending I have none.'

'You don't have any, Martin. You've been told how it is.'

'I've been told nothing but lies! She said my stepfather deeded her estate to the Church for taking my sister into the cloister. But I was born before my sister went there, so I should have been considered before her.'

I sighed. 'Your father had no property of his own to leave you. The estate was your mother's through her father – '

'What difference should that make? I'm her son! It's the son who inherits, not the daughter. I'm not a fool, priest! I'm the heir, even if she was whoring before she married my – ' He stopped, choked, and turned his face away.

So, then, he had come to it at last, that question of his paternity, which he might have doubted years before, if Isabel hadn't been such a competent liar. Should I speak to him now? I wondered.

There was a man coming toward us from the direction of the river. He hailed me. I recognized him as one of the rabble Isabel had hired for her servants in my house. His name was Jerrel, or Gerald; I could never remember which. He came toiling up to us, the mud of the river thick on his bare legs, a look of anxiety on his face.

'*Hlaford, hlaford!* You must come quick! They sent me to tell you!'

'What is it, man? Is your mistress ill?' I had visions of the house afire, Isabel fallen into an apoplexy, or some such calamity, but the man shook his head, waved his arms, and began to babble to me of *se biscop Moris* in his vile London accent.

'What does he say?' asked Martin, who had the grace to look a little perturbed by the possibility of harm to his mother.

'He says Bishop Maurice is ill and wants to speak to me. I thought he was at Fulham, but he must have come downriver this morning. Is he at the minster, then?' I asked Gerald, who nodded eagerly and beckoned me to follow him to the boat in which he'd come to take me.

I might have thought it strange that Maurice, suddenly afflicted, had sent one of my own servants to summon me to him, and by boat, when he might have had a rider out to Westminster in less time. But the familiarity of Gerald's face, the urgency of his appeal, and my own concern for old Maurice made me follow the man to the river's edge without questioning him further. I motioned to Martin to come with me.

Gerald saw this and shook his head. 'No, *hlaford*, he wants only you. Come, come quick!'

'This is the king's courier. If the Bishop of London is ill, the king may need to hear of it. You fool, why didn't you bring your boat into the hithe? It's a swamp here.'

We waded into the water. The river was at high tide, overrunning the muddy fields that spread between the river and the king's palace. I had thought it unwise to rebuild so close to the water, where every year the spring rains brought us perilously close to a flood, but the king would have his house no other place.

Lifting my skirts, I climbed laboriously into the boat, my legs slimy with river ooze. Martin followed, cursing for the ruin of his fine cuffed boots. Gerald took the oars and began to row us out into the channel.

A little way downstream I saw a larger vessel, not Maurice's familiar barge, as I might have expected, but a light ship of the Danish kind, with a square sail and eight oars to the side, useful for maneuvering shallow rivers and creeks. Such a ship seemed more suitable to pirates than to the Bishop of London, but still I suspected nothing. Maurice's servants, or mine, had panicked, hailed the first ship they saw in London harbor, and commandeered it to their service. Poor old Maurice must be near death, though he had seemed hale the last time I'd seen him. My only thoughts were of him, then, my first mentor in England, almost a second father to me, no matter our later differences.

I climbed aboard the ship when we came alongside it, then looked about for Maurice's clerk, his chamberlain, his steward – some face I should know. No one there was familiar, but the man who came toward me had an evil look in his eye. I turned to Martin, who was just about to come up over the rail.

'No, go back! There's something wrong – ' A fist clouted me on the head, Martin was dragged over the rail, our arms were seized and bound, and together we were thrown on the forward deck out of the way of the rowers, who immediately began pulling against the tide to take us downriver.

We passed London by. I'd thought we would. When we reached the bend in the river that hid London from view, the man I supposed was the master of the ship conferred with my erstwhile servant, Gerald, then sent him forward to loosen our bonds. Martin began to rail at him in a voice that cracked with anger and fear.

'You bloody, stupid English pig! What do you think you're about? I'm the king's man! You'll hang for touching me!' He might have saved his breath. Gerald had only enough French to understand 'Get out of my way!' and the captain didn't look as if he were much impressed with Martin's threat.

I sat up, rubbing my wrists to bring some life back into my hands. When I could feel them, I slipped off my seal ring, took my chain of office from my neck, and dropped both into the river.

Martin and Gerald were alike horrified.

'*Hlaford!* What do you do? We mean you no harm!'

'My God, priest! That's gold you threw into the river!'

Gerald made report of me to the captain, who came forward and squatted before me to look into my face. He understood me, if the others did not. After a moment he smiled and said in French that had all the vowel dimensions of Danish:

'My friend priest, you think we are thieves, but the river is the great thief. Now you have lost your treasure, but we mean you no harm. We take you to where you will be quite safe, I promise you. We do not kill priests.'

I said nothing. My blood was rapidly turning to river water, but I could not regret my action. Neither my ring seal, which was a miniature of the great royal seal, nor my chain of office would be used to make some false allegation to the king, or to draw him into any danger. I had as much fear for my life as any other man in such a circumstance, but I could not believe otherwise than that the reason for my capture was to lure the king to rescue me. My own life was of little consequence to any man – save myself – but to Rufus. I began to think who among his enemies would suppose my life or safety would be valuable enough to him, to stoop to my abduction.

Mowbray I thought of at once, naturally, but it wasn't his way. If he felt I was an inconvenience, he would merely have me murdered. Prince Henry? He would attempt to buy me first, as he bought the Cotentin. Earl Hugh, if he thought of me at all, would simply have me butchered in full sight of witnesses. A direct man, Hugh the Wolf. I could think of no one else. I looked at the ruffians who were rowing me to my doom. They were faceless, or might as well have been. Their captain stalked the narrow deck between the rowing benches, urging them to greater speed.

Martin said in a strangled voice: 'What in God's Name is this about? You seem to know. What are they after? Will they kill us, or hold us for ransom?'

'Do you have anything about you that could identify you?'

'No.'

I looked at him. He had a fine head of frizzled hair, made with a curling iron, but under the stress of the wind and the spray from the river even his curls were growing limp and might pass for anyone's. I smiled at him.

'Don't be afraid. They don't want you. When we've gone a bit farther I'll try to make them see they should let you go. But it'll be a long walk back to London.'

He was offended – and curious. 'What makes you think it's you they want? What are you worth?'

'Nothing, now – I hope. In time they may see that.'

'Then what will they do with you?'

I didn't answer. I thought they must kill me if they could find no way to make use of me.

The outgoing tide caught us and carried us along, with the help of a light breeze. The rowers shipped their oars and rested. Food was brought and offered to us. Martin refused it. I ate the hard bread and drank the sour wine, which seemed to meet with the approval of the captain, who came and sat beside me for a time to gnaw a crust of his own.

'Are you taking me overseas?'

He laughed. 'You will know the place when you come to it. They say you're a great man of your king's and know every part of his land, here and over there.' He looked at me, half curious to have that confirmed.

I said, 'What is your name?'

He laughed.

'What is your profession? Are you rich enough to suit yourself?'

'I am a thief, like you, master. We thieves are never rich enough, are we?'

'I will give you gold to let me go free.'

'Some other will give me gold to take you to him.'

'How much?'

'How much do you offer?'

I named a sum I could well afford, and when he smiled and shook his head, I doubled it without pause. That gave him something to meditate on. He preferred to do it away from me, however. Martin came and sat by me as soon as he was gone.

'Did you ask him? To let me go free?'

'We haven't come to that part of the bargaining yet.'

'Well, when will you?'

'What will you do when you're free, Martin, supposing they agree to let you go?'

'Get a horse, somehow; ride to the king; tell him what's happened.'

'Good for you. I'll be gone by then, in the water, or in the ground. Will you say a prayer for me, Martin – after? Will you take care for your mother when I'm not there to goad you to it?'

He folded his arms, looking stark and grim. 'Don't talk nonsense. They won't hurt you. They want you for ransom. They'll send word to the king and he'll pay it. He's fond of you.'

'Yes, I think he is. But it won't suffice. You heard me, just now, offer what would ransom a noble to that sea captain. He had to think about the offer. That means he's been offered nearly as much by someone else. If that someone pays so much for me, will he profit merely by sending to the king for another ransom? I don't think so. I think the man who's willing to pay so much for me means to kill me, don't you?'

He was taken with a fit of shudders. The sun was setting now, and the cool wind that sprang up afresh after the sultriness of the day made our moist flesh seem clammy. The trees on both sides of the river swayed gravely in that breeze and the sail puffed. I studied either bank of the river. There was nothing to be seen but trees and some hint of a swell of land to the steerboard side, which might be Kent. I couldn't remember how far one might come from Westminster in half a day's time. I had never had to reckon such distance before.

The light was failing rapidly. Despite the breeze, the oarsmen were stroking the water again, slowly and evenly. I leaned back against the side of the ship, trying to find a place between cleats and ropes to make myself comfortable. I said to Martin:

'Come and sit by me. We'll keep each other warm when the sun's gone.'

But he wrapped his short cloak closer about him and hunched alone on the other side of the bow. After a time of watching him, I slept.

55

When I woke we were on the open sea and it was nearly dawn; or, at least, there was a lighter streak of sky showing beneath the heavy bars of clouds to the east. The ship was shuddering under a heavy wind, the kind that had wracked our fields and orchards so ruinously that year. The sailors were howling prayers as they pulled their oars; their captain was cursing both them and the wind. Martin sat close by me, his face pinched with fear. I put my arm about him and began to pray.

Presently there was a dispute between the captain and my servant, Gerald. I saw them stand by the mast, their hair and mantelets torn by the storm, their mouths agape. But it was more by the attitude of their bodies and the sharp gestures of their hands that I told their quarrel, for their voices were torn away by the winds. Martin was watching, too. He crept closer, put his mouth to my ear, and cried, 'They want to kill us!'

I lifted my cloak to shield us from the sting of the lashing water. Martin cowered under it. Poor lad, he was shuddering with the wet and with a most sensible fear. I cradled him in my arms, glad for the chance, despite the occasion. He was only just a few months past fifteen. He had thought himself a man, able to face anything fate might offer – anything but a cold and murky death a hundred miles removed from honor or the glory of battle.

The sailors keened like women at the size of the waves. Gerald came crawling forward to us, having finished with plotting our death, and crouched at our feet with his head against my knee, like a repentant hound. The ship began to plunge into trough after trough of heavy water.

We would soon drown or, if we didn't, the captain meant to kill us. There was no hope for me, no hope for my son, cradled in my arms. The storm and the fear must have addled my brains, for in that moment I thought only of telling him who I was. It seemed the most necessary thing for me to do. I left off praying and began to shout:

'Martin, Martin, forgive me for neglecting you! I've wanted you by me from the day you were born! If we live through this, I'll show you my love! I'm your father!'

He jerked back from me. At the same moment we rode high on the crest of a wave. There was a great cracking sound as he cried: 'What? You're lying!' At the same moment there was a scream from astern. The ship dropped and the sea roared over us again.

'I'm your father!'

'No! Liar!'

'Listen to me, before it's too late. Forgive – if you can – no matter, it's true!'

'Liar!'

We plunged again. The steering oar had broken and the steersman was thrown by it, or swept away by the water that roared over us a moment later. Some of the shrouds broke with sounds like those of immense harp strings. The mast began to sway and the sail to swing wildly, its yard crushing the sailors who leaped to secure it.

'I knew your mother before you were born – before she was widowed the first time!' I still tried to hold on to him, but he was fighting me furiously.

'Liar! Liar! You're not! My father was Amiot – '

He tore free from me and tried to stand, but the lurch of the ship brought him down again. If I hadn't grabbed him, he would have followed the dead steersman overboard, but still he fought me. 'Lying priest! I'm not your bastard! Let me go!'

'Would I lie, now? Here? Boy, if we live – '

'I'll kill you! If we live!' He was above me; his face had a murderous look. He lifted his fist, but there was a sickening grinding and a fearful outcry from the sailors. The cruelly twisted mast had cracked and was carried, sail and yards, into the sea. The ship wallowed, nearly overturned; Martin was thrown back from me. Gerald had hold of my legs and was shrieking:

'God save us! God save us!'

I could only cling to whatever cleats and knots of rope were near and bellow in despair: 'Martin! Martin!'

When the squall blew itself out, we were left adrift in a heavy sea without rudder or sail, the crew exhausted. Half the oars had been stripped away. We were shipping so much water that we stood halfway to the top rails in the sea. Several of the crew lay dead; several had vanished along with the steersman. Those still capable of labor bailed water. I lay, half drowned, on the foredeck; Martin had gone astern where the captain forced him to lend a hand with the bailing. Overhead, the sky gave promise of a bright day.

The general opinion of the crew, according to Gerald, who now seemed permanently attached to me, was that I bore responsibility for the calamity, having stirred up the storm by my prayers. Some thought I'd won the whirlwind from the Devil; others thought God had so obliged me. As we floated at the mercy of the swelling sea, Gerald whispered to me:

'They want to throw you overboard, *hlaford*, before you do some other thing. The captain's half of a mind to heed them. Say something to him, or we'll all be drowned.'

I roused myself and sat up. My eyes, nose, throat, and lungs were burning with sea salt; my skin was caked with it. I studied the faces of the men as they worked. What Gerald feared was possible. The crew were ignorant men, some probably not even Christian. Only they knew what use they'd had for me when they took me, but now, with a broken ship, they must blame someone for their folly. Even if they didn't suspect me of sorcery, they'd want to be rid of me; they'd never make the harbor where I was to be a prize. As we were, I was only added weight.

'What's the captain's name, do you know?'

'Godric, *hlaford*. He's an Englishman, though he can't speak decently. From the north country, maybe. He's a hard man, but he may be better than the rest. They're all foreign, or Cornish, which is near as bad. I heard him say a prayer to the Blessed Virgin, but the rest of them only cursed God and you.'

'Go and ask Godric if he'll come speak to me.'

Gerald sidled away to the captain, who stared at me grimly before he gave his bucket to my servant and came slowly forward. There was a welt across his face like the mark of a scourge. One of the sail shrouds must have whipped him when it broke. He was lucky to have his right eye. I put on as calm a manner as I could muster and said:

'God has been merciful to us, Master Godric. We're alive.'

'Some would call it no mercy,' he answered sourly. 'Your dog has sharp ears, priest. Or was it the Devil who told you my name?'

'Do you believe I have special influence with him, captain?' I smiled, or tried to; my face was stiff with salt.

'My men think so. I'm a Christian, so I'll try to doubt it, but your yelling didn't sound like God-prayers to me.'

'I was frightened like the rest of you, but not so much as to forget where to direct my prayers.'

He rubbed his face. 'You know what my men think I should do with you now?'

'I can guess. That's why I wanted to speak to you. Have you given my offer better thought? It should seem fairer now. Unless you meant to deliver me to someone on the Kentish foreland, you aren't likely to reach your harbor. Those who wait to buy me will grow tired of waiting. You've lost your hire.'

He shifted his stance, glancing at his crew, then cocked his head to study me. 'You're a cool one, aren't you? You can sit up and talk of silver as soon as you've spat the sea out of your mouth. Maybe the Devil's got his hand on you, after all. None of what you offer will pay for the mending of my ship.'

'Is that what you want? You'll have it. You may have a new ship, if you like.'

He snorted. 'Just like that? You promise like a Dane, but where would a priest get so much treasure?'

'I can get it, believe me, if you'll only trust me.'

'Trust you! Now, there's the thing: why should you reward us when you're safe on land again? Why wouldn't you just tell your master what we've done and have him hang the lot of us instead?'

'I swear to you by all the saints in Heaven, by the Blessed Virgin, and by my own soul that I won't betray you if you save me from your men.' I held up my right hand to testify to that.

He stared at the hand.

'Godric,' I said, 'you're no murderer. I can read your soul in your face. You're wise to be cautious, but you don't want me on your conscience, or this innocent boy, or my servant, both of whom you'd have to slay if you slay me. Have you ever killed a man? I think not. You weren't always a pirate, either, were you? You're an honest sailor who thought he would earn a simple fee. You didn't bargain for murder; why should you think of it now, when there's no profit in it?'

He frowned. 'Say how you can pay me what you've promised. What's there for you to give me, now you've thrown your gold chain and ring away? I can't ask my men to follow you into some town for the coin. You'd set traps for us. They'd be right to kill me along with you, then.'

I saw he was inclined to let me lead him. I leaned forward eagerly.

'You're right, there is a problem to be solved, but our wits are equal to it. You must set me down near some town, if you can. The nearer Dover the better. I'll go to the town alone and I'll get the ransom, but I'll leave you a hostage.'

'A hostage? Who? This young peacock you've got with you? What value is he to you? He's the king's man, not yours. He told me that straight off, when I put a bucket in his hand.'

'He's the king's esquire, yes. But he's also my son.'

Because we had no steering oar to guide us to a harbor, we could only run aground on a shingle beach sometime that afternoon. There was a village nearby. I could see the top of a wooden tower beyond the trees, which meant there should be a garrison; the king's soldiers, if this were Kent.

Our bargain having been struck with the reluctant consent of Godric's men, I proposed that I should go to the keep, discover our whereabouts, and see to borrowing horses. I would bring back what food and fresh water might be had of the garrison, too.

Godric said sternly: 'You'll go, but not alone, priest. I'll be at your side and I warn you: if you try to trick me, no matter how many Frenchmen there are in that tower, I'll have my knife between your ribs before you can run away. And if we don't return by nightfall' – he lifted his voice threateningly – 'my men will cut your boy's throat and this dog of a servant's, too. Is that understood?'

'Most profoundly, Master Godric. I leave my precious son in your hands, good Englishmen. I won't betray you, have no fear of me. But what if something should delay us? Will your men take sundown for nightfall, or curfew, or what? I wouldn't have my son die and me on the way to you, according to my word.'

Godric consulted with his mates. He was making a show of distrusting me and being fierce with me, but he was as worried as I that his men might lose their courage and cheat him of his ransom. After a moment of consultation he said:

'When it's dark enough to see the Little Plow that stands at the crown of Heaven – when you can see all the stars of it – that's when we must be back again, or you'll cut their throats.' He reached out for Martin's arm, to guide him toward his mate, but Martin avoided him and turned suddenly to dash off across the rough beach, making for the village. The sailors sprang after him with cries of outrage and knocked him down on the sharp rocks. They pummeled him with their fists, then dragged him back again like a slain deer. When he was put on his feet before Godric, the Englishman drew his heavy-bladed knife. I rushed between them and slapped Martin's face sharply.

'You harebrained fool! You're lucky they didn't hamstring you! Try to act like a man now. Your life depends on it. I'm going to the keep – '

'To bring soldiers? To hang them?' Martin's face brightened. We spoke French, but I couldn't tell if Godric understood, so I struck Martin again.

'No, you idiot, not soldiers! Money, horses, food to save our lives. If you care about that, stay here and do as you're bidden.'

'You're going to buy them off? Bribe them? You're the fool!' he yelled.

I turned from him as if disgusted with him entirely. My fury seemed to allay that of Godric. He put his knife away and shoved Martin into the arms of the sailors who had caught him.

'Bind him!' He turned to me, half grinning. 'Thanks be to God I have no children, if this is how they obey their fathers. Priest, if we're going, we'd best be gone. There aren't many hours left until dark.'

When we reached the village, the dogs rushed out on us, snarling and snapping. Godric pelted them with stones until some children and old men came to our rescue. I think it was my tonsure that saved us. We were surrounded and would have been led to the priest's house next to their little church, but I said I must speak to the Frenchmen who held the tower. We were taken there at once. Godric walked at my back, one hand on my shoulder and the other on the hilt of his knife.

The gate porter acknowledged my tonsure, too. He let us in and took us to the constable, who heard my tale with curiosity. I told him I had been bound for Dover when my ship was torn to pieces by the storm. My poor men waited below us on the beach and were in need of food and water, while I must be put on the road to Dover, or to London, whichever was closer, as soon as possible. I would want a proper escort, as I was on the king's business.

I recognized the place I was in. The village was set down on my tax rolls as the vill of Adellum, called Deal by the local inhabitants. It was only a few miles from Dover. More fortunately, the constable recognized me. He had done his castle duty at Dover while I was there and didn't question my right to make demands of him.

'I'll give you horses, gladly, Father,' he said, 'but not until morning, surely. After such hardship as you've endured, youll want a good dinner and a night's rest, and so will your crew. I'll send down for them to come up to us, where they may be fed.'

I was alarmed at that suggestion. A troop of soldiers descending on the sailors would precipitate a panic.

'No, no, Constable! Don't send for them. They must stay and guard their ship.' I laughed uncomfortably, looking at Godric. He didn't understand me when I spoke to the Norman, but lengthy speech with Godric would equally discomfort Constable Drogo. I said to Godric swiftly: 'He means well; he wants to bring the crew up to be fed in the hall. What shall I say to him?'

'That they must stay where they are, priest – if you love your son.'

To Drogo I said: 'Truly, Constable, it's of little consequence, but the men would do better where they are. They have provisions and they've already built their campfire. I fear if you send armed men down to invite them you'll only terrify the poor fellows. They'll think

649

you believe them to be – Danes, or some such marauders.' I laughed. 'Why not let them be as they are? We might have a useless skirmish, unless we take care.'

He shrugged politely. 'They're yours to do with as you will, Father. But come and take some wine with me and tell me how it is with the northern counties. The rains here have all but spoiled the crops, I fear. We'll have hunger. I've already had to lop the hands off two poachers this week.'

Godric sat by me, very uneasy at table with Normans. He gulped his food and wine, his eyes darting around the room like a suspicious hound's. I prayed God he would stun himself with good victuals and fall asleep soon, so that I might tell the constable of my situation. With his aid I might somehow save Martin and forgo the payment of the heavy ransom. I would otherwise have to rob my canons of St. Martin's in Dover of their building fund, which could hardly endear me to them.

But Godric, though he blinked and yawned, kept awake and even reminded me that it was drawing near sundown. I glanced at a window shaft to see the light fading.

'Constable Drogo, I will praise your hospitality to the king himself, but now I must take leave of you for a time. This man and I must go down to our sailors and assure them that all is well with us.'

'Don't trouble yourself, Father. I've already sent someone to do that, and to take them some bread and ale for their supper, too.'

Godric must have sensed the horror I felt. He gripped my wrist. 'What's he said? What's amiss?'

'I didn't know, believe me. I didn't ask him – or tell him – on my mother's soul, Godric!'

'What's wrong?' Drogo inquired, a little put out by our whispering.

'Why, Constable, I – '

At that moment the men who had gone to find our sailors returned to the hall. They reported what I feared: when the men on the beach had seen them coming down through the field, armed and on horseback, they fled in all directions. Most of them had been lost in the twilight, for four mounted men cannot chase a dozen. Three had been caught, one regrettably killed when he fought his captor. They behaved like madmen who expected to be hanged, said the man-at-arms who made the report. It was clear he thought their peculiar response was adequate grounds for inflicting that punishment.

Godric had jumped to his feet the moment the business was made clear to him. He ran down to the lower hall to see who among his crew had been captured. I followed him and tried to make the frightened sailors believe no harm had been meant. I asked for Martin. They looked at me sullenly. Godric spoke to them sharply and they admitted something to him in a whisper. He turned to me, smiling fleetingly for form's sake at the man-at-arms who stood guarding his sailors.

'They say they don't know what happened to him. Arsuf had him in a halter when the Frenchmen came, but no one saw where Arsuf ran. Hold your head up, priest, so these French dogs don't suspect us. I can still put a knife into you, if you betray me. Why are you weeping? You've only lost one son. Since I met you, I've lost thirteen – and better ones, too, by the looks of yours.'

'I don't much care if you use your knife,' I said, but I still flinched when he put his hand to its heft. He nodded grimly at my silent appeal.

'Tell these Frenchmen I'll go down and have a look about for my men, if they'll stay out of the way. They may come out of hiding when they hear my voice, if they haven't run too far.' He touched my arm briefly. 'You're a fool, man. If Arsuf had cut his throat as he should have, they'd have found his body. Your son may still be alive.'

Dawn came. I had slept, but was still unrested. I rose, said my prayers, took bread and wine with Drogo, told him I must go to London now, and at once. An escort was assembled in the bailey yard. While the men were preparing, I went into the neglected chapel of the tower and fell on my knees again to beseech God for the life of Martin.

My beautiful, proud, foolish son, who thought himself a man and was still a child: had he run from the soldiers with the rest, or had he fled from me? Now I repented of telling him. Half the joy I had secretly taken from him was because of his pride, his self-assurance, his arrogance. These were the attributes of a noble, one who would be worthy of the accolade someday, and I had engendered the body that owned them.

I had spoiled my own dream along with his. The very heart of his pride was that he supposed himself the son of a warrior and hero. What ruinous vanity made me reveal myself to him? If he still lived, I would have to find some means to compensate him, perhaps by promise of an early betrothal to one of the king's wards, some little heiress with an estate or two. She would have to be an English girl, but even the best of the young knights were marrying the English now, when they could. I rose and went down into the yard, still weighed down by grief and sending silent appeals to Heaven.

Godric was in the yard, with Martin. They were surrounded by soldiers. The Englishman looked weary and resigned; Martin, shamefaced. I started forward to him, then restrained myself. He avoided my eyes, as if a show of affection from me would be the same as a blow.

I said: 'Captain Godric, you've found one of them, I see. What about the others? My servant, Gerald?'

'Gone, scattered like crows. I found this one hiding in a furrow, as if he expected to take root there. Now you have him, priest, what will you do?'

He looked as if he thought I would command the soldiers to seize him, having regained my son. I laid my hand on his shoulder and said in his ear:

'You need have no fear of me, or of these men. You've done well. The reward I promised you waits in London, if you'll come with me now.'

To Martin I said nothing; I didn't even glance at him for fear of betraying myself with tears. He might have sent Godric to the hangman as well as I, but he kept silent, too. I turned to Drogo.

'Constable, if you find any of our crew still hiding nearby in the next few days, give them waybread and send them on to me in London. I'll repay you for the kindness.'

Two more horses were now brought out. Godric, Martin, and I mounted them, though half blind for weariness, and let the soldiers lead us to London.

We had been given up for dead. Word of our disappearance had gone up to Windsor, and the king broke off his hunting to come and direct the search for us. According to Fulcher, whom I found at the old palace, the king was half frantic for my loss. He had offered a reward of fifty silver marks for news of my safety or the identity of the men who had murdered me.

Even my self-contained Fulcher seemed a little glad to see me alive. We embraced, and he went with me up to the royal tower where the king was.

When I entered the Tower hall with my escort of soldiers, my draggled Martin, and my nervous pirate, there was a momentary silence of tongues, during which interval I suppose a few people must have regretted the sight of me. But the king saw me and sprang up to push through the throng and fling his arms about me. His embrace was like a bear's, but his red face shone like that of a child who's been given a surprise gift as he laughed and kissed me.

Maurice, Robin Bloet, Gerard le Gros, all my friends and fellow clerks surged forward to clasp my hand and give thanks for my deliverance. I was brought to the dais and given a cup to drink while I told a brief version of our tale, identifying Godric and absolving him in the same breath for his part in it.

He stood with his back to a pillar, grinning with apprehension at so many hated, well-fed Normans clustered about him. I gave him special thanks in the king's hearing for having found Martin and brought him back to me, when he had every cause to believe his return would mean imprisonment or death.

Rufus turned to look at Godric, then called for him to come forward. Godric obeyed, as willingly as a hound to a bath, and the king surveyed him so long and so fiercely that I feared he might have him arrested after all. I was about to speak in his defense again when Rufus said roughly:

'Well, you bastard, you deserve hanging. You know that, don't you? But you've spared my priest and my esquire and shown a spot of valor, for an Englishman. For that I'll spare you. Someone give me a purse.'

Robert the Dispenser untied the purse at his belt and set it before the king. He tossed it to Godric, who caught it deftly, but continued to look wary of the gift. Whatever smattering of street and market French my pirate might possess, the king's high, rapid speech was beyond his comprehension. One of my clerks translated it for him. When he understood, he straightened, gave a hoarse shout, and fell at the king's feet, embracing his legs as he babbled.

The amused clerk who had enlightened him said: 'Your Grace, he says you are a true king, even if you are a Frenchman. You're as noble as Alfred, and as just as Canute. You're the best Frenchman who ever lived, and this dog is yours forever, even if you spurn him with your foot.'

Rufus looked both pleased and slightly uncomfortable. 'That's a te-temptation – to boot him. By the F-face, he reeks like a dog that's seen a boar! Tell him to go down to the lower hall and be fed. They won't smell him there.'

'Will you take him into your service, my lord?' I asked. 'You'll rid the seas of a pirate. But if you've no use for him I'll gladly take him, by your leave.'

'He's yours, then. He's too rancid for me.' He motioned me to follow him into a smaller chamber he used for a council room. When I closed the door, he turned and embraced me again, then seized me in a harsh grip and asked:

'Who did it? Who paid that dog to have you taken?'

'I can't say, Your Grace. Godric says he didn't know the man, only that he was a Norman and he met him at Hastings. I believe him. The man was a hireling. Whoever wanted me would have kept safely out of sight until he had me.'

'But who was it? Who are your enemies, man? I'll see they hang. Have no f-fear of that.'

I shook my head. 'Your Grace, my enemies are yours. I believe I was meant only to draw you out of London, perhaps to your own danger and even your death.'

He frowned, still gripping my arms. 'How's that? Did they think I'd come for you without an army?'

'I can't say, not knowing who they were, but it might be that they meant to trick or ambush you, even to do no more than delay you from marching against Mowbray.'

'Mowbray? Do you think it was h-he? I'll have him s-s-split for it!'

'My lord, I do not know. But there are more dangerous men in this world than Robert Mowbray, and some of them smile on you every day.'

He scowled. He didn't like the thought that his friends might be traitors. Only those who had openly offended him could be capable of dishonor. There was no profit for me in naming the men I most suspected: Gilbert of Clare, Hugh of Chester, even Prince Henry. I said:

'We must put this business behind us now, Your Grace. I am safe and not apt to be in danger again. In all likelihood, this was nothing but a foolish jest.'

'The Devil take that jester if I ever find him out,' growled my king, but then his brow lightened. It was easier to dismiss the business if there were no traitors to look for among his friends. 'I missed you, you rascal, more than I can s-say. I'll have to keep you closer to me from now on. We'll stand at each other's backs, eh? Like good soldiers. Now, come and see this letter Mowbray's had sent to me. It's full of impudence! He's spoiled for a fight, and by the F-face, I mean to give him one. His bride must not be too p-pleasing to him!'

He opened the chamber door and shouted for Gerard and the rest to enter.

Within moments the chamber was full of advice on the issue of

Mowbray's defiant letter. Gerard read it aloud; it was an illiterate jeremiad of false lament and rude threats.

'He's gone mad, or this is bait for some conspiracy,' I said when I'd looked at it myself. 'This isn't his speech. He hardly makes speech.'

'Have patience with him still, my lord,' counseled William de St. Carileph.

'Send another envoy. This last has misrepresented you,' urged William de Eu.

'I'll be the next envoy he sees, the bastard,' said Rufus, 'and I'll take him a dispatch that'll burn his eyes out.'

I spent the rest of the day with the king, then went home to Cornhill at Vespers, thinking to change my shirt and let Isabel know I was alive. I found her weeping, with a bruise on her face. Martin had rushed in upon her, struck her, tried to pry open my money box, but, failing that, had fled, cursing us both.

56

The king called up his levies and went into Northumberland against Earl Robert, swarming his host over a land already lean with hunger and soon to be starved when his soldiers had picked it clean. People seemed to believe I was oblivious to the suffering because I still had the duty of extracting the king's due from the land. Let them believe what they will. The poor would have suffered in any case, as the storms and heavy rains had spoiled the crops again. If the earl had been allowed to extend his insurrection into a full-fledged rebellion, the poor would only have suffered the longer. And armies must feed where they march and where they fight. It has been so since the days of Joshua and will always be.

Rufus left the government of the realm jointly in my hands and those of Anselm, determined to ignore the hatred he knew lay between us. I prepared to endure the presence of the man who had ruined my happiness with his interdict and who still continued to preach against me and my friendship with the king, as if I were the most lascivious mortal since Caligula.

Anselm could not get on with anyone of less piety than himself.

Only his sycophantic clerks were dear to him. He had even begun a quarrel with Cardinal Walter and directed his latest preachments to the papal legate, who still remained in England waiting to collect Peter's Pence and, perhaps, the odd bribe for exercising his influence on the king.

To my joy, Anselm himself relieved me of the necessity to humble myself before him daily. He had been given the task of defending the coast of Kent and the southern ports against any invasion from abroad while the king was in the north. He took this responsibility rather more seriously than he had taken his duties as the king's tenant in the past. He remained in Canterbury, and I, in London.

I scoured London for some news of Martin. Fulcher inquired of all the churches in town to see if the boy had taken refuge with one of them, while Godric made a search of the docks, looking for some sailor, or ship's master, who might remember such a young man trying to make passage on a vessel, or even get himself hired as a crewman, but there was no sign of him. Meanwhile, Isabel mourned:

'He called me a whore, my own son! He looked at me as if he hated me!'

'He didn't mean it. He was angry with me. But he lacks something of manners,' I said roughly, for I felt the pain of his offense, too. 'You spoiled him, keeping him with you. If you'd sent him out to a household apart from yourself – '

'He was all I had! And what about you? You talk about manners who have none of your own. Why did you tell him? What business did you have to tell him after all this time? Did you think he'd be glad to hear he's a – a bastard?' Her familiar anger flashed forth at once. She'd been weeping on my breast one moment; now she stood apart and accused me, forgetting her humiliation at the hand of her son. In an instant we were renewing an old quarrel.

'Woman, I did what any man might do who thought he was about to die; I discharged my conscience of an old crime – having traffic with you! God hear me, I now repent of both the traffic and the confession!'

'I'll never see him again.' She wept.

'I think you will. He had no money and he's got no talent, but for polishing armor and wearing fine clothes. He'll come creeping back presently, or else I'll find where he's hiding. He can thank his good angel if I find him before the king does, believe me.'

'What do you mean? What will the king do?'

'With a runaway servant? Anything he pleases, madam. But you may be certain of one thing: he won't have him back in his service again. Our little peacock has lost his chance to be a knight, unless he wins his spurs on the battlefield, which I doubt he has the stomach for.'

'His blood being tainted, you mean?'

I lifted my hand as if to strike her. It was an empty gesture, but she seemed to welcome it. She came closer to present me a better target.

'Go ahead! You've ruined everything else. Beat me, as a peasant beats his wife, or his horse; then throw me out into the street! I won't live on your peasant's charity any longer. I'll go to a convent if I must.'

In the midst of my rage and remorse I had to laugh. 'A convent? You? Oh, Isabel!'

'I will!'

'No. Stay here. I'll go. I've enough on my conscience without putting some cloister to the task of harboring you. Stay – and dry your tears. I'll find your son for you.'

But as Fulcher and Godric did not find him, I tried to turn my mind back to my duties to the king. I had spoken to my lord, both in council and in private, before he went away, on the possibility of a conspiracy lurking behind Mowbray's senseless revolt. I could scarcely name my chief suspect in the plotting, as it was Prince Henry. As far as Rufus was concerned, Henry was his amiable little brother, content with the cheese parings of the Cotentin and to harass Curthose on Rufus's behalf. But I had not forgotten how the prince had come to England in his brother's absence, consorted with various old traitors, and loved to hear himself styled 'Atheling' by the mob.

I began to make inquiry among the men such great lords are apt to forget about when they speak their minds: their servants. Henry's entourage had gone back to Normandy with him, naturally, but he had been served by hands as good as invisible to him both at Southampton and in London. Those men I found and put to question. I say to question, not to torture, which is the device of the inept when it isn't the instrument of revenge.

What I heard from the little men of London and Westminster still did not make good evidence for my case, but it revealed enough bitterness, envy, and rash discontent among certain other men – Gilbert of Clare, Philip of Montgomery, Roger de Lacy, and William de St. Carileph – to make up a full report to the king. I was a little surprised to find Carileph among the malcontents. He was known to be in poor health of late. One would have thought he had supped full of treachery and longed to make a quiet old age, but gratitude was unknown to him and age is no cure for greed. I sent my report to Rufus by my most trusted messenger, Fulcher.

Fulcher reached him before he left York, where the archbishop lent his own considerable mesnie to the host.

King William was never a man to disguise his feelings. When he had finished hearing my message and questioned my brother on a point or two, he turned instantly cold to those gentlemen whom I had named, but he would not have them arrested or questioned. He despised Fulcher's warning that keeping them near him could be dangerous. What followed should have made him doubt the wisdom of his forbearance.

As the host approached the borders of Northumberland, Gilbert of Clare, who was evidently most affected by the king's change of demeanor, drew Rufus aside, spoke to him earnestly, then suddenly fell on his knees as if begging pardon. The king lifted his hand to strike him, then let it fall. He appeared to question Gilbert fiercely, then made a brusque gesture for him to rise and leave him.

There was a woods near the banks of the Tyne where the army was making its camp. It had been the plan of the king to take a party into that wood before sundown, in search of fresh meat. Instead, an armed band of knights rode swiftly into the trees and scoured the forest well.

Gilbert's confession had been of a singular sort. He had warned the king of a body of men waiting in that wood to slay him, men to whose intent Gilbert himself had been a party, but repented of in the final moment. He had indeed begged the king's pardon before he revealed the plot, and Rufus – having his honor charged with forgiving a brother knight at his plea – forbore to punish Gilbert.

Just who the others were in the Judas plot was a secret hidden in the breasts of Gilbert and his king. The woods were empty of lurking men. The searching party returned; the king went into his tent. The next morning the army crossed the Tyne. Nothing more can I tell about this matter. Was there a plot? Did Gilbert invent it in his need to win over Rufus's suspicions? Or – and this I believe is more likely the case – did he invent one conspiracy in order to disguise another and give his companions in crime warning of their lord's suspicions?

The army came to Newcastle. Robert Mowbray had made good use of the great fortress built in '81 by his friend Robert Curthose, when he had pacified Northumbria after the murder of Bishop Walcher. The main body of Mowbray's followers were not in that castle, however, but at Bamburgh with Earl Robert. Those knights in possession of Newcastle lost heart for battle when they saw the extent of the king's levies. Before the siege engines could be set up there was a parley; before the death of a single man in an attack on the gate, it swung up and the castellan surrendered to the king's mercy. Those who occupied the castle were kept there in ward, and the king moved at once toward Tynemouth.

Tynemouth was made strong both by nature and by the design of its architect. It rose sheer above the river estuary on one fork of a twin peninsula. A second headland to its north was crowned by the Abbey Church of St. Oswine, which was protected by a lesser fortress.

The vill of Tynemouth stretched across the neck of the peninsula. The king had no choice but to burn it before he could set out his line of siege. He gave the people warning to be gone first, but as some men never heed what is meant for their own good, there was still an unnecessary loss of life in the struggle that followed. Death excited other pangs than fear. A knight and three men-at-arms were hanged for rape, later.

When the ashes cooled, the king and his army sat down across the neck of the peninsula while his ships cleared its harbor of any vessels that might afford the rebels either comfort or escape. Tynemouth was shut in by land and sea. Yet, it was two months before its castellan, Earl Robert's brother, despaired of his coming to their rescue and yielded himself to the king's will.

Having outwitted murderers who were set to slay him and defeated two of Mowbray's strongest keeps, Rufus rode on to Bamburgh, where Mowbray himself waited.

During the second siege I learned of that attempt on the king's life. I was frantic that those he so easily pardoned, or chose to ignore, might take heart again and conspire against him. If I had been a lord of hosts as Anselm was, I would have marched at once to join my king, but my duty was to serve elsewhere and otherwise. I must hear pleas, collect fines, give dull judgments on brutish men, while he held the great siege of Bamburgh.

I was in the New Forest when I found Martin. There was a case of malicious wounding: a shepherd had driven his staff into the side of another man during a dispute over a sheep, crushing the victim's ribs and causing him to vomit blood.

The shepherds' quarrel had been witnessed by several men from Malwood Lodge, who were now called as the king's accusers against the staff wielder. Martin was among those called.

When he saw me on the bench, he tried to escape the gathering. He was dragged back by the foresters of Malwood, who had no inclination to waste their morning in testimony if the flight of one among them put doubt on their evidence.

Martin was thrust out in front of me. The tall man who had him in charge pushed him to his knees.

'Forgive him, my lord Justice. He's only a boy. The sight of so many quarrelsome people startled him, maybe, but he'll be quiet now.'

I stared at Martin. His face was pale; was it drawn from hunger, too? I realized I was on my feet and sat down again.

'What is your name?' I asked the tall man, who was dressed like a woodsman in green and brown. 'And what is this young man to you?'

'I am Raoul des Aix, keeper of the walk of Malwood, my lord Justice.' He had the accent of an Aquitanian. 'This lad is a friend of my son's.'

'Is he of Malwood or some other place in the forest?'

'He's a servant of our lord the king's, sent to us to recover from a fever. Stand up, boy, so the priest can see you. It may be he knows your face if you let him look at it. Stand up! You've done no wrong.'

Martin stood and we surveyed each other silently. I said: 'I know him. Let him be kept aside when the testimony is given. His behavior puts doubt on his value as a witness. He'll wait for me in the church until the court is adjourned. I'll speak to him then. Someone watch over him.'

When I had disposed of the warring shepherds and other cases of that ilk, I left the collecting of fines to my clerks and went into the cool narthex of the little church. Martin was there with des Aix and several other men of Malwood. They were worried. Martin's behavior made them fear they might be harboring a criminal.

Martin wished to appear defiant, but the number of sober faces surrounding him put a pall on his courage. He went to his knees before me.

I said to the keeper: 'This boy is indeed a servant of the king's. I will speak to him in private, by your leave, Keeper. Walk with me, Martin.'

I blessed myself and went into the nave, which was of the same size and simple design as my church at Godalming. Martin followed me reluctantly. I dipped my knee to the cross at the end of my walk, then turned to him. He flinched slightly and stood well back from me.

'Well, Martin. You've distressed the king with your disappearance and injured your mother with your brutish behavior. If you wanted to prove to them, or to me, that you were never meant to be a gentleman, you've done admirably. At least you've convinced me, though it's a strange way of showing me how little you like being my son. If I were in your shoes and had so detestable a father, I think I would have been at pains to show him my inborn nobility, rather than the churlish peasant ways he might have attributed to himself. You disappoint me greatly. If you've ruined yourself to hear that said, you've succeeded with your plan. What do you have to say for yourself?'

He hadn't much bluster left in him. 'Are you going to tell Raoul – about me?'

'That would be painful for us all; but I will, unless you come with me when we leave here and promise to obey me. Not as your father, which is no matter of great pride to me at the moment, but as the king's minister.'

He wiped his nose with the back of his hand. 'Will the king have me back?'

'The king has better things to consider now than one truant esquire. When he's fought his war he may be in the mood to receive and forgive you. Or he may not remember you at all. There are plenty of young men eager to take your place. Did you suppose your services were unique? I myself find nothing extraordinary in you, and I've known his squires from the time he was first accoutred.'

He flushed. His mouth turned down and his nether lip began to tremble with the strain of withholding tears. He whispered: 'You know what he is.'

I went closer to him so that the men in the narthex couldn't hear our whispers.

'Yes, I know. He is the king. God made him so, as God gave him his nature. It is the part of his servants to serve the king in him – and the better man. If you have done less – or more – it would be better for you if you did not serve him again. Martin, have you done more?' I put my hand on his shoulder but he shook it off.

'No!' His eyes flashed with tears and anger as he glanced back to where the keeper stood waiting. 'No, I've done what was *required*! Do you understand me, *Father*? You should; you know so much about him – his great friend! Everybody knows about you, too, so don't put on a priest's face for me and ask if I've done what I shouldn't.'

'What do you mean, everybody knows about me? What's there to know about me that anybody might not know?'

661

'What they say is an old tale around the court, *Father*: they say you may have your whores, but you're the king's!'

I stared at him so long that he began to fidget and dropped his gaze, his face twitching as if he expected the blow I was tempted to give him. I said as evenly as I could manage:

'I'd thought you still a boy. I forgot how quickly young vipers grow to maturity. Is it because you were jealous of me that you ran away? Because the king greeted me with affection when you thought he should fall on your neck first? Well, you mistake him, and me, but I'll not undertake to explain either of us to you.'

'I didn't say I thought – I said they do,' he muttered.

'Enough! You will come with me now, quietly. And you will do as I bid you, whatever that may be. If you refuse, you'll find yourself under arrest as a vagrant from the king's service. These men will no longer harbor you, which means you'll most likely languish in a prison cell until the king comes home to judge you. Make your choice, now.'

'What are you going to do with me? Send me overseas? I'll go. I'm sick of this land and everyone in it.'

'Whatever I do with you, you'll abide it. A public whipping for desertion of your post isn't something you'd want your mother to witness, I hope.'

He came with me to Winchester, having assured Raoul des Aix that he was cured of his illness and eager to return to his duties. We rode together toward Winchester with my clerks. Martin said very little on the way, though I caught more than one glance in my direction as if he would speak. Whether his furtive expression betokened reproach or appeal was difficult to gauge. I had expected him to burst out in a new tirade against me when he was clear of Lyndburst and the company of that old mercenary Raoul. Like all other young men brought up in his fashion, he might have considered my clerks to be deaf and dumb. But he kept the peace.

I took him to Hyde and turned him over to my novice master, representing him as the son of a worthy widow whom I supported in charity.

'Educate him, if you can,' I said. 'If letters are beyond him, try him with numbers. At the least, teach him patience and his prayers. He has need of both.'

As I spoke I thought the corners of Martin's mouth just began to curl, as if he could almost relish my deception.

*

The blockade of Bamburgh Castle was complete. The king built a rival tower of rough timber – a *malvoisin* to oppose the great fortress on the heights. He garrisoned it with his best soldiers, then turned the governing of it over to Robert fitz Hamon. In spite of the numbers of the royal host, in spite of the 'evil neighbor' that now opposed him, the surly Mowbray, bereft of all hope of rescue from vassals or co-conspirators, continued to defy King William.

Mowbray had provisioned his keep; he had an excellent well. His walls were too high to be breached by the missiles of a siege engine, but he was shut in as surely as if he had taken refuge in a wine jar, only to see it stoppered, waxed, and sealed.

They say he went to the top of his walls and cried out against his former accomplices among the king's host, bidding them be mindful of the false oaths they had sworn together with him. The king laughed at his bellowing, but what did such men as Gilbert of Clare do, or those others whom he had named as traitors to the king and whom Rufus would not yet accuse? Whatever shame such men might have felt for their double treachery, they answered Mowbray nothing.

Summer waned. The pitiful crops were harvested. Bread rose to double its usual cost, and bakers were arrested daily for putting too much leaven in their loaves to make them seem the greater. Minters were accused of shaving coins; theft was rampant. The famished dogs of St. Paul's ran like wolves through the streets until they were clubbed to death by still more famished men and their miserable carcasses flayed and dressed for the pot.

The king, satisfied that Mowbray could do no more than bawl his displeasure from his battlements, left the command of the entire leaguer to fitz Hamon and went into Wales with fresh levies to give aid to Hugh of Chester. Before he went he made his sole offer to Mowbray, putting the words in the mouth of a herald:

'There is a woman in your hall, my lord, who comes of an honorable family and bears a name that is sacred to me. I do not make war on women. Let her come out. I will give her honorable escort to any place of safety she may name in this realm, or even overseas to her father's house. I swear this on my honor as a true soldier.'

The generous offer was refused by the lady herself: Matilda of Laigle, Mowbray's bride, the daughter of warriors.

When the king was gone, however, Mowbray was tempted to come out of his prison. He had received in some manner, possibly by a messenger pigeon, the news that his knights of Newcastle had overcome their wardens and made themselves masters of the keep again. They urged him to come to him. Certain men among the royal host would open their lines to him if he was bold.

The message was a false one, sent to him by Robert fitz Hamon, some said with the king's consent, but Rufus never acknowledged it.

With the prospect of renewing his strength, the earl set forth from his postern gate one night with thirty of his knights. The garrison of the *malvoisin* watched and followed him, sending word ahead to the warden of Newcastle to expect him. The men of Newcastle were too eager. They tried to waylay Mowbray before he reached the gates. There was a rough battle; most of the earl's knights were slain or taken, but he and a remnant of his force escaped and fled to Tynemouth, where the sheer desperation of his attack won him the smaller fortress that guarded the Abbey of Oswine. For six days he held out in that cramped place before the gate was smashed and the defenders routed.

Mowbray fought his way to the abbey church, where he hoped for sanctuary, but there was no strength in that place to secure it for him. Fitz Hamon's men, hot on his traces, dragged him from the chapel and imprisoned him in the cellars of Tynemouth Keep until the king should come and judge him.

At Bamburgh, his noble wife held against the royal force with the aid of her husband's nephew Morel, the murderer of King Malcolm. Their supply of food had all but run out. Fitz Hamon, mindful of the king's respect for the lady and her family, offered her food, but she refused it.

A grim winter fell upon the land. In the west, the king pursued the Welsh into their mountains and blind gorges until the snow made pursuit impossible. As always when they had done their ravaging, the Welsh turned to ghosts and vanished into their high forests. The king came home again, riding a lean horse.

He had no glory from the Welsh and seemed to want none now from Northumbria. He did not go to Bamburgh again, but sent word to Tynemouth that Earl Robert should be taken there and led before its walls with the threat to his bride that if the castle was not surrendered immediately, Mowbray's eyes should be burned from their sockets.

I was astonished. I had never heard the king give so cruel a charge to any man. But he was weary of defiance, and its continuance through the winter would bring desolation anew to a land already twice beggared, by the Conqueror, and by that 'Smiter of the English,' Odo.

When Matilda heard the threat made against her lord, she opened her gate and surrendered to fitz Hamon. Thus, she saved her husband's eyes, but couldn't free him by ransom from fitz Hamon, who brought him triumphantly in chains to Windsor to face the king. Evidently Mowbray believed he would be delivered to the headsman soon, so he spent what he believed to be his last breath in vilifying the king who for so many years had been the object of his unrelenting hatred.

The king heard him with a blood-scalded face, then said: 'I have always played you f-fair, my lord, and I will play you fair now. You're no man for a death of honor by c-combat. You're no bull to be sent to the sh-shambles. You're a bear – and like a bear I'll k-keep you – chained in a pit.'

The Earl of Northumbria was confined in the deepest cell under Windsor tower, still wearing his chains. His wife came to Rufus to plead for him that he be exiled, as other traitors had been before. Rufus refused her.

'Lady, you defend like a T-trojan and plead like a s-saint, but it's no use. Go home to your father. Take whatever treasures the traitor gave you and go. Ask your father to find you a better husband.' He smiled suddenly. 'I wish you joy of the next match. By the Face, if I were a man made for marrying, I'd ask for you myself.'

Matilda de Laigle wasn't a beauty, though she had fine bellflower-colored eyes. She was a great, rawboned, angular woman with a mottled complexion and a Roman nose. She was gaunt from the siege. When Rufus spoke to her, her head came up like that of a horse that smells a boar in the brush.

'Find a new husband? Am I a widow, then? Have you killed my lord?'

The king lost his mirth. 'No, lady. But you're a widow all the same. He's as dead to you as he is to honor. Go and find a better man.'

Now, when the young Morel learned how his uncle had been punished, a great fear came on him that the same measures might be taken against him. He hastened to make his peace with the king by revealing all the secrets of the conspiracy and the names of all who had a share in it. The king heard him in private. He came from the chamber looking as if he had touched carrion.

Morel was rewarded with exile. He went forth from the land of his birth like a Judas, detested alike by the king and by all his former allies. He went first into Flanders, then to Denmark, and still lives, so far as I know, though both his fame as a slayer of princes and his notoriety as a traitor may be alike unknown to those among whom he dwells.

The Christmas Court was upon us, but still the king took no harsh action against the rest of the accused. He waited for them to come to him, as they did, one by one, and confess their crime. Henry de Lacy he deseized of his lands and sent into exile, giving his honors to his brother. Gilbert of Clare he had already pardoned. Hugh of Chester had something to confess, as I had suspected. He paid the king a great fine to gain his goodwill again.

William de St. Carileph took to his bed and died, soon after the New Year. What he may have confessed was confided into the ear of Anselm, who was gracious enough to go and sit by his deathbed, according to Carileph's wish.

Throughout the Christmas season William of Eu stood by Rufus, sat with him in council and at table, upheld his judgments, and condemned his enemies. When we removed to Salisbury soon after Epiphany, the king proclaimed a great tournament to honor the knights who had fought on his behalf. William of Eu was master of the tournament. All the lords who had kept the Christmas Court followed us to Salisbury, and I was commanded to send summons even to those whose time at court was at the Easter season, so there was an even greater concourse than at Windsor. Rich prizes were awarded the victors in the lists, though the king called them all victors who had been true to him.

On the third day of the tournament Rufus appeared under his canopy beside the lists wearing his crown, to the surprise of all who saw him. He made no explanation; gave command for the trials to begin; but before Lord William could send on the first combatants, a knight rode into the field and saluted the king. He was Geoffrey Baynard, son of the lord of Baynard's Keep. In a clear voice he appealed William of Eu of treason against the king, of conspiring to slay him and to give his crown to Stephen of Champagne, the king's cousin!

There was a death silence. Stephen of Champagne! That feckless young man who had dabbled in insurrection at Rochester and been forgiven it as if he were a naughty child. I couldn't believe it. No one, least of all such men as Robert Mowbray and William of Eu, could seriously wish to have such a fool as Stephen for their king when they had a Henry to look to – or could they? I had said once myself that rash men might prefer the rule of a fool to that of a valiant man.

They had once supported Robert Curthose for king. Now, it appeared, they had thought to have two fools to pretend to serve, one in Normandy and one here.

William of Eu denied the charge, affecting great anger toward the young knight who accused him, but there was no retreat from the offer of battle. He turned to the king, and then he saw why Rufus had chosen to wear his crown. He expected to sit in judgment that day. De Eu was denied the service of a champion to fight for him, though he was entitled to that if he felt himself unable to match his opponent. He arrayed himself grimly and went out to meet his challenger.

Geoffrey was young and able. Lord William was better made for beguiling other men's wives in their bowers than setting a lance at the charge. His belly had grown soft and his arm lax since he made himself one of Curthose's rebels at Gerberoy.

He was quickly unhorsed; his defeat was accepted as full evidence of his guilt, though it now appeared the king had been aware of his guilt all along. What was to be his punishment? Exile? A heavy fine, as Hugh the Wolf had paid? Imprisonment, to match that of Mowbray? He was brought before the king. Now he sank on his knees and craved pardon, offered treasure, begged to be sent overseas.

'You are a traitor in three kinds,' said the king. 'You have betrayed your king. You have betrayed your friend and you have betrayed – me. I gave you every chance to speak. Why didn't you? Even those with no more va-va-valor than a h-hen came to me at last and had their say. Mowbray defied me. You – you despised me.'

'Your Grace – ' began Lord William.

'No! I'm not "your grace," or anything of honor to you! I'm that *f-fool* who called you my brother-in-arms again after you be-betrayed my f-father! After you laid plots against me when he died! After you rebelled against me and b-burned Gloucestershire! You came to me again last year with "your grace" and "friend" in your mouth when already you were p-planning this!'

'You talk of honor, always of honor! What is that word to you but something you once heard in a song sung to you by your Irish harlot?' screamed Lord William, his fury suddenly overwhelming his fear. 'Where's your honor when you tax us, your friends, your kinsmen, your brothers-in-arms, as if we were stinking English peasants? You and your whole family were once no better than the rest of us, but now you give yourselves the airs of emperors – you, your father, your brothers, all! We've stood for it long enough. If there's to be someone of your family lording it over us, at least let it be one who can boast that his grandsire married his dam on both sides of the family!'

The king went white, then flushed dangerously. His voice sank to a whisper, but there was no difficulty in hearing it; the field was silent as a church after Lauds.

'You're a getter of bastards, too, by your lady's reckoning. She's complained of you, my lord. Well, there'll be no more bastards. I've a judgment for you. Read it, Chancellor!'

Gerard stood and pronounced the verdict: the lord of Eu was to be deprived of his sight and his manhood, then confined to prison for life. His treason and its punishment were to be proclaimed in every part of the land, so that all men should know that no man, however high he might be, could hope to betray the king and profit by it.

De Eu's steward suffered a harsh fate as well. For carrying his master's messages and withholding knowledge of his treachery from the king, he was to be hanged on a cross at the gates of Salisbury until he died.

Men might have wondered why such an insignificant man as a steward should reap so cruel a punishment when there had been others who did no less and suffered not at all. The answer is simple: that steward of de Eu was none other than William de Alderi, the careless young man who had been the first esquire of Rufus and who had received his spurs from him when he came to be knighted.

57

I went up to Durham after Carileph's death to take inventory of his property and his church's, both now having fallen once more into the king's hand. It was a weary journey to make in late days of January, through a desolate country made more miserable still by hunger than by heavy snows.

Sorry I might be to leave warm fires and a comfortable bed for the icy roads, but I was not sorry to be parted for a time from the king. He masked the guilt he felt for the deaths of William de Eu and de Alderi with a savage kind of good humor. On the day of de Eu's mutilation – which was his death – I remembered a day outside the walls of Gerberoy. No matter what time and hard experience had come between, Rufus felt the same horror for the deed as on the day when he had obeyed his father's command to mutilate Curthose's gallant follower. It sickened me to hear him laugh when Cornard, his jester, invented ribald laments for de Eu in a womanish voice, or to endure the mirth of certain members of his court – Gilbert of Clare and his cowardly brothers, Hugh of Chester, Philip Montgomery – all safely back within the fold.

We came to Durham through a veil of wind-driven sleet, and climbed the slippery road to the top of that steep hill where Carileph had his palace. The village that surrounded it on three sides of the precipice was already shut in for the night. Not even the hungry watchdogs stirred against us, beyond barking from their fetid yards. Across a sprawl of hovels, byres, and sties I could see the shadowed mass of his new church, looking more like a ruin than a beginning that night. I went gratefully into the warmth of the bishop's hall and let his obsequious stewards divest me of my sodden cloak and boots, warm me with braziers, feed me with mutton, and settle me in Carileph's own spacious bed.

In the morning, still feeling some effects of my long journey, I gave instructions to my half-dozen clerks to begin the counting, then went out across the palace yard and through the muck of the village street, thinking to pay my respects to the prior of St. Cuthbert's and to see what manner of architecture might be born from such a worm-soured man as Carileph.

Its size alone might make it impressive, I thought, as I gazed upward at the risk of falling into a frozen puddle. The arcades of the choir wall were well proportioned, better than Maurice's church in London, I thought. As I approached I heard singing; the voices of children issued from the cavern of the choir, which was the extent of the work so far. There were no workmen on the scaffolds, all labor having ceased with the bishop's death. I avoided a pile of scaffold beams and went into the open mouth of the north choir aisle.

The boys of the abbey school were in the choir. Forbidden to huddle together against the sharp wind that whipped them like a lash, they sang the *Exaudi Deus* in thin voices that sent a shudder of remembrance down my spine, despite my fur-lined mantle.

> O, that I had wings like a dove
> For then would I flee away
> And be at rest.

The effect of the words was immediately spoiled by one of the boys' being taken in a fit of coughing. The choirmaster waited until the paroxysm was finished, then stepped forward dispassionately and rapped the boy several times with his wand, a rebuke that the child took without a whimper. I thought of Cormac and myself that first day at St. Vigor. I cleared my throat to catch the monk's attention.

'Your charges are in good voice, Brother, considering their circumstances.'

He wheeled about impatiently, but reconsidered a rebuke on seeing my cloak and gold chain. 'They're lazy today, Reverend Father, but they do well enough when they're put to it.'

'Perhaps you'll be good enough to bring them to the palace later – if your prior permits – to sing for me before the day-meal. Where may I find Prior Turgot?' I had put my hand out to the stone pier beside me and now looked up at it. In a moment I all but forgot my own question for staring at the size, the loftiness, of that pier. Carileph was building a sanctuary for giants! I caught my breath as I imagined what the completed structure must be. The choir alone was as large as many churches. I came to myself, aware that the choirmaster had spoken to me.

'This way, Reverend Father. You'll want to get in out of the cold.' He was eager for me to be gone. He came out of the choir to point me the way to the prior's lodging, then hurried back again, his cadaverous face pinched and blue with the cold. As I crossed to the south side, where the eastern wall of the transept had been finished, I heard him give the cue for the poor, frozen boys:

' "Fearfulness and trembling are come upon me –" '

Old Turgot was prepared to be my enemy from the start. He resented the intrusion of the Crown, and begrudged me every item of information he was obliged to render. Like all his kind, he had come to think of the abbey and its grounds as his possession, though with prudence he frequently attributed its ownership to the Almighty. After a quarter of an hour with him, I decided it would do his soul good for me to make an especially careful investigation of abbey wealth.

When we finished our unsociable discussion, still standing as when I had entered, I asked him to have dinner with me that evening. He refused gracelessly. I asked for the children to be sent. He was about to refuse me that, but something in my aspect warned him not to declare open war on me too soon.

At his ungenerous door I said: 'This will be a splendid church for you when it's finished, Prior. You must take pride in seeing it grow.'

'A man must take pride in nothing save the love of God that's bestowed on him, unworthy though he may be. A great church is a great vanity, the same as a great house. It was His Grace's pride that began this. The old church was good enough.'

So much for the amenities.

By day's end I was coughing like the boy in the choir. The next morning I kept to Carileph's bed, alternately shaken by chills and drawn with fever. For the next several days I was thoroughly miserable. While my clerks did their work on the episcopal ledgers, I was coddled with possets. To amuse myself, I heard the children sing and took pleasure in stuffing them with delicacies from my table, while their distrustful master scowled at this ruin of his good discipline. One evening I fell to an examination of the architect's drawings for the great cathedral.

Since my days as a hod carrier for the brothers of St. Vigor, I had cherished a desire to take some part in the art of building. I satisfied my longings to design and devise to some extent with the simple additions I had planned for St. Martin's, as well as my own house in Winchester. But now, restless with my fever, I perused the lovely tracings of the craftsman's art and seemed to see through his faint lines and notations straight into the reality and beauty of those aisles and vaults, those arches, columns, carvings – the whole expanse of grave majesty of that nave. The image took hold on me, and I went to my chamber window half expecting to see completed what was only just begun.

Perhaps it was because of the isolation and my illness that I was more susceptible to dreaming fantasies, or it may be that my arid soul had been waiting too long for inspiration to refresh it and snatched at illusion for a balm. But as I looked out on that shell of the choir, I fell in love with Carileph's dream – almost I would say as if it were his mistress – which I longed to have and keep for my own.

Carileph! That mendacious wine bibber, that meddler in the affairs of clerks, that gossip, that gourmand, that attender to trivialities! How had this ever taken root from him? Or had it truly changed him? When I imagined he had kept himself from court for fear of being discovered in yet another treachery, had he truly been detained by this invention of a miracle?

God, what it would be to make such a thing come true! To shape it daily and see it grow, out there on the verge of that jutting hill. Compared with that for daring, mere treason was a toy. Even sowing the dragon's teeth of war – the king's way to glory – seemed paltry and unworthy. But to build a monument that would last forever was an enterprise worthy to take possession of the soul!

She – my Lady of Stone – would stand so proudly, taking the winds for her breath and the very sun and moon for her complexion. When the candles were put out, I sat by the window watching how the moonlight changed that yellow-tinged stone to a grey so light that it was nearly as pure as the moon herself. What woman of this earth could I compare her to, my Lady? Margaret of Scotland? Isabel de Montfort? Perhaps, but these were liable to change, to age, frail to ill fortune, to desire. Carileph's Lady, whom I coveted for my own, would never wither, never falter, had one desire – to be! Happy the man who could give her being.

There is never any lapse of energy or diversity of mood in a man that is lost to comment, if he keeps a clerk. Mine may have been of the opinion that it was some woman in the castle who made me shut myself up alone in my bedchamber so soon after evening prayers and descend the stairs next morning with such lassitude. Certain interrupted mutterings of theirs and some wise looks in my direction gave me cause to believe they suspected me.

I rallied, threw off my fever, and reduced my cough and other miseries to mere snuffling; then I made them sorry for themselves with work, which gave them less latitude to speculate on me.

When we left Durham at the end of the month, our pack animals were well laden with treasures of Carileph's which were now the king's. In my own baggage, wrapped carefully in a cloth, I took a treasure dearer than all the rest: the plans and elevations for the Cathedral Church of Christ and the Blessed Virgin.

St. Cuthbert could afford to wait for them awhile; he had waited centuries. Old Turgot might miss the plans and howl for the theft; let him lament. I hardly knew what I should do with them, beyond taking further delight from pretending they were mine. I had no prospects at the time of ever being able to lay true claim to them. I might never live to see Carileph's 'mistress' become my Lady of Stone. But I would see that she was protected – and maybe embellished with one or two slight jewels of my own – until some future Carileph required the parchments of me.

During the time that King William was besieging Mowbray, or pursuing the Welsh fruitlessly in the west, great things were taking place in France. Pope Urban convened a council of clergy at Clermont, an old town of Roman origins in the Auvergne. Anselm and Thomas could not attend with the two hundred or more other bishops, archbishops, and clerics regular and secular who did, they being occupied with our war, but there was such a crush of people in the old town that a scaffold had to be built in the marketplace for Urban to speak to them all.

He made several decrees, among them one once more affirming against the marriage of priests. Then he preached a most wonderful sermon on the desolation of the Christians of the East.

They say he described the holy city of Jerusalem laid prostrate at the feet of infidels, who profaned and defiled the sacred stones where Christ and His disciples once walked. He urged the princes of the West to give up petty strife with one another, assume the badge of the Holy Cross of Christ, and make their wars rather for the deliverance of Jerusalem – where pagans' horses were stabled in ancient churches, where Christians were forced to shameful servitude, where noble men were flogged with whips, yoked with thorns, and like oxen made to pull the heathens' prows.

He promised those who heard him and took up the cross full remission of their sins, and absolution from all obligations of previous vows and debts, from the moment they put on the sacred badge. Those who died in the attempt to liberate the holy city would die as blessed martyrs, destined to go straight to Paradise without suffering Purgatory, and those who survived would gain eternal honor and fame.

This appeal was not a new one; the Conqueror's own father, Robert the Magnificent, had heard and answered a similar one. But Urban's sincerity, the strength of his own personal anguish for the plight of Christians in such bondage, was so overwhelming to his listeners, that no sooner had he finished speaking than he had his first volunteer for martyrdom.

The excitement spread rapidly across the Christian world as the clergy who had heard him returned home to tell Urban's promise to their people. All were summoned to the cause: the rich, the poor, the young or old, warriors, townsmen, cattle drovers, servants. In England, Philip of Montgomery, one of the erstwhile conspirators with Mowbray against the king's peace, was the first among us to take the badge of the cross, which Rufus permitted him to do in lieu of exile. Among our Normans in the home country, Routrou de Mortagne and Walter of St. Valéry, Ivo and Alberic of Grantmesnil, Gerard of Gournai and his wife, even that double traitor, the exiled Earl of Norfolk, Ralph de Guader, had taken fire from Urban's preaching at Clermont.

When I returned from Durham, there was little else talked of at court but how the heathen enemy might be set to flight by the appearance of Norman cavalry, or how their castles, built on ancient and holy ground, might be taken by a Norman onslaught. Anselm was making sermons on sacrifice and holy vows. A good many rogues sewed a cross on their dirty shirts to get them free of debts, their labors, or their marital duties, but there were as many – far more – poor fools who took the call to heart, marked a cross on their tattered smocks with sheep's blood, and ran off into the wild places of the world to starve, convinced they had been ordained by Heaven to deliver Jerusalem.

My son was among them. I went to Winchester to discover how he and another boy in the abbey school had escaped the eye of their novice master, leaving behind them the remnants of the dean's red stole, which they had cut to shreds to fashion their crosses.

I sent a search party at once to Southampton, the nearest port where they might hope to find a ship, and there they were discovered, already with famished cheeks, hanging about the quays, hoping to be enlisted by some knight into his army. They were brought back to Hyde, almost too weak and too dejected to sit their horses.

I saw them both judiciously flogged for their sacrilege of the stole and their disobedience, then spoke to my sobbing son:

'Are you mad? How did you think you could live without food, or money, or even a blanket to keep you from freezing? Did you think of your mother once before you did this stupid thing? Give me an answer!'

'We wanted to serve Christ!' he blurted, weeping as the infirmarian's assistant rubbed ointment into his welts.

'To serve Christ! Admirable! You were living in a house of religion. Might one ask what you thought you were supposed to be doing here?'

'I'm here to be punished – to please you!'

I dismissed the monk and bent over Martin where he lay on his belly scrubbing at his tears with filthy fingers.

'Now – listen to me, my suddenly pious son: I don't have you here to punish you. I don't mean to leave you here forever – God forbid! If you'll just take the trouble to learn to read and compute, I'll make you my bailiff. You'll have a wife with property; you'll ride a horse and wear a fine gown. Then you might even dare to present yourself to the king again and redeem yourself in his eyes. You might still become a soldier, if that's all you care about, or you may find yourself a person of wealth before you're five and twenty. Do you understand me? Is this punishment?'

He shouted: 'I don't want to be your son! I don't want to belong to you! I hate you! Leave me alone.'

I stood up. 'You're my flesh and I won't abandon you to your own ignorant pride. Blood is thicker than what's running out your nose, boy, whether you realize it yet or not. I'll leave you now, if that's what will make you quit sniveling. Learn your letters. You won't escape again. They'll put a watch on you day and night now. Do you have any message for your mother?'

He didn't answer.

'I'll give her your warmest affections.'

In London I met with the same madness, this time from none other than my pirate, Godric. He presented himself to me, wearing a cross, and informed me he had taken a new master.

'They want men who know the sea. They were calling for them down by the German markets. I heard and I couldn't very well just walk by, could I?' He grinned and shifted his feet nervously as I examined his tunic.

'Godric, this is a campaign for fools. I didn't think you were one.' I looked carefully at the material of the cross, to see if any of my vestments had suffered for his religious zeal, but it was made of a cheap sort of stuff, badly dyed.

'Even fools must answer when the Almighty calls them, priest.'

'You're no soldier. What can you do when you get there, supposing you ever do?'

'Oh, I'll not fight the heathen, priest. I'll only be the steersman for such as do. When we've delivered our cargo, we'll come away again, maybe to take on more soldiers. There's more signing on every day. When it's over I'll come back to you, if you still have use for me, that is.'

I gave him a purse. 'God go with you, Godric.'

Free lances, beggars, fools, children, younger sons, and failed men elected to take the cross and go into the wilderness to their death or their glory at the Pope's command. The clever men, the men of power in this world, kept at home. Philip of France still lolled in his adulterous bed; Henry, Emperor of the Germanies, continued his intrigues with his counter-pope; Robert of Bellesme never thought to join his old enemy, Routrou of Mortagne, in any peace pact for the duration of his crusade, but made bloody raids on Mortagne's lands as soon as he was gone.

Rufus laughed at them, scoffed at those who would leave their wealth to the guardianship of their wives or ancient uncles, lay their inheritances open to the greed and pillage of their neighbors, for the sake of men they had no blood ties with, in some land they had never seen.

'They're fools! They're like the camp boys who follow the will-o'the-wisps into the bogs. If someone doesn't drag them out by their greasy scruffs, they'll d-drown ca-catching at phantoms!'

He jeered, or he was angry. The ready knight, the constant soldier ardent for fame, always headlong to be first in any battle charge: he burned to go and lead that fools' army, to teach the fools how to avoid the bogs. He was the man to be their general, not Count Raymond of Toulouse, a man whose honors had not been won, but given to him by an indulgent brother!

I watched the hunger grow in him, the painful ambition to be that Caesar they could say had conquered the barbarians of the East. It gave me sleepless nights and anxious days when he suddenly took Edgar Atheling for his tutor in geography. Edgar had traveled as far in the world as lower Italy. He had watched the tides of the Middle Sea which rolled itself alike against the shores of Europe and the Orient. He knew the Mahometan way of discipline in battle, having taken his path home from Italy through Moorish Spain, where that warrior known as the Cid gave him bread and salt, where the worshipers of Allah ruled over half the land and contended as equals with Christian kings.

'Their horses are as light and quick as hounds, Your Grace, like that palfrey I once gave you. Their riders wear no armor but helms and light shields. They think it shameful to hide behind any steel but that of their swords. And their swords, Will-Rou, must be like the sword of the Archangel Michael! I've held one. I've seen a man take one and split a feather with it as it floated before him. They're so slender and light you could bend one like a willow wand, but the edge they bear – '

Edgar was more than usually eloquent. He itched to go adventuring, too. Rufus took in all his words, a slight smile, half of derision for those heathen ways, half of delight, playing on his lips. Some others that heard him derided Edgar's infatuation with heathen swords.

'If they're that light, they'd break like wands, too, under a good, heavy blade. And those ponies they ride would tire easy.' Hugh of

Chester protested. 'I've seen the like. They're all for show, for racing – not a battle. I wouldn't ride one into a cockfight, by God!'

That put the king on Edgar's side at once: 'I've seen you drunk enough to ride through a cockfight, Hugh. Any h-horse you're apt to ride t-tires easy! But there'd be sport in riding down the rascals and t-testing their steel, wouldn't you say?' He was bright-eyed with the dream.

I did nothing but say prayers daily that he would fall no further into madness. I made certain to remind him every day of the burden he bore to keep peace within his realm. I affected no interest in stories concerning holy wars. I couldn't say: 'You have the Scots waiting on your northern borders, the Welsh on your west, and two brothers overseas hungering to take what's yours away, if you ever turn your back on them.' He knew all that.

Ironically, my best ally in keeping him at home was probably Anselm, who had no interest in the political aspects of Urban's holy war. No desire for victory over the unbelievers moved him any more than a desire for fame. All the things of the world, even those stones over which Christ Himself had walked to Calvary, were of little consequence to his personal vision of good. He saw the world as an accumulation of filth, which men desired without reason. Only in the matter of obedience to the Vicar of Christ did he warm himself to speech, and this he did quite tediously to my way of thinking.

It was tedious to the king, too. He didn't want reminding of Urban any more than of the Welsh. He would never enlist under a papal banner, because it would force upon him what Anselm wished. I thanked God in His wisdom for giving me an Anselm to prate to the king, until I found a better advocate. Then Heaven sent me one.

On the fourth night before the ides of February a partial eclipse of the moon kept everyone awake through half the night with wonder and foreboding. No matter that we no longer believed with the ignorant pagans that a dragon tries to devour that heavenly body from time to time, thus bringing on the eclipse. When the peasants turned out into the streets to bang their pot lids, light their fires, and shout to frighten Moon-Eater away, we of the castle were out on the battlements watching. One couldn't have slept through such clamor in any event, but I confess to something akin to relief for more than the cessation of noise when I saw the moon slowly begin to regain her full light. There had been too many wonders out of Heaven lately.

In Normandy, Robert Curthose may have been awake, seeing the moon eaten by darkness, too. And like any other man, he may have caught the meaning of it. Was he meant to take up the cross? Like the moon, he might wax full again if he cast himself on Heaven's mercy and did God a service. He meant to do it, in the grand manner, but felt himself prevented by that most miserable of practical circumstances – he had drained his treasury dry to toast his friends. He was a pauper.

Some rumor of his taking the cross reached us from Rouen soon after the eclipse; I could only put the effect of his great resolve at Heaven's door. We heard he'd sent an envoy to the King of France, and since there was no war between them, I guessed he might be begging for money. But Philip didn't lend purses; rather he took them.

There was little use in Curthose's appealing to his own vassals; they were already wary of him as a debtor. A wiser man than he might have looked at their wolfish smiles and thought a second time before leaving his duchy to their mercy. He sent an envoy to the Pope.

In a month I received a visitor, one Abbot Jeronto of Dijon, a papal messenger. His appearance at our court was a rude jolt for the legate, Walter of Albano, who was still among us, hoping to gain favors from the king. Anselm, who quickly found reason to quarrel with Cardinal Walter, now lighted with joy to see the humble and pious Jeronto, especially as the abbot immediately favored our court with a set speech against the evils of worldly rule, a subject dear to the heart of our saint.

The king being apart from us for a few days at Windsor, I took the venerable Jeronto aside and heard from him another matter touching on the peace between certain rulers and their brothers. Then I took a good horse on a rough ride to Windsor.

It was late evening when I arrived, but the king and his friends were still waking. Fitz Hamon was there, stripped to his shirt, as if he'd been wrestling; also Prince Edgar; Wat Tirel; Will de Montfichet, castellan of the London Tower; Gilbert and Roger de Clare; Bledry the Welshman; and the fool, Robert Cornard. There were several of the foresters who kept the lodge, and the keeper of the walk of Windsor, all sitting in friendly accord with their betters.

Rufus rose from the table when he saw me. Firelight and torchlight made his face more ruddy and cast an aura about his long, tangled hair. His look was solemn, but he must have sensed there were no ill tidings. He opened his arms.

'I must see Your Grace apart,' I murmured as he embraced me. 'I have some news and a letter from Duke Robert that may please you.'

'Later – when you've eaten. You're wet to the shirt! Rob, fill a cup for this priest before his teeth start to chatter!' Under his breath he asked: 'What good news from Robin? Has he taken himself to a cloister?' Then his face sobered. 'He isn't dead?'

'No, my lord. He wants peace between you.'

He grunted, squeezed my shoulder, then led me to the table. 'Then why the secrecy?'

'He wants something else, too.'

He said no more. I was properly feasted while the conversation took up where I had interrupted it. As I might have guessed, it was about making war on the heathen. This time the consideration was how to provision and equip an army so far from home. I listened as I digested, saying nothing, although the king's eyes met mine several times, as if he dared me to interpose my usual cautions. Bledry sang to them a song he'd made about the supposed habits of the Mahometans, which made the company laugh. The foresters, cut out of the talk, began a dice game at the end of the table. Inevitably, people began to yawn. They'd been up and at the hunt since before dawn.

'You'll bed with me, Raf,' said the king, grinning. 'It's time I heard your prayers.'

I thought Cornard the Fool might have pulled a sour face at that, as I was drawn away to the stairs by the king's firm hand. The rest made beds where they would, near the fire.

When his squires had divested him and departed, the king sat with a wine cup idle in his hand, waiting for me to speak.

'Your noble brother wants to make peace with you, my lord. He feels that with so many sins in the world, the two of you shouldn't add to the number by emulating Cain and Abel. Of the twenty castles you hold of him, he'll grant you full seisin and contest no more with you on the division of their revenues.'

'Well!' He blew out a sigh of bafflement. 'He's just seen God in the Face, or what?'

'In a manner of saying, he has, my lord. He's taken the cross. He means to go to the Holy Land as soon as may be. I have a letter from His Grace Bishop Odo declaring his desire to do that and requesting your aid in furthering the plan.' I read it to him. Jeronto had brought it.

'Ten thousand marks? He wants ten thousand marks of m-me?

For all of Normandy?' Mouth ajar, head shaking, he seemed unable to take it in.

'Exactly, my lord. He'll pledge you all Normandy, with its revenues, for the space of five years, or until he comes home to redeem his pledge, whichever is the shorter term. Bishop Odo seems to have approved the offer.' I showed him Odo's massive seal and scrawl. He glanced at it, then waved it off as if it had an odor. I longed to add argument to Odo's, but there was no need. Everything I might urge on him was already in his mind.

He drank his cup, examined the dregs sourly, then flung it across the room and laughed.

'By God's F-face! Robin was always the man to piss at your feet when you wore new boots! You're another, you damned spoilsport! You're delighted with this, aren't you? Oh, yes! You'd like to see me stay at home like your granddam's dog – leashed to Normandy! – while Robin rides off to fame and honor! Well, you're going to be disappointed, because I'd see him turn a spit in Hell without a napkin before I'd let him get there ahead of me, let alone pay him ten thousand m-marks and kiss him good-bye into the bargain!'

I put my hands into my sleeves, a gesture he detested, and waited for his outrage to tire itself. 'Very good, my lord. I'll inform His Grace of your decision. God go with Your Grace and give you many victories. Who will have the rule of the kingdom while you're away? Will you pardon the Earl of Northumbria and set him on your throne as regent? Or the Earl of Chester? Or your brother Prince Henry?'

He shot a warning finger at me. 'God damn you, Flambard, you take too many liberties with me! Do you say Harry would betray me? He wouldn't! Or, if he tried, I'd wipe him off my throne when I came back, as if he were bird lime.'

'Yes, Your Grace – if you could.'

'What's that? You think I'm a Donald Bane?'

'I think you're the best soldier in Europe, my lord. But even great Alexander had to put his foot on solid land before he could conquer it.'

He advanced with a terrible look, the sort that made the superstitious bless themselves.

I said quickly: 'Nor do I name Prince Henry as a possible traitor more than any other man given such an opportunity to betray, my lord. Who'll take Duke Robert's pledge if you refuse him? A man who leaves a fat purse in the charge of a beggar may expect to find it lighter when he returns, but if he leaves a kingdom –? How if your regent here closed the ports against you? How if no French port would admit you? How if your host was weary and lean with war and had no provision, because the man to whom Duke Robert mortgaged Normandy refused to give you harbor?'

'Enough! That's enough!' He turned as if he loathed the sight of me and went to stand before his war chest. Inside it was his black-enameled shirt of mail with the glimmering dragon, which he must already have dreamed of showing to the heathen. For some time he stood, then he said in a hard voice:

'Very well. You'll have your way with me – you, my uncle, and my d-damned brother. But I'll make you pay for it. Go, tell Robin he'll have his silver. Then go tell my council I'll want ten thousand marks of them, to send a fool to his glory. They're all ripe men. Oh, they'll be glad to give it to you, won't they? If they don't give it willingly – *then get it where you can*, moneyman, but don't take it from my hoard. Be more p-persuasive – d-double the amount! I'll want enough besides to buy up lances, to fill Normandy.'

He came with an ugly smile and put his finger in the center of my chest, poking painfully into my breastbone to emphasize the words.

'You see? I'll be your schoolboy, this once. Let the council know it was all your plan. I'll take Robin's coronet and throne from him and keep them well. When he comes home again and if the heathen let him, he may redeem them – if he can.'

58

The Whitsun Court was like a barnyard for the cackling about my extortions, monster of iniquity that I was. I had made honest knights pawn their chapel chalices, made the churls weep, made simple monks resort to feed on bread and water, all to pay my 'unjust' gelds.

True, the great men of the land still wore golden chains and velvet; the rulers of abbeys and churches were still robust in girth; all their chins were still greased with meat; but they were broken men. One couldn't have told that it was they, not I, who passed the burden of my gelds on to the knights, churls, and monks. I had asked a little gift of each of them. They behaved as if I had demanded their firstborns' blood.

Anselm, as might have been expected, lamented the loudest. He had taken the plate from his monks of Canterbury to make his gift. They didn't bear the loss with the meekness he expected. He made amends by signing over to them one of his manors worth thirty pounds per annum, but still they grumbled. No one was pleased by that transaction, least of all the king, who profited less than the monks. I endured his sarcasm, as well as Anselm's tedious messages concerning my avarice, my effect on the king's soul, the sorry state of the kingdom, and a dozen other matters over which I had little control.

Gundulph came to me privately to see if there was any way the plate might be returned to Canterbury and the manor of Peckham to the archbishop.

'He's an unworldly man, Brother. He hardly knew the value of the plate or the land. Neither are of any worth in his eyes. He's a child in material matters, but a child after Christ's own heart. Now he fears he's betrayed his trust as archbishop, in letting go of land that was entrusted to him, and the plate, he reasons, was God's, not his, to bestow.'

'He's late in his fears. The plate is likely to be melted down by now, and frankly, Your Grace, it's of little matter if it is. Surely Canterbury has more than one set of holy vessels. Archbishop Lanfranc and the late king were both generous to that house.'

Gundulph shook his head at me in sorrow. 'My son, even in such a trifling matter you would oppose this good man. Why? Where did the strife between you begin? If the king goes overseas, you'll be yoked with Anselm to rule the land. It would benefit you to be a little flexible. I know you've had great burdens laid on your back. Why add this? Make your peace with him; see him as he is. He doesn't hate you, personally. I've heard him say he prays for you every day – '

'*Does* he!'

'Yes' – eyes watering as always, Gundulph looked at me soberly – 'always mindful of Our Lord's command to love those who despitefully use – '

'My lord of Rochester, I have not despitefully used the archbishop! I didn't command him to take his monks' plate, or to make a bad bargain for it with Peckham.'

'That is so. But you were harsh enough in your demand for immediate payment to incite him to it. At the least you could express your gratitude, or the king's, instead of letting my good friend know once again just how he has angered the king whom he loves. You'll have need of his wisdom one day. Why not offer him conciliation now and make use of his talents later?'

'His talents? In my opinion the only talent Anselm has, besides his ability to couch the simplest thought in the longest phrase, is to cause the greatest amount of turmoil to the largest number of people for the least reason. He does this wonderfully well! Ask his monks; ask the king; ask, if you will, the Pope, who must be weary of him by now! He exercises this remarkable talent everywhere, and then, when he has offended, he pretends he can't understand why anyone is provoked with him.'

'He is a saint among men, not a courtier.'

'Just so! A saint among men! Alas, we are men here in the court, not angels. We eat, drink, fornicate – make wars on those who oppose us! I mean, the king does what he must and so do I, which is to obey him. Does Anselm think I take pleasure in squeezing money out of England to send Curthose to Jerusalem? I'd rather throw it to the swine. But Curthose will go to Jerusalem and he will have silver of someone to do it. If that coin doesn't come from the king, where will it come from? Who will be our enemy across the Channel, Robert of Bellesme?

'God knows – and you may tell Anselm, if God hasn't revealed it to him – I'd ten times sooner spend the silver to build hospitals, mend the highways, raise churches, and feed the poor. But I have authority only to obey the king with a good grace. That is the part which God has given me to do. When Anselm learns that, he and I may become friends. Until then, tell him to let me be Matthew the tax gatherer at least, and not Judas, in his speeches and letters.'

'Is that how you see yourself?'

'Yes! Anselm and you may not like the analogy, but in my way I try to serve God, by obeying the commands of His anointed king. Let the archbishop try that, and he may find a way out of some of his distress.'

By September the whole wretched business was concluded. The king took the silver I had amassed and went to Normandy with it. His sole thanks to me for it was that he left me instructions to mend the London bridge in his absence, finish the curtain wall around the London Tower, and put a few more courses of stone on the walls of his palace at Westminster before the winter set in.

I found it next to impossible to conscript a labor force out of a famished land to do the work he left me. I called on all those men of the surrounding shires who owed labor service to the town for their land to come to London. I pulled them in by threat and by oxcart. They protested their families would surely starve if they abandoned them at harvest time, poor as that harvest looked to be. I countered with the argument that their families would survive the better, having fewer mouths to feed at home, as the laborers would eat at the town's expense while they did their service.

I put them first to mending the London bridge, which had been half carried away in the summer gales that tore at its age-rotted timbers. The best of my sorry army I employed to finish the curtain wall. In some manner, some of the Londoners looked on this as a frivolous enterprise. In spite of two rebellions in eight years, they could see no use in having a strong fortress to protect the city. Without a curtain wall the Tower was as useless to them as a sieve to bail the sea.

Beyond other considerations, they resented the influx of hungry men to the town whom they were obliged to house and feed. My days were passed in hearing complaints of drunkenness, petty thefts, and brawling between the men of town and shire. I had the offenders whipped, but a whipped man gives little labor, especially when he's half famished to start. In the end I transported the offenders to Westminster, where they were put to labor with less ale and somewhat more bread. The master of the works there didn't thank me for the decision, but he got a surprising amount of labor out of the malcontents. Even I was gratified to see how high the walls of Westminster had risen when frost put an end to the construction.

In the meantime, the king had met his brother at a neutral point in the French Vexin, under the wary mediation of Philip of France. There was great jubilation when the ten thousand marks changed hands. Curthose commanded a celebration that might quickly have eaten up his new-gotten wealth, but the eagerness of some of his followers to be gone on the holy campaign forced him to curtail gourmandising.

He set forth in the company of his cousin Robert of Flanders, his brother-in-law Stephen of Blois and Chartres, and a host of worthy knights, followed by a vast, ragged army of common folk drunk on the twin expectations of salvation and pillage.

The cry they sent up at their going was: 'God wills it! Jerusalem from the heathen!' I am told my king cursed the pious hope and declared he would loosen the teeth of the next man who said 'God wills it.'

One of the men who rode away with Robert was Odo of Bayeux. He had grown exceedingly fat in his old age, like his brother before him. As he was described to me, it took three squires to get him into the saddle. He might have stayed at home in Bayeux, reading Petronius and pinching the cheeks of his choristers; Rufus was too scornful of him to take revenge on him at so late a day. But Odo couldn't endure the prospect of having to call his twice-betrayed nephew 'my lord' again. So, he went.

They took the land route over the mountains into Italy, stopping at Rome to be blessed by the Pope, though not the Pope who had enlisted them. It was Clement who had the mastery of St. Peter's, not Urban. Though Christ may yet condemn him for the presumption, I understand he cheerfully gave them Peter's blessing, as well as Peter's bounty for the duration of their stay.

When they had all but pauperized him, they moved south again until they came to sunny Apulia, the stronghold of the mighty Guiscards, where they elected to pass the winter and harden themselves for war at old Roger's board.

I heard glad news out of Normandy that season. Rufus elected to remain there for the winter and early spring, putting the government into some state of coherence. He drove out those sycophants who hadn't found the courage to follow Curthose and he put decent men in their places.

After the anarchy of nine years it seemed even the anarchists were glad for a respite. Bellesme and all the rest who had fouled the land with strife were quiet, letting their new lord cleanse their Augean Stables without interference. Rufus worked with speed and commendable efficiency. He filled vacant ecclesiastic posts with well-recommended men, replaced garrisons left deficient by the holy expedition, and made a thorough progress of the duchy, hearing the complaints of the common men in his own person. He forgave his erstwhile enemies in the interest of peace. Stephen of Aumale and Robert of Bellesme came to him at Rouen at Christmas, paid him tribute, sat at his table, drank with him, as if they had never taken part in plots against his life.

I think it meant more to him then to have assumed his father's ducal coronet than to own the crown of England. When he came home at Easter to Windsor, he looked and behaved more like the prince I had first learned to love than he had in years. I rejoiced for him. He had been in a chronic state of anger and grief for the mutilation and death of William de Eu. I knew that, if no one else did. It was the chief reason for his sudden desire to go crusading. Now he had expiated his sorrow with a season of successful rule in the land of his birth, where the spirit of his father must have seemed very close to him. Perhaps he had time there to reflect on how cruelty is sometimes a necessary device of good rule, or perhaps he was simply kept so busy he didn't have the time to brood at all.

In any event, he came home a happier man, and I was sorry to have to present him with the Welsh, who were up to their usual business of raid, burn, and vanish as soon as they felt a lessening of strength against them. The Easter Court was brief, late in beginning and too soon concluded. Rufus called up his levies and marched into the west. As ever, the Welsh evaporated at the rumor of his coming. He spent a fruitless time in pursuit of them, then came back to Gloucester for the Whitsun Court where I waited to greet him.

He snorted at the speech I made him on his victory: 'This isn't glory I'm covered with; it's dirt. I haven't had a bath since Easter. Have them bring me a bath, will you?' He brushed aside the greetings of several members of the court and went up to his chamber, where I followed him. I helped him to divest himself of his mud-caked mail, his squires having dawdled below to refresh themselves with drink. When they came he was short with them, flinging them his shirt of mail, his helm, and his boots to clean and ordering them out of sight. The kitchen boys brought up his bathwater; his attendants poured it into his tub. He stripped himself of his shirt and stepped in with a sigh.

'Christ, I ache all over! Is this what it is to grow old? I'm not forty. How did my f-father ma-manage to stay in the saddle all day at his age?'

'We are none of us so young as we were, my lord.'

'It's this damned belly that hampers me, you know! God's Face, do I eat more than other men? Do I swill like old Hugh? No! I work like a pack mule, yet this gut keeps growing. I should be lean as Edgar.'

'Some men are born to leanness, my lord. It's no virtue in them. They can't help themselves any more than – '

'Than I can, to be fat? Or to have these eyes and a f-fool's tongue?' He let himself be scrubbed for a time, then said in a different voice: 'The Devil take that Welshman.'

'The Devil take them all, my lord. Which particular Welshman do you damn?'

'That war chief of theirs, that Cadogan. I was hoping I'd meet him face to face, or sword to sword. He must be made out of mist or else have wings on his heels, the bastard. He vanished every time I came close.'

He rose and stepped out of the tub, then was toweled and offered clean braies, hose, and shirt. He dismissed the attendants and sat on his war chest, gesturing for me to bring him wine.

'I burned him, though. By God, I burned him good! When he slinks out of his hiding place, he won't find things as they were – a taste of his own m-medicine. For every fort of mine he's put to the torch, I've sent ten villages up in smoke. For every fort I've lost, I'll build two. I'll turn Wales into an anthill of garrisons. I may never catch him out in a f-fair fight, but I can shut him up in his cursed foggy mountains. He'll eat his horses next time, before I wear out mine.'

I gave him wine. 'Surely there won't be any need of that for a while, Your Grace. You've won your time of peace. You'll stay the winter with us and enjoy it?'

'Maybe. Maybe.' He didn't want a time of peace. His look was desolate. 'The Scots are at murdering each other again!'

'Fortunately for the rest of the world, they prefer that to murdering strangers. Will you raise levies against them? It's only Red Donald they want to butcher now.'

He made a wry face. 'I owe a campaign to Edgar. He's been croaking "Jerusalem" in his sleep of late. I'll let him take an army up to Dunfermline and put another nephew on the throne there. That should keep him content.' He looked up with a sudden grin. 'Speaking of which, how've you done while I was away? Did you enjoy having the run of things without answering to me? I heard nothing but bad reports of you – which was all to the good, considering who was sending them. You kept them hopping to your whistle, did you? Even Urse de Abitot!'

'He was at the same business with the monks of Worcester, my lord, for which you've reprimanded him before. I only sent him a reminder of your writ of two years ago.'

'And threatened to have his holdings surveyed again, to see if he was paying all his taxes. I heard about it.' He laughed. 'You did well. I never thought I'd see the time Urse would back down from a priest. But he's a thief. You did well to rebuke him. I promised old Wulfstan I wouldn't let him infringe on Church property and I won't, thanks to you. What other news is there?'

'His Grace Bishop Odo is dead, my lord. He died soon after Easter, but the word didn't reach London until last month.'

His voice was toneless. 'Dead? In battle, or for treason?'

'Of a seizure, or some such thing. He left Duke Robert still in Apulia and went to Sicily, most likely to ask for aid from Duke

Roger. He was celebrating Mass at the cathedral in Palermo when he was stricken. He's buried there. Duke Robert finally left Italy and is said to be in Macedonia now, if he hasn't already reached Constantinople.'

The king gazed into his wine cup, then drained it and stood up. 'So – after a lifetime of treasons, one of them goes to Heaven, and the other, to Constantinople. Good riddance to them both! But God should have a care of Odo. He'll be making pacts with Beelzebub behind His back!'

Prince Edgar took his commission from Rufus with grave delight and marched with his nephew Edgar and the king's levies into Scotland after Michaelmas. They had signs from Heaven to light their way north – a comet and a fall of stars. Young Edgar, fired by that display, had a prophetic dream on the way that told him he must go to St. Cuthbert's Abbey at Durham and take the saint's banner for his own. He obeyed. The banner was borne before him into battle, and he – or rather his more seasoned uncle, the Atheling – had the victory over Donald Bane.

Donald was blinded and cast into prison. His confederate, young King Edgar's half brother Edmund, retired to a monastery before the same fate overtook him. In gratitude to St. Cuthbert, King Edgar gave the lands of Coldingham to the abbey and, later, the town of Berwick. He would have had his uncle stay with him, offering him lands and a title in Scotland to befit his royal rank. But the Atheling came home to Rufus again with sworn vows of allegiance from the King of Scots to the King of the English, kneeling at his feet to offer them.

The king received him with such pride and love, praised him so warmly for an enterprise that seemed to me to have had a foregone conclusion – the unseating of Donald Bane had been more than half accomplished before the prince and his nephew even approached the borders of Scotland – that it scarcely surprised me when that praise excited the envy and malice of one of his followers.

A knight of English birth, Ordgar by name, began to mutter tales about the Atheling which spread throughout the court until he was forced to bring them to open appeal before Rufus or be charged with treason, for it is treason to keep treason a secret from the king.

Ordgar told the tale that Edgar, trusting in his descent from ancient kings, was seeking to deprive King William of his crown. He had been met by throngs of worshipful English on his way north, had heard their cries of *cyne-bearn* and *hlaford* without protest, had held what amounted to a royal court at York, once the seat of his most malignant first rebellion against William the Great. He had held another such court at Durham, where he touched people to heal them of their scrofulous sores, as the saintly Confessor was said to have done.

Rufus heard Ordgar to the end of his speech, clutching the arm ends of his chair with whitened fingers while the flush of a great anger suffused his face. It was impossible to tell if his rage was kindled against Ordgar or the Atheling when he said:

'Prince Edgar, you have been charged in the hearing of your peers by a worthy knight. How do you answer this?'

'I have done no treason, Your Grace, neither to you nor to my conscience.'

The king's eyes, heretofore directed toward Ordgar, who stood smiling and confident before him, turned now to Edgar's pale, strained face. There was a profound silence in the hall. Not a man there was ignorant of the great love the king bore the Atheling, though there may have been a few not yet informed of its exact dimension and perversity. If they didn't know, they could not have guessed by the basilisk stare from Rufus to his friend.

The king swallowed and his voice sank as it always did when he made a supreme effort to conquer his stammer.

'This has been a time of treasons, s-since first I wore my f-father's crown. I have lost friends to treasons – kinsmen – men I trusted as I t-trust my own hand. Did you hold such courts as he says?'

'No, Your Grace,' replied Edgar in an equally muted voice. 'Where we came to rest the people flocked to see us, thinking you were with us.'

'You heard them call you – what was it he said? Royal-born? Lord?'

'My lord – I am royal-born.' The pride of those words, spoken so softly and without extenuation, had the force of a shout in that silent chamber.

The king's eyes flashed as they moved when he lowered his head. Those who looked at him from a distance must have imagined them vindictive. I saw they were lighted by a film of tears. He cleared his throat. 'There have been men of la-late who couldn't say as much, yet who would have m-made themselves king in my place, if they could. Did you touch the sores of the King's Evil as he says?'

'Yes, Your Grace.'

'Why did you do that? The healing touch, if a man believes that nonsense, lies only in the hands of an anointed king. Did you tell them you were such a thing as that?'

'I told them I would pray for them and that was a better medicine than any man's touch. But they insisted and held their arms up to me. They were pitiful creatures, my lord. I touched them where I couldn't avoid them altogether.'

'They called him their king and he touched them as if he were royal, Your Grace,' cried Ordgar, vindicated.

'Hold your tongue!' Rufus snarled in a sudden loud voice. To Edgar he said: 'This of the touch is f-foolishness! Only a fool would believe in it. But those were f-fools who came to see you – and fools breed t-treason in other fools with their s-s-su-superstition!'

'I'm not a traitor.'

'That's what de Lacy said, but he fled the kingdom soon after. This man has made a charge against you. On your honor, as a true soldier, will you answer it? If those English didn't think you held yourself to be a king, why did they come to you f-for healing? And if you didn't hold yourself to be a king, why did you do for them what only a king may do, let pass that it was *useless*?' His voice rose to a yell that broke it on the word.

Edgar's face changed. Dark anger took the place of sorrow in it. 'Because I couldn't avoid some of them! And, since you ask me in such a manner as to accuse me, let me say it, too – I *was* an anointed king! Before I was carried out to Berkhamstead to be yielded to your father, Stigand of Canterbury put the Chrism on me!'

'Stigand lost his office.'

'And I lost a crown that I never wore, yet the oil was *there*!' He pointed to his forehead. 'And the English know it. But I never thought treason when I touched those miserable men, I never *did* treason, and I refute the charge this man has brought against me. Let him prove it on me with a sword!'

'Gladly, my lord!' cried Ordgar, and there was a voluble assent from those in the hall.

Rufus sat down, his face drained of color. 'There'll be no trial by battle but by my leave, Englishman.'

I said: 'According to the old English law, Your Grace, the proper appeal of Englishmen to the judgment of God is by ordeal, not battle.'

The king's head snapped around to me. 'I'm all the law there is in this case, priest!'

I bowed my head, venturing a glance at Edgar to see how he had received this; he was unmoved. I didn't like him very much, but my mention of ordeal was a lifeline I threw on the king's behalf to save him. He'd never had the muscle for the lists, and he was four and forty. Ordgar was little more than half that age and had the arm of a broadswordsman, so heavily muscled that it made him seem deformed on the right side.

Edgar's well-greased arm plunged quickly to the elbow in a boiling caldron would pain him, but secret application of a balm of aloes for the three days preceding his showing it to the open court would get him through his ordeal. I could make the king see that and save them both their pride.

Edgar said stubbornly: 'Ordeal is the English law of old times, but this is no court of Englishmen. It is a court of soldiers and I am a soldier. I have the right to ask for trial by wager of battle and I demand it.'

He knew Rufus too well. Whatever the king felt for him at the moment, he wouldn't deny such a blunt appeal to his chivalry. Rufus nodded his assent, and the time and place of the trial were straightway fixed for the morrow.

Edgar retired to the chapel to pray through the night, and Rufus sat in his bedchamber brooding over a chessboard. I was his opponent, or would have been if he had made more than a superficial effort to pursue the game. Rather than put him in check, I removed my king from the board to gain his attention.

'You don't believe he intended treason, my lord?'

He looked at me from under his brows; the lighter eye seemed all but colorless. 'I didn't believe my uncle intended it, either – or Will de Eu. He had an army at his back up there.'

'But didn't use it, except as you commanded him.'

'Maybe he was testing the waters first.'

'Traitors don't test, my lord. They haven't the time. They must strike and prove.'

'Perhaps he struck a bargain with that sprat nephew I've let him put on the Scottish throne, that he'd have the aid of the Scots if he could find support from the English of the north. That would be worth a trial, wouldn't it?'

'I grant you. But you don't think he's done that, do you, my lord?'

He made a little wheeze, as if a laugh had gotten caught in his throat. 'When did you grow to be so trusting and tender of Edgar? I never saw any warm looks pass between you.'

'When did you grow to be so – so doubtful, my lord?'

'Since the last time a friend betrayed me, damn it!' He struck the pieces from the board with a slammed fist. He sat for a moment, staring at nothing, then said: 'No – no, I don't think he meant treachery. I believe – or I want to believe – he's still – Edgar. But an ordinary man can believe in friends. I've learned to my cost that a king can't.'

I nodded. He rose from his stool to pace. It was a lesson he'd gotten in his head, but not in his heart, yet. He burst out suddenly:

'Christ, why did he have to do such a stupid thing as touch for the Evil? A pack of lo-lousy beggars, any ten of whom Ordgar could hire to swear Edgar had urged them to treason! S-stupid! Ordgar did right to accuse him!'

'Then Ordgar should fight him. But what if Ordgar kills him? Will that prove Ordgar is right and the prince is a traitor? You scoff at the idea of the healing touch, my lord. Do you truly believe in the justice of trial by battle?'

'Yes! Why not? There has to be s-some way of settling disputes between men of good birth. You can't have knights calling their brothers-in-arms thieves and liars and just le-let it go. Blood feuds come of that, I promise you. I'd have young King S-sprat down here to answer for Edgar, and all of Hertfordshire ri-rising up to defend Ordgar, if I denied them satisfaction.'

'But what if Prince Edgar loses his battle?'

He paused and sighed. 'I'll exile him.'

'Believing him innocent?'

'Yes, God damn it, yes! I can't do anything else unless I pu— unless I put him to death – which won't be necessary, as Ordgar's bound to *kill him*!' He turned, seized the chessboard, and hurled it against the wall. One of his squires opened the door and put his white face through it, wondering at the noise, and was shouted out again.

'I thought I had done him a good turn, letting him go into Scotland, letting him put his sister's boy on Malcolm's throne. Why did he thank me with this?'

I stood up. 'My lord, I shall never understand the ways of chivalry if Roland himself consented to explain them to me. But if you believe your friend innocent of treason and believe he'll die in the lists – which will prove him guilty in the eyes of all who see the affray – why don't you tell him to choose a champion to fight for him instead? That's allowed, isn't it?'

He turned to stare at me. 'My God,' he said tonelessly. 'Call Edgar. Send him to me.'

I obeyed. When the prince was inside the chamber, I went down into the hall, but not before I heard him shout:

'No! You've had my pride and my service, my love and my honor, and treated them like toys. I'll fight my own wager.'

There was more, but I didn't stay to hear it. Awhile after, Edgar came down the stairs looking defeated and sullen. He motioned to a knight in his service to follow him aside and spoke to him. There were so few English knights at court that one could not choose but know all their names. This one was a Godwine, like several others, a man-calf, with great yellow mustaches and pale eyes. I saw him lift his head and nod several times to what the prince said. When he left Edgar he was smiling.

Ordgar must have been unhappy to find himself facing a man of his own age and weight the next morning; a natural enemy, too. Edgar had chosen well when forced to it. These two English had already drawn swords over a piece of land in Oxfordshire, it seemed.

The whole court was avid to see the trial. The king came late to his seat, his face stiff, his thick fingers picking apprehensively at his neck chains. Edgar sat apart from him in the event of being found guilty. The passage of arms began.

Their weapons had been agreed upon beforehand: lances for three passages, mounted; swords and battle-axes, in case one combatant was unhorsed but still lived to fight. There had been a brief dispute over the axes, as the Norman preferred a mace. At the first charge of horse, Ordgar broke a lance on Godwine, but didn't unseat him. On the second passage he sent Godwine sprawling in the dust, then all but brained him with the haft of his lance when he tried to get to his feet. Things didn't look hopeful for Prince Edgar, or his champion.

Ordgar leaped eagerly from his saddle as Godwine staggered up again. They drew swords and slashed away at each other's shields, until Godwine's blade broke and spun glittering across the field to fall before the stands where the king sat. He foolishly ran and grabbed it up, as if he still meant to fight with it, then saw how he'd sliced through his own hand. He flung it aside as Ordgar came running at him, yelling, with his sword lifted. I closed my eyes and said a brief prayer for his soul, but opened them again at a shout from the crowd.

Godwine had gotten his ax in hand and was a new man. He leaped aside, shouting, as Ordgar's sword was about to fall on his neck, then swung his ax on the sword, smashing it from Ordgar's grip. Ordgar reeled back, almost fell, but he was snatching his own ax from his belt at the same moment. When he got it, the real contest began.

An ax is an Englishman's true weapon. With all others he feels some degree of unease. He's a lout in the saddle, a butcher with a sword. He distrusts the bow and even thinks it unmanly to use it in war; but set him on his two legs with an ax in his hand, and no matter the odds, he'll put all the legions of Hell to shame for pure ugliness.

Ordgar and Godwine hacked at each other, screaming like berserkers, while the crowd about them bellowed for a kill and I felt my gorge rise at the blood spurting from Ordgar's mangled shoulder; Godwine struck him there three times. At last he fell, his arm nearly severed. The king was on his feet at the fall, as were all the rest in the stands except Edgar. Godwine swayed forward to where his enemy slumped and put out his hand to help him rise if he yielded.

But Ordgar, one arm useless and his own death certain, jerked a dagger out of his gambeson where he'd hidden it in defiance of the weapons agreement. Godwine sprang back as it slashed upward toward his throat; then he kicked the treacherous man in the face. Ordgar sprawled on his back with the Englishman's foot on his chest.

'Do you yield?'

'I yield.'

Godwine bent forward. Even Edgar was standing up now. 'Do you confess yourself a liar – and a traitor – false to your oath? Say it, or die damned!'

'I confess – a priest – bring a priest – '

I went down at once to receive his confession, which he could hardly speak with his ruined mouth. Two men lifted and carried him to the king's hall, where a surgeon looked at his hacked arm, but he died from loss of blood before the arm could be amputated and cauterized.

The king gave a feast in honor of Prince Edgar that night. Bledry composed a song on Godwine's valor for the occasion. Rufus rewarded the wounded but ambulatory Englishman with more generosity than met with approval from some of his knights of Hertfordshire, for he invested him with all Ordgar's holdings in that shire, despite claims laid for a portion of them by the dead man's kinfolk.

Prince Edgar sat beside the king again at the high table,

exonerated, redeemed – risen higher in the esteem of his friend than ever, since he first left the fellowship of Robert Curthose for the sake of their love. Edgar might have relished his new-gained position of power. There were those among us, including myself, upon whom he might have inflicted some revenge for the despite in which he had been held. I give him credit for instincts suited to royalty but seldom found there. If the Atheling felt any triumph over his enemies then, he concealed it with a sober look withal. One might almost have supposed he regretted his champion's victory.

59

Edgar Atheling's nobility earned him small credit with that one man whom his piety, more than many another man's, might have wished to please. Archbishop Anselm was dismayed to see the prince so openly beloved by his sovereign king and issued another of his dire warnings on the moral state of our court and nation. There were other specifics to the charge, but Edgar received his due as a corrupting influence on the king and such young men as followed his example in decorum, while I was especially cited for my neglect of the king's spiritual welfare, as well as my 'extortions' from Holy Mother Church.

Rufus countered the old man's tirade with one of his swift rages, finding quarrel with him again for the battle-worthiness of those knights whom Anselm was obliged to equip and send to the king's aid in his campaign against the Welsh.

It was a trivial quarrel and might have been quickly settled in Anselm's favor if the old man had admitted his Kentish bumpkins were not all Rolands, but that he had kept the best of them back for that other task the king assigned to him: safeguarding the southern coast during his absence. It was a commission Anselm had taken and performed with surprising earnestness, even falling into an argument with the papal legate on the matter of its urgency, and Rufus would have been pleased to hear such a straightforward answer. He liked a worthy opponent who could answer him bluntly and to the point. Lanfranc would have done no less.

But Anselm took another turn: rebuked by his king for his shortcomings and finding his own rebukes disregarded, he took refuge in self-pity. He retired to Canterbury and sent word to his friends at court to tell the king that he was now driven by the utmost need to leave his post and go to Rome. Rufus was first baffled by this request, then angrily suspicious.

'What does he mean? What's Rome got to do with it? Does he think the Pope can put his mesnie in trim for him, or what? Tell him to cure his sulks and come to terms with me like a man.'

Gundulph, who bore the message and was probably as much confused by it as Rufus, answered: 'Your Grace, I don't believe the archbishop has that in mind. He says only that he has great need to speak to His Holiness face to face.'

'Why? For what reason?'

'To – to take his counsel, Your Grace.'

The king eyed him narrowly, scratched his beard, and barked his laugh. 'His counsel? On how to manage me?'

'No, Your Grace, I'm certain – '

'Are you? Well – tell the archbishop I have a better opinion of him than he has of me. Tell him when it's t-time for counsel, he's better fitted to give it to Urban than Urban is to give it t-to him. Christ knows, he gives *counsel* better than any man alive!' He laughed again, raggedly. 'And he can't have any sins so black that only the Pope can absolve them. No, let him show me men, on horses that aren't s-s-spavined, be-bearing arms that aren't rusted, and I'll' absolve him myself. Tell him no – and tell him to attend me in Winchester.'

Anselm bore the refusal meekly. He came to Winchester and made his plea to the king in person. He was again refused. It was as if he couldn't hear the words, or had grown senile and easily forgot them. He waited a few days and appealed to Rufus once more. He was refused. The king went hunting in the New Forest for a week while Anselm sat in the royal hall surrounded by his clerks and waited for his return, then appealed again.

The king broke into a fury.

'No! No! And again, no! If you have business with Rome, send a m-messenger, or better yet, say your message to the cardinal legate and let him carry it to Rome for you. It's high time we were quit of him anyway. What is it you have to say, eh? That I've abused you? You've had your will of me in everything. What have I denied you, except a synod, which is un-ne-necessary in any event, because the roads are already so choked with bishops coming and going that a dray can't pass through a city gate without running into a litter of bishop's clerks coming the other way. When have I slighted you, Archbishop? I've given you my trust, made you chief in my council, set you to ju-judge in my place when I was abroad, brought your damned pa-pallium from Rome when you insisted on having it!'

There was a rush of indrawn breaths and a multiple signing of the cross among the pious throughout the hall. I shifted my stance in hope of catching the king's eye, but Anselm only bowed his head and answered doggedly:

'Your Grace has let me give counsel but has not seen fit to take it. I can do no more here. I must go to Rome.'

'To complain of me, because I haven't yielded to your every whim? Because my beard offends you, or my speech is too rough, or my s-sleeves are too long, or my friends not to your taste, or that I don't bless myself and lisp "if God wills it" before I visit the jakes?'

I murmured, 'My lord – ' and got a swift look of spite for it, but my intrusion gave Rufus pause to draw breath and cool his anger. Hugh of Chester was scowling at him; the de Clares looked as if they'd each swallowed a gnat. Anselm stood as before, patiently waiting for the king to conclude.

Rufus fetched a long sigh and sat back. In a muted voice he said: 'Most reverend and holy Father Anselm, the ways of holy men are as much a mystery to me as my ways are to you, but let us put an end to our quarrel, even if we cannot comprehend each other. If I have offended you with my charge concerning your knights, I withdraw all my charges. Send me hereafter such men as you will, however equipped and drilled, and I'll use them as I may. I quit you of all responsibility for them, except to see they come when I call them. Does that satisfy you that I'm not your enemy?'

'I must go to Rome, my lord. This of the soldiers is no offense to me.'

'By the Face, I say you'll never go to Rome with my consent!'

Anselm lifted his head and smiled faintly as if at the pronouncements of a stubborn child.

'Your Grace has all power in his hands. You do as you will, say what pleases you. But what you refuse me today you may grant tomorrow. I will multiply my prayers. I must go to Rome, my lord.'

'Keep him away from me! He means to send me ru-running mad, that's what he w-wants to do. Keep him off me, do you hear?'

'I will try, Your Grace, but – '

'Try? Do it! By God, do it!'

It was difficult to see how I could. The archbishop couldn't be denied his audience with the king if he persisted in asking for it. Anselm had fallen on the perfect way to undermine the king's will.

Each day he presented himself at court, standing humbly among his clerks and surrounded by his adorers, waiting patiently while the king heard other pleas. Every day the king dismissed the court before the old man could come before him, but Anselm had his clerks follow after him to try and press a petition on him.

Each day Anselm spoke to those who surrounded him, quite plaintively: he loved the king; he prayed for his soul daily; he must speak with him on a matter of great urgency. The lay lords, the bishops, were meekly enjoined to add their prayers to Anselm's. Failing to speak to the king, he would then return to Wolvesey and presumably take up those constant prayers once more.

Hugh of Chester attempted to intercede for him, along with a dozen others. He all but reeled backward under the force of the king's refusal:

'No! No! No! No! Is that a all-difficult word for you? Is *he* too deep for simple words? Find me some scholar to render "no" into Greek or Hebrew and I'll say it for him. No! You p-pushed him down my throat, Hugh, you and the Clares, but you can't m-make me s-spew him up again. He won't go to Rome to p-preach against me, or s-stir up fa-factions in F-france against me when I've done nothing to him! He m-may be Urban's to-toady, but he's servant to my crown and I don't give s-servants leave to wander and complain.'

We were removed to London to escape the dreaded old man, but he followed and continued to make himself visible every day. His daily message remained the same: he loved the king; he prayed for his soul's salvation; he must be let to go to Rome. Privately, I thought Anselm had lost his reason. Certainly, Rufus had lost his perspective.

'Love me? Love me and persecute me so? I'd rather have the l-love of the Devil! Tell him that! Tell the archbishop that for all his love, I hate him. I hated him yesterday, I hate him today, and I will hate him the more tomorrow. Tell him!'

Under compulsion I took that message in person. For a few moments after I entered the hall of the river mansion that was Canterbury's home in London, I was uncertain I would be admitted to Anselm's presence. His clerks looked on me as if I stank of sulfur and would gladly have let me kick my heels on the chamberlain's bench until the Millennium. If they chose to humiliate me I must endure it, for the king had made it clear he wanted a report on the archbishop's reaction to his message.

Despite my trepidations I was finally admitted to Anselm's presence a little after None. He came forth from his chapel to speak to me, his myopic eyes blinking weakly, as if he had dwelt in darkness for hours. His face looked worn. I had little doubt what his vigil had cost him. Much as I detested him, I couldn't help but feel a qualm that he might actually kill himself with trying to bend the king's will, in which case we would have a martyr to contend with.

He raised his eyes unwillingly to my face and asked: 'What is your message, chaplain?'

That he didn't address me as 'my son,' or 'brother in Christ' told me in what regard he held me.

'Your Grace must know the message is none of comfort to you. The king rejects your petition and commands you to desist from troubling him with it further.'

'Do I trouble him?'

'Don't you know that you do? Your demands have driven him quite out of his natural character. He is not himself, or he would never have given me the message I'm commanded to bear to you.' I told him the king's words exactly. 'These are not the words of the king I have loved and served for so many years, Your Grace, a king who has a heart incapable of hating anyone but those who do foul murder and treason, and even some of these he has forgiven when they bend to his will.'

He had his staff in hand. He used it as an invalid might to support him to his stool, where he sat down gratefully.

'I wish my words might drive him out of his *unnatural* character. I wish I might have the tongue of a Gregory, to make him realize what his "character" will do for him. It will lead him to his damnation, if it has not already.'

'Your Grace, the king is a man of the strictest honor – '

'The king is a man of rash temper and wicked pride, who lends himself to Hell with interest, like a usurer. And you light him the way to the Pit. They've named you well, Flambard.'

My face grew hot, as if he'd slapped it.

'Your Grace, I cannot contend with you in words. You are the master of arguments. But you mistake your king and you mistake me. I do not lead the king into anything. He is my lord; it follows that he leads me. And the king is a man who very much wishes to do good, to rule well, to make his realm as safe for his people as it was in his father's day.'

'And so he makes constant war? And so he maims and hangs poor men for the theft of a hare? Does he imagine he's doing good when he sends you to rob the churches and abbeys of their plate to fill his war chest?'

'The king does not make war, my lord. He gives war back to those who make it on him. As for those who steal hares, the punishment is hard, I know, but the law was made before our days, and if the king should have mercy on such thieves, we should have none but thieves to abide with. As for the poor, the Gospel tells us – '

'Don't quote Scripture to me, man! You taint it with putting your tongue to it!' He stood up trembling, his filmy eyes wide with wrath. 'What can you know of Scripture, or of your duty as a priest? When do you read it, when say your Office, or your prayers? When do you guide the king, when confess him? What penance do you put on him for his sins? The king is a sodomist well sunk in his perversion. The number of his young men is legion. When have you tried to turn him from his whores?

'You sit at table with them, laugh at their sorry pranks, smile when the king kisses them in the face! Every night you give him your blessing and he takes a lover into his bed the next moment. Every morning you come to hear his prayers and a catamite slips out the door as you enter. You tell me you love him and serve him? I say you must hate him, because you do him no service becoming his office, or yours!'

I thought it as well to leave him then, but as I moved he said in a loud voice: 'Don't turn away from me until I dismiss you, priest, or you'll have no office to serve!'

I faced him again, slowly, remembering how he'd deprived me of Giva.

'Ranulph Flambard, I say you are a disgrace to the priesthood you bear and a traitor to the king you pretend to serve. Behold yourself! Your hands are decked with rings like a heathen's leman. Your gown, your cloak, are cut from a cloth it would shame me to wear, save to the glory of God in His temple. Have you looked on your own face? Your mouth is aslant with a cynic's smile; your eyes look every man insolently in the face. Every woman, too, I have no doubt, in spite of your vows. What are you? A pervert's sycophant, a tyrant's advocate, a betrayer of your brothers in Christ! You – who stand so close to this king, who say you know him so well – you should have been my natural ally if you loved him as you say you do. You – a priest – who were meant to be one of God's lambs, charged with the duty to bring counsel to the wolf in the heart of Man – you have only learned from the wolf to prey on the weak and lick your lips at the smell of their flesh!

'When the king has oppressed the Church, *as he has*, when have you defended her, your natural mother? When he has kept vacant the thrones of bishops and abbots to swell his hoard with their rightful revenues, when have you told him he was in error? When their property was given into your hands to guard, when have you failed to glut yourself with the farming of it? Don't close your eyes to me! Look me in the face!'

I obeyed. He sat down again, still clutching at his staff with either hand, and stared back at me. In a softer voice, as if there were something in his throat, he said:

'We are not allies; but God in His wisdom set us both a task and we have failed it – and Him. Is there any part of your heart not yet so hardened by pride but it can still feel the sorrow of that failure? If there is, someday you will come to know the agony I feel now. Someday, if I live, I will weep for you, when you crawl on your face before God, remembering what He gave you to do that you failed in. I weep now. I was sent to sow the seeds of Christian love and mercy in the heart of a young king, but you, my lazy plowman, failed to prepare the ground for my seed. And so it withers, and the man is deprived of that Blessed Bread he was meant to eat.

'That is more than a great pity; it is a great sin, and I must try to atone for it. That is why I must go to Rome to take counsel of the Holy Father of us all, for my sin, which is as grave as yours. I have failed him. If you truly love this man whom God has anointed to be a king, you will persuade him to give me leave. I charge you to it. I command you to it. Refuse me at your peril. Even your soul must stir a little at the thought of another man's damnation.'

'Well,' said the king when I presented myself to him, 'smock your cheeks and they'd make patches for a virgin's shift. Did he rake you over the coals, unfrock you, or what?'

'I gave the archbishop your words as you spoke them, Your Grace, but he is still determined to see Rome. I believe he will keep applying to you until you grant him his wish or have him shut up in prison.'

'Now there's a thought!' He studied me wryly.

'Not one worth considering, my lord. I was only trying to convey his determination. Why not let him go? It's beneath your dignity to quarrel with this – old saint, let alone attempt to punish him. He has many friends at court. You will hear endless appeals. Why not grant him his wish? He says it's for the good of his own soul he must go to Rome, not to condemn you. Why not let him go?'

He came forward to me, head cocked. 'He has converted you.' He affected enthusiasm. 'Repeat me his sermon! It must have been enough to send Saul tumbling from his ass again.'

'He says I'm a bad priest, which is no news to any, including myself. That's of no consequence, my lord. I tell you now, as I've said before: it is an offense to your nobility to keep the old man here against his will. More: he's a famous scholar, a speaker to whom many an ear will gladly attend if he's kept here. He will be heard calling you a tyrant. Some men will choose to believe it. Left unopposed, he's a dreamer. He says he means you no harm and I believe it. Let him go where he will and put your mind to more important matters.'

He chewed his inner cheek, studying me. 'Well – you know the priestly mind better than I. Tedious old fool! But when he goes, he goes forever. He needn't think he'll keep his throne! I'll have a word to say to Rome about that!'

The next morning the archbishop presented himself as before. The king had met early with his council. They looked grim, or hangdog, as they issued from the council chamber and took their places in the hall. The king called the archbishop to him:

'Reverend Father, you have wearied me much with your petition. If you were a common man, I should say you owed me a fine for the annoyance you've given, but since you are not, I offer you an alternative: you may take your leave of us freely. But you will go as you came: a beggar. I will seize the archbishopric into my own hands and you will never again come before me as archbishop, or any other sort of priest. I will banish you. Do you understand me?'

Some of Anselm's clerks broke into shouts of dismay for this, while some of the king's adherents cheered the king, who angrily waved them to silence. 'Do you understand? Perhaps you'd like to go home and think about it before you answer? It isn't every day a man gives up a throne for a whim.'

'I must go, my lord King, for the sake of my own soul's health, for the sake of the Christian religion – and for your own honor and profit, if you will only believe that. God will protect the throne of Canterbury and in time will put a better man upon it. Thrones and miters honor only those who – deserve them. I must go to Rome.'

The king stared at him. 'You're breaking faith with me. You swore to me. Doesn't that trouble your conscience, Archbishop? Are such things as oaths of as little meaning to you as thrones and miters?'

Anselm looked up from studying his own hands. It was a scholar's question which pricked through his fanatic's brain to the scholar within him. In a schoolroom voice he answered, as to the question of an eager novice:

'Every earthly duty involves in its own nature a saving of duty to God. Faith pledged to earthly matters is given according to the faith due to God, my lord. Faith to God on my part is therefore excepted by the very terms of my oath, which was taken from me against my will. I gave it, unwilling, to a king anointed to be Christ's vicar in this realm. The king is no respecter of Christ's words, or of God's will. I must serve God before Man. He bids me look to my own soul. I must go to Rome, my lord King.'

'You may take nothing with you of the treasures of Canterbury. That includes your vestments, mind you!'

'I will go naked and on foot, rather than give up my purpose.'

The king's face reddened. 'I've never said you must go naked!' He glared at me and gestured for me to read the proclamation he'd had me prepare. Within eleven days Anselm must be ready at some haven to cross the sea, and a messenger from King William would be there to tell him what he might take with him. Anselm bowed his head to that. His companions now urged him to depart the court, fearing no doubt that the king would think better of his word if he stayed. Anselm put aside the hands that plucked at his sleeves.

'My lord, I am going. If I could be gone with your goodwill, it would better become you and it would have been more pleasing to every good man. But not even for your anger will I withdraw myself from love of your soul's health. Knowing not when I may see you again, I commend you to God. As a ghostly father speaking to a beloved son – as Archbishop of Canterbury speaking to a King of England – I would give you my blessing, if you do not refuse it.'

There was utter silence in the hall. The king sat stone still, looking on the archbishop. At last he stirred, his manner almost lethargic. Anselm had shamed him, I thought, though why such a speech should touch the proud soul of Rufus I couldn't say.

'I don't refuse your blessing.' He wouldn't rise, but bowed his head as he sat. Anselm came forward and reached up his hand to touch the head of Rufus, moving the fine hair with his gnarled fingers. He made the sign of the cross above the head of the king, then went forth from the hall, striding like a man from whom half his age had been lifted.

Anselm went directly to Canterbury. The day after he came he gathered his monks and bade them farewell; then, in the sight of a crowd of monks, clerks, and lay folk, he took the staff and scrip of a pilgrim from before the altar and departed for Dover. William Warelwast, my clerk, met him there as the king's man. For two weeks they waited together for the wind to change so that Anselm's ship could sail. On the fifteenth day it did, and Warelwast did that duty which had been given him. He laid his hand on the archbishop's shoulder and declared:

'Anselm of Aosta, in the king's name I restrain you from leaving this realm until you have declared unto me all treasure you take with you.' He then proceeded to search the archbishop's baggage thoroughly, while Anselm's clerks cawed and shrieked about him like so many incensed ravens. After which they were all allowed to board the ship and take their leave.

Thus did the scholar of Bec sail out of our ken. He did not get the satisfaction he may have looked for from the Pope, if he did lodge a complaint against the king, but whether he found that 'peace of soul' he went in quest of, I cannot say.

Warelwast returned to London to give his accounting. Fulcher burst in on me at my house a few hours later. His face was more pale than usual, though he had grown steadily paler and thinner in the time since Giva's death. Osbern had said once, in his unthinking way, that Fulcher was starving himself for grief, but he attributed the cause of the affliction to the recent death of our father. I knew better.

I rose from my stool, prepared to cheer him, and Isabel was already in the act of pouring him a cup of perry, but he burst out at once in angry abuse:

'God help you, what have you come to? How cruel and petty can you be? I would never have believed – but this was your work, wasn't it? I can see your hand in it all the way!'

'What on Earth are you talking about? Sit down, for the love of – Isabel, get him some wine instead.'

'I don't want your damned wine, or your damned hypocrisy! I only want a direct answer from you: did you send Warelwast to abuse the archbishop or not?'

'Abuse him? Who says he was abused? The king himself ordered him to be escorted to his ship, ordered his baggage searched, if that's what you're referring to. Anselm accepted the terms. You heard him say he did.'

'Yes, he had to agree, didn't he? But to ransack his things with a great crowd staring on, as if he were a thief, or a runaway slave – '

'I regret the necessity as you do, but bishops have been known for thieves before this – your patron and mine, the Lord Odo, for example. The property of the see is confiscated to the crown and all of it must be accounted for. Too bad if he took some of it with him.'

'Did anyone really suppose he would? Did the king think it? I doubt it! But there was worse than the mere opening of bags and hampers. Warelwast had two weeks – two weeks! – to make his search. He chose to wait, or was told to wait, until the old man was about to board his ship, when he was saying his last good-byes to his friends, who then had the shame of seeing him publicly humiliated.'

'That was the proper time to do it. Before then it couldn't be known for certain whether he would actually go. Bishops have been known to change their minds, too.'

Isabel said: 'Fulcher, dear, do sit down. You look so ill. Take some wine.' In spite of his continued formality with her, she had formed an attachment for him, based, she claimed, on his fancied resemblance to me in other years. Women are unfathomable. When I was Fulcher's sort of person she had treated me abominably.

He ignored her efforts to soothe him.

'You knew all about this, didn't you, Raf? You enjoyed thinking it up beforehand. You enjoyed hearing Warelwast and the others tell about it this morning. I watched you. That's when I began to know. You're probably enjoying this now.'

'Not very much. I've never found hysterics amusing. Why are you so offended? I never knew you held the archbishop in such esteem. If you'd told me, I might have sent you instead.'

He said flatly: 'God, yes! You might have. Why didn't you, I wonder? You've given me enough other disgusting things to do. Maybe that's why it doesn't seem to bother you. You've had me to do it all for you.'

'Do what? You're rambling.'

'Carry your writs, make your threats, badger holy men in their cloisters – for money, money, and more damned money! But you didn't make me do this. I'd like to think it would have shamed even you to ask me to humiliate that good old man for the sake of your revenge.'

'My revenge, if you choose to call it that, was of *such* little matter to *him*! Compared with what he'd done to me, I'm surprised you think it so harsh.'

'I know – I know. I remember how you were when she died. I felt sorry for you then. But you've recovered *nicely!*' He shot a brief look of dislike at Isabel, whom it startled.

'Have I recovered? You know all about it, do you? You have

wonderful perceptions, brother. You know my heart, Anselm's, everyone's but your own, apparently; but we won't go into that. Look, I didn't separate him from anyone he loves. He chose to go. I didn't take anything from him, or cause the death – '

'You did! You caused Giva's!' He shouted it, and it seemed to take the last of his breath. He leaned on the table, panting. 'Anselm didn't make her die, you did, so don't stare at me like that. You did it with all those babies and all your lies and all your damned ambition.'

I might have struck him, but he fell to his knees before I could raise my fist. Isabel screamed and reached out for him, but he bent over and slid to the floor in a swoon.

'What's the matter with him? Is he dead?' Isabel whispered, standing back from Fulcher now with her knuckles in her mouth as if she'd just seen the marks of leprosy on him.

'I don't know.' I stooped to examine him. 'That explains it. His brow's like an oven brick. Call in your porter and we'll put him to bed. He's been raving out of his head. Go to your 'still room and get him something to cool him. He'll be himself again when he's rested.'

I found I could lift my brother without the aid of the porter, who took fright from Isabel's white face and flinched from him. I carried him to old Trudy's bedchamber and put him on her bed, then sat beside him to examine him more fully.

His skin was dry and hot, his breath rapid and shallow. There were fever spots on his cheeks. I put my ear to his chest and heard a dreadful sound: a sort of grating when he breathed, as if there were sand in his lungs. My anger with him was gone, extinguished almost at the moment it had been kindled. I chafed his thin hands to bring him to life again.

'Fulcher. Fulcher, let's forget our quarrel. You're my good right arm, brother – my conscience. What should I do without you?'

He opened his eyes; his gaze drifted over the room until it came to me. He sighed. 'Everyone at court despises you for what you did to Anselm. They've grown afraid of you, so they may not say so. Only the king praises you, so they must learn to despise or hate him, too. Does that – please you, brother?'

60

My own brother refused to remain in my house. In spite of my efforts to reason with him as I sat by him into the small hours of the night, bathing his brow and speaking every word of conciliation I could utter, he rose at dawn when I had gone to my own bed at last and made his way to St. Paul's. There Maurice promptly put him in the infirmary. When I arrived to inquire about him in the morning, Maurice was very cool to me.

'He will be well cared for here. You needn't trouble yourself about him. Our infirmarian was trained at Salerno.'

'Trouble myself? He's my brother! He's also my clerk, Maurice, so I have a double duty to "trouble" myself if he's ill. Give him over to me and I'll send him down to Dover for the salt air.'

'Your clerk is also a clerk of this chapter, as you are yourself,' Maurice said coldly, and I saw at once I had trespassed on our friendship.

'Forgive me, Your Grace, for my presumption. Will Your Grace permit a brother to speak to his brother clerk for a moment? Only to ask him if he'd prefer sea air to the stink of London, of course, for the sake of his infected lungs? I promise you, I'll not follow him to Dover to persecute him in my notorious way.'

'I've already told him he'll be sent to Fulham when his fever is gone.'

'Fulham. Of course. River vapor is so much more healing than sea air.'

'Do you have any other matter you wish to speak to us about?'

'Maurice – I beg your pardon – Your Grace, why are you angry with me? This dispute between Fulcher and myself is of a different sort and of longer duration than you may suppose – '

'That is not our concern. Do you have any further matter? If not, you have our permission to take your leave.'

'By God, Maurice, I've been your friend for nearly twenty years! Will you judge me without hearing me as the rest have done? I thought you were an honest man.'

He was silent, his gaze fixed on me frowningly.

I said: 'Warelwast did his duty. No more. He acted according to royal decree. The king gave the archbishop full warning that if he deserted his office and the realm in the manner he proposed, he'd be doing so without the royal favor. Yet Anselm persisted in his blind-baby's way to do it, though he knew exactly what the king's words meant for him.'

'You had the man's personal belongings ransacked as if he were some common felon!'

I said it through my teeth to keep from shouting it: 'Yes! I see this is to become the gospel version. Yes, a felon is *precisely* what he should have become when he defied the king. A traitor to his oath and his duty he most certainly became. Yet no harm was done to him and the matter is now ended, whether you choose to believe it was because the king wished it, or Anselm contrived it, and I did nothing but my duty to them both.

'But – *if* I could have done more, Maurice, I would have done! By which I mean, if I could have sent Anselm out to sea naked as Job and afflicted with boils, it would have been my pleasure. If that's what makes you angry with me, you have the right!'

'You are indeed the king's good servant in all things, Ranulph,' Maurice said. 'He must be impatient to see you even now, for which cause you have our leave to go to him.'

Robin Bloet snubbed me in the great hall as I entered the palace, whose shabbiness and neglect were becoming more depressingly apparent every season as it declined and the new royal hall took shape beside it near the West Minster. I couldn't even summon a proper sense of scorn when Robin averted his eyes from me and pretended to be speaking to his chaplain. He only followed after his kind. What more pathetic member of the general herd is there than one who was a rebel in his youth? I bowed to the king, who chastised me:

'Well! So you're finally here. Where've you been, in bed with your hearth girl? You look like a haggard. Come, perch yourself and let's begin. Maurice has excused himself from the council today. Do you know why?'

I shook my head, took my place beside him, and drew out a petition from the bundle proffered me by William Warelwast. The lords of the council took their stools gloomily. The king must have felt a touch of their disapproval, too. I knew he would feel it more than they could guess. He would be sharp-tongued, mostly with me, and I would be patient until he'd discharged his guilt. I prepared myself for petty wrangling.

I was wrong about him. Once order was established and the Bishop of Winchester had offered a prayer for heavenly guidance of the council, the king went straight for the vitals of his critics.

'The see of Canterbury is vacant. Abandoned w-would be the b-better word. I now consider that there n-never was an archbishop between old L-lanfranc's death and this m-moment. Therefore: all writs, acts, orders, and deeds s-signed or committed by – by the *abbot of Bec* – are null and voi-void. Any man unfortunate enough to have treated with him on any matter must now t-treat with me, or risk the loss of what he's gained. Until my clerks a-assure me order has been restored to Canterbury and no inju-justice done to its tenants by their *former false lord,* there'll be no talk of new archbishops.'

There was immediate turmoil. Anselm's worshipers protested the implication that their saint was never archbishop. A few protested on the grounds that the decree would confuse the courts throughout the land. I heartily agreed with them, though I kept silent. Nullifying Anselm's acts would create the worst snarl in the courts since the town of Babel last held a husting. Every clerk who had lost a post through drunkenness, every litigant who had ever paid a grudging fine, every widow still in conflict with an in-law over well rights, would now descend on the court to see if their cases might be remedied. The whole work of the Canterbury chancery would be bogged down in litigation for the next five years, and I would be responsible to see it was set right.

But the king would hear no argument beyond the initial protests of Anselm's friends. By force of will and baleful look he made them understand it was no use to plead with him for Anselm. He turned the discussion to his own imminent departure for Normandy.

'We have demanded of the F-french king that he return to us the Vexin, which is ours by birthright and battle-right from the days of our fa-father – and for which he s-seems to have little use, or he'd not have put it into the hands of his capon son Louis.' He paused to grin at the grunt of agreement he got from Robert de Meulan, great lord of the Vexin, who had recently been obliged to do homage to Louis for his keep on the Seine.

'But poor Philip, what can he do, eh?' asked Rufus. 'His whore keeps him busy by night and his belly by day. He's got no time to defend the Vexin. We offer to do him that service better than his hirelings, or his s-son, and to that end we have demanded of him the border forts of Pontoise, Chaumont, and Mantes.'

There was silence. He had the full attention of those lords who must divide their fealty between him and Philip; the lords of the rich valley of the Seine who would follow him like hounds to the hunt if the Vexin were his quarry.

He sensed their greed. 'Well, now, shall we go and ask King Philip again, in all courtesy? And if he still denies us – *and* if he still puts his b-borrowed wife and his appetite before his honor – shall we do for him what he never had the belly or the arm to do – make his son into a soldier?'

He got a cheer for that, even from old Hugh of Chester, who had just hotly contended with him for the sake of Anselm's true election. All the mighty men of Normandy were eager for a chance to hit at Philip the excommunicate, the taker of bribes, the breaker of promises. They fell into an avid discussion of how the campaign against him might best be begun.

'Well, are you pleased with me?' Rufus asked when we had left the council and gone up to his chamber, where he was divested of his fine embroidered mantle and azure tunic to be made ready for an afternoon's hunt in a rather dirty but more serviceable brown tunic and leather gambeson. He had left the joint justiciarship to me and to Bishop Walkelin of Winchester.

'Are you? I've put it all in your hands, really, you know. I only included old Walkelin to please the Giffards.'

William Giffard, our onetime chancellor, had been insinuated back into the royal favor by the persistence of his kinsmen. There was rumor he'd be chancellor again, if he didn't buy himself a bishopric first. He was said to have set his heart upon Winchester. Gerard had just taken the throne of Hereford.

'Old Walkelin's a sensible fellow,' Rufus said when I only bowed my head in answer to his question. 'He won't give you any difficulty. From the looks of him, he won't give anybody difficulty soon except his sexton. If he dies before I return, you'll take inventory of his estates?'

'Yes, Your Grace. Will you appoint Will Giffard to his place then?'

He pulled off his rings, all but the one that had been Cormac's, and gave them to his chamberlain, who gave them to his steward, who put them in a little coffer while the king cocked his eye at me.

'You wouldn't approve of that? No, I can see you wouldn't. Who'd you prefer? Yourself? I doubt you could afford the luxury of Winchester, Raf – or could you? Have you farmed yourself to riches, bringing in my sheaves?'

I ignored that. 'William Giffard is an amiable man, my lord, but you must own he's a fool.'

'He's a fool, but thanks be to Fortune, I don't own him. Every family must own to its fool. Mine has Robin and that's enough.' His voice took on an edge. 'I'll name whom I will to Winchester, friend; but no man will get it who hasn't plenty of silver to pay for it. I'm going to war, Raf. Not a mean, niggling war with clerks, now, but one that will win me some honor. I want the Vexin and I mean to have it, or I'll not come back to this miserable island. I'll have

Normandy in my hand before Robin comes s-stealing home from the heathen. I'll haul coals for the Devil to have it!' His chamberlain and steward goggled at him for this vow. When he noticed them he drove them from the chamber with a shout of exasperation:

'Get out, you milk-sucks! I can lace my own boots! Now' – he wheezed out a laugh when they were gone – 'they'll go and tell the pious that I've kissed the Devil's arse, the fools. Give me some wine. I should have said there's a demi-devil I mean to hire to haul stones for *me*. His name's Bellesme. Familiar?'

I took in a careful breath. 'You mean to make an ally of Robert of Bellesme, my lord?'

'I mean to employ him. I've set him to building me a good tower on the Epte, at Gisors, to overlook Chaumont. When I've got that and Roche-Guyon, which is being haggled for, and de Meulan's keep, which is mine already, I'll have the Vexin in a vise – and Normandy will be safe to me. Does that give you a notion of how much silver I'll want from your reeves, priest?'

'You'd hire Robert of Bellesme to make a place safe for *you*, my Lord?'

'Oh, he'll do it! He prides himself on making good defenses, and it'll keep him too busy to p-poison me. But he doesn't sell cheap, so see you keep me in co-coin. I may have to hire a taster to sample my mutton.'

He went over to Rouen at Martinmas, leaving me to hear laments from the coast, where his army had been waiting too long for a fair wind. As ever when soldiers are kept idle, there had been some plundering, many charges of breach of peace, and not a few babes engendered too rudely in hayricks. The king hated a rapacious knight and punished some of these offenses harshly, but I had much compensation to make before I could turn my attention to the inventory of Canterbury.

Bishop Walkelin did not survive the winter. He died during the feast of Christmas and I was left sole regent for the king by Epiphany.

I mourned old Walkelin as much as any other who knew him. He'd remained my friend when others forsook me. He was the uncle of Gerard and had been most helpful in getting Robin Bloet and me places at St. Paul's after l.ord Odo's fall. Therefore, it was the more outrageous to me when a foul rumor arose from some undisclosed source which said I had been the cause of Walkelin's death.

According to this malignant report, I'd gone to Walkelin on the morn of Christmas and demanded of him a sum of two hundred pounds in silver to aid the king. They say I interrupted the Holy Mass to do this thing at the very moment when the Divine Body of Our Lord was being exalted on Its paten by the old man's feeble hands. Walkelin naturally rejected my infamous request at once, then prayed to God that He might take him from so vile a world as could contain a wretch like me. Heaven heard him, and he expired at the foot of the altar to my natural consternation.

What can one say about such stupid nonsense? Is it nothing to the perpetrators of this slander that Walkelin died ten days after Christmas in his bed, or that his death was long expected as the result of his age and the sickness that had been devouring his flesh for a year?

I was a witness to his death, to be sure, but far from cursing me for being the cause of the Church's ruin in our land, as the legend has it, he blessed me before he died.

'Now you'll have the whole burden on your back,' he said. 'I'm sorry for it, though it's still a young back and I've done little enough to ease it these past weeks, I fear.'

'You've done more than anyone, Your Grace. You've shown me charity and patience. I thank you for that, and for all the other proofs of friendship you've given me through the years. You almost make me forget my reputation.'

He touched my hand on the bed cover beside his. 'Gerard still loves you in his heart. Young Bloet, too. You must look to them.'

'I don't think so, Your Grace.'

'Look to Thomas of York, then. York has felt itself much abused in the matter of the primacy. Now there's no one at Canterbury, Thomas will come courting you, if you let him. He'd like to exchange thrones, you know. I would commend you to a better friend – Our Lord – but I suspect you'd resent it. Still – ' He made the sign of blessing before my face.

I bowed my head. 'Do I seem lost to redemption to you, too? I hope I'm not, my lord.'

'No, no – '

'You know me for what I am – a tax gatherer. But even one of those came to a good end, the Scriptures tell us.'

He almost smiled, but then a change came over his face, as if he were in pain.

'Shall I call your physician?'

'No! Listen to me, Ranulph. I doubt we'll speak together again. You must be the king's true friend – '

'I've always been that, my lord.'

'No! His *true* friend! Turn him from his path! He won't love you for it. He needs – someone. It might have been me, but that's too late now. I sat by him – '

I thought he wandered. He'd never been the king's intimate. I prepared to leave him to sleep, but he caught me by the wrist with his bony hand and held me. 'Listen to me! I have known his temptation – and overcome it. He may, too. I have had a dream – a vision – some such thing these last three nights – '

I felt a chill from the touch of his cold flesh. He wandered. 'What dream was this, my lord?'

'Why' – he released my arm – 'it was nothing – only – I sat by him in the sanctuary of my church here, at Winchester.'

'No more than that?'

'No more. Except – he said nothing. Nor did I. We sat so long. I thought: Will we sit forever thus and he will not speak and no man speak for him? That was a long thought. Each time I woke from this dream I wept as for a great sorrow. Three times I dreamed this dream. Can you find any meaning in it?'

I shook my head. The feeling of cold must have come from his corpse's hand. It was gone now.

He sighed. 'Nor I. But to dream three times – and I, a dying man. They say we may prophesy.' He closed his eyes.

'My lord, you – you once felt the king's temptation, you say?' This old man? This stick of bone?

A breath for a voice: 'Yes. God forgive me. God – forgave me. I prayed. You must pray for him. Turn him – from his friends – he's a good man, for all of it – ' He slept.

I left him to his rest, but as he had foretold, I never spoke to him again as living man. His confession clung to my spirit like a shroud for several days.

When he was buried, I took inventory of his estates and secured their revenues to the king.

Rufus spent the winter in Normandy, fortifying his keeps, buying up the good opinion of Frenchmen whose allegiance to the French king had been shaken by Philip's sloth as much as by his excommunication. In the spring the campaign opened with a strong assault on the fortress of Chaumont, but while young Prince Louis could not meet Rufus as an equal in the field, while he must fly from him at every encounter, he did not yield what he held. All my lord's military skill could not take the Vexin without the fall of Chaumont and Pontoise, nor could all the silver I might send him buy them. Yet he took many men prisoner and would not let them go for any ransom unless they swore to fight for him alone thereafter, by which means he further weakened the prince's following.

Meanwhile, the mad dogs of Maine were snapping at their own flanks again. The march of incident in that most quarrelsome country was enough to overwhelm the most tireless of chroniclers. Within the past decade they have rebelled repeatedly against their proper masters, first the Conqueror, then Curthose. Desiring a lord of their own nobility, they sent to Italy for some feeble descendant of their most famous count, old Hubert Wake-Dog, only to find that when their new count arrived he was a womanish tyrant who could well abuse his wife, but who lost his senses at any sudden alarm to himself. Hugh the Fainter, he was called.

The men of Maine quickly came to despise him. The Church wasn't long in excommunicating him for his putting away his wife. A kinsman eventually ousted him from Maine altogether by buying up his title for ten thousand deniers and sent him stumbling back to Tuscany. There passed a brief period of quiet in Maine during which the wrath of the natives was turned more against the Count of Anjou than their own lord. Then came the preaching of the Holy Crusade.

The new Count of Maine, Helias de la Flèche by name, was eager to take the cross and slay the heathen in the company of Robert Curthose and Stephen of Blois, his neighbors, but unlike them he soon repented of his vow and stayed at home to make war on Rufus instead.

It came to pass in this manner: Helias came to Rufus, the man he had pledged to serve as his master, the regent for the Duke of Normandy. He made bold to tell him that he meant to depart from Maine on God's business, but said he expected to find it much as he left it when he returned from slaughtering heathen. In his pride he forgot a little thing: that vassals do not inform their masters of such intent, but rather beg their leave to go a-wandering.

Add to his insolence Rufus's well-known dislike for blatant oath-taking, and one has the germs of that quarrel which arose between them. The king spoke as bluntly as he'd been spoken to:

'Go where you please, but don't think you go with m-my f-friendship or my purse at your belt. And when you come home again, prepare yourself for a quiet life. Because the city of Le Mans and the county of Maine belong to me, and I'll have a more worthy steward in your place before you take ship at Nantes.'

Helias was astounded and flew into a passion of self-justification. He demanded a royal tribunal to judge him of his rights to Maine. The king, half angry, half laughing, replied:

'A tribunal? Will you have *me* tried, master? I'll try you first – with spears and arrows. That's the only trial for a m-man of honor.'

'What? What? Will you attack me? I'm a pilgrim! I wear Christ's Holy Cross on my breast, and it's a crime to do injury to any man who bears it! Beware, you'll be damned for it, my lord! The Church will condemn you; all men will condemn you! I'm no Scot you can frighten, or a Welshman you can run into his hole, but God's own soldier! I'll wear His badge on my shield, on my helm, on my horse's very bridle, to let men know my purpose – '

'You can wear it on your shabby arse for all I care!' the king yelled in a fury. 'This is a fool's taunt! Do you want an answer of me? Go home and prepare for it then, instead of taking up your fo-fool's errand! Go! Mend your broken walls! Put a thousand men on top of them with crosses on their breasts! But let me come before them with a thousand lances and we'll see who God favors in this world! Go!'

Helias, knowing what was wise for him, sped home to do as Rufus bade him, but the war for the French Vexin put the upstart out of the king's mind for a time. He let Helias fret over his battlements. Then the venerable Bishop of Le Mans died. Helias, deeming it his privilege to name a successor, chose one Hildebert, archdeacon of St. Julian's, to follow the man who had been set upon his throne by the will of William Bastard. When news of this was brought to Rufus, he erupted into rage:

'I let this fool and his rabble live in peace so long as he didn't step over his borders, but now he comes and as much as pisses on my boots! Does he think I'll overlook this? Go and tell him I forbid the consecration of any bishop I haven't named – and by the Face! – if he offers me any argument, I'll give him the Devil for his bishop!'

Helias heard and could not fail to understand, but he had Hildebert consecrated anyhow. War broke out between the king and Count Helias, and the devil Rufus sent to harass his enemy was no less a minion of Satan than Robert of Bellesme.

Bellesme advanced toward Le Mans by way of Mamers and laid siege to the fort of Dangeul, having met no more than token resistance. But at Dangeul he found himself blocked from further progress. So great was the valor of the men of Dangeul that Bellesme found himself checked for almost the first time in his life. By January he fell back from that fortress humiliated and went to Rufus to stir him up for his assistance in the leaguer.

Now, winter is no time for a leaguer, as any chilblained recruit can tell. There's no forage, little to steal, the wood is wet, and the stiffening winds chill any zeal for fighting in all but the most vainglorious of men. Rufus was sensibly reluctant to commit his mercenaries to any enterprise that might dishearten them. Yet he was unable to make himself refuse Bellesme's challenge to his chivalry. Unwisely, he set forth with an army to fight Helias and the snow.

Helias might have been no Welshman, but he fought like one. He planted detachments in every hedge and hollow; he guarded every ford of every stream and the difficult approaches to every bridge or wood. When the king engaged his men in battle, they rapidly fell back and vanished into their forests as the cavalry advanced. This was no war for mounted men; it was a war for poachers and thieves. The king and Bellesme took nine castles between the Orne and the Sarthe, but from that river to Le Mans the ground remained untrod by their horses' feet.

The king, coming too late to wisdom in the matter, withdrew at last and left Bellesme to hack at shadows for a pastime. Rufus returned to Rouen and took up his other campaign. Though he could never take the chief towers of the Vexin, he laid waste to the land that lay between them, and Prince Louis did not dare to venture from his strongholds to oppose him.

That was a dreadful year for England. From the feast of St. Paul the Simple to St. John's Eve it seemed to rain without ceasing. The crops were spoiled. All the low-lying farmlands were flooded and barren. Cattle starved. Famine threatened, and with that prospect came the flourishing of dread omens: prodigies were born to woman and beast alike, babes that spoke at birth and two-headed calves. The Devil was seen, or heard to speak from certain groves; witchcraft was revealed and old women burned. In Berkshire that reliable pool once more bubbled up blood, and the Black Hunt made the night hideous all over East Anglia.

I had a letter from the prior of Hyde while I was at Gloucester, saying Martin had run away from the abbey school again. I could not break off my business to go to Winchester at once, and by the time I could do so he had been missing for a month. A search had already been made for him throughout the city, and mindful of his last escape, the portreeve of Southampton had been alerted to watch for him, but to no avail. My prior and the novice master were understandably apologetic when they faced me:

'He had become so tractable, Reverend Father Abbot, it no longer seemed necessary to keep a watch on him constantly,' said the novice master. 'Why, only this last month I said to him that if he kept to his studies as he had been doing, he would become a source of gratification to you, his father. He was devout, he was becoming proficient in Latin' – he shrugged his bony shoulders and pulled at his beak of a nose – 'but, unfortunately, he saw fit to run away the day after our talk.'

'He was merely waiting for you to turn your back, Brother,' I answered, thinking that Martin could probably find no better inspiration for escape than to be told he might gratify me. 'Never mind. It wasn't your fault. I'll find him, you may be certain of that. Children have their own cunning, but we may still hope to outwit them, don't you think?'

The prior put his plump hands together as if he were about to offer prayer. 'Reverend Father Abbot, your wits are as keen as any other man's in the kingdom, but this son you name a child is a headstrong young man. However much you and I might wish he could find a vocation for the cloister, if he doesn't feel it himself – '

'Then his prospects are very poor,' I said, perhaps somewhat too sharply, because he flushed. 'Outside the cloister his prospect is starvation. He has no skills that will earn him his bread, and I won't feed an unlettered fool. Believe me, when I bring him here again, he'll have found his vocation.'

I found him. There was no mystery as to his whereabouts once I'd had a moment to think about it. He'd gone back to that Aquitanian huntsman who'd sheltered him before: Raoul des Aix. I took a horse into the New Forest the next morning and found them both at Malwood, a hunting tower some six or seven miles from Brockenhurst. He was practicing at the butts when I rode into the bailey yard. He saw me dismount and started to run, but des Aix caught him and held him by the arm until I came up to them.

'I want to talk to you in private, Martin. Then I'll speak to you, Master of the Hunt. Where can we be alone together?'

'I don't want to speak to you! I've nothing to say to you, except I won't go back to Hyde and you can't force me to!'

Des Aix put an arm about his shoulder as much to restrain as to comfort him. 'Now, lad, remember your duty to the father. You'll speak to him with respect and listen the same way, or I'll clout you about the ears.' He eyed me rather jovially. 'And when all's said – what's your proper title, chapel man? I'm always respectful to the tonsure.'

'Father will be sufficient title. May we go up into the hall?'

He bowed and led the way to the tower, half pushing Martin ahead of him up the wooden steps.

'Get out,' he said to a congregation of spit boys and scullions who were making poor work of cleansing the hearth in the otherwise deserted, cramped hall. Then, extending an arm toward the tables where the scraps of the day-meal remained: 'There's food if you're hungry. When you've scoured the lad, maybe you'll be good enough to hear a word or two from me – Father.' He left us after a reassuring nod to Martin.

I looked at my son. He was dressed in dirty green and brown, tunic and hose, with no sign of a shirt. His chin luxuriated in a new-grown beard, silky and sparse. It was difficult to keep from smiling at the apprehensive way he glanced from me to the door despite his belligerent posture. Des Aix was insolent, but he had the right idea about how to treat the situation. I began in a tolerant voice:

'Well, Martin – '

'It's no use, you know! You can't do with me as you've done before. I'm free of Hyde at last and I'm never going back. I hate it! You can't make me take vows. That's unlawful, even for you.'

'I see. What shall I report to your mother, then? That you've abandoned education to become a – a what? Kennel man? Arrowsmith? Charcoal burner? What honest trade do you mean to practice?'

'Tell her whatever you like. What does it matter what she thinks of me? She made me a bastard at the start of my life, so she can't have cared much for me. Tell her to put her ambitions to better use, such as becoming an honest woman, if that's possible.'

'If you're going to be insolent, we might as well give up talking and be on our way. Get whatever belongs to you here, if anything does, and meet me at the bailey gate. I'll speak to des Aix about a horse for you. You'll find sulking astride is better than afoot.'

'Didn't you hear me? I'm not going with you, damn you! And you might as well save your breath if you're about to threaten me – or Raoul.'

'Threaten? Boy, I don't need to threaten; I only need to say what I want and it's done. If you love him, don't put him in the midst of our quarrel just to accommodate yourself. It wouldn't be fair to your friend.'

'Fair? When were you ever fair?' His voice had been more or less steady, but now it broke on the word. 'What good does it do you to keep me in a prison? What's the purpose, except to prove you have the power to do it? Will you at least tell me that?'

'What purpose? My God, you're my son! I won't have you sink yourself in the mud and be nothing, for the sake of your juvenile spite against me! How can you want to do it, even for that reason? Your mother is a noblewoman. Your ancestors were decent people. Whatever else you think of me, my grandfather was a landed man, not a peasant. Martin, you're the flesh of my flesh, bone of my bone! More than that: look at me! You're like me in more than mere bone and color. The very workings of your brain are familiar to me, boy. Don't you know that, don't you feel it? I left a cloister once, gladly! But not until it had given me what I could use to a purpose. I made myself stay until it did. Hate me, if you like, but hold in your spite and return to Hyde until you've done the same.

'I'm sorry I spoiled your dream of being a hero's son, but there it is: you're not a knight's son and you'll never be a knight yourself. You spoiled that. Yet you can still be a man of some consequence in this world, a lettered man, a man of property. Only try it, boy, and if you don't thank me someday for making you what you were meant to be, I'll – I'll pour a purse of gold out at your feet before witnesses and beg your pardon for having begotten you.' I tried to laugh at that.

'I'd pour it back at your own feet – tax gatherer.'

'I see. Oh, yes, that's very brave, isn't it? You don't know yet what it's like to live in this world with neither a name nor a purse. You haven't lived long enough even to know what the world's about. You're like a yearling mule: your only pleasure is to feed and kick. But someday you'll know. Someday you'll take the coin and welcome, however it comes, believe me!'

Suddenly weary of my own voice and filled with pity for his ignorance, I put out my hand to him, but he backed away from me, shaking his head, his face flushed with anger, his eyes spilling tears of rage.

'Don't touch me! I don't know about your shabby world and I don't want to know about it. All I know is that if you make me go back to Hyde, I'll kill myself there.'

'That's a foolish threat, Martin.'

'That's a promise, priest. Believe it. I'd rather be dead than live to be a – a scavenger, a parasite – a man like you.'

After a long moment I turned away in silence and left him there. I went back to London, where there was still something useful for me to do.

61

The only good news that year came from afar and caused men of every nation to rejoice who heard it: Antioch, the city where St. Paul first preached the Gospel to the Gentiles, was wrested by them from heathen grasp, and Robert, Duke of Normandy, had a part in the victory.

This news was borne to us by ships out of the Mediterranean late in summer. The church bells pealed to receive it, *Te Deum* was sung, people danced in the streets, and more men than ever before were inspired to commend themselves to the Holy Cross, in order to have their chance of glory in the delivery of Jerusalem.

'And who can blame them, now we hear how Heaven itself sends out its Host to help the earthly armies of God? The venture seems safer with angels on one's side, eh?' said Robin Bloet.

'What's that?' asked Gerard between mouthfuls of mutton. We were having dinner together at Windsor to get away from the stench and heat of London, a privilege I felt justified in awarding myself now. In the king's long absence the court had dwindled.

'Oh, didn't you hear? They say when Curthose was about to lose his ground to the Turkish prince, the mountain opened behind the Turks and a ghostly army rode out to the duke's rescue. They were all carrying white banners and they were led – '

'Robin, are you making this up?' He'd had several cups of wine beyond his usual ration, which was generous enough to begin with those days.

He cast me a look of reproach. " – were led by St. George, with the holy martyrs Demetrius and Mercury as his bannerets.'

'Who?'

'Demetrius and Mercury, Ranulph. Or was it George you were unacquainted with? I had it from a reliable source.'

'Your glove maker.'

'A seaman of excellent reputation,' he insisted rather boorishly.

'Who else saw this excursion of the Blessed? Not that I doubt the veracity of such an excellent witness as a sailor.'

'I expect those who had the eyes of Faith saw it and those who didn't – did not. That's the usual way of it.' He was prim, wiping at his lips with his napkin.

'Why, Robin, is that the gleam of dedication I see in your eye, or candle shine? Will you be taking the cross next and leaving all your worldly goods for me to keep for you, in the king's name?'

Our friendship had resumed after a few months of chill, but Robin was still apt to get ruffled if the talk came around to piety, or what should be accorded pious belief, an attitude repugnantly usual in him since he had assumed his miter. He had evidently marked me down for one of Satan's auxiliary demons since the Anselm affair and hoped to please Heaven with the gloss. I was growing accustomed to being blamed for every misfortune from bad weather to the corruption of wine in the vat since I became sole regent for the king after Walkelin's death, yet I resented his hypocrisy.

Gerard said wistfully into the silence that had fallen: 'I only heard about a Fortunate Dew that fell on the Christians in the heat of battle and refreshed them and their horses. It isn't so spectacular as angel armies, but I think I like it better. It has a certain economy with which I'd like to credit Our Lord, if you'll pardon me, Robin. And who was this martyr Mercury, by the way? Ranulph isn't the only ignoramus you have to put up with.'

Robin smiled. 'He was a Cappadocian who suffered for the Faith in the third century. I confess I had to look him up in the Book of Martyrs myself.'

'Oh,' said Gerard, pouring himself more wine. 'One of those.'

'But that proves it must be true. A sailor wouldn't think of him, would he?'

'On that edifying example of proof let us turn the page,' I said. 'Count Henry is paying us another of his unannounced visits without his brother's consent. Gerard, would you take charge of my clerks for a few days while I ride down to Winchester, just to make sure he isn't about to seize the treasury?'

'When you get there you'd better remember to call him *Prince*

Henry – and how do you know he doesn't have the king's consent? They're very close these days.'

'Because the king would have informed me if he had his leave, Robin. '

'Oh, does he still confide every little thing to you? Maybe you can tell us, then: what about his new light of love that's got poor old Edgar Atheling moping at home, savoring repentance again? I hear this one's as pretty as a maid and as rich as Croesus.'

I said more stiffly than I intended: 'He's rich enough. He's the Duke of Aquitaine, and what I hear is that he's been the king's good companion in arms in the Vexin. But that may not be rare enough for a man who likes tales of angel armies.'

'I hear he calls the king his Caesar,' Robin countered, bright-eyed, 'and the king calls him his Anthony. I hear they share a cup at table and a bed at night and that Duke William of the Aquitaine fancies himself a poet more than a soldier and has composed an ode on the king's – '

'Do you get all your news from sailors, Robin, or does some of it come from your other old source, the whores of Fish Street?' I rose. 'I have some letters to write before I go to bed. I give you good night, Brothers.'

Robin leaned back, smiling at me. 'I was only going to say, on the king's victory at Ballon, Raf.' He winked at me over the rim of his cup.

I went up to my chamber, where Fulcher was waiting for me. He had returned to his duties, though he was so gaunt and pale that one might have supposed he'd returned to haunt me, rather than to be reconciled. Good, simple Osbern had worked him around to me when all my letters and appeals had gone unanswered.

I believe I might have had more satisfaction in our reunion if I'd thought Fulcher felt the truth of the old adage about blood and water as I did. But when he first presented himself from his invalid's bed at Fulham, he went down on his knees before me; I knew he meant me to see he was suffering the reconciliation more as a penance than as the opportunity to regain our old affection. When I protested his kneeling, he answered me in an all but airless voice:

'You are my elder brother, the head of our family. You are my superior. I have offended you. I beg your pardon, so I bend my knees. Is there more offense in that?'

'I think you'd like there to be. But no. No, Fulcher, I beg your pardon. We must forgive each other. I'm glad you've come home.' I held out my hands. He rose and took them. We exchanged the kiss of peace as Osbern and my clerks looked on. But Fulcher's hands and his kiss were cold, and his manner toward me from that time was alike cold, patient, and unfeeling. I can't say if it was to lay additional penance on him or on myself that I insisted he become my confessor again.

Now, as I entered the chamber, he rose from before the prie-dieu and faced me, his hands loosely folded before him. I signed to him to finish his prayers, sat on the bed to watch him at it, and blessed myself with him when he said 'Amen.' He coughed almost furtively, turning his head away from the Holy Cross, then presented himself again.

'Shall I hear your prayers now?' he asked dryly.

'Do you think I've deprived so many widows today that I must be shriven before I sleep?'

'Possibly.'

'I assure you, not a single orphan has gone to bed starving on my account for the better part of three days. I'd take pride in that, if pride weren't a sin.'

He never gave my little jests their due. 'If you've no further need of me, then – '

'Not yet! Stay and pour yourself a cup of wine and let me see you drink it.'

He frowned slightly. 'I've no desire for wine.'

'Maurice's infirmarian said you were to have an extra ration every day to restore your blood. You'll have it, or I'll be to blame. Pour for me, too, and do sit down to drink it, please.'

He went obediently to my table and poured out two noticeably unequal measures with the air of a chastened novice. When he offered me the fuller one I refused it and took instead the one he'd meant for himself. I saw there was no more than a swallow in it.

I said: 'Now, lift your cup and give thanks to God the infirmarian didn't prescribe boiled pig's urine, or something with mouse's dung dissolved in it. This is very good, you know. It's from a vineyard in the Vexin. The king sent it to me.'

He sat on a bench against the wall. 'A vineyard in the Vexin. I didn't think there were any of those left now.'

'Yes. But vines can be planted again and will be, when the king is master of that land. Drink it, Fulcher. I *will* take care of you. I remember how you once took care of me.'

He sipped the cup and didn't answer. I was suddenly filled with irritation at his stubborn silence. 'Will you tell me, if you can, just why you're so eager to die? I'd really like to know. I can't understand it. I'm having trouble of late understanding any of my kin. One will be a pauper to spite me, and another will die of grief, or pride, or what?'

His eyes were almost closed, but now at last he smiled ever so faintly. 'Is that what you think, Raf? That I'm dying to spite you? I'm dying of diseased lungs. It isn't very pleasant, but there's no spite in it. Yet one way's as good as another when all's said and done, isn't it?' He opened his eyes and regarded me almost warmly.

'You put yourself on the road to this when Giva died and you blamed me for it. You know it; I know it. You loved her. Everyone knew that, too, except possibly Giva, so there's no use denying it now.'

He looked at me in silence.

I said: 'Fulcher, you loved her, but your devotion to your vows was always stronger than your affection. She would have understood. I even understand and I forgive you. I'm certain God understands and forgives – '

'Has He told you so, brother? Do you get couriers from Him, too, now? What a great man you *have* become.' He was in danger of becoming jocular. The corners of his mouth actually curled.

I said with perfect seriousness: 'I've seen your penance and believe it to be sincere. How could you not think God would see it, too? You never committed any sort of overt act – did you?'

He wheezed: 'Ranulph, don't make me – laugh. It makes me cough!'

'I wasn't conscious of being amusing this time.'

'You're the most complete – hypocrite it's ever been my – misfortune to know. Yet you have your uses. You make me see the depths of my own hypocrisy. Since Elfgiva died I've been trying to forgive you. Now you tell me you forgive me. It's funny – ' He began to heave and cough, wrackingly, desperately.

I was alarmed. 'Drink some of your wine, for God's sake!'

'In a moment – ' He gasped for a bit, then leaned back, exhausted and perspiring, against the wall. He looked at me somberly again. 'Forgive me if I've offended you. I try not to. I really do love you, brother.'

'Drink your wine now.'

'In a moment. I love the life in you, though I wouldn't have it in me any longer; not for all your offices, all your power over – little men, or all your silver, stacked in those chests you hoard at

Winchester. I used to envy you your abilities. Now I pity you for them, truly.'

'Are they so poor, then?'

'Oh, no, they've made you a – a great man. You rule every one of us, now, from the king down to the least beggar. The only trouble is, you want to be loved for your tyranny. You side us about with your convictions, hem us in with argument, charge us with your anger, threaten, beguile, plead – all to make us what we *should* be. How we disappoint you! Such sage advice! Such tender care – and we resent all.' He laughed briefly, then coughed some more.

I rose to fill my cup again. 'This is something too much of a sermon for so near Compline, brother.'

'Then think of it as you must think of Compline, Raf: something to be endured for appearance' sake. Oh, yes, I know you're weary of being charged with worldliness. How could you lack spirituality when the Name of God is in your mouth so often – along with that good advice? But *think* how you must weary us: the king won't marry, for all your urging him. The lords won't give up their hoarded silver to support the king's wars, but steal what you demand from the wretched poor, who won't take your advice and stop dying. Osbern can't be shrewd, or Martin studious. Prince Henry won't stifle his ambition, no matter what bribes you offer him. Even Giva, that wise child you made your whore – '

'That's enough, Fulcher – '

' – wouldn't let you use her any longer to your own harm. She never had an inkling of how many ways you could find to do your soul harm, but she denied you that one, at last. I even offend you with my dying. Yet, you've devoted long years to labor for us all, forgotten what your own life was supposed to be about, while you worked to make us all what we should be.'

I answered him as I would have answered a rebuke in my green years at St. Vigor: 'I thank you for your instruction, good brother. God grant me the grace to amend my ways. Now, shall I take myself off to an anchorite's cell and repent? Who'll take the blame for rainy days if I do? The king makes war in the Vexin, and those grapevines suffer because he *wants* a victory, Fulcher, not because I urge him to it. I disapprove of the waste.'

'Yet you gladly furnish the means to make waste.'

'Gladly? No! By his command and out of his revenues, which are his to demand. And if I didn't do it someone else would – even you, Fulcher, if you were his picked man.'

'Anselm would never have done it.'

'Anselm! Damn Anselm! Anselm is in Italy. So much for him. Please, make up your mind what it is you mean to charge me with: trying to influence the king, or failing to do it. What is it to be?'

'You're at fault for pretending to disapprove of what he does, but condoning his actions by your silence. By pretending you want him to marry, for example, then suffering his – lovers without a word of rebuke!'

'Oh, that's Anselm talking right enough! I, of all the men in the court, with what else I have to do to keep peace and order here – I should stand up in court and tell the king he's a sodomist, like that prating old saint you adore! Fulcher, why should I ruin myself, presenting the king with the obvious? He knows he's a sodomist! It doesn't make him very happy, but he's acquainted with the fact!'

'But you're his priest! You're more than that. You're the nearest thing he's got to a conscience in the world!'

'Well, I'd hardly be that for very long if I did such a stupid, useless thing, believe me.'

'Then you would rather see him damned eternally than risk losing your comfortable life in court? You damn yourself as well by that.'

I looked at him in disgust, but it was futile to be angry with him, for he was still a babe to policy. Death was staring him in the face. Eternity and its consequences were common to his thoughts. It was so with any man who knew he was dying. I went and sat beside him.

'Now, listen to me, brother: I haven't the stuff to be a martyr and I doubt God ever intended me for one. But He *did* intend me for this place I hold in the king's favor. He gave it to *me* – not to Anselm, or to Odo, or to anyone else. Why do you think He did so? Do you believe God would give an anointed king a bad counselor, deliberately? He gave the king his crown, too. He didn't give it to Robert, or to Henry. Do you think God gives a nation to a bad king, deliberately?'

'Yes.'

'Why?'

'To test it. There's Scripture – '

'Christ! Look, what would you have? Curthose is a fool and a wastrel. If he survives the Holy Land and comes home, it'll be a great pity for Normandy, because if he rescues Jerusalem single-handed and the inhabitants of that city give him King Solomon's treasures for his reward, he'll be a pauper by the time he reaches Rouen and he'll pauperize the country again in a year. Coin slips through his fingers like piss through a wicket! Would you have a man like that king in the place of Rufus? Would you want to serve such a fool?'

'Fortunately, I won't have to.'

'Then try to imagine the grieved and beggared multitudes you'll leave behind. Now listen: Henry of Winchester is a venomous snake. He has no friends, because no one can tell his friendship from his hatred. When he smiles, the sextons reach for their spades to dig the graves of those he smiles on. Moreover, he's fathered so many bastards no one can count them, and when he dies they'll make war on each other for his estates until there isn't a man left of them. If his estates include a crown, what will we have here – anarchy, massive rebellion, poisonings, and treacheries worse than any known in William Bastard's time? Not a cheerful prospect.

'This man we serve is flawed to a degree, but in a way that certain great men have been flawed before this. Caesar had his boys, they say. Alexander – the thing is, he's made peace here. He tries to rule honorably. He makes war, but he pays his debts. His enemies fear him, but not his friends. The roads are kept safe, the bridges are repaired, the foreign merchants don't laugh at our silver as they do at the Norman denier. And there *is* hope for him, Fulcher! He isn't lost to hope!'

He sighed and stared at the ceiling. 'You believe that Rufus is the Elect of God here in England?'

'Of course. Why else was he anointed?'

'And that you were put by his side to persuade him by small degrees to give up his vices and breed sons, all to make us safe from his brothers to the end of our days?'

'I wouldn't have put it so, but yes, if you like.'

He shook his head, the smile fading that had scarcely begun at my answer. 'Raf, it isn't our business to make kings, or prevent them, no matter what good purpose we think is being served. That's God's business. We're priests. Our purpose – any man's purpose in this world – is to preserve that thing in ourselves that God lent us. We must try to help others preserve it in themselves, so we'll all have it to give back to God when our days are done. That's our first and last duty to kings – or anyone. And what I fear for you is that in your great care to preserve the – the honor, the *vanity* – of a king, or even in your concern for the stability of the realm, however worthy you make that seem – in the end you'll go back to God with nothing left that's Ranulph; nothing but a pair of grasping hands and a shrill tongue. Apes and peacocks may return as much, without benefit of souls.'

I stood up. 'That's very striking, though it makes little sense. You must put it in a homily and preach it in St. Paul's yard some present Sunday!'

He started to answer but was seized with a fit of coughing that wracked him until I thought his heart must burst from the strain. Against his will I lifted him and forced him to lie upon my bed. His eyes were glazed and his cheeks were patched with red, as if he'd been out in a cruel wind. When he got some measure of breath back he tried to rise, but I pushed him back on the pillow.

'No, you won't go down to that crafty clerks' warren tonight. You'll stay and suffer my company. That's a command, so don't bother to dispute with me.'

He shook his head wordlessly, then turned his face away.

'That's good. That's quite all right. Just be still and sleep. You've done your duty, preaching mine to me. Haven't I always called you my conscience? Be still. Whatever I am, I'm your brother. Don't despair of me altogether.'

I went to Winchester alone, leaving Fulcher under injunction to rest. Having paid my duty calls on my mother and on my sons at Hyde, I went to the castle to find Prince Henry. I found him at the archery butts with two of his knight attendants. He was almost as much a *tirel* as his brother Rufus, though he drew a lighter bow. I watched as he put four arrows into the target center and two more so near, in the red, as would still give a death wound to a deer. His knights praised him.

He saw me and gave over his bow to his squire to advance on me with that lurching, quick-march step he had in common with his brothers. It was as if they each had a nail pressing into their heels, or one leg slightly shorter than the other. He didn't look pleased to see me, but then he never did.

'So – you've come. I wondered if I'd slipped your notice this time.'

I thought there was little likelihood in that, as he liked to trumpet himself too well. He might as well send me a message directly. I wondered if, in fact, he had.

We wasted no time in idle talk, but went straight to the treasury, where, on the previous instructions of the king, I paid Henry his stipend for not pressing a claim against the Crown for the return of his mother's estates, which were given to Robert fitz Hamon. The payment was equal to the rents that fitz Hamon might enjoy from them in a good year. It was in this manner the king chose to keep his word both to his friend and to his brother, each of whom had a claim on the lands. I'd always thought it would be more sensible to give Henry equal lands and be done with the charade, but that was impossible. It was a matter of honor, again.

I waited patiently until the prince had counted his silver in spite of just having seen the treasurer's clerk do it before his eyes. I remembered how the coin was counted that was his patrimony, even while his father lay dying.

When he was satisfied, he gathered up the bags and hauled them away to his private chamber in the castle, then came down into the presence hall again and called me out of the chapel, where I'd gone to say my Office in the meantime.

He offered me wine in the manner of a host, rather than a guest. 'I'm surprised at you, Flambard, troubling with me when you've got bigger game in Rouen, if you only knew it.' His sharp eyes, black as sheep farts, swung up and around from his cup to me without a blink. It was what passed with him for a smile, that arching glance.

'Your Grace mystifies me. What is my game in Rouen?'

'Why, the hunting of catamites. There's a new one – quite a beauty, too. Haven't you heard?'

I sipped my wine and shrugged.

'His name is William le Vieux, and he's got eyes like aquamarines and the handsomest nose in all Europe. You mustn't think I'm smitten with him. I quote my esteemed brother, who also says he looks like Michael Archangel when he takes the field. Does this stir your curiosity?'

'You speak of the Duke of Aquitaine, my lord? I'd heard he was the king's new companion of choice, yes.'

'Companion of choice! Now there's an expression I hadn't heard before. Companion of choice! Yes, they could piss through an oat straw together and not dampen the shaft. Too bad he's a duke. You'll have trouble sending him to a cloister, like you did that page, or "helping" him to a marriage, like you did with Wat Tirel, or even getting him exposed to a pox, as I've always thought you did with that pretty Welsh – '

'My lord, I never did such a thing! What do you take me for, a conjurer of diseases? A thousand people took the pox that summer in London alone. Am I to blame for them, too?'

'I wouldn't be surprised. But you sent the Welshman a gift of leeks by a boy who was pustular the next day.'

'An unfortunate thing. Poor Bledry. But he was lucky. I believe the boy died.'

'Yes. And Bledry retired to his Black Mountains, to sing to his sheep. Well, we've not done with music yet. This new one's a poet, too – and a minstrel.'

'The duke, a minstrel?'

'A *trouveur*, as he would say. His songs are of such matter it were better he sang them in Greek than in French. Will-Rou is much taken with him when he trolls his nasty verses.'

'I never knew His Grace had a taste for poetry, beyond the lay.'

'What my brother has a taste for in this one doesn't come from his mouth. You'd best have him poisoned, Flambard, or he'll cost you more silver than Normandy. He wants to lead an army to Jerusalem, *if* he can go like Alexander.'

'He should be able to afford the journey. He has the Aquitaine and Poitou to draw from.'

Henry pursed his mouth, then tasted his wine. 'Oh, he's got land enough, but he mustn't have put it to farm with a Flambard. Or else he's spent too much on his whores. They say he's got an old convent near Limoges filled with former concubines of his and his father's. He's another of those who'll taste any meat put before him. And he's only twenty-seven.'

I rose. 'If Your Grace will give me leave, I must speak to the constable, then to my prior at Hyde, after which I mean to go down to Twynham on the coast, tomorrow, if the weather holds fair. I've a church in the building there, when I can find the coin to pay the masons.'

'You have more pots to mend than a tinker, don't you? And let no man touch the lead but yourself. Well, that's the way to wealth. If you'll hold tomorrow's journey over for another day, I'll ride with you partway. I'm off to Malwood in the Forest.'

'I would be honored for Your Grace's company.'

While I was speaking to the constable, I saw Henry and his knights striding toward the stables. They took their leave of the city by the south gate street and didn't return until after dark. I questioned a few knowledgeable people about the mystery when I found the opportunity. The prince, I was told, had ridden to Romsey Abbey that day, as he had on each day since he came to Winchester.

What of that? One was tempted to think of that cloister near Limoges of which he'd spoken, but Good Lord, Romsey? With that leopardess of an English princess guarding its door? I began to see a glimmer: Edgyth of Scotland still lived there, under her English aunt's surveillance. Was Henry toying with my little queen? Had he gone courting? I promised myself I would look into it.

62

In August, after much bitter contention, the city of Le Mans fell into the hands of Rufus. His victorious overthrow of its last stronghold, the fortress of Ballon, had put it in his power. He could have crushed the pride of the Centomanians forever if he had been a more ruthless man, for seven hundred knights were held captive in Ballon whom he might have slain. He sent them meat and drink instead and gave them leave to come outside the castle walls on their parole, though his chief captain, Robert de Bellesme, complained that they would escape.

An accord was reached with Fulk of Anjou (always the iron in Count Helias's spine) without Helias's leave. Soon after, Rufus marched through the gates of Le Mans without bloodshed or siege, to hear the welcoming shouts of the inhabitants. It may be that as they had grown weary of their Italian master, now the posturing of their homegrown lord began to weary them, too, and they looked for a more reliable ruler.

Hildebert, the bishop Helias had put on his throne despite Rufus, came to greet the king, who received him graciously. The fortress of the city was occupied by seven hundred of the king's picked men, governed in the king's name by Robert de Montfort. A new royal banner was hoisted to the highest point of the tower, flaunting its emblem of the Transfigured Christ of Lucca.

King William the Younger had achieved the object that was dearest to his heart: he had brought under his hand all the domains that had once belonged to his revered father.

Helias, who had been captured, was once more brought to the king. A different figure he must have presented from the cocksure pilgrim of their first encounter. Bellesme was no kindly guardian. Tall, thin, swarthy, bearded and rough-headed with long neglect of his barber, Count Helias stood before his conqueror a wiser man. The king, as I have heard, opened their dialogue much as he had done before:

'I have you, sir.'

'You do, my lord, if you would have me as I would be had.'

'And how is that? A penitent?'

'A man of honor, Your Grace! I was once lord of this noble country. Fortune has turned against me and I have lost all – but my honor. I ask leave to enter your service now, to be allowed to keep my rank and title of count, if I pledge myself not to make further claim on any land or town until I do some thing the king may deem worthy to make me receive them as a grant from his noble hand. Until that time it will be enough for me to have a place in your following and to enjoy your friendship.'

It was a wonderful speech, designed by its art to appeal to the chivalrous Rufus. He might have risen and clasped Helias to his breast in a moment, but Robert Bellesme and Robert de Meulan intervened and whispered in Rufus's ears by turn.

'This is a cunning man, like all his race,' said de Meulan. 'He'll worm his way to your inner secrets, learn all your devices, and betray you again.'

And Bellesme, no doubt jerking his falcon's head at Helias and de Mealan alike as he said it: 'He's cost you a pretty coin to get him. Will you give him a pension for rebellion, too?'

So the king's impulse was changed and he refused Helias, who showed his true feelings by straightway beginning to rail at the king as he had done before.

'Now I see you for what you are! I would have served you! I would have earned your favor, but now let all men know that what was taken from me by violence I will have back again, unless you mean to shut me up forever, or kill me! Will you do that to a man who would have served you? Ask your ministers before you speak, if you can't decide it for yourself!'

Rufus was nearly strangled with surprise and wrath. He stammered: 'S-son of a whore, will you make me a mur-murderer with words? What will you do? Be off! March! Take f-flight! I give you l-leave to do all you can, and by the Face, if you ever conquer me, I won't come b-begging *you* for grace!'

The count looked about him to see if swords were being drawn against his back, but when he saw there were none he had presence of mind to stand his ground and ask for a safe-conduct through the royal lines beyond the city. Rufus, for all his wrath, remained the honorable knight. He granted the safe-conduct, and Helias made his way, to the joy of his supporters, to his own estates on the Angevin border.

Two days before Michaelmas, Rufus set forth from Maine, sending summons of array to all who owed him service, to take up his war for the Vexin again. On his way to battle he stopped at Conches and there must have seen the great sign in the heavens that astonished and overawed all who saw it in England.

The whole northern sky seemed to blaze and turn the color of blood. I was in London when it happened. The people poured out into the streets when the watchmen gave the alarm, some of them thinking the city must be on fire again, some that the end of the world had come. A few optimists thought it signified Jerusalem had been taken, but most thought of nothing but running about bellowing, or stealing, or fornicating in alleyways with others' wives, until the aldermen and their peacekeepers were driven half mad with trying to restrain them. The racketing lasted half the night, until the gory light faded.

Isabel came running to my chamber, alarmed by the noise in the street as much as by the red light that showed through all our windows. I laughed at her, but in time the effect of the strange glow and the tumult in the streets made me glad she'd come to keep me company. One may laugh at the ignorant for their fear that each miracle of the skies that God affords us for His own purpose signals the end of the world. But that end is an event which will transpire in its own good time, and who, in truth, can say when that time may be?

Isabel and I watched the sky for a while, then closed the shutters and took rare comfort from each other in bed. She wasn't Giva, but then she wasn't the deceitful witch she'd been, either. On a hazardous night when some companionship was needed, one would never know she was more than four and forty.

She seemed to feel kindly disposed toward me, too. 'You're no dotard, yet. In fact' – she administered a light kiss upon my cheek in the dark – 'you are a better man than you used to be.'

I scoffed. 'You've been kind enough tonight. Don't be overkind.'

'I'm not being overkind!'

'You flatter me.'

'If I wanted to flatter you, I'd say you were still as good as you were the first time. That's deceit, which is flattery. I said you were a better man. But I still cherish the boy.'

I laughed.

'Do you remember,' she asked in a seductive voice, 'when we were going to Rouen and you thought I'd ridden off without you?'

'I thought you'd ridden off with some very important business of the bishop's.'

'You thought I'd ridden off without you and that you would never have another chance to have me, because they'd find you and drag you back to your cell and keep you there forever.'

I sighed.

'You came clumping over the hill in my husband's boots, all

covered with mud and horse foam, wild-eyed as a lunatic until you saw me. I would have laughed, but you fell down at my feet in a swoon.'

'I fell down exhausted, madam, from running and walking and being kept awake all night by you, not to mention having been on the road for three days beforehand.'

'There were tears on your cheeks.'

'No doubt. From vexation.'

'You said it was because I tormented you and you were mad in love with me.'

'You have the memory, if not the learning, of a bard.'

'You nearly broke my heart. I fell in love with you on the spot.'

'You had an odd way of showing it.'

'I thought I showed it admirably! I remember we went to the castle and we were eating. You stared and stared at me, so I thought everyone in the hall must see we were lovers. Then, when we heard we'd be separated for the night, do you remember? Your face was so full of want for me, we went straight out of the place and found a solitary hill.' Her hand made a journey down my body. 'You spread the bishop's mantle on the ground, fur side up, and we made love all night long.' She crooned: 'What a lovely thing it was to have a rich fur beneath me and a beautiful boy on top. I felt like a goddess!'

We burst out laughing at the same instant.

The king spent his Christmas in Rouen, having failed to take the fortress of Chaumont from a garrison that could not muster the strength to come beyond the walls to oppose him, but made havoc among his mercenaries by concentrating their arrows on their horses. Several hundred horses of great value were slain, many the only mounts their owners possessed. Their carcasses made a rich feast for the carrion birds and camp dogs. The king was forced to retire from the siege shortly thereafter, for want of fresh air, as the whole field before Chaumont stank like a charnel house.

The saviors of the Holy Sepulcher spent their Christmas at a place called Marrah, in Syria, where their captains quarreled for precedence while the common soldier starved or, as some said, ate the flesh of the dead Turks they had slain in the storming of the city.

I spent the season in Winchester, listening to hints of what a monster I'd become by collecting taxes in an evil year. One would have supposed that no king before mine had ever required his due of the land in the face of rain and famine.

The court was all but vacant with the king abroad. Those who were not already with him elected to stay at home, pleading the bad roads, or fear of being set upon by starving bands of men, although those in England were still less to be feared than those of Marrah.

What good works I had accomplished I heard no word on, and expected to hear none, save from the king himself when he came home. I had finished the curtain wall about the London Keep, and the new palace at Westminster. The foundations for my own church at Twynham – Christ's Church – were laid and the choir was in process of being built. My house at Hyde, the new Hyde that would soon rise outside the walls of Winchester, was also completed, and my mother, Osbern, and his fecund wife, Swanhilda, installed in it, along with their growing brood of sons.

To please my mother on this Christmas I sent for my sons at Hyde to come and spend a few days with their granddam. I sent word for Martin to come, too, but had no satisfaction of it. The foresters of Brockenhurst, Lyndhurst, Malwood, and Ringwood all affected to know nothing of his whereabouts. I should have been relieved as I expected nothing but strife if he made his appearance. But for some foolish reason his absence rankled me more than I would have supposed possible. Osbern took it into his stupid head to try to console me:

'Don't fret about the boy, Raf. He looked well enough the last time I saw him, and if his fortunes worked out the way they were headed, he's found himself a good master at last.'

'What do you mean? You saw him? And didn't tell me? Where? What master has he got? He'll have none without my leave, I promise you.'

'Now, don't be angry with me. I only saw him for a moment, a few weeks ago, when I passed through the forest on the way to Twynham. He jumped a bit when he first saw me.' Osbern smiled. 'For a moment I believe he thought you'd sent me for him, but when he found out it wasn't so, he was quite civil to me. He even asked about you.'

'To know if I were dead yet?'

'Raf, he doesn't hate you.'

'Really? I had the opposite impression. Who's the new master? A poacher? A tinker? Or does he have aspirations to keep sheep now?'

'He didn't have a vocation for the cloister, brother. He had the head, but not the heart, as our old master at Rouen used to say.'

'Who's he following, Osbern?'

'Why, a man he might hope to thrive with: Prince Henry. He says the prince spoke to him when he was – '

'Henry? Henry! He's taken service with the king's brother? What next? Will he show himself to the king and get himself taken to the whipping post for a runaway? Oh, God, what a fool he is!'

'Raf, he's had the good luck to be taken in by a prince – '

'For what purpose? For what purpose? Does Henry know he's mine? Does he know he's the boy who ran away from the king? What does he want him for? What?'

Osbern drew back from me, perplexed. 'Why – you talk as if the prince were going to harm him, or you, through him. Where did you ever get such a notion, Raf? His Grace is a fair man, as I've heard – '

'His Grace makes my flesh creep! He wants a crown! He can smell it! Curthose is away – his brother's heir – and may never come home again, in which case Harry will be the new heir. But Harry can't know that, can he? No, if Curthose does return, there's no help for Harry, so why wait for him?'

'Raf, you're talking treason! You can't accuse the prince of something like that. You have no evidence.'

'Don't I? I know what I know, brother.' I began to pace the room. There didn't seem to be enough air in the room to fill my lungs of a sudden and my heart was quivering strangely. 'I know – I know – '

'What is it you know, for the love of God? Sit down, please do. You look like death all at once. If it was my mentioning Martin that did it, let's forget him, Raf, and – '

His mouth continued to move, but I couldn't hear the sound of his voice. I was gasping for breath, my chest was constricted, and strange pains took hold of my arms and legs. I shook my head to clear it and lost my balance. I heard Osbern cry out: 'Raf! Mother! Mother!' I tried to protest his calling her, but my voice had expired in a dry throat. I'm dying, I thought, and swooned.

When I came to myself, Fulcher was sitting by my bed, saying some Office silently. I felt confused and lethargic. I wanted to speak to him, but couldn't seem to make my tongue move. He lifted his eyes when I sighed and smiled at me.

'So – you're alive. Osbern was half dead with fright when he couldn't bring you around. I told him we're a hardy family; even God must strike us more than once before we die. Can't you speak?'

I could not. I rolled my head on the pillow slightly to signify it. Fulcher put his hand under mine and clasped it.

'Can you squeeze my hand? Gently for "yes," harder for "no"? That's fine. Mother thinks you've had a kind of brain fever. She's bled you rather copiously. I told her you'd been working much too long and hard and I thought you merely needed rest, but she won't take the opinion of one who's never gathered a midnight herb. I hope *you'll* listen to my excellent advice, however, which is to lie perfectly still for a time. Sleep all you like. I'll send word to the king that you're ill and – '

I squeezed his hand very hard. He frowned.

'I'm not to send word? What, then? No, don't try to speak. I'll attend to all you must do. Don't concern yourself. The king will never know you're made of flesh like the rest of us. Trust me. Rest and be strong again. Rest – '

By such soothing he put me at ease, and I slept for a long time. When I woke, my power of speech had returned to me, but not my strength. I was abed for the better part of a fortnight, thanks to my mother's continued leeching of me, I think, as much as to my own debility. Fulcher gave it out that I had severely twisted my knee in putting my foot on a loose cobblestone and could not walk for a few days. All such documents as needed my personal signature he brought home to me, though he had to hold my hand at first to help me make my name with the pen. He turned away visitors adroitly and managed all my court affairs, as he had pledged.

For the first time in my life I had some leisure to think idle thoughts and to dream. My dreams were of such stuff as I would rather not relate, but unlike many another man who comes near death, I found I feared my grave the less for having nearly put my foot in it. What I did fear was not being given enough time to accomplish certain things I meant to do. I had my drawings for Christ Church and those of Carileph's for his church at Durham brought to me, so that I could immerse myself in their designs, to improve the decoration of a door with carvings, and to dream of just how the light would fall from the clerestory onto the stone floor of the nave, lighting the piers and casting the aisles into shadow.

Fulcher seemed both pleased and somehow disturbed by my occupation. 'What is this? You'll burn your brain again with staring at these lines.' He bent nearer to look at my conceit for a doorway arch. 'I didn't know you studied embellishment. This is good. Where did you learn it? There's no end to your ambition, is there? Next you'll want a chisel and maul to cut the stones yourself; then you'll be mixing mortar. Where will it end?'

'In immortality – of a kind. Don't you think? These stones will outlast my evil reputation, if I can live to see them truly laid. How's that for ambition, brother?'

He scowled. 'What's this one? This isn't the nave of Twynham.'

'That's my Lady of Stone.' I rolled the parchment. 'I mean to wed her one day, so if you'll pardon me, Fulcher, I don't like other fellows gaping at her as if she were a bawd.'

I returned to London in a litter, still pretending to have injured my knee, and took up residence in my London house rather than at Westminster with my clerks. There at Cornhill I heard strange tidings one morning from Isabel, who was blunt in her eagerness:

'Ranulph, I'm with child!'

'You're not.'

'I am! I'm past four months. I certainly ought to know the symptoms,' she answered indignantly.

'You're past the age for whelping, that's for certain. You haven't bred in almost twenty years. At your age there's a – a falling off of certain things, as I understand it. That's what it is. Don't be alarmed.'

She drew in her breath, her hazel eyes darkening. 'I'm not alarmed; I'm pleased. Or I was, until now. I'm *not quite* of an age with the Matriarch Sarah, as you seem to think – '

'You lack her sense of humor, too.'

She turned and went out of my chamber. I heard her feet quicken along the gallery on the way to her own room. The door closed heavily. I sighed and went after her, trying to remember to hobble as I entered her chamber. She had cast herself across the bed to weep with more reticence than wrath usually kindled in her. I sat on the bed near her shaking shoulders and put my hand on her head.

'Isabel – '

'Oh, leave me alone! I should have known better than to think it would please you,' she muttered bitterly from under her shielding arm. 'But take heart! I'll probably miscarry. I usually do.'

I stroked her back. 'I'm sorry. I didn't mean to sound – however it was I sounded. You took me by surprise. I thought you must be joking at first, that's all.'

'Oh? And me with no sense of humor? How clever of me!' She shifted her arm so that one of her eyes could peep out, tear-flooded, to accuse me.

I bent and kissed her temple. 'Forgive me. Come, turn over. Let me wipe your eyes.' I accomplished this with my thumbs as she lay regarding me somberly. 'I am pleased – very pleased. But I'm concerned for you. It's been a long time – '

'And I'm so decrepit – '

'No, no – fragile, we'll call it. Very fragile. We must take care for you.' I thought women had a thousand ways of inconveniencing a man, but few of them ever proved fatal. I had killed one woman with giving her a child. I had no wish to take a second victim.

Isabel's mouth moved slightly in a smile. She put one of her hands over mine as it lay along her cheek. 'Fragile is a nicer way of putting it. Almost too nice for you to use to me. I might almost believe you *are* pleased. I am.' Her smile bloomed. 'I'm so pleased, Ranulph! It makes me feel alive again.' But she saw I was still too sober. 'What is it?'

'I don't know. It'll take getting used to, won't it, a child among us? You'll want another servant to oversee the others, and a wet nurse, and – ' I gave it up and shook my head in wonder. 'It's only that death and life have been pressing me for decisions of late, and I have no opinions worth the mentioning. Keep well.' I kissed her brow. 'And see if you can produce us a daughter, will you? I've enough sons, I think.'

The king came home at Easter, bringing with him a host of French knights held in courteous captivity while waiting their ransoms; his sister Adela, Countess of Blois; and William le Vieux, Count of Poitou and Duke of Aquitaine. His company made such a brilliant entry into the city, dressed in their silken gowns and fine woolens, that they might have been assembling for a tourney rather than coming from a faltering campaign in the Vexin.

The lion's share of attention was paid to the young duke. All our curious clerks and our home-fast nobles flocked to see for themselves this pride of the Aquitanians, and the king was as delighted with his court's interest as if he'd brought them a rare beast to gape at. He crowed to me:

'Look at him, priest! Isn't he a beauty? He never wipes his nose on anything less dainty than a virgin's shift, but you should see him take the field. He's Michael Archangel, out to ride down the Devil! God! If I had his tongue the world couldn't keep me! I'd have to turn Pope!' A year in the field hadn't made his own tongue any sweeter to the pious. I thought I heard a bishop choke somewhere, and the two serving boys who hovered over us with platters of baked fish in galantine snickered openly.

Young Duke William could hardly avoid hearing this praise bestowed on him. He turned from his conversation with Prince Henry, seated at the king's right hand, and said:

'All beauty of flesh and of speech must fade, Your Grace. Only valor is eternally fair, in which case I might say if I were as fair as England's great king, then would I be vain of my beauty.'

739

I thought I might just manage not to vomit. The king's grin widened. He turned and lifted his cup to his friend, who preened himself. I could see Henry's face beyond that of Rufus. He looked as if he'd tasted gall in his galantine.

We fed, monstrously well for the Lenten season, and when we were sated, the young duke took a cittern from one of his rose-cheeked squires and proceeded to entertain us like a common jongleur. Despite what I'd heard of him I was surprised at this, as was Robert Cornard, the king's fool, who had evidently prepared an elaborate jest for his master's amusement. He hunched and scowled like an envious ape while the young lord sang to us of perfidious women, as if we were in a bathhouse. Prince Henry caught my eye as it wandered and he smiled very slightly at me. I shuddered and jerked away from his gaze.

What can I say of William le Vieux? His reputation for valor in the field didn't rest in my king's fond estimation alone, but was readily confirmed by less eager lips. His speech was witty, in a manner unnatural to a gentleman; he was said to be the author of the songs he sang, a talent that could hardly recommend him to his peers. His reputation as a formidable lover of women of every shape and degree, as Prince Henry had implied, did that for him, instead.

He was tall and slender with a fair complexion spattered with freckles, his hair frizzed to an aura about his head in the fashion denounced by the Church. He had pale, mischievous eyes under proud, hooded lids and a long, thin nose through which he droned his verses. His voice was slight in song or speech, but pleasant enough, save for that certain cloying tone which attended his flatteries to the king. Even this may have been only the result of his southern speech, which among his kind was peculiarly languid.

His supple fingers plucked the strings of his instrument as deftly as any mountebank's, and when he sang he cast his eyes about at his hearers in a way that seemed to invite criminal assault. I have never in my life loathed anyone so instantly and completely, save perhaps William de St. Carileph.

Throughout his performance the king sat enraptured, his chin propped on a hand, listening to the music with a smile. Whether this smile was fond, absent, or cynical it was difficult to determine. Rufus had no taste for music that I'd ever discovered, or any appetite for erotic verse, exalted or base. The Lay of William Longsword was to him music enough. Yet he applauded vigorously when the song was done and kissed the singer heartily on the lips as he passed to his own stool again. The rest of the company in the hall muttered, laughed, or gnawed their lips in vexation at seeing a wellborn man so disgrace himself.

They were, like Rufus, used to songs of simple butchery, of joyous maimings, of death against great odds on a bloody field. What was to be learned of honor from lays sung to larks and sunshine, of concupiscence and philosophy all uttered in a breath? Fortunately for them, Robert Cornard skipped forth in a moment to soothe their affronted Norman sensibilities with his own impersonation of Fulk le Rechin in search of his strayed bride, always a popular entertainment.

63

I met with the king when that evening was done. As I stood waiting in a corner of his chamber, his squires and chamberlains divested him of his rings, his chains, his rose silk tunic spangled to the hem with golden stars, which ill became his thick body and wind-coarsened face.

He was stouter by a stone than when last I'd seen him, despite what had been an exceptionally active season of campaign. He looked like a bear in vestments, gowned; much more himself when stripped to shirt and hose and seated on his bed, pleasantly scratching an armpit as he held out a gilt-silver cup to be filled with his night draft. The page who was pouring it for him let the cup overfill and splash on the king's hand. He tried to make amends with a towel, but only succeeded in spilling the wine further. Mumbling apologies, he knelt to wipe up the spill from the floor. Rufus drank the wine in his cup, then set the empty vessel on top of the boy's bowed head, which froze the poor fool instantly. He squatted before his master in the attitude of a penitent toad, not daring to move for fear of spilling more wine, until the king shoved him with his unbooted foot and sent him to his rump, sprawling.

'Get out,' he said without rancor, 'and don't let anyone else come blundering in here unless I call them, d'you understand? Claude, you make a wretched page. Be a better usher.' The boy nodded, recovered the empty cup from the floor, and fled.

Rufus sighed. 'Every generation g-gets more c-clumsy than the one before! Where do they breed? Who makes 'em? I had a squire this spring throw himself on his back, t-trying to get off one of my boots! If I'd done such a thing, old Montgomery would have set his h-hounds on me.' He grinned at me suddenly. 'How are you, Raf? How're your brothers, your b-bastards, your one-eyed m-mother, and all your b-burgeoning fortunes at my expense? I've missed your lectures.'

He rose to fling an arm about my neck and beat me on the back with the flat of his hand, as if he were spanking dust out of an old gambeson. 'You're getting grizzled, did you know that? We're going to be old men, priest! Christ's Face, why is it I'll still have to be the ugly one? You haven't lost a tooth or a hair in your forelock yet, have you? Well, there's no justice but the hangman's beam. Come, tell me all your dreary b-business that you don't like to say in council. Then we'll get out the game board. I've got a move to show you.'

I obediently delivered my report on the effronteries of certain sheriffs, the recalcitrance of some abbots, and a general view of the workings of justice throughout the realm during his absence. He listened with interest until I began to expand on the state of his revenues and why they were of less yield than in former years, a matter that he wouldn't receive with the gravity due it.

'The weather has been against the growing of anything but tares, from early spring, my lord. It's been a disastrous year for –'

'– for the crops. This is something like a litany, isn't it? One can get it by heart: 'A murrain on the cattle, Selah, famine in the hinterlands, Selah, so that the rents will be seriously reduced, *in excelsis Deo*. Amen.' He sang the last in a voice somewhat truer than le Vieux's.

I own to being slightly offended. 'Your Grace, God knows I wish I could bring you better report, but –'

'– the weather's been terrible, yes. I've noticed it myself, would you believe it? We who d-dwell in tents like the Israelites can often tell when it rains. Get out the game board and don't "grace" me anymore tonight.'

I obeyed, setting up the pieces on a small table between us. We took stools, drew for sides, and he took the white. He held his hand out over his ivory men as God might have held His over the Jews departing Egypt, then moved the king's pawn two squares.

We played.

'I'll want more coin of you, despite the rain and greedy sheriffs. Don't look pale. It's for a good purpose. Ah! That's what I thought you'd do!' He moved his bishop into the open.

'How much coin, Your Grace? And what is the good purpose?'

'Hear him 'gracing' me, again? I'll want ten thou – thou – move! – ten thousand marks. That shouldn't be too difficult.' He moved his queen out next, leaving his pawns idle. 'You've found as much before, even in rainy weather, eh? Move again!'

I did, irritated by the rude manner in which he was pressing me. 'Yes, my lord. The abbot of Peterborough has just died. The abbey should yield a good return from my inventory. What did you say the purpose for the money was to be?'

'It's for a friend of mine, a s-splended boy! Closer to my heart than my plastron. He wants to go to the Holy Land like all the others. Why do they all want to m-murder heathen when they could stay home in comfort and kill F-french – aha! Check and mate! That's called a Fool's Mate! He's probably got the coin for the journey, but he's loath to s-spend his own. So he's asked for a loan of me, by way of fellowship. Would you like to s-see that move, again, Raf?'

'No, thanks, my lord. Humiliation instructs as well as Aristotle. I presume you're referring to the Duke of Aquitaine?'

He beamed at me. 'Yes! Wonderful boy, don't you think? No, you don't. Very well, play the usurer! Ask me what su-surety I'll get for my loan besides a pair of ki-kisses.'

I said stiffly, 'I would suppose the Aquitaine, my lord.'

He threw up his hands in mock dismay. 'I won't be your granddam! You'd spoil all my hearth tales. Yes, the Aquitaine!' He looked like a schoolboy who'd hoped to astonish his master by getting his lesson. 'Well – what do you think?'

'On the same terms as with Normandy?'

'Yes. I'll have it and Poitou for the price of one lending. And next year I'll have the Vexin, too. Then what will I lack, Raf? What will I lack?'

I stared at him, half piqued, half amused, and began to answer: 'Blois, Anjou, Touraine, Gascony, Brittany –'

'Paris! Paris. Only that. The rest come with it. Now – what do you think?'

'My lord, I never dreamed you meant to make yourself King of France.'

He looked at me for a long moment with his mocking dark eye and credulous-seeming blue one. 'Why not? Has she got one now? What my father began, I'll f-finish.' He seemed to examine what he'd just said. 'There was a time I'd have thought it treason even to think that, but it's true. I'll be a greater man than my f-father before

743

I die – and I won't die trying, because all the f-fools who might have contended with me have gone off to play at Roland with the h-heathen.' He smiled again almost sadly.

'You'll be a greater man than the German emperor if you can accomplish this, my lord. God grant you strength and life to do it.'

His smile went sour. 'Let's just l-leave God out of it, shall we? In any event, He's s-said to be p-preoccupied with another campaign – my good brother Robert's – if you can believe it. S-set up the pieces again and I'll show you how I t-took Rob fitz Hamon last week.'

The Countess Adela, the king's sister, was a quiet guest. Having established her comfortably in the old queen's house on the High Street, dined her once royally, and taken her hunting at Brocken-hurst, the king seemed willing to –

Thanks be to a merciful God Who hears our pleas. I am not forgotten. Fulcher has been to visit me!

I could scarcely believe it was my brother standing in my cell door at first. I've been so long alone, save for my guards and the priest who confess me here. I tried to rise to meet him, but my knees have grown stiff with the cold and so much sitting. He came forward, arms spread, and at my second attempt I threw myself on his neck and hugged his fragile body to me until we both groaned and wept.

'Prison agrees with you more than most men. You've put on flesh,' Fulcher said when we separated.

'There's nothing to do here but eat and dream. You should try incarceration sometime. I may have gained a stone.' I wiped the tears from my beard and embraced him again. 'Fulcher, what does this mean? After all these months –' A sudden fear quenched my joy. 'Am I to be tried? Did they send you to prepare me? What is the charge? Every letter I've written to anyone – the king, Giffard, Maurice, Thomas of York –'

'Thomas is dead, Raf. Your friend Gerard is Archbishop of York now. Perhaps that made a difference; I don't know. I've tried by every means to see you, or send you some message, but no one would let me. Then, yesterday, I was told I might come. Maurice sent me word. Come, sit down again. You're shaking like a willow leaf.' He guided me to the cot and sat by me, still holding my arm.

I searched his face. He didn't look as if he brought fatal tidings, but I couldn't be sure.

'They let you see me! I thought I'd never see anyone again. You can't imagine what it's like, being alone so long. If I hadn't had my pen I'd have gone mad, I think. Fulcher, what does Henry mean to do with me? No – first tell me what happened to the king, to my king. They said he was killed by chance. Is that true?'

He pursed his lips. 'If they've told you that, they've told you all anyone knows. He was at Malwood in the New Forest. They say he shot at a deer and missed. He called out to Count Walter to shoot again for him. Walter's arrow missed the beast and struck the man, instead. They say he died on the instant.' Fulcher gave me a searching look. 'Does that seem feasible to you? I know nothing about the hunt.'

'Wat Tirel? The best shot with a longbow or crossbow in all France, if you believe his own estimate? He shot at an animal the size of a deer and missed – what, was he in direct line with the king? Only a fool would risk a shot then – or a murderer. Did he confess it before they killed him?'

'He wasn't killed. He fled back to Ponthieu.'

'He fled and no one stopped him? In all that party? Why, there should have been – how many? How many people were with the king at Malwood? Who were they? This is strange news, Fulcher.'

'There were eight men of any consequence, besides Count Walter, according to what I've heard: Prince Henry, Robert fitz Hamon, Gilbert and Roger de Clare – '

'Wat Tirel's in-laws, yes. Who else?'

'Their cousin Richard, Gilbert de Laigle, William de Montfichet, and William de Breteuil. The others, the huntsmen – '

'Huntsmen? That Aquitanian, Raoul des Aix – Fulcher, was Martin among them?'

Fulcher continued to look gravely into my eyes for a moment, then dropped his gaze. 'Yes. There were also a number of knights, squires, the hunt servants, archers, the royal guard. Perhaps fifty men in all.' He examined an ink-stained finger.

I said: 'And all those men couldn't catch one Frenchman who'd killed their king?'

'They weren't all in the same part of the forest, apparently. They'd already taken their stands. The king's squires were with him. The chief hunter and his party were near to hand, I suppose. I don't know, Raf. Only those who were there could answer your question. They may have been dumbstruck by the tragedy – confused. They may have only thought of rushing to aid the king and didn't think of preventing Tirel until they saw he was gone.'

'And Henry didn't send someone after him, later? Did no one think this strange in him, not to avenge his brother?' I went to the window feeling numb and ill. A thin, bitter wind blew snow into my face from the embrasure. Despite my little charcoal brazier it was so cold in the cell that the snow didn't melt where it fell, but collected in a tiny drift against the wall.

'Prince Henry was said to be in another part of the forest altogether, not even in his appointed stand. The report is that he'd broken his bowstring and had gone to some shepherd's cot nearby to find the means to mend it.'

'How convenient! And when they brought him the news, he was so overcome with grief he forgot revenge for weeping. Is that it? Is that what they'd have us believe?'

'When they told Prince Henry the news they say he rode straight away from the forest to Winchester and siezed the treasury, then had himself proclaimed king.'

I turned away from the ice-sharp breeze. 'Where's Martin? You've spoken to him? What does he say? He'd have been with Henry, wouldn't he?'

'No. He was left with the chief hunter, along with several others of Henry's entourage. This was des Aix, as you've said. He'd been caught short of men at Malwood, because of the surprise of the king's visit and some verderer's court business taking place at Lyndhurst the same day. I know no more about it than that.'

'But, Fulcher, don't you see how all of this is just too simple? All too convenient – for Henry? Where's Martin now? I want to see him, if you can arrange it with my jailers.'

Fulcher looked at me, how? Pityingly? Suspiciously? How? 'Martin took refuge in Hyde Abbey the next day, claiming sanctuary. He's shut himself up in a cell and won't speak to anyone, not even a confessor.'

'There! You see?'

'Raf, the prior of Hyde says Henry didn't pursue Count Walter because he may believe he already has the murderer of his brother in custody. Everyone knows you quarreled with the king before you took your bishopric.'

I cannot sleep

I cannot sleep I cannot *A porta inferi érue, Domine, animam meam. A porta inferi érue* from the Gate of Hell.

Absolve, we beseech Thee, O Lord, the soul of Thy servant, William, that being dead to this world he may live to Thee and whatever sins he has committed through human frailty, do Thou wipe away by the pardon of Thy merciful goodness through Our

Lord Jesus Christ I have never prayed for him in all these months how is it that I have never prayed O God from the Gate of Hell deliver my soul amen I shall be shut in I shall be shut in forever Martin Martin what have you done *A porta inferi érue, Domine, animam meam.* Absolve, we beseech Thee, O Lord, the soul

There is a dreadful wind rising. This candle burns ill

Absolve, we beseech

Fulcher has come again after a time. I don't know how many days. I have been ill.

'They tell me you haven't been well these last few days.'

'It was the storm. I caught a chill.'

He looked about my cell. 'What's this jumble of parchment? Have you been writing appeals? To the king or the Pope?' He started to touch it.

'No! It's only foolishness. It's how I keep myself entertained. It's nothing. Don't look at it, please. It would embarrass me.'

He looked surprised. 'Have you taken to writing commentaries? There's nothing to be ashamed of in that. Prison has made more than one man a scholar.'

'It doesn't matter. It's all foolishness. I didn't think they'd let me see anyone again – so soon.'

'Well, as I told you before, you may have found a surprising friend in Anselm. He may not approve of you personally –'

'There's an understatement, even for you.'

'– but he doesn't approve of bishops being kept prisoner by kings, or of their being tried by secular courts either.'

'I'd have thought he would be as glad to have me put out of sight as he must have been to be rid of the king.'

'You continue to misjudge him. They say when he heard of the late king's death he wept as if he had lost a son.'

'Then hurried home to reclaim his miter.'

'He came only when King Henry beseeched him, for which Henry may now begin to be a little sorry – and you a little more glad.'

'Yes. Well, I'm trying to learn how to forgive my enemies by forgetting them. Let's talk of something else, shall we? How is Mother? And Osbern and the rest?'

'They're well. They're all in London now. The king confiscated all your property, naturally, but Maurice has been kind enough to give them lodging in one of his own houses here. You see, you do have friends still who think of you.'

'The house on Cornhill too?'

'Yes.'

'Poor Isabel. What's become of her?'

'She's with Mother and Osbern's family. They seem to get on together better than I'd have thought. Her babe is well, too.'

'Well – thank Maurice for me.'

'Thank him yourself. He's here with me to see you. He stayed down in the lower hall only because the constable said you'd been ill. You know how difficult the stairs are for him these days.'

I tried to shake off my languor. 'Here? Please, ask him to come up!'

Fulcher went away and returned in a quarter of an hour with the old man, whose joints were so swollen with age and disease that he could barely lift his feet to take the stairs. A young clerk had him by the other arm. When they had him safely inside my cell, they left us alone. I fell on my knees before my old master and wept. He put his hands on my head in a tentative blessing, then pressed my face to his body. When I had finished weeping, he helped me rise and I helped him to my stool, where he sat in a tremble.

'My boy, my boy, you look so pale!'

'I haven't seen the sun for five months, my friend, except for what leaks through that window.' I knelt before him again and kissed his hands. 'Thank you for coming to see me, and thank you for your care of my family. Even if I were able to leave this place and regain all I've lost, I'd owe you a greater debt than I can repay.'

'Nonsense! I was glad to take them in, and the house was standing empty.'

'If there were any way I could repay you, I would, Maurice. But, as it is, I must ask you for yet more chairty. When I am dead, will you see to it that my family doesn't suffer? Send them back to the Bessin if you must. I doubt that King Henry will take the trouble to look for them if they're out of his ken.'

He seemed amazed. 'Ranulph, you sound as if you think your death is imminent. Are you truly in such poor health?'

I had to laugh, despite my fear and misery. 'Good Lord, Maurice! What man was ever in good health who was the prisoner of a king – especially one who hates him?'

Still he looked askance. 'But no one has said the king means to execute you – far from it! You are the anointed and consecrated Bishop of Durham. The Church simply wouldn't countenance such an act, most especially now that we have our archbishop back to speak for us. No, no, my boy! That could never happen. The king is both Christian enough and intelligent enough to understand that.

Now, get off your knees again and take a seat. I can see it must pain you to kneel.'

I rose awkwardly and sat on my bed. The old fool seemed sincere. He was never able to hide his feelings. If he'd known of any calamitous thing planned for me, he wouldn't have been able to keep it out of his face or voice. But it was possible he was only missing what was there. His eyes had never been good. Now they were rheumy and faded with age. His hearing might not be so acute, either, though he seemed to have no difficulty hearing me. Above all, he placed his faith entirely in Anselm's ability to influence Henry, without once considering the consequences to me of an ecclesiastical trial held before Anselm.

'Maurice, I've had so little news since I came to this place. Fulcher has told me somewhat, but would you please tell me how Ru— how King William came to die?'

'It was a most unfortunate accident! You probably know he was hunting near Malwood Lodge with a small party of his friends. A deer broke cover directly before him. He loosed his bow at it and struck it, but the shot went high. The animal ran past him to the west, into the setting sun. Young Walter of Poix was in the next stand. The king cried out to him, "Shoot, in the Devil's name!" when he stood amazed. Walter shot, his arrow nicked the beast's rack, gadded, and struck the king, who fell without a sound. He died on the instant, with no chance to confess his sins, God be merciful to him.' He blessed himself. I did the same.

'Maurice, you tell that tale as if you'd been there. Were you?'

He was surprised. 'I? No, of course not. My eyes are too poor for the hunt now. But it was told to me by one who was there.'

'Who was that?'

'King Henry himself.'

'But – wasn't he in another part of the line? Wandering, as I heard it, in search of mending for a broken bowstring? My source naturally is not so trustworthy as yours, but this is what Fulcher heard.'

Maurice's brow puckered slightly. 'Why should His Grace have to look for the means to mend a bowstring? His archers would have instantly supplied him with another, or even another bow, if he broke one.'

'Yes, that's so, isn't it? I hadn't thought of that. You know my hunting is confined to waiting for game. But what happened then? They called in the hunt, naturally.'

'Yes. Gilbert de Clare cried out, "The king is dead!" and all rushed in to see the dreadful sight.'

'Gilbert? He was with the king?'

'No, I believe he was with Count Walter.'

'Who did share the stand with the king, do you know?'

'Why – no, I don't believe it was mentioned. But it may have been Robert fitz Hamon. They've companioned each other in the hunt so long, they – they *did* – act together almost as one man.'

We looked on each other for a long moment. He knew my question before I asked it. 'Why, I wonder, didn't the king tell fitz Hamon to shoot, then, rather than Wat Tirel? Or why –'

'I can't answer these questions, Ranulph. I suppose there's no one who can now. Fitz Hamon retired to his estate in Oxfordshire after King Henry's crowning, in the deepest grief. I haven't spoken to him.' He said tremulously: 'Ranulph, why do you ask me all these questions? Walter Tirel killed King William by unhappy chance and fled the country in fear for his life. Why shouldn't he, when he was surrounded by the dead man's dearest friends, mad with grief? You can understand how that would be.'

'Yes. Yes, they would have grieved, wouldn't they? He was the best friend fitz Hamon could ever hope to have. He gave him his own mother's estates there in Oxfordshire. And the Clares – he forgave them their treachery more than once. Wat Tirel had him to thank for a prosperous marriage. Rufus was the matchmaker to that' – I had to smile at the memory – 'to outwit Lanfranc, who wanted him to wed the girl himself. All his good friends – '

I had to move, to rise and pace, or find myself in tears of rage. 'I suppose Tirel must have made his escape when the rest were grieving. You were there when they brought the corpse to Winchester. Did they look properly grieved?'

'Yes, I – well – as to that, the – the body wasn't brought in.'

'What?'

'It was brought, but not that night.' He looked as crestfallen as if he had been guilty of gross neglect. 'They left the king's body in the forest. A charcoal burner brought it the next day, late in the afternoon – on his cart. He'd discovered it.'

I stood still. Maurice sat with his head slightly bowed. I whispered, 'Oh, Maurice – '

'I know, I know. It was an ill deed – ill considered – '

'Infamous!'

'Ill considered! They were confused, frightened – '

'Yes, frightened! I'll warrant frightened. They left him! Even fitz Hamon! Maurice, why am I kept in prison? What are the charges made against me by the king?'

He cleared his throat. 'The principal complaint against you is said to be malfeasance of office.'

'Complaint? Said to be? I asked about charges. What has the king charged me with?'

'The king has never mentioned your name in council. Only Anselm has asked him about you, and according to Anselm, he's said only that you abused the office with your extortions and that you came by your bishopric through simony, both of which are offenses against the Church if they are proved, Ranulph, which' – his voice grew stronger – 'is why the archbishop wants you turned over to an ecclesiastical tribunal, but the king will not allow it.' He blinked at me several times reproachfully. 'You did achieve your office by such means.'

'I paid a thousand pounds for it, yes! Robin Bloet paid five times as much for his. Carileph paid dearly to the Bastard for his. Herbert Losinga bought a pair of miters, one for himself, one for his father. Are those men in prison? Are they about to be taken to a tribunal? If so, let me lead them to it. "Always first," Maurice! That's my motto, if peasants can have them. But I was told the charge against me was treason. Has this never been mentioned to you?'

'No. That was the popular assumption. You're not much loved among the members of the royal council, you know.' He stirred uncomfortably and began to rise with the help of his staff. 'I can stay no longer. I must attend to – '

I seized him by the shoulders. 'You must attend to *me*, Maurice! I'm one of your own! The charge I heard was treason! Now why would someone say that, unless he'd heard it from a very reliable witness – someone close to the king?'

'I don't know! It may have been the heat of the moment that made Henry say it – '

'Then he did say it?'

'No! I mean, I don't know what he said in privacy to his friends, but he never made it a public charge.'

'Then why am I held here? Why won't he turn me over to Anselm? Or exile me? Or charge me with something?'

'I don't know. *I – don't – know!*' In agitation he called out for his clerks: 'Fulcher! Elphrin!'

My brother opened the door at once. By his look as much as his promptness I knew he'd heard us. He took Maurice by the hand and led him out. I waited for him to return and speak to me, but he hasn't. Now I wonder why I was allowed to see him at all. Or if I'll ever see him, or anyone but my jailers, again.

The bells have just finished Matins. Sleet is falling through the window, and it's bitter as a harlot's end in here. My brazier's fit for nothing but smoldering and my candle is nearly spent, but for now I scarcely mind. The chill, the damp, the impending dark, all seem inevitable companions to my fate. I have lived too much in a dream these months alone. It's time I was awake.

Henry doesn't mean to bring me to trial. He doesn't mean to turn me over to Anselm, either. What does he mean to do, then? He's affected to forget me, but he's let me be seen by Fulcher and old Maurice, who can testify if pressed to it that I'm still alive and well. I have this little dread coiled around my heart, cold as Lady Cleopatra's asp: if I were Henry and had such a prisoner to keep as Ranulph, I'd keep him farther off and deeper in some donjon after a while. As deep, maybe, as Robert Mowbray. That is, I would keep him so if I had a thing to hide that he might peep at, and I could not buy his silence.

But he could buy me now for a farthing! My friend is dead and what am I but a starving dog, ready to beg at any man's door?

No! I am the Bishop of Durham! He dare not put me in a grave – though it may be he's put a king in one.

Oh, Fulcher, God, Fulcher, come to me again!

64

Fulcher reminded me I had quarreled with Rufus before I received my bishopric. It was because of the quarrel that I did in fact finally get my heart's desire, but I didn't feel so much gratitude for the benefice at the time as satisfaction in demonstrating my own stiff pride to a suddenly alien and inflexible friend.

The objects of our dissent were two persons so obscure, of such little consequence to the world at that time, that many in the court may not even have heard of one of them. He was one of Curthose's numerous bastards, a boy of about sixteen named Richard, who must have been engendered during Robert's last exile before the Conqueror's death. I know little of his history, only that he had been presented to Duke Robert before he left Normandy and that the boy was left behind, though somehow acknowledged, for Rufus to bring home to England with him. He was too young for knighthood yet, and he was serving as a common soldier in the king's mesnie.

The second person was the Scottish princess Edgyth, and I unwittingly began our quarrel by mentioning to the king Prince Henry's several visits to see her at Romsey. At first he pretended not to understand my meaning:

'What of it? Sh-she's an infant.'

'She was an infant when last you saw her, my lord. She's grown since.'

He laughed his irritating, sharp laugh. 'Are you certain it isn't her aunt that Harry's after, Raf? She was round as a turnip last time I saw *her*. He likes them round and ro-rosy.'

'My lord prefers to take this as a jest, but it's no light matter. The Lady Edgyth is known to the English as their own princess. They discount her father, Malcolm, and prefer to think of her as Edward Confessor's grandniece.'

He frowned slightly, then gave me one of his most ingenuous smiles. 'How inspiring for them!'

'Exactly, Your Grace. The man who marries her will have made himself many friends among the English, if he treats her well. If he should be your brother, who likes to hear himself called "Atheling," he might win himself enough support to – ' I didn't like to use the word *rebel*. *Betray* seemed equally injudicious.

But he took my meaning and didn't like it any more than I thought he would:

'You – you're accusing m-my own brother to my face, who's sworn me fealty – '

'Several times – '

'A good soldier – '

'A younger brother – '

'An honest knight – '

' – who wants you to make him your heir. You said you wouldn't. So what would you have him do next?'

He put his thumb knuckle in his teeth, then began to walk restlessly about the chamber, scratching his neck. His hounds, seeing him rise, went to the door whimpering. He stopped suddenly to scoff:

'But that's nonsense on the face of it! She's a nun! It would be a false m-marriage and they'd both be ca-cast out of the Church, and there'd be the end of his support from these p-priest-kissing peasants. Ha!'

'A very nice legal point, my lord. But the lady isn't a nun.'

He looked at me askance. I smiled.

'I've taken the trouble to inquire. She's never taken vows, nor ever meant to. She wants a husband. You may remember how, when she was a child, she said she wanted to be a queen? That still seems to be the case.'

'Well – by the Holy Face, what do you want me to do about her? Veil her myself?'

'No, my lord. Marry her yourself.'

His mouth opened wide in a child's look of amazement. 'Why, that's good! That's to pay me back for my Fool's Mate, isn't it? Wonderful! But no, thank you, I've better things to do on my way to the grave. I've a campaign to plan, Maine to settle, and soon the Aquitaine will – '

'What about England? It's a small place, but it pays for all the rest.'

'Don't be clever with me anymore, priest. I don't need a tutor at my age.'

'No, my lord. At your age you should be a tutor – to your sons, to make them ready to succeed you in all your own father gave you.'

He drew a great breath and lowered his head a bit, like a wary stag. 'No! That will never be, Raf, so let it be. Now, as to the Vexin – '

But the persistence of Henry's visits to Romsey and his wooing of the frailer-in-loyalty of the king's friends, such as the Clares, had given me too many anxious nights.

'That will never be, my lord? That you have a son? Then your noble and illustrious father must have his hope destroyed, by the son who was most dear to him in the end. He looked for more than campaigns and victories from you. He wanted a royal line to come of his seed, and he gave his crown to you, not Robert or Henry. If you go childless to the grave like the saintly Confessor, your brothers and their bastards will tear apart and devour all that your father – and you – have fought for. We'll have anarchy again and treasons matching those old days, when your father had to find a new bed every night in order to keep from being murdered by his own kin, his own liege men!'

'Stop that! My f-father died a king and I'll die a king – '

'Yes! And your brothers may die so, too. But then there'll be no more kings here! There'll only be petty thieves!'

'Get out!' He threw his wine cup at my head. It missed me and bounced off the wall behind me, but his nervous hounds, taking the noise it made for the signal to attack, leaped on me, snarling.

I fell, warding off the snapping teeth. I heard Rufus bellow: 'Hold off! Hold, dog!' A hound yelped as he kicked it; the second one he seized by the scruff and threw aside, then bent to examine me. 'Are you bitten?'

'Somewhat. On the wrist.'

'Come sit on the bed. I'll tend it.'

I rose from the floor with difficulty, my heart slamming at my breastbone, my lungs seeming not to find enough air. He caught my arm as I would have fallen and led me to the bed. 'Sit there. No, sit! I'll find an ointment.' He went to a battered field chest and searched through the jumble it contained until he found an unguent pot containing some medication no doubt designed for his palfrey. I watched him, gasping, thinking of the first time he'd done such a thing for me. He brought the pot to the bed and took my arm up. 'You're scarcely bleeding.

'You fool,' he muttered as he smeared the fang marks with a thick, dark grease, 'why do you provoke yourself and *m-me* with such non-nonsense?' A laugh. 'I mean to live forever, if you want to know. But you won't, if you go on like this. You're sh-shaking like a custard. Did the dogs fright you so much?'

'No. You've said it yourself, my lord. Neither of us is a young man anymore. I'm nearly forty and no man can tell the hour of his death, not even a king.'

He sniffed and finished his work, binding up my wrist with a cloth. I tried to get to my feet and found myself sprawled on the floor again. I heard him calling his squires before my senses left me.

I woke in the king's bed, along with the hounds that had attacked me. They were worrying their fleas. The king sat hunched at his game board, gnawing at his thumb. In a moment he reached out almost surreptitiously and moved a piece, examined the effect of the move, and muttered, 'Damn.' He looked up as I stirred.

'Stay where you are.'

'My lord, I cannot. Forgive me, I'm much humiliated. Such a thing never happened to me before.'

'Yes, it did. Your brother told me. Why didn't you?'

'It was nothing – exhaustion. It's the same now. I'm quite recovered, however.'

'You're a liar. But sit down if you must be out of b-bed.'

I took the opposite stool. I felt light-headed and drained.

'Would you care to take the side there?' he asked in a moment. 'I think I've just made it so you're winning.' He looked up from under his brows, solemnly. 'I've been thinking about what you said. You frightened the Hell out of me, you know that, don't you? G-giving me dire prophecies, then falling over in a heap like that? Christ!' He flipped his king over with a finger, then rose to prowl the chamber.

He came to rest at last against the wall beneath a window. There was some moonlight to add to the candles and cressets that wavered in the soft air, but I could still not see his eyes. His voice had a deeper note than usual:

'Edgar wants to go chasing heathen. He sent me a petition to furnish him a ship last winter. I refused him – which is why he's avoided court, I suppose. He'd like to have me send a force up to take him and throw him in a donjon, so he could feel the martyr more. But I'll give him his ship in time. Then he'll be gone. I doubt I'll see him again. It's the same with Rob fitz Hamon. He's got more to do with his in-laws now than with me.

'I'm surrounded by people every day, but I miss my friends. Do you know, there're times when I look about and half expect to see Cormac, still? I begin to know how my f-father f-felt when he lost fitz Osbern. N-no one could ever replace him in his heart. That's how I'll feel about you, Raf. You've been my w-warden, my nurse, my f-friend, companion – sometimes you seem about to t-turn into my granddam – ' He laughed, but there was no heart in the sound.

I suppose I must have been gaping at him as if I were a fool. 'Where – why should you feel the loss of me, my lord? I'm not about to leave you.'

'Yes, you are.'

I rose from the stool and asked stiffly, 'Have I offended you so much?'

'Not yet. But it would come. You'd offend me v-very much if I saw you fall down dead at my feet, someday, from overwork for me.'

'But I'm not ill!'

'You'll take your bishopric that's long overdue. Or would you prefer an abbey? After bearing the weight of the whole realm on your back, it'll be nothing for you to have the rule of – what? Take your pick of what's vacant: Winchester, Durham – I can't offer you Canterbury, more's the pity, but how about the abbacy of Peterborough? Or Salisbury? Old Osmond can't last out the year.'

'I'm not ill.' My voice broke.

He didn't answer.

'I am justly rebuked for lecturing Your Grace in the matter of the succession, but this is too hard, my lord. This is – '

'This is nothing to do with that! As a matter of f-fact, you're probably right about what my f-father expected of me. He didn't know all the – the circumstances; at least, I hope he – you're most probably right about Harry and his ambitions, too. With Robin out of the way, he m-might just take it into his head to leave off s-swiving hearth girls and make a reach for my c-crown. But he hasn't done it, yet, and I can't punish him for what he hasn't done. But I'll bear your warning in mind. Name what benefice you'll have.'

I saw it was useless to protest any longer. I thought of the drudgery I had endured, the hatred that had been poured out against me, the long nights spent over ledgers, the weary days spent wrangling for compromise or coin. I thought of my Lady of Stone, waiting for me in the north, waiting for her proper robes, her ornaments, her incense and song that would rise aloft in her praise when I had made her whole.

I said: 'I'll have Carileph's church, if it please Your Grace. I'll have Durham.'

On the morrow of Easter in his court at the new Palace of Westminster, King William formally recommended me to the Archbishop of York for his Suffragan Bishop of Durham and I was accepted.

In May we shifted to Winchester again, in order that the king might visit with his sister Adela, and it was there that I first met the young bastard nephew Richard. He was part of the household guard Rufus left for Adela's protection. I found him a pleasant youth, not without some unhappy physical attributes of his family, but more handsome than otherwise. He was still slender, for one thing, and his legs were of normal length for his body, unlike his father Curthose's. He had pale blue eyes, and his head was clipped and shaved in the best old Norman fashion, but other than that I had no impression of him. He might have been brilliant or stupid without my knowledge, for his only words in my presence were 'Yes, my lady' and 'Your Grace' when his aunt made him known to me. His aunt seemed pleased with him, and Rufus treated him with that offhand kindness he usually bestowed on earnest-looking boys. Prince Henry paid no mind to him at all, so it seemed.

When we had been at the city for about a week, Rufus called me to him one morning and informed me I would keep him company on a brief ride out into the country. I expected this was merely an excuse to get away from the trivial affairs of the court, for which he showed less patience in each succeeding year. We took our leave through the city's south gate with two of his squires and some dozen of his household knights for a guard. As soon as I realized we weren't headed for the forest, I knew we were riding for Romsey Abbey. Since he hadn't offered me an explanation, I was wise enough not to ask for one, but by the look on his face it was a solemn matter we had to deal with.

We were in sight of the little abbey when he called a halt to rest the horses. Leaving his own mount in the care of his squires, he walked aside and leaned against an oak tree to study the walls and bell tower of the abbey in the distance. It seemed an invitation to follow him, so I did. The rest of our company relieved themselves on the vegetation or checked their horses' feet for stones. There was a mild drizzle of rain that seemed just to hang in the air more than fall on our heads, and the smell of the earth was delicious.

He looked uncommonly pale when I reached him. I stood a little way apart and joined him in contemplation of the abbey. I thought of Giva's grave there in the churchyard and wondered if it was marked in any way that I might discover it, after so long a time.

Rufus cleared his throat and asked, 'How do I s-s-speak to her?'

I smiled. 'My lord, it's no great difficulty to speak to a young woman when you've come to tell her something she wants to hear.'

'N-not for you, maybe. What ma-makes you th-think sh-sh – Christ!' He wiped his mouth, then drew a steadying breath. 'I'd le-leaguer Rome to make you Po-pope if you'd do the s-speaking for me.' He glanced at me, beginning to flush. 'I can't! My damned tongue won't. To be a f-fool and an unwilling su-suitor at once is t-too much for it.' He wiped at his face, damp with rain. 'This is too damned much to ask of me! Let's go home.'

'My lord, I'll gladly speak for you! It doesn't take St. Peter's keys to unlock my lips. Let me see the girl first and I promise you, there'll be nothing for you to do but kiss her hand when I bring her to you.'

He snorted. 'I don't think the abbess will let you get as close as all that to the girl, priest.' He gave me a rather sick grin.

'My lord, I promise you, I'll only have to mention your name to the Lady Edgyth. She's eager to be free of that place. She's young, intelligent – from all I've heard – witty, not fat, fair of face – and she has an affection for you from her childhood days. Don't you remember?' I pitied him; he looked miserable. I said carefully: 'It won't be so difficult to – to love her, in time, my lord. When one is loved, one learns to love in return. '

He laughed abruptly. 'What could she ever see, or hear, or know to love in m-me? I'm nothing for li-little girls to dream on. I'm in league with the Devil and the man who had her f-father mur-murdered, if you ask half the kingdom.'

'You're the most valiant soldier in all Europe and she's a soldier's daughter. You're a great king and she's a king's daughter. You're of the new line of royalty and she's of the old. She was made to be your queen, my lord, as if Heaven – '

'Don't sav it! Nothing Heaven ever took a ha-hand in has worked to my good! Let's just go and get it over.'

We weren't especially welcome visitors, not even when the king's name was mentioned. The porteress was a different one from when last I'd tried to gain entry there and so it was probably the effect of my tonsure and quiet bearing that persuaded her to open the gate to us. The king's guard were obliged to remain outside the walls, however. Rufus, beyond giving the porteress one of those baleful looks with which he covered his own confusion, said nothing, leaving it for me to ask for the abbess. All this time a silent congregation of sisters was collecting on the far side of the cloister garth in the shelter of the south wall.

The rain mist had ceased to shimmer in the air and the sun came forth strongly from behind a tattered cloud. While we waited for the abbess to send her consent to see us, a little nun with blushing cheeks came dipping her head to the king and invited us to step into the abbess's private garden, where spring had already sent summons of array to its host, whose flags and ensigns spangled the long grass. The iron gate closed behind me and the king took a breath as if he had been shut up in an oubliette and might never see sunlight again. I cocked my head to the twitter of disparaging birds in an apple tree, and we kept prudent silence until an elderly nun appeared in the lodge walk and said:

'Reverend Mother Abbess will see you now, Your Grace and Reverend Father Abbot.' So, in a fashion I was remembered.

Rufus jerked his head at me to go in alone, then he began to pace the garden.

I entered the lodge to find two women waiting for me; the Abbess Athelfleda and one whom I recognized as Christina, young Edgyth's aunt and the Atheling's sister. We exchanged solemn greetings. Christina favored me with such an accusing look that I might have come to demand their altar silver.

'How may we serve His Grace the king?' Athelfleda asked in tremulous French. She had deeply set, hooded eyes and a great bloodless prow of a nose that must have been bequeathed her by some Danish pirate who had intruded on the chastity of her English mother about the time of the St. Brice's Day Massacre, if her wrinkles were any indication of her age.

'Permit me to speak to one of your wards, Reverend Mother Abbess.' I glanced at Christina. 'I refer to the Princess Edgyth of Scotland.'

'She has done nothing wrong, nothing to be blamed for by you or the king!' said Christina sharply, for which the abbess gave her a glance of reproof.

'I haven't come to blame her, Sister. I've merely come to speak to her – alone.'

'That is impossible!'

'That is imperative, Sister. Alone. And at once. The king is waiting. I believe it will not be the first time the lady has spoken to a man alone here.'

'The rules of this cloister – '

'Are flexible enough to admit Prince Henry. So, now they must admit me. I will suffer someone to stand within hearing of what I say to the lady, however, if she can restrain herself to merely listen and not speak. Is that understood? Then you may bring her. How beautiful your garden is, Reverend Mother Abbess. The king remarked on it as we came in. Your purple field lilies remind me of my home in the Bessin – '

In a few moments Christina opened the door and looked at the abbess, prim-mouthed. Athelfleda said to me: 'You may walk in the garth, Reverend Father Abbot. It's quiet there now, while the sisters are observing their private devotions. No one will disturb you.'

I went out into the shade of the cloister walk and saw Edgyth waiting, clad in a grey gown and wearing a nun's veil. Her stout aunt was walking briskly toward the refectory and went inside, where I expect she kept her ear to the door. As I went to Edgyth she suddenly pulled off her veil and crushed it nervously in her hands. I smiled, hoping to reassure her.

'My lady, I'm very glad to see you again. Do you remember me at all? You were quite young when we last met.'

'You're Ranulph Flambard. My aunt told me your name just now, but I'd have remembered you anyway. Once you were the handsomest priest I thought I'd ever seen.' She bit her lip at that disclosure and added hastily: 'I didn't mean you'd grown ugly, Father, only older – ' Her lip suffered for that, too, until I laughed and took her hand to kiss.

'My lady, I understand what you mean. You've grown older, too, but the addition of years has benefited you more than me. You're as beautiful as your lady mother. Has anyone told you that?'

'Yes.'

'Yes.' I thought I knew who it might have been. 'Lady, will you walk with me? We'll take the northern path, against the sun.' And away from the refectory door. She let me hold her hand over mine as we did so. I saw she clutched her veil out of sight in her right hand.

'Why do you wear that veil if you haven't taken holy vows? You haven't taken vows, have you?'

'No! She – they wanted me to, but I wouldn't! My father never wanted me to be a nun. He told me so.' She looked at the gloomy veil in disgust. 'My aunt says wearing it will protect me from – from – '

'I understand. But a blue one of Gaza cloth would suit you better, wouldn't it? It would match your eyes.'

She said nothing, but sighed for the lack of such an adornment. I led her to the south wall of the abbey church where there were benches set out between the arcades for the sisters to sun themselves on when they took their recreation. When we were seated, I said:

'My lady, I won't keep you in doubt about my mission any longer. I've come to speak to you on behalf of a man who has the greatest respect and affection for you and who would put something on your head better than a veil, if you would allow it. I mean a crown.'

She gazed at me soberly. 'Prince Henry?'

'Prince Henry? Why, has he made you such an offer, child?'

'He wants to marry me. He said he – loved me and a lot of – other things.' She frowned and looked at her lap.

'And would make you a queen?'

'He said – someday.'

'Ah! And what did you say to that?'

'I said nothing. He did all the talking.' Her voice was very low. I had to bend to catch the last.

'Well, that's a very fine offer, except that Prince Henry isn't a king, or likely to become one. He's a comte, which is something like a sheriff here. But perhaps that wouldn't make so much difference to you – if you loved him. Do you?'

'I've only seen him four times in my life,' she said in sudden exasperation. 'My aunt asked me the same question. How can I tell?' She looked at me shrewdly. 'But you didn't come from him, so who is it that wants to make me a queen?' Than I saw the truth dawn in her eyes. 'Will-Rou? Is that who you mean?'

'Would that displease you? You were very fond of him once.'

'I don't know.' She was troubled. 'They say he isn't the way I remember him. He scoffs at God and abuses the Church and – they say he killed my father, too.' Her chin puckered slightly.

'King William didn't kill your father or want him to die. Earl Robert Mowhray had him waylaid and killed for a private grudge. Mowbray is in one of King William's darkest prisons now and must remain there for life. The man Mowbray ordered to murder your father is exiled and possibly dead now, too. Does that ease your mind? I assure you, it's the truth.'

She looked pensive. 'Yes, but what about God and the Church?'

'My lady, I won't lie to you. The king is not so saintly as I would like him to be. But he's endowed an abbey and a hospital to the glory and service of God. He's a fine soldier and he wants to be a great king. Perhaps if he had a good, pious wife to guide him in the matter, he would soon give up his scoffing and the good sisters here would think more kindly of him. Some men, however, you must learn to take as you find them. And you must be out in the world a little in order to understand them. Now, this king who was your friend once may one day be King of France as well as of England, which would mean – if you wished it, of course – that you might be queen of both countries. That's a good deal better than being Countess of the Cotentin. Unless you truly want to stay here at Romsey and dedicate yourself to God. There is nothing that could persuade me to take you out of here if that's what you feel God wants of you.'

'No! I don't want to stay here! They're nothing but old women here, and they do nothing all day but stitch and talk about their miseries!'

I took her hand and turned it palm up, then brought it to my lips. 'This is too lovely a hand to devote to embroidery. It's a hand that should rest in a king's. Do you think you could say yes to King William, if he should ask you for this hand?'

'Does Will-Rou say he loves me?' she asked with affected lightness.

I studied her, still holding her sweet-moist little hand. It was a temptation to lean forward, kiss her baby mouth, and bring her aunt screeching from her hiding place. But Edgyth was naive, as women of good breeding are expected to be, not stupid. She hadn't believed Prince Henry's protestations of love and she was prepared to be wary of mine on behalf of Rufus.

That was good. She was beginning to have some idea of her value in the marriage market. She could easily flatter herself right out of it if I gave her too much encouragement, but her present caution was no harm. The king would better regard her as his consort if she held a high regard for herself.

'My lady, didn't I say I would be honest with you? I want you to learn to trust me and believe that in me you will always have a true friend at court. No, the king hasn't said he loves you. How can he when he hasn't seen you since you were a *bairn?*'

She smiled a little at the familiar word.

'But my master remembers a child he was very fond of, one whose courage and gaiety appealed to his own. Do you recall his visit to your father's court?'

'He gave me a ring. I still have it. We're not allowed to wear such things here, but I've kept it. He let me ride his white palfrey.' Her smile flashed. 'That's what I remember best about him. My brothers were jealous of me!'

'Yes, I recall that, too, as I'm sure the king does. Well, he might have made a betrothal with you then. Your father and mother favored it at the time. Yet he had too much tenderness for your innocence and said he wouldn't be married to a child. But now you're a woman, and I think, if he saw you, he would very soon begin to love you. Do you think you might say yes to him, if he asked you to be his wife now? It's entirely your decision, you know. No one can make you marry against your will – or keep you from doing so, if that's your desire. Then you may wear all the rings and jewels you like.'

She thought about it and swallowed several times, her slight breast rising and falling more rapidly. 'Yes.'

'Praise be to God, my king has found his salvation!' I whispered, and kissed her palm again. I saw the refectory door positively quiver. I rose, letting go of Edgyth's hand. 'My lady, go and get that ring the king once gave you. I must say a word to someone waiting for me in the Reverend Mother Abbess's garden. Come to her lodge in a few minutes and see what joy awaits you there.'

I watched her walk sedately across the garth toward the dorter.

The refectory door swung open and Christina went after her, throwing me a look that made me laugh aloud. I returned to the abbess's lodge, passed through it finding her gone, and went out into her garden.

It was empty. I ran to the outer gate, which was open. The king was nowhere in sight, nor was his palfrey, or his guard. I ran to the far side of the church wall and looked down the northern side, then back to the extreme of the south cloister wall. My own horse was still tethered to a post there, but otherwise I had been abandoned.

65

My solitary ride back to Winchester should have cooled the anger that boiled in me, but when I came into the king's presence it flared up again like an oiled torch, making me reckless to the point of unreason. I forgot he had people about him. It might have been Prince Henry, or a choir of devils; I neither knew nor cared.

'Your Grace made good speed in your retreat!'

I think he smiled. 'You made pretty good s-speed yourself.'

'I never heard you were so adept at running away. You must have flown out the gate as soon as I left you.'

'Priest, I went away. I didn't fly, or retreat. You're out of breath. Le-let's go in and have some wine.' He scattered squires with a gesture and took me by the arm. We were in the cavalry yard near the stables. He pushed more than led me aside in the direction of the tower stairs.

'Why did you do it? You gave me your word! I gave it to that girl!'

His fingers dug into my arm. 'I did not g-give you my word. No! I never did that.'

'You led me there, you made me think you were serious, you sent me in to speak with her. I count that as good as a promise. What else would you call it?'

He sighed. 'Well, no man can keep all his promises. But it isn't the same as giving my word, I prom – I assure you. I thought I could do something I f-found I couldn't do, after all, then I thought of a b-better way to do it and s-so came away. That's the end of it.'

'A better way? What better way? To do what?'

'To g-get an heir. That's what this was all for, wasn't it? You didn't expect to make me be-bed that girl to my p-pleasure, or hers, did you? But get an heir – that's easy. I'll adopt a nephew. Christ knows, I've p-plenty of them.'

'Yes. All bastards!'

His color rose as he glanced about us to see who listened. Then he made a show of wry amusement: 'Well, then, you can't say I've never done a good deed. I'll make one of them le-legitimate.'

'I see. And who might that one be?'

'Why, young Richard that's Robin's get will do well enough. He shows promise, don't you think?'

'You could be satisfied with that? To take your brother's neglected *bastard* for your heir?'

'Ranulph – that's the end of it.'

'No, there'd be much more. Besides naming a bastard for your successor over two legitimate brothers, you'd be breaking your sacred word again – and to someone of more consequence than a mere priest or cloistered girl. I mean the word you swore to your brother Robert to make him your heir if you died without legitimate issue. Or did you suppose he'd gladly step aside for a bastard he didn't know existed until last year? He's a little bit of a fool, but not so much as that, and the end of it, my lord, is that you'll have broken your word, no matter how fine a line you draw between a mere promise and a sworn oath!'

He grabbed me and pushed me against the stone wall. 'What do you know about it? You couldn't understand the d-difference between the two if I d-drew it for you in b-blood. Now, h-hold your tongue before it r-runs you to your ruin.'

'I think it's already done that, with your help. Surely at Romsey they think I'm the very ruin of a liar and fool. Is that what my new place is to be, as your fool? Will Robert Cornard lend me his cap and stick when you send me to tell the men who've already betrayed you twice that you're adopting your brother's bastard to be their future king? Shall I have to tell it to the King of France, who sent you Cornard? I can't do Fulk of Anjou for him, but I can make a pretty imitation of – '

He struck me across the face with the glove he held clenched in one fist. I saw in his eyes that he might as easily kill me, but though he raised his fist again, he let it drop. He struggled to speak and achieved a bare whisper: 'I owe you nothing now. But I can show you what a king's word means. I gave you Durham. Go and take it while you can.'

I stepped back, almost falling against the steps. There were tears in his eyes and I felt my own sting with them. 'My lord, I – '

'Do you doubt me? Do you think I'll c-come and tu-turn you out, once you're there, or t-trump up charges against you? Put the offer on another f-footing, then – one you sh-should understand. Give me a th-thousand pounds sil-silver for it and it's yours. That's cheap enough, isn't it? I've p-paid more for a g-good horse!' He pushed past me and went up the stairs to the hall.

I looked about me. Everyone still in the bailey was staring up at me, though they had all had the care to stay well back from us during our dispute. I descended and walked through them to the stables, took my horse, and rode to my house outside the walls.

My mother bristled with outrage, Osbern and Swanhilda were terrified, and Fulcher was grimly silent as we went about packing all the household goods to be moved to London. Fulcher was astonished when I told him to count out a thousand pounds in silver from my various household accounts and have it put aside to be sent to the king.

'He didn't mean that and he'll be even more angry when you remind him of it. Think of what you're doing! Besides beggaring yourself, if you break with him you'll not have a single friend left at court.'

'I won't need a single friend at court. I'll have to be in it only once a year – at Christmas. I can take the chill for that time.'

'You're behaving like a child and thinking like a fool! The Bishop of Durham is a member of the royal council. You'll be in court when he wants you there, but you won't be able to achieve a thing there, or in Durham. There are people who've waited years to get revenge on you. You'll find yourself accused of everything from – from boundary incursions to robbing pilgrims, and without the king there'll be nobody to defend you.'

'He may not defend me, but he won't let them eat me whole, either.'

'Are you quite sure of that?'

'Yes. He doesn't make wars – or promises – with peasants. It's beneath him.'

'Oh? He's burned quite a few peasants out of their hovels in the Vexin. Perhaps he just didn't notice they were there.'

'He's said he won't burn me out – and he won't.'

Fulcher stared at me in despair and shook his head. 'It's past belief! He's thrown your whole life of service back in your face and you'd still take his word for that. You still love him! Very well, I'll be quiet, but just try to remember Carileph, will you, as you go off to be the hermit bishop?'

I removed my family to London, putting them in with Isabel, who was now great with child and confined to bed most of the time for fear of miscarrying. She was chagrined to find herself being invaded by two women, but she put a good face on it. Mother did her part to smooth things over by immediately curing Isabel's constant indigestion and declaring herself to be her midwife. The promise of yet one more grandchild delighted my mother almost as much as the prospect of late motherhood enthralled Isabel. So, to my relief, there was no war among the females of my house.

On the nones of June I was consecrated Bishop of Durham in St. Paul's by Thomas, Archbishop of York, with Maurice and Robin Bloet assisting. Thomas had required no profession of obedience from Carileph, nor did he of me. The king remained at Winchester.

Robin Bloet surveyed me afterward and remarked: 'So, now you have it all, your heart's desire. Or do you?'

'I am content.'

'I wondered. We'd begun to think, Gerard and I, that you'd never ask for anything, that you were content as you were. Is there some message you'd like me to convey to the king for you?' He knew about the rift, naturally, though he hadn't been one of the onlookers in the bailey.

'You may tell His Grace that I pray for his health and continued strength daily.'

'Yes.' He glanced about to see if we were monitored. 'It's interesting. You were no sooner gone than he began to make a great show of affection for that nephew – Richard, is it? He's suddenly up at the high table, getting teased and gibed at, having gold chains hung about his neck one moment and an ale pot poured in his lap the next. They say it's sure he's really Duke Robert's bastard, but I've since heard someone say he looked so much like the king, one could almost take him for his own – which I thought quite enough to make the judicious weep. And yet, the next thing heard was that someone said the king spoke of adopting the boy at the next Christmas Court, which is utter nonsense, because the king has said nothing of that to his council. Yet – he has taken the lad up so closely as to put a blight on his friendship with that peacock from the Aquitaine, who's now ready to pack himself off home without having gotten whatever it was he came for. Do you know something of any of this?'

'Something.'

'I see. We are in an expansive mood, aren't we?'

'What does Prince Henry say about Rufus adopting the boy?'

Robin pursed his lips in thought. 'Why, nothing I can recall. But he smiles on him, so I don't suppose he's too concerned.'

'God help him, then. The boy, I mean.'

Hearing no call to return to court, I did what seemed both right and agreeable to me: I went up to Durham. This occasioned something of a crisis at home, as Isabel had believed she would accompany me there, despite the rapid approach of her lying-in. When I forbade her, she felt certain I meant to abandon her.

There is no way to try logic with a gravid woman. In the end I left Isabel weeping and my mother darkly hinting that we would either bring on the babe's birth untimely and kill it, or mark it with our strife and suffer the consequences later.

I took Fulcher aside before I set out, gave him a somewhat more slender purse than I should have liked to bestow, and said: 'Try to make her lying-in as comfortable as possible. Buy her cloth for a new gown and swaddling clothes. Tell her how it is I can't have her up there with me before I'm installed. Say to her that I give her this house with all its furnishings to do with as she likes. Tell her if the child is a male to name it – I don't care what she names it, so long as it isn't Amiot or Beelzebub. Tell her I love her, the fool. Say I'll come for her – to see her, that is – no later than Christmas.'

I reached Durham in a gusting summer wind that had almost cleaned the filth between my new residence and my new church, by which I mean that collection of squalid huts, pigsties, and duck paddles that passes for a village. I promised myself that as soon as it was possible I would have that indefensible heap of humanity and animal life removed farther down the side of the hill and put a curtain wall around the hill's crest, between castle and church. Unless God had changed their nature, we hadn't seen the last of the raiding Scots, and I never meant to fall victim to their pillage.

My arrival was unexpected despite outriders. The floors were littered with unclean straw, the ovens cold, the servants goggle-eyed with confusion to see me, a dozen clerks, and my baggage servants. Food for our need was sought at the abbey, and in a little while a procession came, buffeted by the wind, bearing bread, fish, cheese, butter, honey, ale, and about enough wine to turn a virgin's cheeks rosy. This was to stay us only until the kitchen was put to order and a decent meal prepared. Prior Turgot didn't make the difficult journey himself.

In a short while a flock of women from the village were herded through the door and began a grand cleansing of the presence hall and my bedchamber. I astonished my chamberlain by calling for a bath in the middle of both a week and a day and amazed him further by wanting soap and by wishing to tend to my bathing alone. I saw I would have little trouble establishing myself as an eccentric worthy of legend.

By early evening I had begun to smell mutton roasting and to feel that satisfaction of being in a place truly mine, not the king's or another man's. I unrolled the drawings for my Lady of Stone, and while dreaming over them and waiting for my supper, I may have drunk too much of good Abbot Turgot's wine, no doubt thereby depriving some worthy monk of his ration with which to wash down an altar or soothe a toothache. I was not, however, drunk.

I thought it would be pleasant to visit my Lady as the sun was setting, to hear Vespers sung in what portion of her was already built. I left my chamber and hall, walked through the miry village, collecting a suitable number of idiots, children, and dogs to make my passage notable, and entered the open end of the choir, still unscreened.

The stones of the choir aisles were beautiful; the great carved piers had a warm hue, almost golden when the western sun shone upon them, and they were new-washed with the windblown summer's rain. I touched them, leaned to embrace them. Their long shadows were as deep as sighs. Because the sanctuary was still open to the world, birds had nested at the tops of the pillars. Their throaty murmur was the only Vespers that would be sung there that day, it seemed. The monks of St. Cuthbert's were singing in the cloister, around the shrine of their founder, temporarily resting there. I found myself much relieved. For the first time I had my treasure all to myself, after so much dreaming on it.

Carileph did one good work in his whole life, starting that magnificent shrine. I would do another in finishing it – my beauty, my wonderful Lady of Stone. She would reign over all the churches of the north, and when West Minster itself fell back into the fens it rose from, my Lady would still stand proudly on her hill.

I walked the brief aisles of the choir in peace, entered the sanctuary, and turned to humble myself before its altar. When I rose again an amazing thing happened. I, at least, was amazed, and so were several dozen doves that had gone to rest on the ledges above me: I began to sing the antiphon to the Queen of Heaven:

> *Ave, Regina caelorum,*
> *Ave, Domina Angelorum:*
> *Salve, radix, salve, porta,*
> *Ex qua mundo, lux est orta:*
> *Gaude, Virgo gloriosa,*
> *Super omnes speciosa,*
> *Vale, o valde decora,*
> *Et pro nobis Christum exora . . .*

One who has not tried this at full voice in a high-walled, empty place of sounding stone, free of snuffling monks and the choke of ill-burning cresset oil, cannot begin to imagine what a glorious feeling of power and exaltation that song brings forth from the heart.

There was a great, terrified flapping of bird wings overhead as the trespassing doves fled the sanctuary to take roost in the wooded hillsides that flanked the river below. I heard a soft, communal sigh behind me and remembered I had brought pilgrims to Vespers. For their sake as well as my own I lifted my arms and my voice again. I could almost feel my Lady stir. It was as if I were slapping a newborn giantess into life. She breathed with the soughing wind that always comes to that hill at sundown. I saluted her:

> *AVE, Regina caelorum!*
> *AVE, Domina Angelorum!*
> *SALVE, radix, SALVE, porta,*
> *EX qua mundo, LUX est orta!*
> *GAUDE! Virgo gloriosa –*

'What in the Name of the Many Wounds of Christ are you *doing?*' bellowed another voice behind me.

I wheeled about – I admit to being badly startled out of my ecstasy – and nearly fell. Prior Turgot stood at the western end of the choir. I recognized him at once, even though the glare of the low-hanging sun nearly blinded me and made him seem twice his size. From his stance, fists on hips and great sandaled feet braced well apart, he might have been the Angel of the Sword, sent to expel me from my paradise.

'I'm singing to Our Lady,' I said. 'I may have been about to dance for her, in the fashion of King David. Would you care to join me?'

He came forward a step, his chin thrust out as if he had a mind to thump me like a rude street urchin who had offended him.

'You're drunk, or you'd know better than to try your insolence on me, man. I can have you whipped for this sacrilege, or worse. Who are you?'

I was happy to tell him, as he'd either grown thick-sighted or forgetful of our last meeting. 'A man. A happy man. The vicar of Godalming. Dean of the chapter of St. Martin's in Dover. Archdeacon of Twynham. Abbot of Hyde. Sole chaplain to the king, tax gatherer, extortionist of the meek and holy – Anti-Christ, maybe! I am Ranulph Flambard, Bishop of Durham and your new abbot, Turgot! Didn't anyone tell you I was here?'

On the third before the nones of July, the feast day of St. Romulus, bishop and martyr, the holy city of Jerusalem was taken from the heathen by God's warriors and bestowed upon Godfrey de Bouillon, who was elected king there. Rumor had it that Robert Curthose was first offered the crown, but refused it out of modesty. They say it was then proffered to none other than Edgar Atheling, because of his ancient and honorable lineage, but he too refused it, saying he could not live out his life so far from his ancestral home even for a crown. How exceedingly like them both!

In July word was brought to King William as he hunted in the New Forest that Count Helias had broken his parole and was attacking the royal garrisons with such vigor that he was in a fair way to reclaiming all of Maine to himself. They say the king laughed to hear the news. Peace would have begun to pall on him by then. He had been overtaken by the messenger as he was setting out from Lyndhurst to the Brockenhurst woods. Still mounted, he put spurs to his horse's flanks, curveted him, and cried:

'Let all who love me follow me!'

And all who were with him had little choice but to obey. They rode at a good Norman gallop from that place to the coast of the Test estuary ten miles away. A storm was boiling up out of the southeast as they came to Hythe on Southampton Water. Winds lashed the waves and tossed the sorry vessels of the little fishing village against the quays. The astonished fishermen protested when Rufus ordered them to man boats and carry him over the water to the port where the ships were. Even the hardiest of his loving friends were alarmed to think of risking their lives in such frail boats and counseled their lord to wait a bit, until the storm had blown out.

'We must support our friends, my lords!' the king yelled above the roar of wind and water. 'The mad dogs are barking again!'

'This is no army, Your Grace,' cried Robert fitz Hamon. 'Our friends will last until the wind sinks. We'll drown if we try these rotten tubs now!'

'Kings never drown, Robin! Believe it! Trust me and you'll see the winds obey me!' After which, without waiting for a seasoned hand to steady it, he jumped off the quay into the nearest boat and by a miracle managed not to overturn it. As if some magic had stirred to answer the confidence in the king's voice, the wind promptly abated. All the lords, knights, and fishermen then scrambled after him, oars were put out, and the hunters made over the estuary to an old, worn-out cog they found in port, which Rufus boarded with no more pomp than a nithing escaping into exile. He commanded they put to sea at once and was obeyed, as a king who has God's Ear – or the Devil's luck.

They put into port at Touques early the next morning, hungry as wolves. All the inhabitants of the town rushed down to the harbor, seeing a ship under sail come in from England, and found the king laughing at them from her 'castle, demanding food and a horse.

The first person to offer him either was the curé of the village, who gave him his half loaf and his elderly mare. The king accepted both with courtesy and made his way to Bonneville, surrounded by his friends on foot and a horde of admiring villagers with whom he traded jests like a tinker.

At Bonneville he feasted, sent out summons of array, soon collected his army, and set out to find Helias at Le Mans. But the boastful count, when he got word of the king's notable crossing and hearty reception, took fright and deserted his capital, leaving it in flames. Rufus pursued him with fire and sword across the county, finding each time he drew near him that Helias had fired his own stronghold rather than yield it to his lord. From Vaux to Oustillé, from Chateau-du-Loir to Mayet fled the Centomanian, until he came to a fortress he felt he could defend and there sat him down expecting a vigorous assault. He wasn't disappointed, though there was an unexpected delay.

The royal army arrived at Mayet on a Friday and the next day began assembling for storming the walls. But the little curé of Touques who had accompanied them at the king's behest, and who must have been bursting with self-importance for the familiarity and affection the king bestowed on him in exchange for his gift of bread and transportation, made bold to remind Rufus that to make such an attack on such a day would break the oath of the Truce of God, as it had been set out at the synod of Rouen in '96.

'What's this Truce of God?' asked the king suspiciously, pretending he had never heard of it.

'Why, Your Grace, the holy synod decreed that no man make war on another from sunset on a Wednesday to sunrise on a Monday, nor on any feast day to the Virgin, nor the feasts of the Holy Apostles, nor from the Sunday before the beginning of Lent to the – '

'When in the name of – when does He let me make a little war, then?' (I can imagine as if I were there how he must have looked as he said it: a little angry and impatient, but half ready to burst into laughter at the effrontery of the priest.)

'My lord, between a Monday morning and Wednesday Vespers, if they don't fall on a feast day to the – '

'Virgin, or the Apostles, yes, I see. God drives a bargain like a Fleming, would you say, Father?'

'God desires peace between men, not war, my lord.'

'Is He so kind to the heathen? He'll never get His Sepulcher back,' said the king, who had not yet heard of the deliverance of Jerusalem. 'I believe He was a better general in the days of King Saul and the Amalekites, but no matter. God's done me a favor, for once. I'll do Him one in return.' The assault was delayed until Monday, to the wonder of Robert de Bellesme and his kind, no doubt.

The king had his men fill up the dry motte below the bailey with great heaps of wood to make a bedding for heavy beams that would support his siege engines to the walls of Mayet. But the men of the garrison saw his intent and flung caldrons of burning coals down on the wood, setting it on fire and almost setting light to their own walls, too. The resulting heat and smoke were a torment to both sides on a hot July day. The king put up his engines as near the ditch as he might and flung stones over the walls.

The men of the garrison responded in kind. One of their stones fell so near the king that it startled his horse and almost threw him, but he got control of the beast and yelled his defiance at the enemy:

'More to the left, you fools! To the left! I'll stand for you!'

The next stone fell closer and crushed the head of a man-at-arms who had run up to steady the king's destrier. From the walls came a cry:

'There's fresh meat for you, Red Will! Take it to your kitchen and have it for your supper!'

Then the king's rage broke: 'Fresh meat? Fresh meat? That's something you won't taste again this year! I gave you God's Truce, you motherless bastards; now I'll give you mine! When you want fresh meat again, come to Le Mans and ask me for it!'

He drew off his army and set them to laying waste to the land: uprooting every vine, felling every fruit tree, butchering every beast, trampling the corn, leveling the walls of every barn and granary – ravaging the whole country, which was very rich for a league around Mayet, as his father had once wasted Mantes.

Count Helias, when he knew what ruin had been worked upon him, came forth from his –

Fulcher has been to see me again. I know now what I only felt in my bowels before. I shall never have my freedom from this place unless it be to go to a worse one. Oh, God, from my own gift –

66

I will set this down and then I'll have finished with my vain history which no man may read. It doesn't matter. God never intended me for a Gregory of Tours, much less an Augustine. My brothers came to me yesterday and brought a visitor I thought I should never see, told me a tale I thought I should never hear.

I've been sitting here since dawn, watching the shaft of thin sunlight that falls through my window make its slow journey across my walls. I meant to write of the last year of King William's life, of our reconciliation at Christmastide, of his magnanimity to the men of Maine after the ruin of Mayet and his grief for the sudden death of his nephew Richard in the New Forest only a month before his own.

But these things I must let go by and tell another thing, except my weary brain which got no rest in the night can do nothing more useful than search after the words of a song that Cormac used to sing. There were Irish names in it that won't come to me, but the burden of it drones in my head like a lamenting bee:

These are the arrows that murder sleep.

It's a woman's dirge for her slain lover, I suppose. It's hard to tell with Gaelic names. He was a foreigner:

It came to me out of a foreign land.

Something here about her love for the dead. Something something have fled for me

> And Oh! my peace is fled.

My peace is fled, yes. She was a king's daughter. In her old age she still remembered and grieved for him. The Irish women are said to be very free with giving of their loves, as apparently Cormac's mother was. He said once his father was a Welshman. How could that be and he still count himself Irish? I'll never know if he was truly a prince in his land, as the old brother at St. Vigor said he told them. It's probably not true, but it's years too late to go asking.

Why won't the damned words come back to me? I've heard them a hundred times, but not one stave:

> These are the arrows that murder sleep.

The last:

> Chaste Christ! What sorrow is like to mine?
> My heart is weary and fate is strong.
> These are the arrows that murder sleep
> Every hour the cold night long.

Now, there's a triumph of sorts: the sun must be halfway to its meridian by now and all I've got to answer for my time here is a single stave of a song about people who mean nothing to me!

It was yesterday about this time that my door opened and Fulcher stepped through quickly, glancing behind him. He was followed by a cowled monk thrust through the doorway by my brother Osbern, who had him by the arm. The look on Osbern's normally pleasant, foolish face was so grim it was almost comical. I let my pen drop and stood up, expectant but confused. In the moment I first saw the cowl I thought my brothers had succeeded in smuggling Isabel in to see me. I was about to say as much when Osbern jerked the hood from the person's head at the same time Fulcher said:

'All right, filth! Do your duty!'

It was Martin under the cowl. He had a bruised face and a swollen lip. His eyes were glazed, red-rimmed for lack of sleep. At Fulcher's command he went down on his knees, then threw himself at my feet.

'What's this about? Martin? Fulcher?' At the moment I asked I began to know the dread of an answer. I thought of lifting Martin up. He was sobbing. But an instinct born of looking into my brother's drawn face kept me from it. I asked again in a sterner voice: 'Martin, what is it? What have you done?'

'Forgive me!'

'I can't forgive you until I know your crime.' His head was tonsured. 'Have you taken vows, then broken them? Deserted the abbey? This is very serious. You're no longer a child – '

I looked at my brothers and saw it was worse yet. I sat on my stool again, feeling slightly foolish and impatient with them. They'd brought him to me to judge, but were chary of naming the charge, which was grave enough to warrant a beating. I felt my heart descend into my stomach as if I were the felon.

'Martin, raise your head and tell me what this is about. Are you a thief as well as a runaway? Have you lain with a virgin and been caught? For God's sake, stop that moaning and speak!'

'He didn't run away. We took him from the abbey,' said Fulcher.

'Forgive me, Raf, but I made use of your seal – and your name – on a letter we put in the prior's hand, at Hyde.' He smiled. 'You may not be loved there, but an abbot's an abbot, even in prison. We gave the prior to understand that you must see your son and he released him.'

'Did he have to beat him senseless to make him go?'

Fulcher answered with toneless indifference: 'No. We did that for him later.'

'You?'

'He wanted to run away, the first night out of Winchester.'

'Father – ' Martin's hand touched my foot. Had he ever willingly called me by that name before?

Fulcher kicked him in the side. 'Tell him, now. Tell him what you told des Aix, what you told your confessor, what you told me!'

Martin howled in anguish: 'It was an accident! I never meant it! I was aiming for the deer, but it changed course and I hit him, instead!'

'Who? Hit – who?' I already knew, but I snatched up Martin's head by the forelock and shouted in his face: 'Who?'

He shrieked: 'The king! The king! The king!' and fell down sobbing as I let go his hair. I stared at Fulcher.

'That's not all of it,' he said.

'What more can there be, for Sweet Jesus' sake?'

Fulcher's words escaped him without voice: 'Tell him, Martin. Get off your face and confess it like a man.'

Martin obeyed, pushing himself up to his knees. He'd bloodied his nose, but he spoke with more calm now, though his breath was cut off in spasms that jerked him from time to time:

'We were at Malwood Lodge. We'd come from Brockenhurst the day before. We hadn't gone to the stands yet, because the king took sick after the day-meal that day. It was Lammas and there'd been the usual gorging and drinking. A woman from Lymington brought the king a loaf that only he ate. His bowels griped him and he vomited, later. Count Robert fitz Hamon wanted to send for the woman and question her, but the king wouldn't have it. He said it was a spoiled onion. Fitz Hamon wanted to send to the city for a doctor – '

'Don't drag this out like Roland's Ride! Just tell what you did,' Osbern said impatiently.

'No, let him tell it as he will, now he's started,' I said. I didn't want more sobbing and writhing on the floor. I nodded to Martin, who wiped his bleeding nose on his sleeve and continued:

'The king had a dream in the night, something about being bled – '

'How do you know what dreams he had?' I asked. 'Were you lodged with him?'

'No! He cried out so loud, everyone in the tower heard him. He – called for light and made his friends stay by him until daylight, talking to cheer him. Everybody in the place heard about the dream before morning. Count Walter was telling it before the king came down from his chamber. The dream was that he had a doctor to bleed him, and when the lancet touched him, his blood shot up like a fountain, so it covered the sky and turned it dark.' He shuddered and swallowed as if he might turn ill at the thought.

I waited. I knew the secret dread Rufus had for his own dreams, how much he wanted an interpreter to put a good light on them. He would tell this one, certainly.

'The next morning, he came down to the hall saying he was better and wouldn't be questioned about it any more. We had a holy service, broke our fast, and the king held court in the bailey, until time for the day-meal. About Sext, a monk came from Gloucester with a message he said was from Abbot Serlo of St. Peter's there. He read it out. It was the tale of – of a dream that one of Serlo's monks had had. It was – it was like the king's, in a way, but worse. He – '

'Tell it!'

'He dreamed that the king went into a chapel and – and laid hands on the Holy Image of Christ! He tried to eat it, gnawed at it, until Christ struck him with His foot and he fell down, and out of his mouth poured fire and smoke that rose until it covered the light! It was a horrible dream! Men blessed themselves when it was told, but the king laughed. He said to Count Walter: "Do this one justice, eh, Wat?" And Tirel said, 'I will, my lord." '

'What did he mean by that?'

'I think he was teasing Count Walter for having taken his own dream too much to heart and talking about it even to the huntsmen in the bailey that morning. Tirel got red in the face, but he laughed, too.'

Tirel had much to be embarrassed about. It had been his arrow, gadding from a glancing blow on the antlers of a stag, that had struck the king's nephew and killed him a month before. He'd been exonerated of any blame for the incident, but he must have been very eager to ingratiate himself afresh with Rufus, who had truly grieved for the boy he'd once threatened to make his heir.

'Go on.'

'Well, the king laughed and said to his dispenser: "Monks dream for money. Pay him something." He said to the monk who'd read Serlo's message: "I'm surprised at Serlo for sending me this. I always thought him a good old man, but I think it's very simple of him to put the dreams of his snoring monks into writing and send them to me, when I'm weighed down by real matters. Does he think I'm like the English, who give up their journeys or their business because of the dreams of old women? I thought better of him!" And then everyone pretended to think the dream was foolish but fitz Hamon, who asked the king if it wouldn't be wiser to return to the city, where he was better guarded. But the king mocked him and gave instructions for the hunt.'

'So, now we come at last to the hunt!'

'It didn't begin until evening. The king stayed a long time at table, laughing, talking. He ate and drank a great deal, too, as if to make sure everyone knew he'd recovered from his sickness. He and Prince Henry made wagers on cockfights in the hall, then went out to test a new palfrey the prince had given him before they left the city. It was a present for his – for his birthday.' Martin's head drooped again as his voice died to a mutter.

'Did he receive my gift before he died?'

His face twisted. He began to weep silently. I glanced at Fulcher, who looked down on my son with the most bitter distaste.

'Well?'

'Yes, it came that afternoon as we were preparing to go into the forest. I was near the king then, because – because I'd tried to beg his forgiveness.'

'You spoke to him?'

'Yes, and he – he said I was a fool to do it! He said: "I knew you at sight, you blockhead. I know all about you. You should be ashamed to show yourself a fool, with such a clever father. Don't you know that if I acknowledge you, I'll have to deal with you in a way you won't like? Take yourself off and grow a beard, or something. I won't have back a man who deserts me. It's bad for the discipline of my boys." He went back to lacing his boots that he'd loosened while he was riding. It was then the smith came from Twynham with your arrows. Everyone in the stable yard came to see how they glittered in the sun.'

I had hoped they would please my friend, who had shown me his forgiveness so generously. I'd had the half-dozen arrows especially made, with silver-gilt tips and scarlet fletching. The shafts were striped in gold leaf alternating with scarlet: the king's colors.

'Was he pleased?'

'He held them up for all to see. Then he gave Tirel two of them.'

'What?'

'I think it was – by way of forgiving him, maybe. 'You'll take the stand next to me,' he said to him; then he gave him the arrows. 'The sharpest arrows are properly given to him who deals the deadliest strokes.' It seemed to make Count Walter happy, but not fitz Hamon.'

'Get on with it,' Fulcher said. 'I scarcely think we have to know everything the king said, or thought, especially as you're not fit to interpret his thoughts for us.'

'He was a forgiving man!' Martin cried, his voice breaking on the last word. 'He even forgave me. When everyone was mounted and moving out of the bailey – he called out to me as I was running to take my place with des Aix – I was his archer that day. I stopped as the king rode by me and he put one of – one of your arrows in my hand. "Keep it,' he said, and went by me." He choked again.

'Give him some wine, Osbern, or we'll never hear the end of his tale,' Fulcher said.

'I would have kept it – I would have kept it all my life!' He leaned against my knee, weeping. I might have wept with him in other circumstances, but I was empty of all feeling. The child in whom I had once taken vain pride had destroyed the man whose friendship had shaped my life. I pushed Martin's face away from my knee and said:

'No more weeping. Just tell what you must.'

He sighed. 'We made for the Canterton Wood. It was so late in the day, the keeper felt that was the only walk where we might find game. His beaters were already out in the northern wood, coursing their hounds. The king was in the prime notch, where the game might be driven to him most naturally. Tirel was in the stand to the west of him. Gilbert de Laigle and Sir William de Montfichet were farther to – '

'Where was Prince Henry?'

'He went into the eastern wood, beyond the Canterton Road. I never saw him until after – after. The sun was low and the light was blinding unless you kept your eyes straight ahead. Ralph and I were on the hill above Tirel, to the left of the king. I had nothing to do but hold a second bow for Ralph and keep watch for game. I could look as far down the line as de Laigle's notch, where his white hair caught the light. I thought he'd never have a hope of killing anything unless he wore a cap, since the deer must be able to see him as well as I.

'It was so quiet for a while, I could hear Raoul breathe. He had an arrow already nocked and was listening to the sound of the hounds across the marsh. I took out the arrow the king gave me, turning away from Raoul so he couldn't see me fit it to my string. He didn't like it if I looked bow-hungry, as he said.

'The stag broke from a slot in the far side of the wood, just across from Tirel – coming straight on for him. It was a bad shot for him. He held his draw, to see if the stag would turn the natural way to the west, where the trees opened up around the marsh. Then, almost at the same time he shot, another stag broke from cover near the king.

'It wasn't a good shot for him, either, but I saw him draw to it and hold for a moment, then shoot. I heard Wat Tirel curse, but I was watching the king's deer. He'd hit it, high on the shoulder. It didn't stumble, but it changed course suddenly, running across the path of the other stag.

'The king yelled: "Shoot, Wat! Shoot, in the Devil's name!" He didn't know Tirel had already done it. Raoul des Aix left our stand and ran a little way downhill, to see if he could make the mark, but he couldn't; it was too far by then. All at once, Tirel's stag came at us, plunging up the hill. I jumped up and took aim without thinking whether I should or not! My moving startled it. Just as I let go, I remembered it was the arrow the king gave me that I'd shot, and all I could think was: "Now I've lost it and I'll never find it." Then I heard the stag hit the ground behind me and Raoul came running back.

'It was him that killed it, but the first thing he did – he hit me in the face with his fist, for forgetting my place. He'd have kept on hitting me, but we heard the king's archer screaming: "The king's struck! The king's struck!" And – and then Raoul shoved me aside and ran down to him. I picked myself up and ran after him, because I couldn't make sense out of what Roger said. How could the king be struck? How – the deer had passed too far above him!

'When I got to the stand, I saw the king, lying on his side with his right arm doubled up under him. His left arm was flung out and he was still holding his bow. He didn't move and – and nobody offered to touch him. Raoul was angry. He grabbed Roger by the neck of the shirt and he shouted: "Who did this? Where did it come from? Was it you?"

'Roger started to cry: "I didn't see it! I didn't! The sun was in my eyes!" And they were into a wrangle with each other about how the sun shouldn't have been in Roger's eyes if he'd been where he was supposed to be. Then Wat Tirel came and fell on his knees before the king – and turned the body over. The others in the western stands were coming in, too, but I didn't see them, or anything, except that – except that the king was dead!' The weeping that escaped him was like a hound's whine.

'He – his eyes were still open – and his mouth, too. He looked – just surprised. He'd taken hold of the arrow as he fell, to pull it out, and he broke it, or his fall broke it. I could see the feathers sticking out from his fist. Everybody saw them, but we just stared, until de Laigle said – I think it was him – "Oh, Christ, Wat, what have you done?"

' "Nothing. I've done nothing." He was shaking his head like a fool. De Laigle jerked him around and yelled at him: "He God damn well couldn't have shot himself, could he? Look at the fletching!" Then fitz Hamon came running and he was like a madman. He wanted to kill Tirel right there. De Laigle and Montfichet had to hold him back. He cried like a woman; he said that if they were murderers they might as well kill him, too, as he'd rather be dead with Will-Rou than look on their faces any more. And all the time Tirel kept saying he didn't do it, that he'd only shot once and then at the stag before him. But nobody believed him – except me.

'When Prince Henry came, there was more shouting, this time

from the Clares, because Tirel was their sister's husband, and – and somehow in the middle of that Tirel got away. I think Prince Henry let him – maybe for the sake of the Clares. Maybe because – I don't think he cared – whether it was murder, or an accident, or anything! He – nobody was paying any attention to the king!

'They shouted for the keeper, shouted for their horses and their squires to come to them, shouted for – shouted –

'I slipped out of their way. They didn't notice me. Not even Raoul remembered me then. Nobody knew I'd had one of those arrows for a little while but the dead king, so I crawled into the underbrush a little way up the hill and waited until they rode away.

'They left him on the ground where he fell, you know! As if he were – nothing. I waited to see if they'd come back for him with a litter, but they didn't. Nobody came. I went down to him and sat beside him to brush the flies away from his face. I closed his eyes and held his hand. I told him – told him I was sorry – '

He bent forward until his head touched the floor again.

'That's enough,' I said.

'More than enough, I'd say,' Osbern said bitterly. 'And he kept it all to himself, instead of coming to us at the beginning, which might have saved you from arrest!'

'No. No, I don't think so. If I'd heard this at the first, I might have thought Henry suspected me – or thought he could find a way to lay his blame on me,' I said. 'You see, all this time I've thought Henry was behind it. When the king's death followed so close on Richard's, when Tirel was named in each case, I thought he'd cleared the way for himself to take the crown before Curthose came home – and I was to be implicated in some way, when he'd had time to think how to do it. But now I see it's as Martin says. Henry simply doesn't care who did it, or how, or why it was done. Enough for him that it was. That's all.'

'Then why have you been arrested at all?' asked Fulcher, still frowning down on the bowed head of the weeping Martin.

'I don't know.' I felt very tired all at once, as if I had been laboring up a hill for hours. 'Maybe only to keep me from demanding an inquest. He had the Clares' honor to think of – and they had their brother-in-law to defend. Honor – honor. What do they mean by it? You say Tirel's gone overseas? And the huntsman des Aix, too?'

'Both gone and not likely to come back to give evidence.'

'And Martin told des Aix what he'd done?'

'It was the Aquitanian who got him safely back to Hyde. Like all the rest, when the deed was done he didn't concern himself with the how or why of it. Only to get safe away.'

'A wise man. Well, Fulcher – you must get Martin out of England somehow. The longer he stays, the more likely it is this will come out in the open, and when it's known, Henry will have to act. Perhaps a pilgrimage can be arranged; to Rome, or somewhere.'

'To Hell with Martin!' said Osbern. 'You're the one we'd better get out of England now.'

I shook my head. 'I don't think that's likely. I'll petition the archbishops, but I doubt that Anselm is in any hurry to try my case.'

'Forget petitions! You can make those until you fall into senility. Anselm and the king are already at odds, and Gerard isn't the best loved Archbishop of York we ever had. Neither of them can aid you, if you can't help yourself.'

I was a little astonished at the determined tone of Osbern's speech. He wasn't always the fool. I glanced at Fulcher.

'He's right. You must deliver yourself, Raf.'

'Deliver myself from this place? The strongest keep in the kingdom? There isn't any way – is there?'

My mother has sent me the gift of a cask of good red wine

67

Thanks be to God and my mother I am free!

Fulcher writes this for me, but he will be a good scribe (yes, that, too!), as I am half dead from coming down that damned rope. No! That blessed rope!

Who would have thought it of my little mother? When she heard her sons speaking of how they might get me safe away, she said nothing, but went and purchased a rope from a chandler and coiled it up inside that cask of wine – Isabel's gift out of her own purse – as neatly as if it were a seal ribbon.

I wasn't warned; there was no time, with the constable's man prowling in my chamber, looking into the hampers of clothing and food that accompanied the cask. Only the generous amount of food prompted me to invite my captors to be my guests at an impromptu feast, for what else could I do with a ham and a whole saddle of roasted mutton?

Poor lads! Their work is dull and the weather's cold. What else should they do but accept my hospitality? The king is overseas, and who is to say they mustn't accept a drink from an obliging prisoner?

I didn't even see the rope until my honored guests had lapped the level of the wine halfway down the cask. We'd knocked the head off in order to dip into it with our cups, so they might have seen it and been as startled as I. But I hid my delight in my sweet mother's craft and filled cups for them no sooner than they'd drained them. Oh, it was a splendid dinner! I never had a better, even when I feasted the papal legate and sent him to bed with a bathhouse whore!

When they were snoring on my table, I carefully drew out coil after beautiful, wine-soaked coil of that good rope, measuring it ell by ell. There was only one blight on my joy: I could see it wasn't near long enough to take me from my window to the ground. It must serve, however; I only need add to it with linen strips torn from my bedclothes. I took a knife and began to work, fearful that one of my guests would wake to a call of Nature and discover me in the act of escape. But they had supped too well of me. They slept like happy swine. If they hadn't been cruel enough to leave two of the garrison on duty outside my door, I could have gone straight down the stairs of the Tower.

When I had my bed strips secured to the rope with a multiplicity of wine-wetted knots, I tied one end to the window mullion, having set open the shutters and latched them to the wall. The icy wind gusted through my cell and put out both candle and cresset, leaving me fumbling in the dark. Now, more than ever, I feared the waking of the guards, but I couldn't yet throw myself on the mercy of the rope and plunge to freedom.

First I must make safe my precious chronicle which has kept me sane through these near hopeless months of solitude. No nosy clerk of the constable's could be allowed to paw through those pages, which were as inward to me as the very chambers of my heart! I tied the end of the rope about my writing box and leaned out the window to see if my rescuers were below.

Out of the wet darkness their pale faces appeared like ghosts looking up to me: Fulcher, Osbern, even Martin. I let my burden over the edge of the sill and sent it to them tenderly, praying some weakness in my knots wouldn't send it plunging to the stones of the bailey where it would be scattered and exposed.

(Fulcher is smiling. He thinks this is all very foolish. But I say that this is the child of my brain and no less dear to me than the children of my loins.)

It was delivered safely, though it had begun to swing alarmingly in the wind before Fulcher caught it. When I felt the weight of it leave the rope, I sighed a prayer of thanks and turned to my final business. I could hear a voice below, hissing instructions to me. Hurry! Yes, but first I must put on my vestments, my sacred robes that had cost me so dear, which had been carefully laid away in the small chest at the foot of my narrow bed since I came to that place of penance and reflection. I was – and am – the Bishop of Durham! I would not go forth as a thief in the night. If the rope and linen parted and I spattered my brains on the stones of the yard, I would at least die in the dignity of my office. Besides which, the green cope alone had cost me nearly twenty marks, and no toady of Henry's, no Will Giffard, nor any other of his stripe would have it to wear from me, unless they stole it from my corpse!

I put on my miter and took up my staff. I couldn't find my gloves in the dark. I thought they must have fallen out of the folds of my cope and lost themselves in the shreds of bedclothing. Never mind; I took my staff under arm, climbed upon my stool, grasped my lifeline, and squeezed myself through the window.

(Fulcher laughs now. It wasn't easy! In the months of sitting, with no occupation but writing, eating, drinking, and brooding, even you might have gained a bit of weight, my brother. I must have gained more than a stone.)

I lost my miter, trying to work myself around the unyielding mullion; then I began my descent. I was too desperate to be terrified of the tremendous height – or else too terrified to be anything but desperate enough to brave it. Thank God it was dark! If I'd been able to see clearly how far I had to fall, my senses might have deserted me. But all I could see was the glimmer of the wet stone wall in the moonlight.

The stench and chill of the river fog rose up around me. I slipped on the wet rope. Then my pains began. I had never tried even my youthful weight on a rope. I had never, since my days as an oblate, used my hands for any menial labor. I could never have imagined the insupportable weight of my own body on the tender skin of my fingers and palms.

I wrapped my legs around the rope, beat my knees painfully against the wall, slipped, swung out, slipped again. My teeth were clenched so hard that I can still feel the effect of their grinding in my temples. I slipped again. I didn't seem to be very far from my window and already I was in agony. I heard Fulcher whispering urgently:

'Get it between your knees, Raf! For the love of God!' And then I began to slide dreadfully, the wirelike hairs of the hempen rope cutting into my palms like knives. I held on as long as I was able, but our bodies are such fools! They fear death, but they'll risk it in a moment to save themselves from a little pain. The flesh of my hands felt as if torches were searing them; brands burned my knees, flamed against my shins, as the hemp whipped against them. The stones of the Tower wall blurred before my eyes. I cried out and fell, striking the ground on both feet, then falling backward at once, full length.

I might have split my skull and finished the business, but my wise brothers had heaped straw under my window, even as I had been ladling wine down my guards' throats. I lay more dead than alive, both ankles either broken or severely strained, my arms nearly pulled from their sockets, and my hands paralyzed by the burns that seared away the flesh of my palms.

Fulcher clapped his hand over my mouth to stifle my cry; then he and Martin lifted me, half swooning, and carried me away to the river stairs. Osbern went before us with a lantern, mindful of whom we might yet meet by surprise, however many bribes had been paid. Swan and her children were waiting for us at the bottom of the stairs. There was a boat tied alongside. My brothers and my son put me into it, guided Swanhilda and the children aboard, then leaped in and took the oars.

'Where's Mother?' I cried when I saw them dip the oars.

'She, Isabel, and the children are taking another ship than ours.'

'Isabel? The children? What children?'

'Your children, Raf. Have you forgotten them?'

I was abashed. I had, in truth, put them entirely out of mind the last few months. 'But – it's dangerous for them to travel alone, without protection of a man. Why did you let them? They'll be found out and taken – robbed at the least, if there's anything left to rob me of.'

'I doubt it,' said Fulcher. 'It was Isabel's idea. She and Mother needed time to gather your household goods. They'd have been of little use to us here, tonight. And aren't you being the least bit ungrateful to Isabel? She's going to board ship as a noble widow on pilgrimage to the shrines of France, with her children. Mother's to be her servant. They're taking as many of your valuables as they can without exciting the suspicion of the ship's captain. But the Countess of Lyons should be allowed a few luxuries without its seeming strange to him.'

'The Countess of Lyons?'

'She thought you might have forgotten. She said to remind you she still had a claim to that title from her late husband. I hope you won't complain of the cost of this to me later, brother. There are two ship's captains to be satisfied; passage for the lot of us will come at double the usual fare. Your servants in London have been paid to take a slow pilgrimage of their own up to Durham. Those in Durham are on their way to Winchester, and those in that city are making for London. It's a whole army we've put on the move to keep them from being questioned about you, until we're safely gone. We hope the trick will save their lives as well. Also, take into consideration the bribes I've paid to the constable's lieutenant to allow us to bring you clothes and provisions – '

'Yes, yes! I'm grateful, grateful! What use is silver if I'm dead?'

'Exactly. Only, I thought you might not think so when we're in France and you look into your household chests.'

'Sweet Jesus, I know you've done more than your duty to me, Fulcher, and I mean to find some proper reward for you – somewhere.'

He looked at me with his usual wry smile.

(Yes, just as you do now, my brother – my conscience – but I *will* reward you!)

Now – what else is there to put down? We're on a ship bound for La Tréport, which is presently in King Henry's hands and a damned dangerous place to go near. Ships may already be on the sea after us from London. If they are, why, we must outrun them! We'll buy horses and ride straight for Rouen – if my rescuing angels have left me the silver for it – I jest, Fulcher. We'll ride if I must be tied to my saddle, brother. There'll be no time for litters and leisurely journeys then.

We'll find Duke Robert and let him know we're his loyal servants. By St. Michael's angels, he should be glad to see me! He's needed someone to put some iron in his spine since he came home from his holy war. He's got reason to fight his little brother now: he has a wife and a child on the way – the first one born on the right side of his blanket!

'Well, then I'll be his new Odo! I'll put fire in his belly again! If he can fight Henry as he fought the heathen, he can win his kingdom back from that thief of crowns, and when he does that, he'll win me back – '

*

Here my brother Ranulph went silent for so long a time and with his eyes squeezed shut so tightly I thought it must be from the pain of his many injuries. But as I was about to put away my pen he opened his eyes again, letting pent-up tears fall down his cheeks as he whispered:

'My Lady of Stone.'

What he meant by that I cannot say, but the way he said it was more tender than any word I ever heard him speak to child or woman I have known. He sleeps now. The coast of France is near.

These people I wish to thank, who lent me books, or helped me to find research material I might otherwise have missed. The generosity of friends is no small thing to a writer who will go wandering in obscure eras among all but unrecorded people. I thank them profoundly, but hasten to say that no blame must be attributed to them for whatever use I made of their books.

They are: Donald Baker, Librarian, the Willard Library; the Reverend William E. Stark, pastor of St. John's Anglican Church; the Reverend Joseph Ziliak, pastor of Nativity Church; and William A. Gumberts, all of Evansville, Indiana; the Reverend Canon Gordon Berriman, Hon. Vicar Choral, Durham Cathedral; Marilyn Hird, Reference Librarian, Durham University; and that archivist of St. Paul's Cathedral, London, whose letter and name have been lost to me, but whose graciousness has not.

Most especially I thank my husband, Kilburn Durham – history buff, mediaeval weapons-architecture-military history expert, proof-reader, grammarian, cartographer, calligrapher, whose brains I have picked without a qualm, whose tranquillity I have disturbed, and whose opinions I may have sometimes disputed and flouted to my loss.

M.D.